50P

CW01163403

The Torn Tiki

QUAVELS BY THE SAME AUTHOR

The Feather Chest (1996)
THE ARK *of Ao Tea Roa* (1998)
The Torn Tiki (1999)

The Torn Tiki

A Quavel

by
Miguel Orio

The Pentland Press
Edinburgh – Cambridge – Durham – USA

© M. Orio, 1999

First published in 1999 by
The Pentland Press Ltd
1 Hutton Close,
South Church
Bishop Auckland
Durham
England

All rights reserved
Unauthorised duplication
contravenes existing laws

ISBN 1–85821–686–9

Typeset in Melior 10/13
Printed and bound by Bookcraft Ltd., Bath, England

*To the Memory of
Herman Melville,
the Avatar of
Freedom of Thought
in American Letters.*

Disclaimer

All names, places, events, professions, characters, dates, plots, bibliographical data, technical and scientific references, as well as philosophical, religious and mythological interpretations, except those historically verifiable as part and parcel of the public domain through the Fourth Estate, are totally the product of my imagination. Any similarity with anyone or anything, anywhere, must be regarded as purely coincidental or accidental. Of course, this being a quavel, that is, *qua*si + no*vel*, like the other two components of the trilogy 'The Hermit Islands', its fictive *intelaiatura* does not necessarily warrant any dogmatic adherence to facts in any human consortium that may have ever existed under the leaky umbrella of either general truth or personal beliefs. The opinions, declarations, statements, invectives, actions and the like within the realm of infinite human dysfunctions must be regarded as those belonging to personages and protagonists only. The writer is only the retriever, the collector, the assorter, the printer of what all characters have done in search of an author. That has been rather easy and fun. The most difficult and frustrating process in the publication of this book has been that of finding a courageous publisher in a free society. It is well known that, according to Simone de Beauvoir, 'L'écrivain original, tant qu'il n'est pas mort, est toujours scandaleux.'

M.O.

Acknowledgements

The author gratefully acknowledges the following. Although he tried his best to contact every source for permission to quote beyond the normally assumed parameters of fair copyright legalities, in a few cases no reply was ever received because of either changes of address or other reasons such as death, bankruptcy, callousness and obscure international agreements.

Ms Alison J. Ressler for the difficult preparation of the American typescript.

Dr Graziana Lazzarino for a critical reading of the first draft.

Dr Frank Vecchio for furnishing reference material relating to academic and religious institutions, as well as for suggesting cleansing moderation in stylistic convolutions.

Mrs Jeanne Zachman for securing conventual contacts at the very inception of my first idea.

The Head of the Department of History at the University of Victoria at Wellington, New Zealand for providing academic information.

The Waitangi Tribunal Staff for generously sending basic and periodical publications.

The staff of the Kippenberger Military Archives and Library, Queen Elizabeth II Army Memorial Museum in Waiouru, New Zealand for duplicating archival records.

The publisher Bonz Verlag for kindly permitting the author to quote extensively from Dorothea Norman Jones, 'View Point from New Zealand', in *Money, Food, Drink, and Fashion*, ed. John Beebe (Fellbach-Oeffingen, 1983).

Mr Tim Smith for generously compiling bibliographic material on medical matters, and for kindly exchanging views on controversial issues by correspondence and telephone.

Sister B., Monastery of XXX, for charitably providing the most important and scholarly material on the humane philosophy of life engendered by St Francis and St Clare of Assisi, as well as for subtly proffering constant encouragement, quintessential poetic inspiration and the most tender source of global sisterhood within the Rule through which she is dedicating her whole life to Obedience, Poverty and Chastity.

Mr Mark Grant for allowing quotations from *Anthimus' De obseruatione ciborum* (Devon: Prospect, 1996).

Ms Carol Christiansen, Permission Manager, for quotations from Herman Melville, *Moby Dick* (New York: Bantam, 1953).

Harcourt Brace & Co. for quotations of excerpts from Giacomo Casanova, *History of my Life*, transl. Willard R. Trask (Baltimore and London: The Johns Hopkins Press, 1966).

Mr Paul Moon for excerpts from *The Occupation of the Moutoa Gardens* (Auckland: Paul Moon, 1996).

Many other institutions and persons, who have preferred to remain anonymous, for their vital contributions to my completing the last volume of 'The Hermit Islands'.

yomey
ikubaku ka aru
yo mijikashi

                    Masaoka Shiki

And we are here as on a darkling plain
Swept with confused alarm of struggle and flight,
  Where ignorant armies clash by night.

                    Matthew Arnold

Es gibt überhaupt keine höhere Form
des Bekenntnisses zu einem Volk,
als is seiner Sprache zu schreiben;
selbt wenn man schlecth schreibt.

                    Heinrich Böll

Oh! royal is the rose,
But barbed with many a dart;
Beware, beware the rose,
'Tis cankered at the heart.

                    Herman Melville

Foreword

In the bitter ecclesiastical *tremendum* of 1520, the preacher John Agricola admitted gloomily that he was "coming to understand what manner of thing man is, flesh is, trust in men is". *The Torn Tiki* fiercely rebellows this and similar observations, both participating in and transcending the genre of Jeremiad in which they find their most terrifying, pristine affirmation. In this, the final, zenithal panel of his neo-Boschian *The Hermit Islands* triptych, Orio continues his devastating critique of Occidental imperialism in the new world order, mercilessly amplifying it until even the most callous reader can detect its susurrating, subaural leifmotif.

The Torn Tiki – like its two predecessors – revels in history *sub scamno* in the finest Lutheran tradition, chronicling the development of its chief protagonist, the Croat-Maori Komaru Reti, from his work as an idealistic but pacific student of Ao Tea Roan history to his ultimate apotheosis as a revolutionary anarch, revanchist and Ensorian Redeemer. Reti's youth and inexperience mark him apart from his older literary progenitors in *The Feather Chest* and *The Ark of Ao Tea Roa*, the serene Pilot and misanthropic Peter Darby, whose immundane *khaibit* throws a pall of horror over the two later volumes; and yet the themes which are so potently treated are encountered throughout the trilogy – the *frisson* and ultimate breech between a love of pacifism and a hatred of injustice, the dilemma of the exile either to retreat from the world or to struggle with it, and perhaps most challenging of all, the daring contradistinction between conventional Western romantic stereotypes (which restrict and parody individual behaviour) and incestuous relationships (which liberate it). It is almost as if Orio were sardonically emphasizing the *diablerie* of the cycle through the desperate efforts of its doomed hero, the young Jacob to his predecessors' Abraham and Isaac.

Komaru and his sister Mahina, heirs to a Maori-cum-activist, become the crystalline shewstone through which we view their country's peculiar political physiognomy, a starkly dualist environment where Maoritanga co-exists uneasily with a spurious engrafted *ancien régime* so bent of bribing key dissentients into betraying their racial cause that, as Mahina asseverates, "our Islands are simply a geographic expression existing as an afterthought". The cynicism and political disillusionment elicited by the tergiversation of Maori leaders creates an atmosphere of acute disgust at the Weimarite impurity of mainstream debate, a samsaran recognition that "nowadays there are no tragedies as in ancient Greece, but only accidents caused by hedonism".

Reti falls into an ambivalent relationship with the *amoureuse* Melissa McTavish, a fiftysomething advisor whose nyphomaniacal propensities unsatiated by her marriage find a new release in her insouciant, remote *protégé* with her psychiatrist husband Bill's overt consent. Superficially a pleasant *divertissement*, the author's prose insidiously undermines our faith in the union's wholesomeness, implying a process of corruption, indeed of betrayal: "she [Melissa] had broken a paradigm by infusing into a Maori the drive of lust". Komaru, seeking patronage and support for his campaign against the wilful neglect of the Treaty of Waitangi, finds himself in a bewildering *mésalliance* with an incontinent, shallow couple ("their illness is not Maori, you know" satirically comments Komaru's friend Whina of a hostel of recovering dipsomaniacs) whose materialistic liberalism can never satisfy his increasingly Sorelian manifesto in whose lexicon lust and pederasty have no place and where "democracy" savours more of vitiating ochlocracy and baseless compromise, a world away from his enobling, irreclaimable dream of a Maoritanga where "death does not deserve to be treated as royalty", and *virtú* holds the balance.

Much of *The Torn Tiki* is a superb disquisition on how impossible a Ba'athian-style synthesis between the two cultures is, on how dialectic merely leads to the consolidation of supermajoritarian *schwärmer* control. A Melmothian vista of *déraciné* misery is evoked by Reti's description of the Maori plight: "A Polynesian . . . is like a Jew. He can 'live' comfortably in any part of the world, but he can only 'be' wholesome in the land of his ancestors". Other catalysts for this horror of *détente* emerge: his father, a World War II veteran afflicted by alcoholism, dies leaving him with a concise "Moral Testament" whose twenty-four page "innocent eye" text-and-glyph account of the nineteenth century Palmerstonian invasion instils in Komaru an almost Elijan wrath; and, most controversially and yet tenderly of all, we are treated to the delineation of a brief, incestuous *affaire* between Reti and his homecoming sister – an antinomian passage as parabolic in its manner as Matthew 19:11, "Not all men can receive this precept, but only those to whom it is given". In a sense, both anagogical and existential, the reader is made witness to an act of congress every whit as subversive and bodly *inciviste* as the fatal romance between Winston Smith and Julia in *1984*, or the world-shunning lovers in Conrad's *Victory*; even bolder is the narrative's impassioned assertion of the "rightlessness" of such relationships, their very antithesis to the datum of democracy: "Love can thrive only in a dictatorial relationship, in a master/slave bonding". The eponymous *tiki*, a symbol of purity worn religiously by Reti's sibling, is contrasted deftly with the lascivious Melissa's habitual use of prophylactics: at best a *Doppelgänger* or fetch of *tiki* honour. The conclusion to this primal, ineradicable syllogism leads Mahina to anchoritical escape in the United States of America, and Komaru to the brink of regicide. Rogernomics, Lange and Maori Council palliatives divide the nation, and only a stillborn act of irredentist defiance on the eve of the millennium remains to the matriculated terrorist, a *de profundis* expostulation against the collective insanity of both Government and People.

The Torn Tiki brings The Hermit Islands Trilogy to an elemental, conflagratory close; and yet it is not a close: the very essence and plenum of Mr Orio's *roman fleuve* is its cyclical skepsis, its mesmerising assault against the easy certainties of anthropocentricism, modernity and monoglot Anglo-Saxon *Kulturkampf* which embed the soil of his beloved Ao Tea Roa, his spiritual heartland, like so many dragonsteeth; certainties backed by the black-suited security operatives who shadow Komaru ("the sun") throughout the imminent eclipse. Those of us who live in the guilty metropolitan centres of former empires will find its fearful portrait of colonial sin all too recognizable, too vividly implicatory of the Ship of Fools in which we are still sailing, of the innocence which is as far from us as it is near to Orio's "seeing visionary"; and when his sister Mahina affirms that "I am Polynesian, an island spirit sailing the waves of affection", who will gainsay her?

Jonathan Grimes

Preface

With this quavel, the trilogy titled 'The Hermit Islands' is complete. In the 1986 outline, the original subject-matter had not been parcelled into three volumes since it encompassed an entire story to be structured into chapters only, without any hiatus that now requires three individual titles, namely, *The Feather Chest*, *THE ARK of Ao Tea Roa* and *The Torn Tiki*. Although the *motus animorum* of 'love' remains constant within the delicate framework of contemporary Maori life and culture in Ao Tea Roa, each volume contains unrelated protagonists and different human relationships. Thus, each title covers independent situations and characters.

As the whole narrative of the trilogy amounted to nearly 5,000 typewritten pages, the feasibility of publishing the work under a single title was remote. Except for the now defunct interest in James Michener's 'rediscovery' of that vaguely defined area at the bottom of the world and in the staging area for nuclear games about two generations ago, people had rarely heard of human concerns for natural phenomena such as El Niño and El Grande that had constituted two filaments of the whole web framing *The Feather Chest*.

Although the quavels had been outlined and, except for the last one, mostly written in 1986 at a ranch north of Benson, Arizona, the process of dismembering the first complete draft into three separate ones took place during my world travels until the early 1990s. Regardless of the resulting triadic structure, it was a matter of either keeping the entire narrative unified through identical names and personalities of the main characters and their rôles in interrelated plots, to be published in three consecutive parts, or of dividing the total work into three independent quavels. Each of these would display autonomous protagonists within diverse unities of place and time, though cohesively related by the main themes of Life, Love, Death, Freedom, Justice and other chimerical themes pursued by humans engaged in ennobling their Earthly enterprises in spite of peculiar historical and cultural constraints deeply rooted in Ao Tea Roa.

I opted for the latter solution, even knowing that this would somewhat weaken the original structure of the quasi-epic work on the one hand, though strengthening the cohesiveness of each independent quavel on the other. As I am about to release for publication the third volume of the Pacific trilogy, I feel it proper to make known some personal and difficult aspects of my writing activities. Why? Simple.

Until the age of 27, I had never written a single sentence in English, except perhaps in questionnaires sent to me when working as an interpreter for Morrison-Knudsen in Northern Brazil. The rather intimate account of my fight against psychological obstacles, being these not necessarily unique in the life of a single human being, may render other people in similar circumstances stronger in their determination to overcome writer's blocks and persevere in following the goals born in their hearts.

First, there is no archipelago known or called The Hermit Islands. There is only a 'Hermit Island' in the Bismarck Archipelago, about 500 miles north of and along the same longitude as Port Moresby, Papua New Guinea, and about 100 miles WNW of Admiralty Island. I chose this title for the trilogy, first, because the name occurs in *The Feather Chest*, as well as in *THE ARK of Ao Tea Roa*, and also on the basis of the fact that, within the Polynesian triangle, these islands – dozens of them now designated by Western geographers and colonial politicians as 'New Zealand' (*sic*) – were the last to be reached by the Morioris, Maoris and other Polynesians during and after the reign of Charlemagne (i.e. from the ninth century). These islands were also the last to be colonized, through brute force and the one-sided use of firearms, by immoral political 'agreements' between the highly literate heirs of the Magna Carta for 'Home' consumption and by the deceptive displacement of long-established 'mythological' practices among illiterate, though highly cultured, Aborigines.

Finally, the designation of 'hermit' was adopted because of its original, though complex, derivation from a Greek etymon meaning 'desert' in modern parlance. As there is no desert understood in geographic terms within Ao Tea Roa, the label is meant to point out that, unlike other modern political entities that acquired freedom from 'British' oppression during the 20th century, from India to Kenya to Fiji, Ao Tea Roa has been and still is a 'hermit', that is, an involuntary recluse among the so-called civilised nations that insist on considering Maoris as barely surviving biological entities, on Earth.

Although no Maori 'white-looking' children have ever been taken away from their families, as done in Australia since 1880 for the sake of integrating them into the mainstream of British culture, the Maoris are psychologically worse off than the Native Australians, the American Indians and the Hawaiians, to mention a few people who succumbed to European colonialism around the Pacific Rim. They have been first brainwashed into believing that they are the real owners of their *whenua*, as well as pacifically 'integrated' as per James Michener's *obiter dicta*, when in practice they were and are still isolated from the rest of the dominant 'moral' world because of remote geographic location and their own 'philosophy' of non-violent confrontation. The consequences of ensuing alienation are frightening, for Ao Tea Roans, both Maoris and Pakehas, are among the former colonial nations displaying the highest percentage of suicide, particularly among the young. It suffices for Westerners to glance at any international newscast via European TV sources, from Deutsche Welle to the BBC and French stations, to barely detect at the bottom of the screen a minuscule scratch of land normally covered by white clouds that bring cold, rain and depression. New Zealand is simply the colon of Australia in the anatomical atlas of the Earth. As brutally defined by Peter Wells, in 'The Tasman triangle', *The Australian's Review of Books* (February 1998), p. 24, 'NZ is a kind of joke country.'

Nevertheless, as done every year, Maoris keep on denouncing the Treaty of Waitangi of 1840. During their last activity in front of Buckingham Palace on 6 February 1997, they related once more their chronic grievances at great financial expense, personal sacrifice and public derision by bemused tourists, mostly Americans taking advantage of low-season tours during the boreal winter. On that day, however, something historical occurred, almost as an *umbra futurorum* cast on the charade staged later by British conservatism before Buckingham Palace on the occasion of the death of Diana, Princess of Wales seven months later. As reported by the rather sedate *The Times* on page 3 of the following Sunday edition, 'In the letter [delivered to the Privy Purse door of the palace], the Confederation of Chiefs of the United Tribes of Aotearoa requested a meeting with the Queen to address Treaty of Waitangi grievances.' There were no bombs *à la* IRA, no burning tires *à la* South Africa, no rock throwing *à la* Palestine, no actions of violence whatsoever. These Maoris, after all, were descended from forefathers who, during the so-called Maori wars, naïvely respected the Christian Sunday to worship the Lord, though the British took advantage of it and attacked the Maoris, who had believed in both chivalry and the gentlemen's agreement.

In fact, Eru Manukau, spokesman for the Confederation of Chiefs, made sure that Maori grievances were presented in the most 'British' parliamentary fashion. Of course, the Queen and her burdensome 70-year-old image were not in residence, since *de Maoribus non curat lex...Britannica*. Nothing was accomplished on the surface. But something unique took place in the deep structure of the British apparatus of blind conservatism. For the very first time in history, 'The Maori ceremony delayed the changing of the guard ritual in front of Buckingham Palace by about half an hour,' as 33 minutes of 'suspense' among the 'Bemused crowds awaiting the daily changing of the guard ceremony.' Thirty-three minutes that transformed the course of history for The Hermit Island and initiated the pacific progress of inevitable transition from colonial and insulting 'New Zealand' to Aboriginal and pristine Ao Tea Roa. That day, Big Ben stood psychologically still for 33 minutes. The last vestiges of the British Empire has dissolved symbolically into a *fait accompli*. The shadow assigned to Queen Victoria by Dobson in 1840 had been re-incorporated into the mythical substances allegedly left in trust to the Maoris after the Waitangi 'Trick', although in reality grabbed by real estate speculators, pathetically *naïve* missionaries and cruel military cadres. In essence, the Maoris had been left with only traditional Polynesian values in their souls shielded solely by dignity.

Before analysing my writing process, it is necessary to make a *mise au point* with regard to the medium of expression, normally one's 'mother tongue'. Modern English, unlike most, if not all, literary languages, presents some problems of 'variation' not only in spelling, but also in semantics and syntax, not to speak of cultural peculiarities tied to a particular nation where English is the ONLY or at least the primary language. This variation is not unlike that occurring in the transition from Classical Latin to Vulgar Latin and the resulting Romance languages. *The English Languages* by Tom McArthur, in fact, is an example of the linguistic parallel situation, describing the pluralism of English(es) as for Vulgar Latin at the end of the Middle Ages, just before the emergence of individual national languages from Vulgar Latin.

It would be otiose to refer to other synchronic and diachronic variations, be they regional, social, professional or 'translinguistic', and noticed within a 'politically correct' monolingual nation such as the USA, regardless of whether people speak and write languages other than English, from Arabic to Chinese to Vietnamese, not to mention solidly entrenched 'ethnic' languages from Ebonics to Navajo to Spanish. These differences are 'internal' because of geographic, historical, religious or racial reasons. I refer only to different types of English as siblings in the same family. In essence, one could conceive of an unknown English 'parent', through known daughter languages, such as British English, American English, Canadian English, Australasian, South African, Indian, and so forth.

English, as the language of so many diverse nations, thus, presents salient variations that at times create difficulties of presentation at the creative and editorial levels. I envision a time in which an editor or an author may be forced to declare in a Preface something like, 'This book was written in "X" English', where 'X' stands for a markedly different language, as may be said even nowadays of British versus American English. And even here, it is obvious that, when British English is used, one could even state that it is 'X' English or 'Y' English, as in the case of Oxford English versus BBC English or Soho English just to mention other allo-Englishes of intralinguistic nature.

In the case of American English, the breakdown into subcategories is normally not required unless needed for scholarly or theatrical purposes. In fact, when an American, assuming the writer was born and reared in the USA, writes a novel, naturally the language is American English, though the contents may betray some features typical of a certain author according to various factors. However, when the author writes about, say, New Zealand, how can the 'realistic' expressions of a 'Kiwi' be handled in writing for some aspects of lexicon, spelling, syntax and even 'jargon' that is actually 'New Zealander' or even 'New Zealandese'?

For critics who declare that in New Zealand people speak and write 'British' English, one can dispute their assertion with concrete evidence, especially at the 'sound' level, or immediately at the written one, by comparing, say, an issue of *The New Zealand Herald* and one of *The Times*. Or one may even cite variant cases of group interaction, as in the case of 'forced' contact for whatever reasons.

When this variation, however, is carried to the written level, the situation may become more problematic. In fact, in the first two volumes of this trilogy, I first wrote in American English for the simple reason that I was in Arizona and Colorado, respectively, where I interacted in everything through the language of the country. Besides, I had assumed and hoped that my work would be published in the

USA. Thus, I wrote in American, well, perhaps I should call it cerebral European American, because I automatically carried over 'Latin' syntax and lexicon since it was 'natural' for me to use Romance etyma rather than others from Anglo-Saxon stock such as 'select' instead of 'choose'. Nevertheless, I was careful to observe to some degree the realistic expressions contrasting American with New Zealandese. Thus, when American characters wrote a letter, they observed American cultural rules, excluding, of course, what I considered misspelling steeped in ignorance, such as 'supercede' instead of 'supersede', though the former is 'accepted' and thus sanctified by callousness. I also avoided non-grammatical hypercorrections that have become the norm since Thoreau's *Walden*, as in 'I see young men, my townsmen, whose misfortune it (*sic*, emphasis mine) is to have inherited farms ...' (p. 8). In some cases, I even used certain features to stress the degree to which some graduates from high schools and even college employ their mother tongue gone to the dogs of non-prescriptivism. Of course, I would have never dared to appeal to a generation of Americanoids à la J. D. Salinger or Kerouac, even if I had spent a few centuries among them, for my glottal genes were made mostly of 'printed' English, and not of phonic ones. Similarly, I did employ realistic features for New Zealanders, for no one in Australasian English would use American and vice versa, except for some incidental media expressions acquired via the gossipy airways of CNN.

At that stage of my rather freshman experience, if not subconscious ambition, in literary pursuits via a language other than my 'maternal' one, many problems arose as a consequence of what happens to culturally displaced persons. There are situations that create unique phenomena of alienation in the psyche of a Terrestrial affected by events of war, political dissension, social upheaval, personal conflict or even merely chance stemming from Wanderlust or quest for the Self. I refer to two main problems. One deals with exile, and the other with the medium of expression imposed by circumstances.

In 1991, a seminal book, *The Exile and the Writer* by Bettina L. Knapp brought to the attention of the learned public, and in particular to the community of writers, a phenomenon that, although not unknown in general, had never before been studied in depth and systematically. Professor Knapp examined the impact of exile on writers within history, literature and mythology, after analysing the various types of exile on the basis of a select group of authors in both Western and 'Oriental' cultures. By limiting her analysis to a Jungian approach, Knapp recounted critically the 'Exoteric and

Esoteric Experiences' of several writers who tied their fates to the consequences of being uprooted from their native countries.

The phenomenon is complex, for there are variables of all types involving age, language, political factors, not to speak of religious and psychological constraints. Although Knapp confined her analysis to a small group of 'literary cases', she nevertheless set the course for 'the exile as a fundamental form of the human condition', and, in addition, she was the first to create a paradigm of differences and similarities classifying types, orders and relationships.

According to Knapp, exile may be involuntary or voluntary. History is replete with instances of this dichotomy, from Greek and Roman times (to speak only of Western 'civilisation') to modern cultures. After the generalised presentation of this dichotomy, a new element is introduced: 'exoteric exile' versus 'esoteric exile'. For the former, Knapp gives examples from Greece and Rome down to the Cultural Revolution in Communist China. In all cases, the exoteric exile involved 'a permanent physical departure from the natal land and banishment to areas outside the boundaries of the [home] country.' This was not always so, since during China's Cultural Revolution an individual was forcibly moved, say, from a city to a distant farm or factory where the intellectual or professional exchanged the pen (brush) for a shovel (hoe). The esoteric exile, however, was 'a withdrawal on the part of the individual from the empirical realm and a desire or need to live predominantly in their inner world.' In a more physical sense, this difference is one between the centrifugal and the centripetal.

Even at this point, one can imagine how these variables can occur, whether the exoteric exile can be either voluntary or involuntary, while the esoteric may not be so unless as a consequence of the former, and thus rather marginal. When all these variables are coupled or contrasted with the terms 'extraverted or intraverted', it follows that a complex mosaic emerges within which the concepts of exile 'may be explored with regard to human development only after nomadism gave way to a sedentary mode of life.' Within this mosaic, actually a kaleidoscope showing many mathematical combinations of type of exiles (both as a concept and as expressed by an individual), it is obvious that one can study a large variety of human phenomena in all cultures.

Among all these dissective variables and factors, there is, however, one thing missing: the language factor. It was not Knapp's task to consider the rôle played by a 'creative' language used before and after exile, as a dynamic process, that created a new dimension leading to a non-genetic means of communication, as in the case of Joseph Conrad switching from Polish to English after and during the interaction with other languages such as Ukrainian or French. Here another 'paradigm' could be sketched by bringing into projection the rôle of several idioms in the development of a writer. Thus, the following questions could be asked: as a consequence of exile, whether voluntary or not, did an author continue to write in his 'mother tongue' or did the author start to write in a NEW language, whether by choice or by the force of events? Here, answers may create additional questions regarding the new language used for a literary 'career', for there is quite a difference between whether a writer switches from, say, Polish to English (Conrad), English to French (Samuel Beckett), Russian to English (Vladimir Nabokov), and so forth, whether the writer had written or published anything in the 'mother tongue'. And there is no point in injecting the dimension 'firstness', that is, whether the writer had to start from scratch in a new language environment, as in the case of Conrad.

Thus, this difference is more pronounced when one shifts, say, from Chinese to English (Lin Yu-tang) or from English to Japanese (Isaiah Ben-Dasan). There is no need to make a comprehensive inventory of historical cases as examples of languages caused by exile as a dynamic process. What is more important and relevant in this Preface is the concept of the 'orphan of the mother tongue' with all its psychological, physical and emotional implications. In essence, 'language' is a poor term to express that bundle of painful rejections, adoptions, adjustments and adaptations that an individual has to make or to suffer, whether consciously or not. This is also a function of the age when a person becomes an exile, a critical one being whether it is before or after puberty. That age is a rough dividing line beyond which a physiological and psychological barrier, a 'foreign accent', is kept forever or not, along with 'native' morphosyntactic and idio-cultural vestiges versus the superimposed new cultural structures.

It may be said now that there is a certain correlation between freedom and variation or multiculturalism, if not polyglottism. Lack of freedom, particularly political freedom, accounts too, if not more strongly, for a similar consequence. In practice, a new dimension can be created in the analysis of literature. While, in the past, literature could be observed along historical times, thus creating a history of literature, nowadays, within an ever-increasing period of production, one can sketch a dynamic 'geography' of literature, this being the result of migration of people, and most of them by involuntary exile. The phenomenon can be studied, thus, not only with regard to writers alienated from their own formative cultures, that is, transculturated for whatever reason, but also observed and existing as protagonists or characters within a work of literature whether within either one's own mother tongue or a different language.

Although the concept of 'orphans of the mother tongue' has existed for some time under different designations in various languages, its latest actualisation for writers was historicised by Giorgio Pressburger (himself an orphan of his mother tongue) in *'Scrittori orfani di MADRE LINGUA', Corriere della Sera* (21 November 1996). In it, the author presented just the concept and the basics for the phenomenon with examples taken from Nabokov, Conrad, Beckett, Eugene Ionesco, Italo Svevo and other well known literary figures, though, ironically, not Giovanni Ruffini, the first modern Italian who preferred English in writing several 'Victorian' novels as an exile in Scotland, France and Switzerland. The case of Joseph Brodsky is just the most recent one for an involuntary exile from the Soviet Union in 1972.

More complex cases are listed, such as that of Marino Strombathelyi, who switched from Hungarian to teach Italian literature at the University of Trieste, to Agota Kristof, a Hungarian writing in French. As regards the former, the tradition is long for those academicians or scholars from Bronislaw Malinowski (from Polish to English) to Roman Jacobson (from Russian to English). Academia is replete with similar cases all over the world. Amazingly, the reverse trend in both directions is nearly unknown, except for an exiguous line of teachers or journalists beginning with the Scottish (and semi-Americanised) scholar Lafcadio Hearn (Japanese to English) and the New Zealander Rewi Alley (Chinese to English), just to mention a few extreme cases, though easily recognisable among older *literati*, not to speak of spies such as Kim Philby and Richard Sorge swimming in a bouillabaisse of Hindi, Arabic, Russian or German and Japanese via English. In the USA alone the phenomenon is well known in connection with those émigrés forced to adopt a new language, from Jerzy Kosinski to Vladimir Nabokov. Of course, some *déracinés* like Eric Maria Remarque in the United States continued to write in their mother tongue, as seen even in Israel until fluency allowed them to venture into Sabra Hebrew, quite a feat for most, though not as for others who never had a genetic language continuum floating psychologically or religiously in their mind, until it surfaced as a former repressed dream within a culturally conducive *modus scribendi*.

At times, however, it is amazing to witness parallel phenomena among writers who, although in voluntary exile, keep on writing in their mother tongue. It suffices to remember here Heinrich Böll and Aleksander Solzhenitsyn, born a year apart at the end of World War I, but aeons away from each other culturally. Nevertheless, they were close as literary phenomena in the exploration of their souls, as the former wrote in German and the latter in Russian.

Böll fell in love with Achill Island, Ireland, which he first visited in 1954, a Utopia that perhaps represented physically his innermost view of mankind: bitter flavor, jagged cliffs, wild beaches reflecting the melancholy and rough soul of Ireland itself. In the rather little known 'Irish Diary', Böll opened his soul to the world from the hamlet Dugort accepted by him as his second Vaterland.

Solzhenitsyn, although he first left East for West Germany after the brutal experience of his involuntary exile in Kazakhastan, was only able to reach the USA in 1976, where he continued to write in the wilds of Vermont. It is significant that both writers sought a new refuge away from the city and even the treacherous glamour of university life. Both wrote along parallel lines, analysing the human condition *vis-à-vis* war, freedom, despotism and the struggle to keep sanity in check by continuing to write as a reflection of anguish, undoubtedly a cathartic and unique experience. In their cases, as they had already written in their mother tongues, they kept on doing so in spite of living so close, respectively, to the confines of Irish people in Dugort and Americans in Cavendish.

In Nabokov's experience, his alienation was more complex since he switched from Russian to French and then to English. Similar is the case of Elias Canetti. Unlike Beckett, who refused to write in his mother tongue (English, already superimposed onto Irish) and preferred French for both political and aesthetic reasons, Canetti presents a more complex case. It is futile to attempt a label for his literature, regardless of the language he used. Would he be the psychological product of Austrian culture, Bulgarian life or Sephardic Judaism on his father's side? Do British historians classify him as a British writer for his having lived in England so long, although writing in German? How far can the concept of 'Home' nationality be invoked to classify people on political foundations?

A case in point is Katherine Mansfield, born in New Zealand and raised partly in New Zealand, and in England. As late as 1956, she is listed in the *Encyclopaedia Britannica* as a 'British writer'. No wonder! The few lines dedicated to her in the *EB* are so perfunctory that she seems to appear as a freak in the history of New Zealand literature. One has to read A. O. Orage's *On Love* to understand the psychologically complex life of a woman who stands in Kiwi history like a tower of literary uniqueness, and I doubt that even New Zealanders have ever read the most intimate 'Talks with Katherine Mansfield at Fointainebleau', exuding Mansfield's interplay with English, French and German cultures through her troubled personal life and her peripatetic literary career.

Again, it is futile to make a detailed display of persons coping with the painful task of abandoning a mother tongue to survive in another means of expression. Many a time such people were ridiculed whenever a few minor slips floated along the written syntagm, not to speak of the 'accent' always emerging especially in unguarded moments of relaxation. Even Conrad was regarded as an anomaly. In spite of what Albert J. Guérad, Morton Dauwen Zabel, F. R. Leavis, Robert Penn Warren and others had written about Conrad as a giant in 'English literature', the ex-Polish student of medicine at the University of Kracow, even after the First World War, was not thought of as a novelist, in spite of having published his first novel in 1895, but a 'literary freak since he wrote in a language he had not learned until he was a man.' These words by Quentin Anderson, an admirer of Conrad's, in the Preface to *Lord Jim* indicate his scorn for those who have never learned a foreign language, not to mention writing in it to create great works of literature.

Finally, what should one say of George Tabori or Salman Rushdie? Or of, say, R. R. Narayan and Keri Hulme? Are they British writers because they wrote in English? Well, their literary souls may have been Hungarian, Hindu or Maori. Or does a soul have to be British in order to write in English? Varro spoke of *Homo trilinguis* to designate the humanist able to write in Latin, Greek and Hebrew. Masilius did the same for Greek, Latin, and Gallic. And Ennius, born in ancient Calabria and thus a speaker of Oscan at home and of Greek at school, had to express himself in Latin after Roman imperialists invaded his country. Are these 'Latin' or 'Roman' writers?

Perhaps literature, for the purpose of both *delectare* and *instruere*, has reached a level of 'mass targeting' and a stage of specific aglotticity where it is illogical, or at least superfluous, to attach an adjective of nationality to writers and their work. As the Earth becomes smaller in so many ways, a 'native' language too as a 'genetic' medium is becoming rather irrelevant – witness the incipient 'stenographic' attempt to codify basic e-mail 'language' via upper case signs and punctuation marks of a standard American typewriter. In practice, this list of codes transcends every national language, though it lacks the poetic creativity of the traditional 'uterine' *signifiant*. What counts is its *signifié*, and the resulting *semeion* as a product of the mind and the heart untied to accidental cultural constraints that, one must admit, dominate the mass media, namely 'English', the Latin of the Middle Ages before it fragmented into well-defined 'national' languages. In any case, a writer's place of birth is purely accidental for the physical person until he is freed from it for psychological and other reasons. Witness the 'Italian patriot', Ruffini, who did not hesitate to state, 'Je ne suis guère Italien que de naissance.' The Gabriele Dante Rossetti tradition alone in England had sanctioned that topobiological accident.

Amazingly, with regard to English, two antithetical phenomena have occurred in the history of European literature since Victorian times for political reasons. On the one hand, one might say that this 'self-exiling' tendency of 'genetic' language began with James Joyce's *Ulysses* in Zurich, in which he seemed to have been writing in English mostly as an unconscious habit, though trying to break away from it by injecting into his 'mother' tongue languages such as Italian, Latin, French and others, almost according to a mind register operating at the moment of jotting down his ideas on paper. Indeed, Joyce seems to have been on the verge of departing from 'English', particularly in *Finnegans Wake*, the quintessence of 'quavelism', by handling it nervously, as if tied to it by fate through his fingers while his brain was working languagelessly or within the plurilingual Indo-European framework of his genes. Was Joyce's latent departure from 'only' English a subconscious reaction to having taught it for so long in Trieste? It is relevant to note that, when he was an exile in Trieste, culturally Italian or at least 'Romance', the city was under Austrian political domination. As a matter of fact, even the Baedeker guide of pre-First World War refers tourists visiting the Venetian regions to an Austrian edition in German. That was the period when Thomas Mann was fantasising about polluted water in order to write *Death in Venice* before beginning his exodus all over the West, including the USA. Nevertheless, he always wrote in German.

On the other hand, particularly in the case of a voluntary exile as a sign of political protest, the earliest manifestation of a deliberate act of defiance against 'Fatherland' is witnessed through the life and literary career of Ruffini (20 September 1805–3 November 1881), the very first 'orphan of the mother tongue' in the wake of Rossetti, who fled to Scotland via Malta. Ruffini, who is almost forgotten in Italy, is still studied by contemporary critics as a product of British culture, the latest being Allan Conrad Christensen in *A European Version of Victorian Fiction: The Novels of Giovanni Ruffini* (Amsterdam: Rodopi, 1997).

Thus, the eternal question: when does one become an Italian as distinct from, say, a Greek or a Roman? An answer is difficult, otherwise it is possible to state that Archimedes and Caesar were Italian. Is Ruffini, a unique phenomenon in 'English' literature, though never included in any encyclopaedia such as the *Britannica*, an Italian? He admits to being one only by birth, but his Italy was a nation *in posse*, a nation he dreamed of as one distinct from Piedmont, a French-protected region of mountaineers who had never been heard of in 'Italian' letters and arts until the Savoia family spread out by sheer force all over the peninsula.

Finally, people who remember the classic drama three unities of time, action and place, might wonder about the last one, 'Why the South Pacific?' Who knows, really? Probably, I was in search of Utopia, a place, a habitat still uncontaminated totally by European self-destructive enterprises in the name of colonialism. That is why at the Forbidden City in Beijing I had apologized loudly for the evils brought to China by white people. Analogically, I had read a lot, and in many languages, about the Pacific seas since I was a teenager, from Jules Verne to Emilio Salgari to Robert Louis Stevenson. Joseph Conrad, Jack London, Mark Twain, Frederick O'Brien, Herman Melville and others came later. Did anything 'juvenile' emerge surreptitiously in my childlike soul during the isolation of a sun-baked Arizona ranch surrounded by the Catalinas and the Whetstones ranges, away from the life-giving seas of my memories? Or was it the subconscious *saudade* of my Tyrrhenian wine-coloured waters attracting me toward the presemeiotic dwelling of my soul? Will I ever know anything about the ineffable mystery of being compelled to write? And for whom? Probably mostly for myself, for everything is ephemeral, dispersible along the tides of time, lost forever into the stellar dust of generational irretrievability.

As to the theme, the subject-matter I selected, Maori freedom from oppression, its similarity to the Basque and the descendants of Oscan civilization, as well as to other cultures still enslaved by the vestiges of political colonialism, is very close in spirit. Only details may be different. The human condition once more, in Ao Tea Roa in particular, has detached itself from the European counterpart only in terms of latitude, exactly at its antipodes. When two extremes extend toward each other, the fate of historical recurrence needs no explanation. But, unlike those European ones, Pacific fates are not beyond the boundaries of no return, for they are only a couple of centuries old, too young to be obliterated by aeons of callousness. If the Jews persevered in grasping their freedom in the land of their ancestors after 20 centuries, Maoris and other Polynesians, from Hawaii to Tahiti, will have all the chances to reacquire their *whenua* and dignity in a consortium of intelligent, pacific and industrious human beings.

Never as before after the Waitangi 'Trick' was the Maori movement as alive and vibrant as it is today. What is needed to implement the restitution of Maori faith is an act of contrition through the unselfish cooperation, the intestinal fortitude, the total admission of past wrongs on the part of the non-Pacific world that, as for the Republic of South Africa, hope is not lost. Will the wishy-washy United Nations have the knowledge and the wisdom to take a hard look at its humane conscience, if it has one? Or does one have to wait until the waves of the tsunami departing from the original coasts of Hawaiki disperse themselves along the shores of the Long White Cloud during the 21st century?

M.O.

Introduction

Although the following lines were written when the last volume of 'The Hermit Islands' was first drafted, in terms of exposition providing the background for *The Torn Tiki* alone, they may also be considered as an introduction to the entire trilogy. When this was conceived in the early 1980s, the idea of exploring, and possibly applying, some Jungian views to a pristine, monolithic culture struggling to escape the yoke of a solidly entrenched colonizing organization seemed to appeal to my then-tentative perception of archetypes. Their application to so-called 'primitive' culture in general was still to be verified in the process of analysing rarely studied communities in the wake of the Second World War. Regardless of whether Jung's theories were a *'feu de paille'*, I could not escape their influence on my formation as a writer analysing the human landscape of vanishing cultures.

As I was concerned with the matter at hand only as background for the proper understanding of a people's culture, and not for a specialised study by a professional, my examination of Maori traditions, necessary for the delineation of a 'quavel', proved to be challenging for the entire South Pacific area that had been exposed to traditional psychological interpretations. In a way, it was a matter of picking up the pieces of shattered 'Aboriginal' psyches and trying to re-assemble them to create a new mosaic of functional reality. It would have been too presumptuous, and even absurd, to envision in detail Maori life before it was 'discovered' as an independent and self-sufficient living system on Earth. This attempt at a 'quavelistic' internal reconstruction, nevertheless, was challenging in Ao Tea Roa, also known as New Zealand, for both geographic and accidental reasons that constituted a unique laboratory hosting specimens of ideas, feelings, beliefs and other non-tridimensional entities held as 'sacred' by 'Natives' untamed by white civilization.

For working purposes, it is useful to isolate three main themes permeating the culture of 'The Hermit Islands', namely: the search for a *mana* symbolised by a Father-Figure within a wide range of conceptual visions; the quest to understanding 'Western' love in 'complementary' antithesis with non-intellectualized Polynesian Eros; and the struggle to escape the *tragic* perception of daily life at the 'edge of the Earth'. The element of 'tragedy', however, should be understood in Classical terms, and not in vulgate interpretations of accidental misfortunes as often related by the Fourth Estate in tabloid journalism. Whether Maoris conceived 'tragedy' in Greek terms is beside the point. As specimens of observation by Westerners for the past two centuries, Ao Tea Roans already possessed a cosmic consciousness of their existence in a Universe of unknowns as expressed by their spirals of both Earthly records and galactic patterns. The recollections by Frederick Edward Maning, although subjective, still remain a pristine source of *Old New Zealand*. In 'The Hermit Islands' most characters share all of these near fatalistic tendencies within the social turmoil stemming from political and historical events, though the binding element is clearly 'Wars' as the universal opprobrium to which humans were exposed all over the globe within the 20th century, ironically when in Maori life all armed conflicts had ceased. Therefore, the two faces of a cultural Janus reflected on the minds of cosmically conscious biological entities on Earth – Life and Death, Love and Hate, War and Peace, and so forth – shone also constantly onto the souls of those who had the misfortune of being forced to carry the stone uphill along Sisyphean trails.

In particular, the search for the source of Life, as perhaps encapsulated in the Father-Figure, is the most prominent among those attempts flowing with blood and tears during the existence of sensitive people. This feeling of alienation was caught by a unique woman, namely Dorothea Norman Jones, in her epic-making 'View Point from New Zealand' (in *Money. Food. Drink. and Fashion and Analytic Training: Depth Dimensions of Physical Existence*, ed. John Beebe [Fellbach-Oeffingen: Bonz, 1983]). In just three and one-half pages, she condensed a whole description of a major human behaviour dictated by geography, history and political forces acting inexorably upon the 'prisoners' of The Hermit Islands.

The following paragraphs offer an inkling of a problem to which the inhabitants of Ao Tea Roa, both Maoris and Pakehas, have been conditioned sadly and tragically by the fate of colonialism, although there seems to be a certain hope of redemption from such a state of affairs because of the explosion of instant communication via satellite, from transmission of facsimiles to e-mail and cheaper transport by sea and air:

Jung has said that the land influences the people who live on it.

I spent my first 17 years in New Zealand before I left for 40 years to work in Britain, India and Africa. I have been back for twelve years, and I have been interested in the people who have lived on it for the last 150 years, the period since it was first settled by Europeans.

It is a very austere land, much occupied by mountain ranges and volcanoes in the North, with rocky coasts and the sea never far away.

In Europe I always feel that the land is friendly to human beings and that the mountain villages seem as though they belong. In India I felt the land was actually hostile to human beings and would like to destroy them. In New Zealand I feel the land is quite indifferent to human beings. It is as if the mountains look down on the human life and simply do not notice it. The mountains endure depredations such as the burning off of their forests and consequent erosion and flooding as though they will always be there and human life will pass away.

There is a marvellous 'untouched by man' quality about some of the mountains where man has actually never been. Snow peaks in the South Island with names such as Chaos and Cosmos have this quality.

This character of the land and the extreme isolation of the islands of New Zealand from the rest of the world have had a strange effect on the people. You really feel you are on the edge of the world and may drop off. The recent airplane disaster in Antarctica [28 November 1979], in which a DC–10 on a science flight to the Antarctic crashed on Mt Erebus with the loss of over 250 New Zealanders, English, Americans and Japanese, made that feeling even stronger.

You cannot get further away from the rest of the world. Although air travel is very quick now, and you can be on the other side of the world in 30 hours or so, it is still very expensive. Easy going and coming is only possible for the young who can work their way round the world. The majority of the young do seem to do this in the late teens and twenties. But for the rest of the people a trip away is the ambition of a life time which most can only do when they retire.

And so the whole culture shows the effects of this isolation. Both Europeans and Maoris, who form perhaps more than 10% of the population, have lost their original culture, and the country is in the early and painful stages of evolving a new culture of its own.

New Zealanders of European origin – English, Scottish, Irish and Danish [and some 'Italians' presumably from the Kingdom of the Two Sicilies, as per 'scholarly' observations made by Colleen McCullough in *The Thorn Birds*] – have now lived there for 5 generations, as have some Chinese. In the last 30 years there have been many Dutch settlers and refugees from Europe.

The Europeans who arrived in the early and middle part of the last century, those pioneers who burnt off the forests and broke in the land, seem to have been people well rooted in family life, firmly supported by the culture of the land they came from. But with each succeeding generation, the supporting structure seems to have become weaker and people more rootless, and I think the quality of mothering has progressively declined. The fifth generation has been left very uncertain of who they are.

This may explain the strangely immature state of many of New Zealand's young men of European descent. In spite of being married, they seem to be fixed in an adolescent state. They have time only for rugby or other sport and spend their time drinking with the boys in the pub and are never at home. They do not seem able to mature into responsible husbands and fathers, and so even if the marriage does not break up, lonely wives have to be both mother and father to the children. I have often wondered why so many of the women between 40 and 50 look so masculine, and why maternal looking women in this age group seem so rare.

I asked one or two experienced psychotherapists about this and they said two factors may be responsible:

(1) The economic depression of the late 1920s and early 1930s led to a 'failure of nerve' in many men who found themselves unable to fulfil their expected rôles as successful breadwinner.

(2) The 1939–1945 War effectively removed many men, so that the women had to function as solo parents.

Perhaps as a consequence of these factors, women became managing and masculine looking; their femininity receded. This had a profound effect on the children: the girls found femininity much devalued and the boys remained dependent and immature. One might expect this consequence when the image of a good father is entirely absent from the family, and the mother is a woman whose mothering qualities, if ever there, have been suppressed by the need to act as a controlling father. In turn, the immature men have become absent fathers and the girls who failed to find their femininity have become unmaternal, managing mothers. This does not, of course, apply to the whole population, but is a definite trend.

The Maoris, on the other hand, have lived in New Zealand for six or seven centuries, since their ancestors made the great, three week long journey by canoe from Polynesia, a tremendous feat of navigation, to the land of the Long White Cloud where they settled mainly in the warmer North Island. They were able to retain their tribal structure well until the last thirty years when, for the first time, Maoris began coming into towns and working in mainly unskilled occupations. Though from earliest times there have been distinguished Maori members of Parliament and even Cabinet Ministers and orators.

In the last century there were battles about land. The Maoris have a great reverence for nature. They revere mountains and trees and rivers, and the tradition of good mothering; and the family, being the great concern of Maori women, is traditionally strong. But this family is a very extended family, and the *marae* is a sort of tribal home where all members of the tribe belong and to which they are always welcome to return. There, the Elders are greatly respected. At a family gathering, all sleep on mattresses on the floor of the *marae*, and there is a great feeling of belonging together.

The younger Maoris have suffered a great loss of such roots by leaving the tribal lands and coming into big cities to find work. In the cities they are often lonely and get into trouble with drink and bad company. [The film *Once Were Warriors* gives an overview of the brutal drama about life in the urban Maori ghetto.] Of late years there have been great numbers of unemployed young Maoris and the emergence of gangs and warfare. The Maori Elders themselves are making determined efforts to create urban *maraes*, places in cities where young lost Maoris can feel at home.

As regards the two factors responsible for the New Zealand situation, that is, 'The economic depression' and 'The 1939–1945 War', one should add, however, another one that, unlike having a similar negative impact on Ao Tea Roa, could be considered of positive value, namely, 'The drastic sociopolitical changes attempted in the mid 1980s' during Lange's term as Prime Minister and the ensuing experiments known as Rogernomics. The Socialist 'dress' characterised as State Welfare for generations was being shed in favour of privatisation and other trade and labour restructuring leading to a freer choice running the lives of a people who for so long had believed in a 'Father-Figure' government for lack of an independent, aggressive, 'capitalistic' approach to everyday life.

Of course, every drastic change accomplished as a *coupure épistémologique* implies pains. In fact, agriculture and animal husbandry suffered along with construction, trade and union power. But the crisis was surmounted when New Zealanders realised that their culture was a better one than before by accepting a modicum of biculturalism integrating both Maoris and Pakehas. This realization was felt when the 1975 paper structure of the Waitangi Tribunal became a functional reality in the late 1980s, yielding tangible results in the 1990s, and consequently people began to envisage and accept the possibility that new 'canoes' of co-existence could be held afloat and even navigate with the cooperation of both races for a peaceful and prosperous nation. In fact, Maori representation in the political arena increased to the point that one came to see how discriminatory the continuation of having special seats for Maoris was – the traditional four established a century earlier – rather than for anyone to be elected regardless of regional or tribal constraints.

Again, Dorothea Norman Jones explains the phenomenon along historical lines:

> English people coming out to settle in New Zealand, having been told that it is just like England, feel strange and only then begin to realize how much they have been supported by their own tradition and culture, when it is no longer there. There is more sun, higher wages and life is easier, but so much is missing in the psychic atmosphere. Yet the absence of tradition and the small population (just over three million) would make new ideas about social experiments possible in a way that could never be possible in older countries with larger populations, if any one had any new ideas. Superficially, the culture seems a very materialistic one, unleavened by spiritual influences in the cities and towns. However, in quiet backwaters one finds many individuals who have retreated from this kind of world and who live by very different values.
>
> As the only Jungian analyst in New Zealand, I find that the average New Zealander has deep suspicions about the shadow side of life and denies this side in every possible way. Expressions of anger are unacceptable socially, and what your neighbors think of you very much governs what you do. People are surprised and

bewildered by the outbreaks of violence and gang warfare, and call for more law and order to suppress them.

In fact, New Zealanders of European origin find it very hard to believe that there is an unconscious at all. This is perfectly understandable in view of a past when the settlers were occupied with felling trees and making pasture land and only had time for practical considerations. Even among present day New Zealanders there is a tendency to disparage any kind of intellectual activity. Most of my analytic patients have been people from England, Europe or United States of America or New Zealanders who have lived in these countries. One could say that Jung's description of how man of this age is more and more out of contact with his unconscious is well illustrated in New Zealand.

But in spite of the fact that the Behaviourist school has dominated the teaching of psychology there for a long time, I have lately been delighted to find that young psychiatrists and students of all kinds are, on their own, finding what they seek in Jung's ideas.

To synthesise the characteristics permeating each component of the trilogy, regardless of the sensuality found in each of the three quavels, in the *The Feather Chest* the search for the Father-Figure is dominated by the relationship between Peter Darby, of European descent, and his half-sister, Emere, of both Maori and European stock. One could, thus, label the whole unity of cohesion as 'emotional' or, better, 'emotive', in spite of the fact that Peter tries hard to suppress that normal component of humankind, while Emere fights to manifest it more *Maoro*.

In THE ARK *of Ao Tea Roa*, the interaction between The Pilot and Titiwai, the two Maori protagonists, is more intellectual than anything else. The Pilot is more mature than Peter, perhaps because he was tempered in the African and European theaters of war. The former fatalistically accepts a utopic mission though he knows that THE ARK, as the abbey of Monte Cassino built and rebuilt as a Utopia so many times during 15 centuries of upheavals, will suffer the same fate, when other people will attempt similar Sisyphean tasks.

Unlike the emotivism and the intellectualism permeating, respectively, the preceding two quavels, in *The Torn Tiki*, a surge of spirituality displayed by Mahina may appear at first deceptively baffling among and along lives of extremely disturbing human behaviour, but is later operative enough to take them along divergent paths and definitive isolation from the 'normal' world. Although different in means of pursuit, the spiritual element, departing from a state of confusion and despair, gradually and slowly makes its way toward an epiphany in which total alienation from the functional world, whether symbolic or real, crowns the end as the only solution to Earthly life.

Coal Creek Canyon,
Gilpin County, Colorado, USA
12 November 1997–28 February 1999

Chapter 1

On 29 July 1991, the weather in the extreme south of New Zealand's North Island was at its abnormal zenith of winter meteorological coincidences. The wind was reigning supreme in Wellington, thus, its nickname 'Windington'. A combination of rare atmospheric patterns had developed and settled in the area, where the temperature was barely above freezing. State Highway 1 from Waioru to Taihape and State Highway 49 from Waioru to Ohakune were closed under 15 centimetres of snow. As Komaru Reti rode the bus to Wellington on his four-hour return trip from Wanganui, he saw pellets of hail blowing nearly horizontally against the windows of the Beehive, one of the Capital's governmental buildings. When he got off at the corner of Victoria and Harris Streets, he sensed that the windchill factor must have been below zero centigrade. Once he reached the café in the mezzanine of the public library, Komaru felt psychologically ready to resume his daily research activity after a quick midday 'dinner'. He was rather traditional in his food selection – a bowl of tinned toheroa soup, a sandwich of brown bread with Vegemite and a cuppa.

In spite of the comfortable journey, he felt tired, for he had spent the whole weekend in Wanganui as a house guest of Dr McTavish. His wife, Melissa, had planned to help edit the first draft of a manuscript for a Master's Degree at Victoria University, where Komaru had conceived the idea of delineating the legal attempts made by Maoris in the process of defending their *whenua*. Well, it was a matter of marrying history and jurisprudence. Nearly two centuries of British verbiage were clearly in favour of the Crown, as 'recorded' in the *New Zealand Year-Book*. It was Komaru's ambition to sift through records of a painful past in order to extract the Crown 'legalities' that since 1840 had obfuscated the veracity of Natives' rights.

In Wanganui, the course of events had suddenly shifted from the planned editorial activities to an unexpected development of intimate deeds. During the previous few months, whenever visiting the McTavishes Komaru had detected chemical reactions in the air, though he had dismissed them as stemming from a lack of social companionship ever since he had left Auckland for Wellington. These two cities were different at all levels. While Auckland was the unique center of Polynesian life, Wellington appeared as a cold assembly of bureaucratic buildings pullulating with Pakeha mentality and behaviour. His friendship with the McTavishes helped compensate for being away from familial and familiar surroundings.

On several occasions, ever since Komaru had met the McTavishes at the monthly meetings of the South Pacific Peoples Forum, Melissa seemed to exude a non-Pakeha femininity of extreme sexuality at the threshold of impending menopause. From the few hints given by her husband, a psychiatrist, she had left England after suffering a trauma as a young woman in search of herself, had travelled a lot, and had met her husband in Australia before settling in New Zealand. In recollecting the physical exploits of the last few days, Komaru nearly dozed off at the library desk covered with reference materials. His mind was in turmoil, for he had become Melissa's lover. A blond Pakeha, she was probably old enough to be his mother, but her energy was that of a female in her 20s. And Komaru was only 25.

The whole affair had been brewing in the back of his mind only as a possibility under Melissa's 'European' womanhood made of casual wear, of subtle perfumes, of accidental body contacts, of 'Maori' proximity, and other signs leading to symptoms of a powerful attraction on both sides. Komaru's only dividing screen of 'respect' for an older person, and a Brit at that, was becoming more transparent from day to day, until finally, on Friday evening, it had vanished to reveal an uncontrollable desire pouring from Melissa's electrifying body in instant sexual interaction. For a while, there had been some touch and go situations, which, again, Komaru had wanted to put aside as perhaps manners of behaviour among good friends. A couple of times, on his departing after an evening meal or after attending a lecture, Melissa had hugged him rather tightly. He had felt a pair of small but hard breasts jutting from under her tight blouse. And he had detected an intriguing perfume as if emanating from a wild beast in heat.

On Friday evening, Dr McTavish was not at home. Komaru was told that he had to attend a weekend meeting of some kind in Palmerston North. Thus, rather than having evening tea at home, Melissa suggested eating out. For her, this was a rare occasion, since usually Kiwis don't dine in restaurants. She had stressed that he was to be her guest, for she reminded him that he was a student on a strict budget. He did not resist the invitation. Moreover, Wanganui restaurants did not have Wellington's pretentiousness.

Melissa had given Komaru an option. Would he like to dine at *Michaels* or at the *Cosmopolitan Club*? What was the difference? She explained that *Michaels* featured a modern cuisine with emphasis on New Zealand tastes for the adventurous. The *Cosmopolitan Club* stressed homestyle Kiwi meals. Both, of course, were 'Licenced'. Well, Komaru had never developed a taste for alcoholic beverages. He could tolerate an analcoholic beer from time to time, and that was all. His genes had not yet been superseded by those which, unfortunately, most Maori people in Auckland had adapted themselves to after a few generations of Pakeha blood pollution. Melissa explained also that she and her husband were members of the *Cosmopolitan Club*, where guests were welcome.

Komaru assumed that the *Cosmopolitan Club* would be a safer place to dine, not so much for the rather puzzling turn of events that called for him to escort the wife of an absent male member, as much as for that of being seen by Maori activists at other 'open' restaurants. Wanganui was still a rural, almost backwoods town in comparison with larger and more sophisticated cities, he thought. Yes, of course, Wanganui boasted of a Polytechnic Institute, but this was not Auckland University or even Canterbury University. Thus, he did not feel too hesitant to opt for the *Club*. There was nothing sneaky or suspicious to start with. He was a protégé of the McTavishes, who saw in him a bright human being in excellent physical shape. Nearly a bull-looking individual, he seemed the result of an optimal training in sports, though lately he had resigned from all Pakeha and Maori teams calling for brutal activities. He did not want to risk bodily injuries, for he had planned to spend all his time studying political matters without any interruptions of ephemeral glory on fields of athletic competition. As analysed by Dr McTavish in informal or casual meetings, however, Komaru seemed to betray some characteristics pointing to the consequences of a youthful Attention Deficit Disorder. In spite of a repressed hyperkinesis, however, Komaru tended not to defend himself or even to react whenever something negative was attributed to him. He heard but did not pay attention to criticism, even when this was done fairly. And he hated to decide on anything in the presence of a female.

That is why, when confronted with a selection of food in public places, he would remain indifferent. He knew that at the *Cosmopolitan Club* he could navigate through 'Kiwi' food all right. Except for soul food of Maori tradition, New Zealand had never and probably would never develop a cuisine of its own. Basically, it was a matter of choosing either British victuals or Maori dishes. He would feel hopeless only when confronted with some situations that tried to emulate a European pseudo-sophistication in New Zealand's attempts to become civilized even after all the efforts made by the 'Galloping Gourmet'. Graham Kerr himself knew he had failed in his missionary culinary efforts, and that is why he had directed his work toward a more traditional missionary outlet, that of preparing souls for an eternity of bliss in Christian heavens rather than at table of gourmands. Nevertheless, Komaru made an exception for some Italian food, especially when this was centred around vegetables and seafood. There were many points of similarity with Maori food, but this was so only for Southern Italian dishes. Under no condition would Komaru eat anything 'Northern' Italian, real or fictitious, for he could not stand the sweaty smell of Parmesan cheese. He associated his revulsion with his lactose intolerance, though he explained to himself that it was based on the fact that the Northern Italian dishes to which he had been exposed in Auckland could be anything covered or cooked with Parmesan cheese, since this tended to kill the original taste of the food components, analogically with the French, even though modern refrigeration reduces the need to hide the taste of rotten meat and fish with sauces. Of course, his 'allergy' was totally psychological since cheese contains no lactose. This is rapidly consumed by lactid acid bacteria in the process of fermentation.

Komaru barely remembered what he ate, for he noticed immediately that, as he was the only Maori in the dining room, some people glanced at him in a rather puzzled manner. Was it because he was a Maori or because Mrs McTavish behaved in a rather 'informal' manner? Who was that elegant lady paying so much attention to him? Indeed, Melissa barely touched her mutton pie washed down by one glass after another of undistinguished house wine. Komaru wondered whether she would be able to drive home safely. He had struggled to finish eating a plate of *koura* 'crayfish' accompanied by a watercress salad and a couple of *kumaras*, undoubtedly the essence of soul food, though prepared as a Kiwi one. He had drunk water.

It was a strange dinner, not so much because of the spurious combination of the items selected, as of the amused look of the Pakeha waiter compounded by the fact that Melissa talked throughout the meal as if in a trance. Her wide-open blue eyes seemed to look far away as if lost in a dream. And she asked so many questions about him, his family, his health, his 'romantic' life. Was this affecting his studies? He laughed openly and this puzzled Melissa. But he did not explain anything. Lately, as he was in the midst of an affair with a young Chinese woman, he had no extra time to waste in Romeoing. Thus, for Komaru that approachment by Melissa, for whatever reason she may have had, was hardly an introduction to a weekend session of editorial work. He hoped that perhaps it was her attempt to put him at ease. When he heard that her husband would be away for the weekend, Komaru had expressed a jolt of surprise beyond the casual one, and had looked at her in a different way. She had X-rayed his brown eyes, as if trying to read his mind. He had withstood her penetrating look rather defiantly and had not lowered his glance until she did so first. She knew he had noticed her as a male looks at a female: either a victim or a conqueror. Regardless, Komaru had not anticipated the storm by which he was caught upon arriving at the McTavish residence. He only remembered, after she undressed in front of the fireplace in the rumpus room, that under the heavy silk gown she wore around her belly only a gold chain carrying a small *tiki*. And her *mons*, although shaven closely, betrayed some incipient gray hair.

That Wellington Monday, normally one of recapitulation, of synthesis, of planning, was rather different. The four-hour bus trip from Wanganui had helped him relax somewhat and meditate on the sudden shift of relationship between a man and woman, and in particular between a youth full of vigour and a housewife starving for vulval penetrations.

The traumatic experience, though not unpleasant, had shaken him emotionally, for the world around him had suddenly assumed the face of the unexpected, though vaguely anticipated by subtle signs of possibilities and even probabilities. Nevertheless, he had hoped to outline the structure of his historical essay. The idea had been born upon returning from a year of study at East China Normal University in Shanghai in 1988–89, the academic year that had changed a whole century of brutal interaction among humans.

Among several aspects of Chinese life during that academic year, Komaru had been exposed to a multisecular culture from the didactic to the scientific. As a collateral activity, mostly as a hobby-type of investigation covering even *feng shui* among others, he had acquired an incidental belief in Chinese numerology for the first arabic ten digits including the zero. This number, in antithesis to any tradition to which he had been exposed on elementary Western arithmetic, for the Han was since time immemorial the homonym of efficiency.

Amusingly, it did not jive with the everyday life on the campus of the university. Even water was lacking from time to time for weeks. At the cafeteria, food had to be prepared in a way calling for the minimum use of water that, in an emergency, was substituted by beer. And rice steamed in Tsing Tao tasted like hell. Nevertheless, the evening meetings with Chinese students in the dining hall were always exciting and even amusing, for a Maori in China is often regarded as an African.

In Shanghai it was the number '8' that made people crazed whenever it was displayed on anything, from dormitory rooms to car plates, the very few driven by party officials. Of course, the number '4' was already known to him as a pseudo-*tapu* almost immediately on arriving in China, for it never appeared anywhere of importance. Thus, he understood, for example, why he would climb from the third to the fifth floor of his dormitory, whether there were only four floors, including the ground level, in the Foreign Student Building. The American and the European systems of counting floors still co-existed here and there, only to create confusion in the downtown-buildings along the Bund, particularly in those where old elevators worked from time to time according to the intermittent presence of electricity. Ironically, he had a room on the fourth level, although this was labelled the fifth floor.

In a course on ancient China's traditions Komaru had also learned the psychological value of the number '9'. This was considered as the representative of yang, the masculine and positive principle in nature. For whatever reason, that number was regarded as the equivalent of eternity and auspiciousness. This was baffling to Komaru, if not scary, because in previous tentative studies in the causes and frequencies of wars, that number came up all the time, although during his life so far, the number '9' did not register any significant happening. Perhaps he was not perspicacious enough to recognise the positive value of that last single digit in traditional mathematics, although in classical Chinese architecture the number 9 occurred often in sequential multiples, as, say, '9999', corresponding to the number of rooms in the Forbidden City. When he visited Beijing, he found out, among other things, that the Temple of Heaven measures nine *zhang* in diameter. Finally, among the various figures involving '9', very often its multiples displayed the signifier whose signified was a sign of luck. In fact, according to the *Book of Changes* (*I Ching*), '9 × 5' means 'dragon in the sky', which is a lucky sign *par excellence*.

The list containing the mythology of '9' is long, including the number of women an emperor was entitled to in multiples – 9 concubines, 27 servers, 81 maidens, and so forth. He wondered how an emperor could cope with all those females, particularly concubines, and when in Beijing Komaru laughed at a situation dominated by just one single concubine, which he translated mentally into a 'mistress' *more Britannico*, or *amoureuse more gallico*. The concept and its actualization in Ao Tea Roa, of course, were not new. Maori men had always shared part of their adult life with more than one 'espouse' without ascribing a complex relationship calling for specific social labels.

Naturally, that custom was a normal 'affair' in precolonial times. Although the social ménage continues, particularly in rural areas, it did not cause any painful dysfunction as this was also considered a Pakeha import associated with the best expression of literature such as novels, dramas, poetry and the like. Even opera, whether soap via TV or more sanctified like those Italianate concoctions on the stage, was highly accepted and enjoyed vicariously as fiction for lack of European sophistication. Royalty, affluent people, celebrities and others of similar privileged position apparently were destined to deal with concubinage as a matter of fact. That is why, although unmarried, Komaru wondered what Melissa's rôle could be in his immediate life, if any. She was only a '1', and that had already begun to affect his concentration on delineating the essay concerning Maori life in the 20th century, the most destructive time sequence in European as well as in Maori life. The difference was that Europeans, and the British in particular, had survived at a great loss and had even obtained benefits from conflicts. Maoris, on the contrary, had barely survived without any apparent improvements to their original claims, although the extablishment of the Waitangi Tribunal in 1975 began to act as a palliative for Maori and Pakeha race relations. In spite of wishful thinking, Maoris were still colonials. All visible and marginal changes were simply cosmetic. The soul of Maoritanga was as oppressed as before.

That afternoon in Wellington vanished slowly between vagaries going back to Melissa and thoughts emerging in numerology for a compact synthesis of historical events. By late afternoon, and rather accidentally, he had summarised segments of political feats by being almost forced to select only three main points out of 'nine' emerging as a magical number. Thus, he decided to adopt '9' with the intention of later expanding those historical stations three times as a function of beginning and end. But how to label those two extreme points? After all, they were connected with biological entities since, whatever the events taking place within those parameters, humans were always responsible for everything. All conflicts are born in the minds and the hearts of biodegradable and finite Terrestrials, from the most inconsequential feelings of incipient fear to global wars. Thus, Komaru named those two stations as a function of Birth and Death, perhaps the most frequent words occurring in the lexicon of Mankind. Even by assigning one of the terms to each biologically conscious entity just once and multiplying it by each mind and body ever existing on Earth, the resulting figures went into the zillions. Being selfish, he did not include non-human entities because he assumed that, say, paramecia do not think in terms of beginning and end. But what about snakes? Well, there were no snakes in Ao Tea Roa. Perhaps he could include sheep. But, then, no computer on Earth could calculate word frequency on the basis of past non-human animals gone forever. Besides, how could he include *moa, kuri* and 'Moriori'? He dismissed plants, for they don't think. Or do they? Obviously, being prodded by his own conviction, and that of five billion followers believing in him, that he could think and calculate, he briefly noted certain phenomena as puzzling as an ideological calendar contained between the end of the First World War and the Tiananmen Square episode of 'misunderstanding' that had avoided, for half a century, a Third World War.

By discarding 1909 as a non-relevant year on the international scene, although the seeds of long-range Yugoslavian anarchy had already been planted by the Austrians to germinate 90 years later, Komaru assigned 1919 as the first step in the short ladder leading to unique phenomena that changed Earth and the Solar System forever. To contain his analysis on the basis of a short list of components, he avoided a dyadic platform of operation since this could be misinterpreted as a naturally antithetical formation. He also dismissed a tetradic structure of departure leading to a Chinese conceived unlucky situation. Consequently, he settled on the first step of 'world' history, mostly European, as follows:

1919 –   Birth of the Comintern
          Birth of the League of Nations
          Birth of Fascism

For Komaru, the main evils of 20th century historical events could be expressed at the incipient stage of that triad. The fact that 'world' history was synonymous with European chronicles could not be a mere coincidence, as the First World War was over, and the League of Nations was rather optimistic. President Woodrow Wilson, the American new face on the block of power play, had in fact said on Valentine's Day: 'A living thing is born, and we must see to it what clothes we put on it.' Well, Wilson's child must have been born with an Attention Deficit Disorder, for that child did not pay attention to the fact that three weeks later Vladimir Ilyich Lenin created in Moscow a Communist organisation via the Third International, or Comintern, a structure destined to change the world during the life span of a European human. Seventy years? Two weeks later, Benito Mussolini created the *Fasci di Combattimento*, basically Fascism in antithesis to the Comintern. Ironically and surreptitiously, within a few weeks a triad of oppositional organisations had already germinated to create chaos. Indeed, there were some voices already crying in the wilderness of decrepit Europe. One was screaming in the very heart of Germany, where Oswald Spengler had just published the first volume of *Der Untergang des Abenblandes*. That work, by the now almost forgotten prophet of doom for the Pakehas of Western civilization, was for Komaru like a modern Nostradamus anticipating the passing of white callousness to be followed by the birth of a new civilization, that is, Maoridom. Oh, Komaru thought, how could Europeans believe in those organizations leading to potential world disorder? Yes, New Zealand *had* to believe. The horror of Gallipoli was still fresh in the memories of every family, and in England the anguish of doom began with the Battle of the Somme, where 58,000 soldiers had been killed on its very first day. That was the equivalent of the entire Maori population of the time. Later, the losses suffered in one single day in August 1945 in Japan would be minnows in comparison with the losses experienced by all the fighting powers on a single day on the Somme.

But Komaru did not forget what was happening in countries where idealists were fighting for other causes. Indeed, a few weeks after Mussolini created the *Fasci di Combattimento*, Emiliano Zapata, one of Komaru's private heroes, was killed by the forces of oppression in Mexico. To him, Zapata was not a 'rebel', but a patriot just like those who, 70 years later, continue to fight for justice in Chiapas, as described by Cecilia Rodrigues, US Representative of the Zapatista Army of National Liberation.

Before darkness set in during that winter day, Komaru left the Parliamentary Library after deciding not to stop at the Alexander

Turnbull Library to verify some data. The weather was not conducive to peak performance analysis. He attributed his physical condition to the sexual marathon in which Melissa had engaged him from Friday evening to Monday morning. Besides, after sketching the first historical station as a function of 'Birth' and 'Death' of historical events, his thoughts turned to the meaning of those two physiological labels containing between them something called 'Life', the most intangible, if not absurd, segment of biologically programmed 'envelopment'. By the time he left the bus stop at the corner of Courtenay Place and Cambridge Terraces, a wild idea suddenly occurred to him. It dealt with Birth, thus Life, and Death as End of whatever constituted a segment of Time. These synchronic points were connected with Time along which he had structured the whole 20th century: 1919, 1929, 1939, ... 1989. He did not want to speculate in terms of 1999. At that time, he did not discard the possibility that, meanwhile, another 'world' war could develop intentionally on the part of sick people or just by accident. Actually, there was no need to even use the term 'world', for a war nowadays covers the entire planet immediately with the help of scientists who are conferred a Nobel Prize to wage war and later another prize for 'peace'-fying it. Everything was so logical that Komaru blamed the brain for having developed itself as an instrument of destruction.

He had attended a lecture given by Christopher Willis, who maintained that the human brain was completely different from that of any other animal. Komaru had laughed at that statement by remembering the comment made by the bishop's wife when in London she had attended a lecture by Charles Darwin on humans descending from the apes – 'Let's keep it a secret'! What a discovery! Had the brain been not 'astonishingly different', then were humans supposed to be closer to which other animals? To sheep or pigs? In either case, New Zealand was an ideal country for both Pakeha and Maori.

Amazingly, a long evolutionary step supposed to have started billions of years BP had resulted in creating the only brain housed in *Homo belligerens*. This brain, to compensate for its chip on the shoulder in being smaller than that of other animals, had 'evolved' to use its structure in terms of the most complex function: War.

Even microbiology, through an examination of cytoskeletons and microtubles, substructures hiding throughout their cell cytoplasm, had failed to explain the brain's inability consciously to account for its own lack of consciousness. Komaru thought that this was at the very root of war since the era of dinosaurs, who were extinguished not by natural upheavals but by fighting among themselves in spite of possessing a complex and 'intelligent' brain. Humans were next in line for 'fighting' survival. So many billions of years to find out that the brain was an 'end' in itself! Komaru hoped that no one would hear his conclusion, for he could be taken to Wai O Hine, the only mental facility still operating within a prison at nearby Lake Alice, for psychiatric observation. Nevertheless, he was convinced that the brain was so selfish that it had invented the concept of the 'mind' to fool itself and every human ever to appear on Earth.

By the time he entered his flat, the most illogical thought assaulted him. The brain had dumped its responsibility onto his mind and created a reflection of a prosaic question asked often by any human being trying to extend its terrestrial existence into eternity: Is there Life after Death? But, he asked himself, Why another Life, Life No. 2? Was one not enough? And would this Life end again like Life No. 1? Who wants to go through another traumatic experience? Well, anyway, the question was not a new one for Pakehas. They had the right to fool themselves any time. There was no problem among Maoris, since the cessation of biological activities among them never presented any difficulty. Maoris would enter their Rangi where they would meet all those who had sojourned on Earth before. The problem existed among Pakehas, as well as those who believed in not only one after-Life, but also many lives through reincarnation and the like. Everything was logical, possible, intriguing when the issue was studied in terms of all the religions, of all the philosophical systems, and whatever humans concocted to fool themselves. From philosophers to psychiatrists to *tohunga*, there was nothing new. These people fooled paying listeners in order not to fool themselves.

Suddenly, however, his brain switched a neuron in a different way, and, thus, he asked himself something frightening, namely, Is there Death after Life? But, of course! The 'evidence' was unassailable. Only a fool would question that. But the question was not related to the normal assurance of a biological phenomenon. The very fact that the question could be formulated posed an intriguing problem. It was something puzzling on the basis of definitions, for Death implies the cessation of Life. Then, again, why another Life, a second one? Rather baffling. Why should one acquire a Life, give it up at a certain time, and then re-acquire it for whatever reason?

Komaru was simply confused, to say the least. Why would he think of Death that, in his triadic examination of history, represented just the end of a period, whether real or fictitious? Nevertheless, he was sensing Death, he reasoned, merely as a reflection of an artificial segmentation for an historical essay. Thus, he tried to dismiss the whole sixth sense feeling of the impending as simply a product of his tired imagination.

At his flat, however, the question began to obsess him again. Is there Death *after* Life? This was different from a similar question, Is there Death *during* Life? Or, is there Death at whatever end of Life? He tried to define both Life and Death, after dismissing the other subquestion, Is this Life I am living now No. 1 or some previous number? Have I ever experienced a previous Death before acquiring this Life? On the basis of his definitions, which he kept to himself, he was convinced that Death does not exist in any form related to a temporal or biological point, for only Life could exist or could not exist at all. Along that line of 'reasoning', the whole cosmos was always full of 'Lives', or, better, entities, whether spiritual or abstract, existed *in posse* until they become *in esse* wherever biologically possible in certain surroundings, as on Planet Earth or any other cosmic locality permitting a substantiation called Life.

Consequently, for Komaru, Life never ceases since it is always somewhere waiting in the wings to express itself as a work of art, of faith, or simply an accident like rape or a social incident like marriage or whatever encounters of sperms and ova are called in different cultures. It is an accident that humans are regarded as the carriers of Life under certain conditions, from a home to a laboratory. As a matter of fact, certain entities are never 'born' on Earth, though they have a 'Life' somewhere orbiting in a 'holding corral' even before a foetus is actualised.

Komaru concluded that the question, Is there Death after Life?, does not make any sense, for the simple reason that Death has never existed as an independent entity, does not exist anywhere, and will never exist as a tree, a rock, or a star does. It could not exist even as a concept because it would be the consequence of an organism tied to Life. The two terminals excluded each other, even though one of them, namely Life, could exist at any time somewhere for an indefinite time. And when Life existed in any possible way, from the chemical to the dogmatic to the philosophical, it was nothing else than a state of mind and, thus, illogical. In fact, a stillborn child by any medium is spared the traumatic experience of going through a materialised 'Life' on Earth. Why not leave it wherever it has always been 'alive' without being imposed on an absurd stage called Death? Does a foetus *in posse* ever have a chance of deciding for itself in advance whether it is an advantage to savour the pleasures and the torments of a Terrestrial existence? In essence, for Komaru the very concept of Death, coinciding with his Maori upbringing and personal reflections about his existing on Earth, was an invention of those biological entities who are unable to conceive the fact that for a while their human components are assembled and then recycled during a journey called Life regardless of Death, since this does not exist *per se*, to the contrary of Life, which can be tangible in different forms along a continuum of eternity. And he wondered how many people before him had thought the same way. Of course, Sigmund Freud was a parvenu by saying that 'the aim of all life is death'. Before him, John Keats had written to Fanny Browne, 'I have two luxuries to brood over in my walk, your loveliness and the hour of my death'. From Greek and Roman thinkers to Renaissance and modern philosophers, the list of thanatologists is so long that even Schopenhauer is but a speck in a rosary of *angst*.

Komaru was baffled by this sudden discovery nevertheless. And bothered, too, for it sounded like some kind of cheap missionary preaching by the various religious organisations hitting Ao Tea Roa since pre-Waitangi days. How could he, the self-styled 'guerrilla' of the 21st century, accept such nonsense? How could he discard whatever permeated everyday Life via a most frequent event called Death, from obituary notices to accident reports of all types, or even suicides afflicting especially the youth of Ao Tea Roa? He must have been wrong somewhere, for he also remembered that he had placed humans at the centre of the Universe. More than that, he had connected Life only with humans. He felt ashamed of himself, for he had not included animals, plants, chemicals, minerals and a host of things subject to a process of beginning and ending, be these called Birth and Death, with Life between them. Why not the ...

He was happy the telephone interrupted his thinking. He had time, however, to consider all his theoretical suppositions as a bunch of stupidities. Life, as Death, was more complex than anything he had just considered as a matter of intellectual speculation. Could it be Melissa? Perhaps he should have called her first and just say hello. No, of course, not thank her for a 'pleasurable' weekend. He felt ambivalent to the whole thing, for he had never entered the vagina of a white woman. Different feelings, subtle fragrances, tactile reactions, smooth encounters of sliding tissues, variable temperatures surfacing in never conceived before locations revealing themselves as erogenous zones emerged clearly during enhanced performances. Or was it all in his mind? No, of course, for Melissa was a revelation at all possible levels of interaction. She knew exactly every physical and physiological part of him, as if she had already analysed him as probably only her husband, a doctor in internal medicine first and then a psychiatrist, could do. So, in just one weekend, Komaru had experienced the sensations of a theoretical lifetime. Or were they a copycat of a Previous Life?

Chapter 2

The telephone call had come from Wanganui. Melissa was on the line. Her voice, barely audible, sounded like that of a person who had just woken up from a deep sleep, though the clock by the phone stand showed only 21:00. And her voice betrayed a hesitant rhythm of mellifluous cadences between hoarse grunts, as if she were trying to clear her throat of clinkers of satisfaction, and petulant hints at renewals through smacking her lips as if she hungered for his kisses.

During a single weekend, Komaru had first undergone an intensive course in 'Frenchy' osculation. As a Maori youth, he had desultorily tried to alternate *hongi* adherences with labial licking and rubbing, but the nasal reaction to his affective manifestations always took a place of priority and prominence in his gratification from epidermic contacts as a foreplay to other stimulating enterprises. After all, the *hongi* was deeply ingrained in his genetic system, while European kisses were Johnny-come-latelies introduced by the wives of missionaries, along with other techniques of arousal a few generations past.

It was his encounter with the Chinese girl, Ling-ling, that made Komaru aware of something definitely an export from West into East. When he tried on her something he would not do with Maori girls, that is a kiss as per what he had heard or read about, Ling-ling recoilled particularly at the idea of having a non-normal appendage, like a tongue, introduced into her body. No French kiss, no matter what. Although in China she had been exposed to some basic experiences in amatory enterprises by a couple of boyfriends, she did not know anything about 'dual' kissing. She allowed Komaru to place his lips on hers, *bucca clausa*, with the intention of further explorations Komaru had never tried before, but Ling-ling did not react invitingly. She actually felt a certain tickling of disgust, in spite of not being a *tabula rasa*. Since she had been introduced only to genital connections, she could not understand Komaru's fixation for other sources of arousal. She even suggested to him, with great modesty, first to touch her feet, then caress them with his fingers before engaging in lingual promenades even under her soles. This made her go into a delirium and a series of orgasms, as when she even placed herself in a position for a tighter spot, a ritual that Maori warriors performed with the children of enemies defeated in battle. And she was so tiring! That was like the customary brandy at the end of a heavy meal. Apparently, the pressure of Komaru's tip onto the frontal parietal area at the bottom of her vagina was extremely pleasurable.

But no, no kisses calling for a surrogate introduction of a tongue into her mouth or, worse, hers into his or whatever! And, of course, he did not dare to try on her fellatio, and neither cunnilingus in her. But the reason for the latter was not 'cannibalistic'. It was purely 'hydraulic' and olfactory for, when Ling-ling reached a pan-orgasm, she discharged at least a decilitre of 'vaginal' fluid covering Komaru's pubic area with a shower of an acrid and viscid emission. She told him that she was a Manchu, a Chang like the defunct American puppet in Taiwan, and not a Han. Undoubtedly, Komaru concluded, Southern Asian females, like Maoris, did not dispense such a generous portion of clarified butter. That was a prerogative for men. Komaru's discharges, as he was told later by Melissa, were special since, rather than being a jet of fluid like a syringe's, they were dispensed as a series of soft pellets that made her scream after ingesting them avidly as if gulping sterlet caviar eggs one by one from a silver spoon. She, however, smacked her lips soon after. Melissa and Ling-ling at least had something in common, though through different orifices.

The more traditional and exciting 'kiss' a Chinese man would perform on a woman, and nowadays even on another man, was a type of *hongi*, that is, a monorhinal affair calling for a man to press his nose on any of the two female facial cheeks while the nostrils inhaled the female fragrances of soft epidermis, real or imaginary. During this process, the man usually lowered his eyes as if savouring an appetising dish and, in fact, at the end of the Chinese '*hongi*', undoubtedly a Northern Hemisphere phenomenon, from the Eskimos to the American Indian, he smacked his lips as a sign of appreciation. This last act signalled the end of the rhino-facial intercourse in a sonorous manner, not dissimilar from what a diner does sucking the last drop of watermelon soup signifying the end of a Chinese supper.

In collating Ling-ling's, instructions with Melissa's performance, Komaru thought of the Japanese, and the 'egg exchange' illustrated in the film *Tampopo* came to his mind, a parody of the *tapu* kiss in public. The Japanese, with a quintessence of refinement in their amatory culture, had reached a compromise to fool the movie censors. The two actors never touch each other's lips. The Western rôle of the tongue was performed by the raw egg, a rather dangerous affair in case one of the two lovers had gingivitis or, worse, a periodontal infection with loss of blood. Would it carry the possibility for an HIV transmission? Komaru laughed in remembering the question once posed by Dr McTavish when he casually told him how healthy his teeth looked. Was he fishing for information on the status of his health to protect his wife and, thus, himself?

But the thing that intrigued Komaru was the result of his quick comparative analysis of the oscular transaction. He concluded that the kiss was definitely Western, even if detected in recent Maori traditions. Pakeha missionaries, Catholic in particular, and these were French like Pompallier since pre-Waitangi days, reflected onto their pagans some characteristics of the daily cannibalistic ritual of the Mass. And Maoris felt at home. Maori navigators had left the Southern Easter shores of Asia millennia ago, and there was definitely a genetic memory surfacing in human interactions regarding eroticism, and thus sex. The mouth was for speaking, breathing and eating. Oh, and drinking, of course. Komaru's ancestors did use their lips in conjunction with teeth to eat and drink, though particularly to suck the warm blood from the *vena cava* of enemies killed in combat. Thus, French kissing was basically an antipasto to cannibalism. Indeed, at times Komaru, being taught to savour Melissa's saliva and feel the thousands of lingual gustatory glands as deep as the back palate, had bouts of atavistic fear. Was she planning to eat him?

Melissa was simply superb. In a few days of patient teaching, she had applied all her knowledge in order to collate her thin and sensitive lips with Komaru's full-bodied and hot mouth. At first, Komaru had not understood the rôle of labial activities as a prelude to anything else manifested by Melissa. Only later during the weekend was Komaru instructed about the proper coordination and synchronization of other components in the oscular process, since this involved the teeth, the tongue and the palate, as well as the type of contact calling for suction, licking, biting and a host of refined *minutiae* that, yes, he could recall but not describe even to himself.

He just wondered. The very first lessons were confined to the external buccal area before they were applied to the internal one, where Komaru had to try the mutual adherence of tongues, first in static amplexes and then later in sliding, twisting and embracing fashion. When the whole sequence of variations called for sucking each other's tongues, the resulting effect was for him a revelation of total stupefaction. And to think that the operation took place only within his head, the most sacred part of his body. Indeed, in the beginning, when Melissa started to caress, then cup, and finally hold his head with both hands, at first he reacted as disgusted and violated in his very *tapu* of a unique persona. But then, after resigning to the aggression by a female in heat, he just went along a network of pristine sensations. Oh, Europeans were simply decadent, he thought. And, for whatever reasons, the face of his sister flashed onto the blinding screen of his subconscious. He wondered whether she had been exposed to American refinements of that sort. After all, Americans were European imports. As a college student in Portland, Oregon, had she acquired trans-Atlantic manners of European stock, or was she still a Maori girl educated at the Auckland Girls School under the dictatorial guidance of a prissy Mistress? Had Hollywood moved that far north, to the campus of the Transpacific University?

Strange, he reflected. In a way, Melissa was a missionary of a sort, imparting new mores to indigenous heathens. And in recollecting her lean body at work in the kitchen or at play in the bedroom, Komaru went over some of the verbal barrage of questions with which Melissa assaulted him in the heart of Maoritanga. In reply, he even felt bold enough to ask her a few things of his own, one being about her rather exotic name. Unusual, he had told her. And she replied that *Wanganui* too was unusual. For whom? Her name for him, and the name of the city for her. When Komaru told her that both names were 'foreign' in his stock of traditional Maori lexicology, he gave her an immediate explanation about his name. Well, that was simple. In Polynesian, Komaru meant 'Sun', yes, a source of light and warmth. In Ao Tea Roa, basically a cold country in comparison with the original place of departure for his *iwi* many centuries ago, his name had been chosen by his father almost as a liaison with his ancestral *whenua*. It was a long story along the recounting of his *whakapapa*, and he promised that one day he would tell her more about himself and his family. For the time being, *Wanganui* and *Melissa* were to be analysed first, the former for her sake, and the latter for his own.

He knew that in his culture every name was tied to a fate of some kind. And the two names were undoubtedly foreign, smack in the heart of Maoritanga. In fact, during the afternoon of the R and R Monday, while he tried to concentrate on his research work, both the 'weekend' city and its female inhabitant recurred a few times in connection with their pronunciation and meaning. There was nothing Maori in them, not even for Wanganui that, at first glance, in print or when reaching the careless listener, would evoke a Polynesian significance. It was merely a phoney Pakeha invention. He told her, during the short pause he was allowed to rest in bed or at the dining table, that the present 'Wanganui' designation is one of the results of early phonetic transcriptions made by explorers, missionaries, traders and the like. Komaru always felt and 'heard' that name as 'Whanganui', that is, the dyad of *whanga*, 'large' or 'long', 'wide', etc. and *nui*, 'river'. He knew the history for the corruption of the name yielding at the same time Wanganui for the city and Whanganui for its river flowing into the Tasman Sea of North Island.

There was nothing new in Ao Tea Roa in connection with the existence of false doublets affecting the toponomastic of indigenous traditions. Ao Tea Roa seemed particularly susceptible to hosting a large platform of schizzy situations in people, animals, plants and things. For Komaru, every schizophrenic appearance on maps and documents was the result of political issues. It sufficed to take a look at early records showing *h*-less names that were imposed on 'natives' by publications such as *An Encyclopaedia of New Zealand* and *Bateman's New Zealand Encyclopaedia*. Additionally, there were two corollary and complementary items connected with those transcriptions. One reflected the ironic situation that near the *h*-less Wanganui City there was, and is, another river spelled with the -*h*-, namely, Whangaeku, as its riparian town also written Whangaeku. The other item was that the '*h*' is not an isolated sound *per se* in some 'dialectal' variations, as in Cockney, whether with or without the *h*-sound. In Polynesia, the 'wh' is a digraph representing a single sound, not a sequence of two. Melissa became bored with Komaru's explanation, but he insisted on continuing. And she listened by gluing her palpitating body to his recuperating one. He even went to the bathroom to rest a while and to gain time before another marathonic jujitsu. Unfortunately, he nearly froze to death in that British lavatory. Why in the world do English people keep their inner sanctum so frigid? To save on the heating bill or to limit their stay there strictly to the essential? Was it the consequence of a Victorian tradition?

Upon returning from the toilet, he began to lecture, and this time he looked for comfort near her supple body, where her belly radiated an anticipatory invitation beyond skin contact. The Whanganui–Wanganui variation, an important issue in Komaru's psyche, was not unique in history and geography. It started with the unawareness of the original shape for land colonized by the Maori – was their new *whenua* two islands, three islands, or how many? Of course, Maoris had never had any problem in identifying and labelling each of them.

But Pakehas, after a series of tentative classifications, first settled on three: North, Middle and South, before finally accepting and still using a North Island and South Island of colonial New Zealand by relegating tiny Stewart Island to the rôle of a dot among the total of at least a dozen 'political' islands, not counting others of uncertain 'dependency' and 'protectorate' status.

In Komaru's way of explaining dysfunctions for tagging physical entities peppering the Pacific Ocean, he accepted the double standards imposed on Wanganui for the city and Whanganui for its River, the near-by National Park, the Whanganui-Rangitikei, and other features. It was not a phenomenon present only in North Island, for in South Island there is also a Wanganui (var. Whanganui) River about 40 miles south of Hekitika. One is thus mystified by the fact that the memory of Jock McKenzie, a sheep rustler, is immortalized via Mackenzie Country, but Mt Mackenzie in Fiordland owes its label to Sir Thomas Mackenzie. Between the two Pakeha 'pioneers', the confusion of spelling and geographic designation is one more phenomenon characterising the mental status of the Hermit Islands inhabitants: each individual life runs on two tracks, not necessarily parallel to each other.

But Komaru had no problem with the Maori language. He knew that a hypothetical *'wanga'* did not, could not, exist in Polynesia. Besides, the ancient history of Whanganui was unambiguous among Maori. Known originally as Petre, after Lord Petre, one of the directors of the New Zealand Company, it was established in 1840, the same year the Trick of Waitangi had been performed by 'governor' Hobson. By 1848, its population was 156. In this number one should include *mirabile dictu*, a group of Italians that had been parachuted in the area to introduce the *Pedinculus humanus* var. *mediterraneus* as described in *The Thorn Birds*. The original *Pedinculus humanus* var. *polynensis* had already been exterminated by the Maoris even before the *moa* as a source of protein along with the bat and the *kuri*. It was a necessary enterprise since the missionaries were slowly succeeding in imposing a Christian *tapu* on human flesh. The 'Italian' variety released, upon squashing it between dentals or molars, a new flavour recalling *olio di oliva extra vérgine* that seemed to appeal to Maori taste. As a new source of protein, the imported variety became the perfect antipasto for a *hangi* party.

Thus, Wanganui is still known originally for three things: the introduction of lice by Italian settlers shanghaied by the New Zealand Company from Strómboli (although Garibaldi had not yet invaded the

Kingdom of the Two Sicilies, and thus there was no political Italy yet); the duality of its name in the phoney attempt to accept Hobson's statement: 'We [British] are one people'; and an exporting centre of Maori mummified heads to a museum in Florence, Italy, as a *quid pro quo* for allowing 'Italians' to cultivate the *pedinculus* on behalf of the Maoris. Amazingly, the Pakeha dealer in Maori heads, Joe Rowe, underwent the Scottish Maiden syndrome, for his own head was chopped off, mummified and kept by Wanganui area Maoris. Pakehas had not yet nearly understood the powerful retribution of *utu*.

That evening, just before receiving the telephone call from Melissa, Komaru recollected episodes of the encounter with her. He simply could not believe that a 50-year-old female (or was she younger?) could release and employ so much energy and skill in sexual enterprises. Was she taking oestrogen or anything else dispensed by her doctor–husband? Of course, he was thinking 'Maori', for at 50 a *wahine* is usually obese, toothless, morose and satisfied with daily tasks involving household activities. Melissa was an unchained fury from the very beginning. She exuded waves upon waves of magnetic attraction. Between pauses calling for washing herself, eating and lying in bed spread-eagled as in Leonardo's *Homo-metron*, she just talked and drank Cardhu. This was an expensive item in Ao Tea Roa but she believed in that Scotch concoction. She said that the bottle itself represented an erotic image or her receptive personality by displaying four ovals, one on every side, one per each possibility of welcoming a *phallus paratus*. And Komaru was happy not to venture into that metaphoric glassy partition, for Melissa's orifices were, to the contrary, moist anytime either by saliva, Bartholin's glandular secretions or Hong Kong ointments that allowed, depending on each of the four localities, a rather easy access after the initial hurried fumbling in positioning complementary organs. Only the navel had remained perforce unpatented.

Melissa was indefatigable, petulant, but superb. When Komaru assumed that a truce was in order on the basis of his wrongly assumed recent prowess, Melissa would casually and then intentionally manipulate him delicately, then more forcefully, and finally more wildly, until he responded unconsciously to her demands of drawing blood to the veins of his appendage. She would begin with her fingers by shaping them into a sugar cube pincer. Then the palm of her hand would massage his scrotal area, to which he would respond nearly instantly. Next she would switch to her semi-open lips by blowing puffs of hot breath. The opening of her mouth would allow first a touch and then probing with her delicate lingual tip before finally allowing the whole tongue to swish any engulfable part of his lower body, switching from sphere to cylinder and from sensitive areas to protuberant bones around the inguinal area before ending at his toes – and starting again backward. Did she assume he felt pleasures as a Chinese woman does?

And she talked, and drank, and talked. She would explain why she liked single malt spirits. Apparently, Cardhu took a few minutes – and she first stood in awe in front of the bottle holding it like an infant on her bosom before removing the cap as if praying before the sacrifice – to reach her ovaries which became inflamed with passion, and consequently they could be hypothetically soothed only by some powerful jets of hot semen. Of course, everything was psychological. Komaru wondered if really she could feel the wetness of him, and even the temperature if any, but did not dare to ask. In Melissa's imagination, no other liquid could do that trick, not even a vaginal douche of barley water as recommended by the third edition of the *Encyclopaedia Britannica* (1767), as her husband had told her. She informed Komaru that a century later Victorian women wasted a lot of barley in futile concoctions. For her, barley had only one function – that of being used in the distillation of Cardhu in Knockando, Aberlour, Banffshire AB38 7RY, Scotland, UK. She even remembered the road leading to Knockando: the B9102. Amusingly, the first Cardhu distillery was established in 1824 when John Cumming was first 'licensed', and she coupled often the Freudian *Knock* and *Cum*ming soon after releasing her multiple seizures by screaming to high hell, for in both Knockando and Cumming she saw psychoanalytic reflections, particularly by remembering her Latin gerund in *-ando*, which she pronounced by 'rhyming' it with tango.

Well, Komaru had studied Latin and Greek, and she told him she had done that, too. Then Melissa elaborated on her preposterous tango 'rhyming', because, she explained, except for mango, the tango, after a few Cardhu shots, was the perfect preface to further introductions. She said she would try a cocktail of Cardhu with mango juice. Of course, Komaru reflected, she must be drunk. He had never heard of that brand name and neither had he danced that rhythm. He could not understand anything European behind a Maori *waiata* after an analcoholic beer or two.

'European?' he had asked. 'I thought it was Argentinean.'

'Well, yes and no, for the tango was born in Italy and then exported to South America before World War I.'

And, remembering her school Latin, she explained that *tango* was the first person singular of the present indicative of *tangere*, 'to touch'. So, 'I touch' became the first free body dance to break all the barriers of previous European ballroom dance by allowing two bodies to touch each other as if glued by the poetic and sensual rhythm of that transfusion of music. The torsos became one – only the legs were free flowing in all possible variations, including the landing of a frictioning thigh over the *mons Veneris*. That is why Pius X had placed a ban against destructive social influences caused by the tango. Even the Kaiser had forbidden all officers of the German army when in uniform to dance that lascivious tune.

The tango topic led almost to the first 'intellectual' fight between them, because Komaru challenged the Latin of the term, unless accepted purely as a coincidence. In fact, Melissa was lectured that, in Maori, *tango* is a verb meaning 'to take up', 'to hold' and similar acceptations, undoubtedly a more descriptive and close description than Latin from grabbing and at times even groping a partner while dancing the 'Argentinian' tango *à la* Rodolfo Valentino.

Melissa confuted that assumption by saying that so far no one had proven the 'export' of the dance from Rotorua to Buenos Aires. Komaru counteracted that a complete study of the dance should cover at the comparative level the duplication of the term in General Polynesian, since *tangotango* means 'to keep on holding' anything, including a female, or 'to use', 'to handle' a woman. Only in Samoan, according to Margaret Mead's imagination, is the term *tago* [tango] closer to Classical Latin meaning 'touch' as in *noli me tangere*. At that, Melissa would tell Komaru that his negative imperative meant nothing to her, since he was her possession, and thus she could touch him anytime and anywhere, whether in a horizontal or a vertical position.

It was so funny! Melissa had never learned of any serious cultural stuff in a horizontal position. When she talked, however, she was always astride him as if prodding him to a gentle gallop. She used to ride in the country around Cambridge. And she talked and drank until spilling some scotch on him. And then she would fall into a catatonic stage for a few hours when Komaru would get up to shower, eat and try to sleep.

On the second day, Melissa spoke about herself. She first gave him a lecture on the meaning of her name. That happened when, in unguarded or sleepy moments, Komaru would call her 'Melitta', rather than Melissa.

'I'm not a coffee pot! Melis-s-s-sa, please!'

'Sorry, Melissa!'

'But, why do you call me Melitta at times?'

He explained that in Maori there is no 's' sound, and that automatically he switched to the closest substitute in the dental order.

'No 's' in Polynesian?'

'No, in almost all Pacific languages. There are only a few vestiges here and there, as in Samoan, but I frankly do not know whether the Samoan "s" is a fossil from a Proto-Polynesian stage or an import of some kind deriving from languages in contact. Incidentally, when I studied Greek at Victoria University, I became aware of certain language phenomena in Hellenic dialects alternating -ss- with -tt-. I think in Attic your name must have been Melitta on the basis of a Maori comparison.'

'Yes, of course, I did not particularly care for Greek, but my father insisted I take it. Well, he was a Professor of Classics at Cambridge, that stuffed shirt town. The only books he kept by his bedside were C. T. Lewis, and Liddell and Scott. But why is it that you are able to pronounce the double "s" when you address me correctly but not when you use the -t-?'

'Who knows? Probably because in Maori we don't have the so-called double consonant.'

'Uh, please think of me properly, for I want to enjoy myself before my husband kills me. Do you know, anyway, what Melissa means in Greek? Too late, anyway, for I already stung you, and you seem to like my pot of honey.'

'A bee?'

'Yes, a bee.'

'But, what kind of bee?'

'Sorry, I don't know, but you could ask Sir Edmund. I bet there were no "Italian" bees in Greece 27 centuries ago, although my name was also that of one of the priestesses of Delphi. That is why I consider you my slave. I know fate.'

Of course, Komaru assumed that she was drunk. However, the thought of her husband, the *tertium quid*, surged unobtrusively in Komaru's mind. And, for whatever reason, by interacting with a woman who had lost all her inhibitions he felt excited. But did she need alcohol to reach a stage of physiological freedom? She did not think so. Alcohol was for her only a reminder of an age when she was unaware of her own sexual liberation. She did not need it any longer, but it gave her pleasure via the flavour of Cardhu. She was a traditionalist.

'Your fate? You mean a domestic threat? Your husband?'

Komaru was puzzled. Where was Dr McTavish? And when would he come back? He did not like to get involved with a Pakeha wife, although he knew that Maori men had been raped by wives of missionaries even before they were considered 'One people' by the Treaty of Waitangi. Well, at least if one believes Frederick Edward Maning in his *Old New Zealand*.

'You see, Komaru, I don't know why my father insisted on giving me the name of Melissa against my mother's wishes. Perhaps he had read Aristotle's Orlando Furioso or seen Dosso Dossi's Melissa painted in 1516.'

'I think it is a euphonic name, very pleasant.'

'Thank you, you know how to proffer compliments, but the fate of Melissa, the wife of Periander, is not.'

And thus she spent nearly an hour relating to Komaru the historical account of the second tyrant of Corinth in the sixth century BC. Although the story was informative, Komaru struggled to remain awake, for he was exhausted. He thought of the soporific technique applied by mothers to a restless child before falling asleep: reading a fable. He vaguely remembered segments of a complex drama about Periander, a combination of Nero, Casanova and Nixon *avant la lettre*. Actually, Periander was a humanist, an idealist, a poet, though living a life of intense physical sensation and experimentation through his concubines. The problem stemmed from his loving his wife morbidly, and thus he succumbed to the false accusations of his seraglio women whom he used and disposed of much like political adversaries. In the typical fashion of a Greek tragedy, before this was institutionalised on the stage, he was overwhelmed by fits of jealousy under whose spell he killed his wife in cold blood. Leaving several children of tender age in his household, she was missed to the point of deranging Periander's mind in spite of trying to create a surrogate political despot through his favourite son, Lycophon. When this son died under mysterious circumstances, Periander became extremely despondent and found relief for his unhappiness by killing himself.

'When did this happen?', asked Komaru.

'In about 585 BC, if I remember my history, at least according to Herodotus.'

'My goodness!', exclaimed Komaru, 'and does it have anything to do with your husband? Where do I stand in this unexpected mess? You know how we are regarded by your people in Tory Wanganui?'

'Of course, I know. But, unlike the mythological Melissa, I have no hidden treasures my husband would like to find after my death. I only have one, and you already know that. Don't you worry. Even if my husband kills me, I doubt, actually I know, that he will call a necromancer, for he is perfectly aware of what I possess below my navel. Surely, it is golden, but unlike the people in Wüttenberg's church yard, he will not call up ghosts to question me.'

'Sorry, I am afraid I don't understand what you are talking about.'

'You will in time. Please bear with me. My husband is an exceptional person. Moreover, he likes you.'

The Monday evening telephone call in a way clarified certain puzzling things, though it also presented others.

'I trust I am not intruding calling you at home.'

Komaru nearly laughed at her. Who was intruding on whom?

'No, of course. Actually, I was thinking about you, uh ... about us. Now what?'

'That is why I am calling you, for I noticed that this morning you were on edge. You...'

'Sorry, I was afraid that your husband could return at any time. And I don't like creating an atmosphere of cheap antagonism, especially here in Wanganui, where violence against "foreigners", i.e. Maoris, flares up periodically. You know how constables disregard any civil rights rules when they become emotionally involved in protecting their white women.'

'Oh, no! Again, there is nothing to worry about. And you are neither German nor Japanese. Regardless, my husband does not believe in Mediterranean emotionalism. We are British, if you forgive me this expression of self-complacency.'

Melissa was referring to two episodes of social hatred, race discrimination, and physical violence. They had taken place during the First and Second World Wars.

'Yes, it may be so, but, regardless of your husband's personal view of life, I am a Maori. And I know I could be lynched, for I am a student of history. Besides, just imagine if by any chance I happen to land on the operating table of a surgery room at Queen Alexandra Hospital. Do you remember what happened to Rodolfo Valentino just because of appendicitis? Incidentally, I assume that he has not come back yet from wherever he had gone.'

'He should be back at any time. And I think that one day you and us could create a threesome. I mean it.'

There was a long pause. Komaru was shocked, as if someone had touched his head with the *pounamu* battle club of a dead chief for the sake of creating an irretrievable *tapu*. He was so incensed that he raised the tone of his voice.

'Do you mean to say that you are going to tell your husband about me?'

'Well, not specifically so, not about you. You see, he and I have been exploring the possibility of revitalising our sex life by injecting into it a new dimension. Purely an academic matter. So, the idea is purely mine. I love him very much, and I would do anything to make him happy.'

'Listen, Melit..., sorry, Melissa, don't you dare tell him anything about me, well, about us. How do you think I would feel when meeting him, especially in your presence?'

'But, naturally, I would never reveal anything to him, though I am free to tell him that I have a lover. No name. He would love to hear that because, you see, that way he could get excited at the idea of, well, not to participate in anything. He just likes to watch.'

'To watch what? I don't understand.'

'To watch me making love to a man. Perhaps probably even to a woman. I still don't know. We are at the talking stage. As a medical doctor he is exposed to and tempted by a host of women who find him attractive. But, you realise how his professional ethics binds him to a strict adherence to the Hippocratic Oath.'

'For Heaven's sake, Melissa, if you ever tell him anything about me I shall disavow everything, and I'll take you to court for trying to denigrate the Maori character.'

'Komaru, please, you will see that nothing of that sort will ever take place. It will be up to you to decide if one day you change your mind. For the time being, let's accept the status quo on an incidental basis.'

'OK, let me use the American pragmatic consensual agreement as adults, even if it sounds somewhat vulgar. I was wrong. I had imagined something more noble. You know, it is difficult to grow up as an orphan. My mother died when, as a young boy, I was beginning to become aware of womanhood as a shelter to the baffling aspects of life. The other female around me was my sister, of course quite a different situation.'

'So, did you see in me a surrogate mother?'

'Perhaps. And did you see in me, what, a son? Did you ever have any children?'

'Unfortunately, no. Could you not tell that I have not had any? Not even Cesarean? Uh, you said you have a sister.'

'Yes, but this is irrelevant. I barely know her, she has always been at school here and there. I haven't seen her in three years. We rarely correspond. She is in the States. Sorry, may I come back to your cryptic way of recounting history? Why did you say I was neither a German nor a Japanese?'

There she went, keeping him on the phone until late in the evening. And she talked almost uninterruptedly. Only once it seemed to Komaru that there was a pause as if someone had come into her bedroom. He guessed it was her husband.

Melissa first spoke about an ugly episode of the First World War, when the local newspaper, *The Triad*, kept on fomenting discord among super-Christian Wanganui subscribers through an Editorial. In Wanganui, the Boston of New Zealand, they read that 'sexual perversity of the grossest and more pitiable sort is commoner in Germany than in any other country in Europe, and has its necessary part in every social scandal. Adultery is quite as prevalent there as elsewhere, and virgin brides are certainly far less plentiful ... than they are in France and England.'

Komaru wondered. Was she reading or quoting from memory, or simply paraphrasing? But that had happened nearly three generations past. Adultery, explained Melissa, becomes null and void as a concept when there is a blind scale holding a spouse on each plate. As soon as the weight of tacit agreement levels the plates, all morality vanishes into the convenience of selfish opportunity for both sides. Of course, at that time there was only gonorrhea, chancre, syphilis and other routine ailments. Now there is AIDS. Each moral generation adds a new disease, but prevention entails precautions.'

'But I did not take any precautions.

'I did that myself, since I did not know you well. As regards myself, don't worry. My husband tests me periodically.'

The last statement baffled, actually stunned him, for he was unable to ask why. Did her husband check on her or on himself?

Komaru's puzzlement was derailed by her continuing to relate episodes of the First World War. In Wanganui, a butcher of German extraction, a certain Heinhold, had first been crucified with accusations of all sorts in the local papers. Then 3,000 Wanganui citizens defied twelve constables by destroying the butcher shop. A piano company, she was not sure about its name, perhaps the Dresden Piano Company, had to change its name to Bristol Company, and even so that did not stop riots of all sorts. Only British firms were allowed to furnish musical instruments. On 15 January 1915, a certain Gaudin living in Apia, Samoa, under New Zealand jurisdiction, was found guilty of philosophical treason and condemned to 5 years of hard labour.

However, the most clamorous case was that affecting a renowned professor at Victoria University. He was also known for blowing the whistle about the teaching standards based on personalities, rather than on solid scholarship. Melissa gave details of all sorts, and Komaru wondered whether his studying at Victoria would affect his career, for that university still carries the stigma of the most blatant case of injustice. The professor, named George William von Zedlit, had been accused of treachery and had become a *cause célèbre* compared with that of Captain Dreyfus in France. Unfortunately, there was no Zola in New Zealand. And the professor died quietly after suffering the most humiliating blisters of dishumanity. British patriotism normally is manifested more outside Europe, and New Zealand, as a vociferous and immature child attached to the umbilical cord of Mummy Albion, exaggerated the whole thing just for the hell of being placed on the map of international loyalty.

Komaru thought that something was congenitally wrong with the Pakehas colonising Ao Tea Roa. Super-duper patriotism of the basest kind, mostly borne by vulgar masses exploited by demagogues, also became rampant in the Second World War. The worst episode of 'misunderstanding' took place in a concentration camp at Featherstone holding Japanese POWs. In a riot apparently caused by poor administrative procedures calling for forced labour, 48 prisoners were machine-gunned to death, and many more were wounded.

'Enough!,' said Komaru. 'What do you want to prove?'

'I was just speaking of "recent" times, just two generations ago.'

'Yes, but we don't have to speak only of recent times. I know what happened to Maorihood after the Treaty was signed. We Maori carry psychological scars that have become genetic. In Wanganui alone, Governor Fitz-Roy had to rely on a garrison of 800 army men just to "protect" the Pakehas. That was pure invasion. Wanganui has ever since carried the burden of a touchy co-existence between the two races. I wonder if there will ever be an *utu* to be satisfied by younger Maoris learning history. That is what I plan to do. And do you think that you could frankly help me in editorial matters trying to uncover injustice?'

'I shall try, Komaru, for both recent and past episodes of political violence in Wanganui will not happen again. Wanganui has changed.'

'I doubt it,' replied Komaru, 'for it still remains as the symbol of the most Maori city in Ao Tea Roa. The spiritual essence, its *wairua*, may be dormant, but not gone away. Read the local papers. I just glanced a few times at the *Wanganui Chronicle*, particularly at the Saturday issue. It looks like it is published in Bath, not in your city. The most British and useless items are published just to keep alive the confrontational spirit under the first garrison quartered there by Governor Fitz-Roy. But anything can happen again, anytime, particularly after the rôle played by Ken Mair, the leader of *Ahi Ka*, in 1985, and by the activities of the Waitangi Action Committee. By next year *Te PuniKokiri*, "Ministry of Maori Development", may begin a new era of awakening.'

'Komaru, when you give me the first draft of your work, we will analyse it objectively. Sorry we put it aside for the time being. Actually, I'm not sorry. I feel that we have shed all the formalities of polite society. I am sure it will be better for both of us this way. Once the flesh is hung to "stay", we will not be tempted by it as much if not as a necessary victual for the senses that dominate us.'

And once more Komaru reviewed Melissa as a human being. She was not a feminist, and neither a prissy Briton. Who was she?

'May I ask you, has your husband returned?'

'Yes, he is showering and shaving. He always does that before he takes me to bed. I look forward to being played by his sophisticated and intellectual manner of dealing with a human body beyond that of his profession. Good night, Komaru.'

He hung up the phone without answering. He was simply confused, but also prickled by what she had proposed to him earlier. And thinking about the possibilities of engaging in something unorthodox, he felt excited. He wondered what Dr McTavish would do to his wife. And, to fall asleep after being aroused by imagining another man in the bed he had left in the morning, he masturbated hard. In the process, he soiled the sheets. A thought occurred to him. Had Melissa changed her sheets? Or had she kept them unchanged to keep the scent of Polynesian glands for the benefit of her husband's aphrodisiac needs?

Komaru laboured to fall asleep. How late was it? Oh, time for the late news. Thus, he turned on the TV1 from Auckland. And, how exciting, the TV announcer had mentioned that 10 years had gone by since the Prince of Wales had married a certain Diana. A few shots had been flashed on the screen showing scenes from Canterbury Cathedral. Komaru wondered how a 19-year-old kindergarten teacher could be a match for an old wolf. A marriage of convenience, like that of the McTavishes? Oh, the weather had been capricious. It was snowing on the Canterbury plains. Two different types of Canterbury at the antipodes of each other. How long would the weather of a Canterbury wedding remain fine? Except for that of the Queen and Prince Philip, on the surface the 20th century had not been immune to bad weather for several generations of British royalty.

Chapter 3

The political European summer of 1991, crowning the unexpected revolution that dissolved the Cold War in 1989–90, did not affect Komaru's view of the history of the 20th century as a concept, although he anthropomorphised it to the point of considering it as a lunatic lost in mental confusion and going in circles like an errant. A whole century of grandiose ideas, of toilsome social experimentation, of real and imaginary fights between Hawks and Doves, the whole complex of human suffering had collapsed into a Black Hole of futility. As for the Gulf War interlude, Komaru felt it was an inconsequential skirmish. It only served to prolong the agony of the Iraqi people in coping with lower standards of living.

Was that a foretoken of what could happen in Ao Tea Roa? Were the prophecies of Te Whiti to be nullified by similar developments in Maoridom? Had anyone won or lost anything? Had society changed in any 'positive' direction? Had Everyman in the streets of the cities, in the buildings of metropolises, in the squares of rural villages of First-, Second-, and Third-World countries received any benefit in a material way or just peace of mind?

Komaru tried to make sense of the Pakeha world, the very world that in the past had made fun of and condemned Maoris when they were in constant strife for survival. He laboured to collate his reflections, as filtered from antipodean theaters of European and Asian events, onto Ao Tea Roa. Yes, a slow ascension of Maori rights toward a climax of some kind was proceeding independently of any confrontational collapse between Communism and Capitalism. But for how long?

Suddenly, the whole apparatus of political and militaristic operations had become boneless. What would take the place of the old structures? And what would the results be for the people? For Komaru, only one thing seemed to progress in common everywhere, from the North to the South Pole, from Kathmandu to Timbuktu. An explosion of information, yes, through the computerisation of old traditional methods, had become nearly global. And its results? Crime against and by school children, the replacement of old dictatorships with new ones, the dissolution of basic social nuclei, the paideiaisation of higher education entrusted to software designed to atrophy the brain, the spread of AIDS, the saturation of ... The telephone ring interrupted his stream of thought.

'Yes?,' said Komaru. His tone was clearly rude.

'Hello, this is Dr McTavish. Am I interrupting anything ... exciting?'

'Oh, no, how are you, sir? I was just trying to complete another section before meeting Melit ... sorry, Mrs McTavish.'

'I am glad she can help you. You see, I think that she always wished to have a son. Her maternal instincts, unfortunately, are confined to, shall I say, vicarious activities.'

Komaru thought that Dr McTavish was talking in riddles. What was he saying? Or was he being sarcastic?

'I think Mrs McTavish is not only helpful but also patient and ...'

'Well, sorry to interrupt, I am on a strict schedule. Actually, you too have been very helpful to her. You just arrived at the right time. Oh, listen, I am coming down to Wellington next week. May I take you to dinner?'

'But, sir, I would be delighted. However, it is me who ...'

'Again, listen, I will call you in a few days, so that we can have a good chat. It has to be in mid-week, because, as you know, I am often very busy on weekends.'

And he hung up without even saying goodbye. Komaru felt nearly insulted. But then he reflected that the rather brusque behavior displayed by Dr McTavish was due to his being under stress of some kind. After a few minutes of pondering about that sudden social call, Komaru forced himself to sit down and proceed with his sketch of 20th-century history based on number '9'. He hoped that it would develop into a thesis for the partial fulfillment of requirements called by the Examination Committee for a Master's Degree in History at Victoria University. He tentatively delineated the triad as follows:

1929 –   Birth of the Vatican State
            Birth of the Depression
            Birth of Modern America

Komaru had a lot of difficulty in sketching a triadic enclosure of the 1920s, for the intrusion of a World Religion based on dictatorial foundations was a new component in modern times. Yes, he recalled Islam along 'imperialistic' lines, but it had not become institutionalised behind the law of a single autonomous nation. Catholicism, although older than Islam, had surged globally as a first only in modern times behind a series of dogmas beginning with that of the Immaculate Conception. By placing the decade along a continuum was Komaru able to notice that the USA had emerged, along with the Vatican State, not only as a world power, but also as a crucible of ideological tenets that in the long run became more important and seminal than any others, including Communism, ever conceived and developed within the 20th century. At the same time, for him, Earth had been understood as an 'integrated' system that had acquired some sudden paradigmatic traits derived from slowly grown syntagmatic phenomena orchestrated by the speculative minds of human beings concerned with the only living room orbiting the Sun.

In essence, Komaru could not admit to himself that, within this uniquely fragile dwelling, two apparently unconnected religious and social structures could be built to last in spite of their intangible architectural components. The first, dealing with the birth of a foreign power controlling the people of Italy at the centre of their very government, the Vatican, was indeed unique in the annals of Mankind. Ironically, the 'Vatican' had been *de facto* a mind-controlling institution that had enslaved millions of people for 19 centuries. In particular, Komaru wondered how Italians could accept a *vipara in sinu*, that is, the creation not only of a political system but also of a religious dictatorship based within Italy, a country that was barely a teenager among world powers. The parallel between Italy under a pope and Iran under an ayatollah was frighteningly clear. The Lateran Treaty signed on 11 February by two despotic governments created an oppressive social precedent for the purpose of consolidating a dictatorship of the soul. Mussolini had sold the Italians' freedom of religion by using the obliteration of freedom of speech within a monarchical system reeking with the stench of blood spilled in the process of wiping out the guerrilla movement of Southern Italy through summary executions.

Thus, from the north and the centre of Italy, three different evil winds, namely, the monarchy, Fascism and the Vatican, had destroyed the remaining ideological skeletons of democracy inherited from the Greeks in pre-Roman times. In thinking about that unique *ménage à trois* controlling the bodies of Italians through conscriptions, their souls through the cannibalistic ritual of the Mass, and their minds through the 'Mussolini ha sempre ragione' dogma in papal fashion, Komaru was grateful to his father, whose personal *whakapapa* gave him a background for mental hygiene, as well as an understanding of a people who, also for 2,000 years, had endured a series of infallible and mythological precepts. Through his father, Komaru had developed an affection for 'his' Italian people, whom he considered as brothers and sisters in the shadows of psychological impotence. Simply, both in Italy and Ao Tea Roa, vicious governmental 'authorities' had brainwashed generations of citizens through dictatorial edicts.

But democracy was not dead. As a matter of fact, democracy was making itself evident as a consequence of the Depression in spite of its initial negative impact not only in the USA but also throughout the Earth. Ironically, it was a Republican government that hosted the germs of change on the Petri dish of social revolution. Although sporting a Republican president of sorts, that is, President Edgar J. Hoover as inaugurated on 4 March, American politics was dominated by a Democratic Congressional majority. In practice, Hoover played the rôle of a person who had to dig his own grave before being executed and interred by the will of the people. The 1920s were fertile ground for the planting and germination of ideas that later led to the development of social reforms and slow racial integration, later leading to the establishment of civil rights.

Amazingly, it took an economic vacuum, worse than the Russian Revolution that changed the face of Europe in the batting of an eyelash, to create the foundations of a new America. In fact, without Hoover and a Depression, the West and later the whole world would probably still be mired in a status quo of general stagnation pervading 'intelligent' organized societies. But, more amazingly, only a few people may have noticed that, although the NAACP, the American Association for the Advancement of Colored People, had become 30 years old, its practical effects had been amputated by sheer political power and the miseries of the First World War. It took neither a street fight nor an act of violence to begin the effacement of the last vestige of slavery and to wake up from racial despondency, but the projection of the performing arts to initiate the long process of social awakening.

If there is a place where this change began to unfold, it should be clearly named Harlem. Within its ghetto, still 'landlorded' by whites, the 1920s witnessed the flourishing of subtle political assertion. Who would have thought of, say, Duke Ellington as a mere pianist using his fingers? He was touching his soul through the artistic expression of his mind along with Bessie Smith, Bill Robinson and others. The Cotton Club, Barron's and Leroy's were not only physical enclosures hosting musicians and singers, but also subtle revolutionaries defying the naïveté of white people through art. And 'African' arts became a means of fighting within the confines of Harlem that in practice were the public squares and streets of tomorrow. It suffices to read between the lines of a simple statement made by Langston Hughes to grasp the anguish of a soul and the hope of a heart: 'We younger Negro artists ... intend to express our individual dark-skinned selves without fear or shame. If white people are pleased we are glad. If they are not, it doesn't matter.' What he really meant was: we don't give a damn. We shall overcome.

Komaru made a parallel between that subtle political manifesto and several ones made by the Maoris through nearly two centuries of white oppression. He felt that, read carefully, Hughes' statement represented the Preamble to freedom, the first step along a difficult and bloody path. Thus, although Hoover had promised 'a chicken in every pot, and a car in every garage', it took a Depression and a new president to rip apart the fabric of American capitalistic society in order to initiate the long walk to become two generations later Martin Luther King's march into Washington, DC.

Finally, Komaru thought that, as the Depression had furnished the grounds for the birth of a small-scale democracy in the USA, Communism had ironically created the climate of opinion for the development of global 'democracy'. As a matter of fact, it is even possible to assume that without the establishment of the 'evil empire' of latter days, world democracy would still be languishing under the capitalistic power of American tycoons, the same ones who, in the 1920s, sent federal troops to quench workers' rights not only in America, but also in nearby nations starting with the Naco, Arizona, affair 'to protect American lives and property' from the farts of Mexican frijoles in Naco, Sonora.

Dr McTavish called one morning and left a message on the recording machine. Komaru had spent all day at the Turnbull Library, where he had drafted an informal 'Manifesto' that on the surface had nothing to do with his MA thesis. Months earlier he had been asked by a few close friends and activists to work on a preliminary programme delineating the International Year of the World's Indigenous People insofar as the Maoris were concerned. Although more than a year away, it required plenty of planning ahead. The relevant aspect of the Year was the fact that Ao Tea Roa was to host most activities 'at home' in 1993, as declared by the UN Assembly in December, 1990. The theme would be 'Indigenous People – A New Partnership'.

The message from Dr McTavish was clear. He was sorry he could not make it for dinner. Would Komaru, however, be free for supper the following day? There was no need to reply unless the answer was negative. He would pick Komaru up at 17:00 in the lobby of his apartment complex. And he had suggested that a necktie would be in order. That suggestion sounded more like a warning. Where was he planning to have dinner, at *Orsini's*? And, he wondered, is Melissa coming along? And what was her husband doing in Wellington smack during the winter?

Komaru did not hide his nervousness. He did not know what to expect from that invitation. Was it to be a meeting? If so, it sounded more like a business one, not the least social. He hoped that he did not have to cope with French food. He tolerated German cooking, but this was rarely served anywhere in Wellington. The preponderance was Italian, often disguised under either 'Continental' or 'Northern', which could mean polenta, cannellini bean soup, tomato-based salads, breast of turkey Wellington, baked potatoes and chocolate mousse. This was, of course, American-Indian food. The rampant spread of Asian cookery had also been accepted by Kiwis under the less discriminatory label of Asian, and not 'Oriental'. The adjective 'Asian' was actually a larger umbrella under which some people began to place both New Zealand and Australia since these were neither European nor African. Although Australia did not mind being regarded as part of Asia, New Zealand violently opposed that association, and favoured rather Antarctica. Ironically, no one recalled that Maoris had originally departed from Asia.

The surprise came out of nowhere when Dr McTavish parked his car near the *Great Expectations*, a restaurant Komaru had only heard about for having won a 'Taste of New Zealand' Award in 1989. He immediately knew what to expect, for the place was operated by a smart owner interested in bridging race relations via culinary enterprises. Komaru was glad to notice that the establishment was BYO – no need to decline alcoholic beverages. Amusingly, the menu featured a 'home made ice cream in a brandy snap basket'. He only hoped that Dr McTavish would not consider and treat him as Pip in Charles Dickens' *Great Expectations*.

The menu indicated also that the chef was bound to employ only fresh New Zealand victuals. Komaru noticed that the selection could appeal to both Maoris and Pakehas, as well as to the cosmopolitan clientèle inhabiting the capital. Thus, he felt immediately at home by selecting Pork Wellington, basically a small ham stuffed with diced *kumara* surrounding the bone cavity and presented on a platter like a cornucopia-shaped dish garnished with very thin apple 'chips' and watercress. That was Maori food, too. The waiter served Komaru with a flair by carving a perfect slice of meat and filling the centre with the 'veggies.' The bone had been removed before baking, and only the lower end stuck out as a reminder of a former life. The glaze conferred upon the served portion a colourful image of a balanced dish that looked more like a *nature morte* composition than '*hangi*' food. Plenty of manipulation etymologically, Komaru observed mentally, though the arrangement on the dish was made only with knife and fork. No fingers ever touched the food, contrary to the modern trend calling for 'arranging' edible items on the plate, rather than placing or pouring components of a meal on a dish with serving silver. Komaru once more had observed that, in Pakeha restaurants nowadays, fingers did all the walking in the kitchen before reaching the dining table. Cooking had become a matter of assembly plant techniques by stressing flamboyant colours, Jackson Pollock design, collage structures and mumbo-jumbo serialisation of vegetable-fleshy bits and pieces with scattered flecks of exotic fruit in casual arrangements.

At *Great Expectations*, however, the main dish selected by Komaru was excellent, for the whole former swine – was it a boar or a sow? – came accompanied by fresh ginger julienne lacing the subcutaneous area in contrast with the thin and soft hide wrapped in bacon strips before being completely enclosed in puffy pastry. That was a super-duper feat of structural engineering. The dish was ingenious by bringing into one single expression of cuisine the British Beef Wellington tradition – unknown in Ao Tea Roa – into Polynesian territory. Yes, the emphasis on race relations was visible, at least at table, for the vegetables were Maori, and the spices definitely Asian.

Dr McTavish selected a smoked salmon mousse by adducing his avoidance of bad cholesterol carriers. And he ate sparingly, particularly after the jazz band flooded the atmosphere with sterilised tunes. Komaru was glad that Melissa was not part of the supper reunion, for it became a business meeting slowly and nearly casually. It seemed to Komaru that the inception of the band music signalled the purpose of the get-together, for what followed in the conversation, actually a monologue, revealed one of the most intriguing proposals for a 'business' partnership. And, although the tables at *Great Expectations* were rather close to each other for anyone tending toward claustrophobia, Komaru felt insulated against over-receptive ears since they had been seated at the far corner of the salon, but close enough to the band whose music functioned as a soundscreen between Dr McTavish and the other customers.

What followed was the quintessential sublimation of race relations, as if taking the rôle of dessert, which Komaru had declined because of the brandy lacing the ice cream. Dr McTavish concluded his meal with a chunk of French bread and Ferndale brie. He told Komaru that his only exception to a low-cholesterol diet was a necessary ingredient to a good digestion. He had acquired that habit in Europe, where wine and cheese crown a normal meal much better than the American TV-advertised chemical product to be taken after eating chicken cacciatore. He went further by explaining that Ferndale *brie*, made in New Zealand by a French company, was much better than the imported variety because it was fresher and 'biologique' since sheep could eat chemically free grass year round, while in France pollution was inching its way into the complete food chain, including the milk around Brie. Although pasteurisation destroys the individual characteristics of the milk, it prevents what happened in England in 1988 when *Listeria monocytoneges* was responsible for the death of many people after they ate either brie or camembert.

Good Heavens, thought Komaru, he must be a rather sophisticated person. Dr McTavish, in his late 60s, had roamed the world before settling first in Wellington and then in Wanganui in order to stay away from the dredges of the large cities. When the band resumed playing after a short break, Dr McTavish had finished his French-style dessert followed by tea. To keep him company, Komaru had nibbled on a coconut pudding of some kind devoid of animal milk. As a jazz tune became slow and soft, Dr McTavish shot straight from the hip. Komaru laboured to grasp first the phonic medium and then its meaning.

'I know everything about you fucking my wife. And I am glad about it because ...'

A waitress had approached the diners suggesting the *Great Expectations* dessert, but only green tea was in order for Dr McTavish. Apparently, for him that concoction had therapeutic properties. Komaru followed suit automatically, for his mind was numb. But, in that interval, Komaru was able to catch his breath. And the story began to unfold in near clinical terms.

It was late when Dr McTavish dropped him at the kerb of his apartment complex. Komaru barely remembered how the evening went by under the near-magic spell cast on him by a man who was obviously a cultured person and an affable human being. What did Dr McTavish see in Komaru? A son? A screen? A target of some kind? Perhaps it was the last, since it is well known that a characteristic of New Zealand manifested by Pakehas was a constant feeling of insecurity stemming from a capital sin of some kind committed by the first settlers. The parallelism with the Trokosi people along the Volta of Ghana was not unwarranted for, even after three or four generations of missionary culture, barely pubescent girls were still expected to become sexual outlets for the priests of dishumanising cults. Not to speak of some Southern Italian vassalage in villages and towns in which a wrong performed by someone could be transferred for a whole century until paid by descendants who had meanwhile moved to Northern Italy, or even Germany as guest-workers. Geoff Murphy's film *Utu* was one of the first expressions of this state of mind affecting both Maoris and Pakehas, a flow of subtle and unforgettable 'responsibilities' that could now transcend race. And, while Maoris were beginning to be used as excuses for being blessed with the holy water of repayments, Pakehas espoused the necessity of unburdening themselves for wrongs committed generations earlier. The situation was not unlike that of Australians *vis-à-vis* the Aborigines. There was some pronounced difference, however, between the two former colonies. New Zealand was a *mea culpa* nation. Missionaries had done their work well, since Australia could be labelled as a 'Look at me, Adonis nation'. This way Australians would not account for 'one of the darkest chapters in the history of British colonization' as stated by Charles Barrett and A. S. Kenyon in *Blackfellows of Australia* as early as the beginning of the 20th century.

Komaru was simply puzzled. What were the McTavishes doing in Ao Tea Roa? Was their 'style' of life a way of repaying debts, of going through life through hedonistic activities in order to maintain an operational minimum of mental health, or simply a consciously devised 'philosophical' *modus vivendi*? And why had they chosen Wanganui as their *locus vivendi*?

When Komaru turned on the lights in his study-living room, he suddenly remembered he had not read the afternoon mail he had retrieved in the lobby. He had postponed reading even his sister's letter on whose envelope two stamps displayed the American flag. He also noticed the red light flashing on the recording machine. So he first turned it on and listened to the message of a Salvation Army officer calling him from Auckland. It just said, 'This is Miss Wood from the Army. It is about your father. Please call our Parnell Office at your earliest convenience.'

The number she had given corresponded to that usually called by him from time to time whenever business matters were to be expedited in connection with the Social Services Centre on Churton Street, where the Bridge Programme for Alcoholics was located. He already knew Miss Wood, with whom he had corresponded a few times about his father before he had been recovered for treatment on Rotoroa Island. It had not been easy to have his father admitted to that Residential Programme. A month earlier, Komaru had phoned him, and on that occasion signs of improvement had been noticed with regard to a gradual return to 'normal' life. Komaru felt guilty for having put his father aside, away from his home in Pakakura. And, being wrapped up in his studies, Maori activities, and the preparation for the 1992 Year of Indigenous People, he nearly forgot that his father was still alive. He had assumed that the Salvation Army would take care of everything, and that one day his father would return home fully recovered, Meanwhile, Melissa had taken him away from his routine life. He had found a 'mother', but had forgotten about his father. Of course, he would call Miss Wood first thing in the morning.

He was tired. It had been quite an evening under the nervous scrutiny of the restaurant owner who, although not telling Dr McTavish to clear the premises, waited patiently until the couple left. All waiters and the jazz band had already gone for the night. *Great Expectations* was known for staying open late, without any rigid closing hours, but not THAT late, for it was nearly midnight.

After brushing his teeth, Komaru went to bed, taking with him Mahina's letter. He missed her because she was the last woman left near him in the Auckland area. He had no one on his mother's side he knew or could remember, and his father's *iwi* were all in the Bay of Islands.

Dear Brother, Kia ora!

I am sorry I haven't been able to write earlier. Being busy with the summer session I just could not think of anything else but course work in order to have additional credit hours. Now, by taking whatever is required during my senior year – I haven't yet decided what beyond the departmental list – I should have enough hours to graduate in 1992.

Thus I have postponed my vacation this winter, sorry, this summer, for here in Portland it is SUMMER, simply a paradise weather-wise as Americans say. Perhaps I am selfish, but the thought of spending a month of vacation, where? in Auckland or even in Wellington as per your invitation, does not appeal to me. Oregon is at its best now. I simply want to rest a little and decide, or attempt to decide, what to do with the rest of my life.

I am happy that two years ago I changed my major from English literature to philosophy, for one can always be engaged in literary activities after acquiring philosophical training, though not the reverse. Meanwhile, I have discovered I am interested in many things, through psychology, poetry, ethics, and, please don't laugh, religion. I took a course in comparative religion as an auditor, that is, without credit, and I enjoyed it immensely. Actually, I regarded its contents along both historical and philosophical lines delineating what fellow humans have been doing in order to find out what they are and how they can live on Earth. Next year, I plan to take additional courses, including one on Catholicism. Perhaps I can 'convert' you into studying that subject-matter. Please don't think I am funny, but I can now begin to understand what missionaries tried to do in our country, and here I refer to the idealistic missionaries, not to those escapists who sought a way of living by treading on the bodies of our *iwi*.

Enough of myself! What have you heard about Father? I am concerned that he has not replied to my last two letters. I know that the A. A. Programme is good, and that they have a 90% success rate in treating alcoholics. But what about the rest? Have you called him recently? You know how expensive it is for me to call him from Portland. Besides, at Rotoroa they don't accept telephone calls unless they are first screened. I don't like to waste my money by leaving messages. Please tell me something about Father. In the last note he sounded rather depressed.

So here I am, planning to spend my last summer in the States. I shall try to travel a little, perhaps to Canada, but alone it is not wise. Although Oregon is not as dangerous as California, it is important to join a friend. Unfortunately, Tanya, my roommate, has gone back East for the rest of the summer. So, here I am, but not inactive. I have been consulting with the college infirmary to refer me to a plastic surgeon. You know that I would like to take advantage of the American techniques to try and solve my problem once and for all, one way or the other. I understand that at the University of Washington Hospital they have a good department where 'plastic' operations can be performed on an experimental basis. Personally, however, as I grow older, I think 'that' problem is not as much as it used to be when we used to swim along the beaches of Waiheke. Do you remember the old *pa* at Putiki Bay? I miss it. You see, Oregon beaches, except for a few spots, are overwhelming. They are so different from ours, huge, cold and full of flotsam. At least what I have seen so far. You know I don't care for romantic notions of nature. But at times I dream of the days we spent in our own backyard and our schoolmates.

Please write. Although life on campus is busy, I feel lonely. In addition, there is a cultural abyss between me and American students, much more than me and the Pakehas. It is a double social ditch difficult to cross because, although pleasant, kind, and easy-going, American boys are so immature, materialistic, and, sorry, rather shallow culturally. Please, forgive me. I love America. It has no complexes at the everyday level. Only politically they tend to assume that they are at the centre of the Universe. Nothing seems to worry them. They don't feel threatened by anything except their own fragility when it comes to spiritual matters. The boys in general are *tabula rasa*. The girls are mostly interested in their bodies. They know everything about it, in and out. I rarely hear them speaking about any past or any future. They have no inkling about their *whakapapa*, and what counts is the most immediate gratification of the senses, but without any full consciousness of their actions. I hope I am not too critical, or wrong, sorry, uncharitable, about my hosts. But both boys and girls follow the *carpe diem* life apparently unconsciously. Tomorrow for them is as blank as their past. The Atlantic their forefathers crossed seems to have washed out any vestige of genetic memory. Not so, however, for the Asians, mainly the Chinese and the Vietnamese who thrive here on the West Coast. I associate more with them, for they are always aware of their past by reckoning, as we do, in thousands of years. That helps me to consider them as links in a chain holding me more firmly tied to an anchor of inner stability.

I hope I haven't bothered you with my vagaries. After all, perhaps only you can understand me. So, tell me what you are doing. Are you still playing the rôle of Don Quixote? If so, have you found a Sancho Panza to feed your horse?

Aroha,
Mahina

Komaru thought that Mahina had not changed at all in her addressing him as an equal after spending three years in America.

The same nasty little sister trying to make subtle fun of big brother. He only detected, between the lines, a tinge of sadness, and even depression, in Mahina's account of her life in Oregon, in spite of regarding that state as a pleasant spot on Earth. Anyway, he consoled himself, one more year to go. She would come back. Father will have a woman again to hold together whatever family life was left in a motherless *whanau*.

Chapter 4

The day following the supper with Dr McTavish, Komaru felt exhausted, much more than having spent a weekend with Melissa, although, after the initial exploration of sexual curiosity, she began, well, not to slow down, but to fall into a routine of activities, including preparation of meals, reading and criticism of Komaru's drafts, editorial suggestions and sessions of self-examination. Melissa also felt free to open up toward Komaru, as if he were to analyse her through her body rather than her mind.

He forced himself to get out of bed, drink two cups of green tea and nibble on some kiwi fruit, rind and all. He was not hungry, probably because he had too many things on his mind. What to do first? He remembered to call Miss Wood, but intentionally waited to do so because he anticipated problems, and he did not want to get upset before drafting at least another triadic segment of history. This time he had to deal with 1939, and he just could not think of any other component beyond the single one. That was enough to jot down ideas for later expansion.

Then he recalled reading Mahina's letter. Sister was somewhat depressed. He would answer in the afternoon. My goodness, she had changed. Even her language had become Americanised at various levels, including spelling. Of course, she was an American student, and she had to adopt the rules of the country. And he felt sad about her medical condition. How had she managed to function among dormitory student? Was it why she had declined to join a sorority? He had nearly forgotten about her situation. He hoped that she would be helped at the University of Washington. The New Zealand government has promised to assist her with a special subvention assigned to Maori citizens unable to be treated in their own country. A few feminist organizations were behind that promise.

He had to first stand by his schedule to formulate a near cabalistic theory that could perhaps be utilized for an MA thesis in historical accidentality. He knew that in history one could theorise on anything. But would he be able to fool his MA committee? The era of von

Zedlit had vanished a long time ago. Things were becoming very serious. And he cared, for he hoped to apply any knowledge to what he had in mind on behalf of his people with the help of the legal system being slowly, but firmly, developed with the assistance of Maori solicitors and barristers. He planned to meet Moana Jackson, Founder and Director of the Maori Legal Services, since Jackson himself had studied at Victoria University and, in addition, had obtained a Law degree from Columbia University, a centre of excellent studies creating even future presidents of the USA. And America was the country *par excellence* that had the right to consider itself as the most litigious society in the world. There were more attorneys in the US than Maori inhabitants of Ao Tea Roa.

By noon he had finished a draft of his '9' theory, a temporary one. He knew it was rather a stretch to fit any Chinese numerical superstition. Moreover, what was there about that magic number? Was it not just the opposite? He rationalized by convincing himself that it was just a way of considering himself lucky to follow a syntagmatic flow of narrative before paradigmatising it into an item of novelty. But deep in his heart he began to doubt about it, because he felt that the whole thing started to leak like the '*Blitz*' theory in *The Structure of Scientific Revolutions*. Thomas Kuhn had been debunked a long time ago. Nothing could happen from nothing, and whatever apparent sudden surge of a new paradigm was actually the end product of a slow, invisible, constant happening that found itself in the proper environment to create itself. The analogy with anything latent waiting for a sponge of platinum for the proper catalysis was not unwarranted. The proof was given by the sudden dismantling of the Berlin Wall and all the consequential developments that led to what could not really be a *coupure épistémologique*. If this could be accepted, then it took nearly 30 years, hardly an epistemological break.

1939 –   Inception of the Second World War

At this point, Komaru was resigned to the fact that he could not extract and delineate a 'triadic' enclosure of main political events polluting old, decrepit Europe and the entire planet. He just could not make any sense of the European madness allowing human beings to witness the absurd carnage based on 'philosophical' principles. And at that point he thought of his sister. What good was philosophy to sanction the tenets formulated by Nazi Germany? Would his sister apply her knowledge of philosophy to understand the behaviour of politically, or even religiously, indoctrinated masses? He was able to understand, though not to condone, the beginning of the First World War as a result of European royalty playing deleterious chess games on monarchical boards. *The Guns of August* by Barbara Tuchman had 'pacified' his anguish in his quest to grasp events leading to still more carnage after barely 20 years of 'peace'. What were 'The Guns of September'?

Komaru tried to analyse the behavior of each European nation along a continuum made of giant ellipses, that is, a series of dots more or less touching each other. Whenever there was a gap between them, that void could be conceived as 'peace'. But these gaps were so few and so small that it was difficult to conceive of peace *per se* as an autonomous entity. It seemed to him that peace could be understood only as an absence of war, and not the reverse. When he tried to project European antagonisms within his own country, well, he distinguished first between pre- and post-oppression. Yes, in pre-oppression, Maoris fought among each other along a trail of survivalism. It was purely a matter of surviving within a hell of a country onto which his forefathers had been dumped by either fate or intention. But he could not forgive those who would label the Maori people as 'savages' because of those tribal skirmishes. As if European tribes had been immune to mass slaughter! He remembered in particular a highly biased publication by a certain Carl V. Smith, who wrote *From N to Z* to explain the presence of New Zealand as a nation to both New Zealanders and 'visitors'. For Smith, after the first 'discovery' made by Tasman, 'New Zealand lived in peace with no outsiders to interfere with the Maoris' national pastime of massacring themselves ...'. He had made several notes about European views of how people regard their enemies. On a second note card, Komaru had found another quotation saying that Maoris 'are only a few of the many peoples who have been reported as absorbing strength from their enemies through the medium of blood, flesh, heart, or broth. In general, the cannibal's object was to increase his own power, but in a number of instances the act was intended as the ultimate demonstration of hatred or scorn. As recently as 1971, a member of Black September, accused of assassinating Wasfi Tal, the Prime Minister of Jordan, declared "I am satisfied now. I drank from Tal's blood". Eyewitnesses confirmed that he had not been speaking metaphorically.' When Komaru found the rest of the cards, and in particular the preceding one containing the statement above, he was glad to see that the quotation had been lifted from Reay Tannahill's *Fresh and Blood: A History of the*

Cannibal Complex. The sarcastic comparison between Maoris and Europeans was beyond comprehension. If massacring each other was a Maori pastime during spells of peace as a normality, what could one say of Europeans massacring each other as a chronic *modus vivendi* along a continuum where each dot of the historic record barely allowed humans to detect a rare space of peace between them? Theoretically, the food supply problem, solved in part by Napoleon's Appert for packing meat, could be avoided at great savings. After each battle, warriors on both sides could feed freely by utilizing the bodies of their enemies or, better, of their comrades as a sign of respect and gratitude for having given their lives for a noble cause. In a very finite world like Earth, that would make a lot of sense. Of course, heads of government, generals, chaplains blessing the living and the dead on both sides of the trenches, and politicians should be offered choice morsels. Bones could be utilized instead of those from Argentinean cows to make chemical-free calcium tablets for anyone affected by moral osteoporosis.

Thus, in his consideration of each decade ending with a '9', Komaru just gave up for the 1930s. How could he integrate all the neurotic 'happenings' in spite of Jean Renoir's *Grande Illusion*, the last moral film just before the inception of total madness? From Franco's takeover of democratic Spain and Fermi's splitting of the atom in January, the whole decade was a calendar of inconceivable events culminating in the expulsion of the Soviet Union from the League of Nations. What a farce! The League had already died years earlier for the simple reason that most nations had formalised and accepted the Geneva Convention as a code of war. It was no pun to state that the League had a 'conflict of interest' and, thus, it had *Gone with the Wind* of war. As long as 'civilised' nations agree on how to conduct a war based on a gentleman's agreement, *Homo sapiens sapiens* is doomed and should be labelled *Homo belliger insipiens*.

And, to top off the immorality of the Nobel Prize for Peace from nations exporting arms to warring nations on both sides of the trenches, that is, Sweden and Norway, that year the prize was not awarded to anyone. That proved once more that war is the norm, and peace the exception. Komaru felt that, until this concept of fatalism is obliterated by more logical thinking, humans have no right to inhabit Earth. Komaru viewed the '39' stop along an ellipsis between 1919 and 1989 as a mid-point within what normally is assumed as the life span of an average individual in Western Europe. Other humans did not count. They were simply slaves of themselves at the mercy of a warrior God who had passed his torch on to the Greeks and the Romans in a sequence pausing with the Prussians until it was entrusted to the German people as inheritors of bellicosity for their *modus vivendi atque carnificiendi*.

Meanwhile, Komaru was trying to make sense of Melissa's matter-of-fact review of recent events.

'My husband was so delighted to talk with you last night. Perhaps he and you could continue knowing each other this coming weekend, here, at our home.'

The phone call gave him a jolt. He did not like being interrupted while working, but then he thought he could be civil enough to play the game of polite social interaction. Besides, he had already sketched his notes for '1939', so it was fine to take a break.

'Hello, yes, oh, well, he is quite a bloke. Phenomenal. You see, I think that the advantage of being British, what I mean, of descending from such a race, is to utilise manners deriving from a long tradition of formalities and *savoir faire*. We Maoris have barely begun to join the human consortium, so ...'

'Komaru, please stop that nonsense. You are at times so contradictory. Or do you play with sarcasm? What is a British tradition if not haggis of a dozen tribes? Like yours. Only we have been blessed with a central power to give a cohesive consistency to my people. Basically, there is no difference in looking at your people. The main cleavage can be seen in the fact that your tribes spent centuries in isolation. Ours roamed the world because of whatever reason, so ...'

'Melissa, please, so early in the morning, I just can't ...'

'Sorry, I will cut it short. Can you come up this weekend? Bill will cook supper, and the three of us could talk in the evening. But during the day we can begin to go over your work. What do you say?'

'I don't know. Actually, why don't we postpone our ... meeting until next week? I'll call you about it. I am afraid that I might have to go to Auckland on a personal matter.'

'Oh, I love Auckland. We used to live there, but then Bill felt it was better for us to move to the country. It is more conducive to his work. And he likes the area around, especially the rivers, the parks, you know. Ehi, why don't you and I spend some time in Auckland during the summer? So exciting, so ...'

Komaru cut it short. The reference to Auckland made him decide not to waste any time and, first things first, the next day he took the train to Papakura. His father's home was in the care of a neighbor who was kind enough even to water the garden from time to time. But the orchard looked unkempt. The back fence was torn down. Some old newspapers were scattered here and there among the shrubbery. Thus, he spent two days in preparation for his departure to visit with his father after meeting with Captain Bickhard, the Salvation Army coordinator of the Social Services.

The Salvation Army made its presence known in Ao Tea Roa as early as 1883, when two teenagers, like Mormon missionaries, were sent by its founder, William Booth, from England to help humanity through Christian social work. Although its membership is low in comparison with that of other countries such as the USA, not more than one percent, the Army is solidly entrenched in both Pakeha and Maori life, particularly for its work with alcoholics.

The early history of the Army records a tough time in being accepted by the populace. Vociferous women were on their way to obtain a right to vote, and emotional men could not tolerate seeing young Army people in blue uniforms and red flashes invading their 'freedom' of religion through cadres. The very fact that the Army had officers in rank as high as generals down to lowly 'privates' offended the masses. Several Salvationists were even arrested by 'regular' army members of the government for meeting in the streets. The militarisation of church activities, of course, was not new, beginning with the Society of Jesus in Spain to the Church Army in England. The power structure was pyramidal as in any despotic system. After all, they were 'soldiers' who had signed Articles of War and volunteered to fight for Christ.

After more than a century of service to the souls and the bodies of those people raising their psychological status from colonists to New Zealanders, things had changed meanwhile. Service to disadvantaged groups and other human wrecks was recognised unofficially even by what used to be a model Socialist State taking care of every need, from bread and butter to social pensions and earthquake insurance. In fact, the state relies on the 'Army' in areas of social policy where the government usually fails as a consequence of political bitching. In essence, the Salvation Army functions like a 'Red Cross' whenever and wherever life imbalances develop by accident or design. The organization is a poor prerogative of advanced nations at home or abroad. Ironically, the Salvation Army thrives where the most absurd cleavages of social classes exist among the richest nations on Earth. And it operates where, in theory, there should not be any need for their existence. In the final analysis, the Army validates the failure of a government to take care of the dredges of humanity. That is why, in the former Soviet Union or in any other dictatorial environment, it was and is impossible to have a 'salvation' military organization.

The theme of 'salvation', of course, is not forgotten within the framework of Christianity, that kaleidoscopic mosaic of an absurd corporate organisation whose history gave the *modus operandi* to Wall Street daily life: takeovers, mergers, wars, spying, conversions, alliances, defections and disinformation, to maintain a few techniques of defense and offense, are common to both Christianity and Wall Street. In the former case, one saves the soul; in the latter, the dollar. Amusingly, if not amazingly, the Salvation Army does not believe in the 'holiness principle' while both Christianity and Wall Street do. Proselytising, naturally, is part of the game, since genetic transmission of faith is not yet part of any laboratory experimentation. A Christian gene has not yet been isolated. The traditional 'Army' is not as aggressive as other sects, like the Mormons, especially in Ao Tea Roa, since they arrived before the Christian warriors in blue uniforms. The Mormons have the *jus primae indoctrinationis* based on the fact that their *Book* was the first 'gospel' to be translated into Maori. Quite a feat, whose difficulty was lessened by simply adapting English semantemes to the scanty phonic inventory of Polynesian. The phenomenon is not dissimilar from what the Greeks did in creating a tool of work via Latin. The whole 'military' terminology, from 'angel' to 'bishop' in English, is simply Greek through a glottic development with the help of linguisticians, the priests of deception, performing field work among heathens.

That fine morning, Komaru left the bus at Queen Street and decided to walk all the way to Parnell. So instead of taking Bus 63 from the downtown terminal, he skirted the University Campus along Waterloo Quadrant, entered Gittos Street via Constitution Hill, crossed Parnell Road at Earle Street, and reached Churton Street. He wondered: who or what was Churton? Undoubtedly, not a Maori anyone or anything.

At the very beginning of Churton, the Army office looked rather uninviting among the idiosyncratic display of shapes, styles, colours and activities through which the oldest, and the once proletarian, district of residential Auckland received a new lease on life after years of near 'ghetto'-like isolation on the other side of the railway. The 'Beverly Hills' of Auckland could now receive Queen Elizabeth for a bowl of Maori food at *Antoine's*. Komaru wondered how such an 'old wolf' could command high prices from restaurants to shops to residences by simply wearing sheep's clothing through cosmetic work. The 'Medina' of Auckland lacked only a minaret to act as a beacon. But this was on the drafting board, waiting for someone to finance it.

Captain Bickhard received Komaru immediately. And he got straight to the point. His father could not stay any longer at the Centre.

'But, why?'

'Well, we have already treated your father, a model patient. Psychologically and medically he is completely out of the woods. I am positive that he will never revert to alcohol as a palliative to his unhappy life. The problem is that he may last only a few more months on Earth.'

'I am sorry, I don't understand. You ...'

'When your father was admitted, he already had advanced cirrhosis. His liver had been taken over by nodules that have altered the organ.'

'But is there not anything we can do to save him, even an organ transplant, or ...'

'Mr Reti, let me see here, your father is about 68 years old. Apparently, he had been drinking steadily for many years, probably for 50 years. You yourself must have been conceived when he was an alcoholic. What do you know about his family history or your own? At any rate, this is a matter to be discussed with the doctor when you visit your father. But, there are already complications. Plenty of malnutrition, living alone. I do not know whether there are other factors, including constant use of medication. Incidentally, do you know exactly when your father started drinking?'

Komaru could not tell Captain Bickhard everything in one meeting. His father's life was not simple. Two marriages, both wives dead. Or at least so he was told.

'His file shows some gaps here and there. I don't quite understand. You know how popular the alcohol gene is in the generational process of transmission. At any rate, what I am telling you is just ... shall I say, informal. The multiple causes of cirrhosis are not known. We are positive, however, that the major one is alcohol abuse.'

'I assume that it is the cause. He started drinking in Italy during the Second World War. He mentioned in passing how the cold nights spent in the frozen trenches were made shorter by the wine left by the Germans in the Sangro River area.'

'Sorry to hear that. Anyway, there is nothing else that we can do. When you talk with your father, you will decide whether he would like to go home and, basically, wait for death among his family or in a hospital, actually a hospice, for terminally ill patients. Beyond the body, there may be something else that is not subject to decay, and that ...'

'Captain Bickhard, sorry to interrupt you, but have the doctors said anything regarding, well, what I mean, how much time my father has left?'

'I don't know, but depending on proper nutrition, rest, periodic removal of fluid, and ...'

'What kind of fluid?'

'The fluid of the blood that is lost in the abdominal cavity. It may press against the diaphragm and interfere with breathing.'

'But you spoke of proper nutrition, too.'

'Yes, that can prolong life for a little longer, or at least may make it more comfortable. You see, I am not a medical doctor, but I have learned a lot about people like your father. They develop similar or nearly identical symptoms. As regards proper nutrition, your father has already been placed on a well-balanced protein diet, plus high doses of vitamin A, B-complex and D. Even K, since this cannot be stored in an abnormal liver. Finally, folic acid helps too. In a properly controlled environment, your father can live a little longer, but comfortably. However, he has to be watched since even simple water can shorten his life.'

'Water?'

'Yes, because it is a liquid, of course, and as such it increases, along with salt, the fluid build-up in the body.'

Komaru thanked the captain, who referred him to the administrative wing of the office. There were financial aspects to be taken care of, mostly token ones. The Army, after all, was not a profit organisation. Could Komaru provide for whatever could be done in case his father decided to either enter a hospice or go home? Of course, he would, especially after consulting with his sister. She had one more year of college, and after graduation she could return home and take care of Father.

The most immediate task, however, was to visit with him at the treatment centre. He made all the arrangements via a telephone call. Relatives of patients had to plan carefully any visit to the island. It was not a resort.

In Auckland, Spring was in the air. Soon, the new year would witness activities of both local and national importance. After all, Auckland was THE Polynesian hub of the Pacific, the crossroads between Sydney and the Asian ports. There were plans for the construction of a tall tower like the ones in Seattle and Atlanta, with a rotating platform for a restaurant, though in Auckland the utilitarian aspect was stressed to placate the criticism of disgruntled citizens who opposed the 'American' invasion of the New Zealand sky. It was felt that the tower would serve as a beacon and add safety to air navigation. Oh, the new Maori university, the new Maori TV station, the new Maori cemetery, the new ... He stopped thinking. The cemetery. That was something to be discussed with his father.

On the ferry to Waiheke Island he read the current issue of the *Gulf News*. So much stress on tourism. And plans to enlarge this and that with the intention of attracting overseas visitors. But things had changed. These visitors were not British, and not even European. References to organisations, names of tours, and the like sported Asian names, especially Japanese. Komaru noticed that, in addition to toy autos made in Japan, the people themselves looked different. 'Americans' were not to be seen as often as in past years. And more Chinese, Vietnamese, Koreans and other 'Orientals', as still referred to in tourist publications, had simply invaded Auckland.

From Oneroa Beach he hired a taxi to Man o'War Bay. He could have taken the Waiheke Rural Mail Run minibus, but he liked to see some of the places where his father used to take him and Mahina when they were so young. It was almost a sentimental journey. More motels, tourist agencies, kayaking centres and new vineyards peppered the area. He was simply impressed by the *vitis vinifera* spreading over the most unthinkable terrain, where once towered *kauri* trees. Was New Zealand going to abandon farming and ranching in favour of vineyards? And who would drink all that wine? Not Maoris, for sure. He learned later that the projected export market was not Europe or America. The new target was to be Singapore, Hong Kong, Japan – even Australia.

At the roadblock west of the Man o'War Bay, he met an employee of the Salvation Army sent by Mr M. V. Kaheno. At the jeep trail end, a motor boat was waiting for Komaru. Miss Wood had organised the trip to the very last detail. The 7 kilometre crossing took about 20 minutes. At the western jetty of Rotoroa Island, the personal assistant to the director welcomed him with her Toyota.

'*Haere mai*, Mr Reti, welcome to Rotoroa.'
'*Ae, e ...*'
'Miss Walker, or just Whina.'
'Whina? You don't look that old!'
'My mother was an admirer of Dame Cooper. I bask in her fame.'

'Forget the Mr business, sister. Just Komaru.'
'Now I see, you are bringing sunshine to our misty island.'
'How is my father?'
'Emotionally, a mess. He does not drink any more, and neither does he crave alcohol. One hundred percent recovered, but that is not all. Physically? Well, Mr ... sorry, Komaru, why don't you first unpack at the guest house? Then, after dinner you may see your father. The meeting with his doctor is tomorrow at 10:00 sharp. The director will see you in the afternoon.'
'Thank you, Whina. You sound like someone from the North. Ngapuhi?'
'In part, yes, but my *whakapapa* is still confusing. My grandfather was an American Marine. I was born in Kaikoe.'
'And what are you doing here? Why not the Mayo Clinic?'
'Well, I prefer to be here. Most patients are brothers and sisters. Maoris. And their illness is not *maori*, you know.'

Komaru was assigned a small but comfortable room. New Zealand-style, mid-1940s. The electric blanket was a blessing. The fog emanating from Waiheke Island that day was miserable. To the south, Ponui Island looked lonely.

He removed his shoes, lay down on the army-style metal bed, covered himself with the electric blanket, turned it on, and tried to rest. The calm silence was almost absolute. From time to time the muted sounds of engines from high-speed boats and ferries drifted along with the fog onto the buildings of the sanatorium complex.

He fell asleep. And he dreamed of his family, of his school years, of his upbringing in Auckland when the city was beginning to experience the growing pains of immigration. And the turmoil of coping with the dualism of his soul in a Pakeha environment. How relaxing was Papakura away from the city centre.

A friendly knock at the door woke him up. He felt hungry immediately. What time was it?

'Come in, please.'
'Mr Reti ... sorry, Komaru.'

Whina stepped on the threshold. She had changed into a dress.

'Would you not like to spruce up and meet your father?'

It was three o'clock. Komaru had slept through dinner. He was hungry, but relaxed enough to anticipate a calm encounter. He had not seen his father since Waitangi Day. And he felt a bit guilty.

Chapter 5

'Mr Reti, oh, sorry, Komaru.'

'*E* Whina, *tomo mai ki roto!*'

'You must have been exhausted. Tried to wake you up for dinner. No answer.'

'Thank you for letting me rest. It seems that certain days conjure up a stressful series of events. I ...'

'Your father is anxious to see you. He is quite a bloke. At times I detect in his eyes a spark of penetrating malice. An intriguing one. He looks at me like an X-ray machine. He simply wonders.'

'But, why? You mean wondering about your person as a female?'

'In part, but he just cannot figure me out. It is almost a love–hate situation. Your father attracts me, not at all sexually, but from a psychological standpoint. He is inscrutable. Only once has he asked me direct questions. However, you know, it is strictly forbidden to allow feelings to take over professional distances between staff and patients. He was simply puzzled during the first days of his treatment about me as a human specimen. The fact that we spoke nearly the same dialect did not convince him to open up.'

'I must confess that I myself am puzzled by you. You said your grandfather was an American Marine?'

'Yes, but let's go. I may tell you more this evening after tea.'

She left him at his father's room. He knocked, opened the door, and stood by the threshold as if waiting to be invited to go in.

'*E, Papa.*'

'*E, Tama*. You still speak Maori. At least in monosyllables. Come in, *haere mai!*'

'Shall I say, what, *he roa te wahi i haere mai ai ahau kia kite i a koe*?'

'Hell, we are becoming bastardized. Aren't we?'

'*Papa!*'

His father was sitting in a rocking chair facing the Waiheke Channel. On the windowsill a pair of binoculars rested by a large map of the area. The sun was beginning to set over the airstrip serving the

Stonyridge Vineyard. Komaru could see with naked eyes sections of the Cowes Bay Road following the contour of the island. Flocks of birds flew into the sun toward the Onetangi reserve. The whole area was peaceful, except for some distant rumbling of jets on the western horizon.

Their *hongi* was mute but long, warm, intimate. Komaru's nasal passages aspired the odor of ancestral *whenua*, the stream of blood relationship, the breath of trust. And the pores of his skin exchanged invisible particles of flesh intimacy. How different was the touch from that of Mahina years ago. Hers felt smooth, silken, almost creamy. Here Komaru felt the roughness of manhood and the terminality of a long *whakapapa*. Mahina's nose was to be licked with moist lips. His father's was to be pressed by humming lightly within the confines of a generation gap trying to cover a bridge created by the ravages of time.

The initial hesitant conversation took a long time to assume the character of a flowing dialogue. Komaru's father was obviously in a sad mood.

'So, *Tama*, who would have said that in my old age I would be a prisoner of the British Army? Of course, this is to save my pagan soul. But they cured me, at least from wasting my pension on spirits.'

'*Papa, e Papa*, how are you?'

'Well, can't you see for yourself? I can now start a new life. Soon I'll be released. What for, and where to, I don't know. What do you say?'

Komaru felt a stab in his heart and tried to change the subject of conversation.

'I just received a letter from Mahina. One more year, Dad, and she will be back with us.'

'Us? Do you mean to say that you are coming back to Papakura?'

'Possibly. I myself should finish my thesis soon and ...'

'And then you would place all your dreams of ... independence aside and abandon Wellington for a stifling suburb to watch me die?'

'Please, *Papa*!'

The rest of the afternoon was difficult for both father and son, but as the sun slowly sank under the forests of Waiheke, Komaru had detected that a certain tranquillity had surrounded his father. When Komaru turned on the light by the door, he saw several paintings by the bookshelf. He was happy to see that his father was painting again. A few carved figurines were lined up on the telly.

'I am glad you have gone back into work. I had forgotten to ask you if you needed any art supplies. I could ...'

'No need now. I should be dismissed in a week or so. You know, tomorrow both of us will be at the staff meeting for the usual details of ... Army discharge. Of course, that will not be like that of the 28th.'

'Twenty-eighth?'

'*Tama*, you do belong to a generation of ... sorry, what I meant, you know, the Maori Battalion. And you have studied history? Of course, Pakeha history ...'

A knock on the door interrupted that mocking tone of observation. Whina entered and asked Mr Reti Sr to follow her to the dining room. Komaru, however, had been invited by the director of the complex for an informal tea. Tomorrow Komaru would have time to spend with his father, and the day after tomorrow the motorboat would come to pick him up at the quay.

'That is fine, *Tama*. We are going to have breakfast together first thing in the morning.'

The tea with the director and some of his staff was pleasant. In a way, it was an informal get together as a prelude to the more formal meeting to take place at 10 o'clock next day in order to conclude all formalities leading to Mr Reti's dismissal. Thus, after thanking everyone, Komaru left the small private dining room and tried to find his way back to the guest quarters.

'*E*, Komaru! Are you lost?'

Whina was in the hallway.

'How did you like our "island" tea?'

'Delicious. The fritters were simply melting in my mouth. In Wellington you don't get fresh fish as in the past. Most things are sold frozen.'

'But here we get fresh food from Waiheke fishermen. And some of our own patients catch a few goodies from time to time from the quay. Oh, incidentally, would you like a cuppa before retiring? I am off duty. And the lounge is rather quiet this time of the evening.'

Her invitation sounded genuine and friendly.

'Sure, thank you. No fly cemeteries, please. I ate like a pig. The Army seems to have good cooks.'

The lounge, a combination of library, dance hall and waiting room was nearly deserted. In one corner a middle-aged man was browsing among old magazines rather nervously. When he found whatever he was looking for, he left in a hurry.

'So, Komaru, you now have a chance to ask me all the questions you want. Not professional ones, of course. I noticed that you are rather curious about me.'

'Well, frankly, since you have been handling my father's case for nearly everything, I was just wondering what you learned about him.'

'But that is a matter for my superiors to assess; I mean doctors, psychiatrists, and so on. Sorry.'

'However, you have come to know him, haven't you?'

'Yes, of course, but before that perhaps you would like to know a few more things about me.'

'Oh, go ahead.'

'You remember yesterday when you asked me about my dialect, I told you that my grandfather was an American Marine.'

'Yes, but what?'

'I also noticed that you looked at me in a strange way. Was it the dialect you were interested in, or my *whakapapa*? And why?'

'For my professional reasons. I am working on a thesis for an MA degree in history and ...'

'And you found in me a specimen of research?'

'You see, there is something about you I just can't put my finger on.'

'My grandfather?'

'Perhaps.'

'Does it show?'

'What?'

'My race. My one-eighth contamination.'

'Contamination?'

'My grandfather was a Negro. He met my grandmother in Wellington soon after the riots caused by white people making no distinction between Maoris and Negroes. I am sure you know THAT history.'

'I do.'

'Does that tell you anything about me?'

'A lot, sister. And how does my father enter into the picture?'

'He is a racist. Not *vis-à-vis* the Negroes, but with regard to whites. Actually, for him whites are worse than Negroes.'

'I am sorry. But, incidentally, why do you refer to your grandfather as a Negro?'

'Why not? Have you never read any papers or books published in 1944 in Wellington?'

'Yes, but nowadays that name has assumed a connotation of ...'

'Please, Komaru! So you would refer to me as what? Actually, the papers were rather kind, because Pakehas referred to them as niggers. But officials elevated them to Negroes. The rest is ... history. From Negroes to Blacks, Black-Americans, Afro-Americans, African-Americans, Africans and so on. I laugh. Do you know what I am at present? A multiracial, which means nothing, although Pakehas call my 'type' a Maoratto, that is, a Maori Mulatto.'

'This world stinks, doesn't it?'

Komaru thought of Melissa. God, if his father knew what was going on between him and her and, worse, being entertained by her husband!

'Whina, has my father's, say, behaviour or whatever interfered with any relationship between him and doctors, nurses, and others?'

'Yes, and that is why the director would like to dismiss him as soon as possible. Sorry, here I have already sinned.'

'I appreciate what you have just told me. That will help me to outline a program for my father's final days.'

'Komaru, he loathes the Pakehas more than anything else. You see, he ascribes his condition to them. He says that he feels like a Chinese poisoned by the opium smuggled by the English into their country, in spite of the fact that it was illegal in England. He is unhappy about not being able to secure some books on 19th-century China.'

'I can understand.'

'But not to the point of dreaming that one day all Pakehas will have to leave Ao Tea Roa. The English left India, and will leave Hong Kong. Why not Ao Tea Roa?'

'How?'

'Ask him! Also, ask him how he can distinguish between a "pure" white and a range of quarters, eighths, etc. When an exodus will take place, who can determine who is going to go? Am I supposed to go to America or to Africa?'

Next morning Komaru had breakfast with his father in the main dining room. It was cafeteria style, but some people could be served at their tables on request, depending on their medical condition or a particular diet. In essence, Komaru and his father agreed on a plan of action with stress on the financial situation. The farm that had been sold during the Rogernomic period had created quite a modest sum of savings. The house in Papakura was free and clear. Mahina was on a government fellowship for gifted Maoris. Komaru himself was on a bursary at Victoria. Financially, the situation was nothing to brag about, but enough to ensure a comfortable life for a few more years. Sooner or later Komaru would have to look for employment. The big question was Mahina. But, of course, it was assumed that she would get married sooner or later, or at least get a teaching certificate and secure a post somewhere in the government. At the idea of anticipating a marriage for Mahina, he felt funny. Who? She was just a child. Plus, how could she become a wife, unless she met an exceptional mate? Father seemed to have forgotten that Mahina was not a normal female.

The breakfast conversation was productive since they had left aside all personal views and concentrated on practical issues. They agreed on a plan to have his father back at the Papakura home, from which he could take the bus to visit the clinic and the doctor whenever the excess fluid would develop later. A part-time nurse would visit him every day, and 'meals on wheels' would be delivered by the local organisations taking care of senior citizens. Later, if necessary, hospitalisation could solve the more complex problems of the liver disease depending on the course of the illness. It was a matter of hanging on for a few more months until Mahina came back from America in June after graduation. Meanwhile, his father would do his best to attend the last, 'his' last meeting of the Maori Battalion scheduled for 3–6 April 1992, at the Sports and Conference Centre of Rotorua. For Komaru's father, that Reunion was of particular importance since the Host was B Company, his own. Who knew how many more Reunions would take place later? Tentatively, the 19th would take place in 1994 at the Turangawaewae Marae in Ngaruawahia but, of course, he knew that he would not be alive at that time.

By 10 o'clock the Retis were at the conference table of the Rehabilitation Centre. Two doctors, a psychologist, a nurse, the Director, the Financial Trustee and a secretary were present at an efficient and rather short session. Paperwork was circulated, examined, discussed and some sheets were signed by responsible parties. A final date for the official dismissal was not established, but it was hoped that Komaru would inform the centre as soon as his father's home was ready to receive him in cooperation with the local clinic in Papakura. As Spring was approaching fast, and thus the new rehabilitation programme was to be initiated, the director asked Komaru not to extend, for whatever reason, his father's stay beyond the end of September.

Thus, Komaru spent the whole day with his father. They walked along the beach, mostly silently. At one point, his father removed his shoes and followed the water line as if looking for a piece of *rimu* or other hard wood washed ashore. He would use it for his carvings, which at times took part of his daytime activities. Supper was served, by special arrangement, in his father's room, and Whina acted as a kind of hostess. It was typical 'Maori' food: *toheroa* soup, steamed pork with cream of *kumara*, watercress with a vinaigrette type of dressing and broiled apple slices in vanilla sauce. There was little talk. Komaru felt a strong sense of anguish. He had understood that the responsibility of planning for the last segment of his father's life would not be an easy task. But he counted on his sister. She could help, should the illness be a long one.

In the morning, he got passage on the Salvation motor boat, which took him directly to Waiheke's ferry terminal, and from there to Auckland. This time he took the train directly to Wellington. There was a lot of mail in his box, and two telephone calls: one from Melissa and another from her husband. Nothing special. They were asking him to call whenever possible. Perhaps he would like to spend next weekend in Wanganui. This time, Dr McTavish would be happy to host him and even prepare a good meal without interfering with Komaru's work, should he be ready to bring any portion of his MA thesis for criticism by Melissa.

Thus, the next day he decided to go back to his studio and either the Turnbull Library or the Public Library to verify some data. Both libraries were in the process of developing computerized programmes of direct access by a combination of modems with a telephone line. Komaru was not ready for such luxury. Besides, he preferred to touch, smell, read and finger through the books and periodicals. Standing by a square monitor at times developed in him a quasi-stance of discomfort that created some blackish, round little dots dancing in front of his eyes. He spent only one hour at the Turnbull, where he took a few notes.

By evening, he had drafted the segment dealing with the post-Second World War part of his theory, by isolating three cardinal items deciding the fate of the world.

1949 –   Birth of Modern China
            Birth of Twin Germany
            Birth of NATO

The end of the 1940s witnessed the creation of two POTENTIAL super giants, namely, China in the East and Germany in the West. The fact that Modern Germany was born as a twin did not make much difference to Komaru because he thought that the German people, hosting the highest concentration of bellicosity in their genetic baggage, would sooner or later recover from that freak of a political nature and recombine their two fractions to become the mightiest industrial and military nation after China east of the Atlantic river. And the Chinese people, hosting the lowest concentration of bellicosity in their genetic baggage, would nevertheless recover from 30 years of internal and external strife to create the most powerful economic and cultural machine in competition with the whole West.

Komaru took a little time to recall the militaristic difference between *Homo germanicus* and *H. sinensis*. The former was forever the inheritor of the fighting tradition for the hell of it, while the latter was a pacific entity based on a millennium dedicated to the refined enjoyment of life in spite of all the difficulties stemming from the usual natural and human vagaries of existence. Thus, in the Germans Komaru saw a *Homo belligerens in esse*, while in the latter he detected the *Homo pacificus in posse*. As regards the germinal status of Germans, well, he did not bother to go into deep analysis about it. He knew that the world was full of twins, be they East–West or North–South. Even China, with the Southern appendix of Hong Kong and Taiwan, thus *de facto* a North and South China, was a temporary situation as was Vietnam, Korea and, for horizontal orientation, Cyprus, Guinea, Timor and the like.

However, in the case of Germany (and 'Sancho Panza' Austria), Komaru felt the weight of the 'Education Paradox' since its citizens were the most university educated people on Earth, and, nevertheless, the most homicidal under the wings of organized warfare and racial intolerance. How could a nation of aesthetic, literate people enjoy reading romantic poetry and listening to Beethoven and Mozart time and again, while at the same time sending children to concentration camps? Chinese people, probably the most illiterate per capita among superpowers of destruction, on the other hand, displayed a tradition of pacifism. Amazingly, they never had a Schiller in their *whakapapa*. Komaru wondered whether there was a correlation between higher education and higher bellicosity. Or, perhaps, was Christianity at fault somewhere, while Buddhism and Confucianism acted as pacifiers? Could one conclude that Christianity was for whites THE religion of, if not the excuse for, war through possessing all the genes of bellicosity, responsible for all the most destructive wars, and defiantly oblivious to all the precepts reached by its founder, Christ, for the sake of self-destruction? Komaru became afraid that Christianity and Humanity were simply antithetical to each other when analysed from a purely philosophical point of view. In essence, Christ had been turned into an excuse for humans to kill each other since the Donatist schism at the beginning of the 4th century in northern Africa. Everything else to the contrary was merely a 'Chinese' paper tiger.

Above the whole mosaic, Komaru saw China as the baby boomer

of the 20th century. In the following one, China would become the most powerful nation in the world at all levels, surpassing the USA economically, the whole of Europe culturally, and all the religious organisations put together spiritually. For Komaru, China was the invisible hand that, when Earth became saturated with all its Gaean dysfunctions of a social nature, would become a model of efficiency, order and stability. And all the remaining nations on Earth would rely on China to continue their meager existence until the selenisation of Earth, a fate that cannot be avoided, especially if nuclear weapons continued to be stored as a cache of tools for mass-assisted suicide. The whole scenario of human disintegration, after all, was well on its way. Decrepit Europe, including the remains of the Soviet empire and, ironically, Canada for genetic reasons stemming from the defunct British empire, was dying of old age in the hospice of Euro dreams. The USA, in spite of its 'Jupiter complex' under the umbrella of naïve democracy, had acquired an immunisation deficit syndrome made of technological palliatives that only served to delay the opening of a giant Pandora's box of social disarray through *panem et circenses*, like basketball courts where drugged spectators watch millionaire players place a ball into a ring. Japan was just a cadet in the noble family of mankind – and this cadet could only become an impotent clergyman, a doomed warrior or a usurious banker. The rest of the world, including New Zealand and Australia, could be regarded as a Third World agglomeration of allo-nations that would never fly into the Sun. This was particularly so for the 'Latin' nations in all corners of Earth. They had allowed Christianity to emasculate the analytic recesses of their minds and had become social eunuchs in spite of the potential riches surrounding them. Brazil was just a prototype. Africa and the rest of Asia were irrelevant on the stage of humanity.

Finally, as to NATO, Komaru thought that it only gave ideas to the Russians to create similar organisations in order to crown the whole northern hemisphere with nests of nuclear 'Titans' ready to take off toward Hell. From Canada to Turkey and from England to America, as well as under the oceans, in the air, and in the bowels of the Earth, mankind had succeeded in planning and was beginning to create a network of communication systems governing the tools of mass suicide. The ancient Romans would never have conceived the ridiculous adage of 'Si vis pacem, para bellum'. Nuke nations had simply been fooled and duped by the Caesars' complex of inferiority. France, as its avatar, still reads its *De bello gallico* as a daily breviary to keep its mental sanity in check.

Komaru was not satisfied with the style and sequencing of the outline for the section dealing with '49'. Most concepts would be at best confusing to most readers, unless they already had in mind what he had conceived and stored during the last few months of analysis, In part, the unsatisfactory drafting of that historical decade within his frozen paradigm was ascribed to the fact that Mahina's letter, received the previous day, had disturbed him a lot. Part of the plans regarding his father's return home had been shattered by what Mahina wrote in the second paragraph of her letter, apparently as a result of a sudden decision.

You see, I like the States, and Portland in particular. It is a dynamic community that reminds me of the little I know about Christchurch for its climate, both physical and intellectual. There are many cultural facilities and parks, and, being a city at the hub − of the Pacific Rim, it promises to be a stepping stone between Ao Tea Roa and Europe. But, more than anything else, it provides a shelter to me personally. By knowing what I think I do about our country, a boiling cauldron that could explode at any time, within its limited and confined cultural and historical constraints, I, perhaps selfishly, cannot fail to select Portland as a substitute for what I would expect in Auckland, and in particular any of its satellite districts like Papakura. So I decided to do anything possible in order to stay in the United States, and perhaps in the Portland area or the west. This may also solve or at least attenuate my problems by eradicating the limited facilities of New Zealand. I, in essence, would detach myself from the hard times I expect for our islands, their potential turmoil affecting women like me, and do my best to get a job and one day become an American citizen. Which will not be easy. But there are ways. I have already applied for a part-time position in the university library. Although, as a foreign student, I can only work there temporarily, I hope nevertheless to one day obtain a permanent visa. But, by deciding to spend the rest of my life in America, it does not mean that my psychological problems will disappear. It is a toss up between living among people with a superiority or inferiority complex. You know, there is no other nation in the world that believes in being at the centre of the universe as Imperial China used to feel. From politicians to Wall Street CEOs, most people are convinced and act as if America was chosen by God to lead the world in everything under the invisible canopy of democracy to finance the pursuit of human happiness. Sadly, they seem to assume that their sheer power of material nature will last forever, and that the dragon of social upheaval can be chained by technological complexities run by an educated society. This has created a polarisation between functional superstructures and basic structural foundations. While the former shine in uncontrolled progress at all levels of daily life, the latter, made of moral clay, are sinking slowly and undetected in the mire of materialism and violence. Only an infusion of spiritualism could hold all the societal infrastructures as a cohesive body for a little longer, but I doubt that this will ever happen. You as a historian have undoubtedly been confronted with examples of past America-like callous social organizations collapsing under the dead weight of their own presumptuousness.

New Zealand's complex is antipodean, that is, one of inferiority. And here I don't need to elaborate about the delusion of grandeur permeating both Pakehas and Maoris except people like you, the Zapatistas of Ao Tea Roa. I am amazed to witness how a Kiwi can live a whole lifetime confined within a dreamlike suspension by refusing to accept reality. Do you think that our ovine culture can export frozen lamb legs forever at one dollar a kilogram? If Kiwis knew! When I was in Seattle I heard a joke among University of Washington medical students, who, hearing that I was from New Zealand, kidded me to hurry up and 'go home' before a local computer magnate bought it for cash. Of course, they had no idea whatsoever that Maoris would not see a penny from the sale proceeds, for the transaction would take place between the Crown and American CEOs. Then, what would happen to the Waitangi Tribunal? Transform it into a museum displaying tattooed Maori heads next to those of Merino sheep to attract American tourists to another island like Puerto Rico, Guam, Samoa and the like?

Komaru felt that his sister's depressing letter was the second step in a possible series of stressful events and setbacks that had begun with his father's illness. Too many little things had started to pile up. How could Mahina abandon her father in his care? Or, more frankly, how could she leave him 'alone' after father died? The few distant relatives and close friends could not possibly replace her as the closest blood fulcrum on which he could rotate his hopes for his mental health. He needed a reliable nose on whom a *hongi* could be placed in complete trust. What had happened to Mahina? Was an *atua* of some kind repaying him for associating himself with Melissa, a Pakeha devil enveloping him with angel wings of immediate gratification and even a smattering of pride?

He decided not to reply immediately. Besides, he had to wait for his father's new life in Papakura, the ancestral home. Thus, he spent the rest of the week in a restless fight against himself to overcome his tendency to procrastinate and tackle some of the most demanding tasks confronting him. The two telephone calls from the McTavishes were in the back of his mind. The doctor appeared to him a genuine potential friend, one that, to be frank, could help him even from a medical point of view in connection with his father's situation. But Melissa was beginning to inch her way into his mind as an enigma. He tried to go over what Dr McTavish had told him at *Great Expectations*. What could he expect from that relationship? Was he to become a pawn in a crazy game of human interaction or just an accidental cog in an infernal machine of fate?

Chapter 6

Looking at the calendar in his bathroom, Komaru was suddenly struck by the thought that soon Father's Day would be observed on 1 September, that being the first Sunday of the month. That Pakeha tradition had already begun to spread among Maoris, especially among those who had intermarried with so many nationals from all over the world. Being Maori was becoming 'cool' in the parlance of youth. As Maoris began to be recognised and respected, if not from fear of a transracial *utu*, as the people of tomorrow, barriers started to be indented as the first step for a long-term erosion. Komaru knew, however, that a 'Berlin Wall' effect could not take place. And neither a drive *à la* Desert Storm. President Bush would not give a damn about any hermit island of the Pacific. Ironically, the Pacific had made him a hero for having been shot down by the Japanese. But, after all, America was the country of heroes. It was so plagued with new mythologies deriving from sport subcultures that the 'hero' had become one of the most frequent word to be read about or heard on TV for the most banal accomplishments, even when one had succeeded in surviving against all odds. Ao Tea Roa, by following that type of reasoning, would be a country of heroes for having not only reversed a trend of extinction, but also by overcoming survival and paving the potential way to become free at home. At least they would become the avatars of what in theory could happen to the ghosts of the Australian Aborigines, to those of Chatham, Tasmania, not counting those all over the world intentionally wiped out by militaristic 'civilisation'. The Romans could be proud of having their imperialism revived by the British, the French, the Spanish, the Portuguese, the Dutch and others all over the world. Was it coincidental that all those nations were Christian? Komaru, although a student of history, could not place his finger on another parallel example among Moslems or Jews or whatever. Of course, Hinduism, Buddhism, Confucianism and other 'Oriental' beliefs were simply pagan. Was it accidental, however, that these religions, being unlike Christianity, had never entered the annals of history as having their 'armies' engaged in deliberate genocide? Tarik's crossing his own strait in 711 had been child's play and had actually erected in the long run a wall against Medieval cultural stagnation in at least a corner of Christian Europe.

Komaru had gone astray with his 'reasoning'. He tended to fall into vagaries of philosophical history. He had even reached a hasty conclusion stating that wars seem to be a derivation of Christianity, not to speak of inter-Christian conflicts that make the 'proof of the pudding' totally etymological as to the meaning of proof.

He felt better about topics of attention crowding his mind when he decided that 1 September would be the date for his father's return to Papakura. Thus, he only allowed a couple of days to investigate an item discussed or, better, clinically outlined by Dr McTavish at the restaurant more than a month earlier. He recalled a cryptic sentence.

'You see, Mr Reti, actually, may I call you Komaru, since you could be my son, Melissa is a nymphomaniac. Have you ever heard that term?'

'Yes, it can be actually read about it, in parallel cases. Once a politician from the Labour Party used it right here saying that New Zealand unions are like nymphomaniacs since, soon after they obtain something, they start all over again. They are never satisfied.'

'Well, the parallelism has some merits, but I hope that workers' unions are not affected medically as a nympho, sorry, a nymphomaniac is. Melissa is one of those "open" cases that, unknown to most, present a baffling medical problem. Like having a headache and taking aspirin as a palliative. Unless you find the cause of a headache, you simply go on indefinitely without any hope for treating the patient. Melissa reached a point of no return more than a generation ago. She was at the stage of becoming insane in England, before roaming the world teaching English and trying to understand herself as a female. It is a long story.'

That evening, Komaru learned quite a lot about both Melissa and Bill. They were phenomenal people, an exceptional married couple, a unique association of two human beings that had come out of the closet, though still not for open consumption. Not in New Zealand, anyway, since that country offered the McTavishes a new lease on life by permitting them carefully to blend among the Pakehas via a solid profession and among the Maoris through a genuine interest in their culture, Thus, in anticipation of returning their call, Komaru allowed himself one or two hours of research in order to learn about

Melissa's 'medical' condition. What the doctor had told him seemed far-fetched, and Komaru wondered whether Melissa's husband was himself a psychiatric case.

Komaru had thought that spending a few hours in one single library would answer some of his questions about nymphomania. Dictionaries offered only circular meanings. Even medical lexicological reference books were parsimonious in explaining, or at least defining, the affliction Melissa once called a blessing to be indulged in to the utmost. She considered herself a biological machine to be disposed of like any other terrestrial animal. For her, sex was simply a matter of thermodynamics. For her husband, it was a current reflection of natural behaviour inherited from protozoa and paramecia, who apparently have the most exciting reproductive life on Earth. Humans had undergone the result of a curse that, according to a Mexican doctor, had punished them enough by splitting their original androgynous structure into two parts: male and female. The Mexican doctor had even studied in detail Aristophanes' views in Plato's *Symposium*, where a string of terms in later English gave modern biologists a list of things to ponder about, from androgynous to hermaphrodite to gynandromorph. Zeus apparently had been offended and had utilized an *utu* rather than a permanent *tapu* on the so-called human race. He did not want to obliterate it, for how could he be remembered had he done so? Thus, he simply and magnanimously employed the ante-literam Solomonic justice method by splitting the original humans vertically and horizontally. The brouhaha caused by liberation movements creating lesbians and gays was a compromise. There was nothing new. After all, how could Sappho be remembered on the basis of a few fragments and passing remarks in historical notes by ancient unpaid journalists uncovered in Egyptian papyri? How could Zeus ever anticipate that in 1962 some charred remains of papyri found at Derveni would prove the dishonesty of a Plato in burning Diagoras' book for his own niche in history, and in the process conning the Athenians into condemning Socrates to death?

As usual, Komaru went astray in his research. He just could not stop at a determinate point that was necessary not only to avoid wasting time and energy, but also to concentrate on a particular subject. Although intellectually he knew that he could spend a lifetime on a particular topic, he would spread all over creation merely for the sake of learning in a geometric progression. Thus, instead of spending only a few hours, he employed two days at the Turnbull, at the University Library, at the National Library and at the Public Library.

Just before making final arrangements to take his father to Papakura on 1 September and surprise him with a little Father's Day party in near-Pakeha style, Komaru had found out a lot about nymphomania, though not necessarily a definite answer to its existence as a medical phenomenon or, better, a human problem, if any, from a social point of view in prissy New Zealand. Meanwhile, he had come across a preliminary study based on a telephone survey of women, mostly Pakeha. The tentative results indicated that in sexual activities Neo-Zealanders were rather straight-laced. There was a qualification about the Maoris since they were regarded as culturally 'divisive'. Thinking of Melissa and her husband's sexual mores, he laughed, for he felt antithetical to 'divisive'. He could not find a term for it, and he used the faulty 'catalytic' in place of conciliatory, no, better say coordinator. But, of course, the McTavishes were not New Zealanders. The final survey would take a few more years, in spite of the fact that the Auckland University Medical Society was surprised by the openness of the response. Well, over the phone, anyway, people invent baloney just to experiment and enjoy the vicarious pleasure of what they would like to do and never did, if not answer prickling questions. What Komaru found out about nymphomania was rather revealing, and he laughed at his own Freudian adjective, and even funny in connection with British prudery in pre-Victorian times.

He learned that the current term 'nymphomania', applied loosely to a host of sexual behaviour manifestations, displayed, or suffered, by women in all cultures is, at best, still misunderstood, if not regarded unfairly in spite of constant interest by some segments of the general public. The 'classical label' *furor uterinus* is misleading from a medical and historical standpoint since the Latin term appeared only in the 18th century, as related below, though the malaise as recognised by Lucretius in *De rerum natura* simply as *furor* without any adjectival specification. Satyriasis, the male counterpart to nyphomania, on the other hand, does not seem to concern the guardians of morals or medical scientists as much as nymphomania, unless men affected by 'excessive' sexual drives commit crimes against society through rape or other deleterious actions within the legal and moral parameters of a specific culture. Although the psycho-physiological 'condition' affects potentially half of the world's population, to Komaru it seemed that it was concentrated in the USA. The most confusing terminology, however, is found in Michel Foucault's third volume of *History of Sexuality*, where he says that 'Satyriasis in women[!] is sometimes mentioned.' Komaru had no time to refer to the original French, and neither to Soranus' *Gynecology* in the *Corpus Medicorum Graecorum*. However, a most fantastic work titled *Porneia* by Aline Rousselle confuted Foucault through her detailed and fully documented knowledge of the Classical world, particularly evident in Chapter 4, namely 'On virginity and hysteria'.

He found out that, while the terms 'nympho' (an American abbreviation of nymphomaniac) and 'satyr' are the two faces of a sexual 'Janus', the nominal suffixes to each male and female counterpart are unbalanced to the detriment of women. This could be construed as an aspect of professional male chauvinism going back to a tradition of views that, either intentionally or accidentally, discarded the logical contrast of 'satyriasis' versus analogically created *'nymphiasis' or *'satyromania' versus 'nymphomania'. While the noun-suffix -*iasis*, from Greek, is used for an unspecified disease related to the characteristic prefix for a male, the suffix-*mania* is reserved for a more specific disease attributed to females affected by 'mental and physical hyperactivity or disorganization of behavior', as Komaru read in almost any medical or psychological dictionary.

The analogical creation of terminology to the detriment of the female, therefore, has forced her to carry the stigmatic suffix of 'mania', undoubtedly a medical term for both a psychological and a physiological dysfunction, though without giving details on the interaction, if any, between the two basic types of affliction. The proof, if valid, lies in the fact that in English the term 'satyriasis' was accepted in print as early as 1657 according to most English language dictionaries, while 'nymphomania', kept in the limbo of ignorance for fear of moral pollution, was made public in print as such only in 1775 through the *OED*. Thus, it took more than a century to devise and accept a disparaging suffix to describe for the female situation an analogical component as the gender counterpart to seemingly identical human dysfunctions. In fact, a Don Juan or a Casanova is not regarded with the same sense of 'disapproval' as is a Cleopatra, the Roman Messalina, Catherine II of Russia, the 'Italian Messalina', i.e. Queen Joanna of Naples, or even a certain Peggy Guggenheim for their 'excessive' sexual activities, according to a pamphlet published by Cauldwell in 1947.

In the process of analysing what both laypersons in general and professionals in particular label 'nymphomania', there emerged several 'whys' with their collateral adverbs of time, place and manner, giving explanations that are often in conflict with each other as a function of historical and contemporary trends or, better, of past and present assumptions in the medical and social sciences, not to speak of literary and pseudo-literary interpretations. The tendency, as understood and recorded so far, has been one of regarding the whole enigma as a single item in terms of inception, development, and, rarely, full treatment.

Historically, nymphomania has been compartmentalised into neatly defined niches according to mostly subjective premises. For example, as regards its sphere of existence, nymphomania has been placed within the domain of either psychology, psychiatry, medicine, sociology and even demoniacal compartments, just to mention a few main headings, as Komaru found out by scanning back issues of *Sexology*. In terms of roots, on the other hand, the tendency, if not the post-Freudian tradition, has been 'extremist', that is, either/or. This is in conflict with the school of thought that objectively departs from premises that in sexuality everything is a continuum. There are no frozen stations anywhere along the way.

Although Komaru's research was not extensive, he would guess that no 'final' agreement had been reached as to the medical condition and its treatment, if not prevention, for the 'disease' seems to lie beyond the evolutionary sphere of *Homo curabilis*. Thus, one can only navigate through schools of thought ascribing the condition or the disease to one extreme or another, that is, whether a case of 'nature' and, therefore, 'genetic' at one end, in opposition, not in contrast, with 'nurture' or environmental constructs at the other. Komaru did exclude that, even by considering extremist views, what may have been an inception at the 'nature' level, through genes, may have gradually shifted to the 'nurture' end of performance. In other words, what is born within an individual female and, thus, latently present within her genetic paradigm, may erupt at a certain chronological point as a full manifestation by becoming a consequence of the environmental and a domain of 'nurture'. In a way, this causes a flow along the syntagm of daily life until it becomes chronically operational as a *modus vivendi in inveterato amplexu sexuali*.

After two days of intensive browsing in three libraries, Komaru concluded that, even at the classificatory stage *vis-à-vis* the dynamics of nymphomania, it is not easy to approach the subject-matter with total confidence and hope for comprehensive results since each case is unique within a general framework of reference. The reasons for this uniqueness are several. First, although nymphomania is either born within or acquired by an individual, it is always subject to the 'action' performed by another party, whether that party is a man (a normal occurrence), another woman (a frequent possibility) or surrogate entities such as non-physiological 'tools', namely vegetal or non-biodegradable penile substitutes such as vibrators among the most sophisticated devices offered by modern technology. Of course, *le délire de toucher* is the most efficient and least expensive means of avoiding an external source of manipulation, as well as less likely to cause infection and internal damage. Another factor for uniqueness is that, fortunately or unfortunately, the life of a nymphomaniac, a human being, is rather short and, thus, as for any other human phenomenon, not observable for a period longer than a century at best, unlike some other terrestrial living organisms, such as a bristlecone pine (3,000 plus years) or even a rock (about 3.7 billion years).

Meanwhile, previous studies of cases have rarely been correlated comprehensively even within a single culture. Consequently, nymphomania has become and is still a taboo subject. Anyone willing to consult almost any reference material, from a single dictionary of the English language to an expensive medical dictionary, will be given a one-sentence definition indicating an anomaly such as an 'excessive' or 'abnormal' amount of female sexuality and, thus, a rather negative portrayal of something projected along a subjective axis of normality from which a woman goes astray.

But, what is normal? No one has so far had the 'vision' or courage to define what is acceptable in human sexuality, except by espousing religious or moral tenets of dubious pan-human values. These rather moot considerations or beliefs, that in print reflect a literal collation of previous assumptions, are frozen and will remain frozen in description for a long time because, even terminologically, they are the products of popular ignorance, of subjective institutional codes and of scientific callousness. Among 'culturally literate' and sane individuals nowadays, there is a fairly comfortable belief that in human sexuality everything is in a 'Heraclitean' flux. This is particularly true in a woman's life that is constantly being readjusted to a kaleidoscopic pattern of feelings, emotions, and dreams as a function of conception, gestation, parturition, child-rearing and menopause.

By assuming that 'abnormal' sexual activity has existed since 'prehistoric' times, since allegedly womanhood has not changed for at least a quarter of a million years, it may be possible to speculate on the birth of any term within the already mentioned Judaeo-Christian, if not the Judaeo-Christian-Muslim components overlapping each other in the West. One should not forget that Europe without Islamic cultural contributions would still be in the 'dark' ages. This pan-cultural mosaic imposed itself, by the book or the blade, on most 'Western' cultures to render humans perhaps schizophrenic, paranoid, if not allo-anthropic, as a function of a 'higher' degree of civilization through religious dogmas.

Some analysts may even go to extremes by stating that 'Western' religions have changed the face of mankind, but few mention the fact that half of this mankind has been affected the most, namely, women. Why? Because women, as most mammals, possess a hymen as an ID to womanhood, though, unfortunately, unlike in guinea pigs, once 'deflowered' the hymen does *not* reseal the vaginal aperture after each reproductive period. And reading about this impedimentum, for whatever reason, Komaru's thoughts went to Portland. Did Mahina still possess it in Portland? How strange, he reflected. This is an exclusive primacy of the female. No other entity can boast the same privilege or curse. Whether this is a relevant consideration in the analysis of sex is beside the point unless evidence can collate human nymphomania with similar unquestionable conditions, whether medical or psychological, among elephants, squirrels or paramecia. However, one should keep in mind the rôle of the hymen in all societies, particularly in those where young women are subject to a host of indignities ranging from the avuncular 'toe' in defloration, not to mention infibulation and 'female circumcision', all being false terms for mutilation of the body and tampering with the mind of innocent humans. In Ao Tea Roa, the taking care of the hymen was done as a normal 'operation' by a girl's *kuia* through the usage of a *whakakai* called 'ahiwharau', basically a *pounamu* pin worn by a male relative as an earpendant and employed on the *puhi* on demand, according to Makereti.

On the second day of his research, Komaru, by confining his investigation to the English language, could assume that the written term 'nymphonamia' was born in the USA under God during 1775, and is, thus, as American as motherhood, apple pie and baseball. It later appeared in England through a translation from Latin made by a certain Doctor William Cullen, an eminent physician who died in 1790. His translation of a text appearing in English as *Nosology* was published only in 1800. Anyone who would like to learn more about Dr Cullen, a fantastic teacher and a prolific writer, can refer to the 9th edition of *Encyclopaedia Britannica*, especially for the influence he received from the philosophical and medical doctrines of Dr

Hermann Boerhaave of Leyden, who had written all his scientific works in Latin. Komaru wondered whether Dr McTavish knew of Dr Cullen's work.

It never fails, thought Komaru. Historical records seem to confirm Henry Ford's dictum that 'history is bunk'. Under the entry 'nymphomania' in the *OED*, nothing is shown as a record before 1800. In fact, all records referring to and including the term are of later date, though the explanations given are, if not condemning, at least amusing. Without taking the space to provide bibliographical references that the finicky reader can find directly, it suffices to mention just a few sentences referring to nymphomania. The standard explanation is 'a feminine disease characterised by morbid and uncontrolled sexual desire'. Other references quote records such as 'in a few cases, the attack has degenerated into nymphomania', 'the girl ... in whom the cerebellum was absent suffered from nymphomania', 'though nymphomaniac symptoms are constantly present when young females are insane', and so forth. Not even animals are spared uncharitable descriptions of their sexual mores. As late as 1900, according to the *OED*, in the prestigious *The Lancet*, one may read that 'It [satyriasis] is practiced upon mares ... which have nymphomaniac tendencies'.

During the afternoon spent at the Public Library, Komaru consulted the 3rd edition of the *Encyclopaedia Britannica* covering 1788–97, during which both male and female 'aberrations' were included, but with a difference: the male disease is entered as 'satyriasis', but the female one as *furor uterinus*. The latter is what the term for nymphomania was before Dr Cullen's translation from Latin. Or, perhaps, there may have been a term in English, but it was not used for fear of polluting the souls of Anglophones. It was also customary to record in Latin anything that was too risqué, as in translations from foreign languages such as Chinese or Sanskrit. Thus, *furor uterinus* may have been created by analogy with exciting Classical Latin terms such as *furor poeticus, furor loquendi, furor scribendi* and others. Komaru made a Xerox copy of the entry to discuss for fun with Dr McTavish.

After reading that entry, beginning with 'The *furor uterinus* is in most instances either a species of madness ...', Komaru did not know whether he should laugh or cry. But, as a History Major, he knew that, for the sake of objectivity, one should not entirely blame our forefathers for assuming a rather deep-seated 'happening' in the uterus since, rather recently, even in college textbooks on human sexuality, one may learn a new geography or, rather, a new topography for the *terra incognita* of half the human population. This can be inferred by collating the type of orgasms felt by women as a function of the sexual organs even before speleologists came upon the 'G-spot'. And Melissa had one easy to find. Well, at least she guided him wherever she thought it was located.

Indeed, Melissa could identify several locations on the map of her sexual pleasure, a prerogative apparently denied to her husband. These were related to a triad, namely, a 'vulval orgasm', a 'uterine orgasm' and a 'blended' orgasm (compliments of the Osterizer). The latter allegedly combined the two former orgasms. However, what had happened to what precomputer-age housewives knew, unlike Melissa, about their 'clitoral' and 'vaginal' orgasms? Apparently, they were parts of the comprehensive 'vulval' orgasm, within which a clitoral orgasm was never vulval, while the vaginal could also include the clitoral. A privileged hierarchical position has always its kudos.

By the end of the second day, Komaru knew that the *furor uterinus* described by the ancients was not solely a product of their imagination. The reason for the uterine orgasm was the 'repetitive displacement' of the uterus and consequent stimulation of the peritoneum. Apparently, whoever described and categorised the different types of orgasms must have had a good informant. 'Hey, honey, what are you feeling?' 'Just a moment, sweetie, I think I am experiencing a vulval orgasm, but I am not sure whether it is clitoral or vaginal. Oh ... no ... it is uterine, up, up and away, in my beautiful balloon, just a beautiful *furor uterinus*. Thank heavens I am allergic to barley water!'

In trying to reach a conclusion, Komaru relied on the 1947 pamphlet by Cauldwell. This was very difficult to examine under the Cerberite eyes of a prissy librarian female who was probably undergoing a vicarious orgasm. Komaru felt that, although medical science seems, perhaps rightly, to be cautious to come out freely in the open, pathological foundations of nymphomania have already been considered for at least a century as a consequence of a physical condition or dysfunction. This, again, can be only inceptual and leading later to the psychological stage of the 'mania'. In essence, although it may begin in or be triggered by the 'body', nymphomania can later shift to become paradigmatized into the mind. Of course, the reverse cannot be discarded lightly. This was presented succinctly by Cauldwell's study that Komaru was able to duplicate in a nearby coin-operated machine when the librarian left him alone just before the library closed for the day.

Nymphomania appears to arise from a disordered personality – a mental disease, and the physiologist would say that this resulted from glandular dysfunction or brain pathology. Of this latter there seems little doubt. In support of this is the statement from the *Archives of Neurology and Psychiatry*:

> Whether the type of (brain) tumor presented is an extreme rarity among patients with symptoms of nymphomania or whether there are other similar cases which have gone unrecognized is impossible to ascertain until psychiatrists and neurologists direct their attention to the possibility of the existence of an organic lesion in the sensory area of the brain in patients with nymphomania.

Many of the so-called *symptoms* of hypersexuality are strictly indicative of the reverse – or hyposexuality. And, even though the physiologist is logical when he looks for glandular disturbance, the psychologist is right when he seeks a foundation in the measurement of the duration and force of mental processes. Likewise, the sociologist is not far afield when he studies behavioristic patterns. The pathologist pursues a logical course in his suspicions of a brain tumour or other brain disease. The psychiatrist and the neurologist admit all of the possibilities suggested by the several other specialists and are justifiable in their contention that the mind acts as the receiver of the various end results and that therefore psychotherapy, or mental treatment, is indicated.

And, here again, Melissa came in as a proof of her sexuality. Could it be that yesterday's nymphomaniac can be seen as a 'highly sexed' woman who in the past did not have a chance to express her sexuality liberally and freely? The sexual liberation of females using the Pill since the 1960s had in a way shelved certain male/female interactions through normally accepted, or at least tolerated, legal associations. Otherwise, several Hollywood stars, who preferred to copulate under the sanctions of holy matrimony, as in the case of Elizabeth Taylor, rather than through shacking up as Marilyn Monroe did, would have been classified as nymphomaniacs according to old sociological views.

Was Melissa's case one of fighting her husband's potential impotence with mechanical gadgets of all types obtainable even at a hardware store or through the help of a third party, as Komaru thought of himself? Or was it something flaring up in 'advanced' nations? Was the absence of 'love', atrophied by Hollywood, responsible for a palliative through endless sex? In American society, as in other highly industrialised countries permeated by bored humans carrying over genes from Sybaris, the phenomenon seemed endemic. Why? *Taedium vitae*? *Carpe diem*? Lack of spirituality, defiance of established double-standard political systems, or a subconscious desire for self-annihilation through potential AIDS? Komaru felt a chill in his spine. He had not used any prophylactics. Was Melissa safe?

When Komaru went home late in the evening, for, being tired, he had stopped at the *Spice of Life* for a relaxing meal, he gathered all his notes and began to ponder about the two days of research. He felt ready to meet the McTavishes, for he felt stronger about their life style, but there remained big questions. Is nymphomania a mental dysfunction, a purely physiological abnormality, or what? Or can it begin at either level and then shift from one area to another? Moreover, is it monogenetic, polygenetic, or complementary? And how does it impact an individual, a family nucleus or society at large? Perhaps by analysing and engendering some respect for the female going through a private hell every hour of her life, it may be possible to find a *modus tolerandi* so that life on Earth will be less of a pain in the uterus. And, to accomplish this task, Komaru felt that men should feel equally responsible since they can help. After all, a woman affected by nymphomania can be a reflection of a man or men desirous to come half way towards their sisters objectively and even charitably if necessary. In that connection, Komaru was at a loss to consider himself either a hero or a martyr.

One way to formulate a constructive process of understanding and healing is that of coming out with personal experiences, as in his case. This was not only difficult, but also extremely delicate and painful. He could guess that most men interacting with nymphomaniacs may be married and in search of sexual novelty, if not excitement, outside the peaceful, though at times dull, routine of marriage.

Komaru felt that, so far, the analysis of the subject-matter had been confined within both narrow synchronic and short diachronic parameters. He felt it important that the inquisitive journey should not stop at the Freudian station, or at Krafft-Ebing's, Cullen's, Boerhaave's, Galen's, Aristotle's, and so forth. There is no question that a 'nostalgia' film in black and white may lay some foundations for inspiration and avoidance of old pitfalls, but what does one gain by retracing the footsteps of old trails? The diachronic analysis should take humans beyond the usual stations of 'written' records. How? Simply by analogy with what paleontologists, anthropologists and archaeologists do with physical evidence. The search for today's mysteries surrounding nymphomania should climb back along a trail of 'billions of years of microbial evolution' by performing a dance of comparative and historical analysis, a mystery dance brilliantly performed along the evolution of human sexuality.

Komaru had checked out for a week a most fascinating study of mankind in the 20th century, namely, Lynn Margulis and Dorion Sagan's *Mystery Dance*, just received at the Public Library. By scanning some key paragraphs, he knew that it would be rather significant to go back billions of years in trying to scrutinise nymphomania with the discriminatory probing of medical doctors, psychologists, psychiatrists and case workers dispensing modern versions of 'barley water' as a substitute for matrimony. This is clearly inadequate to solve the problem. This problem, long the domain of male analysts, is now being tackled by females. Melissa seemed to have a sixth sense in addition to a comparable intellectual and professional formation. After all, it was both her mental health and sexuality at stake, and thus it was proper for her and other women to take care of their own business.

As a matter of fact, only they, being women, are entitled to understand nymphomania that, from now on, should be referred to as 'fossil sex' or 'paleo-sex' for therapeutic purposes, for pleasure, for mental hygiene, or for whatever reason if not just for the heck of it, as long as they do not interfere with 'environmental' constraints. Whether this 'paleo-sex' is caused by a 'tumour', endocrinological dysfunction, a stroke, an impotent husband, an early trauma (rape, child abuse, incest, etc.), is beside the point. Once the 'phenomenon' becomes 'in', that is, paradigmatic, ingrained, fully physiological or even 'genetic', well, it is there, and there is no point in burying one's head in the sand of Sartrean '*mauvaise foi*' of self deception or shame.

Thus, for Komaru, the basic formation of professionals studying nymphomania should include considerations going back to a paleo-stage of 'evolution'. For these activities, should one pose questions such as why, when and how did the female animal develop a hymen? Or did other lower animals lose it at some stage of evolution? What is the rôle of oestrus in female mammals that lost the 'periodicity' of such physiological process? Is paleo-sex triggered by a 'fossil' remnant of such oestrus subject to whatever causes its 'flow', whether physical or mental, in any direction? What is the rôle of ovulation? Research records show that, even before the onset of ovulation, a woman may be affected by paleo-sex. And what is the rôle of orgasm?

Is it the obverse of frigidity, and thus a weapon of defense, or a hindrance in paleo-sex? Finally, is there a correlation between IQ and PSQ, that is, *Paleo-Sex-Quotient*?

Suddenly, Komaru was struck by a strange thought. By any chance, was Melissa 'in love' with him? How could she be when so often she told him how much she loved her husband, how intelligent and cerebral he was, such a god to revere? She also told Komaru that, unlike her husband, he was 'special', whatever that meant. Actually, thinking more deeply, he asked himself whether Melissa mentioned him as 'special' in comparison with her husband alone or with other men. And how many? Would knowing an exact figure make any difference?

The element of 'love' became a puzzle for Komaru. He believed that in the periodic table of human emotions, feeling, sentiments, passions, and so forth, there was an empty square, for everything was apparently known about that element except its nature and relationship with *Homo eroticus*. He knew that he had never loved anyone, and no one had ever loved him. In Melissa's case, 'love' could not enter into any paleo-sex 'behaviour'. When love affects a nympho, it apparently 'cures' the mania. In this case, it is doubtful that the pathological dysfunction ever existed. It may have been a fossil remnant that was removed through introspection (oh, the dismantling power of etymology!) or even painful conformation with the social mores prevailing over 'selfish' necessities. But for how long would this delicate balance last in an affective association? Would the family ties be relevant enough to overcome the dormant 'genes' of paleo-sex that are always latent in a healthy female?

Komaru felt grateful to his protective *wairua* that he was not in love with Melissa. His association with her was one of discovery, both trans- and intraracial. He was just growing up along the edges of an old European culture transplanted onto his own that the tradition of love had not yet contaminated totally. And he wondered if the trumpeted legend of Hinemoa was not only merely a reflection of genetic memory acquired before the Maori canoes left Hawaiki carrying along not only the *kuri*, but also something that the Chinese had in their mythological stock as later transplanted into Japan and also Ao Tea Roa before the Western variety was imported along with the Bible and its subconsciously cerebral and refined cannibalism.

Chapter 7

September had always held a special fascination for Komaru. In approaching the occurrence of the Spring Equinox, he took a weekend off from the various tasks in which he had been engaged. He spent nearly 3 weeks, beginning with Father's Day, to settle pending issues. The Papakura home had been spruced up, his father had fallen into a routine life, and the visiting nurse had established a pattern of relaxed chores. Dr McTavish had helped, pulling strings informally, by establishing contacts, dispensing advice, suggesting nutritional possibilities and encouraging Komaru to hold steadfast to stressful reality. The originally planned supper at Wanganui had been postponed several times for one reason or another.

When Komaru left Papakura on the morning of the 19th, he felt relieved that, until Mahina's return, his father could live a more or less tranquil life, except for the constant monitoring of the fluid build-up caused by advancing cirrhosis. The garden had been returned to normality. All the rooms had been repainted except for Mahina's. She did not want anything to be done under any conditions. Thus, while the rest of the house looked more mature as adapted for grown-up people, Mahina's study/bedroom remained almost childlike in its decorations, contents and memorabilia. Komaru had nearly forgotten how possessive his sister was of her things. She barely allowed him to enter her place, especially after the innocent relationship of sibling childhood had been superseded by a transitional reorganization of interaction. Komaru had to knock first and wait for permission to enter.

That change in etiquette had become more evident when Mahina approached the age of twelve. Always a skinny child, by that time she had begun to put on some weight, her limbs became longer, and the flesh around her bone structure acquired a gentle rotundity. Although as children the two siblings had been free to see each other in casual nudity, after Mahina approached puberty her bust problem became more evident. Without a mother or any other female to either counsel or protect her during that critical stage of development, what had started as an annoying anomaly to be rectified as soon as she could undergo plastic surgery had become a major issue. It caused Mahina to create a life of both introspection and adaptation to extreme privacy that was understood by her classmates and friends as a European legacy via her mother.

She had been born with a third nipple that, as long as it stayed the same size as the other two, presented no discomfort or concern. It could be looked on as if it were a mole or a growth to be excised in time. Had she confided in her Headmistress or any other woman, probably by now she could have been treated successfully or palliatively. Only once, at the age of 10 months or so, before her mother died, had she been taken to the local Karitane clinic. At that time it was felt that it would be better to wait until puberty and then decide what to do if a third breast should develop in a parallel fashion with the other two. But then no additional analysis was performed after she became motherless.

As Mahina grew up, she nearly forgot that she was different, although she became extremely careful to avoid situations that might reveal her medical condition, particularly at school. A couple of times, her father vaguely alluded to her breast as something that could be taken care of when she became an adult. Komaru, who had become familiarised with his sister's problem, nearly forgot it too. Being a few years older than Mahina, Komaru left home for school in the normal sequence and was absent from Papakura. And, meanwhile, Mahina had learned not only to take care of herself, but also to assume the rôle of the mistress of the house with all its responsibilities, including washing, tending the garden and incidental cooking normally done by her father.

The whole thing nearly came to a crisis when Mahina had received a scholarship from Transpacific University in Portland, an institution that had developed a strong programme of 'catholicism' attracting foreign students. Actually, the adjective 'foreign' was later changed to 'international' to minimise the discomfort of being considered a stranger in a 'catholic' environment. The fact that the university was Catholic, of course, was nearly incidental, if not redundant, because there were many Catholic institutions on the west coast, even one in the same city, namely, the University of Portland. But it attracted students from all over the world, especially the Pacific Rim. Strangely, Mahina was the first from her country to apply for admission and the only one ever to land on that north Pacific shore. Among the international students representing 34 countries, she was the only Ao

Tea Roan. In a way, she was happy not to be 'checked' by the familiarity of co-nationals abroad.

There had been only a period of anguish soon after she had applied for admission to several institutions on the west coast. She had to undergo a physical examination to obtain a student visa. But the doctor appointed by the US Consulate in Auckland did not make an issue of it. The student was in perfect health, normally developed, highly intelligent and so forth. At the bottom of the medical certificate she had simply entered a sentence under 'Observations', namely: 'Miss Reti possesses an extra breast located nearly over the left ventricle of her heart. Although developed as much as the other two, the breast does not indicate any potential dysfunction affecting the academic life of a student'.

That declaration had created a strong peace of mind for Mahina. After developing her breasts during puberty, that had, incidentally, started nearly 2 years later than for most Ao Tea Roans, Mahina had accepted her physical status and adapted herself to daily life, including normal dressing and wearing anything like any other teenager. The only exception she had made was in avoiding extremely tight shirts and an occasionally worn fashionable sweater imported from Italy. And she never needed to wear a bra. The other two breasts and nipples, being rather medium in size, framed the smaller one inconspicuously as a small cone between two larger ones. Only rarely would her *tiki* press or rub against what she had named 'the third eye'. Much later, when she became aware of her sexuality and of areas subject to erogenous stimulation, did she discover that 'the third eye' was extremely sensitive to the touch. While the two normal nipples reacted as expected in a healthy teenager, the third one displayed a larger protuberance in proportion to its base, particularly when fondled. That abnormal reaction had first taken place when she soaped herself during showers, and then later when, just before leaving for Oregon, she had checked for any lump or growth as part of her health campaign against breast cancer. In her self-examination, she had triggered a wave of warm feelings all over her body, while a languor had descended below her navel before acquiring the characteristics of an orgasm. And that was all although she had not done it intentionally.

Before Komaru left Papakura on the 19th, the anniversary of the right to vote granted to women in 1893, he looked around his sister's room, mostly at photographs taken here and there, and observed her in a different light. He wondered, for he missed her and her constant pricking him with mocking and nearly derisive criticism. She was smaller, and often she asked for his help in household chores during the summer. And he was always patient, gentle, affectionate. Only lately, after going through the confusing and revealing series of 'international' contacts starting with Ling-ling, Komaru could not help imagining what had happened to his sister. Portland, Oregon, was not far from Hollywood, and the feminist revolution had reached its highest peak of pathetic freedom. He felt comfortable that, in his instinctive feeling of protection toward the only female he could trust, Mahina was attending a Catholic university that called for a non-mainstream-type of American education, where campus life was not regulated by the cheap philosophy of pulp magazines sporting disgusting centerfolds of hair growth. He wondered why Asians were reluctant to be photographed displaying pubic hair. But had Mahina carried genes from whom? The Yugoslavian or the Maori stock? Ling-ling was blank except for paleo-vestiges of once protective barriers against weather, insects and disease. Melissa underwent periodical depilatory sessions, not necessarily for health or aesthetic reasons, but to eliminate any interference in the epidermic contact with a partner. For her, the skin-to-skin contact was a most exciting experience, particularly when she used creams and lotions fomenting pleasurable gliding movements in all directions without creating epidermic eruptions of reddish spots. He did not have to follow suit in Melissa's preparations, for his race had been spared unnecessary 'pelury'.

Spring was already in the air, and he reacted to nature's awakening in an analytic way. The relationship with the McTavishes had generated in him a hedonistic approach to daily life, though he knew that he had priorities, from the 'Movement' to his studies. Not that a career in history was the primary purposes in his life, but he hoped that it would give him a solid foundation in his fight to recover Ao Tea Roa from the indignities of political and psychological rape. And, after deciding to stop at Wanganui on the 19th, perhaps for the weekend, he called first. Dr McTavish was happy to hear from him.

'By all means. Stop by any time. You have apparently forgotten that you are not a stranger here.'

Komaru's life had changed meanwhile. He became 'automobilious'. As a token of appreciation for taking care of so many things, his father had 'financed' the purchase of his own pick-up. In driving to Wanganui, he had taken the road through the Whanganui Park, then he zigzagged by the river along rural routes for the pleasure of touching base with the land of his ancestors. And he thought of Melissa. During the last meeting, she had absorbed half a bottle of Cardhu, but had poured out a most significant segment of her life as lived before she met her husband in Australia.

After graduating from the University of Cambridge with a degree in History, although she did not say when or at what college, she had found that England was not the place for a woman to find a pleasant job in spite of feminism. Through the help of her father, she had secured a position in a vanity press in London. Because of her classical language background and knowledge of French and Italian, she had first become a PA to a rather unscrupulous individual milking money from naïve individuals hoping to become famous through writing. She later became a copy editor, an activity she enjoyed because she was extremely curious about foreign countries, travel, expeditions and the like. She developed in her blood the masculine traditions of the 'abroad' when the British Empire had begun to agonize soon after each former colony cut the umbilical cord with Britain. And it was this kind of activity that triggered in her the wish to leave England in order to roam the world. She had read so many manuscripts by individuals who had been all over the globe, and particularly Africa. After reading books such as *Out of Africa*, *A Passage to India*, and so many others, she could not remain in England. She decided to go somewhere. How? Well, she succumbed to the most popular syndrome, that of teaching English abroad. And, via an agency, she was hired and dispatched to Japan when the currency exchange was extremely favourable to the pound sterling. Being paid in yen was not a lucrative activity, but she was learning a lot.

In Japan she became an extremely mature and independent woman. It was Japan that had released whatever had chained her to an anguishing situation derived by accident. As a nanny for the family of a professor whose wife had died, she had been happy to take care of children when she was barely 16. It was pleasant to be engaged in household activities, not only for the sake of the two small children, but also for the 10-year-old niece of the professor, whose brother's family was on sabbatical in the USA.

And then something traumatic happened one evening. The brother of the professor on sabbatical, a drifter who had spent his youth in Amsterdam during the hippie era, used to come to visit with the niece, just to say hello. He brought candies and had a cup of tea generously prepared by Melissa. One evening, the former hippie, who had meanwhile cut his hair because of a job as a dishwasher in a restaurant, dropped by unexpectedly. Melissa smelled trouble. He was clearly intoxicated. The evening was hot and sultry, during that October Indian Summer. Melissa was wearing a comfortable, sleeveless chemise that helped her to bear the stifling atmosphere. The two children were asleep already, and she was watching the telly with Heather, the 10-year-old guest.

That evening developed into a nightmare. The hippie, for she had blanked out his name after the trauma, had blocked the door after locking it with the security key, ripped the phone from the wall and went into a sexual rampage. Melissa just could not think straight, and rather than exposing the children to scenes of violence, submitted herself to the most degrading series of sexual aberrations after begging Heather to increase the telly volume and just watch *Upstairs, Downstairs*. Even though she cooperated with him, he brutalised her to the maximum in all possible ways. There was no way to stop him. And when she thought that he had exhausted himself with all his exploits, he tried to do the same with his niece, a frail and sickly looking girl who was nursing a cold. Heather's undies were ripped off along with everything else she was wearing. The brute was nearly ready to enter her when Melissa took the andiron from the fireplace and hit him straight on his head. He passed out. Had she killed him? Who cared? Meanwhile, the children in their bedroom had awakened and started crying. The noise and the crying had alerted some neighbours who had called Scotland Yard. When the police arrived, the attacker was beginning to recover, though bleeding profusely.

When he came out of the hospital, a judge gave him 14 years in gaol, one of the harshest sentences ever imposed in London. And when he was released, he began to look for Melissa, trying to get his 'revenge' for unfair treatment. That October night sealed Melissa's fate forever. She was taken for extended treatment and observation for, although violent copulation with the hippie had shattered her psychologically, internal vaginal damage was not extensive since she had often had obstetric examinations during the onset of her difficult and irregular menstruation at age 14. It was, however, her being brutally sodomized that had caused permanent lesions, with later bouts of hemorrhoidal complications. For a long time until adulthood, defecating was an excruciating process, especially after eating rough food, which in time she learned to avoid.

Later in her social life she had become nearly a recluse. When attending university, she did not date anyone, she refrained from attending parties, and she just followed a course of studies with her parents' encouragement until a position was found with a vanity press. And when she left for Japan after becoming bored by routine work in preparing manuscripts for publication, she knew that she could feel safer. Teaching English in a private institution abroad was mostly a platform for securing respect and gratitude, particularly in Asian countries, not necessarily for becoming affluent. English was sought by both students and executives who had the complex of being monolingual. It was felt that, by not knowing a foreign language, a 'salaryman' would place his company in a condition of inferiority. Ironically, it was American English that most CEOs sought, and not British English. But Melissa adapted herself to that particular demand. Moreover, she compensated for her lack of American linguistic pragmatism with her refined personality, for Japanese men found in her pristine and formal behaviour something similar to Japanese female traditions in manners. American female teachers, with their outgoing and sport-like approach to education, tended to smash barriers of pedagogical traditions by stressing routine techniques. Not carrying as many centuries of academic background as their English cousins, American female teachers had no complexes regarding the language they taught and made their own impromptu rules in the classroom. Emphasis was on learning how to speak American, not on writing it, for the Japanese, accustomed to engineering precision, would stumble whenever spelling, grammatical and logical analyses, punctuation, parenthetical sentences, use of auxiliary verbs and the like were placed under scrutiny for consistency and logicality. American was the language of democracy, and thus open to all idiosyncrasies generated by a fluid society in contraposition to frozen Japanese.

Japan, thus, had become Melissa's refuge. At first, things went fine. She had arrived in Kyoto, the spirit of Japan, which she found a fascinating city. The American presence was felt in almost every sector of business, tourism and even food. And during those 2 years of Japanese experience she had the opportunity to develop a philosophy of life, except that for a long time she doubted she would become a normal female. She knew that she could not and would not ever become a mother. She also knew that teaching in a private Japanese institution would not lead anywhere in terms of a career. Thus, she went along that type of teaching English and in the process she also learnt a lot of Japanese history, culture and 'Oriental' philosophy. Nara was only 40 kilometres away, and there she spent nearly every weekend. And it was in Nara that she met a Japanese man, a literary man, a poet, a rebel, who changed her into a sex machine. In Nara she became an unusual woman, and for the first time in her adult life she enjoyed becoming and being a biological system yielding to herself an indefinite amount of physical pleasure. Only much later in life did she begin to question her own motives for having men at her feet like toys to be used and disposed of without any scruple, any apology, any guilt. True to her name, Melissa had become a queen bee.

The evening Komaru stopped by the McTavishes on his return trip to Wellington, he had a few surprises. First, Melissa was not home, actually not even in New Zealand. She had gone to Brazil as soon as Komaru had returned to Auckland to take care of his father. Three weeks had gone by, meanwhile, and Melissa was still in Brazil, where apparently she was having a jolly good time. But, why? His host told him that later in the evening they would have a good talk. Thus, after Komaru refreshed himself and rested a while, he spent a long evening at supper, first in the dining room annexed to the open kitchen, and later in the rumpus room.

The meal Dr McTavish had prepared was a revelation in many ways. Komaru knew that he was a superb chef by avocation, but had no idea of the dedication with which food was studied, prepared, presented, eaten and talked about historically and culturally. Komaru had heard of Graham Kerr via TV programmes resurrected and modified according to the fashion of nutritional concerns, and in Dr McTavish Komaru saw a 'senior' Kerr spending an evening of excitement by creating an atmosphere of amphytrionic and hedonistic *mise-en-scène*, nearly theatrical. In fact, Komaru, seated by one corner of the dining table already set with colorful plates and glasses on a tablecloth that looked like a mixed up American flag, was in awe. Not drinking wine, Komaru nursed a tall glass of orange juice while the doctor performed feats of culinary preparations on the other side of the counter. Komaru was simply fascinated, and he wondered what kind of man was there in the kitchen that looked more like a chemical laboratory than a typical New Zealand utilitarian cooking room.

All the appliances were 'American'-looking, like those seen on TV shows, from cabinets to lighting to pots and pans hanging from the ceiling with indirect light reflected on the French copperware. When Melissa was in the kitchen, she rarely used any of the facilities now employed by her husband. The walls surrounding the large appliances were lined with shelves full of spice tins, bottles, little mortars and pestles, while tall glass containers were shelved in one corner. What did they contain? And Dr McTavish talked about his activities while preparing different things at the same time. It was a sequence of movements with the dexterity of a ballet dancer, between the refrigerator equipped with an icemaker to the sink, to the gas range, to the pantry, and the wine cabinet.

'I know you don't drink, Komaru, but, you see, the alcohol evaporates quickly. Only the flavour remains. Like eating and enjoying grapes.'

'I must confess that I am fascinated. You should be on the stage of Auckland TV1. You would be a successful star.'

'I? Not me! Cooking is a very private affair, more so than, say, bedroom activities. It is only for the initiates, for refined stomachs and minds. You see, I have nearly reached a state of social perfection, finally. In this household, I take care of the stomach, and Melissa takes care of the ... uh ... mind.'

'But, about Melissa, sorry, why Brazil? What happened?'

'It's a long story, but she chose Brazil in order to undergo plastic surgery. Something she says she had to do for various reasons. So, when she heard you would be away for nearly a month, she decided to cross the Atlantic and take care of several things. The last time I talked with her on the phone, she was high, that is, in the high phase of her bipolar syndrome, which she keeps under control with lithium whenever she does not drink. Mixing the two would be nearly suicidal. At times, I wonder how she survives.'

'I must admit that Melissa is a fantastic woman. Does she suffer ever in any way?'

'Yes and no. But her intense life devoted exclusively to her mind, sorry, I should say body, allows her to go through life in a safe way.'

'Wasn't she happy then here in Ao Tea Roa ... sorry, New Zealand? Couldn't she do here whatever she needed? Was she ill? Why plastic surgery?'

'Oh, she had a list of things. And in Brazil the cost is much lower. Although she has in England an income derived from the estate of her parents, now deceased, she went to Brazil for economic reasons, as well as safety ones.'

'Sorry, I just ...'

'Well, let me check the oven, I am going to explain. First of all, she wanted to have her breasts enlarged. She always felt hers were small, and not like those of Maoris who at the age of 14 possess busts like Sophia Loren's. Besides, they had begun to dry up, shall

I say, at her age. They don't have the elasticity and the shape of youth. So, I guess she felt that you would like them better. Probably she is doing that for your, shall I say, pleasure.'

'I, sorry, well ...'

'That's fine, Komaru. When she comes back, for a while she will be, well, out of commission, for the silicone injection takes a long time to be integrated into the sensory paradigm of touching and caressing. I know, as a doctor, besides, that, although enlarged breasts look to some more sexy and statuesque, they nevertheless shift when manipulated for excitement or whatever. Think of an extremely ripe mango whose seed nearly floats under the skin. According to the Viennese psychologist Melanie Klein's theory of 'good breasts versus bad breasts,' the silicone ones do not constitute the real thing particularly towards breast-fed children's bonding with parents. Melissa had been bottle-fed. Oh, let me see, we must be ready now, matter of seconds.'

He was referring to the artichokes being broiled and then served as an antipasto. To Komaru they smelled like burnt Maori vegetables left too long in the *umu*.

'Here we are. All right, please help yourself.'

And for Komaru a small surgical operation began on how to handle and eat those crustacean-looking vegetables with hard leaves surrounding a core that had been removed. But the taste was excellent, although some filaments remained between his teeth nearly indecently.

'I must confess, this is the first time I have eaten this thing. I assume this is Italian.'

'Oh, no, I will tell you later. But first, please, while you eat, and take your time, let me finish my Melissa story. Had you noticed her puffed eye bags, actually under her eyes. Complications of drugs, medicine, lack of sleep, allergies, a host of dysfunctions. So in Brazil she is going to have that type of swelling removed simply for cosmetic reasons. I want her to be happy. Melissa is for me nearly a sublimation of womanhood. The main reason, actually, for Latin America is her face. She is undergoing facial treatment, well plastic surgery. When she returns, you will see the face of a 25-year-old woman, uh, I should say, your age. She will be a new face on the block. This is vaguely called a facelift, though there is some truth in it because, after a while, the lift will begin to sag into sudden wrinkles. But for a few years, that will be more a faith lift than a face one. Sorry, I see you are through. Let me serve the next course.'

And there Komaru saw a plate placed on the table with a fragrant lamb meat, no, probably a hogget. With all the appearance of a crown for 'Queen for a Day', like those American TV shows seen only in black-and-white via programmes dumped by Hollywood on the market of Third-World countries. And the new potatoes, the mint jelly, the Maori spinach.

'Thank you, Dr McTavish, you must have worked all day long. I appreciate your preparing Maori food. I feel more at ...'

'Oh, wait, no, go ahead, about Melissa. The reason she underwent a facial uplift is different. She will tell you that herself, I am sure. And upon her return, I will have to be at Mangere to be sure that immigration authorities will not create problems. Her face on the passport photograph will not look much like her real person. She will be completely different, for also the nose will be changed. In essence, she will not possess an ... English face any longer. Her nose is being reshaped into a French one, a bit turned up backward. That will make her feel more secure. She is always afraid of being recognised by the bloke who spent 14 years in gaol. In England, she could be protected by a restraining order, but not abroad. He wants to get even with her. He feels that Melissa provoked him when she was 16 and instigated the sex rampage. Probably he will kill her if he ever finds her. How do you like the lamb? Oh, you said Maori food. Well, wouldn't you put pork before lamb?'

'Yes, of course, but according to my father, in my home it was lamb, not pork. My mother rarely cooked pork for whatever reasons. I can't recall details, for I was only 4 years old when my mother died. The tradition, however, remained. Well, anyway, this European food still seems to find difficulty in crossing the Atlantic, am I correct?'

'Wait, let us have some dessert, and tea for you. I will have a glass of wine. Good for the heart. Yes, both in North and South America, people do not appreciate lamb. Probably this has to do with a misconception of food flow between continents, though all culinary boundaries by now have been eliminated. What I mean, simply, humans have reached a stage in which it is difficult to speak, say, of "Italian" cuisine versus industrialized nations found in any city of the world – or the reverse. Here in Wanganui, take a look. Is the *Pizza Hut* American? Even at *Michaels* you can have anything you find in Florence. Thus, the old food can be detected only in "regional" cuisines, as all immigrant cuisine in New Zealand and Australia. As a matter of fact, Australasian cooking is a pot-pourri of the culinary practices of the proletarian world, from convicts' tradition to sophisticated Chinese intellectuals forced by Mao to flee their country. Australasian diners are confronted daily with a Petri dish without knowing it.'

Komaru barely had time to enjoy the dessert that consisted of French-looking soft tortillas filled with sliced apples and burned with a flaming liquid of some kind. He did not like them. But he tried to become interested in Dr McTavish's exploits. After all, he was so kind to expose him to what?, sophisticated dining. With Melissa, eating was just like stopping at a petrol station to fill up and gain new energy for the following trip to the bedroom. And he told the doctor about his aversion to parmesan cheese. It simply disgusted him.

'Oh, I understand. You must have an allergy of some kind, though not a lactose dysfunction. Probably a genetic situation. What do you know about your *whakapapa*?'

'Not much, especially on my mother's side. I hope one day to take a trip to Europe and find out. She was Yugoslavian.'

'Of what ethnic group?'

'Sorry, I'll have to ask my father next time. I never thought about that. Meanwhile, who knows what is going on there after the Berlin Wall consequences. But you see, going back to cheese, I can take some when fresh, like ricotta, but not the parmesan. Do you think I may have had a trauma of some kind? I don't know, except that I am afraid I'll develop a skin rash whenever I am confronted with so-called Northern Italian dishes. I always smell a faint odor of, sorry, dirty socks, as I did when I tried some polenta. Which is actually not Italian anyway.'

'I know. I wonder what the Italians would eat had it not been for the conquest of Latin America. I think that Columbus was sent to America by Florence's Chamber of Commerce to revitalise Italian cooking. Otherwise, at this stage, Italians would still eat like Roman shepherds and the myth of Italian cooking would not have produced an Elizabeth David.'

'So, you think that we can't speak of "national" cuisine any longer?'

'You are right. A national cuisine, made up of an assembly line of dishes prepared with a variety of components from all corners of the world, is a contradiction, an insult to the intelligence of sophisticated diners confronted with kangaroo *sukiyaki*. As there is no national cuisine, except in Third-World countries, clinging by necessity to "regional", if not a family, one. Modern communication has destroyed individuality in everything, except perhaps in some particular human relations like mine with you and Melissa. Tomorrow, I would like to take you for a boat ride. Let us take a day of rest and fun. And talk more about her, the only woman that ever provided me with the most exciting family life. And you are helping her to strengthen it.'

Komaru was still confused when he tried to fall asleep that evening. It was the first time he was spending a lonely night in that household where he felt like a stranger. He was in the guest room, and Melissa's absence made it look like sleeping at one of the *marae* in the Bay of Islands where, as a product of Maori father and a European mother, he could not identify himself with anything or anybody. That night he missed Melissa, as he always missed his mother, of whom he seldom spoke with anyone, except with Mahina.

Chapter 8

It was an intense weekend that Komaru spent at the McTavishes. Although sad for having left his father alone, he was comforted by the fact that soon he would resume research for his MA thesis in Wellington. Meanwhile, he could rest and organise a week of work on the following Monday, this being Labour Day following the Daylight Saving on the last Sunday of October. Melissa, whom he had not seen for nearly 2 months, was scheduled to arrive that Sunday. Only in retrospect was Komaru able to grasp the full meaning of the events affecting him and the McTavishes. First, the good doctor of bodies and minds, near retirement, had insisted on being called Bill, at least in the intimacy of his home. That Saturday, Bill and Komaru agreed to take a short trip on the Austral 'Mississippi', for the Whanganui River can boast of parallel cultural traits for Maoris and Pakehas as the former does for American whites and African-Americans. Of course, the parallelism ends there since, ironically, the Maoris had not been imported from Africa. They had been there since time immemorial.

It was an exhilarating spring day at the edge of November, when Wanganui begins to savour the glory of an incipient summer along the Whanganui. Although Bill often took his own canoe for exploring and sailing up and down the river, starting from different locations to downstream destinations, that Saturday he preferred to board the *Otunui* paddle steamer simply to relax with Komaw. They drove first to the City Marina under the City Bridge, left the car near *Quay Café*, and at 10 o'clock they sailed up to *Holly Lodge*, where they stopped for dinner. Rather than returning immediately, they remained in the area where they walked along the stream until the steamer took them back to Wanganui in the early evening.

Komaru had not had the time before to re-explore what, as a teenager, he had done with his father and Mahina. In 10 years, things along that stretch had changed somewhat, for efforts had been made to promote the amenities of the area to attract tourists. Memories came back like the projection of a black-and-white movie depicting both the history of traditional Maori culture and the attempts made by Pakehas to 'colonise' the river embankments before motorways and railways began to cut across the valley toward the north. Bill and Komaru leaned indolently on the rail of the upper deck, quietly looking at the remnants of old *pas* dotting the riparian hills, as well as the crumbling structures of abandoned Pakeha farms still surrounded by old cottonwood trees incongruously emerging among the native vegetation. It was during the return trip that Bill resumed his monologue as both a continuation of information on what he called Melissa's 'Japanese experience', as well as a short account of their encounter in Australia before settling in New Zealand.

Melissa's first year of teaching in Kyoto had gone well, considering the rather initial lonely stay in a city of people living in the past. In time, however, she made a few friends among the expatriates, and even some Japanese. Nothing intimate, of course, for she was still under the long spell of the trauma suffered nearly 20 years earlier. She had become a sexual vegetable, afraid of even looking at herself nude before a mirror. Only after meeting a Mr Oba in Nara did she begin to change, discovering in her body a gold mine of unexpected and surprising female sexuality. Although resisting it as if afraid of remembering the psychological and physical pain suffered when she was a nanny, the Nara exposure to the artistic and materialistic tradition of that brief empire acted as a catalyst in her psyche. The 'Pompeiian effect' had acted as a subtle erotic purgative removing from her mind all the mental blocks keeping under control a volcano of emotions.

Bill was not exhaustive in sketching through short sentences and long pauses what Melissa must have related to him over the years. But Komaru sensed that the outline of the 'Japanese' rebirth of his wife sounded more like a preparation for her return from Brazil. Apparently, she enjoyed the Latin-American stay after undergoing a series of 'cosmetic' operations. Why so much time spent there? Komaru asked himself. There seemed to be something fishy about the whole thing. Just for a breast augmentation and the removal of eye pouches caused by Wanganui weather? Oh, of course, Bill had also mentioned a facial lift.

Obasan was a mature man, whom Melissa had met in front of the Nara railway station, where a Buddhist monk stood as immobile as a statue holding a wooden bowl. When Melissa stopped by the monk trying to find some change in her purse, she found only a few large bills that she did not intend to give away. After all, her salary was barely allowing her to live in a Spartan way. When she apologised to the monk in English, the monk did not react at all. Actually, he seemed to recoil a little as if afraid of being too close to a foreign devil. And a woman at that. He stood frozen with his inscrutable eyes lost far away toward some deer grazing in the meadow across the main city street. She then decided to try her Japanese to ask for directions, for she had left the city guide on the train. In essence, she wanted to show the monk her friendly attitude. She was sure he would at least indicate the general bearing for the Temple of the Great Buddha at the Tōdai-ji complex.

'Tōdai-ji-yuki no basu wa koko desu-ka?'

She was not sure whether her asking for the location of the bus stop among many was correct. But, again, no reaction at all from the monk, who seemed annoyed at the request.

'Hell!', she said.

The rather loud ejaculation could not escape the attention of Kazuhito Oba, who happened to walk by. He retraced his steps, stopped next to Melissa, and with a rather intriguing smile addressed her in perfect British English.

'May I be of assistance? Are you lost?'

'Well, not quite.'

She smiled at him and explained her situation. And he was generous in elucidating why the monk did not seem to react, for this was not supposed to either beg or thank anyone. By training, he could not even have the slightest contact with any human being, and particularly with a woman. As regards the bus, according to Obasan, there was no need to take any. She could just walk straight east, then take a left at the Government Building, and three blocks later she would see the West Pagoda, just 150 metres from the main entrance of the temple complex. When she started on her way after thanking Obasan rather perfunctorily, he approached her at the same rate of walking and talked to her once more.

'Incidentally, I happen to be on my way to the Daibutsu-den. I have to take some photographs of the reliefs around the Bronze Lantern. May I escort you? I would be delighted to be your guide.'

And so Obasan become Melissa's Virgil. From then on, during several weekends, Mr Oba showed her nearly the whole of Nara's area, where in less than a century humans had succeeded in building an array of temples, pagodas and other buildings. It was a *tour de force* rarely accomplished anywhere on the face of the Earth under the sprint of a hedonistic drive reaching a *floruit* in music, paintings, sculptures and landscaping. It was not difficult to imagine a still silent *joie de vivre* lingering all over the huge parks away from the hustle and bustle of the large cities. For Melissa, it was something like beginning to live vicariously in an Asiatic Florence when it was still in medieval garments.

Mr Oba was what one could label a Nippon hippie, though sophisticated enough tactfully to display a mature intellectual formation. Living alone in Kyoto, he invited her to his small shoebox house not far from the Craft Centre on Shijo-dori in the Gion quarter, the most notorious geisha quarter. And there Obasan introduced her to an anachronistic reconstruction of daily life as it could have been during the Renaissance in Florence. When he respectfully asked to address her as Melissa, rather than Miss Featherstone, she agreed readily, though asked why.

'Well, I just cannot think of a stone having the weight of a feather, except in the sculpture of the birds surrounding the temples.'

It was a curious compromise, for Melissa stuck to her original way of addressing him as Oba without the *-san*. She just could not pronounce his first name, that to her sounded like an initial Italian profanity followed by an imperial suffix. And so, regardless of vocatives, Kazuhito took Melissa under his wing of protection by offering her a cup of Java coffee, and strangely not tea, at a 'bar' kitty-corner from the Gion Hotel. That cup of coffee broke the ice of Melissa's natural reserve compounded by her fear of opening up to any man.

The rest of the story was rather foggy in Bill's account of Melissa's awakening of her sexual personality. Kazuhito saw in her a natural clump of clay, potentially ready to be molded into a work of art. Apparently she had undergone a slow, gentle, though nearly computer-programed schedule first of humanisation, and later of endo-physiologicisation. She simply allowed him to remove the coat of fear and disgust still covering her psyche. And Kazuhito was gentle, patient, perseverant. She appreciated everything at each step of his artistic approach to build for himself a white goddess, for Melissa had the body of a 'Swedish' actress except for her breasts. These were Japanese enough not to count at all as a source of erogenous possibility. Finally, one day Melissa had allowed him to break her cocoon, from which she saw the petals of her emotions scattered by the winds of the unexpected into a new life. *Sic incipit vita nova*, she thought with apologies to Dante as she remembered the course on medieval literature. And Nara was 'medieval' enough to create the proper atmosphere of refined poetry through which she began the journey toward the most sensuous life leading later to total freedom. Like a small God, Kazuhito had sculpted a new Eve, and had blown onto her a puff of total womanhood. He had been nearly sadistic, taking his time in every movement of his hands, of his body against her, of his breath around her face. But that progressive and calculated way of preparing the pyre for her own internal consumption was rather puzzling to Melissa, for he never kissed her on the mouth as she would have expected at least when she took the initiative, for Kazuhito had the lips of an Apollo. Even his teeth were perfect. Finally, one day she understood. Matter of culture. That was against nature, or was she wrong? In contrast with English, and particularly American mores, the rôle of nudity in Japan was a contradictory affair. After participating in some public bath ceremonies with her female colleagues in the mixed company of Japanese friends, she convinced herself that group nudity triggers no apparent emotion. It seemed to her that totally naked Japanese people acted as if being in public conferred upon them an additional coat of skin, an invisible robe of complete privacy. She even formulated a rule of nude behaviour as a function of arithmetic. When alone, a Japanese is mystic. When in the company of the opposite sex, he or she is an artist of copulation. But when among a group of three or more, the Japanese become invisible under normal circumstances, not including, of course, promiscuous parties of degenerate individuals, as in Tantric Masses. How could one ever think of such a vulgarity? Would she ever be free to allow anyone, except her husband or lover one day, to see the tattoo in red and blue depicting a pair of wings around her navel? Oh, she thought, the stupid errors of youth, the indelible burdens of curiosity, the frivolous marks of fleeting conformity!

In trying to recollect the various phases of Melissa's struggle to find herself in Japan, Bill reminisced about some of the psychological regurgitations he caught, particularly when she made love to him. In the beginning, he was rather annoyed at having to hear about the prowess of her past lovers. She would go into details about acrobatic techniques, comparative sizes (was Mr Oba of Hainu stock?), repetitive motions, hand movements synchronised with intracoxal probing, and the like. Bill knew of that surrogate aphrodisiac that women seem to take sadistically as if needed to perform better by applying their reflections of things past. He often asked himself why Melissa, rather than concentrating on him and herself, would need to return to past exploits by third parties. Did women realise how debilitating that reminiscence could be in affecting the performance of the new toy in their hands or in their cavities?

At any rate, it was a fact that Obasan, after completing a basic course in her boot camp training, had created in her the *summum* of her sensuality to the point that he could not cope with her any longer. She was so powerful in her contractions that, despite the fact that he pressed himself against her, enveloping her body with all his limbs, she would expel him at the very moment she needed to keep him within her. And she was puzzled at what she later construed as Tantalus' torture in the act, and later torment in recollection. In fact, when Obasan and Melissa would go on an outing, at first she would sit in the sun and relax morosely as if neglected by him. Later, when ionised, she would become feverish, nervous, restless. Her very presence was supposed to trigger in him a constant initiative to enter her at any cost, particularly when, surrounded by the tranquillity of nature, he would shift into a poetic mood of reflection and meditation. In addition, she would prompt him into speeding up and increasing his rhythm of Debussy sea music into a Rossini cavalcade. Had he taught her the wrong purpose of human ultraproximity or had she misunderstood the whole lesson by equating incipient love with a demonstration of sexual Olympiads? Puccini had never entered her mind.

Of course, there was no love on either side. The problem of performance insufficiency on the part of Mr Oba become so acute that she never thought it was not him to be blamed. No single person in the world, unless substituted by a computerised robot, could cope with her. And Kazuhito himself had become so psychologically devastated that he even contemplated suicide when he found out that she had started dating other men regularly, mostly Japanese, including a *sumo* champion she had met in a coffee shop. And he had brought along a whole classroom of nine students for a single night's performance on the ring of the training school. That night, Melissa scored eleven points, starting with the *sumo* teacher, followed with the maximum respectful ceremony by each pupil, and sealed by the teacher again as a token expression verifying that his *sumotori* had performed well. None of them had been expelled from her ring.

When Melissa tried to enroll her own English-language students, the Institute fired her. She had lost control not only of her *décor*, but also of classroom activities – arriving late in the morning, unprepared, absent-minded, tired. She would even act defiantly, trying to rub her body against some timid men recoiling in the chairs while smiling and hissing with embarrassment. On top of that, she started to drink even in class from an open tin of Pepsi.

Having run out of money after charging her credit cards to the maximum, she answered an advertisement in the English-language daily, and in a matter of days she acquired the basic skills to become a strip teaser to the tune of American rock music – which she abhorred. She even excelled in pushing drinks onto her Japanese customers after changing her initial job under the maternal guidance of a Mamasan who saw her as a potential gold mine. And Melissa herself found out that, by making about 50 pounds sterling an hour when the yen was nearly 250 to the American dollar, she could enjoy life in the most hedonistic way. It was her revenge on men, though she did not know that, as she did not realise how she had slipped into working in a bath house. At first, she assumed that her rôle was not that of a prostitute. She had begun to be just a *yuna*, that is, a 'hot-water girl' helping travellers to relax in the *toruko-buro*, most commonly known as 'soap-land' district. As a blonde, tall, blue-eyed nymph with long hair flowing on her niveous shoulders, she seemed to have detached herself from the 'European' murals surrounding the pools of the bath houses. And, thus, for nearly a year Melissa slipped slowly into a world where she was both a queen and a slave. She could command both men and a high salary, and at the same time she was the slave of a cunning Mamasan who would threaten reporting her to the British consular officers and high Japanese officials, for her visa and working permit had expired. She knew that that type of frenetic life could not go on indefinitely. She subconsciously hoped for something to happen, and, luckily for her, when one day she sought a doctor to treat her for a nasty yeast infection, she found out that her vagina was on the verge of a total prolapse.

Amazingly, while in Kyoto, Melissa had never understood the cleavage between the sacred and the profane in Japanese culture. She often remembered Kazuhito. In trying to 'know' Melissa, Dr McTavish wondered why she had learned, through her Japanese Pygmalion, that Kazuhito's people must have been infected by the moral standards of Islam, for, whenever nudity was at issue, its being banned in public was identical. The amusing thing of it all was that Japan, unlike Moslem countries, did not possess a Koran or a Mahomet. What was it that inhibited a Japanese from kissing in the open, or displaying thighs, buttocks and breasts as easily as whites would? Was it something the Japanese inherited from the Chinese, along with writing and everything else coming from the heart? Only after meeting her husband-to-be, Melissa finally understood the kiss taboo stemming from the avoidance of germs and bacteria, a tradition cast in history after having lost its original meaning. After all, why do Chinese and Japanese still stroll here and there wearing surgical masks as easily as American women wear lipstick and rouge? In fact, Bill explained that germs and bacteria residing in the gingivae could be transmitted to a partner through bleeding gums. For him, that possible exchange was more deadly than HIV in the long run since, as the human head is attached to a body, it is possible for the infection to travel through the bloodstream to the heart, whose valves would be contaminated to the point of causing a heart attack. Melissa was not convinced by that rather naïve explanation, for it seemed far-fetched. However, Bill, as a doctor, did believe in that theory.

'You see, Komaru, Japanese people register the lowest incidence of heart attacks.'

'But, is this not because of their low fat diet, such as fish and rice?'

'Yes and no. I still think that both gum diseases and fat food in America contribute to creating a silent pandemic among Americans of Japanese descent, as other ethnic groups. They succumb to cardiac arrest.'

'Then, Bill, where or when did Melissa learn to kiss so expertly?'

'That was something she acquired later, after transferring the, say, locus of her erotic imagination from the vulva to the mouth. It was an alternate solution to her tired reception hall. That happened in Australia.'

'In Australia?'

'Correct, where she went for R and R. That is when I met her, although she had already given vent to her nympho syndrome. But that is another story. Her Japanese gynecologist had informed her that, in order to stop the advanced prolapse of her vagina, and her countrymen from the spread of something beyond a yeast infection, he had contacted the British consul in Kyoto. An officer visited her at the YMCA, where she had taken refuge while nearly completely intoxicated with alcohol in spite of taking penicillin. When she refused to leave Japan, the consular officer threatened to report her situation to the Prefecture Police. After all, she was practically a *yona* in a nation that had abolished prostitution a generation before. Besides, she was 'working' without a residence permit. Would she like to be interned in a local rehabilitation centre among Japanese women?

The following day Melissa took a flight for Australia. In a week she had secured a job as a telephone operator in a resort area being developed along the beach north of Port Douglas in Queensland. And there Bill, learning to secure a PADI scuba dive certificate while vacationing along the Great Barrier Reef, one day met Melissa in the main lobby of the Queenslander Hotel. That was 12 years past. They had then moved to New Zealand, first in the Auckland area, then in Wellington, and finally settling in Wanganui. They had been living, as in a Hollywood script derived from the most popular romance fiction writers, as a married couple ever since. And, indeed, they later got married in Auckland, when she realised that she had become a fully developed nympho. And he, as a voyeur, had finally found a lovely woman willing to be pushed onto his colleagues the same way Dr Kinsey had done with his wife Clara in Bloomington, Indiana. Both doctors had a few things in common. Skirting homosexuality, they were studying the human male barely exiting from his sex cave in a world of predetermined behaviour in black and white. And both doctors in essence had embarked on that kind of scholarly excuse to keep their mental sanity in check. But in Dr McTavish's case, it was his way of getting excited at following closely her receptive activities and listening to her screams of pleasure when she was in bed with other men, not necessarily one or two at a time, but in a series of consortia under the wings of the 'Ramanui' Athletic Club.

'Do you mean there is an athletic club at the Ramanui Lodge?'

'Oh, no, of course. That is a fictitious cover for securing a rented facility there where the management is unaware of our monthly meetings in nearby cottages. It is a "family oriented" group obeying strict rules of membership. I myself take off from Wanganui during weekends in order to coordinate the monthly get together. You have to rent music equipment for the band, a trailer to carry supplies and so forth. We love being in the open within the welcoming arms of nature. The Whanganui Park area is the best in New Zealand, still pristine and unexplored. The Seventh Day Adventists, the Mormons, the Ratana Church and similar straight-laced organisations have not yet discovered us. That would be the day, for we have among us a French Catholic priest who prefers same sex interactions. He is crazy for teenage boys.'

'Dr McTavish, how can you allow that in ...'

'Of course, no one under 21 is admitted to our club. And, since single membership is rare and only as a guest when introduced by a colleague for a weekend only, Maurice, I mean the priest, brings some men's clothes and looks for small women to be clad in them.

When female companions, mostly young wives, agree to be entertained, they wear boys jeans and shirts. And the priest never looks at his partners, ah, frontally. He just places a baseball cap on the young woman's head and dreams of drawing with a lipstick Harley-Davidson motorcycles between their scapulae.'

Komaru could now understand how certain aberrations could be simply 'child's play'. He did not know that Jesus the Nazarene had said, 'Sinite pargulos venire ad me!' He began to doubt the sanity of intelligent and respected citizens living on the fringe of dementia praecox. He thought that Maori warriors in pre-Cook times and Greek praeceptors in classical eras could be regarded, in comparison, as models of virtue.

By that time the steamer's horn had signalled its approach to the Marina Quay, just after passing the river curve by the Moutoa Gardens. The sun had begun to set past Queens Park and Cooks Gardens. The surroundings looked so green and peaceful. And the evening so tranquil at Bill's home near Victoria Park. It was time to relax. Tomorrow they would leave together, driving their individual cars. Komaru would return to his flat. Bill would continue to Wellington International Airport to pick up Melissa.

Strange, thought Komaru. He was growing up too fast for a young man in his early 20s. He had not been invited to the airport to welcome Melissa. After all, having seen her dissected in her very soul, Komaru imagined that husband and wife needed some seclusion as in a happy family. There were things in a Pakeha ménage that called for the inalienable right to British privacy in a public place. What may take place in the sanctity of one's home was simply another matter. Walls of a dwelling seemed to have been invented not necessarily to protect morals. Rather, to engage in destroying them. They had been protected for centuries by the Magna Carta.

At his apartment, Komaru found a lot of mail on a table of the entrance way. The manager had been kind enough to clear the box nearly every day, or whenever it became full. Among the usual end-of-the-month bills, bulletins from various organisations and advertisements, Komaru found two letters that, even without being opened, seemed to require immediate attention. One was from Mahina, and the other from 'the professor' at the University of Auckland. Komaru could guess the contents of the latter missive, but not those of the former. To get rid of what he thought was a routine affair, he read the latter. Thank Heavens it was short, though rather disturbing. He had been remiss in 'reporting' to his Auckland friends on the status of certain special developments at the Waitangi Tribunal, as well as the Centre for Maori Affairs. Moreover, the professor was wondering about two things. The first, was Komaru's recent absenteeism in dealing with the Wellington research (which meant 'cell-status quo') and the other was an innocent question regarding his association with a Pakeha lady. What did he know about her? He had been seen with both her and her husband, though lately she had disappeared from the Wanganui scene. Where had she gone and why?

That had upset Komaru for, after all, no matter what that lady could be or represent, that was none of the professor's business. It was simply a private affair stemming from an encounter that had taken place in one of the meetings at which many Pakehas, feeling guilty about what their ancestors had done to the Maoris, or even trying to be on their side in case anything erupted as a social upheaval sooner or later, had participated in their efforts to cement genuine inter-racial relations. There was one final observation. 'I have been told that you volunteered to sketch a recipe of ten points to be circulated in teaching our young generation not to forget the traditions of our political *whakapapa*. After all, you are a student of history, and we don't have many like you. Have you sketched that recipe?'

No, of course, he had not. Between his father's illness, the research for his MA, Melissa's intrusion into his private life and the financial situation he had put other things aside. Now, with a vehicle to take care of, including taxes, petrol, maintenance and permits, he needed to secure a job. He would apply for a part-time position at some of the tourist agents advertising for a docent to lead European and American visitors desiring to see some New Zealand locations in North Island. He decided to work on the decalogue in the morning. And not to get upset, for he had a sixth sense about his sister's letter, heavier than usual and carrying three times the usual postage, he decided not to read it until first finishing a draft for the professor's evaluation in the morning. Thus, he went to bed and, in spite of being rather upset by the scolding received from Auckland, he soon fell asleep. He had found his comfortable bed as welcoming as an old shoe. Confucius' *Analects* had fallen on the floor barely opened by the bookmark between pages 122 and 123.

Chapter 9

The paperback edition of Confucius' *Analects* made him trip on the floor the next morning. Bad start, he thought, and he laughed too. After 26 centuries, that Han made people stumble over themselves. The European tradition, from Marsilio Ficino to Baldassarre Castiglione to Niccolò Machiavelli, was the product of freshmen compositions. The Roman thinkers on governmental, political and ethical standards were just amateurs, even after standing on the shoulders of Greek philosophers like Socrates and Jewish thinkers like Jesus. Gibbon had left a good analysis of their cowboy mentality in comparison with the Chinese position of gentlemanship, of which only some filaments could be detected in the fabric of the British tradition, in spite of all the evils they had unchained in Sino-European relations. Komaru apologised to Arthur Waley, whom he considered a unique genius integrating philology, history and philosophy into the tapestry of scholarly objectivity.

The vintage reprint had split between pages 166 and 167. He picked it up and took it to the kitchen corner table where he laid it after inserting a pencil as a marker. He thought of Mahina. She would have screamed if she had seen him doing that. For her, a book was a living organism. She acted as a Buddhist does in front of an annoying fly. For Komaru, however, even a hardback edition was a utilitarian tool to be disposed of whenever convenient. He believed that in a couple of generations all books would become fossils, except for those dug by bibliologists here and there as from the sands around the three libraries of Alexandria. He did not even wait to have breakfast after taking a shower. Thus he read what had accidentally caught his attention.

> Duke Ching of Ch'i asked Master K'ung about government. Master K'ung replied, saying, Let the prince be a prince, the minister a minister, the father a father, and the son a son. The Duke said, How true! For indeed when the prince is not a prince, the minister not a minister, the father not a father, the son not a son, one may

have a dish of millet in front and yet not know if one will live to eat it.

Unbelievable, he thought, how modern, how universal. That was Chinese politics as manifested in full at Tiananmen Square. Only the name of the actors had been changed. The number '3' as a footnote by Waley referred the reader to the bottom of the page.

Figure of speech denoting utter insecurity. Legend makes Duke Ching haunted by the fear of death.

And Komaru thought about his father, the conversation with him before leaving Papakura, and the total obedience sworn to him in spite of disagreeing with his views on the future of Ao Tea Roa. Why was Confucius not included as one of the textbooks to be studied in every elementary school? But, how, when schools in certain technologically advanced countries require children to go through a metal detector? What had happened to authority and citizens relying on their 'prince' for security and safety?

The next few lines under Paragraph 12 of Book XII were short, but complementary and conclusive to the preceding Paragraph 11.

The Master said, Talk about 'deciding a lawsuit with half a word' – Yu is the man for that. Tzu-lu never slept over a promise.

And at the end of the line, number '1' took Komaru to the note at the bottom of the page.

He never agreed to do anything that could not be done till next day; for during the night circumstances might alter and prevent him from carrying out his word.' Such is the interpretation of the early commentators. Chu Hsi takes it in the sense of 'never putting off till tomorrow.'

Shang Tzu's Su Chih had anticipated by six centuries the concept of 'dilatory government' through the practice of cunctator Fabius Maximus.

Komaru's tendency to procrastinate whenever important decisions had to be made reminded him of Shanghai, where he was first exposed to Confucius' thought in a more formal way than the little he had acquired from his professor, Li-ping, at Auckland University and later from Ling-ling informally. It was December 1988, in the ground level classroom of his dorm, where at times lectures were held by *ad hoc* visiting instructors. It was a class for foreign students, including

Canadians, Americans, Nigerians, Kenyans and other English-speaking students. In Chinese 'philosophical' thought, his instructor was a Christian in his 60s who had gone through the hell of the Cultural Revolution. He could not speak English, and neither would he read the Pinyin systems for Romanizing Chinese ideograms. Thus, the lecture on Confucius was delivered with the help of a young woman who spoke excellent British English, but, when it came to interpreting technical terms, she turned out to be a disaster. She had never read anything by Confucius in English. Everybody was so embarassed, particularly when his *Analects* were presented, though that term was never uttered. Komaru knew, however, what the title was from the contents.

Confucius' tenets had suddenly acquired a certain popularity among students as a consequence of an international conference of Nobel Prize winners in Paris a few months earlier. The topic was 'Facing the 21st Century'. At the conclusion of the conference, the participants issued 16 points as if they had been given directly by a Scandinavian deity. One of these was: 'If mankind is to survive, it must go back 25 centuries to tap the wisdom of Confucius'. Erza Pound, thought Komaru, would have a hard laugh vindicating his Pisan *cantos* born in an open-air 'gorilla-cage'.

Well, Komaru felt that was simply an exaggeration, if not a misreading of Confucian thought. The fact that the statement had been formulated by Nobel Prize winners could not warrant anything except presumption, particularly since none of the laureates knew Chinese, and neither philosophy, religion, or the history of ideas. But they had a thorough knowledge of economics, physics and chemistry, as if these subject-matters could rescue a rotten humanity from despair. The very title of the contents for the several subject matters covered by Confucius presented problems of all kinds, particularly for what in the West one understands for '*Analects*'. Komaru remembered at least four or five interpretations given by the young lady who, through no fault of her own, seemed to have lost face, and indeed the following day she was replaced by a man who had collated the Chinese works with both French and English 'translations'.

When Komaru asked him why the term '*Analects*' did not ring any bell, he knew of them via James Legge's selection as another case of a term that, once in print, go stuck forever. This happens from time to time here and there, even in operas, whose titles remain cast in bronze in the annals of musicology. The prototype of this phenomenon is the case of *La forza del destino*, known universally in English as

'The Force of Destiny', instead of 'The Power of Fate'. The illiterate translator who equated *'forza'* with 'force' knew of no intellectual terminology except the brutal one, and likewise no difference between Gypsy 'destiny' and tragic Greek 'fate'.

In spite of Professor Legge's excellent translation, though Komaru preferred Wiley's, a better title for the work in question would have been something like 'principles of ethics' in human relations or enterprises, 'ethical foundations', 'ethical dialogues' or even 'suggestions for ethical living' or whatever. Regardless of the title, and in spite of his admiration for Confucius, Komaru had placed the 'dialogues' along a parallel axis with Plato's, several evangelists', not to include Latin and Renaissance thinkers. Why go back 25 centuries to ONE SINGLE pseudo- and absolute problem-solver? Komaru could not understand how Nobel laureates, just for holding a diploma and a cheque, could make such a blank declaration *ex cathedra* of a pompous and phoney erudition.

If Confucius had been so great in solving the problems of Mankind, why had it taken China 25 centuries to emerge from the pit of glebe servility in spite of the fact that, as early as 350 years after he died, his thoughts had ascended to state ideology? Komaru felt that Mao's Red Book did more in one generation than Confucius in 100 to give and apply the most cathedratical lesson in survival on behalf of the largest society of humans for so long on the brink of extinction. Confucius, however, left an indelible mark on Komaru's psyche through his disciples, as Mark, Luke, etc. did for Jesus. In particular, Komaru remembered Chu Shi (or Xi) for having recorded one of his Master's principles on never waiting for tomorrow. And that is why, by forcing himself to perform, he sat at the computer desk and drafted the document for the 'professor', who relied on the generation style of the 'young lions' for easier communication *à la* Kerouac. Komaru, however, resisted the Professor's suggestion and kept a dignified style appropriate to a Decalogue.

The Decalogue of the Maori Warriors

1. We, Warriors of Ao Tea Roa, are hereby organised as a fighting unit on the basis of our Polynesian genetic stock *whakapapa*.

2. We have sworn to assert our inalienable *whenua* rights by using any means at our disposal.

3. We shall begin our liberation war by first reoccupying the

480,000 acres of land stolen by the Crown in Waikato for the purpose of creating an International Court Case.

4. We shall then repossess all our *whenua* invaded by British troops in Taranaki and the Bay of Plenty.

5. We shall bring to trial at an *ad-hoc* International Court whoever is morally and legally responsible for destroying the sanctity of Parihaka.

6. We shall hold accountable any Pakeha descendant for depriving many Maori *iwi* of legal ownership in their ancestral *whenua*.

7. We shall require compensation for all the Maori land taken for roads, airports, harbours and other public works from Muriwhenua to Rakiura.

8. We shall force any person or institution to make full payments with interest for any Maori land and any other property without satisfying the terms of sales contracts.

9. We shall require that *whenua* put aside for Maori reserves be conveyed to us as promised in vain during two centuries of political oppression.

10. We, Maori Warriors, shall never cease to uproot white supremacy regardless of the consequences in Ao Tea Roa or throughout the British Commonwealth.

Signed: _____ Date: Waitangi Day, 1992

After re-reading the document, he made a few changes here and there, and by mid-morning he took the lift down to the office of the rental administration from where, after paying two dollars in cash and being sure that no record of a sender was left, he faxed the decalogue to the home of the professor in Auckland. Then he retrieved the document and went back to his flat, where he burnt it in the sink of his lavatory. By the time he opened the door, the phone was ringing.

'Greetings from Auckland. I happened to be at home for dinner. Can't stand American assembly lines of so-called mass victuals. Thank you for the draft. I only glanced at it. Let's go over it point by point. I can see immediately that your "style" is more like that of a barrister such as Moana Jackson than that of a historian. You should have studied law but, of course, I would not have known you.'

'Should I take this as a compliment?'

'As you like it. Now, Komaru, it is difficult to really devise the proper language as if it were to be sculpted in stone. If this document is to be left in trust to posterity as something sacred to be revered by generations of Maoris grateful to their ancestors, surely you can be more specific. But, you see, there is nothing new here. You know that Doug Graham has been reciting these litanies of complaints for at least the last ten years.'

'Sure, I know. But, as Treaty Negotiation Minister he just cannot climb any platform of debate sporting an SKS automatic rifle. He is a "progressist": and that calls for patience. If he succeeds in bringing to an end the Ngai Tahu settlement, well, that could be regarded as the first step in the long walk to a final agreement. But I doubt it. You see, sir, you are not old enough.'

'Then what? Have you consulted with some of your elders? Do you trust any of them?'

'Yes and no. There is quite a difference among them. For example, consider on the one hand Tau Henare, the Maori Affairs Minister, and on the other Hepi te Heuheu. First of all, the former is too young. The latter has been ill for a while with diabetes. And on top of that, he has been brainwashed by the title of "Sir". As a Crown pawn, though honest and sincere, how can he operate without being accused of ingratitude?'

'I can understand. Any other leader?'

'During the last few years I have consulted with Matiu Rata. Yes, he has been instrumental in the formulation and implementation of the Waitangi Tribunal legislation, but he is too much a gentleman. Probably he has read Confucius. Do you think that as founder of the Mana Motuhae Party he can succeed in anything substantial by being tied to the Ratana Church?'

'Perhaps not. He is too ethical for what you plan to do. It looks like you learned a lot in Shanghai besides Chinese culture.'

'And you, as a historian, seem to surround yourself only by an intellectual aura of activism. We Maori need to discard the concept of pacifism, although I myself as a neo-Confucian abhor violence. Besides, I grew up believing that we had the best race relations in the world. What a lie! Just the opposite, because the very fact that we are constantly reminded of that maxim means that we have been submitting ourselves to a position of meekness. The best race relation is one in which no one should even conceive of any degree of idealistic status quo. And here I don't refer only to the Pakeha versus Maori relations. Take the case of Kiwi paranoia about Asian immigrants, not necessarily going back to Seddon's times. I would not be surprised to witness contemporary cases of Lionel Terry's "Yellow Peril Syndrome" leading to the shooting down of Chinese citizens living in Wellington.'

'God forbid! You are right, Komaru. I can see how this kind of discrimination can create problems among Maoris. My wife at times relates to me how the mental health system has failed a large segment of the Maori population. Many of our people have been deprived of self respect. Percentage-wise, they are found in psychiatric wards, prisons, and relief organisations in larger proportion than Pakehas. As a doctor, she hears of distressing signals affecting our country, particulaly when Eurocentric values are used to analyse our cultural identity dysfunctions.'

'And suicide. What does your wife know about it? How many death certificates may she have written ascribing death to natural causes or accidents rather than suicide?'

'She does not speak about it. I know, however, that she is in close contact with Mason Durie who, in addition to local experience, has acquired expertise in Canada. It seems that some Maori youth seeking the status of their elders overcome by dejection prefer to kill themselves subtly and away from society. In practice, they follow in the footsteps of the Moriori, with the difference that they spare the British the indignity of using their own bullets. Only the means changes as an act of defiance. While my wife's compatriots exterminated the inhabitants of Chatham Island directly, they still do similar things indirectly through the silent process of fomenting social disparity. I am ashamed of my English in-laws. One day historical Nemesis will have an indigestion of retributions.'

'Thank you, sir. I hope I did not give you a hard time as an undergraduate.'

'You did, actually, but I enjoyed it. After all, one generation gap has produced "young lions" like you that in my youth couldn't even dream of not conforming to missionary indoctrination. Well, let me see, the composition is not bad of course, the spirit of the contents is extremely demagogic, though also, sorry, corny and visionary as it is intended to be. However, I detect something childish, if not repetitive and non-sequential.'

'I am grateful to you for the frankness with which you have interpreted it.'

'Fine, ring me up and let's get together in my office when you come up to see your father after Christmas.'

It was almost time for dinner. Oh, the bills to be paid, not many, but he had the new ones for the truck he had transferred to his name: the insurance, the NZAA and the title. He was happy with himself, for he thought that he had accomplished a lot in one morning. He changed his mind, however, when the American stamps on a letter showed up at the bottom of the correspondence. Oh, sister, he apologised, how could I forget you? No, he decided to read it in the evening as a dessert for what he was going to have for tea. How could he follow in Fabius Maximus' footsteps? After all, he was not at war with Mahina.

So, he decided to watch the telly about the post-Gulf War situation, the Yugoslavian unrest, the Libyan crisis and the usual policing of the world by American troops as if they had been designated by God to save humanity from what He was unable to avoid. No, he told himself, I am not going to open that letter. I'd better clean up the draft of the outline for the 1959 chapter.

And this he sketched, for it did not entail any mental strain. It was simply what he could give Melissa whenever she rested from her return journey. He wondered about her. How would she look? What had she learned in Brazil? After touching the key for PRINT, he obtained what he thought was rather too short and unconvincing.

1959 –   Birth of Modern Cuba
            Birth of Modern Tibet
            Birth of Modern France

The crowning '9' of the 1950s at first seemed deceptive to Komaru since each component of other triads did not display any apparent trait of interconnection. However, after taking stock of all the political and technological phenomena taking place in the most prolific decade of the century, Komaru began to understand how Cuba, Tibet and France were the result of a world shaken to its very soul.

Starting with France, it was a total metamorphosis of the colonial status quo preparing the terrain for the American suckers in the ensuing Vietnam 'conflict'. The Korea interlude had not been a good teacher in spite of President Truman's didactic efforts. The political eruptions in Africa were understood only as the necessity of preparedness for more atomic testing after the Soviet Union exploded its first A-bomb. France would follow suit and for a generation would soil the Pacific with radioactivity. The French chip on the shoulder was dusted off temporarily with the election of De Gaulle to his royal seat of government.

The Chinese protection of Tibet started an emotional wave among nations who had forgotten their own 'cultural' attachment to similar situations. The USA, in particular, could not see any reason for a Chinese effort to push Tibet into the 20th century through education, higher standards of living and other amenities freeing the Tibetan underdogs from the parasitism of monks and nuns to the detriment of freedom from hunger and ignorance. Very conveniently, America did not remember a similar 'protection' for the Philippines, Puerto Rico and even the Hawaiian Islands. None of these had any cultural ties with the USA, unlike Tibet that for centuries was an integral part of China at many levels of culture and civilisation.

As for Cuba, freed from the typical political and financial support of dictatorships peppering the Caribbeans, the only fault displayed by Fidel Castro was that of succeeding in his revolution. Those TV viewers who remember Walter Cronkite's evening news reporting on Cuba knew that, sooner or later, the CIA would pull the carpet out from under the feet of every idealist trying to elevate the dignity of banana republics to a level of humanness. But, of course, the Soviet scare was always around the corner. And too bad that affluent tourists could not buy a Cuban virgin for ten dollars any more. The Hemingway *feu de paille* had been extinguished with the sweat of those who had accepted the tough reality of acquiring moral independence in spite of parasites playing domino in Miami under the wings of Social Security paid by American taxpayers.

Komaru simply could not remain unemotional. He knew that the end of the 1950s encapsulated a host of complex phenomena taking place during that decade. Those were the Eisenhower years, during which the American populace was well fed and entertained, as well as afraid of losing a high standard of living. Money was flowing. But people were beginning to lose elbow room. Thus, the beginning of the space race. A childish game had started between two superpowers wasting basic resources to the detriment of the world's freedom from hunger and disease. The seeds of irreversible social policies had been sown. A philosophical revolution was making its way among those Third World countries screaming for independence of the mind, of the soul, of the stomach. The world had changed forever. The 1950s had opened the door to chaos in spite of computer technology looming on the immediate horizon, a chaos of the spirit that could only be swept under the rug of callousness.

He browsed over those few pages of outline for Melissa. She had a superb knowledge of English. Born and reared in a scholarly environment, and keeping in touch with 'home' via *The Times Literary Supplement* and the *London Review of Books*, she kept herself *au courant* of most European movements dissected through the Carthusian tradition of British intellectuals. Not that she believed in it as an infallible and impartial documentational corpus, but just enough to be informed even when, say, the Booker Book Award was decided upon without anyone having read most of the competing publications.

It was early, in the pre-intimate relationship with Melissa, that Komaru had asked her why she would be so interested in espousing the Maori cause. She went into a long explanation, in which he believed, saying that as a white person, and British in particular, it was an act of penance for all the evil brought to Ao Tea Roa by colonial imperialism. She told Komaru that she represented, as a Committee of One, Queen Elizabeth II, formally begging Komaru, also as a Committee of One, to forgive Great Britain for all the torts inflicted upon all the Maoris of Ao Tea Roa. And Komaru felt more than intrigued and later convinced, since there are many idealists who try to reverse the course of history. At least that was the explanation between two historians studying their discipline from the antithetical points of view that, extended to the infinity of justice, merged to blend into an epiphany of Right versus Wrong.

The telephone call from Melissa arrived when Komaru had begun to open Mahina's thick letter that had been lying on the kitchen counter for a whole day. He had left it there almost as a dessert to be enjoyed in the privacy of his affection for his kid sister, the lamb of the family. That is why he had planned to have tea first, and then go over the 'American' feminine jargon acquired on the West Coast of America. What could Mahina say in such a heavy missive, semi-opened in a brown envelope and not in the usual light grey one displaying the Transpacific University logo? Mahina had affixed a label for both the sender and the addressee. The tightly bent metal clasp, in addition to the sealing fold, conjured up a mysterious content. Had his sister dispatched AIR MAIL a document of importance? And paid $1.19, which meant about NZ$2.00?

On the phone, Melissa's voice was soft and seductive.

'I am ... baaack, brand new outside and inside. All for you as before. And I am dying to scratch your skin, for I have long nails. Oh, those Brazilian *sertanejos, cangaceiros, moços*, oh, they had no manners. Just *martelos pneumáticos* for a quickie. But you ... Now I know. You are special, because I love you!'

Komaru had not even had the time to catch his breath and utter anything, even what he thought of saying for the sake of common civility.

'Ah, *e*, Melitta, *kia ora*. Sorry, Melissa. Welcome back! How ...'

Blank, pause of puzzlement on one side, attempts to decipher unspoken utterances on the other. Of course, Komaru thought, she must have at least a couple of Cardhu thimbles circulating in her blood system.

'Oh, Komaru, that tough *cachaça*, so unrefined, even with lime as a *pinga*. The Scots are the saviours of humanity.'

Poor Melissa, he reflected. And he simply wondered why humans had to rely on external palliatives in order to fight insecurity, boredom or simply find the courage to face the world for what it was. The tone of Melissa's voice was sensual, her tempo slow and hesitant, her diction scratchy and fragmented. But her desire was clearly burning the telephone wires. And at that thought Komaru nearly laughed, thinking that perhaps she was using her cordless phone, which she carried even in the shower when she called him in moments of self-induced delirium. And that he hated. As a matter of fact, he never felt comfortable knowing that the other party of a conversation would be sending radio signals for anyone to hear, and to enjoy, via a scanner. And Melissa could be really 'vocal' free of charge.

'How are you? Where are you?'

'At home, in my ... in our bed, stark naked as if waiting for you to take over, oh, no! first look at the new female panting and drooling and foaming at both mouths waiting to be brutalised by you, monster of the Long White Cloud. Sorry, I am drinking now, holding a mirror in front of my face. Do you remember the extra fat and muscles pushing the excess skin drooping from my upper lids, and the puffy bags under my eyes? They had become so unsightly after the series of intense orgasms you caused in me. Well, nearly gone. I take you from now on without worrying about puffy eyes and ...'

'Swell, sorry, congratulations!'

'Swell? No! They don't swell any longer.'

'What I meant, fine, wonderful. "Swell" is a term my sister has learned in the States. During her last phone call, she used that word instead of "you know", the current Americanism for morons, filling 75 per cent of any dialogue. The president of the university there has forbidden students to say "you know" any more. So, they utter something between "so" and "well", such as "swell", along with "cool" ... But, frankly, I had never noticed anything unpleasant or, shall I say, repulsive. Hardly noticeable as a normal ... consequence of the ageing process. You know, sorry, well, what I meant, you are aware of the fact that I am a historian. So the body, and your body, writes its own history every minute of its life. So ...'

'Age, hell! You had not noticed anything in my face because you were interested in anything below my nose, barely pausing at my breasts. That is why, and I am younger now and ...'

'For how long? Aren't you suffering meanwhile or do you ...'

'First of all, I did not suffer at all, anaesthesia, you know. A few temporary scars, yes, but actually, I had a ball spending the rest of my parents' estate pursuing all the possible pleasures in Brazil. You know, with the devaluation of the *cruzeiro*, or *cruz*, or whatever, the British pound could buy half the State of Minas Gerais, or at least the Pampulha Club near Belo Horizonte. Oh, well, the new upper lids will last several years, but the lower ones will be forever, if I take good care of myself.'

'Incidentally, why didn't you tell me you were planning to take that trip to, where, Brazil?'

'As I said to Belo Horizonte, north of Rio de Janeiro, at a private resort clinic. An old coffee plantation transformed into a repair shop for the older daughters of Venus. As a matter of fact, the name of the rebirth institution is As Crianças de Venus. Oh, wait, let me turn to my right. That damn mirror. I had hoped Bill would install it low on the wall.'

Komaru remembered THE mirror, nearly 2 metres long, in a gilded rococo frame lying by the wall at an angle on the woman's side of the bed. He recalled why she told him she did not want it affixed to the ceiling.

'No, better this way. You see, I don't enjoy seeing Bill's back for his is flat, not as plumpish as yours. Oh, yours is more exciting, but then when I mount you I can't see much unless I twist my neck or use another smaller mirror. Too complicated. The lateral approach is more rewarding. Besides, I am afraid a ceiling mirror would fall and shatter itself on my face. Oh, you should see my new face, although there are still a few black scars. New Zealand's earthquakes had already disfigured many noses, and eyes.'

'But you rarely open yours when you ... well, when you reach an ...'

'Oh, Komaru, of course, I let my imagination take over to compose a visual symphony of remembrances. Actually, a fast parade of peak performances I first enjoyed in Kyoto. Oh, Kazuhito, and then the *sumotori* school, and ...'

'But then where do I stand? Are you using me as a sponge of platinum?'

'No, no, no! You are the best, you are a magician, you are the Paracelsus of Polynesia. Of course, from now on you have to be patient at first, and gentle and careful. Because things are still sore. It will take 3 months for the breasts to be handled the way I taught you. They are perfect. I always wanted them lifted that way. The only problem now is that I have to wear a brassiere, and buy a new wardrobe, well, just for the blouses. Sweaters are still fine, more "Italian" looking. Benetton sexy. Yes, the "dairy" look, for you to suck, but extra gently, they are so sensitive, sore as hell.'

For whatever reason, Komaru glanced at Mahina's letter, still unopened, and thought of her teenager breasts. And Melissa's that once were similar. However, around her aureolae one could detect some small wrinkles, like erosion mini-drybeds departing from the nipples and effacing themselves after crossing the brilliant purple circle surrounding the centre of the mammas. A perfect target for playing darts of Cupid games. He tried hard to remember the name of the British psychologist who had written a long article in *The Times Literary Supplement*. Was it a certain Dr Ringbell? According to his theory, men living away from the normal human consortia enjoyed playing that game as a surrogate to the real game in flesh and blood, especially in the military as an alternative to homosexual outlets. Although Dr Ringbell was known for his homosexual exploits, he actually spoke of therapy. According to stories circulating among the survivors of the 28th Maori Battalion fighting in Libya, Dr Ringbell would begin his analysis of shell-shocked patients by inserting a thermometer into the sphincter of his casualties. Then a finger for testing the rôle of the prostate gland in a pre-psychiatric examination. Undoubtedly, *Myra Breckenridge*, had it been written earlier, could have been a basic textbook in premed course. Among Maoris, the last stages of internal medicine never took place, except for darts launched impromptu even when the ghibli blew Sahara sands all over creation. Dr Ringbell was the perfect embodiment of S&M that made General Wavell's tea rather bitter.

Damn, thought Komaru after registering a certain stirring of sensation all his toes. He did not really care about Melissa's mammillary 'rebirth'. Had she destroyed his infatuation with Sandro Botticelli's *Birth of Venus*? Komaru wondered where the artist had obtained that giant *pipi* shell. Even St James of Compostela could not provide that background. So, for what purpose had Melissa enlarged her breasts? Probably, Ao Tea Roa had been transformed by the British into a huge dairy farm, but women were not cows. New Zealand had never really welcomed a Dairy Queen among sheep. Well, at least not until females reached their 50s. Could they not stay in socialist pens as long as possible, like veal specimens? Again, only in Italy, and perhaps even France, could veal provide hungry males with real gourmet flesh.

Melissa was obviously proud of herself. Oh, when could he 'come up'? The language was clearly Freudian. She knew that he and Bill had talked a lot during her absence. And she was eager, even anxious, to 're-veal' to him her 'newself', for she had undergone five basic procedures in just 5 weeks. Oh, yes, first a facelift, then an epidermic resurfacing and forehead lift. Of course, the most sexy operation was the breast augmentation through the injection of silicone from under the armpits. The Latin term 'augmentation' shocked Komaru, a strict language purist. Why not either 'breast increase' or 'mammillary augmentation'? Well, that was the fashion. And Melissa gave him a dissertation on the subject. How exciting it was when the female therapist began gently to massage the new product! When he anticipated a long monologue, he asked her to wait a second.

'Listen, let me grab the phone in the bedroom, then I will hang up ...'

'Where are you?'

'In the kitchen, having a glass of rice milk.'

'That soya concoction? Where did you acquire that habit?'

'In Shanghai. I could not drink Tsingtao, the only fluid most people took to fight dehydration.'

He took his time, undressed, lay naked in bed, turned off all the lights and listened to her. On the fourth floor of the Majoribanks apartments, the Kent Terrace traffic noise of the evening rush hour had almost subsided. Komaru was floating in reminiscences. Melissa and Mahina were coming and going on the screen of his subconscious. The sequencing of the two images were puzzling to him. He could not consciously understand the superimposed images of the two women. But then Ling-ling came into the picture as a *'Dea' ex machina*, and Mahina was blanketed out as if he had touched the 'delete' key of his mental computer.

'You see, Komaru, I am a new woman outside. I also thought of undergoing a hysterectomy, but I was advised against it, for that operation has been abused, especially in the States. A survey made years ago by a consumer group found that most doctors engaged themselves in that surgery when their weekly load was slack. Indeed, for what? Nothing has ever gone out of my vagina.'

Komaru nearly choked to death trying to repress a malicious comment. Although he had begun to care for Melissa as a human being, at times he felt used and abused. Nevertheless, he thought of the legions of natural and non-natural speleological probes entering and exiting from her. In that connection, it reminded him of a legal term regarding an easement for a right-of-way secured by Pakehas to cross over Maori land, namely, the 'right of ingress, egress and regress.' That technical language devised by the Crown would ensure that the British be the *de facto* owners and the Maoris 'servients'.

'I wish I could write a thesis on the subject. You see, whatever we know about the social rôle of the breast in advanced societies has always been analysed by males. One should, of course, write at least three parts, one for the West, another for the East – and here probably an encyclopedia would not suffice – and one more for the rest of Earth. Africa alone would be *terra incognita*.'

Komaru made an effort not to yawn. Strangely, Melissa had not mentioned Ao Tea Roa. Well, after all, what kind of impact would New Zealand's mammillology have on humanity, which meant male fixations above the waist?

Thus, Komaru become more attentive when Melissa started to cover the subject along Christian historiography. She mentioned a 15th-century painting, by Giovanni Busi, representing St Agatha, recognised by both Catholic and Anglican believers as per *Vitae Sanctorum*. The painter had depicted St Agatha carrying her breasts, probably size C according to American standards of measurement. The two pink grapefruit-like breasts were placed on a glass tray according to perfect anatomical exactitude, with proper precautions made by portraying the tray with a 5 millimetre border to avoid the falling out of the two hemispheres onto the table by which Agatha was standing. With her right hand, she seemed to probe her right breast for possible cancer growth. Her forefinger and index finger, slightly indenting the fat tissues and muscles, are a masterpiece of perspective representation historiographically accepted after Italian artists had emerged from the two-dimensional tradition through the final efforts of Paolo Uccello. *Melissa, damn it, I am falling asleep.* But she talked about Agatha, a Sicilian, of course. How else could a woman living above the 40th parallel possess breasts like hers? It is a fact that bra manufacturers export 90% of their product in size A, except for Bavaria, north of the butter/oil gastrogloss. The degree of virginity apparently was not a factor. Oh, what a painter! The left breast showed the delicately pink-painted nipple to a 30-degree inclination by natural gravity. Had Isaac Newton by any chance substituted apples for breasts to be politically correct? And why that brownish branch of, what, a soft reed as a symbolic *phallus flaccidus*? For tickling? An enhancing tool before electronic devices were invented?

Poor Agatha, a lady of such noble descent as per her Greek etymon, resisting and fending off all advances by Roman soldiers, the armies of civilisation, died a martyr and a virgin, in that order. What a waste. But, unlike Egyptian pagans, she became a saint. What else could she get from life beyond a Polynesian *hangi*? Island cultural traditions seem to be similar, regardless of latitude. Thus, for the last 17 centuries, Agatha has been venerated by leery Sicilians in various paintings antecedent to later *Playboy* breasts designed by Jack Cole to Dolly Parton's specifications. That was what teenagers from both Catania and Palermo started to fantasise with before pulp magazines began to display cow udders as the *summum bonum* of femalehood. Ironically, if not amusingly, Agatha's breasts were at times misinterpreted in some paintings as two bread buns, and so in some churches of Palermo on 5 February one can witness the blessing of freshly baked breads to commemorate the torture of a stubborn female who kept her chastity at any cost. Gabriele d'Annunzio, however, used to have *'le mammelle di Sant'Agata'* for dessert as prepared by his cook, Santa Clara, for his master, San Francesco. They consisted of two white custards sprinkled with powdered chestnuts.

Actually, for Komaru there was nothing new except the photographic veracity of 20th-century techniques, because the paintings representing Agnes Sorel had already foreseen the Latin trend. How else could Italian film directors become famous via *cinéma vérité*? By the reign of Charles VII, not to begin with Greek and Roman times, breasts had been accepted as classic in size, shape and colour. Three requirements: high enough to be cupped even by a seminarian, off-white like 4 per cent milk and exactly round like an oversized wild apple. The whole period, beginning with Italian orchard products in the early Renaissance and ending with the French Revolution, exhibit those breasts as the most erotic expression of art. Or even the most artistic expression of eroticism. And Melissa had those natural breasts, English mammas complementing a dolichocephalic head as if her large eyes had descended onto her bosom to take the place of her aureolar area. Komaru had admired them, perhaps because they reminded him of Mahina's, though not for sexual inspiration.

For him, Melissa's breasts were what Komaru had not drunk from as a child – he had a Maori wet nurse, for his mother was dry. Of course, Mahina was blessed, or cursed, with an extra one. That was a modest endowment in comparison with, say, Artemis of Ephesus, who had 24 of them. But Mahina had a trinity of possibilities. Would one day a lover hold her lateral breasts with his hands while sucking the nipple of the third one?

When Komaru awoke from that dream, he realised he had fallen asleep while listening passively to Melissa. She must have hypnotised him with the story of St Agatha. He wondered whether his mind had recollected *le mammelle di Sant'Agata* as the dessert described by Don Fabrizio in Lampedusa's *Il Gattopardo*. The phone receiver was off the cradle, Mahina's letter lay on the floor by the receiver, and only the bathroom night light had come on automatically.

He was ashamed of himself. Why had he dreamed of so many breasts, past, present, future, real and mythological? And, shifting his question on a general plane, he asked himself why does one dream? Of course, humans did not have to wait millions of years to be told a lot of baloney by a Viennese Johnny-come-lately. After all, the oneiric tradition had been around since Earthlings had grasped the concept and the reality of their own consciousness, the very one that allowed them to confer upon themselves a label of Humanness. As a matter of fact, a 'label' is the first rite of autobaptism for the selfish reason of detaching oneself from all other biological entities in the Solar System, a needle in a haystack of baffling and useless inquiry, the pastime of philosophers and astrophysicists.

As to Freud, did one have to believe him saying that dreams are the camouflaged fulfillment, the surrogate realisation, the vicarious actualisation of an aborted desire? From the little Komaru remembered from his undergraduate psychology course at the University of Auckland, he knew that, if Freud had been born and raised in Ao Tea Roa, he would have developed all the complexes of inferiority typical of all Kiwis, both Maoris and Pakehas. And, therefore, Freud would have concocted a completely different commercial theory, since he would have known from his childhood that old pre-Waitangi Maoris used to place the fattest breasts on the very top of an *umu*. That was a simple Newtonian principle, since the fat would drip slowly down on the other body parts, such as the arms and ribs of muscular men, a self-basting culinary technique.

At least Agatha's breasts were apparently saved when cut from her body before it was roasted on an open pit like St Lawrence's. In fact, the 'Freudian' tradition, starting in the Renaissance, continued down to Zurbarán's times. Had Zurbarán, who specialised in exalted religious themes, gone to Sicily to celebrate the saving of Agatha's breasts as spare parts in severe burn cases, he would have realised that the 5 February was not just an accident of history. At that time of the year, all almond, plum and apple trees have already bloomed out, scattering their petals around the Bays of both Palermo and Catania (that was a sister city compromise). Amazingly, when the Sicilians re-enact St Agatha's sacrifice, at the same time in Ao Tea Roa a rape ceremony was also performed by British descendants. Because of the time difference, the re-enactment of a stuprum celebration in Waitangi at 7:00 p.m. was coincidental with the 7:00 a.m. beginning of the celebration for something similar in Sicily, had New Zealand been anthropomorphised. An attempted stuprum in a Mediterranean island and another in a Pacific one were not a simple coincidence. However, as yet, Ao Tea Roa had not been sanctified.

Chapter 10

When Komaru woke up suddenly in the dark, he glanced at the lighted clock dial that seemed to display 5:10. Strange, he thought. No daylight seeped through the plastic blinds of the bedroom window, a normal sign of dawn in late Spring. And no traffic noise reached him from the usually busy city thoroughfare during the morning rush hour. When he turned on the headboard reading lamp, he realised that it was only 2:25. The alarm hand was over the hour hand of the clock, and this had confused him. Well, he was now wide awake. Finding himself in his familiar Pakeha bed again had triggered in him the old student routine of early morning risings. But not that early! He decided to call it a night.

He went to the bathroom, washed his hands and splattered his face with cold water but, rather than hitting his work desk in the 'rumpus' room, he opted for a return to bed. The absence of natural light from the window on the left side of his desk forced him to take a few more hours of rest and meditation. But this time Mahina's letter lying on the floor changed his plans. 'Yes, sister, all right,' he said aloud, as if she could hear him. 'Sorry, I have been amiss. I'll listen to you.'

He retrieved the letter, lay in bed after placing another Pakeha pillow against the headboard, and gingerly completed opening the large envelope, almost as if savouring the invisible company of Mahina in-the quiet intimacy of *whare* recollections. At times, he missed the *kainga* type of night accommodations, where the entire Maori family slept in a single room, accustomed to the gentle breathing of familiarity, the body odor of proximity, the accidental touch of genetic membership. And everything was so natural, these matter-of-fact cultural habits that were slowly vanishing from the *marae* of old Ao Tea Roa. He recalled how nudity was never thought of as a sin or an embarrassment. All natural acts among the family were just a function of being human, and never did anyone manifest what in post-Christian times could be construed as improper. As a matter of fact, Komaru could not think of any Maori word approximating the vocabulary for lust. And even when aroused by Melissa, he kept for himself some kind of sexual dignity that puzzled her. Yes, his body would react under the hormonal drive of his youth, but his psyche remained Maori enough to make Melissa ask him whether she ever excited him. European 'literary' and fabulistic traditions were not at the foundation of the 'hot' relationship between the two lovers. In practice, Melissa was an accomplished musician skillfully playing an instrument of pleasure. And, as an instrument, Komaru performed many functions, from one of simple procreation, as for most Maoris, to one of complex eroticism. Maori bodies and Pakeha minds were always a world apart when they tried to 'integrate' themselves. Never had the so-called 'race relations' been such an abstract concept derived from phoney essays in futility as in the McTavish household. Komaru fought so hard with his refractory mind in trying to remember the name of a British scholar who stated that the so-called best 'race relations' trumpeted by politicians had always stopped on the threshold of a Pakeha bedroom or of a Maori *whare*.

Mahina had written about 20 pages on both sides of an American college notebook bound by wire spirals. In detaching them, some pieces of paper were still attached as elemental fringes of monolateral decorations. Did Mahina write, not type, of course, in classrooms, in the laboratory, in her dorm — where? Her minute writing betrayed a calligraphic style of potential spirals. There was no date.

Browsing quickly over the letter, Komaru deduced that Mahina had written at different times, over many days, probably even weeks. And the alternation of various pen colours, including black, blue and red, provided a supposition that was later confirmed by the many tempos of sequences — calm, quick, nervous, quasi-stenographic with corrections and crossovers. A couple of pages were written in pencil, a heavy graphite used for drawing. A few smudges here and there indicated how the pages were folded, opened and refolded several times.

This time Mahina wrote mostly in English, actually in American, although incidentally carrying over the Maori location of adjectives and the absence of plural morphemes. In the past, she had always written in Maori, but that was only for brief messages on postcards or short notes. She had now written some kind of moral testament in diary form. Maori words, however, were spelled by following the rules of Classical Latin, with superscripts for vowels. Komaru remembered that mania of vowel length marking since her days at the Turakina Maori Girls' College. From the very first couple of sentences, Komaru noticed that he was reading not a letter about perfunctory matters, but the product of a mature mind. In essence, he detected some kind of barrier being placed between his childhood sister and his sibling of adulthood. The past had become simply poetic. Reality was something that he could not assume so easily in the behaviour of the only female relative he could blindly trust. And his heart started to ache thinking of her. He had never felt that way. Why?

My dear Tungāne,

First of all, please forgive me if this time I write in English. You see, I tried several times in our language, but I simply cannot express concepts and thoughts developed within, and connected with, my 'local' life. Aotearoa at times seems so far away that anything normal Downunder becomes artificial. It would be stupid for me, and insulting to you, to adopt the phonetic transcription of English into Maori phonemes whenever I can't find corresponding items in everyday language. Thus, be it either English or Maori, but only if I am at home. Here I am, and I feel psychologically abroad on the one hand for the things of my heart, though a Yankee for pragmatic purposes. I want to avoid what the British did in lexicology by accepting Latin stock – what? Eighty-five per cent – for the language of ideas on their island, besides later doublets splitting humans into populace and gentry after 1066. I don't want our Maori *reo* to follow in those footsteps of *calques*. Moreover, after more than 3 years in an 'American' environment, I already feel contaminated to the point of being more comfortable in a hybrid 'English' since, in order to avoid the standard question – 'Where are you from?' – I bluff my way through social situations displaying a phony 'British' accent. By now I could probably pass as a New Englander 'language-wise' (how do you like this 'adverb'?), an American proletarian barbarism. Now, I shall follow some kind of topical order, not necessarily in order of priority. Just at random.

Pāpā. How shall I thank you for taking care of *Pāpā*? Although he has not given me the details of his return home, nor anything about the ramifications preceding and following the move, he has written just enough for me to grasp his state of mind. I was tempted a few times to call him or even to take the first flight to Auckland, charging the fare to my credit card (amazing, here students can get one simply by placing a telephone call), but for just a short visit between Tuesday and Thursday on that island?

You know how he referred to it once? 'Te motu matenga.' I can understand. And all personnel, 'whakahemohemo'. Poor Dad! The manager of the sanatorium wrote me twice after I inquired about the situation in the early stage of Dad's confinement, and he did not encourage me to incur the expense of that journey. He said that you were more appropriate to the case. Now, am I wrong in assuming that for Dad it is only a matter of months? Will he be strong enough to last until winter, sorry, American summer, just after my graduation? I hope so, because I selfishly need a few more months to solve important problems. More below.

And he is so depressed. And cryptic. At times, particularly when he writes in our *reo*, he drops hints about episodes of his life, but he never elaborates, as if he is either afraid of hurting me or himself – or both. This is especially so in relation to his Kòrčula experience, the sentimental journey he took there, and meeting *Mamā*. Undoubtedly, he is perturbed by things he does not want to tell me. He goes around in circles when referring to her in answer to questions I have asked him, either specifically or in passing. When I left home, I was not yet mature – or curious – enough to learn more about her. I know she never spoke our dialect. I hope one day to extract from you whatever you remember about her. You must remember better than me, sorry, I.

Americans take pleasure in breaking grammatical rules. But lately, as I grow older and think about, although I don't hope for, motherhood, I simply wonder. No bonding with a woman, a female, a mother, a sister, in the past! And none on the horizon – more below – for the future. I think that women – to use an Americanism – get the short end of the stick from birth. Men don't have to worry about producing offspring with all the physical and psychological implications. Sorry, I digress. Back to Dad. Why did he leave the Bay of Islands and his *iwi*, as if intentionally becoming an exile in his own *whenua*?

I hope that during the time you recently spent with him, you had the opportunity to learn more about our *whakapapa*. When I look at myself, and when I am asked if I am of Greek descent, I wonder why, though I infer some of the genetic crossovers, but only up to a certain point. For example, have you ever explained to yourself the background of our tribal name? Why is our 'family' name RETI? Although I have checked here and there, even in Tregear's dictionary, I am at a loss to trace a clear line of continuity. Yes, *Pāpā* told me when I was barely a teenager that our records had been messed up by so many social upheavals. It was simply difficult to uncover a 'real' genealogical background. I hope that one day I'll be able to spend some time in the Papakura Resource Centre, Te Hukatai at UA, the Turangi Public Library, and the Turakina Maori Girls College. This last institution, as you know, could perhaps shed some light on my early education. I could check in their photographic records for my own effigy, since Pāpā seems to have either hidden or destroyed the old albums. And if he has, why? You see, that might explain my own anatomical anomaly. Is there a family secret, a skeleton in the closet as Americans are fond of saying?

Me. No, no dice, as I learned this jargon in democratic America. And I wonder how the ancient Romans would reconcile their Cesarean ALEA JACTA EST! What I mean, I decided to remain for the rest of my life exactly the way I was born and the way I am. I don't have to explain in detail, you can infer the missing squares in my personal paradigm.

It took, of course, some time, but I decided that it is not wise to risk complications for the sake of becoming 'normal'. In consultation with Dr Beyers' staff at the University Health Center, as well as with the Counseling Services on students' physical and mental health, at the end of the Summer Session I underwent a series of examinations at the University of Washington School of Medicine, Department of Plastic Surgery. It was almost a Catch–22 situation (have you read that 'philosophical' novel?) because expenses would be paid by some local welfare associations if, and I say IF, I could be certified as a 'student with disability'. The problem was that, when I applied for admission, I should have declared my case to the Coordinator of the Office for Students with Disability at that time. Had I done that, I probably would not have been admitted. And now I just can't do that. Nonetheless, in Seattle, which reminds me in part of Auckland if this city could have a focal point of any kind, like a public square or a system of popular parks, a panel of specialists threw the ball back at me. The removal of the *tertium quid* could, in the long run, create an unknown process of 'blockage' (whatever they called it) during lactation – of course if I married, got with child, etc.

One way or another, I would never expect to join a nudist camp or serve beer in a topless bar. And neither motherhood. And what would I say, 'Oh, darling, you love me and you want to marry me? Okie dokie. Wait a minute! One, two, three. Take a look! How would you like to cope with an extra *in medias res*?' Solution Two:

'Oh, you see, one day I got burned by the accidental spilling of coconut oil while frying fritters in Papakura. You know, that is what could happen on the wrong side of the tracks, that group of near-Brazilian *favelas*, that conglomeration of Maori districts close to the Great North Road.' So, if I did not pass the test with the first suitor, try again before or after removal?

Komaru, sorry, please don't feel despondent for me. But, you see, if I had a mother I could ... no! And I can't talk with Dad. Why add sorrow to his miserable life? And, actually, well, who says that I am going to get married? To whom? An American? A diluted Maori? A tolerant Pakeha? No! Sure, I could marry with the understanding that I would never have children so as not to spread the variation of my species. How? Taking the necessary precautions each and every time my husband (my lover? or who?) felt the need to tantalise me? Or should I be spayed like a puppy bitch?

Would I ever, then, feel normal? The irony! Yes, I know OUR father suggested calling me Mahina because of that stupid coincidence. July 21, 1969, when here it was still 20 July. What a joke! A small breast for Man, a giant problem for Mahina. Well, I am determined to find out anything that might have created me this way. I have scanned in vain literature on Polynesian anthropology – race, migrations, radiation and so forth. The variables are so many, topped by the most obvious, incest. The seed for this tormenting doubt was planted in my mind indirectly and casually by the barrage of questions from both the Student Health Center counselling director and some doctors in Seattle. In the former case, no one could release my health records to anyone except the director, who felt it unnecessary because of the Privacy Act, though I think he did not want to stick his neck out on account of the possibility of having the TU incur the expense. In the latter case, I was unable to furnish any coordinated answers since I, that is, me, Mahina, don't know much. Is it not frustrating not to know where you come from, even within the 'open' family structure admitting children into our *iwi* regardless of specific fatherhood or motherhood?

Et de hoc satis. You see, Latin, which you felt so unnecessary in our school, comes in handy at times to shove under the rug the clinkers of bitterness. I am so happy I did study it because, instead of taking Latin like all freshmen here, I was given credit. And in its place I took other courses, you remember I wrote you about them years ago? *Qualis mater, talis filia*? Or what? Do you recall the baffling meaning of 'The father has eaten sour grapes and the children's teeth are set on edge?' At any rate, please do not ever, ever, ever refer to me or my situation under any circumstances. It is a very private matter. Just think of me as if I was born in Tibet with a third eye.

The giant step, my own, not 'Fe-kind's'. I have coined this lexicological opprobrium by eliminating the 'male' of female. Adam's rib is simply a fable, though I accept it for reasons given later in this letter, if I have time and space. You see, I can now understand, in retrospect, why I declared my major as philosophy at the end of my 'freshwo-' year. I must be a, what, an élitist of some kind, a lucky one to have indulged in that option without regard to a pragmatic career, for what can one do with a BA in Philosophy? I know, for my selfish reasons, for the time being. I am so happy, for I was groping in the dark. I now hope to see some light. You remember from previous letters that I took several courses in religion, actually religion*S*, after one in comparative religion. Months of confusion.

But, first of all, I was never influenced by anything connected with the fact that TU is Catholic. In fact, when I entered it, I was determined to remain, if not an atheist, as agnostic as possible. Or perhaps I was subconsciously in search of something I did not know how to label. I was lucky to land here, a liberal, free, excellent institution. Both Ao Tea Roa and New Zealand will take centuries to reach a degree of 'academic' balance like what I feel here. Especially Victoria U., where you are supposed to get an MA in History. How are you coming along? What was I saying, oh, yes, no pressure of any kind has ever been applied to students, and for sure not on me. After going through Judaism, Christianity and Islam, among other collateral variations, I concluded that they are the same. The differences between them are accidents of history, culture, language, geography and perhaps even diet. As a matter of fact, each religion borrowed from the other and finally blended their beliefs and traditions. I did not know, for example, that Francis of Assisi had been incorporated into the Hindu list of gods as a healer. Conversely, Hindu divinities were accepted as Christian martyrs. The intermingling of ideas, culture, etc. is impressive. But that examination of them made me a 'religious' person first, on the threshold of mysticism, for which, really, religion is unnecessary. Perhaps it is a matter of terminology imposed by the legality and the imposition of Latin on the West, under which we Polynesians are still suffering linguistically – what I mean lexicologically, through the application of English transphonetically. What an atrocity!

I wish I could talk with you seriously, as I have with some professors and graduate students, most of them on their way to becoming priests, a lucky breed of people who have solved all the intimate problems of life and death. Thinking of what we, that is you and me, learned through the Ratana Church, well, though not our fault and neither Dad's, makes me shudder, though it could have been worse if that had been a place of Mormonism – which I consider sociologically to be the actualisation of a most utopic accomplishment, though philosophically a mumbo-jumbo of subtle militaristic tenets worse than the extremist Muslim indoctrination movement initiated with drums across the Strait of al-Tarik. When religion is spread by drums, and now bullets, what can you expect but blind indoctrination as in Ireland? Oh, yes, the Ratana. Not that I chastise it, no. I did not know any better, though, again, in retrospect its affiliation with a political side dish undoubtedly gave me a certain pride of Maoriness beyond Anglicism as the other solution since there was no bridge between Pakehahood and Maorihood in the name of a single God. At that time, I felt that God was British, spoke English, and was a male chauvinist. At least my childhood God was Polynesian, spoke Maori, and was chauvinist as well in my favour. That was logical, was it not, though I did not realise at that time that God cannot be culturally chauvinistic. Well, I had not studied philosophy yet. In fact, when I took Oriental Philosophy, I slid into Confucianism, sans God. Then I retraced my steps via Ancient Philosophy that I audited for fun, from Plotinus to Neo-Platonism, and for credit another course with stress on Augustine (quite a bloke, he should have been a politician advising David Lange in place of Roger Douglas), Anselm, and Scotus, down to Ockham (did President Nixon use a rusty razor to cut his own throat?).

Oh, Komaru, in studying the history of philosophy I felt as if I was entering a crystal palace full of blinding light at midnight. If I were God I would require that each head of state pass an examination in philosophy. I wonder whether Reagan knew of the discipline. At present, Bush is for me an enigma, though for sure he is conducting what could be construed as a crusade against Islam though not for the purpose of defending Christianity. Again, there are no spice routes threatened by Moslems, just petrol. And again, within Islamic religion astride the Gulf. What a mockery!

At present I am cramming a lot of theology, both for knowledge and enlightenment. Next semester I plan to take Philosophical Theology to explore the interaction between biological reason and religious faith, of course the Christian tradition.

And, since I don't have to beat around the bush (the American one), nor prepare you psychologically, I now feel strong enough to inform you that I have DECIDED, and don't get mad, but I plan to become a Christian, a real one, and that specifically means Catholic ... if I pass the tests outside the classroom. This may shock you, I know, but if you love me as 'Komaru' (after all I cannot live without your light), you will understand. What a surprise to realise that you are a Sun, the only star in my life, and me a miserable little Moon tied to the Earth as a battery of energy. And I am studying hard. With the help of Dr Marston, a Professor of Theology, I have secured and am digesting the *Catechism of the Catholic Church*, an 800-page tome that at first looks so ominous or, better, discouraging. But then I am concentrating on the section dealing with Baptism, the first of several Sacraments, the basic one leading to the others. It is the Baptism for adults, though I feel like a baby in anticipation of converting to Catholicism. Actually, it is not really a conversion because at present I am nothing, so that I feel that at Christmas, in a few weeks, I shall be born properly in the chapel of the university.

Listen, I am not jumping off in midstream. I know EXACTLY what I am doing. I went through every possible doctrine, from Hinduism to Buddhism and even Sufism. This I found at the origin of biological thought as the quintessence of incipient intelligence. The problem is that in part it has been appropriated by some sects of Islam, but if properly analysed as a mode of conduct and as a breviary of personal happiness, Sufism is not that different from Catholicism. So this is, shall I say, a refinement of other thoughts, though complex and comprehensive. Once you believe, all your afflictions of the spirit disappear, and all the problems of the heart are solved forever. The pageantry, the mysteries, the traditions of Catholicism are basically irrelevant, if not tied to 'vulgar' ceremonies having their roots in pragmatism (like burning incense to dispel the awful odor of catacomb-stagnant air, though in every ancient rite you find vestiges of fire and smoke, and so forth). Plus the fact that, if for 20 centuries these external manifestations of Christianity have endured and cemented generations of terrestrials all over, there must be something true in them to last that long.

And don't tell me that other 'religions' are older. Yes, but they were not, I think, 'catholic' enough. Not that Catholicism was born in a restricted area of tolerance, but can you envisage Europeans living like Hindus, or ancient Egyptians practising Islamic beliefs, or Romans Shintoism? Of course, now I know that, unless you believe in a polygenetic theory of 'beginning', there must be only a monogenetic explanation, regardless of terms, labels, and pageantry. How can one believe in Catholicism without ancient Persia and Judaism? And how can Islam exist without both Christianity and Judaism? *Idem* Mormonism and all the various commercial sects down to the Seventh-Day Adventists and Scientologists. Really, an open-minded Catholic can regard these offshoots like stray faiths feeding on the same tree of knowledge.

Sorry for the tirade, but I had to write someone, for I feel as if a burden is being lifted from me. And that has nothing to do with my condition. So what, I am not a cripple, and even if I were I would not mind or care because my heart is at peace with myself and itself. Besides, who is as perfect as a Hollywood model of fleeting illusion? Komaru, believe me, but with religion, for me now the fountainhead of pure philosophy (just the opposite of what I thought earlier), I shall become purified of ephemeral concerns. Komaru, do YOU understand me?

'Hell!', said Komaru aloud as if Mahina had been in the next room. No, I can't understand you. You have been brainwashed by a bunch of football players wearing black tunics. Goddamit!

He was furious. He felt cheated, destroyed, abandoned. His hands were trembling. And his heart was throbbing in his throat as if he were choking. He was going to lose, what, he did not know what. She was not going to die or stay away from his *kainga*. Fine! Let her become a Catholic. So what? Would she eat only *pipi* on Friday instead of mutton? And receive a few milligrams of New Zealand wheat from a Paten? Wasn't she allergic to wheat? Would she become cannibalistic again like her ancestors, eating the flesh of God, no, of Jesus? And drink His blood? Actually, he admitted to himself that he did not know much about religion, and Catholicism in particular.

He felt thirsty, got up and, after tossing Mahina's letter on the floor, made tea, gulped it down, and returned to bed. Hell, he talked to himself, I still have ten more pages to read. What a morning to begin working on one more chapter. How can I ever finish that stupid thesis? Can I give anything to Melissa? He decided to finish reading the American missive.

My Senior Thesis. During the Christmas break, which is not as long as ours, I plan to work on an exciting project for my thesis. Well, I had not planned to write one, but my advisor felt that, as an honour student, I would greatly benefit from delineating something parallel to my religious, no, actually, my spiritual awakening because I thought at times of my childhood, permeated by a strange *wairua*, though a good one. The title? Tentatively – 'Elements of angelology: probing the first universal'.

Of course, it is only a temporary title, but the subject-matter is exciting, elevating, illuminating because I have to deal with angels as the first concept of universality among humans. Simple. Maybe the first concept was that of self-awareness, i.e. the grasp of consciousness, but if so I can still equate it, or cram it into angelology. I begin to believe that the grasp of consciousness is triggered by the awareness that an individual has a collateral 'person' in the form of spirit. That is, all beings on Earth are spiritual entities from the very beginning regardless of the concept of soul. Impossible to explain in writing, but the whole thing started when I began to learn some ancient history about Persia. Would you believe it? The earliest records for the 'existence' of angels go back to what is, ironically, now called Iran.

You find it amusing or ironic? I could not believe it. I can't go into details, but I assure you that I have found the concept of ἄγγελος in each and every culture I have analysed, even in the most 'primitive' one such as that of the Land Dayak in Borneo, not different from the ancient *yazatas*, *fravashis* and *Ameshas Spentas* of Zoroastrian creeds. And, by any chance, do you remember what Dad used to say to us as children when we were reminded of *atua kai-tiaki*, our own guardian spirits? Why were we told by missionaries about *anahere* when we already had them at home? Did anyone think of the etymological atrocities involved in deriving *anahere* from English *angel*, and this from Latin *angelus*, in turn from ἄγγελος, when Polynesian *atua kai-tiaki* had been roaming the largest ocean on Earth? Of course, this is a matter of terminology, but what intrigues me is that angels may not have been created by God at all, since He did not need them as, what, bodyguards, messengers, foreign agents to protect biological entities. I am toying as the idea that angels are born at the same time with humans, like an invisible appendage. Then, if performing good deeds, they are allowed to retire and live forever and wherever a superior Being thinks they deserve a reward like eternal life. Otherwise, they become similar to our own *atua kahukahu*, i.e. devils condemned to perform evil actions, mirrors of our biological matter. Excitingly enough, if not disappointingly, I came across the Swedish mystic Emanuel Swedenborg, who claimed that angels were originally people of flesh and blood but he never mentioned anything about the original conception as a dual entity, i.e. spirit and matter, in which I believe. So you see, I still have a new theory, my own, to work out. And, contrary to Rudolf Steiner, I do not distinguish between angels and spirits. As in our own culture, they are identical, they mean the same, regardless of hierarchy – which is not needed. If democracy was ever born anywhere, it was not on Earth. God did not need an army beginning with privates and ending with generals. Now I can explain to myself why, when Terrestrials are about to die, they see an angel floating around, etc. Nonsense. What they see is themselves, that is, the other side of their face, as a Janus, ready to leave Earthly matter completely and finally to remain spiritual after temporary Life. Thus, in a way, it is not a matter of whether there is Life after Death. No! Life continues via the angel/spirit that had been chained to flesh and blood. At the risk of 'sinning', I can state that at Death there is a resurrection for each individual worthy of undergoing that process of eternal freedom. One does not have to wait until Doomsday to listen to trumpets. Sorry. I had better stop here. Please don't think I am on drugs. Here the university is free of everything, including alcohol, cigarettes, and ... yes, sexual promiscuity. At least in my case. We are, indeed, protected by angels.

My future ...

Komaru simply folded the letter before he completed reading the last three pages. He was just shattered by his sister's 'philosophy'. He did not feel like wasting any more time on nonsense theories that stank of Medieval neurosis. Moreover, he had a project to work on. Mahina, the Moon of his psychological Solar System, was beginning to bother him as a sibling appendage. So stupid that she should have been named in honour of a lunar expedition coinciding with her birth. She must have become a lunatic for sure. July 21, 1969. What? Could she not have been born either later or earlier? 1969. Well, there she was, and that reminded him that he had not worked at all on the '9' project for many weeks now, his theory of historical coincidences. He had to, if he was to give something new to Melissa. He did not want Pakehas to assume that Maori 'P.T.' was only theoretical. Thus, without even thinking of replying to Mahina's letter, he forced himself to outline the year 1969 no matter what. That morning was the inception of the Austral Summer Solstice. The following day sunshine would be one minute later toward Cape Reinga. He wrote '1969' and continued to sketch without even thinking that it was the Year of the Moon, alias the Year of Mahina.

1969 – Birth of the Moon
        Birth of Modern Libya
        Birth of Activism

As Komaru's academic advisor often reminded him in discussions with regard to student events that took place in 1968, a privilege of youth is a lack of modesty. This moral fault has always surfaced at the beginning of social revolutions born in academic circles all over the world. That year, in France, history repeated itself and spread throughout many university campuses like wildfire. For Komaru, however, there seemed to be little in the past to prevent one from acting as a meter of comparison, and he did not care to learn from mistakes. He did not think twice about the fact that his sister had been born on 21 July 1969 (New Zealand time), that is, 20 July, USA time.

And so Komaru anchored Mahina to the triad of 1969, though only for family reasons, and not for his thesis, however coincidental or irrelevant it might be. His sister, after all, had nothing to do with history, though he simply could not dismiss her presence so easily. So, he concentrated on the birth of the Moon. Of course, 'birth' to him meant registration on the anagraphic book of human accomplishments, regardless of its probable futility *vis-à-vis* benefits deriving from its orbiting in the junk-filled backyard of Earth. The more stress was assigned to that desert satellite just for being there, the more it constituted for Komaru an action like a latter-day climbing of Mount Everest. The billions of dollars spent on that accomplishment! That money to make the Earth more comfortable was another expression of callousness on the part of those nations who, like the USA and the Soviet Union, had placed themselves at the centre of the universe without thinking about the resentment of starving nations that one day would cause the selenisation of the Earth itself. In essence,

Komaru thought that the destruction of the Moon's privacy gave humans a preview of what the Earth will look like sooner or later as a consequence of human folly.

The inclusion of Col. Khadafy into his exponential triad of that year's relevance was dictated by the need to anchor himself to an astrological projection of the Moon onto the Earth. After all, the 18-year-old despotism of King Idris I of Libya was overthrown in a bloodless coup by a junta lead by two idealists, one of whom was Khadafy. Arab nationalism via revolution was spreading throughout the world in a geometric progression. Would similar political movements take place throughout the Pacific islands still under the yoke of European colonialism? He dreamed of himself as of a potential Khadafy in Ao Tea Roa. Libya and New Zealand had a lot in common, including a history of exploitation and oppression. After reading Knud Holmboe's *Desert Encounter*, Komaru was so shocked by Italian colonialism that, comparatively, in terms of population, an Arab Holocaust is now part of history. Graziani had been the avatar of Hitler's Nazi atrocities. Then the Italians had been kicked out of Africa by the vagaries of the Second World War. The 'British' would be kicked out of Ao Tea Roa sooner or later as they had been from India and South Africa. Or would the Pakehas prefer to integrate themselves as they did in Kenya and other African countries?

Time was on his side, Komaru believed. While he thought of himself as a theoretical Khadafy, who would be his 'partner' like Col. Schwirrib in Libya? Mahina? Now that vague hope, even symbolically, was more unlikely than before, for the 'Pakistani lesson' was still fresh in the memory of those people bringing politics into a family such as Bhutto's. Besides, Mahina's forthcoming conversion to Catholicism could detract her from her previous dedication to freeing Ao Tea Roans from the last vestiges of British colonialism. Then, who, Melissa? How could he dream of a Pakeha as a second face of his political Janus coin to be tossed up in Wanganui, a rural town that, although boasting a technological institute, lacked the political centrality of Auckland or Wellington?

He put his 'foil' partner aside for the time being, though he believed that a 'recently' arrived Pakeha from the 'mother' country, like Melissa, could be above suspicion. She would be regarded simply as one of those Christian ladies who, feeling guilty for the social status of the indigenous people, spend their lives in relief work activities to secure an easier passage to paradise.

Thus, Komaru concentrated on the last component of the triad. He knew that '1969' could not realistically be considered as the 'Birth of Activism' on a global scale, for that movement had begun a year earlier in France. But it did apply to New Zealand. The spread of 'unrest', from Blacks seizing the Student Union at Cornell University and the occupation of campuses from Columbia to Madison to Berkeley, 'Black Power' had attracted all colours, including white and yellow. From the pacific Woodstock festival to the violent taking over of Japanese universities, 1969 had peaked and become a symbol for the whole decade of youthful challenge to a past of injustice all over the world, and had been reflected onto Ao Tea Roa as a light of concern. Of course, anything happening so far away from those hermit islands takes years to be 'seen' at all levels. However, the seeds of what had happened in France, Japan, the USA, Italy and other countries had already been planted Maori-style with a silent stick into fertile soil. It would take some time to witness the germination of all the social 'turmoil' beginning at the Raglan Golf Course and at Bastion Point. The gates of freedom had been opened just a little in order for Komaru to delineate the following two decades of events in global history and the overlapping three decades on the stage of Ao Tea Roa's call to Polynesian 'arms'.

Chapter 11

As the Wellington Spring of 1991 gave way to the Christmas inception of the Summer and of the year of 1992, Komaru's mind began to be burdened by an ever-increasing series of stressful tasks to be accomplished as per his programme of activities. One of them was the International Indigenous People Festival to be held in Auckland. These items loomed over him as soon as he woke up in the morning and created a throbbing pain around his lobes, as if they were about to detach themselves from his forehead. He would become immediately aware of a host of things to be done, of responsibilities to be fulfilled, of chores to be attended to carefully and comprehensively.

First of all, under the shock caused by Mahina's letter, he re-appraised his family situation, then his academic programme, and finally his political commitments, not necessarily in that order. He vacillated between wanting to reply to his sister's 'confessions', writing her an *epistula ad hereticam*, and wanting to ignore her altogether. After all, by embracing Catholicism, Mahina's actions in his emotional opinion were tantamount to renouncing Maorihood, and perhaps even Maoridom. That was a slap in the face of a whole world of family values. It was bad enough to espouse an alien religion to start with, a system of beliefs completely antithetical to the mores of Polynesia, but to espouse Catholicism! It was absurd! He felt that he had overestimated Mahina's intelligence. She must have discarded all the genetic stock of a whole continuum of innate *sine qua non* tenets of spiritual life supports. That was like betraying a whole *whakapapa*. At the same time, Mahina's concern about her birth and infancy lingered in his mind. Was Mahina seeking some kind of haven of mental sanity? He had tried a similar solution to the mystery of his own life. In fact, he recalled some of the books he had read in Shanghai, where he tried to connect China with Japan in the spread of 'philosophical' religions along the various phases of Buddhism. Yes, the family tree, the ancestral ties and the genetic chain of psychological roots were necessary for his psychological stability.

He searched nervously among his books and finally found Suzuki's

Manual of Zen Buddhism. Had Mahina read anything by Suzuki? In the eighth century, Japan already had many centuries of Chinese culture in its stock of philosophical thought. Call it religion, he told himself. Yoka Daishi, that is Yung-chia Ta-shih, also known as Hsuan-chiao, had already composed, among others, *Cheng-tao Ke.* This un-'Anglicizable' title could be rendered as a song for the actualisation of the Way, in which the philosopher tackles the concept of the *whakapapa*:

> When the notion of the original family is not properly understood, you never attain the understanding of the Buddha's perfect 'abrupt' system ... [As to the rest of us,] they are either ignorant or puerile ... They are indeed idle dreamers lost in a world of senses and objects.

No, Komaru would not solve his problems by procrastination. No, Mahina, taken for granted as a standard of female purity and familial devotion within his *iwi*, could not be dismissed as easily as evacuating an indigestible meal of boiled *toheroa* after taking an enema. So, she remained in his belly as a dead weight that would make its presence clearly known by ascending into his brain each and every time a pair of dark eyes shone in the face of a female teenager crossing his path during his daily activities. Mahina's semblance had been imprinted in his active consciousness and frozen in time without any awareness that meanwhile she must have changed in body and mind. At times, when Komaru coveted Melissa's slender and fair body barely punctuated by two small jutting protuberances on her torso, there floated Mahina's figure of the girl barely emerging from childhood along the seashore of Papakura, particularly during the last family outing on Youngs Beach, where Maori teenagers defied the police by discarding bathing suits. Those were the days of innocence when hormonal regurgitations had not yet burst out of his system. His voice was still soprano, and when frolicking in and out of the water his body seemed still hermaphroditic in the collective psyche of Maori *hapu*. The third eye, barely detectable as a large mole or an incipient *moko* left barely sketched by a capricious *tohunga* on Mahina's body, had become a distinctive trait of difference between the siblings.

In spite of snapshots occasionally received from Oregon, Komaru would remember his sister as she was when she departed from Mangere Airport nearly 4 years before. That day she was wearing a pair of grey flannel slacks and a black parka over a blue school jacket. It was cold in Auckland in July, but she would soon arrive in Portland in full uniform of Pakeha conformity. Her look, sad and somber, had become imprinted deeply into his guts by overlapping it on that of his mother, whom he barely remembered. Only the porcelain oval photograph on the *Waikumete* cemetery tombstone could be compared with the image left by Mahina at her departure. The two effigies were like transparent recollections kept apart only by the realisation that the older one, frozen in time, had gone away forever, while the younger one lingered more vividly through a symbolic generation gap.

The older Komaru became, the more cognisant he felt about the need to retrieve, through imaginary eye contact, an icon of female relationship. And so, by fooling himself along the selection of a rather cowardly – as he sensed – mild solution, he avoided the thought of preparing an intensely conceived letter of reproach for Mahina's proposed conversion simply by sending her a postcard saying that he had received her long letter and that he would reply later. Meanwhile, he feared the coming school break that included so many memories blending Maori traditions with Pakeha festivities. The long stretch beginning with the Summer Solstice would include Christmas, which he abhorred; Boxing Day, an insulting display of charity toward poverty-stricken families; the New Year's 'white' day; the interminable January of traffic jams, crowded beaches, noisy camping on sacred Maori land; and preparation for subtly 'celebrating' Waitangi Day on 6 February, a day of mourning. Those were weeks of deep depression, of powerful pain, of unabashed anguish. And now? Being a slave of Melissa, he was subject to the uncontrollable magnet that would wipe out all daily problems simply by attracting all his weakness through her Circean femininity. Melissa! Did he need another 'M' in the alphabet of his emotive inventory? Did he not already have Mahina, and Mama, and Maorihood, Maoritanga, Maoridom? How could he accept the 'abruptness' of change from the first utterance barely articulated on the lips of his infancy as a universal?

During his last encounter with Melissa, Komaru discussed that physiological phenomenon with her, a historian born and raised within the Collingwoodian paradigm of British historiography. Komaru had at first contraposed his views, retrieved from Kuhn's sudden change theory in the emergence of scientific revolutions, which Komaru transferred to any other change, mutation or 'conversion'. Yes, the paradigmatic break could be sudden, 'abrupt' as in the Buddhist attainment of Nirvana, but Komaru discounted the 'out of nowhere creation' of anything. Either one is what one is or one becomes what one could after a long meditation experience or 'revelation'. Yes, it takes only one step to cross a threshold, but that step could have been the last after walking a long way. A resolution impromptu was never the action of a mature, thinking mind. And that is what he was pondering when he answered the telephone. His father had told him that he had decided to take care of three important things: the first was attending 'his' last Maori Battalion reunion; the second concerned his burial at the Auckland Maori cemetery; and the third dealt with the Papakura home in order to facilitate the inheritance transaction while he was still alive.

'*E Tama*, how are you doing?'

'*Ae, e Pa*, as well as a Pakeha.'

'You mean with all your *manawa*?'

'Of course not, *Pa*.'

'So you are still a Maori?'

'Oh, Dad, what else can I be?'

'I thought that by now you had been indoctrinated by colour blindness. I assume that you are still planning to take over our *whenua*.

Komaru felt a sharp pain in his heart. Had his father sensed anything 'different' in his behaviour?

'There are ways and means of bringing Hawaiki to Ao Tea Roa. I am still learning. I have plenty of time ahead to ...'

'But not me. Although I can still cope with daily tasks, I think that this is my last summer. And that is why I now ask you to take care of family chores. After all, you are my *Tama*.'

'*E, Pa* ...'

'First, please write down whatever you need to remember. You know I don't like to write much. I shall arrive in Rotorua on April Fool's Day so that I can make a fool of myself for a whole week with the memories of the 28th Battalion. The organising committee couldn't do a better job in selecting Rotorua, my last platform of Maoridom before leaving for Cape Reinga.'

'*Pa*, ...'

'*Tama*, let me talk business. I have already booked a room for you and me at the Grand Hotel. Sorry I could not afford a better place, but it is comfortable enough. We can take our meals at Cobb's. Oh, I wish I could invite Mahina, too, but I know she just can't move during her last semester. It is rather ironic that Rotorua has a sister city right at the door of Mahina's American home.'

'Sorry, I did not know ...'

'And neither does Mahina. That is Klamath Falls, in Oregon. And she once visited it. Still a wild place, except for its downtown. Anyway, we shall talk about it when you come up. I count on you to take me to a few places. How is the truck?'

'Drinking petrol like a Yankee, but a blessing.'

'Yes, I hope you can take me to the Murulka Urupa at Ohinemutu. At first I thought I could be buried there among my comrades, but it is so lonely there in the middle of nowhere, although I understand that a few trees have been planted on the opposite side of the obelisk. It looks like it was erected at the hypothetical centre of a larger plan to accommodate those who are still left, or perhaps other Returned Services from a future war.'

'Like hell, *Pa*. No more Maori are going to fight in Pakeha wars, and ...'

'Sorry, *Tama*, that is why I prefer to be buried in a civilian cemetery, namely the Waikumete.'

'Among Pakehas, or because of Mama?'

'Well, yes and no. Perhaps you don't know that, through the efforts of Haaki Walker, the Chairman of the Waitakere City Council Maori Committee, Waikumete is in the process of cutting out a special section for a cemetery according to our own *kawa*. He is still working out some details in order to include the various tribal differences for a single *urupa*. Of course, we Maori will take care of administration and maintenance. That means you, for I shall be gone. And if our *urupa* is not ready by the time I fly to Hawaiki, you shall be sure to bury me there. The removal of Mama should not be difficult in case you plan to put us together, even in a single plot.'

That reference to his mother made Komaru fall into a state of shock. His father rarely talked about her. The subject-matter was *tapu*.

'Of course Pa, ae. I am happy to hear that. Well, but, can one place a cross there? That would be quite an accomplishment. An integrated cemetery, the quintessence of perfect race relations through Mama?'

'It will be your task to be sure of that. You are a Maori, aren't you?'

'What is a Maori?'

'Whatever you think of it, and that will make your mother Maori, too, regardless of her being a Yugoslavian and a Christian. Actually, I don't know whether one can refer now to her as having been a Yugoslavian. She should be regarded as a Dinaric, through her mother's ancestors.'

'But wasn't she born in Kòrčula?'

'Yes, of course, but ... listen, *Tama*, I will not spend a lot of money for a complex European *whakapapa*. I shall brief you and Mahina at the proper time. Europeans are simply crazy, worse than our own northern tribes. Meanwhile, speaking of you and Mahina, I decided to transfer the title of our home to your names. This way the inheritance situation will be clear and less expensive.'

'*Papa*, no, please, what I mean, thank you, but I would like to not have any share in it. Please change the title on behalf of Mahina only. She needs security and I ...'

'I know you can't stand Papakura. It is not Bucklands Beach, but neither is it K-Road. Anyway, we shall talk more at a later date.'

'In a few weeks I plan to drive north ... you know ... Waitangi.'

'Wasting your time or shaking hands with the governor?'

'Yes and no. I will tell you more about it. Goodbye, *Papa*.'

His father hung up silently. Komaru sensed that he must have offended his father. But he had no intention of spending the rest of his life in Papakura. It reeked with regimented real estate activities. No, he did not like to be tied to material possessions. Besides, by relinquishing his share to Mahina, he would ensure that she would be there to function almost as an anchor of tradition. Or what? He was confused. Unless Mahina had different ideas. She at times hinted at not being able to re-integrate herself into Aotearoan life. She spoke of the States, of which she was highly critical for its crimes, discrimination and the like, but still as a place where one could hide and live on peanuts. She was already talking like an American. Although he could understand her desire to blend into the melting pot of the young nation, he nevertheless wanted to have her near him. He needed her, though not exactly knowing why.

The thought of preparing himself for a week of intoxication with Melissa wiped out any other concern. He was increasingly becoming addicted to something that was so un-Maori: lust. And in that connection he made a mental reference to Rotorua's legend of the Pacific Romeo and Juliet. That was pure romantic love. And he had never experienced that particular dysfunction, though he planned to learn more about Hinemoa and Tutenekai upon meeting his father during the first week of April. He was suspicious that the Maori legend of the two lovers was simply a missionary magnification. Actually, most people believed it was a 'true' story before it was transferred into a novel and a movie by changing Rotorua into Boston, and reversing the social classes, in order to have a proper Hollywood finale.

Just before leaving for Wanganui, he received a rather nasty letter from Mahina. The content was short and to the point. Mahina was knocking at the door of his conscience. Did she deserve a perfunctory postcard containing an architect's sketch of a future Auckland Tower like a copycat of the Seattle Space Needle? She did not care about Aotearoa's being influenced by Western architecture, or even its adaptation to hybrid technological contamination for the sake of appearing civilised in the eyes of the cultured world. Who cared? No matter what, Auckland would still be spreading horizontally all over one-quarter hectare block units like sick cells without any plan of intelligent and humane design for functional urban living. The largest Polynesian city in the world would never become a city with aesthetic toponymics like a San Diego, a San Francisco, a Seattle, a Vancouver, or even a Portland, Oregon, where Mahina felt integrated as a part of the anthroposcape. Her campus alone would make humans feel vibrantly alive and in total communion with nature. But tourists visiting Auckland cannot relate to any pleasant landmarks worthy of being remembered, photographed or talked about. An Italian traveller would find it impossible to find a historical piazza, a French a promenade boulevard, a Japanese a meditation park. Urbanistic design had never immigrated to New Zealand, as if it had stopped west of the Tasman Sea by more sensitive Australians. The few existing 'empty' spaces in Auckland are always without people as if these were afraid of becoming accessories to an 'impersonal' city.

In Portland, Mahina had become an interpreter of humanised nature in consonance with a balanced sense of habitat. She felt that the extreme 'touch-it-not' policy of conservatism had created a generation of Pakehas too naïve, if not mentally incapable of conceiving any artistic plan beyond that of a purely utilitarian city criss-crossed by motorways. These were actually functioning like 'Berlin walls' delimiting ghetto boundaries of Polynesian areas teeming with Tongans, Fijians, Rarotongans, among others, and even Norfolkians being satisfied with a loaf of socialist bread, a chunk of unexportable tough mutton and a tin of warm beer. She was critical, overly critical, Komaru thought, because she was mad at him, her only brother, in whom she had confided much more than in her academic and spiritual advisor.

That was the catalyst for Komaru to write a letter that he would mail on his way to Wanganui. Maybe she was right, but not THAT right, to preach Americanism across the Pacific. Ao Tea Roa was not Arabia. So, he sat at the computer with the intention of firing off a missive of retort, but by the time he finished he had written a bland and rather short letter with neither head nor tail. On the one hand, the budding historian in him had planned to draft his reply along a chronological axis of cool reasoning, though, on the other, he succumbed to feelings that forced him to handle Mahina as a fragile creature, deserving extremely tender care. How could he boss his sister, the only window he had from which to look down into the bottomless pit of his heart? He missed her. He looked at the two photographs of her on his 'service' table. The first had been taken at the Mangere airport upon her departure for America. She was 19 years of age. A scared looking baby crow with sad eyes posing for Komaru's camera with affection and puzzlement. The other had been sent by her a few weeks before. She had been invited by some American friends for Christmas dinner. The large Christmaas tree in the background seemed to dwarf her with all its trinkets hanging among polychromous lights. She had changed physically. She was a woman now, betraying an intelligent face of independence, an assertive posture, a look of modest maturity. But her eyes were the same. Barely smiling over a tinge of innate sadness. That was the first photo of a Catholic Mahina. She appeared to be at peace with herself. And Komaru felt a sudden premonition of total loss. He consoled himself with the idea of seeing her at the beginning of winter. But, deep in his bowels, he sensed that he had lost her forever, except when he remembered her within the indelible parameters of innocent childhood. But he played the game with himself. He was determined to write her with the never lost authority of a 'big brother'.

My dear tuahine,

You. You win. As usual. Because you are my tuahine. Not Mahina. If you were just Moon, I, as Sun, could burn you. Or let you freeze to death. You, tuahine. But you can sense what I could have written, can't you? Especially on selecting Catholicism, the worst religion on Earth. The religion of the absurd. The religion that appropriated the beauty of spiritualism in order to indoctrinate blank minds into regimented zombies. Your choice. Particularly if that decision will make you happy. Now, the prosaic.

Yes, I concur with you that it is better not to tamper with nature, especially when, by trying to bring this to so-called normality, one may trigger the inception of abnormality in the future. Oh, the body! Does it have a future? Moreover, as you seem to have stubbornly decided to spend the rest of your life as a Catholic, you will find for sure a *modus vivendi* consonant with your own philosophical training. But this is what I do not understand. I am convinced that a philosopher, either a generalist or specifist, cannot be compatible with being a 'religionist'. But, you win. Nearly 4 years of undergraduate training, for what? To accept a bunch of dogmatic mumbo jumbo? Again, you win.

But, perhaps you have chosen the right way, one that will solve all your problems, including the physical ones. I assume that you believe in being reborn somewhere, sometime. Strange, some time ago I was talking with an 'international' student from Tibet. He was telling me that having a 'body' (incidentally, are you still using father's *tiki* as a pendant to mask your third eye whether over your shirt or under it?) automatically calls for rebirth. So, why does one have to be a Catholic? He was telling me that being in possession of a body is a continuous process, not only merely in operation on Earth, but also throughout what you know better than I as the Universe. I don't pretend to understand it, though I accept it 'as is' without being a Catholic. Otherwise, how could I imagine the billions of galaxies containing billions of 'worlds' that are inhabited, and each of those worlds can accommodate all the people who were born, who have died, and who will be born again and forever? Of course, you agree too, I reckon, that the inhabitants of these worlds may not be like us. In fact, I believe that as holders of spiritual essences, we Earthlings may be the most inefficient containers. We leak at times, we burst under the smallest pressure, we disobey all the laws of cooperation. I am even convinced that we are among the lowest forms of intelligence (incidentally, do you distinguish between intelligent and non- intelligent LIFE? Such a stupid concept! Who is going to draw a line between an IQ of, say 89 and 90?), sorry, in comparison with other forms of 'intelligence', particularly with regard to spiritualism. And I am sure that you know that one does not have to be religious in order to live an admirable Earthly life according to spiritual tenets and ethical principles.

I know I am erratic. But I am simply talking with you. I cannot establish a dialogue at present. Perhaps when you return home, we can explore some common ground of understanding. Meanwhile, from the courses I took in China and what I have read, I cannot accept the theory that Man is the highest form of 'evolution', as Catholicism seems to imply, for I believe that, yes, there is a much higher form of, well, call it LIFE, outside the temporary container of the human body. You see, we refrain from calling it 'life' because it implies death. It is there, forever riding in a chariot from which we are being watched like rats in a grandiose cage of experimentation, exactly the way we watch zoos, and labs, and military parades and battlefields. (I was talking with Dad some time ago about similar matters and he, of course, on the threshold of life and death, knows more than you and me combined.) I laugh at people who worry about how one day Earthlings will react to the arrival of so-called ETs. Psychiatrists will probably make a mint by soothing the fears of panic. Oh, how wrong they are, for there are a couple of things they don't take into consideration. The first is that 'The Chariots of the Gods' will never be so stupid as to land on Earth (of course, they do in your case, sorry, what I mean, for Catholic believers, if not for Christians in general – do you include Mormons?). It's like asking a royal lady to enter, say, a snake pit. Who wants to be destroyed by associating with humans? Perhaps only angels, but you said that these were first humans before becoming celestials. The second thing is the most childish 'wishful thinking' of megalomaniacal 'scientists' who, by acquiring a more comprehensive knowledge of the universe than 'primitive' people, assume that the Earth is mature enough, ripe, ready, to be contacted by extra-terrestrials. How stupid it is to waste so many resources on radio antennae and similar contraptions in the hope of capturing 'alien' messages. The Arecipo syndrome is the quintessence of human frailty, particularly in connection with the concept of time. How can a spiritual being – your 'angel' – become associated with time, which is only a physical concept within a certain social institution?

I am sure that you have experienced a dream whose time unit is much larger than the 'physical' time during which you lived the dream itself.

And, forgive me again. How can I talk with you by letter? Anyway, it is only a matter of a few months. Meanwhile, I will take care of Dad, who plans to attend the Rotorua meeting in April. He considers himself already dead, since he has made plans to be buried in the Maori cemetery, to dispose of the house in our names (I don't want it, it is all yours), and other things. Please forgive me. Be happy, but don't leave me alone no matter what you plan to do. I don't care if you become a Buddhist or a Zoroastrian or a follower of Scientology. As long as I can see you, I can keep my sanity in check. And best wishes for your angelology project. Have you found out who your guardian angel is? Regardless of my skepticism about angels (what race are they?), I must confess that he is very tolerant and protective. You would not believe it, but I said 'he' because mine is an American Indian from what is now Brazil, perhaps a Tupí or Guaraní. Don't ask me how I know about him and how he heard of me. I don't joke. Lately, especially, I've gotten involved in, shall I say, social activities that are unheard of among us, that is, among our *iwi*. I am learning a lot about Pakeha decadentism, sybaritism and subconscious moral suicide. Ao Tea Roa is reaching a point in which Pakehas are running scared. They know that their days are finite politically. Oh, I have been keeping away from my early scaramouches, but, of course, I am 'legally' active. Pakehas nowadays go more than halfway to create anything we mention at the drop of a hat – cemeteries, universities, tribunals, TV stations, Maori language centres, land research and so forth, including the release of old classified documents once sealed in special archive rooms. And when we barely mention something about *tapu* on a certain parcel of *whenua*, lo and behold, they withdraw their intention to build. I don't know how much and what you read about New Zealand. You told me once that in Portland a newspaper vendor received the Sunday edition of *The Herald*. Too bad you can't get OUR papers. Anyway, a few more months and you will be home. Meanwhile, I'll report to you after seeing Dad at the Rotorua meeting.

As ever, your loving tungane, triple AAA (where did you learn 'Aroha × 3'?)

Komaru

Komaru did not go over the draft on-screen. He did not feel it necessary to place the macron over the vowels. But he hoped one day to buy software that contained dedicated 'Latin' vowels, rather than having to stop and select them from a separate entry. With his sister, he could afford that informality, though he knew that Mahina was a stickler for correct graphic representation. At any rate, he was not happy about the letter he had finished. He had been too accommodating, as if losing his usual prerogative as a big brother 'protecting' his sister. So, just before touching the PRINT key, he felt like pricking Mahina with a PS, an envoy for the sake of reminding her that he was still in possession of the *mana* of primogeniture.

PS. I hope one day that you become the first Maori woman to be sanctified by the Vatican State. After all, no one has ever become a saint in Ao Tea Roa. Can you imagine a Polynesian teaching now to prepare a *hangi* in Heaven? (What kind of diet do angels and saints follow up there?) In spite of 'Thornbird' philosophy, we must still be pagans. What did the pope see here years ago as a potential? Maybe Katherine Mansfield? Too bad I missed him, you know, I was in China worshipping Mao's saints on a Rewi Alley scholarship.

Chapter 12

The New Year's Eve that Komaru spent at the McTavishes was a mixture of everything he might have conceived if he had the wild imagination of a Borgia, the sexual freedom of a de Sade, the anguishing nihilism of a Kafka and the mental derangement of a Freud. There could have been other components, ranging from pure hedonism to refined decadentism to hermetic Tantrism. But nothing that took place that night implied anything forceful, deceptive or planned. Actually, the whole extended weekend was interspersed with episodes of subtle irony, of mute fun, and freelance individualism through the interaction of an erotic crew of explorers on a no-return voyage into consciously self-destructive pleasure. Amazingly, Komaru felt that the 1 January would mark the inception of a mega-year of enterprises covering all literary and theoretical fantasies punctuated by some pragmatic verifications limited only by mathematically infinite physiological possibilities.

Komaru did not know that, should he have required those prerequisites to integrate himself into an evening and a night of baffling and mind-altering relationships, he could play the game satisfactorily. Well, at least with regard to Bill and Melissa, though with respect to his own range of adaptations, he tended to underrate himself. Only later during 1992 did Komaru see himself in retrospect as a medium between Melissa, the insatiable nympho, and Bill, the potentially impotent. Komaru had become the *tertium quid* at their psychological mercy and physical exploitation. Not that he minded that, for the 'happening' of that night, astride two hypothetical Austral astronomic segments, turned out to be so revealing, as if he had been spelunking into his guts, mostly under the temptation of grasping near-immediate gratification in a chain reaction. The discovery of indifferent expectations for adventure was becoming the very essence of his manhood, housed in a machine made of flesh and blood. And mind, heart, stomach, eyes, smell, touch. And conversation through a language of easily assumed flow in all theoretical directions, most of them new, a flow from the in to the out, and from the out to the in.

The evening of his arrival, Komaru was greeted by Melissa at the top of the stairs. The light emanating from the windows of Dr McTavish's laboratory, a detached structure that was originally the laundry copper shed before remodelling, indicated that Melissa's husband was working on his usual research: suicide as the purest and only expression of freedom in New Zealand. Ironically, Dr McTavish had, well, espoused the only true universal dictum of a dictator, namely, Mussolini's tenet that 'there are freedoms, [but] freedom has never existed'. For New Zealanders, there was an exception to the dictator's generalisation for, according to Dr McTavish, a self-destruction psychiatrist, Hermit Islands' inhabitants, both Maori and Pakeha, displayed that essential way of escape from despair. According to him, New Zealanders were the most mentally balanced terrestrials, since they carried a chip on each shoulder. That created a *contradictio in terminis* because, again on the basis of statistical analysis, during the period beginning in 1974, the year the psychiatrist began his research, and the end of 1991 (pending a few more cases to be entered in the Public Health Report the next day), there was an average of 382 suicides per annum, plus 2,674 hospitalizations for aborted suicide. Apparently, the 15–24-year age group represented the highest risk. Of course, there were so-called accidents of an unexplainable nature, particularly among females who, in practice, chose means of destruction for which they were not skilled enough. Since Dr McTavish's arrival in New Zealand, the rate of successful suicide (a murderous alliteration in the minds of morbid linguisticians), had increased by 400 per cent. Youth Affairs Minister Deborah Morris, as well as 'workers' Jill Petts, Pam Corkery and Muriel Newman, began to scream for help. It seemed that mostly women cared to analyse the unique situation placing New Zealand rather close to European nations traditionally regarded for endemic similar problems, as Hungary and Scandinavian countries.

Dr McTavish had heard Komaru's lorry in the driveway and had told him to enter the house. The downstairs door was unlocked, so he could just holler to Melissa. And she welcomed him as soon as he rang the bell with a series of egocentric expressions. She was wearing a pair of red hot pants and a green halter. From the bottom landing, Komaru saw her standing at the top of the stairs as if an interior decorator had placed a blonde amazon against the background of the upper landing, whose wall contained a mirror framed by Father Christmas decorations – plastic flowerlets and red pistils along green ribbons, and little lighted bulbs among them. And Melissa stood there like a barely dressed Nike, though just for a while.

'Come in, stranger. I missed you. Did you miss me? Never mind. Do you recognise me? Do you still want me? Look!'

In so saying, she raised the bottom part of her halter to uncover a work of art, a pair of perfectly shaped breasts. And, while holding the halter with her left hand, she cupped her right mamma up as if in place of a single bra. By that time, Komaru had reached the landing. He immediately noticed that the two breasts looked somewhat stained, or rather veined, by some greyish streaks departing from under the armpits. Her nipples were larger, but they displayed some radiated rays of filaments just below the skin as if this had been stretched in a pyramido-conical fashion.

'Touch me, but gently. Do you like them? No, lightly, please. They are so sore. It will take some months of healing, of adaptation, and I have to wear a brassiere for a while.'

Komaru, if not embarrassed by that clinical self-examination, was somewhat annoyed. He had not opened his mouth to greet her. And when he attempted to say something, she brought his face to hers, trying to kiss him gently. It was at that moment that Komaru saw her face. It was different, with black and blue patches around the neck, along the forehead hairline, under the eyes, on top of the eyebrows. When he embraced her, by placing his cheek along hers, he also noticed her hair along the left ear patched up. But the skin was smooth, shining lightly under the obvious sun tan. And, when she tried to insert her tongue into his mouth, he resisted. She was a different Melissa, like an inflated rubber doll he had seen in sex shops along K-Road in Auckland.

'Happy New Year!,' Komaru was finally able to utter.

'Not yet,' she replied, 'because I still want you to close this year for me as I often thought of you on the surgical table of Dr Tavares. For a while I starved. I was consoled only by my social nurse through her deep massages. Barely satisfying. You see, my frontal body is still very sensitive. Can't take the weight of anything for the time being. Come with me. Bill is working, and he will not come up for a while.'

'But, Melitta, sorry, Melissa, I haven't even washed up. Oh, here, my belated Christmas token of ... appreciation.'

He had left on the little table two packages containing gifts for her and Bill. His overnight case was still in his lorry. And in it was the manuscript for the historical outline of his MA thesis.

'Oh, thank you. I'll open it later. Go ahead, the lavatory is ready.'

But Komaru did not go there, for he needed the toilet. It had been so hot that during his trip he had drunk a lot of lemonade and orange juice. He had just flushed the bowl when Melissa disturbed his privacy.

'May I come in?'

'I ... I am still washing my hands.'

'Just fine. I'll dry them off for you,' she hollered from the threshold of the toilet.

Then, she entered it and removed her halter. Komaru wondered what in the world she had in mind, though the handwriting was already on all four walls. Not that he was squeamish about the rather unromantic environment for acts of female aggression, for in the past he had been confined to nearly all types of erotic spaces. Melissa was unpredictable from the very beginning of intimacy. From the sand dunes of South Beach to the plastic floor in the garage and the public library seminar room conference table, she had enticed Komaru to satisfy her whims at the drop of her shorts or at the raising of her skirt, for she never wore any undies anywhere.

Once, she said that, even if made of gauze like cotton from Egypt, or Arizona's Pima County, panties would tend to harbour germs, bacteria, yeast cultures, contaminants, particularly in public toilets, taxicabs, tramway benches, airline seats, and virtually any place hosting her muscular buttocks. When Komaru tried to contradict her, saying that undies or even light pads would actually stop any infiltration of such curiosity seekers, Melissa retorted by adducing a different reason for avoiding wearing anything between her cavities and the flow of air. She changed her tune by saying that a shield between her legs would render her warmer, and even hotter than her normal state of being. That constantly higher temperature would cause in her an uncontrollable drive to be quenched only by a douche of semen.

This Komaru could not understand, since warm plus warm does not normally result in pellets of refrigerated yogurt. That is what Bill explained to him during the short cruise they had taken on the Wanganui. He told Komaru how, at times, while working in his 'psychocell', he would see Melissa sitting on a landscape rock, appearing spaced out, hot and morose, with her head down, cupping her *mons* with one hand and spreading liquid vitamin E along her *coxae* with the other hand. In that exalted condition, she would restlessly wait for him to come out of the studio, to be calmed down on the first couple of steps leading upstairs. Her intense bitchiness would even twist the meaning of rejection into one of position by screaming at her husband, *Vade retro, Satana*!

There was an understanding between Bill and Melissa. She would never, never, disturb him while he was engaged in research. And he, too, after the first months of marriage during which she had 'dated' both friends and strangers, had never interfered with her urgent needs. She had told him from the very beginning that whatever she had to do with her body – since it belonged only to her – was strictly her business. At first, Bill could not understand how she had to 'return' to her Japanese conditioning, but, then, he put aside all his confusion when he realised that he alone could not cope with her. He had only asked her to inform him of her activities for various social and health reasons. And she agreed totally. She would at times take her little Toyota and park by bars and quay hangouts simply to dream of possibilities, and at times engaging in quickie entertainment. Even the local constables had come to know her as the *putaine respecteuse* after she had told them that she never took money from anyone. She regarded herself as a Mother Teresa of a sort, for she not only gave money or work referrals to jobless and illegal aliens in exchange for attention, but also she felt a Christian compassion to 'help' Chinese sailors and Tongan drifters starving for transient and white flesh. Was it a French philosopher who had stated that, to reach sanctitude, *les avenues du Seigneur sont infinies*?

One thing she insisted on besides security for the place of action – protection. She had brought from Japan a plastic 'medallion' representing the helmeted head silhouette of a Trojan soldier. On its back there was a square pocket secured by a small flap lined with a strip of Velcro. The Japanese 'tiki' was large enough to contain two prophylactics, which she carried at all times. Originally, the Japanese medallion was used by liberated Kyoto geishas to carry a rice powder puff, but some smart ones substituted a latex protector for the puff. AIDS had made Kyoto the Minamata of the entrance bay, and the conversion from a rice powder touch-up to a sealed packet of one or more *kondomo* has revolutionised the Asian market with the approval of local health authorities. The fact that the soldier was a Trojan had escaped the notice of many pharmaceutical companies, although some American entrepreneurs had tried to obtain a patent for the health 'tiki', that would hang for dear life from a silk cord or a leather shoelace. Unfortunately, in Washington the Patent Office refused to consider the idea because the Trojan was already a symbol of an ancient American hush-hush two-syllable utterance proffered by pre-women's lib teenagers. An alternative, rather than the Trojan, was the sketch of Casanova's silhouette. Although the original Casanova linen sock received a patent, the hanging container was never accepted by any American company. No high school teenager or grade school child would risk her open air 'reputation' by branding herself a free receptacle on demand, in spite of the fact that the careful female would avoid fumbling through a purse, a backpack or a brassiere to open the door to a guardian angel. But Melissa carried the 'tiki' all the time, just in case. At first she did not think about unfolding the wings of the guardian angel. It was Komaru who later insisted on wearing that precautionary sheath of latex, especially after he found out that she could potentially have been with anyone minutes before receiving him.

So, when she entered the toilet, Komaru saw that she was not wearing the halter. In its place there were two hemispheric floaters that seemed not to 'belong'. He thought of St Agatha. Although lying on the tray that the painter had used as a receptacle of display, the two breasts were more natural looking than those exhibited by Melissa. Logical, he thought. They were natural, real, even in two dimensions, and more exciting. But Melissa had a penchant for shifting her focus of attention from one pair of round spheres to two more normal ones, for she had lowered the toilet seat, removed her red hot pants, placed the contoured rug surrounding the bottom of the stool on top of the closed seat, and kneeled gingerly on it by placing her forearms on the water tank.

'Please,' she said, 'this is not my favorite fashion, but for a while it will have to do. And don't touch my breasts. Bill has tried but hasn't succeeded. He is thicker but shorter. You are slimmer and longer. Much better for the G-spot. You should have no problems.'

Komaru had seen his face reflected in the mirror hanging above the stool. He looked puzzled. And, during a moment of hesitation in trying to understand what Melissa was talking about, he wondered why anyone would hang a mirror in a WC. He then asked her.

'Don't waste any time. I am on fire. Oh, yes, the mirror. So that, by moving it away from the wall on one side, I can reflect myself on the other mirror above the sink. So I can look at buttocks, as I can look at yours now. No, drop your pants to the floor.'

Komaru was rather annoyed at the idea of indirect examination but, under the circumstances, he decided to go through with it as quickly as possible. After all, he had been starving, except that on

~ 164 ~

Christmas Eve he had called Ling-ling for a quick translation from Maori into Cantonese – which she handled skillfully in spite of possessing an extra tone. He had felt a bit guilty for having cheated on Melissa but, after all, there had been no declaration of loyalty. And now after hearing about her behaviour from Bill, he didn't think twice about performing as speedily as possible. The problem was that he simply couldn't. What in the world, he thought. Am I in the right place? Yes, he was probing the majora gently. There was no mistake. He was not trying to enter the *vicum caecum*, since Melissa did not like the haemorrhoidal consequences. Besides, after being sodomised so violently at 16, she had never been normal, in spite of being patched up internally. Scars acted up from time to time, depending upon her diet. Although the *kuri* fashion represented two alternatives *more Maoro*, he stuck to the reverse missionary tradition, though ironically it had always been the normal Maori position, as in *Quest for Fire*. After all, everything in New Zealand was upside down, wasn't it?

But the problem was not one of topography. It was a matter of impedimenta. He knew that he was around the minora, but, although he felt the copious generosity of Melissa's viscosity, through the compliments of Dr Bartholin, he was simply stopped by a barrier. And she screamed as if in pain.

'Oh, come on, Kom.' She had used her term of endearment by reducing three syllables to one. Which he did nearly immediately. She felt his pellets around her, but the process was mostly an external one. And a messy one, for which she grabbed a couple of Puffies from the box lying on the water tank between her forearms.

'Wow! *Puxa a vida, rapaz. Você tinha fome!*'
'Sorry, what is happening?'
'Oh, I learned some Brazilian down there. I said you were starving.'
'I don't mean that. Have you dried up down there or what?'
She laughed.
'That is my present to you. Tonight, after supper, I shall present you with a unique dessert. First, we are going to have a light meal. You know I would like to cook, but Bill has no confidence in my abilities. The main meal will be tomorrow at noon. But, again, for tonight's tea, I will be in charge. I will ...'

Suddenly Bill entered the toilet room. He didn't even blink an eye.
'Well, I am glad that you are apparently having fun. Please forgive me.'
And he left quietly.

Komaru tried to open his mouth. He couldn't. But he did not feel any reaction. He had become insensitive to what he considered British superiority. Yes, he thought, the English are not only sophisticated, but also tolerant.

'You really excited me for nothing. Like a precocious child. Not your fault. But, if I had told you, you would have felt self-conscious. And even a second time would not help.'

'Help what? And what were you supposed to tell me?'

'You see, during the last few days in Dr Tavares' *clínica*, after I had savoured all the tropical fruits as compensation for the pain and medication of plastic surgery, I accepted a bonus offer from the good doctor. He told me that, under anaesthesia, he examined me all over and found that apparently I had been abusing the natural propensity in welcoming guests without any rest for my organs. I had simply become too wide. That could be one of the possible reasons for my needing constant adoration I should have been born in India near the Black Pagoda at Konārak in the State of Orissa. So, when I came out of anaesthesia, Dr Tavares suggested work on the minora and the hymen, on the house. He said I had been such a good patient. All the staff had reported excellent cooperation. And this he did. Rebirth. As I was before the last time I baby-sat. Starting from scratch, as they say. I learned that expression in Japan. Obviously, the Japanese had American English instructors. So, tonight we are going to have fun. New year at midnight, new life, new sensations I'll give you the *jus primae noctis* because Bill simply could not do that. But, first, let me take a bath and a shower. Meanwhile, you can visit with Bill in the rumpus room. Then I will cook. Do you like Italian food? Of course, you do. I remember what Bill once prepared for you straight from a book by a certain Bugialli.

'Yes, I think so. In fact, he told me that, although he possesses many books on Italian cuisine, he prefers male authors and cooks. This means that there aren't many of them in England. Bill is so particular. He can't stand women in the kitchen. He thinks that they cannot possibly do justice to Italian cooking. After he started reading a book by a Marcia, no, sorry, Marcella, he got so disgusted with her patronising tone in giving directions that he simply tossed the book, an expensive one, in the dust bin. Tonight, however, he is making an exception for me.'

When Komaru entered the rumpus room, Dr McTavish got up from his armchair and greeted him effusively. Komaru felt at ease immediately. Yes, he thought, that household was a strange one, but apparently friendly, hospitable, and sincere.

'I hope you had fun with Melissa. She likes you so much. Actually, she loves you, thought she is not in love with you. We love each other very much because there are no secrets between us. We even thrive on vicarious experiences. Well, how do you like the new Queen Bee?'

'Well, I ...'

'Sorry, what about a lemon cordial or a fruit juice? I am having the most faithful: G and T. Quinine is very good for me. I am always afraid of a malaria recurrence. Psychological, of course. I got it in Northern Australia in spite of all the pills I took.'

'A lemon cordial would be fine. Thank you.'

'You know, you are lucky you don't drink. And you don't smoke either. You are going to become a centenarian very easily. Oh, incidentally, how is your father?'

Komaru briefed him on the latest developments having to do mostly with the cirrhosis advancing rapidly. They spoke about the Maori problem of alcoholism and related social difficulties.

'You are fortunate that genetic forces have not affected you. Do you know how old your father was when he started drinking?'

'Not exactly, but very young, when he also started smoking.'

'Then, yes, I remember, you said once he was with the Maori Battalion in the war, wasn't he?'

'Yes, indeed.'

'It figures. Hemi was right.'

'Sorry?'

'Oh, James Baxter. Of course, you were a child when he died. 1972. Probably you haven't read his "Returned Soldier". Just two lines to synthesise the evils brought home after the greatest evil of all. I think it reads as "The boy who volunteered at seventeen/At twenty-three is heavy on the booze."'

'Quite right. My father. And most members of the Battalion. I hope that he will last long enough for his last meeting in a few months in ...'

'Here I am. I hope you boys did not miss me. And how do you like my kitchen uniform?'

They had gotten up at the sudden apparition of a Melissa dressed as if ready to join a chorus of the Folies Bergère. High, spiked heals, black silk stockings held in place by garters at mid-thigh, red G-string barely covered by a black lace miniskirt of transparent organdy; a black semi-corset holding the lower half of her breasts in place by virtue of some gravity-defying apparatus; long, red, lace gloves reaching nearly to her arm pits; a high, propped up coiffure of her blond hair held in place by a red and green branch and flowerlets of *pohutukawa*. And she had a Japanese-style medallion hanging from her neck, a majolica figure representing something like a Trojan soldier.

'Oh, Mel,' said Bill. 'You are simply adorable. I love you, honey.'

Komaru nearly exploded into a laugh. Was there any conscious relationship between the Greek etymon and honey? Dr McTavish's tone was full of affection to the point of sounding sticky.

'And I love you. You know that! And I love you, too, Kom.'

She had gotten hold of him tenderly, pressed her torso against his lightly, placed her right cheek on his, and then pressed her lips against his after wetting hers. And she held him for quite a few seconds, while whispering into his ears something that sounded like French. No, it must have been Brazilian. So many nasal vowels in two sentences. Then, releasing him, she said in a normal tone of voice: 'You are special. I love you!'

And Komaru remained speechless, not so much because he did not know what to say, but as if instantly 'maced' out by a wave of strange perfume. What in the world is it, he wondered. Well, Melissa had brought from Brazil *uma droga de Carnaval*, one of the several types of scents that Brazilians spray each other with through *uma bomba* in order to express exhilaration and greetings at carnival time. But, what was it? It was Bill who solved Komaru's puzzlement, for, thought not embraced by Melissa, Dr McTavish, having noticed the exotic fragrance, asked her pointedly what she was wearing.

'Well, you see what. Something comfortable for the warm weather. Besides, I feel better this way in the kitchen, light and breezy if I am to cook, don't ...'

'Yes, honey, I think you are simply adorable. But I was referring to the perfume.'

'Oh, I bought this from a witch in Juiz de Fora. It is distilled, though crudely, from a tropical animal to prepare the best Witches' Ointment. Oh, darling, would you bring me one, but light. I don't want to get too hot.'

'Of course, honey,' said Bill. He got up and came back with a shot of Cardhu. Straight. No water, though at times she added half a jigger of Fiuggi. She believed in Michelangelo's therapy to dissolve kidney stones.

After a couple of slow sips, Melissa went into a long explanation about her perfume. Bill was nearly enchanted, even excited, at the details she gave while lying in an odalisca fashion on the main couch. Komaru was intrigued, though somewhat skeptical. However, the intensity of the fragrance was affecting his stomach. Like the smell of cheap anisette, though whatever Melissa wore was permeating the room more subtly.

'I was told that the black people of Bahia brought the formula from Africa, perhaps Ethiopia, though the civet can also be found in Burma and Thailand. The *viverra civetta* secretes a yellow liquid from her sexual glands, and this is used to concoct almost anything aphrodisiac. Of course, I don't need that, but I felt that it could prepare the atmosphere for dessert later. Don't worry. I have diluted it to the maximum because, as you may know, it could lead to nosebleed and even death.'

Komaru sat on a chair transfixed. Bill was smacking his lips as if his G and T had absorbed some of the scent emanating from Melissa's body. He was also salivating and looking at her with enlarged eyes. Had he taken anything before the G and T? Strange, thought Komaru, the scent was more floral than animal. Nevertheless, it was inebriating. And, amusingly, he felt hungry for food. The lemon cordial had stimulated his salivary glands.

'Any music, honey?'

'Yes, but not too loud. I have to concentrate on the tea.'

'Shall I play any of the Brazilian tapes?'

'Well, no, tonight perhaps something relaxing. Why not some Benedictine chants, no, too monotonous. Well, yes, spiritual but, please, no American jingles or oversweet stuff. Maybe something by Britten, just to complement the season? Which reminds me, maybe while I cook could you boys remove and store the Christmas tree?'

The *pohutukawa*, artificial, of course, made Komaru somewhat sad. He wondered how that Maori weather predictor could have functioned like a Christmas tree for Pakehas. He tried to recall whether it had bloomed in November, rather than in December. Would it be a long, hot summer? How could an Aotearoan bush become related to the birth of a Jewish boy in the northern hemisphere?

'Bill, sorry, oh, thank you! I miss the pine tree, even one from Norfolk.'

She had appeared on the threshold of the rumpus room all red in the face.

'Oh, already down! Bill, darling, do you recommend that I wash the macaroni?'

Meanwhile, Britten's tape had begun to play 'Freezing Winter Night' as part of *A Ceremony of Carols*. The treble voices were blending harmoniously with the harp notes of Opus 28.

'Not necessarily, honey. Only if you so want. Probably it is recommended if imported from China.'

A bell went off in Komaru's head. Made of wheat? Calling for a sprinkle of grated cheese?

Melissa returned to the kitchen where she engaged in alchemistic enterprises. Of course, she was safe since she was using her mother's cookbook published in 1953. The author, Nell Heaton, had been a pioneer in compiling that sort of work in a country barely emerging from the culinary 'middle ages' of a world war.

'Sorry, Komaru, would you mind helping me select the sauce?'

He was happy to leave Bill to cope with the plastic Christmas tree. Actually, he was curious about what in the world Melissa was going to do for evening tea.

The blue book lay flat, opened to page 323. The first entry under 'M' was very illuminating.

> MACARONI (Fr. *macaroni*). A paste made from wheaten flour: a characteristic Italian food, though made in other European countries. Macaroni is divided into two classes: *paste lunghe* and *paste tagliate* (known in France as pâtes d'Italie). Paste lunghe is shaped into various lengths and thicknesses, known as vermicelli, tagliatelle, spaghetti, etc. Paste tagliate is macaroni made into various decorative shapes, such as rings, stars, crosses, letters of the alphabet, etc. Some of these are available in this country.

Komaru had seen a package of 500 gram pasta marked as CAPELLI D'ANGELO, a very thin string of spaghetti-looking pasta, lying by a large pot into which Melissa had put water, salt and cooking oil.

'I assume, Komaru, that I can proceed according to how to cook, although they are not listed on the long variety, What do you say?'

'I suppose so, Melissa. Rather a spiritual food, ideal for the season. After all, it was an angel who announced impregnation to Mary. Am I correct?'

'Yes, of course. We are going to eat his hair. The angel must have been a blonde. What sex, incidentally?'

'Come on. Does it matter? I assume they are bisexual, according to their own needs and to those genders with whom they interact. Of course, I do prefer male angels. I wonder if they are immune to terrestrial diseases.'

'You mean AIDS and ...'

'Of course. Oh, let me read.'

TO COOK. There is no need to wash the macaroni before cooking and it is never soaked. Throw into a pan of boiling water (salted) and boil for 20 min. at least. When tender, drain and rinse in cold water under a running tap, then reheat in a colander if the macaroni is for garnish or to be served with a little melted butter, or else reheat in sauce. Can also be used in milk pudding (see under this heading) or as a soup garnish.

Under 'Variation for Use' Komaru read a long list of possibilities from 'curry sauce garnished with peas' to 'Mayonnaise or French dressing and garlic'. He begged Melissa to avoid anything containing cheese because of his allergy to lactose.

'Oh, dear. Perhaps I should use an Italian sauce. What do you say?'
'Excellent, I see one on page 444.'

Komaru scanned it quickly and, having found no cheese (though butter), he opted for it. It looked rather exotic for an Italian sauce, for it included at the end some sherry and tammy.

'Kom, please ask Bill to come here.'

When Bill came in, the angel hair swill was being washed under the tap. The concoction, after 20 minutes of cooking, looked like a paste for old fashioned wallpaper. Obviously, the BBC documentary was wrong about the pasta growing on trees in Swiss valleys. The strings, once too regular, had vanished into a fondue type of meal.

'Bill, what do you think about adding tammy? Why?'

Bill looked at page 494 and suggested that the tammy could be done without. He had read: 'A kind of woolen cloth, also known as "taminy", used for straining fruit syrup, liquid jelly, etc.'

Obviously, 'tammy' had been intended as a directive of some kind. Perhaps it meant to strain the sherry before serving the angel hair dish.

And that was the meal that made Komaru sick to his stomach the whole night after he had interacted with that fantastic couple during the process of a very difficult digestion. However, he had been able to follow Melissa's directions step by step under the bemused scrutiny of a drooling Bill waiting for his turn.

When Komaru woke up early in the morning, he heard his stomach rumbling against Melissa's buttocks. The noise seemed to be a counterpoint to Bill's snoring on the other side of the bed. The towelette Melissa had obviously thrown on the *kauri* floor was spotted by some dark brown stains. Blood had coagulated on it, and it had dried up after assuming the shape of a small Spanish National Guard hat. Komaru picked it up gingerly by one corner and entered first the toilet, where he left the congealed cloth, and then the bathroom across the hallway. It was the first day of the new Gregorian year. Through the open window, the air was already blowing warm from the Tasman Sea. He thought of the beach. He felt like walking along the sand dunes among the *maram* grass, eager to touch the soil of the earth, regardless of scratching the soles of his feet. He would not feel any pain. He had been conditioned by the roughness of nature. But not as much as he thought he should have been after spending a whole night acting like a robot lubricated by sweat, saliva, blood and semen. He needed to take a long swim to clear the pores of his skin and the doubts in his mind.

Chapter 13

Walla Walla, Washington
31 December 1991

I am still at Tanya's home. By now you must have received a few postcards from here and there, the first posted from Tillamook, on my way to Walla Walla (this has to do with 'water' or streams – I wonder if there is any connection with a proto-Polynesian source, you know, the 'wa-' root). In Tillamook I visited the cheese factory. It reminded me of home. I know that in reading these lines about milk and cheese you may become sick. Sorry. And strange. I do not have that reaction to milk products. Don't we possess related genes?

Anyway, Tanya and I are spending 'Xmas' (American pragmatic spelling) at her parents'. You may remember Tanya – she and I were roommates during the sophomore year abroad programme, in Salzburg. And we have been friends and roommates at Woodbury Hall ever since. Tanya is quite a girl. She seems to have solved all the problems of the world, and her own. In her attempt to escape the hard life of her family – generations of farmers in rural Washington – in Europe she decided to become a medical doctor. Probably she had been influenced by the status of European doctors, so different from ours. But then she changed her mind after deciding that she could do a much better job among non-humans. So she is taking pre-med courses to pursue a career as a veterinarian. This takes her back to her family traditions, especially as she feels more at home with large animals. So sensitive, particularly toward horses. You know that during our year abroad we visited England, among other places. And there she decided that horses deserve a better understanding of their lives than they now have, for whatever reason. I personally feel that those quadrupeds are exploited like servants for hedonistic purposes. Well, except in France. In Lyons I saw horse meat steak advertised on a restaurant menu. That looked like reading about the flesh of a tribe other than ours listed for consumption at a *pa* after surplus captives were killed a few generations ago during our own skirmishes.

I had hoped to receive a letter from you before I left the campus for the winter holidays. Nothing. I don't know what to say, particularly since I may have been influenced (a sibling sixth-sense?) by a short note from Dad. You seem to be undergoing a crisis of some kind. If so, what is it? Since I open up to you, can't you do the same? Are you still trying to change the world single-handedly? Have you spent any time with Dad recently?

At times, realising that this is my last semester in the States, I feel somewhat restless, confused, if not worried, about what to do next. I cannot continue drawing funds from Dad's savings. In addition, you know that my bursary help will cease at the end of June. And, coming back home, what then? How can I reintegrate myself into Ao Tea Roa, not to mention New Zealand, after absorbing so much American life and thinking? I hope that you can help me, since I have mixed feelings. I often feel that our Islands are simply a geographic expression existing as an afterthought. The few news items I can get from the American media (nothing on TV, of course) about Ao Tea Roa clearly tell me that, as far as Americans are concerned, we do not exist at all. Only sporadically is some reference made in passing to either minor political or tourist activities, and when so always as a reflection of Australia, or even Fiji, after later events have uncovered the shame involved in the abduction of 'white' Aboriginal children. Nothing about our *whenua, iwi,* Waitangi. We Maori seem not to exist in the American press, except in the Sunday edition of *The Oregonian* advertising cheap holidays in the travel section. I used to subscribe to *KiwiPhile*, a homemade information monthly trumpeting the allegedly superior (and cheap) life in New Zealand. What a dream from naïve Americans! Although published in California for local consumption, I doubt it has any impact anywhere and, if so, only among either expatriates or youth desirous of discovering a phoney Shangri-la south of the equator. Anyway, I discontinued that periodical since I felt that, although sincerely compiled by utopian romanticists, it did little to describe the real situation resulting from the Waitangi rape.

Sorry. I am somewhat distraught, uncoordinated, sad. As everyone in this farmhouse just outside Walla Walla (the fields around are cultivated for sugar beets) is asleep, I sense some kind of 'longitudinal' longing. Here it is night, a little snow on the ground, and very quiet. We are in full winter, in the inland. I know that it is already afternoon of the 1 January in Wellington – sunshine (I watch the weather reports on CNN), warmer than here. But where are you? In Papakura with Dad or in Wellington among your books? Dad has mentioned that you have made friends with the family of a psychiatrist in Wanganui, a certain Dr McTavish. Is he a Kiwi? He has been kind enough to help Dad in the process of his transition from 'Devil's Island' (Dad's last label for the sanatorium, undoubtedly unjust) to Papakura. Puzzling. How come? You never wrote me about that contact. Knowing your intellectual (you call it genetic) aversion to whites, what happened? What kind of family are they? Do they understand us? What do they say about the rôle of the Waitangi Tribunal? Do you still think that this is a long way from Nuremberg, which incidentally I visited during my sophomore year? What I remember best are, sorry, its pastry shops and little gingerbread houses. One of these miniature houses was under the Xmas tree for Tanya. She was raised Catholic, as was her mother. And guess what Tanya gave me for Xmas? She feels so close to me because she knows I was baptised, so she gave me a book, namely, *A Short History of Christian Thought* by a certain Linwood Urban. I found it informative, thought there are some gaps here and there. Undoubtedly not a philosophical work, nevertheless it presents the contributions of Kierkegaard (my present hero) with regard to the rôle of the individual's relationship with God (I hope you don't laugh – yes, you say that God is not needed in the present world, that you never had the pleasure of meeting him, and neither have I, though I KNOW that I will). But, you see, I am going beyond K., since I feel that no man, sorry, no woman is an island, even in religion. Just last semester, before my conversion, I discovered Friedrich Schleiermacher. He stressed the community of believers, rather than the individual one, in a fellowship of Christians (call it the Church or whatever). There cannot be billions of 'single' communities, for now I believe in the circular interaction between and among humans united in continuing the effort made by Jesus to change the world through Love (please don't laugh at me, I am serious – after all, aren't you doing something similar starting with our *whenua*?). And how is your MA thesis proceeding? Do you think that your analysis and understanding of 'white' history can help you?

Oh, dear brother, I wish I could talk with you at length! I have read so much and studied philosophy (the religion of the soul) as a key to understanding myself. And, like Tanya (she is even becoming, well, not possessive toward me, but 'protective' – after all, she feels she influenced a pagan like me to understand life, love and God), I begin to solve great problems for my existence on Earth. Please do not assume that I have betrayed you and 'our' Maoridom, but I think I have the right to follow my own path. I have but one life, and not a 'normal' one, since I see myself as a deviant and, thus, I want to proceed in a way that I consider less stressful and individually within people, a community of humans who for thousands of years have followed common interests.

I plan to return to Portland in a week. Meanwhile, Tanya and I, weather permitting under the influence of the Japanese current, plan to take short trips to neighbouring 'cultural' areas (something like our own *pas* destroyed by civilization) and Vancouver Island, Canada, particularly Victoria, didn't I tell you? I have a driver's license so I can drive Tanya's car when she gets tired, on the right side of the road, of course. Will I be able to drive at home and do you have an automobile? What happened to Dad's lorry? I find so many similarities between us and the Indians. When I tell Tanya about that, she says that I don't look 'native'. She states that I have the look of a Southern European tanned by the sun. I don't know what to say. Incidentally, she knows about me, well, why I wear my large *tiki* all the time, even when I shower. The first time she saw it she thought I had a lipoma. Then I explained everything to her, and she accepted me as a normal person. She even got funny, saying that I was privileged to be overendowed with a spare part in case of breast cancer, the scourge – if not the historical Nemesis – of American feminism, as a slap in the face of contemporary 'liberated' existence.

I don't know who fared better, they (the Indians) or us. I've visited ruins here and there, totem poles, fishing villages. It's depressing how their culture has been wiped out in the wake of European occupation. Tanya descends, actually, from a Russian family on her father's side. The Russians used to live nearby barely more than a century ago, as in Alaska. Tanya's family is now handling a farm where they raise, in addition to beets, also peas and carrots, which are then packed at Walla Walla Canning Company and Libby's.

As I said, Tanya has solved all her problems. She knows where she is going during her life and afterwards. She has changed a little since I first met her at the dorm. She had some kind of misunderstanding with the RA, sorry, the Resident Assistant, in connection with a boyfriend. After that, she just resolved to drop all typical activities of the boyfriend culture permeating the life of college girls. Horror stories. We Maoris are more puritanical than the Chinese and the Muslims. At least from what Americans see in me, or what they don't. Although I have participated in some interactions with boys at a superficial level (the normal functions of integrated college life), I have never been able to understand their tendency to regard learning as an opportunity for the disintegration of morals and family values. Of course, this university is not 'normal' in comparison with what students do, say, at UCLA, at the University of Colorado, or at other progressive institutions infested with drugs, promiscuity and playboyism. I know that I am regarded as an 'oddball', but not so much as if I had attended some other institutions.

Komaru, please write to me. I am anxious to go back to Portland to find some of your letters. Tell me about you, father and everything else. I miss you and your bossiness. I think that you are the best brother I could ever think of, even if you changed so much after spending a year in Shanghai. Just think, I attended Mass on Xmas day with Tanya's family. So fascinating in a church not so far from the Washington penitentiary and an unofficial brothel for illegal Mexican workers. And I remembered that you spent Xmas morning in 1988 visiting Mao's tomb in Tiananmen Square. One could find some connections based on idealism for both Jesus and Mao, undoubtedly great men if seen within the context of aching humanity.

After Mass we had dinner with the extended family. Touched by their generosity, the naïveté of rural relatives, the mixed feelings of uneasiness toward a New Zealand. No one seemed to know where it is located and, once told where, they wondered why people would live so far from everyone else on Earth, and what language we speak. They complimented me for speaking English so well!

So I plan to post this letter tomorrow, though it will not be picked up until the second. Meanwhile, I will read some of the books I borrowed from the local public library and the Walla Walla Community College. As you know, the best course I ever took was one on comparative religion. Others followed. Although I have already decided on ONE religion, I am still uncovering parallels all over the world between Catholicism and its universality and other spiritual movements undoubtedly born from interior analyses. For example, when I read quotations from Lao Tzu and Chuang Tzu, I can't distinguish between Taoism and Christianity. Concepts such as non-violence, awareness, acceptance, wisdom, virtue, solitude and others are found all over. Then why Christianity, you might ask. At present I think that Jesus must have been influenced by eastern thought. Maybe he travelled to India. Amazingly, a 'Westerner' like Mother Teresa is now carrying her ball of spiritual life into the east. What is new? Not much, especially after discovering the fantastic works of Thomas Merton. You should read him. Ironically, he died 'accidentally' visiting the East while working for peace. I say 'accidentally' though some friends thought it was a set-up to get rid of a pacifist while the States was trying to contain Communism. Who knows? The forces of materialism and dictatorship recur periodically to silence humans who are trying to make a better world. Well, the Romans considered Jesus a rebel and a threat to imperialism. And this happens every day all over the world. Think of South Africa, or of all of Africa, as a matter of fact. Yes, you say, think of Ao Tea Roa to start with. Charity begins at home, yes, I know your thinking. But what can you do? Either you fight the whole world or you withdraw from it.

Well, I had better stop here. I trust I am not bothering you with my thoughts, or should I say my soul. As father has fewer hours left on Earth, whom else can I count on? So, let me finish by saying that, for whatever you are doing at present, I am going to pray for you. Please don't laugh. I am learning how to pray, particularly before and after reciting the Rosary. Tanya's mother was kind enough to give me a mother-of-pearl rosary for Christmas. It is a mind-relaxing device, in addition to creating an atmosphere of communion with millions of other people touching beads of psychological similarity all over the world, regardless of religion. You know, Moslems, Buddhists, Taoists, and so many others use similar expedients, though the process can also be followed mentally. How can I tell you what is going on in my mind and my heart? Yes, I say heart, replacing what we have been taught in our culture as the seat of all feelings, sorry, not replacing, but perhaps adding to our Maori belly for courage, belief and dignity.

So I hongi you for a delicate and warm exchange of sisterhood while I hum lightly the familial and familiar notes of trust, respect and aroha. So strange, I haven't touched the nose of anybody for so long that I feel funny after so much, shall I say, abstinence.

Here one exchanges the touches of lips and cheeks. I don't think that lips can smell the related genes flowing in our Polynesian veins.

Incidentally, what kind of blood type do you have? I am curious because a year ago I gave blood to the infirmary. Amazingly, I found out that my blood is A positive, the same as for a large segment of Western Europeans. I was so surprised that I asked for a second analysis, which confirmed the first. In my biology class I learned that most Polynesians have Type O, the same found among American Indians and Eskimos. Sorry for the digression.

Write me soon, and again aroha from American Indian land and your A+ sister,

Mahina

Only weeks later, around the 20 January in connection with Wellington's Anniversary Day, was Komaru able to recollect and analyse the New Year's events in Wanganui. He had aged 'socially' more in a few days than in many years of introspection. He knew that it was not a matter of 'retrocognition', for he was not subject to paranormal phenomena. He preferred to think in terms of retrospection as an objective analysis about a fully conscious experience undergone at the McTavishes. He looked at 'historical' facts in retrospect, and he laughed at this concept for, after all, as a historian his whole psyche was always floating in retrospection. But, was this not an introspection, a reflection, a dissection of remembrances?

Komaru admitted to himself the possibility of smashing himself unconsciously against a wall of retrospective falsification, a mnemonic error in recalling and crystallising an event or a series of events. He even considered whether the falsification could be intentional, not only for some of the past, but also for the whole of it, resulting then in a distorted vision caused by a series of true and false 'blended' memories. In addition, he considered the possibility of his own past reality for, far from being 'transparent' in matters of deconstruction, it could be distorted and thus ambiguous along an elliptical process. He wondered what the psychiatrist McTavish would say about the omission of painful-to-recall facts in free association during psychoanalysis. No matter what, Komaru could not lie to himself, regardless of seeking an escape valve through philosophical methods of phoney Husserlian phenomenology, as well as a possible memory safety net tended by Hegel and held by Heidegger. As a historian, Komaru was forced to accept the more or less shaky paradigm of tangible reality in order to perform as a reasonably sane individual among a myriad of doubts.

So, he proceeded chronologically, beginning with the informal 'Italian' supper prepared by Melissa. The main dish of pasta took him back to the porridge made of dry *kumara* that his paternal grandmother used to feed him for breakfast during his childhood. Of course, Komaru did not sprinkle any grated cheese, as requested by Bill, in the hope that the pasta would be more palatable. The rest of the meal was a blank space in his recollection, but the discussion that took place after dinner came back to his mind vividly.

'Well, Melissa, honey, that was a good Italian dinner. Those people take food so seriously, as if each meal were the last before an execution.'

'Sorry, darling, I think I overcooked everything.'

'No problem. Digestion is easier that way. Tomorrow it is my turn. It will be a day of rest. Late breakfast, beach outing, afternoon lounging, Mozart and then, while Komaru discusses his project with you, I'll prepare the first dinner of 1992. Just think of a peaceful New Zealand away from Yugoslavia, Iraq, Central America, and the like.'

'It seems that we are cut off from history,' interjected Komaru, 'and I wonder whether in this era of fast communication we are really at peace morally.'

'Is not morality a question of geography?' said Melissa. 'If humans prefer to destroy themselves through warring as in primitive Ao Tea Roa, why should we suffer? Let's enjoy life now and forget war, history, and deranged humans.'

'But, Melissa, how can we? Do you think that my ancestors engaged in war, instead of making love, for the sake of pure maliciousness?'

'No, of course, but why not change the subject in favour of bonobo philosophy?'

'Yes, honey, why not?'

Zoology had never been a favourite subject in Komaru's education. After all, animals living in his antecolonial memory house were very few. He had never studied the sex life of bats and glow worms. But it did not take him very long to be instructed in pragmatic philosophy. Melissa had removed the pillows of the corner sofa, pulled the seat toward the centre of the room, and in a fiat had created a king-size bed. Then she placed the pillows against the sofa back after spreading a beach blanket on top of it.

'All right, bonobos, let us make love, not war.'

'Oh, honey, so generous of you. And, Komaru, please feel free to help yourself any way you like. Don't be bashful. We have no inhibitions.'

It did not take long for Melissa to get rid of the few clothes she was wearing. In a jiffy she first sat against the back of the sofa, then slid down the middle of it lasciviously while Bill removed his slacks, shoes and shirt. For whatever reason, he kept his socks and underwear on.

It is said that life is made 99 per cent of sequential syntagms flowing along the highway of normality and 1 per cent of impromptu paradigms emerging abruptly here and there. There she was, Melissa, tanned, hot, lying down with open legs as if trying to cool hot spots in anticipation of sweaty epidermic contacts.

Komaru timidly followed suit. On his left, Bill was observing him as a psychiatrist observes a confused patient. He was actually bemused, smiling subtly, and looking at Komaru's shorts. Melissa had opened her arms as if encouraging Komaru to be embraced maternally. Her movements were so slow and studied that Komaru felt as if he was watching a movie at half its normal frame speed.

'Come to me, Komaru, make love to me slowly, gently. I have already lubricated myself to make it easy for us. Dr Tavares must have performed a heavy-duty mending operation.'

She bent toward Komaru, who refrained from looking at Bill. And she pulled Komaru's shorts down slowly while blowing her breath around his loins. Meanwhile, the palms of her hands skimmed him so delicately that he reacted nearly instantly. And Melissa dropped herself backward, carrying Komaru with her. His chest bounced on her breast, and she moaned with pain.

'Sorry, I am so tender. Please hold yourself up with your arms.'

This he did, as if imitating a Galapagos iguana doing pushups, though he was distracted by observing her mammas. It was a different Melissa sporting two incongruous half balls of Dutch cheese floating under a thin skin. They were undoubtedly in the way. Where were the tiny breasts that once dotted the spacious bosom of a blonde athlete? The similarity with cheese ball halves made him somewhat sick. Diarrhea. Nausea. And Bill waiting in the wings. He had removed his shorts, too, and he showed a rather small appendage, semi-lost in a large puff of black hair. But he looked soft and pendulous. And he glanced at Komaru's with a tinge of incredulity, for Komaru reminded Bill of the scale on which a Pompeiian was resting a *phallus paratus* as depicted in the famed mural of the Vettii house. Thus,

Komaru gingerly adapted to Melissa's body like a Marine recruit ready to begin pushups under the scrutiny of a drill sergeant.

Nevertheless, he was extremely affectionate toward Melissa. It was in part his assumption that he should have taken his time in foreplay activities. And he kissed her on the lips when she opened her mouth, exhaling the hot breath of desire. She glued her tongue to his while pulling him into her. Was he applying some of the introductory steps he had learned from her during their very first encounter? Or was he wary of Bill's presence, taking his time 'loving' her as a welcoming woman who obviously liked him? Perhaps Komaru was subconsciously showing off by playing the rôle of a romantic Hollywood actor on the stage of the absurd. Melissa's husband was the producer, the director and the supporting actor in a surrealistic movie.

Then she placed her lips on his left ear and softly whispered terms of endearment.

'Kom, I love you. You are special. With you it is different because you care for me. And you don't hurt me. You are so considerate.'

Komaru thought that Pakeha conception of 'love' was probably medieval, but its realisation was extremely liberated. He was discovering the unusual in British culture imported against the will of his ancestors in order to civilise backwoods Ao Tea Roa.

'Take your time, Kom. Gently. You hurt me a bit this afternoon, and I am so tender. And Bill is eager to follow in your footsteps.'

Komaru almost laughed in her face. Perhaps he should have used his toe to overcome Dr Tavares' embroidery, as done in some tribes of Africa via avuncular help to deflower a virgin. And, taking a look at Bill, he saw him almost foaming, anxious to be given the American 'OK' signal by forming a circle with the thumb and forefinger, a very obscene gesture in Brazilian culture. The situation was becoming rather amusing. Polynesian mores had vanished into thin air. Pakeha expectations were lingering through Bill, now observing almost every detail after approaching Komaru too closely for his comfort, while Bill was still pending, nearly lost in the large clump of curly black hair.

It was Melissa who, in a way, tricked Komaru into the final stage. Although she was obviously affected by a pleasurable pain manifested by a series of powerful orgasms, she applied both hands to his buttocks and drove him home in a single burst that was reflected onto Komaru quite sensorially. And he rested on her breasts, though uncomfortably. They were shifty, in the way, somewhat artificial against his own breast. Why in the world did she have to have a so-called breast augmentation? Oh, at least she could have selected a smaller size that could be cupped like Ling-ling's, still hard and sensitive. Melissa did not seem to react at all when Komaru caressed her skin, except when probing the right nipple, which became visibly enlarged. But the nipple looked corrugated as if there was not enough skin to cover it naturally. Breasts, and Melissa, and Ling-ling. And then Mahina inserted herself between the two. He was first intrigued, and then bothered by that intrusive vision. He had never even imagined a Polynesian trio of mammas, so ephemeral in size that by the age of 20 they become naturally as large as what Melissa had reached artificially. Oh, yes, St Agatha. And the whole mammalogical tradition sped by while he eased himself out of her in a puddle of himself and of her, helped by the solicitous offer of Bill handing him a bunch of Puffies, Product of New Zealand. But didn't Melissa use white ones? This time they were pink. Then he realised that they had been blessed with the result of Dr Tavares' reconstructive inventiveness, for which he was very well known among Japanese women whose prospective husbands required proof of virginity.

And so Komaru recalled Bill taking his turn as soon as space was created beside Melissa. The condom was still hanging from Komaru when Melissa, obviously knowing what her husband expected, turned herself over in *kuri* fashion and, when she set herself barely in position, Bill grabbed her by the hip with both hands and plunged into her like a mini pneumatic drill. She started to moan immediately, nearly screaming, something she had not done with Komaru. The whole congregation sounded artificial, like the repetition of a routine process. In fact, Bill had taken only a minute or two, as if he were being watched by a referee counting the seconds of the whole performance at the rate of four strokes per second. No words were exchanged. Komaru was first shocked, then intrigued by that *coitus a tergo*, so fast, as if Bill was afraid of losing the flow of blood along his penile veins. Was that love between a husband and wife? Or something he had seen in a movie, oh, where?, yes, a *National Geographic* documentary on the lives of lions in Tanzania. The male would snarl at the female, grab her neck with his mouth, wave his tail nervously, and perform his reproductive duty so fast that one had to be extremely attentive to see the whole function. Of course, the lion could repeat his performance every 20 minutes or so. Could Bill do something similar once a week?

The answer was provided later during the night, when Komaru found himself in the bedroom, with Melissa placing herself in the centre of the bed like a naïve cocotte ready to be sacrificed to Priapus. Komaru had just come out of the shower when he saw Bill opening some panels behind the pillow propped against the headboard.

Melissa had meanwhile changed into a new Circean uniform consisting of a black laced brassiere, bikini undies, and incongruously long red stockings held by black garters. What amazed Komaru was the fact that she was also wearing black pointed and spiked shoes, shining on her feet like protective armor. On the left nightstand a bottle of Cardhu was already open. Had she not drunk already a whole bottle of Australian wine – what was it, oh, yes, a Shiraz from Coonawarra recommended by the *Wine Industry Journal*. Bill preferred Australian wines after being indoctrinated by Eric Rolls, for him the dean of Epicureans in the entire southern hemisphere.

'Honey, can you put your glass away?'

She hurriedly tried to gulp the drink before moving over and, in the process, she spilled some Cardhu on her breast. Komaru, standing by the bed wearing a large towel as a Polynesian pareo, rushed to her aid, grabbed a corner of the sheet, and tried to dry her off.

'No,' she said pulling the towel away, 'use this, but gently. Oh, what happened to you? Have you lost weight?'

Obviously, she was drunk, but in a mellifluous way true to her name. Languidly, snake-like, contorting her body, she waited for a ritual while Bill, after removing some contraptions from behind the bookcase headboard, tried to attach them to her wrists. They were fake chains made of plastic. And she did not resist. Likewise, Bill proceeded to tie her ankles to the bottom footboard, while Melissa held Komaru close to her.

Now she was tied in that silly American posture of eroticism. Bemusedly, Komaru did not understand the purpose of that *mise-en-scène*. For what? To excite a lover? And how could she move her feet safely while sporting 5-inch spiked heels? Highly dangerous. Were they a tool of defense in case of theatrical aggression? Meanwhile, Bill had brought out a cardboard box and had dumped out a small arsenal of toys – different sizes of latex substitutes, operated by batteries (and plenty of them) in several sizes and shapes, carrying the letter A in various sequences. And some small tubes of lubricant, plus a jar of an American product branded Heavenly Glide, Water Soluble. Finally, he retrieved something Komaru thought was a king-sized rosary with about seven plastic balls strung by a silkish looking cord.

'Billy, daaaling!'

'Yes, honey.'
'The balls!'
'Which ones?'
'Komaru's.'
'Ask him, but be patient, wait for ...'
'No, stupid daaalin. The iron balls, the ...'

Komaru understood. He had brought as a Christmas gift a set of Iron Balls made in China, bought in the open market west of the refectory at East China Normal University. He had gotten them as a souvenir, as well as to massage the palm of his hand and release tension. What in the world did Melissa want them for, since her hands were tied to the bed?

'Where are they?'
'In my jewelry drawer.'

Bill handed Komaru a small blue box containing two balls, one slightly larger than the other. He had barely used them, and he had even kept the 'directions' for use and maintenance. In fact, on the last page of the instruction booklet he read quickly:

> If it is to be unused for a long period of time, coat it with wax or grease for sealing and preservation.

> Manufactured by
> Iron Balls Factory, Baoding City, Hebei Province

'Daaalin ... Billy. The feather. And Dr Ruth.'
'Sure. Komaru, just wait a second.'
'Wait for what?'
'I'll tell you. Just a sec.'

Meanwhile, Melissa had spread herself as if ready to be photographed for the centerfold of *Playboy*. And Bill took a fingerful of Heavenly Glide, dubbed the labia minora gingerly, and also the majora here and there. Finally, he took the feather (what was it, an African ostrich's?) and spread the pomate delicately all over. Komaru felt as if holding a box containing St Agatha's shrunken breasts. He tried to be still because the metallic sound emanating from the Chinese box triggered Melissa's interest in them.

'Michelangelo, that is enough. Kom, the balls.'
'Sorry ...'
'What she means, you insert them there. Ah, the small first, and then the other. Don't hesitate. She knows how to suck them into the right place. In Europe this kind of pre-penetration, according to

Casanova, was very popular in the 18th century. The hollow balls, however, were solid gold, rather expensive toys used mostly to compensate courtesans without offending them by leaving money as for common prostitutes. This way the lover would simply leave the balls *in situ* as if forgotten, and then the woman would remove and sell them at a good price. Of course, the whole thing was dangerous for inexperienced women. Often a barber had to be called to extract the balls with a pair of crude forceps. Magnets were not yet an accepted means of retrieval as done nowadays, via a vibrating dildo made in China by the same export company.'

'Would it not hurt her if ...'

'Hurt, hell, go ahead, you already went through. Did you not an hour ago?'

So Komaru removed the smaller one, and in handling it the sound of Salvation Army Christmas bells on street corners spread over the bed. St Melissa, ex-virgin with the compliments of Dr Tavares, and now martyr compliments of her husband and lover in residence. Amazing, Komaru thought, how mythical Mother Nature of Anglo-Saxon families provides for proper apertures to be gulped so easily. After all, does it now allow the head of an infant to go through? But then how can Melissa expel them? Is it not extremely dangerous, he thought. Of course, he did not remember that the patient had a medical doctor in residence. But, did he have a set of magnetic forceps?

The contact between the two balls triggered a muted tone when Melissa started writhing within the constraints of the plastic chains. The music increased when Bill inserted a circumcised black dildo glistening with a perfumed oil. And, after turning on the switch for the mechanism therein, the cacophonic tune was nearly submerged by Melissa's screams and babbling expressions. Who says that Sybarites bred only in Magna Graecia, nymphos in Burton's seraglios, and witches in Salem? Undoubtedly, the British Empire had left quite a legacy still operating in QE II's Commonwealth.

'Out you go, Bill, come to me Kom!'

He had been ready for the last few minutes, although somewhat nauseated by the smell of alcohol emanating from Melissa's breast and breath. However, his honour was at stake. After all, he was the honoured guest of civilised people, of refined professionals, of respected citizens. And he thought of the yin and yang located within Melissa, for the two enamelled blue balls showed the black and white Eastern symbol of reproduction, of life, of universality. The Chinese ideograph represented the 'God of Longevity', The king of the "Threasures",' to 'Strengthen the ball players and make our country powerful.' The Chinese translator of the Chinese logo had even made a spirant of the dental explosive in order to anglicise it for export reasons. Melissa had applied some of the contents in the 'directions' booklet in a novel way: 'According to the Chinese traditional medical theory of 'Jingluo (jingluo refers to the main and collateral channels, regarded as a network of passages, through which vital energy circulates ...)'. So that when Komaru was stopped midway by the larger ball, he got hurt and imitated Dr McTavish's speed method simply to finish off quickly. He just could not oppose flesh against enameled steel. And even so, in spite of the awkward missionary tradition propped by a pillow under Melissa's buttocks, she became an Indian goddess as if she had been endowed with extra legs and arms. In the process, the echo of the ball music reverberated light through the body to the point that, placing his left ear in the middle of her breasts, Komaru could faintly hear two tunes, 'one sound high and one low', intermingled during Melissa's convulsions. Oh, those damn Brazilian breasts, thought Komaru, floating under him and making him nearly seasick. How he missed the pointed pressure of the former nipples against his own athletic and hairless breast. Ling-ling now could score a victory, and Mah. . . oh, no! how could it be so when *Quae sunt aequalia uni tertio sunt aequalia inter se*?

Oh, how relieved he felt when he turned onto his right side to remove his protective godlet. And in so doing he observed Bill, who had no need to wear one. After all, he was her husband. Could she get pregnant? Of course, if she had not been spayed a long time ago. But she could still become infected at the drop of a ... condom, the most important contribution made by mankind to femalekind in order to make Hippocrates go bankrupt and Malthus happy. And then Bill began to strap some metal chains converging on a ring into which he had inserted himself. Limp, yes, but Melissa, obviously accustomed to a rite of staging up, had begun to kiss him there avidly so that in a few minutes Bill felt circumscribed by the ring that kept everything in place just to explore the already lubricated neighbourhood. And, as Bill repeated the submachine gun performance in a matter of a minute, Melissa reproduced the previous sequence of moans, screams, babbles and bites. Obviously, she was faking, but so well that Komaru nearly felt excited. But he went to the shower again. Polynesians seem to start dying out if they stay away from water longer than an hour.

When he came back to the bed, Bill was sound asleep facing the window wall toward the Chinese gooseberry tree garden. It was hot, and with Bill covered with part of the sheet, Melissa glued her belly to his buttocks, while hers were left uncovered and exposed toward Komaru's side like a split Mexican papaya. Thus, silently he slid down next to her on his left side and tried to fall asleep. But it took a long time to do so, for as an adult he had never slept near two people, and Pakehas at that! His stomach was still acting up after the Italian macaroni dinner. And his mind was in turmoil. There he was, near two geniuses, a historiographer who had scored the highest marks at Cambridge as a follower of Edward Follett Carr, and a psychiatrist who had helped Carl Jung to carve inscriptions of pseudo-Indian Tantric mottos on Swiss rocks.

Just before falling asleep, Komaru remembered Mahina's letter written at the end of the year. She was asking him if he had spent his vacations in Wellington among his books. An ocean away, a whole universe between them. And the hope of being able to reply to her under the drive of retrospection. But what could he tell her? On the one hand, he was angry at her describing so easily her feelings about a new spiritual life. How could she fall among the wolves of Vatican Monarchy? He would be tolerant and understanding, of course, but straight to the point when it came to telling her off. But when he thought of himself and what he had been doing lately, he became anxious to return to Wellington for a billion reasons. He would, however, remain in Wanganui another day to discuss his thesis with Melissa. Then in Wellington he would finish the two or three more outlines for the last decades of the 20th century and of the British Empire. Except for Hong Kong, Ao Tea Roa would be the last, the *coup de grâce* to white colonialism.

Chapter 14

The first weekend of 1992 was for Komaru one of revelation about human nature as he viewed it in himself and in others with whom he interacted. The week that followed presented itself as a social container into which fell several items calling for action, or at least for analysis. First of all, Mahina's impact on him, already lingering in his mind with ever-increasing frequency, became his major concern in spite of the physical distance separating them. The psychic distance, however, had become non-existent. Then there was his father's situation, appearing more darkly on the horizon of immediacy, which rendered him nervous and jumpy. Next, the 'McTavish vortex', into which he had fallen consciously and selfishly, began to spin more densely and quickly around his libido. There was no question about the almost tangible mesh surrounding him, particularly since he began to feel toward Melissa some sentiments of neurotic attachment deriving from immediate comfort. Other prosaic, pending matters weighed on him in concert with the deadlines and responsibilities involved in the completion of his MA thesis. For some time he had not been working at all on his outline – he had gotten stuck at the acme of the 1970s, and the synthesis for 1979 loomed nearly as an abortion from his mind. In fact, he admitted to himself that he had a writer's block, though it was not necessarily a mental one. He had succumbed to emotionalism, if not selfish interest. Melissa was palpitating in his subconscious not as a succuba during his sleep, but through one of various incubi, although clearly a pleasant and powerful attraction deserving his admiration when he was fully awake.

By the middle of January, after putting aside physical distractions of a hedonistic nature, he forced himself at least to produce a historical and near-cabalistic view of the decade. He was not happy with the results. He even thought that the artificial parceling of historic events – which by now he labelled subjective vicarious retrospections – was for 1979 the weakest so far in his attempts to paradigmatise slices of human events.

By the end of January, he had tentatively accepted what he printed from the computer as follows:

1979 –   Birth of Modern Iran
         Birth of Modern England
         Birth of Modern Central African Republic

History, Komaru began to believe, is a therapeutic tool in the process of inventing a different happening, even the reverse of 'real' records, as long as it helps someone to feel better. Oh, Komaru thought, if only this or that had taken place the opposite way, or had not happened at all! And so he convinced himself not only of non-historical facts, but also of things that could take place in the future. For the past, what was the difference as long as the future could be built as a utopia? Could the past invent the future? Why not sketch '1999', the near apex of a decade leading to 'The Birth of Modern Ao Tea Roa' as a reflection of things to take place for Maoris seeing a *pan-umbra futurorum*? Or could the future forget the past? Too bad that so many had suffered and died in either voluntary or forced processes of life and death. He thought, who knows what really happened in every fight, war, or revolution within the minds of participants who could never tell the survivors anything comforting, such as 'I died happy' or 'I died in a state of bliss'?
And thus Komaru, in anticipation of a new, childishly conceived millennium beginning at 00:01 of Gregorian year 2001, selected three more corners as antithetical to one another as possible, and apparently not connected with each other unless analysed within the giant framework of faceless humanity, that humanity wearing a worn-out Etruscan mask of countless *personae* on the permanent stage of Greek tragedy.
Iran came up as a source of retribution against powers supporting the opulence of a Shah who had wasted billions of dollars in resources for his own egotistic aggrandisement. Similarly, Nemesis had taken care of Bokassa. The Central African Empire and Iran had suffered the same fate. Not that the ensuing political system was better, but at least it conferred upon 'mass-people' a psychological anchor of intangible freedom even at the risk of their starving under the new regime. Khoumeni, in spite of Foucault's panegyric, and Dack, notwithstanding the CIA's blessing, could not perform a miracle overnight, but they could tell their people that they were free of the schizophrenic superpowers dictating colonialistic policies thousands of miles away. The impotence displayed by the USA, as an example

vis-à-vis the takeover of the American embassy in Tehran, was just one of the things to come all over the world. In Latin America alone, the Nicaragua 'syndrome' was one bead along a rosary of people's power. Then, Biafra, Cambodia, Vietnam, Poland, Quebec, Ireland, Wounded Knee, Chile, Basqueland, Ethiopia, Corsica, Angola, Molucca, Panama, Mauritania, Rhodesia, Uganda and others too numerous to mention were just beads along a recitation of many people's fight against political injustice. Amazingly, New Zealand was never reported on by the international press for anything relevant taking place Down Under, Komaru thought. What does one have to do to be noticed? *Quo usque tandem, Britannia, abutieris patientiae nostrae?*, he told himself. Would an Australasian Catilina get up sooner or later somewhere in front of the Beehive not to shoot bullets but to shout 'Pakeha henumi!' all over Aotearoa? Where had the spirit of the Bastion Point Golf Club hidden itself waiting for a rebirth?

One of the amazing things Komaru began to wonder about was the power of retrospection for the most recent history he was analysing with regard to Melissa. And retrospection overwhelmed him in a matter of hours, taking him from Wellington to the morning he woke up in the McTavishes' bed. That night, when Komaru was awakened by two warm hemispheres rubbing against his belly, he behaved almost as if in a dream. Melissa was knocking at the door of his manhood, and he reacted quickly when he was grabbed and led into a cleft of hot and moist flesh. He was reminded of the flytrap seducing giant insects for slow digestion. He took his time without even thinking about wearing anything. What was he to fear? Making her pregnant while Bill apparently was asleep on the other side of Melissa? But then, as soon as Komaru finished, Bill grabbed Melissa by the left shoulder and started his routine hammering. That surprised Komaru, for Bill must have raised his erotic antennae in expectation. In fact, Melissa had positioned herself for Bill's favourite approach. For whatever reasons, her husband must have had an aversion to missionary indoctrination. And the king-sized waterbed vibrated even after Bill dropped exhausted on his side. Komaru wondered why Pakehas had to invent a water mattress, making him almost seasick on dry land. It must have been something cultural, for Queen Victoria had used a rubber mattress filled with hot water during her final illness.

'Honey, you did not ..., what I mean, Komaru did not wear anything. Why?'

'Oh, sweetheart, sorry, I didn't think about it. I was asleep, I ...'

'But what about me? Swimming in Polynesian juices. That takes longer for me, you know. I could barely make it. Next ...'

'Was it unpleasant? And I doubt Kom is infected by anything. Are you, Kom?'

'Sorry, oh, no, I ... thought that she had taken care of herself.'

In fact, Komaru, except for Melissa's normal state of natural lubrication, had not detected any signs of thalamic partnership. Who was faking what? Was Bill that old already? How psychological, if not psychotic, was his relationship with his wife?

'Honey, it was simply delicious after Dr Tavares was put aside. Like a little death, earth to earth, flesh to flesh, and the sharing was so refreshing. Between the two of you, I feel really full. It is so gratifying! But I promise you ...'

Komaru could not continue listening to that domestic exchange so early in the morning. So he got up, went downstairs to 'his' room, showered, dressed and, in waiting for his hosts to descend from the crop-sharing garden of joy, looked for some writing material in his case, and began to write a letter to Mahina. The beginning was difficult, not only because he rarely wrote by hand after being conditioned by a word-processing system, but also because his mind could not change so quickly from a triangular, physical exploit to a dyadic, sibling dialogue. In anticipation of receiving mail from the States, and one for sure from Mahina, Komaru had planned to tell his sister what he did not have the guts to say in his last letter. That had to do with her conversion to Catholicism. He simply began to be obsessed with that thought. And he lowered the boom on her. Actually, his letter was an attempt to put on paper what he later would transfer onto a computer screen before printing.

Wanganui, 1 January 1992

Dear Mahina,

It is the first of the Pakeha year, and ironically I am spending it as a guest at the McTavishes. Who are they? Friends, well, nice people. Mrs McT, a historian who preferred to become a housewife, and I met at one of the Pacific Forum meetings. To make a long story short, she and her husband have become my friends. He is a psychiatrist who, through his professional contacts, has been helping father. And she is helping me with her criticism of my theory on the meaning of history as seen by one of its victims. Well, I don't consider this cheating, for my ideas are original, though probably corny. Her father was a retired Professor of Classics at Cambridge. They have connections in Wellington, and I hope that through them I may get a post at the Waitangi Tribunal. That is why I am trying to lie low. Indeed, I plan not to attend the Waitangi Day – expenses, and the usual fake ceremony, and the pharisaic atmosphere. I prefer to visit with Dad later when he attends the 28th M.B. meeting in Rotorua.

Here in Wanganui things are quiet, though I detect in the air some kind of restlessness. But, I, myself, am resting. My hosts are asleep upstairs, and later we plan to go to the beach, probably to Castlecliff. This is not an exclusive resort area. I don't know if you ever heard of it, but Bill, i.e. Dr McTavish, told me it is popular with backpackers and young people. He informed me that his wife likes to walk among them almost as if trying to recapture her youth as it was in Brighton, England, when things were more conservative. She is kind of a liberated lady, trying to enjoy life almost hedonistically. But, Mahina, she is sharp, intelligent, beautiful, generous, and can be affectionate. I must confess that she is the first Pakeha female whom I see from a human and humane point of view, though at times I am baffled by her, well, iconoclastic position regarding England or, actually, Europe. She is *a*religious in the traditional way, but she is extremely conversant with the thoughts of Buddha, Confucius and, you may not believe it, Clare of Assisi. Although I am writing this now, I plan to transfer my thoughts via the WP.

So, another Pakeha year ahead. Today, after breakfast (incidentally Mrs McTavish is the worst cook I have ever come across, even worse than you – I remember when you cooked once for father, and had forgotten to remove the skin of the beef tongue, sorry, I'm trying to be funny – I love you, you know) as I said we go to the beach, lunch at the Wing-Wah (I miss Chinese food, and it is cheap there – I'll play the rôle of the amphitryon for a change, with my meager finances), rest in the afternoon when she will take a look at what I have been doing so far. Actually, it will be mostly a discussion on the meaning of history. Does this exist? And if so, what is it for us Maoris? And, mercifully, Bill will cook tonight. He is a gourmet cook, a historian of anything that enters the mouth for pure gustatory reasons, not so much for dietary purposes. And then tomorrow I'll drive back to Wellington.

OK, sister, I have been thinking of you and your recent religious propensity. Well, I know that Americans are, or can be, religious, even fanatical, but you are not in the South. I do not know what to say but, first of all, you mentioned, briefly and some time ago, God. I am sorry, but I don't see why one should include It (sorry, is It for you a male?) in any religion. Or, ever, regardless of It, is God (whatever you conceive it to be) necessary? I mean, what is Its function or purpose? When was It invented and by whom? Of course, I know from my Oriental philosophy course that in certain cultures Its presence may explain the formation and the existence of the Universe. I am no scientist, but I am simply unable to explain Its rôle in the Universe (supposing there is a Universe). Did God create itself to create a Universe or was the Universe already in existence before God? If this last supposition is right (and who can say that?), then why God? If it is not, God must have a hell of a time (sorry!) to create a Universe out of what? Nothing? And for what purpose? I repeat myself, I know. Was It so masochistic to engage itself in that mastodontic enterprise leading to the creation of humans along with many other biological dysfunctions? Obviously, there must be a connection between the Universe and God, but I don't know in what direction. Is there a causal explanation of why God should exist in the Universe? To me it does not make any sense. As Wittgenstein wrote, if I remember correctly, this stinking world is simply a big question (and I might add not a Big Bang), and I doubt that an answer to this question must be causal, particularly with regard to the question of Life and its meaning. Can you tell me why, my dear sister, you are in the Universe? Of course, as this exists, whether in reality or in the imagination of thinkers, do you ever wonder how it is? I am seriously asking you because you are studying philosophy. Now that you have embraced Catholicism, I am more puzzled than before at how you may be able to explain my questions. Do you have a working hypothesis? If so, does it jibe with so-called scientists'? What I mean is, how can philosophers (and among them I include religious people shoving all their beliefs under the rug of God) and physicists co-exist and explain one single phenomenon on logical grounds? Some time ago I read somewhere about the infallibility of popes defying all the laws of nature (and of God, I presume). I refer, for example, to Marian dogmatism. Of course, I consider dogmatism the easy way out of anything. I simply cannot conceive of you as an individual accepting dogmatism *vis-à-vis* physical laws. Do you believe in the so-called Immaculate Conception? OK, parthenogenesis is possible. But have you come across Pius XXI's declaration that Mary was assumed into Heaven bodily, even supposing there is a Heaven for chauvinistic believers? Surely, many other religions have their own heavens – are they integrated systems? Also, does it mean that this Mary, once reaching Heaven, is what, a substitute for God, or an associate who finally took feminists' rights from Earth to Heaven? I wonder what Carl Jung (or Germaine Greer, as a matter of fact) would think about having full equality between male and female monarchs sharing the administrative duties of souls. Will it be a cooperative affair? If so, then why so much aversion to allowing females to share power first on Earth and then in Heaven? Is Vatican imperialism only patrilineal forever?

So, dear Mahina, I do not know what to say. I do not question the emergence of *Homo religiosus* (sorry, the language of male chauvinism is not only anthropological). This does not bother me. Humans have the right to become fools, or mystics, or whatever, but for God's sake (please forgive me, I do not intend to use a semantic pun), you, my sister, a Catholic? Have you ever studied the HISTORY of Vatican imperialism, in reality an absolute monarchy for 2,000 years? I pity those poor Italians who for so long have been subject to colonial rules emanating from the Vatican in Rome. I often spoke with Dad about his impressions of Italians. Of course, during the war there was hardly any time to look around and make a sociological analysis, but then, when he went back 20 years later, he simply could not believe how Italians could function at the mercy of black-collared autocrats, worse than the powers of evil in the Pentagon and the Kremlin. It is theoretically possible that the political actions exuding from these last two forces can change one day for better or for worse, but I can't think of the Vatican except as a monster crawling out of a few hectares of land to choke a nation (is it an autonomous nation?). When you visited Italy during your Salzburg year, how did you find its inhabitants? Are they so brainwashed in spite of being a people of artists? That is the problem, that art reflects reality, and that is why the richest concentration of art is housed in the Vatican. What a joke!

I almost thought of sending you a book. It is simply shocking to read about the inheritance Italians have acquired through the biological and psychological influence of a priests-to-popes range of prelates. I refer, to name just one, to *The Love Affairs of the Vatican* by Dr Angelo S. Rappoport. I doubt that your library has it in the history section. Perhaps I contradict myself by adducing history in matters of faith, but that book should be required reading for anyone wishing to join Catholicism. The accounts of that monarchy operating in the wings of human souls are enough to make one wish that the Vatican as an institution be obliterated from the face of the Earth. Nowhere on Earth, indeed, is there anything comparable. Horror stories of murder, incest, torture, fraud, warring, persecutions, you name it, all the most vicious acts ever concocted by *Homo ferox*. They are all found in the unique existence of the most inhuman powerhouse against the dignity of fellow Terrestrians. Just think about what the British monarchy did to us in a couple of centuries. That is child's play. Multiply that period by ten for time and a billion for perversion. People like Nero, de Sade, Hitler, and the like would have found no place in the Vatican, unless accepted as 'saints' in comparison with what Vatican despots have done, particularly when Italy was trying to break the chains of medievalism in order to confer upon Man a token patina of intellectual and political freedom. In essence, Vatican prelates had inherited all the negative aspects of Roman imperialism, with all its disastrous consequences, wiping out entire cultures all over the world; fragmented and infected with the *morbus vaticanus*, from all Latin (*sic!*) American nations to the most recent displacement of Pacific indigenous life. The more I think about it, the more I feel that all wars have actually been conflicts tied to religious tenets, and among these the most insidious, most revolting, most horrible have emerged from the Vatican, replacing a whole system of native accomplishments with a process of conquest for the sake of saving pagan souls. Probably I shall be dead by the year 2000, but you may be around to see that that Polish actor will concoct some new dogma modifying the political system of Heaven to accommodate feminists and Third-World saints. I would not be surprised if a new bodily transfer will be made with the help of NASA to take Mother Teresa into Heaven. Such is the fate of believers, and here I mean Catholics who implicitly accept all the garbage thrown *urbi et orbi*. There is no other imperial centre in the entire world for similar religious institutions. Not that religion *per se* is evil. No, an implicit 'religionism' is probably part of becoming and being human. As a matter of fact, and here please don't faint, if I were to espouse a religion (call it so), I would embrace the Islamic one, for it is more a mode of life like Confucianism, plus, of course, an adaptation of modern necessities in order to contain the disintegration of moral values as you can witness yourself in the USA. As a matter of fact, I envision that Buddhists, Confucians, Jews, Christians, Muslims (and God knows who else!) will one day be united for the sake of survival in a rotten world. This can only spin in orbit when one day social upheavals and dwindling resources can prolong life on Earth with total cooperation among them. I think that this idea, which is not mine, was already outlined many centuries ago by, you would not believe it, an Italian, the irony! I refer to Giovanni Pico della Mirandola (late 15th century), a humanist and philosopher. I don't know how he survived the black hand of the Inquisition. Probably because he was protected by the Medicis. Of course, the Pope prohibited the publication of his best theories. Pico had been influenced by Savonarola. And I assume you learned in your Catholic university what happened to him – strangled and burnt at the stake by order of the pope.

Oh, I hear Bill coming downstairs for breakfast. I shall continue this in Wellington.

After spending the whole of January in Wellington, Komaru had forgotten the letter he had handwritten in Wanganui to Mahina. It was after the celebration of the Wellington Anniversary and after receiving cards from Mahina along with the long letter from Walla Walla that he decided to tackle 'Project Sister'. Some of his procrastination was due to the distraction brought by the latest imperial manipulation in the 'Gulf War' by the Americans. Komaru did not know the facts, but he did not blame Saddam Hussein for attacking Kuwait. Actually, Komaru felt that the Iraqi president had been tricked into launching an expedition on a medieval institution after receiving carte blanche from the American ambassador. She had stated that the USA would not interfere with neighbourhood squabbles. The poor lady did not think about what she had created by ignorance of *lavabo manus meas* policy. The about-face by Bush resulted in wasting billions of dollars and thousands of innocent lives in order to keep the British monopoly of BP and American oil a few cents below fair market value. It was undoubtedly a pyrrhic victory and further incentive for those espousing extremist views of Moslem fundamentalism all over Asia and Africa. Yes, Komaru thought, it was a storm in a glass of water, as well as an opportunity for imperial powers to test new weapons, just as the Nazis had done in Guernica before the Second World War. Komaru wondered whether Desert Storm had laid the groundwork for the so-called Third World War in the long run.

In re-reading the Walla Walla letter, Komaru could not help but feel somewhat deceived. And so strange. Across the Pacific, two siblings were trying to establish psychological contact with each other while engaging in diametrically opposite enterprises. Komaru, although studying himself within the McTavishes generous home, in retrospect felt as if he had descended into an abyss of confusing behaviour. He did not blame his hosts, for he enjoyed the experience, but this, when seen within his Polynesian mores, appeared as an out of control 'Desert Storm' in the haziness of his mind. Komaru knew he had crossed a line in the sand of his Maori values and traditions by getting enmeshed in a pleasurable, selfish, powerful network of carnal knowledge. In essence, although he had never indulged in drugs, he felt as if he had succumbed to some of them triggering in him an addiction for the simple purpose of having them. He felt hooked, and he enjoyed every minute of the addiction. The original excuse for frequenting Melissa's intimate salon of Venus had passed to a second level. The very thought that he could possess the total and full psyche of Melissa gave him a sense of power. He felt inebriated by a heavy dose of aphrodisiac magnetism. Melissa's perfume was only a corollary. It was her body that dominated his everything. At the same time, knowing that he had become a slave of a Pakeha female had created in him a feeling of rebellion against something, though not against women. He even thought of dominating them from now on, though at times he had doubts. He, thus, reacted unconsciously by attacking what he could, and the topic of religion, Catholicism in particular, prompted by Mahina's correspondence, became a target for an emotional outlet.

He re-read Mahina's letter several times, going over it back and forth in order to make sense of her new relationship with him. He just could not understand that his sister was 'praying' for him. The American English spelling and the phonetic similarity alternating an a/e in that verb confused him. Was the act of praying a substitute for preying on the gullibility of weak minds? And what was Mahina praying for? To save him from going astray?

Meanwhile, Komaru had received a short letter from Mahina in answer to the one he had sent her on his way to Wanganui. She had become offended by the PS he had affixed as a semi-jocular envoi. She reacted calmly but forcefully enough to assert her independence and freedom of thought.

'Yes,' she had written, 'I felt I had lost in you a large portion of my genuine siblingness. Why did you have to make fun of me hoping that I would become the first Maori woman to be sanctified by the Vatican? You haven't yet realised how serious my beliefs are. And I hope that from now on you'll behave at least as an adult, regardless of the blood ties that are binding us emotionally and genetically. If I did not care for you as a sister toward a younger papa, I would have stopped even writing you. But I have for you, as ever, my most genuine feeling of aroha, the ancestral power of affection regardless of distances, languages, and traditions. Until now there was only one place, beside that of Papa, hosting you for moral support. Why do you have to spoil that sanctuary of trust?

PS. For your edification, I have to remind you of the rôle of Suzanne (Mary) Aubert who founded her religious order smack in Wanganui. Is it possible that, when you visit that city to engage in your historical activities, you have forgotten the Daughters of Our Lady of Compassion? Yes, of course, she was born in France, but she spent all her adult energies to make of Ao Tea Roa, and Wanganui in particular, a better world. Is it possible that, in WANGANUI, you haven't heard of her as a possible saint? What are you doing in that Maori enclave, anyway, besides toying with a few ideas of abstract history? Is Mother Mary Aubert not part of real history?

PPS. May I also suggest that, rather than criticising unjustly the contributions of European nuns and monks, you express a token of gratitude to them for their trying to bring to the attention of the civilised world British despotism? As an instance, why don't you visit the Archives of the Auckland Catholic Diocese and read the second volume of *Storia della Nuova Zelanda* by the Benedictine Felice Vaggioli? He spent seven years of 'hard labours' stemming from the Earl of Glascow's determination to wipe us off when our population had reached the bottom, barely 40,000 left on both islands. Do you know that s.o.b. sent an emissary to Italy, bought all existing copies and burned them (except for one still hidden in Auckland)? If you have the guts, why don't you build a monument to Brother Vaggioli in Auckland, rather than having your Department of History raise funds to erect a statue to the general who destroyed Montecassino, where Brother Vaggioli left his youth for the backwoods Ao Tea Roa?

That PS and PPS did it to Komaru. In fact, it took him back to

Wanganui's beach where he spent the late morning with the McTavishes. Melissa had bought a new bathing suit, if one could call it that. The G-string-like apparel in red had created quite a sensation mostly among white bathers. For the Maori youth loitering in search of excitement, Melissa had become a source of wonderment. For the few Americans, who had pitched their tents at Castlecliff Camp, where Bill had parked his car, the Pakeha Aphrodite was a common phenomenon as on California beaches. But the new, oversized breasts sported under a rather ill-fitting top was not so usual even among Californians. A small crowd had surged around the trio simply for the sake of curiosity. And Melissa, knowing that she was at the centre of attention, glowed in self-importance. Those new breasts 'Made in Brazil' could compete even with Maori ones. The problem was that Maori females regard anything above the waistline of their pareo as a normal anatomical necessity for feeding babies. Besides, they would not be so stupid as to lounge in murderous sunshine triggering melanomas. But Melissa, the queen of bees, had become the queen of the beach.

'Honey, should you not apply any cream for your skin?'
'Oh, yes, darling. Kom, would you help me with my shoulders?'
'Of course.'

She lay down on the towel and Komaru applied an Australian product all over her shoulders. In so doing, he noticed the black label of her bra top was sticking out. So he tucked it underneath the garment.

Then she got up and informed Bill she was going for a walk along the beach. Bill and Komaru remained under the Lavazza coffee umbrella with the intention of resting, and even sleeping in the open. The Tasman breeze was soothing. They needed to recover from the nocturnal celebration. But they began talking about Melissa.

'Oh, how happy she is!' Bill said. 'She needs constant attention by men. Her *id* level is so low that, even after the night we gave her, she is still unsatisfied. Look, do you see how she turns her head back to be sure she is followed?'

'By whom?'

'By the boys. I would not be surprised. That is her first outing as a refurbished mantis.'

'Mantis?', asked Komaru.

'Oh, sorry, the preying mantis. You know. I hope she will be discreet. This is a small place, and I simply can't risk putting my practice in jeopardy.'

'Do you mean she is going to ... to engage in ...'

'I hope so. That is why she underwent all that painful plastic surgery. To extend her age of functionalism. I trust she carried her purse, oh, her Japanese Trojan amulet.'

'Yes, she had tied it to her left wrist. The leather pouch beneath it looked full. I noticed it.'

'That is my only concern. The rest is all hers. What can I do or, better, what can WE do?'

'Do you mean that after all we did since yesterday she is still, well, hungry?'

'Sadly so, I should say. Komaru, even for me, and I have studied her medical condition thoroughly, she can keep her mental sanity only by a constant and daily dose of sex. I tried everything, even considered the possibility of performing a clitoridectomy. She would have agreed, but that would not change her. Everything is in her brilliant mind. Besides, I would be the loser, not she.'

'Sorry, I don't understand.'

'Well, Komaru, haven't you noticed the oversized clitoris protruding between even the majora before she becomes wet? It is one of the reasons I like her.'

'No, I haven't had the opportunity. Well, if so, is it a peculiarity of the white race?'

'Oh, no. It is Melissa's. Probably she is a vestige of a paleohermaphroditic specimen. Next time, ask her for an inspection, or just play around as part of your foreplay. She would not mind it.'

'The problem, Bill, is that she does not allow me to engage in foreplay. She can hardly wait to welcome me in a matter of seconds. But, now that I can remember, I helped her once or twice to dry off, but saw nothing.'

'Surely, once she is wet, her clitoris nearly hides between folds. Try before. Incidentally, do you know why the French like snails?'

'I guess I do, but, coming back to your attempt to, say, make her normal, why did you say that you would lose? You mean she would put her ardor apart?'

'No, of course, as I said, she will always be a super nympho. But then I would not benefit from her making love to me.'

At that point, Komaru felt intrigued. He looked at Bill pointedly, asking silently for an explanation. And Bill obliged.

'You see, Melissa's clitoris is long enough so that, as an erectile tissue, it can act like a mini toy in flesh and blood. And she can enter my diaphragm enough to give me pleasure. Not long enough to touch my prostate, but psychologically that special foreplay has established in us a unique dyad of rare sex. The trick is not to make it moist. Once it becomes so, it retracts like the *tio* neck you catch at low tide. The only thing I made her promise me was never to use it on anybody else. The source of infection in that mini toy can be deadly. As I say, I use Melissa's extended tool for my own gratification, for I would not allow any man to play with me. My career, in that case, would come to an end. That is why all gay psychiatrists are forced to live in a closet. Only Dr Kinsey had the courage to do anything he wanted. But he was famous and he even indulged in hiring a prostitute with the excuse of acting as a voyeur for research purposes. She had a full 2-inch long clitoris. By the way, do you see her anywhere? Did she not go north toward that group of fishing boats?'

'I think so, but I am not sure. I see, however, that the entourage seems to have vanished as well.'

'I would not be surprised. I am accustomed to her ... , shall we call them, peccadilloes. But it was not so when we first started to go together in Australia. I simply could not understand, even as a medical doctor and a psychiatrist, how she could do that to me when she constantly told me how much she loved me. And I knew that she could be an excellent wife. It just is what it is. I finally understood her predicament, and mine, after we clarified the matter on a beach like this. We had sat at an open-air bar. We had made love all night, and that was years ago when I could compete better, age-wise. And Melissa started, between drinks, to use her subtle techniques, movements, cloth shifting, etc., to attract the flies. Then she asked me whether I would mind if she went with an Italian tourist to his motel room a few metres away. That Ay-Tee apparently wanted to show her some new underwater apparatus to photograph fish. Of course, I did not mind. So, I continued reading a book I had about, you would not believe it, Australian wines. By the time I had read a few pages, I noticed that the Italian crowd had diminished. Was Melissa going to overstay her fishing expedition? It was almost time for supper. Thus I went to the motel, and there, the sub equipment room was full of Sicilian studs in different poses of engagement. I was speechless. You know, we British have the blessing of remaining aplomb even on the verge of being innocently decapitated. The amazing thing is that I myself became sexually excited seeing her between two youths vying for position. So I stayed in line waiting for my turn, *nature*, for Melissa's Japanese amulet lay empty on the nightstand. I counted seven boys in their 20s. I was already 46 or so. And when it was my turn Melissa received me with the most affectionate word of encouragement, but, while I swam in a flood of *mascarpone*, and as I detected the *hircus caprinus* of sweat, I became nearly impotent to perform. However, Italian inventiveness came into play. That was the so-called Florentine 'fine hand' that helped me to kindle the fire of desire for Melissa, waiting patiently for relief. Well, while I was in her, a beautiful young Sicilian Samaritan entered me so pleasurably that all three of us climaxed at the same time under the applause of the whole crowd. I was a virgin no longer. And pleasure exceeded pain. After that discovery our fate was sealed. We established our own rules of social behaviour and, in essence, we joined the club.'

'The club?'

'In general, the club of modern youth. Oh, we are also members of two clubs, but I will tell you more about that later. I see she is coming back.'

And that she did, sweating in the noon of the Tasmanian sun. Her body was covered with sand and dry weeds. Her arms and legs were black and blue. Her hairstyle had disintegrated into hanging strings and her bra label was hanging out, but she was happy. The Brazilian miracle had worked out beyond expectation.

Chapter 15

The Waitangi Day of 1992 came and went on a Thursday. That day Komaru stayed home. He had been distraught by attempts made by Wellington to emasculate the old tradition of 'celebrating' the Treaty in the historical 'Far North' in order to keep Maori purists away from possible activist demonstrations. An 'official' function on Wellington government grounds would easily be controlled by the local police force. In addition, it was felt that a larger participation of diplomatic corps members would work as a safety device to ensure a peaceful function. The absence of the old Waitangi flag pole in Wellington would also help to nullify attacks on the New Zealand flag.

On the evening of the fifth Komaru had disconnected his telephone, and on the sixth he deferred checking his mail in the lobby of the building. By turning off the radio and the TV, and by lowering the window shades, he gave the impression of not being at home. He made no noise of any kind except to flush the toilet once in the morning. He did not even shower or cook. And he remained in the nude all day long.

He next fasted, drinking only fruit juices, while forcing himself to analyse and synthesise the meaning of a date that had occurred 153 times to remind Maori political opiates of the rape suffered by the last pristine and wholesome Pacific culture, which was eventually destroyed by British imperialism. He felt that colonialism was still alive and well through a subtle new technique of interaction disguised as good race relations trumpeted as the best in the entire world. But on the occurrence of the sesquicentennial two years before, something had snapped in his soul. He finally understood the new Pakeha game. Whites had suddenly become very accommodating, cooperative, unctuous, and even submissive for the sake of surviving and enjoying the good life they had built up at the expense of the entire Maori civilization. They had no intention of going through the 'Portuguese' Calvary syndrome as in Angola and Mozambique.

As long as they could, Pakehas would not rock the boat. After all, the whole 'justice' system was in their hands. They could control the submissive Maori mind, conditioned by two centuries of monastic-type obedience, as long as possible. Between returning 'Home', that home now polluted by Commonwealth 'colours' and 'staying on' *à la India*, pathetically kept alive by Paul Scott, the latter solution would be better, especially for those possessing real estate which was drastically undervalued on the books of appraisers. After all, who would own 'top' homes, say, in Auckland, the largest 'Polynesian' city in the world? For sure not the Maoris on Kohimarama Road or Victoria Avenue. Even adjacent islands, traditionally regarded as far away and second-hand citizen enclaves such as Papakura, were beginning to be disposed of by the almighty trans-Pacific dollar. A case in point was Waiheke Island. When he went through that island to visit his father at the sanatorium, Komaru simply could not believe how the property values on that 'Maori' island had changed. New 'commuter' bedrooms had replaced the ancient *kauri* forests. The Pakeha pioneers had done their homework generations in advance.

Yes, things had changed a lot, but it was still a long shot to assume that the average Maori would one day be regarded au pair 'portfolio-wise' with a Pakeha, if ever. When Komaru was enrolled in the history' 'honours' courses at Victoria University, he began to analyse the topsy-turvy and farcical charade with which Pakehas had succeeded in brainwashing the Maori 'intellectual' élite as a pawn in the hands of the white majority. Historically, this was nothing new, for he remembered how the Romans had done something similar by granting the '*Romanus sum*' palliative to Africans, Dalmatians, Iberians and the like. History was replete with cases of secondary citizenship 'enjoyed' by colonials in their own land. The Roman-of-Rome concept is still alive in the dialect of modern day mythical Italy as 'romano de Roma'.

Surely, not all Maoris had been indoctrinated so easily. Only those aspiring to acquire the material goods possessed and enjoyed by whites dreamed of equipollent political rights. The fools! But many activists remained in the wings of the smoke-in-the-eye stage, despising the tangible wealth they could reach after fighting, begging and convincing a tribunal that their forefathers were the rightful owners. Not Komaru, no, he would not submit to that kind of forced meretricious approach in order to assert his inalienable rights. The clue to his penetrating analysis of a 'new integrated' society – he laughed at honors conferred upon those demonstrating deeds of such *mise-en-scène* – trying to phase out the limbo of political armistice surfaced almost as a joke in his consciousness with regard to the Waitangi Tribunal. He simply could not understand or accept the sequence of those two words, a perfect case of semantic *contradictio in adiecto* in any syntactic flow. For Komaru everything had been encapsulated into a lexical dyad in which 'Waitangi' had been adjectivised, and thus emasculated, to confer a parvence of Maoriness onto the 'Tribunal' since its inception in October 1975, through the Treaty of Waitangi Act. Ironically, to the best of his recollection, no one had associated the etymological force of *wai* plus *tangi* in connection with the whole political affair, for *wai*, 'water', and *tangi*, 'funeral', although true, would have sounded too depressing – the death celebration of the whole body of water surrounding Ao Tea Roa.

Worse than assuming *wai* as 'water' would be to confer on *wai* the meaning of 'memory' or 'recollection', rather than a geographic connotation. The death of memory, of Maori history! But his father kept on reminding him, when he was too young to grasp the essence of the full value, that slowly 'waitangi' would fade into oblivion through materialistic pursuits and through the naïve adherence of 'aristocratic' Maoris to Pakehanism via a royal decree of sorts prepared by a London *travet* thousands of miles away. Even as a motherless teenager desiring to become something in the world family for lack of an *iwi* one, Komaru worked hard to understand that world of injustice.

Thus, he mentally went over some of the key literature that had influenced him; seeds dropped in his psychic field while he was growing up in a world of confusion. In particular, he remembered Ballara's *Proud to be White? A Survey of Pakeha Prejudice in New Zealand*, and he asked himself whether a similar survey could be, or had been, made in Ao Tea Roa as well, for, any time people read 'New Zealand' anywhere, automatically this meant WCC, i.e. White, Christian, Colonial, while Ao Tea Roa was always associated with Maoris. The introduction to Ballara's survey was a revelation, if not a masterpiece of wishful thinking, for its author, Hiwi Tauroa, had stated that 'The message of this book is that the Treaty was not a fraud'. How exciting! And who had ever said that it was? Without putting in doubt the sincerity of Ballara's ecumenical efforts, a noble view of *faute de mieux* in the mid 1980s, Komaru asked himself, why then a Tribunal? Does it not imply a bringing to justice and obtaining reparations upon finding someone guilty of wrongdoing? Yes, of course, he thought. The problem was that he saw in the Tribunal a reverse structure for the functioning of its operation. Who was judging whom and what? At best, only Maoris could preside and dispense, with plenty of tolerance and compassion, justice to the Pakehas who had had the bad fortune to be dumped as either convicts or civil servants, or later as adventurers, missionaries and so forth, by accident or design, onto Ao Tea Roa. There was no New Zealand. That was created later by displacing Ao Tea Roa. Indeed, Komaru dissected everything from a perspective that projected things onto mirrors of genocide and moral holocaust.

Nevertheless, Komaru, rather than giving political asylum retroactively, assigning land to that scum of white humanity carrying a chip on its collective shoulder of superiority, and finally welcoming them as born-again Kiwis, accepted the reality *de facto* by convincing himself that Maoris now only have recourse by fighting to regain what was theirs to start with. The token Maori components of the predominant legal apparatus was visible, and risible, in his thinking paradigm. Who was judging whom?

Rather than a Waitangi Tribunal, for Komaru a more realistic label would be Waitangi Clemency Act toward Aggressors who had created and maintained a social atmosphere of political oppression for two centuries. Well, Pakehas had to admit and declare that it was the Maori being forced to obtain certain rights for which, illogically, they had to fight uphill battles of all types involving historical data, legal records, Crown despotism and a host of procedures kept in stock by white colonialists. That is why Komaru had dedicated himself to the Waitangi Action Committee, participating in the compilation of the mimeographed *Te Hikoi Ki Waitangi 1985* under the coordination of Hinewhare Harawira. In particular, although still 'young', he worked on 'Te Hui Oranga o Te Moana Nui A Kiwa, 1986' to welcome guests from Tahiti, Belau, the Marshall Islands, Kanaky, Australia, Great Turtle Island, and Asia. He still treasured the photographs taken in 1985 of The Maori Embassy, a fragile wooden shack with the moral strength of steel, and of the Hikoi leaving Takaparawha, passing through Orakei Marae, and the Hikoi at Oruawharo Marae.

Thus, on 6 February he reviewed many of the mimeographed 'registered publications' hastily stapled under a green cover and mailed from Newton all over the world. Among the various publications, now so difficult to find even in libraries, he particularly treasured *Ko Matou Nga Kaitiaki O Aotearoa*. What he read on page 16 had taken place merely 60 years before: 'In 1932 Ratana took a petition to the King. Asking that the Treaty of Waitangi be honoured the King did not want to see Ratana because he was not interested in us Maori'. What an insult!

In reading that record, he decided to study history since he saw in it an inventory of lies, deceptions and frauds that gave him a framework from which to dismantle that apparatus, and then devise proper counter techniques of destruction. When he was in his second year at Victoria University, an article by Sandra Coney in the *Dominion-Sunday Times* (18 September 1988) gave him the final impetus to dedicate his life to fight, to resistance, to a war against past wrongs. The atmosphere of revolution, that brought Pearl Buck's Chinese condition to the forefront of dignity and respect, had soaked him after seeing the Mao miracle. If Mao had done that for nearly a billion people, could he not do something similar in a toy nation of less than 3 million? He would fight, alone if necessary, the whole system of oppression by joining it. And that is why in 1992 he would try to be hired by the Waitangi Tribunal for whatever position available. Ironically, as a Maori he would be given preferential treatment, since it was now fashionable to rekindle the sheep station spirit of 'our Maori' protectionism. Even white teenagers and sexually frustrated housewives in what sociologists regarded as a 'straight laced society' competed in flirting with a Maori 'hori' the same way that Californians welcomed American Indian status in building relationships through government guidelines of affirmative action. The information furnished aseptically and periodically in the self-glorifying publication *Te Manutukutuku, Te Roopu Whakamana I Te Tiriti O Waitangi*, kept him informed, as an outsider, of possibilities. Now Melissa would help, and he laughed at being able literally to screw his way up to that post in Wellington. They surely had money in those deluxe offices. The only thing he did not like was to be thought of by Melissa as an opportunist, for he liked her. He did not want to hurt her, ever. He only hoped to join the Tribunal staff on the occasion of its 21st birthday, namely, 11 October 1995, with the hope of understanding and grasping the legitimacy, if any, of its existence and function. What a front! He thought of the four pathetic Maori members of the Parliament kept for decoration in a white hall of supremacy astride the 20th century. In particular, he wanted to challenge the so-called 'Spirit of the Treaty' as discussed in typical legalese of self indulgence by W. H. Oliver in *Claims to the Waitangi Tribunal*, beginning with 'The Tribunal's task is to test [!] the action of the Crown, as set cut in a claim and as sustained by its own inquiries, against the principles of the Treaty'. Crown hell, he thought, using an Americanism freely ejaculated on TV screens. Where am I, he screamed aloud when he read it soon after meeting Melissa in

1991 at a Pacific Forum meeting. What legalese mumbo-jumbo invoking the Orakei of 1987 and even borrowing the Boldt decision (*United States v. Washington, 1984*) 'recognising the sea-fishing rights of a group of North American Indians who were also protected by a Treaty'! The parallel between one single treaty, the only one in his *whenua*, by a Crown, and a US Government that had disregarded and dissolved each and every 'treaty' it ever made, was like comparing a mouse to an elephant. The dissimilarity in everything comparable had been whitewashed in order to confer a *prima facie* on the outcome of Maori rights through an uphill battle against an anachronistic Crown on the deathbed of colonialism.

That night, Komaru slept little. Only in the early morning was he able to drift in and out of a much needed sleep. But at 06:00 the alarm clock blasted him out of his morning dreams. He had forgotten to switch it off. Thus he got up, hooked up the phone and went back to bed. Well, the phone started ringing immediately. And who on Earth was it? Melissa's voice, though soft, pierced his mind.

'Kom, what happened? Why was the phone disconnected? I was so worried that you had been involved in yesterday's skirmishes with the constables.'

'Thank you, Melissa, sorry, I just needed to be away from everyone. Simply ...'

'Even from me? Are you all right? You sound so distraught!'

'No, actually, merely sleepy.'

'You know, I thought that yesterday you would surprise me with a visit for a change. Even Bill was concerned. After all, do you know that we haven't seen you in a month?'

'Sorry, too many things and I haven't yet finished the last segment of the thesis. What we discussed on the first of the year has perturbed me. I just seem to run along two different tracks. But I shall rework the whole thing in terms of your suggestion. Rather than defining history on the basis of universal and abstracts tenets, I shall try to extract what history has been as a consequence of its purpose in Ao Tea Roa. In fact, yesterday I finished the outline comprising New Zealand in the 1980s. I plan to consider Ao Tea Roa in the 1990s, if I live long enough for this last decennium of the 20th century, as a crucible for our freedom.'

'Good! It seems that you have caught what I hoped you would uncover by yourself. That night you began to grasp what my professor at Cambridge used to dispense by questioning facts, both real and imaginary. And you seem to be able to delineate a thesis along what did NOT take place on one side, thought it did on the other. Kom, enough of that. I miss you. When are you coming up?'

'I hope soon. Please convey my regards to Bill. Tell him that it is a pity Casanova's theories have never entered the curriculum of a history department.'

And that took him back to that first day of the year in Wanganui. It had been a memorable afternoon and evening and night. What an indigestion of food, discussions, music, eroticism, theorising, and exploration of the body, the mind, the soul, in every direction.

After a quick lunch and a short rest, Melissa had come down all showered and fresh looking into the guest room, where Komaru was trying to organise his papers in anticipation of a review. She was wearing a flowing organdy dress like a Greek *peplos*. Her long legs were bare against the back light of afternoon sunshine pouring in from the northern window. Sleeveless, oversized, loose at the waist, the *peplos* smelled of wildflowers. She had let her hair down, though somewhat curved concentrically toward her chin. Her nails had been freshly painted with a different color, a dark red, approaching the coagulated tint of a chocolate pudding. And, of course, she was holding a glass of Cardhu. This time Komaru was glad that its burned oak smell was overcome by Melissa's body lotion overpowering the perfume emanating from the gown. She came in like a lioness scouting for food. And she was hungry.

'Sorry, I trust I am not disturbing. Have you rested well?'

He nearly laughed. Who was asking him? He had done nothing at the beach, except talk with Bill about European literature of the Baroque period. And Casanova. In trying to get up from his European bed, he was prevented by Melissa, who pushed him down. And her drink spilled on his pareo.

'Oh, I am sorry, Kom. Let me wipe you off.'

And she removed it by snapping it away, leaving him on his back unprotected.

'My goodness, you were sleeping. The little baby!'

So saying she started to dry him off with his own pareo soaked with scotch. At first the feeling was refreshing and mildly comforting but, after a few seconds, the damn thing started to burn. What proof was it? Ninety? Forty-five percent alcohol? Komaru had never learned the schizophrenic system of designating the alcoholic content of anything, but he knew it was strong enough to act on him.

'Oh, sorry, no, stay put, don't get up! I did not realise that scotch would burn your skin. I'll take care of you.'

And she simply climbed astride him as if mounting a horse. For the first time Komaru noticed that her legs were slightly bowed, or perhaps it was her way of approaching an equine. And she did not even remove the flowing dress. She just tossed the front of it over her head like a reverse hood. The caryatid was now fully alive.

'Gingerly, please, I just took a bath, and I am dry' she uttered through her veiled mouth. That was for Komaru a novel approach since, although her body was naked, her head had disappeared into a ball of organdy. It was for Komaru like trying to contact an alien from a UFO. But she did not have to see anything, for she knew Komaru's body as well as her Cambridge horse. One thing that bothered him was her breasts. They hung down on his upper torso bouncing against his throat, nearly suffocating him. And he thought of Ling-ling with her rosy buds jutting onto his lower torso. And, no, not of Mahina, of course not. He apologised to himself. That was Melissa's fault for having increased those bouncing appendages. For what? They were in the way, especially in the coming spasm of a joint expedition. They simply created an unwanted space. But the other thing that assailed his brain was how hungry she was, or seemed to be. How was that possible after what he was told by Bill on his way home?

Bill actually laughed all the way. He knew of Casanova referring to a *comte de six fois*. Well, Melissa had actually been a *comtesse de sept*, not *de six fois*, for he had counted seven beach boys throwing kisses at her when the trio left the Lavazza shades.

'Well, don't you feel refreshed?'

Yes, of course, he felt so everywhere except where he needed it most. And he hoped that the absence of the Trojan soldier had been replaced by the septic properties of Cardhu. Those Scots must have learned something from the ancient Romans who, however, used garlic, moldy bread and Tropean onions to protect themselves from Gaelic guerrillas.

'Go ahead, change your pareo. I'll be in the rumpus room.'

In retrospect, Komaru went over the discussion with Melissa while Bill started planning supper to celebrate the first day of the year. Now he had on his desk the outline for the 1980s. He could soon see Melissa and show it to her as part of lived history. He also had in mind outlining the 1990s as a possibility. He reviewed the former decade, the first lived by him as an adult concerned with his own land. This was not a physical entity. It was his own mind tied to the fate of a people who, like the Phoenix, had risen from the ashes of opprobrium *in extremis*. There was nothing he could do for the 1980s. They had occurred. But could he do anything to write his own history' in the 1990s? Thus, he polished the outline with the intention of seeing Melissa upon his return from the meeting of the 28th Maori Battalion in Rotorua.

1989 –   Birth of Modern Europe
         Birth of Modern New Zealand
         Death of Communism

Upon re-reading the sketch for the last triad of his historical essay, immodestly thought of as unique in the annals of human events, Komaru was struck by the coincidental framework delimiting the whole 70 years, that is, the fact that this period, corresponding roughly to the life span of a Western individual, is comprised between the Birth of the Comintern and the Death of Communism. So much effort toward nothing. So much blood spilled by humans for the vain purpose of creating a better humanity! Was it worth the fight? Komaru was rather pragmatic. Too bad, he thought, that millions of people had died in vain. Within the life of John Q. and Jane Q. Smith, assuming that they were born on 1 January 1919, quintillions of dollars and rubles had been spent to return to Square One. 'Frankly, my dear, I don't give a damn.' Komaru saw himself as a Clark Gable in the latter-day film of Earth gone with the Wind. Scarlett was humanity with all its caprices and vanities. What remained under the ashes of the 20th century was a barely visible patch of green shoots among which a few positive accomplishments were discernible.

One germinating blade of hope was the birth of a new Europe. The irony of it all was that no one had anticipated what took place, and more importantly no one understood how it happened, during the summer of 1989. The Virginia Farm had no inkling whatsoever about the fertilisation of ideas quietly covering the soil of revolution.

Amazingly, as 1939 had initiated a process of European disintegration leading to the chaos created by Nazi policies and the birth of twin Germany, it was this very disintegration that initiated, *sans le savoir*, the catalytic process of reshuffling the cards of political games. Komaru was at a loss to understand what happened in East and West Germany during the Summer of 1989. He felt that probably no one will ever find out what really happened, except that it was something dictated by 'People's Power'. It was undoubtedly a European football game played by Poland and Hungary in a field with Gorbachev as the referee. The Berlin Wall was the 50 yard line. And the supreme irony was that the Americans played no active part in it.

Nevertheless, a few dates mark some of the mysterious and invisible hands that threw the ball across the 50 yard line. By 10 October after an uneasy summer that started with the futile movements at Tiananmen Square, Honecker had already lost control of the game at a meeting of the Politburo. The Leipzig demonstration 6 days later forced him to resign on 18 October. On 9 November, East Germans were told that they could cross the Wall any time at any place. Although still physically intact, the Wall had crumbled overnight. And, along with it, East Germany, in spite of a new Constitution to be written soon after deploring German submission to Moscow and setting 6 May 1990, as the date for municipal elections.

But East Germany was not alone in the process of rewriting political history. Bulgaria, Romania, Hungary, Czechoslovakia and the whole Eastern bloc had actually created a psychological group that could be called Euroglasnost, particularly after the movements initiated in Poland years before. People's Power had accomplished miracles almost bloodlessly, except for the Romanian swan song of Ceauşescu. Europe was not the same, particularly after the disintegration of the Soviet Union. The 'Evil Empire' had vanished forever and, consequently, 'democracy' had begun to inch its way along with the usual initial confusion of blinding freedom and its consequential waves of crime, economic disarray, hunger, devaluation of currency, rampant prostitution and whatever else happens when a sudden transition from dictatorship to democracy takes place. Luckily, that situation was avoided in China through the courtesy of those naïve students who allowed themselves to be killed in order to maintain stability in a country that had become the most capitalistic one in the world. After all, disturbances like those in Tiananmen had also taken place in capitalistic America, as in Colorado a couple of generations earlier when peaceful Italian miners were shot to death along with women and children by the forces of order called in by capitalistic forces. And China was no different. Had the students succeeded in winning the *papier mâché* revolution, China would have undergone a process of disintegration similar to what took place in the Soviet Union and Yugoslavia. Forty years of struggle to acquire peace and dignity in China would have been lost to the warlords of opportunism waiting in the wings. In essence, the students demonstrating in Tiananmen Square under the instigation of the Taiwan government had died to save China from chaos. Those idealistic students were the real heroes.

One day, when intelligent democracy, if needed, can be established in China through real People's Power, those heroes will have a monument to their memory facing Mao's portrait.

As regards the Birth of Modern New Zealand, well, Komaru had no qualms in stating that, since Waitangi Day, Ao Tea Roa was being shaken in its very governmental core along political and economic trends. He attributed the main change to the issue of race relations resulting in an ideological discord and the dramatic resignation of David Lange as Prime Minister in August. Three factors contributed to create major revisions of internal policies, namely, the increased fragility of racial harmony, the rampant inflation and unheard of unemployment.

The new PM, Geoffrey Palmer, at 47 years of age was confronted with significant problems compounded by the re-election of Roger Douglas, of 'Rogernomics' fame, whom Lange had sacked the previous year as Minister of Finance. In part the international position of New Zealand had become strained after Lange's visit to Yale University in April. He had declared ANZUS virtually dead, but still some navy ships are purchased from Australia, a feat confirming the schizophrenic attitude of a 'baby' anti-nuclear nation regarding visits of nuclear-armed ships in New Zealand ports.

At the same time, privatisation had created initial havoc in Michener's 'paradise' run by the state, particularly for institutions like the Post Office, several petroleum companies, and even the services of New Zealand Shipping Corporation, the most vital link with the world by carrying 99% of value for import and export products. On the positive side, one could witness the election of Helen Clark as New Zealand's first female Deputy Prime Minister. It had taken longer than a century for a woman to become a prominent leader in spite of the fact that New Zealand women were the first in the world to be granted the right to vote.

Even long-range proposals were designated to implement what *de jure* were always supposed to be Maori property, as in the case of a 'progressive assignation' of fishing quotes to Maori groups designated to obtain 50% of their rights by 2008. And, finally to implement these rights, a so-called 'Wall of Death' drift-net fishing was banned within the 370-kilometre exclusive economic zone.

Yes, a Modern New Zealand was being born, but Komaru felt that it was still a long way from reaching the psychological status of political freedom. The Head of State was a foreign woman who spoke no Maori, namely, Elizabeth II, a queen living at the antipodes of Ao

Tea Roa, as represented by an Archbishop. Church and State, as in Britain, did not do much to grant relief to a chronic oppression imposed by the Trick of Waitangi. The parallelism between the Birth of Modern Europe and the Birth of Modern New Zealand was not unwarranted. Which of the two political entities would become mature adults in the first twenty years of the third millennium?

Chapter 16

'You see,' said Melissa, 'there is a problem in our universities today. This problem was identified and put forth more than a generation ago by my professor at Cambridge.'

Melissa nearly went into a reverie about Professor Carr, whose lectures she attended on different occasions, though particularly and faithfully from January to March 1961. At that time, barely 18 years old, she possessed an extremely receptive and analytical mind. Komaru calculated that Melissa was now about 49 years old.

The problem was one of curricular activities, though not confined to England. Ironically, as the world began to shrink through increased communication facilities, the learning of foreign languages dropped in direct proportion to the expansion of English as a lingua franca of commerce, politics, transportation and, of course, education.

'You are right,' rejoined Komaru. 'As you know, Professor Carr is very well known at Victoria through his work, and I am still fascinated by his *What is History?* As a matter of fact, that book is still the very first on the list of recommended texts for History 419, specifically, course 2137, "History and Theory", taught by Mr Michael Burns.'

'So cogent,' observed Melissa. 'But, how much stress was put on theory?'

'A lot. In fact, Mr Burns nearly forgot about history *per se* and concentrated on theory. I felt he knew that theory determines history, and not the reverse. And that directed me into creating a new theory, though not necessarily as a new philosophical re-evaluation of my field, but as a means of delineating a technique of analysis. That is why, under the influence of my Chinese infatuation, or call it subconscious indoctrination, I came up with the "Proof of Nine".'

'I understand you, but I wonder what your MA committee will think of what you are doing. Incidentally, who is your director, and the other readers scheduled to evaluate your work and sit on your examination board? And how often have you met with him?'

'You mean my advisor? That is a she. Dr Liesel Barnes. She has been approved by Professor Kramer, the head, as my supervisor. You see, Melissa, my present work, as you know, is so iconoclastic that I tread on thin ice. But she is the best to judge my theory because she is particularly interested in New Zealand history first, and in intellectual/cultural history second. And this second field has determined my trend of thought because, as a corollary, Dr Barnes has been teaching and working on Maori–Pakeha relations, the Treaty of Waitangi issues, and colonial exploration and travel.'

'But these peripheral areas seem to be excluded from what I have read so far in your outlines, though they loom in the distance.'

'Yes, but she, sorry, Dr Barnes has undoubtedly grasped my main effort. And she accepted me because of the fact that I can read Latin, studied Greek, speak German and have a working knowledge of Mandarin. That has dispelled what, as you know, Professor Carr said with regard to glottal parochialism.'

'Yes, he shocked his colleagues in his last lecture when he declared that candidates should not be allowed to sit for an honours degree without the proper knowledge of modern languages other than English. And you are lucky, Kom, you are a chosen student.'

Melissa, after re-adjusting her peplos, poured another shot of Cardhu and fell into a distant reflection for a few seconds.

'Incidentally, how old is Dr Barnes?'

Komaru was caught, well, not exactly off guard, but he was disturbed by the sudden question. How could he know?

'Frankly, I don't know. Probably about your age. A mature young lady. Why?'

'Oh, I was thinking. Of course, you are lucky, for you speak Maori.'

And here Komaru became confused. He did not understand the *sequitur* of Melissa's investigation that had little to do with his theory on history. Then, as if returning from a longer pause of reflection, she in part solved Komaru's puzzlement.

'My question is not about her person, but with regard to her position *vis-à-vis* the political dimension of history. I wonder whether she belongs, formation-wise, to either the middle years of this century or to the last years of the 19th century. Would you say she is liberal or conservative?'

'Hard to say, but I would guess that her academic formation is conservative, while her mind is liberal. She is a problem-solver who individualises concrete difficulties in order to seek practical solutions. She often mentions Sir Lewis Namier's lectures at the same university. I detect in her a certain mature love for "actualism", if I may say so. She undoubtedly rejects Professor Oakeshott's vision of empiricism by quoting him as saying, I can't recall exactly, that we historians sail an infinite, chartless and deep ocean. She must be a poet because her gift of imagery is superb, especially when she speaks of healthy skepticism *à la* Schopenhauer. I would even say despair when she mentions our being tossed somewhere containing neither a point of departure nor a known destination. Basically, she sees us historians as fighting to keep afloat and on an even keel.'

'I think I like her. She must have grasped the very essence of history, My father, a classicist, had a dim view of it. He used to confuse me by repeating time and again that history is but the exclusive domain of an individual, and thus subject to changing his own existence as a function of protean political codes. Thus, for him history could not possibly exist because of the infinite atoms of unanalysibility.'

'Oh, my goodness, then what am I doing?'

'I would not worry, for you have injected into your theory the global political dimension of this elusive field of inquiry. I know that you are well enough equipped to handle your work with the hope of reaching a harbour, and to stay afloat in both academia as an intellectual exercise and in life as a matter of survival. And your exposure to Chinese culture is, or may be one day, the key of the 21st century "unknown".'

'Thank you, Melissa, but my Chinese exposure is very light, though I count on a young Chinese lady to help me explore the political and cultural background of the only nation on Earth that has been alive for 5,000 or 6,000 years uninterruptedly. Amazingly, for us Westerners, the most revealing document to approach this unique human phenomenon is not the product of a historian, but that of a scholar who grew up intellectually away from a department of history. And, *Dieu merci*, he wrote in English.'

'You mean Dr Needham?'

'Of course! I bought several of his volumes on the Bund for a few pennies. The most fascinating reading because often they are not found in academese.'

'And, amazingly, historians tend to shun that work since they feel it is tied to China. At least that was the trend at Cambridge in my time. For my professors, China was simply a non-political entity, in spite of the warning launched by Edwin Pulleybank in *Chinese History and World History*. You see, at that time we Brits were swimming along the glory of the post-Second World War. China was only 5 or 6 years, not centuries, old politically. And Taiwan was protected by the American fleet. We were still insulated like Taiwan, protected by a vestige of an Empire. Thus, China was regarded as a thin stream barely running parallel to the larger one of humanity. How things have changed, even in our kitchen, from tofu to quail eggs. Even Bill says that ...'

Bill had come downstairs to the rumpus room wearing a black-and-white apron, and even a white chef's hat.

'Sorry to interrupt you academicians. I shall be in the kitchen for some time. We shall go "Home" tonight, Melissa, thanks to Mrs Ortiz. There they are beginning to wake up in another year while our troops and airmen are playing in the sand of the Persian Gulf.'

'And Mr Bush, the CIA fellow, challenging Allah for the sake of petrol. Daaarling, Kom is simply fabulous. I feel as if I am back at Cambridge.'

'Not me, I was in Kuwait enjoying Coca Cola, the only safe drink we could afford. You would have gone nuts. A contraband bottle of a Canadian spirit cost a 100 dollars.'

'Well, this is what New Zealand charges for my Cardhu. I wonder why.'

'Well, political games, would you not agree? Anyway, you could come up and set the table in an hour or so. It will be a home-cooked dinner.'

He left in a hurry carrying in his hand a book.

'Sorry, Komaru, I think we were in China, weren't we?'

'Yes, and coincidentally, when Bill spoke of Mr Bush, I remembered where we international students were taken as tourists to Beijing. Mr Bush used to be there almost every evening, a rather seedy looking place not far from Tiananmen Square. I remember the tall ceiling, the fans swirling, the ordinary tables and chairs, the kitchen seen through the order counter. But, Melissa, the food was good. And the people patronising that place were always puzzling. That was the impression I got the first time, and the second when I went with my Chinese Professor of History. He was, you would not believe it, a Christian, a Baptist, who was a survivor of the Cultural Revolution. He used to tell me about his mother, who had had her feet bound. Obviously a member of the Chinese 'aristocracy'. And he used to point out to me the members of the spy ring who frequented the restaurant. He even mentioned that one day Mr Bush's Chinese year, at present swept under the rug, would be exciting reading if he ever writes about it. Of course, that may never be possible for obvious reasons.'

'Amazing, a fantastic career by a man of action. Shot down by the Japanese and in charge of shooting down anything running against the gain of oil exports and imports affecting Texas. Democracy can always be invoked, anyway, in order to protect family values, wouldn't you say so, Kom, under the aegis of the Almighty Dollar? In Gold they trust, after all. Oh, Kom, I am getting sleepy. Forgive me. Oh, well, why don't you keep Bill company? And call me when supper is ready. And, Kom, I ... I love you.'

He thought she must have reached a level of intoxication that had affected her mental faculties. Then he remembered the old Latin phrase, what was it, *in vino veritas*? Actually, it should be in Cardhu, an ablative of the fourth declension. Bill must be proud of his forebears for having shifted from proletarian *cerevisia* to a *liquor spissus*. Ovid and Horace would have approved. After all, any contribution to humanity is, like history, the product of an alembic. All the Arab and Greek historians could not be wrong.

By the time he reached the landing by the upstairs corridor, Melissa had stretched her legs on the sofa. He had taken with him the research papers. What would he do with them? She had not read them. But she had not forgotten.

'Komaru, please, leave them here by the coffee table. Thank you. I promise I'll read them carefully, but first mail me the last part, the 1980s. Here, thanks.'

At that she grabbed him by the arm. He resisted. He just could not change horses in midstream, but he had misunderstood.

'No, no, Kom. I am sleepy. Just a kiss, a soft one as the first one I taught you. But touch me on the cheeks, see how my eyelids are younger and fresher?'

Komaru caressed her softly on both cheeks with his large hands, first rubbing his big fingers under her eyes and then lowering his palms around her mandibles after starting with the four fingers from the bottom of her ears. Dr Tavares had nearly competed with the Creator successfully, for her face was so tender and babyish. The streaks of brownish and black were still apparent here and there, as if trying to disappear in post-scar dots of self-absorbing stitch points.

'Thank you, Kom, thank you. Now, go and help Bill. And, please, can you set the table yourself? When supper is ready, call me; actually, come and fetch me ... Kom, you really know how to kiss so tenderly, like a brother to a sister. You have learned fast. Oh, leave your nose for your sister, you do have a sister ... and you told me once that you are very close to a Chinese girl, what is her name, Limplimp, Liglig, oh, yes, Lingling ...'

It was several weeks later that Komaru, in his apartment in Wellington, recalled the rest of the evening. For the first time, Melissa had shown herself intoxicated and revealed a human being depressed, gloomy, distraught.

In the kitchen, Bill barely noticed him when Komaru sat at the counter. He was so busy among a cohort of gadgets. And the fragrance of various olfactory components was permeating the whole main floor. Then he turned and saw Komaru browsing through a cookbook.

'Sorry, Komaru, I hadn't heard you. Well, how did it go?'

'You mean the meeting? Just fine. But not Melissa.'

'What, is she sick?'

'No, well, I don't think so, but she suddenly became so ... depressed, sleepy.'

'That happens when her cycle is low. I bet she has not taken her pills lately, trying to stay high. But then she collapses. Excuse me a sec. That is Elisabeth, my culinary friend.'

'But you told me you never use recipes compiled by women.'

'You are right, but Elisabeth is an exception I make because her book is the only one about the table of Britain. No one else has ever done anything like that.'

'Not even the other Elizabeth? With a zed, I think.'

'No, amazing, isn't it? The difference between a *zed* and an *ess* is enormous. Ortiz took the best of British cooking to the world at large, but David did the opposite by bringing into England the outside world. Had it not been for those two ladies, Europeans would think that we at Home are still in the caveman stage chewing barely seared meat. And we would not know the healthy diets of the Mediterranean, particularly of Italy, keeping a prejudice against garlic and onions, broccoli and olive oil, eggplant and peppers. Even Melissa now tries to apply some of the health theories into practice, but she just can't cook. The problem is her irregular adherence to what stabilises her mind.'

'You mean the alcohol?'

'No, the opposite, although the Cardhu does not help. You see, Melissa is a manic-depressive, but mostly in the morning. When busy, or when she takes her pills for bipolar disorder, she can function nearly normally, or, I should say, she may enter a phase of normality that can last weeks and even months. That is when she can cook better, she can engage in complex creative activities, grandiose plans and the like. Her energy level becomes higher than mine, and I must confess that I take Ginko-biloba and ginseng and ginger, the three brain Gs. Then insomnia comes in and, consequently, she undergoes bouts of depression. Since she met you she has been high and happy. But you cannot stay around every day, she knows that.'

'Then what does she do?'

'You should ask what I do, or she and I do. We go to the club, I talked with you about it, and sometimes I will send you some literature about it.'

'Please, not now, I am so busy with my thesis.'

'I meant in the future. Oh, the menu. Here is what we are having tonight. Please get that pencil there and help me remember the sequencing of things. All right, for a starter, sorry, I mean an appetizer, we are going to have marinated salmon. Already in the fridge to set. Typically scotch. After all, *naissance oblige*. I once met Dennis is Woodtli, the Head Chef at Lochalsh Hotel, in Kyle of Lochalshm, of course, where else, Highland. Oh, can you set the table? Informal, everything is there on the sideboard. I know you don't drink, but place for us all the glasses. The first for the Pouilly-Fuissé. You are doing well. Oh, I was saying, Melissa, a brilliant mind. Basically, she can function normally, exceptionally. Our own PM had the same condition, and Mozart, and that is why she adores him. Churchill would not have won the war if he had not been treated.'

'With what?'

'We don't know exactly with what. But probably lithium carbonate, which was still experimental.'

'Oh, the serviettes. Then the main dish in your honour is pork. At home we don't use it too much, but tonight, simply loin of pork with apple and onion purée. The recipe is from Brian Prideaux-Brune of Plumber Manor at Sturminster Newton in Dorset. Don't worry about the vermouth Noilly Prat. The alcohol disappears quickly. And I use no heavy cream, I know about your lactose dysfunction. And Melissa wants to stay thin. She says that only a slender woman can enjoy top sex. And I agree with her. The nerves of sensitivity are not buried in fat.'

'Doesn't lithium interfere with alcohol?'

'Well, perhaps, though now she is taking something else. There are different names for what in the US they call Depakote, which I get directly for my clinic. Basically, it is a brand name form of Divalproex sodium to be taken orally in tablets of various milligrams from 125 to 500. There are side effects such as drowsiness, dizziness, etc. in addition to sleep disturbances. And alcohol does not help, of course. Once Melissa got ill after eating a well-roasted barbecue beef. The charcoal turned out to be interacting negatively, and she vomited all day long. Oh, Komaru, you see, for the raspberry soufflé I line the mold with olive oil, not butter. And, oh, the avocado salad, with radicchio invented by MacSween, at Oakley Court, no red wine vinegar. So you can eat everything.'

'I am sorry you have to go to such trouble for me.'

'Well, you deserve the best. I want you to be one crowned by an intellectual dinner just for tonight. After all, one cannot plan many of them in one's lifetime. When Melissa wakes up we relax by either talking or watching a film. Lately, I have discovered Lina Wertmüller. What a director and writer! I think that perhaps you would like to watch one of her films contrasting the North and the South of Italy sociologically. It reminded me of this country, the Pakehas and the Maoris.'

'Thank you, I have noticed that our own producers tend now to tackle the racial relations via celluloid. But I feel that at times they consider us noble savages being redeemed by white civilisation. They fail to put into projection any Maori hero along a list of Men to Remember. If you make a list of the most remarkable people on Earth, say, ten of them, no Maori shows up. And even one hundred or a thousand.'

'Do you have a list of ten?'

'I could make one up, I don't know.'

'While we wait for Melissa, and no hurry, whom would you include?'

'Let me see, maybe we could make one together. Why don't you start ... first? After all, you, as a Pakeha, have a chronological advantage. I can't go farther back than Kupe.'

'All right. Let me begin with Buddha, then Jesus, and then St Francis. Then, well, Martin Luther, Freud.'

'Rather intriguing. Chronologically perhaps, but in terms of importance, what? Do you include, say, Homer and Julius Caesar?'

'No, of course. What have they done for the sake of humanity? I prefer St Augustine and St Benedict, particularly for New Zealand. And you?'

'Undoubtedly Mohammed and Karl Marx. And Mao. They constitute my favourite trio.'

'Evident enough, why not? But I was thinking on a pan-Earth plan. Personally, I think differently.'

'How?'

'If I had to select my own trio, for my own mental sanity, I would choose first the Marquis de Sade, then Casanova, and Carl Jung.'

'Wow, now I understand why you keep those books by your bedside.'

'With an exception. I used to have Freud, but then I switched to Jung after I spent some time at his Swiss retreat. Not that I agree with his theories, though not completely. But I have espoused his *modus vivendi*, though only for the sake of survival. Jung, first of all, was so narcissistic that he required immediate medical attention. Which he did by himself by breaking away from Freud, embracing Tantrism, polygamy, actually a seraglio living style.'

'My goodness, I begin to see parallels.'

'At that time Jung was far ahead of the modern liberation style of living. And he was able to fool so many people by transforming psychoanalysis into a phoney Dionysian religion, actually a cult, that allowed him to enjoy females with his wife's agreement. His charismatic personality allowed him to do basically what he wanted. And people were hooked by his inventing concepts that the Chinese had already used with different words, you know, the animus, anima and so forth.'

'Yes, I had noticed that. Jung, however, made so many ideas known to the West through his basic essays on Oriental "religions".'

'More than religions, Jung had concocted tenors of living to suit his ever-increasing childishness by hiding behind Socrates' budding nazism, though I think I am being a little uncharitable. Too early to evaluate his rejection of Freud and Christianity in favour of an Aryan "cult". Anyway, he made a lot of waves among the young, as I myself was. At that age people are susceptible, as I assume you are now. What do you say?'

'At present I am still under the influence of Marx. He was the quintessence of Man's reshaping of Man with a piece of paper and a pen at the British Library. And, just think, it is amazing that as a Westerner he spread his gospel more effectively than, say, St Paul throughout the East, a first in "geographic" intellectual influence.

What a contradictory person! At times I think he was bored with life and so he concocted his social theories to get even with humans for, you know, that snob was the antithesis of the proletariat, the heartless lover of mankind without having ever entered a factory or talked to the peasants in the fields. I think he was the most conservative aristocrat of the 19th century. It is so ironic that Chinese communists don't know that Marx had a horror of a "purely proletarian set-up".'

'How true! And, indeed, only Freud understood him, but Freud would not analyse Marx for fear of destroying a fallacy. How could Freud analyse Marx's daughter's suicide after knowing of a father who would not practice what he preached to others outside his family? That is what happens in American politics: no one ever speaks evil of a fellow Republican. Can you imagine a Ford refusing to pardon a Nixon?'

'Eh, are you getting hungry? I think I am going to get Melissa.'

'Go ahead, I am going to fill the water glasses. Still hot here.'

And supper went smoothly, pleasantly, almost romantically because of the candles Bill had asked Komaru to light. The music Komaru had selected from among the CDs blended in a quiet atmosphere of soft notes – preludes, études, nocturnes, impromptus, fantasies. Chopin was simply magical in an age of rock. And Melissa, slowly awakening from whatever had forced her to sleep before supper, was glowing in the reflection of the nearest flame trying to see Komaru through the amber liquid slowly decreasing between morsels of a Scotch–Maori dinner: echoes of European decadence permeating an atmosphere created to make life more tolerable.

It was Melissa who broke the individual silences into which all of them seemed to have indulged by thinking of a human consortium subject to the vagaries of life: a few moments of tranquillity among the pressing deadlines created by Man in order to make things better, more lasting, more equipollent for humans. How foolish to think of that! And why at an evening party? Why do humans congregate at a dining table in order to grasp from life the essence of happiness? Why is it that humans need to eat and drink in order to allow the brain and the heart to float in reminiscences of past good and hope of future bliss?

'I am sorry, daaaling, that I left you guys alone for so long. But I dreamed and dreamed. I can't recall what. And what did you people do?'

'We talked and made an inventory of those humans who remain

in history for better and for worse. Then we selected our trio who at present enrich our lives and inspire us to higher deeds.'

'How courageous!'

Bill and Komaru listed their current heroes and then asked Melissa to list hers.

She hesitated and timidly declared that she is set on Oriental figures. For her, as Bill knew, the platform of her soul was located in India, China and Japan. It was simple. Hinduism for her body, Buddhism for her mind and 'Clarissism' for her spirit. She also explained that there were peripheral tenets circling around her according to situations and people. She spoke highly of Confucianism, Shintoism and even that blend of Judeo-Christianity which she just could not split into absolute single entities. In addition, she injected Mohammedism to the last dyad as a natural offshoot, for without Judaism there would be no Christianity, and thus no Islam.

At that, Komaru got inflamed since he was studying the Koran. And he started asking questions of Melissa, but Bill interrupted the analytical trend by suggesting something less engaging.

'Shall we watch Wertmüller?'

Melissa approved. She had not seen the Italian Pakeha–Maori movie. She was curious. And down in the rumpus room they got comfortable to watch what Komaru felt was a parody of Ao Tea Roa social life as lived around Sicily.

The scenery could have been anywhere around the Coromandel peninsula, and the theme was an essay in social class relations. She found it fascinating, starting with the intriguing title, namely 'Travolti da insolito destino nel mare blu di agosto'. Yes, the only change should have been from August to January. The rest was perfect. And the language difference between Northern Italian and Sicilian was almost like one between English and Maori. Of course, the English subtitles helped, but the film could have been understood even without them, except for the section that Melissa found extremely exciting. That was when the blond Italian goddess, who resembled her so closely, offered the only *primitia* left in her as a symbol of total love toward a modern Odysseus. The Circe had repeated the offer three times – 'Sodomízzami'. And Melissa looked at Komaru intensely with her mouth open, while Bill was glowing at the idea of witnessing something new, exciting, unique just once. A thought crossed Komaru's mind. By any chance, had Dr Tavares applied his mending surgery beyond his call of duty?

Chapter 17

Returning from Papakura, where he had left his father after the conclusion of the 18th Reunion in Rotorua, Komaru became aware of 'terminality' for a loved one. This surged clearly, though calmly, into his heart and mind. There was no doubt that the days spent during the first week of April were the last that his father would enjoy among his former comrades at arms. At age 68, after two marriages, a complex life of tribulations, of fights within himself and against deranged human beings, sadness and resignation had taken over. Recollection of events that had happened half a century before blended with the immediacy of one more event looming inexorably on the horizon – death due to cirrhosis, a form of suicide through a slow process of disintegration among various forms accepted by society. Any other suicide would not have been approved by the society in which he lived on the margin of intentional anonymity. Besides, Komaru's father did not like to give the press the opportunity to describe in detail every small morsel of self-programmed dying. He knew that, unlike the tacit approval among Maoris who never indulged in morbid cinematographic records, Pakeha reporters took page after page of newspaper space in order clinically to account for all the gory details, titillating the boredom of Australasian life. What else could they write about at length? The cost of lamb, the arrival and departure of ships and airplanes, the speed of a horse breaking a record or the projected new Museum in Wellington? Life was drab in The Hermit Islands at the edge of the Earth. If anyone would stop or limit freedom of the press describing suicide in details, then some local newspapers would have to either declare bankruptcy or enlarge their advertising section for used automobiles, real estate auctions and extra columns of bereavement in both English and Maori. Komaru's observations were mostly silent and personal, though real and frightening.

The mayor of Rotorua had greeted the Returned Servicemen with 'tangihia ratou i mahue atu i rawahi', 'paying homage to the unfortunates [!] who were left behind overseas'. Komaru's father was not sure who was really unfortunate, one dying a slow death for 50 years or instantly on a battlefield. Was his half a century sojourn in Ao Tea Roa that fortunate or was it full of lingering anguish in seeing his *whenua* basically the same with regard to Maori rights? Yes, changes had taken place, but he regarded them as cosmetic in comparison to political metamorphoses taking place in, say, South Africa where world opinion supported boycotts at all levels. Would this world ever apply similar measure on behalf of Maoris? Who gave a damn? After all, these forgotten islands with a sprinkling of 'natives' were merely a matter of curiosity in connection with Chinese gooseberries. What else would, say, an American know about the last pristine culture on Earth, the remains of what used to be Ao Tea Roa in spite of piano sonatas on solitary beaches and *waiata* manifestations lamenting the good old days of wild fights via Hollywood?

Komaru took his father here and there along a sentimental journey to ancient settlements of past freedom, though mainly to Whakarewarewa and Ohimutu. The brief meeting with Paki Inia, representing the Federation of Tribes of Te Arawa was, for Komaru, an official introduction by his father to his inheritance of duties towards the *whenua* of his blood. Revelations, hopes, and adherence to the unwritten decalogues of an undeletable *whakapapa*.

In particular among many 'contacts', some live, others dead, was the recollection of Dr Patrick Eisdell Moore's contribution to helping Maori soldiers in Italy, later associated with other activities at home. In fact, rather than working in a comfortable 'medical' environment, Dr Moore preferred to spend his professional life among Maori children at Te Puia and other locations along the east coast where he established clinical centres to help the deaf.

There were, of course, fewer veterans than at the previous 17th Meeting, but their presence was revived through the usual photographs taken along the calvary of the Second World War. From one taken on Alexandria Quay in Egypt to another in Trieste, the road had been long, bloody, painful. The snapshot of the three Bennett brothers took his father back to the absurd battle of Cassino and the suicidal attack near its railway station. Another photograph taken by Lieutenant Reti, Komaru's father, showed the 'Group of Six'. It was September 1943, at the inception of the Italian campaign. The rains had made the roads impassable even to jeeps like the one stuck behind them. Komaru's father took a look at every one of the five members, with a particular interest in the officer standing on the extreme right of the snapshot, Jim Henare, the late Sir James. How young and proud he was in his 'Eisenhower' jacket! And his penetrating eyes betrayed some baffling look of doubt, if not of despair, through a strong sense of determination, that only a born leader can display silently. Gone, like the *moa*.

Where had the others gone, Wally Jones, Wally Wordley and Ben Christy? Would it not have been better for his father to have disappeared into eternity without suffering the anguish of carrying the burden of a family secret as a consequence of a war, compounded by alcoholism, depression and liver disease? But then he would not have produced Komaru, on whom he had imprinted a high sense of belonging to Maoridom along a continuity of responsibilities. Komaru, he knew, would do as a son what he as a father could not do any longer. Mahina, well, she was a woman, and as such she was to be relegated to 'Fourth World Women' for he saw no hope for his daughter as a member of an oppressed group WITHIN another oppressed group in traditional Ao Tea Roa.

Finally, his thoughts went to Sir Apirana Ngata, the patriot responsible for organising the Maori Battalion, and to Padre Wi Huata, whose moral force was stronger than his Anglican evangelism, for he became the cohesive gene keeping the spirit and the soul of Maoridom alive, especially through the constant use of the Maori language that had never been heard before along the iter of tears between Alexandria and Trieste. And the old animosity by Pakehas against Ngata was dispelled in the process of historical re-evaluation. What else could Ngata do besides calling for volunteers in order to constitute a Maori Battalion? It was a matter of future political survival for better or for worse, though the Gallipoli lesson had not helped those who died in the Dardanelles. Who got sections of land after the First and Second World Wars? Would Ngata now be proud and feel re-vindicated for his controversial actions resulting in 336 deaths out of 2,227 soldiers by knowing at his Rangi that his policies would be continued by the Ka Awatea formation of the new Ministry of Maori Development? And would he laugh at himself by seeing his effigy on a 50 dollar bank note?

When on the 6 April Komaru and his father left Rotorua for Papakura, the last lines of the Maori Battalion marching song lingering over the area assumed a ring of novelty, for Komaru made a few mental changes. Some veterans were singing

> You will march, march, march to the enemy

> And will fight right to the end
> For God, for King, for Country, *au e*
> *Ake! Ake! Kia Haka e!*

Was God satisfied that his father had marched and killed for Him, as well as for a distant King, and for what Country? Komaru retained the old Maori warriors' ejaculation: 'Ake! Ake! Kia Haka e!' 'Fight on, fight on, for ever and ever!' The genes of his *iwi* were flowing fast in his blood. There was nothing new in the genetic process. The only difference was fighting not for a White God, a White king, a White Country. With apologies to Corporal Anania Amohau, Komaru pledged to himself to fight for the Maori cause, regardless of any label ascribed to it.

In Wellington, after hiring a nurse in Papakura to take care of his father during the last stage of his life before entering a hospice in Auckland, Komaru reviewed his mail – letters, bills, newspapers, bulletins and other end-of-the-month items. He gave priority to a large envelope carrying only a Wanganui PO box number. What could it be?

WANGANUI WIDE WORLD CLUB
January 1992 Newsletter

Thank you for your interest in the WWW Club. While the United States and its 'allies' are engaged in skirting a new wild adventure in the Persian Gulf, we residents of Wanganui have just founded an organisation designed to counteract the traditional restrictions born with missionary 'social' indoctrination afflicting New Zealand. Since its informal inception last year, our Club has acquired a membership whose existence has deep roots in people who consider themselves free spirits exploring Wanganui Lifestyle. 'This is Well Worth the Journey.' We believe that Wanganui is the right place for our Club not only because of its historical traditions of quality education and cultural heritage, but also due to a function of geography. Many people have been relocating in Wanganui because of its temperate climate, low cost of living, and no traffic jams, among many advantages, such as our proximity to Wellington, not to mention other natural attractions within a few hours drive. We work very hard to create a relaxed and non-threatening social environment within which self-select people welcome others sincerely and warmly.

Before you read the second part of this newsletter, please consider and analyse carefully some (tentative) general rules.

MEMBERSHIP

1. The club membership is limited to couples, though occasionally the presence of a single guest is possible on an *ad hoc* basis.

2. The Club does not provide for exclusive single membership.

3. We are a Club where the focus lies on the interaction of couples, not a place for singles to meet.

4. The relationship creating a 'couple' is very loose in the sense that it may be made of married, unmarried, that is, legally or socially bound by permanent or informal ties.

5. We are a non-profit organisation and no member receives any compensation. Thus, every dollar is expended for the group.

6. Group 'heads' are board members elected to hold seats and to conduct club business. All board members, and occasionally other non-members, donate their time and services to render the operation of the Club possible.

7. Whenever expenses are incurred by a member on behalf of the group, they are reimbursed.

8. Whenever funds from yearly dues accrue beyond meeting basic requirements, the money is used to enhance regular or special events.

9. Membership is open to anyone regardless of race, religion, social status, age and other general characteristics that have been typical of New Zealand's open life style. However, there is nothing cast in stone since rules may be changed as a function of 'political' and social trends, provided that normal adherence to healthy habits, such as no smoking, no drugs, and no diseases assurance is abided by the honour system.

10. This rule is the most important one and it relates to the unquestionable acceptance of 'No!' Our members are extremely sensitive to this absolute and unbreakable rule. This means that no member will ever apply any pressure on anyone to 'partake' in anything. Anyone violating this rule will first and discreetly be confronted with the case. If necessary, regardless of 'legality', a

member clearly accused of disregarding 'Rule 10' shall relinquish membership and physical presence immediately and without any recourse. Once the confidentiality of a relationship between and among members is tainted for any reason, nothing can recreate mutual trust. In our short existence, no one has ever broken this rule designed to ensure security, comfort and freedom of individuality.

INTRODUCTORY REMARKS ON GROUP BEHAVIOUR

As regards the 'mechanism' operating at an actual social meeting, first timers will probably choose to sit with their mates at one of the various tables provided for watching others, relax with a drink or simply wait for a 'happening'. Normally, one notices no 'cliqueish' crowd formation for any reason, for members tend to mingle. It does not take long to welcome a smiling face to introduce himself (and at times herself) asking for a dance. Although men initiate the invitation, ladies are hardly shy.

You will notice plenty of touching, hugging and kissing. You may wonder whether people expressing physical manifestations have already 'experienced' all those partners with such a display of affection. Maybe yes, perhaps not, for it is difficult to know what has happened in the minds of the 'players'. Moreover, no one cares as long as such manifestations are mutually accepted. Circle members are calm, warm and balanced people who generally develop friendship before or concurrent with advanced interludes.

Probably you aspire to meet one or more couples sharing mutual desires. This is the ideal situation, though it may not be always the case since at times personal preference may impede unanimous indulgence. Thus, you may feel apprehensive to become acquainted with someone that you did not phantasise about as a play-bloke or play-sheila. Try not to let such thoughts interfere with simply making a new friend. Also, try not to stifle your partner's interest even though one's feelings don't align along your own feeling that as a couple you need to pair up and 'swap' directly. Be realistic. Each person may have some intimate and preconceived notions. Just because a sheila does not care for the short and balding husband of a high-spike shoe wearing wife that he has his eyes on, does not mean one must be denied or the other suffer. In other words, bilateral compatibility is not a requirement to enter into a relationship, for it is quite common for one side of the couple to develop an intimate relationship while the other enters simply a friendship. As in any human relationship, honesty is the best policy. Only when someone is misled will hurt feelings occur. Finally, there is no requirement to provide an explanation for disinterest in another. A simple 'No, thank you' with a smile of appreciation is usually accepted graciously without the need to justify anything under the general umbrella of 'Rule 10'.

THE WANGANUI CLUB LIFESTYLE

We are a group of members living within a two-to-three hour driving distance, meeting for the common purpose of an enjoyable lifestyle upon mutual consent, and not a group that expects one to conduct the lifestyle with each and every person one meets. It is one's choice to become involved to whatever degree one likes without any expectation or criticism. For example, some ladies may be apprehensive to consent to dance after viewing some of the physical interaction that may transpire on the dance floor. This may take place when a gentleman makes advances. These should be made with regard to the sensitivity of the ladies' feelings when a gesture of disapproval looms in the air. If concurrence is noted, then the 'initial' problem of 'resistance' or shyness can be understood. After all, no one can blame a bloke for trying a sheila who is 'available'. This can be inferred particularly whenever probing a woman who likes risqué exhibitionism through provoking 'lingerie' or suggestive body contact. However, no one should ever take anything for granted. The degree to which one participates in anything is strictly one's choice. In fact, many find contentment simply in discovering a new dance partner for unusual rhythms such as the tango, or a conversationalist with common interests from cooking to poetry to loom weaving. Many members are and remain 'just friends'.

As an evening of dancing comes to conclusion, one may catch wind of an after social party or two. The club at times sponsors an after social party. However, not all parties are club-sponsored. When they are, they are restricted to active members where visitors are never invited. The reason for this is to protect the privacy of club members in a totally relaxed environment. Club-sponsored parties abide by the rule of consent and general courtesy. Of course, there is no guarantee should one opt to attend.

TRIAL PERIOD

In reflection of your experience, you may come to find uncertainties or questions influencing your decision to join. If you find discomfort in the lifestyle after exploring our club, it is probably not a good idea to join. Being comfortable with the lifestyle and the ability to let your partner 'go' without reservation or undue anxiety is paramount.

If personal comfort is not an issue where the decision is whether or not to join our club, please review what you expect from a club. With most clubs like ours, the ability to link up with partners is highly probable. You don't normally have that probability by going to a church service or even a bar. If that is your desire, most any club will do. If you are looking for 'more', consider the old dating adage: 'Fine, now that we have done THAT, what else'?

Well, you will find out that our club excels among the few ones existing in North Island. Of course, we may not be aware of all existing 'underground' clubs for the simple reason that New Zealand society has not yet accepted the incorporation of non- profit organisations of this type on the national level, especially among Maori *iwi*. In our society, we are still aeons behind what in other cultures is not only admissible but also encouraged as an outlet to married life frustrations and behind the scenes deceptions.

There is MORE, but things may not be too obvious to the casual observer the first time. You have to look for lingering and not too obvious mores. It is not easy when you are caught up in the emotions of HOW to fit in. Try to recall conversations you heard at 'normal' parties beyond the normally expected. Dinners, outings, movie-goings, exploring common interests, etc. may give you a clue about your seeking something else looming in the wings of personal 'liberation'. We have many members who share not only partners, but also find friendship and share mutual interests beyond sex. Was it Chekhov, who in the second act of *Uncle Vanya* declared: 'A woman becomes a man's friend in this order – first she is an acquaintance, then a mistress, and only after that a friend'? Of course, Chekhov was reflecting the male chauvinistic view of the period about a 100 years ago, but many female members have rewritten this observation by simply saying that a man becomes a woman's friend in this order – first an acquaintance, then a lover and only after that a real friend forever. In certain cases it happens that you meet someone in a position of trust – whether or not known mutually or unilaterally – such as professor/student, banker/client, doctor/patient, constable/neighbour, etc. When that occurs, simply avoid mentioning or recollecting anything beyond the most immediate relationship until, and if ever, any of the two parties feel comfortable to disclose any present or past non-Club association. Any serious member will never go around saying 'You know I met the pastor of St Ophelia at the Club?' If it is your desire to maintain a separate identity for your 'regular' social life, you may find some of our genuinely interested-in-you people intrusive and disconcerting. Remember Rule 10!

✦

After returning from Rotorua's meetings in which his father had participated, Komaru could not help but compare the 'Club' atmosphere among members of the 28th Maori Battalion with one envisaged at the Wanganui Club. That first part of rules and regulations governing a group of human beings had made him uneasy. How could it be possible for humans to organise and enjoy a club devoted to hedonistic purposes? Of course, he knew that he would never join. The reasons were obvious – he was single, he did not want to meet anyone who could identify him in the future for what he had in mind politically for fear of being blackmailed, he did not like to share anyone with anybody, even if his partner was a temporary association for whatever reason. Plus, he had planned to finish his work at the university, take care of his father, cooperate with Mahina, and a host of other things. Besides, from the sexual point of view he 'had' Melissa. And he recalled that she in essence was 'acting' as a member of the Club, which at that time he did not know about. But even without the Club, Melissa did anything she wanted to do. Her 'club' was a medical condition. And Komaru tolerated her behaviour silently, and undoubtedly confusedly. What could he do? When he started working with her, he had no idea whatsoever what kind of person he had encountered.

Now, reflecting over the absurd ménage, Komaru rationalised by telling himself that in practice he was a member of the McTavishes Club. No dues, no by-laws, no newsletter. He even thought about having Bill as president, himself as vice-president and Melissa as secretary-treasurer. Besides, from time to time, Komaru would see Ling-ling who, meanwhile, had become a friend to the point of confiding in him how she was experiencing plenty of race discrimination in Pakeha New Zealand. The old 'yellow peril' fear was subtly 'inching' its way once more, though not because of miscegenation but because of the fact that 'Orientals' had started to compete with Pakehas in all endeavours of business, commerce, education and even culinary arts. It was well known that the most brilliant minds at Victoria University were Chinese. This created an atmosphere of reverse competition to the point that a *numerus clausus* was often invoked when, on the basis of academic performance, bursaries had to be given to Asian students. Therefore, a reverse and subtle process of affirmative action on behalf of whites was applied to the detriment of justice and official laws. Normally, Chinese and white 'relationships' were tolerated in terms of 'visibility'. However, when a Chinese and a Maori became associated, even in terms of friendship, the Maori was chastised by Pakehas for fear of seeing a political and racial alliance detrimental to the status quo.

Amazingly enough, the second part of the newsletter contained grains of truth. He skipped reading here and there, stopping when he found elements of truth with regard to the social and sexual lives of New Zealanders who, in Komaru's view, would not be concerned with being considered as the islands of Cybele but those of homosexuals on a *per capita* basis. This tendency in New Zealand was, for Komaru, more noticeable as a function of the stress placed by politicians on race relations for which prizes and diplomas were dispensed particularly by the Race Relations Office on 6 February. The 'One Love Unity Celebration' had just begun to be organised with the hope of being implemented every year beginning with 1993. King Bob Marley could be invited to Wellington Carlaw Park every year to dispense awards through reggae and dances.

> In your pursuit of exploring social/sexual activity beyond the confines of a monogamous relationship, you will experience factors that make us humans so unique. You may acquire in the process the ability to reason, experience new emotions, and become aware of a sex drive which often becomes aroused by others than your chosen or current mate. This is particularly true for females when oestrogen levels drop at menopause and likewise when the testosterone decreases for men at their climacterium.
>
> The arousal part is a normal healthy human factor. Flirtation and discovery of mutual attraction doesn't automatically disappear after entering a dedicated relationship. Cultural diversity pervading the world either provides or suppresses interaction outside monogamy. In the Western world, of which we are part in spite of belonging geographically to the eastern hemisphere, the propensity is to suppress. Ironically, we are still in the Victorian era for different reasons, and especially because anything that takes place

in Europe arrives to our Hermit Islands after generations. This is particularly so because most immigrants are chosen from among the most conservative, even from Britain. Amusingly, in England we witness the most evident non-monogamous tendency in every sector of private and public life, from heads of government to members of royal houses officially presiding over religious functions.

At this point Komaru took a break. He had detected Dr McTavish's language style, for he remembered his discussion on the boat along the Whanganui to a place where members used to congregate. Thus, to clear his mind, Komaru decided to check his mail. He took the lift to the lobby, where he retrieved several items, including a letter from his father, one from Melissa and another from Mahina. The one from his father surprised him for he rarely wrote. He used to be in touch with his son via phone.

Upon returning to the apartment, he decided to finish the second part of the WWW newsletter for the simple purpose of disposing of 'excess garbage' before opening the mail just received. He anticipated replying to what he just got in the mail, and the thought disturbed him somewhat because he could anticipate what the contents would be. Thus, he hurried along the reading of the Club philosophy of proselytising.

Since childhood we are taught and are surrounded by 'exclusive partners' standards. These, of course, are always potentially moot, especially when male partners become absent for many years, particularly during overseas wars. There are more 'casualties' at home than in the battlefield whenever marital partnership is altered by patriotic exploits. For whatever reasons, many feel that something is 'wrong' or 'missing' for a fulfilling life with just one person – a view that could be disproved in certain communities such as monasteries, convents, prisons, army barracks and the like. Often such feelings form the basis for a break-up in the relationship where there is too much demand on one person to satisfy every desire. This is specially true in households where the female spends most of her time engaged in the usual chores, though nowadays some relief is granted by having two breadwinners, a situation already potentially open to joining a club to avoid the usual temptations of deceptive nature, and therefore the destruction of a status quo sanctioned by church and state.

Such destruction is usually unfair as what is being expected is humanly impossible to deliver. Many look within themselves and view in others' behaviour/compulsion a need to expand beyond the confines of 'just one' in an age bombarding us with explicit situations in movies, TV shows, magazines, etc. This challenges the so-called status quo and often brings up emotional questions such as 'is there anything wrong with me?' Surrogates such as masturbation or joining a culinary club don't seem to answer intimate questions. Of course, in most cases there is nothing wrong with an individual possessing the intelligence and the freedom of a normal human in the information age. The social standards of New Zealand, although regarded by most psychologists as 'straight laced', trigger questions that are not 'human-oriented'. They may derive from faulty polls manipulated in the laboratory of wishful thinking. In reality, the standards are oriented such that the emotions are protected in society by jealousy and insecurity that create hosts of patients for psychologists who need them to keep their sofas warm. Consequently, truly felt desires for another human being, to whatever degree, are artificially squelched. The result is usually frustration leading to anger. The utilisation of ability to reason, thus, to understand these emotions and to conclude that 'more than one is OK' is what 'swinging' (to use an American term) is all about. It is easy to understand this concept, but not always so easy to comfortably practise it as the same emotions compelling people toward what they may react against. Of course, one should not exclude from the general view particular situations in which one partner is affected by either nymphomania or satyriasis.

Here Komaru reflected a little. He wondered whether Bill had cooperated, or even designed, the club to maintain family stability. Then why Komaru as a *Deux ex machina*? Was he being used as an alternate source or, by any chance, had Melissa found something different? Komaru remembered Melissa's refrain 'You are special'. Was there any element of 'love' in any of the relationships fostered by the Club? He continued reading as if looking for an answer to his question.

Often damage is brought into a relationship because one or the other yields to powerful sex drives, particularly under special circumstances, such as intoxication through alcohol or drugs, not to mention the real or phoney use of aphrodisiacs such as perfumes of animal or vegetable sources. Of course, reading about or emulating other humans' activities act as a powerful tool of vicarious pleasure. Usually these 'affairs', resulting in deception and lies, once revealed, have devastating effects except perhaps when these affairs are consummated among friends above any suspicion, for it is felt that a friend never betrays anybody. In examining the feelings associated with such events, it is often discovered that 'hurt' is not so much due to the 'act'. The most painful is the violation of trust due to the secretive circumstances, as well as the jealousy that someone else found your partner desirable. In other cases it is the risible reaction on the part of common friends who know everything but would not reveal the deceptive situation. It is easy to understand violation due to deception, as well as to receiving a bill from a doctor regarding the treatment of a vaginal infection or venereal disease that could not have been caused by a cautious partner. What becomes confusing for some is a mixture of jealousy and 'fair play'. The 'victim' becomes angered not only because his or her mate found someone more enticing, but also no one found him or her attractive in return. Also, often confusing are feelings of 'pride' that someone else found a partner attractive and the 'victim' was denied the pleasure of experiencing it. Not to think of the usual feeling of lack of gratitude for whatever one partner had done for the other at great sacrifice to make the other happy by providing a wonderful family, a home and the like. Therefore, a club like ours provides the opportunity to explore interludes beyond the monogamous relationship in an environment where the factors of deception and deceit are absent. Members participate in activities as couples by providing an umbrella of total honesty.

Komaru skipped several pages of logistics, tentative schedules of meetings here and there, safety involving couples leaving children at home, and other practical considerations. He then turned to some preliminary considerations that in part repeated previous things or elaborated on others.

PRELIMINARY CONSIDERATIONS

If you are uncertain whether the WWW Club is for you, here are some items to be discussed with your partner. In talking about the Club, try to be open and honest. Expressions such as 'I'm not sure', 'I would like to experience it first to find out' or 'I wonder how you would react if you saw me in the arms of so and so' are not valid answers. The extent to which you have shared intimate relationship experiences outside your 'normal' relationship will also determine the amount of firm yes or no answers. Logically, no partner would ever propose a unilateral relationship such as 'I would like to have male friends from my high school days' by selfishly keeping the husband tied to a monogamous relationship, and likewise for men in parallel situations.

The following 'decalogue' is just a tentative list of possibilities.

1. I would like to have pleasurable experiences with others.

2. I would like for my partner to have pleasurable experiences with others.

3. Other intimate, pleasurable experiences will not threaten our relationship.

4. It is not disturbing to me, or I would enjoy finding out that my partner is attractive to others.

5. It is not disturbing to me, or I would enjoy that my partner is attractive to others.

6. Our relationship is stable and secure enough to permit the discovery of others we find attractive.

7. One would not be jealous or upset if only the other made a 'connection'.

8. We can talk about experiences and be honest with each other about our feelings and reactions. Of course, certain items of 'comparison', such as 'His is much bigger than yours' or 'You have never satisfied me as much as X or Y' are not constructive topics even though they reflect realities, if not the very purpose, of joining a club.

9. The decision to try swinging is agreeable to both where one or the other is not just being 'tolerant' or 'understanding' in lieu of true feelings.

10. I shall not interfere with my partner's sole judgment except when obvious danger may stem from a liaison affecting the family or business.

If you answered 'yes' or 'maybe' to all of these questions, it is probably safe to attend a social without damaging your relationship. If either of you had some definite no-responses, swinging is not for you.

Komaru was interrupted by a telephone call at that stage of reading. He decided not to answer in order to finish the esoteric reading of applied psychiatry to place humans close to bonobos, the closest allies in sexuality. He then proceeded.

Human sexuality is a multi-faceted gem where, by adopting the WWW Club lifestyle, many unique aspects are experienced or shared for their own sake. One advantage of swinging is that it does permit enjoying certain sexual aspects that may not be practical in a couple's relationship. A couple's understanding of such often reinforces a relationship, in a way like 'having your cake and eating it too'. No pun intended. Of course, these notes are not intended to become part of a treatise on human sexuality. A few examples are given below so you can get a feel for the diversity of possibilities whenever you participate in a party. Much of this is 'universal' among different clubs outside New Zealand. However, the impact of recent immigrants, particularly from the former Soviet Union and Yugoslavia, has begun to spread in North Island. Consider, thus, special interest groups, such as those of Indian or Tibetan background associating 'religious' traditions as in the case of Tantrism. If you are unsure about a private party you have been invited to, it is better to ask first than be embarrassed. Please consider the following carefully.

CASE HISTORIES

1. You want to indulge in your first interlude. You feel uncomfortable with the presence of so many others. Simply close the door, and your privacy will be respected. Be advised that some other parties request that the doors NOT be closed.

2. You and your partner have discovered a couple you wish to mutually share or be in the same room with or without others. Again, just close the door.

3. You are in a room with multiple beds. One is vacant and others are waiting for a place. The door is left ajar and you will be asked if it is all right to come in to use the bed. You decide one way or the other. In essence, you may accept one couple and reject another for any reason.

4. You have no objections or desire to be watched. Possibly, invite others to share your experience. With the door left open, you will imply an invitation for others. Of course, it is your decision whom you allow to participate since Rule 10 overrides everything at any time.

5. Orgies may occur when people congregate as an open group so designated in advance to experience the collective activities of indiscriminate sex. There may often be interaction between members of the same sex as well as heterosexual engagement. Orgy variations take place when and where several participants focus on pleasuring just one. This often occurs where a woman hosts multiple male partners to participate. However, one may 'stand by' to see if she is receptive. Hot tubs, for example, often provide the ideal setting where hands move about freely to provide additional touches or caresses to couples openly displaying affection or suggest interest in anyone to indulge further. Of course, in the case of hot tubs it is extremely impolite, if not rude, to allow anything to be released soiling the whole tub. If these activities offend you, simply leave the area. No one will be offended. Or, if you just want to observe, you are free to remain at a comfortable distance and even help the crowd by bringing drinks or whatever needed by the participants.

6. Display of nudity and/or risqué attire are very common, especially as the party progresses. If you like flirting or showing off this way, it is a great place to do so. Just because you are on 'display', however, does not warrant free license for anything. However, do expect advances. And remember Rule 10, even when all appearances seem to allow obvious interactions.

7. No photographs, video, and/or sound recording, requests for personal family names, addresses, telephone, faxes, etc. are ever asked in a group of more than two individuals or couples unless clearly offered without expecting that the information be accepted.

We hope that we have answered ...

Well, that was quite a reading. Komaru felt that most possible human interactions within the whole range of sexuality, from the traditional to the most unusual as per all manuals of erotica in all cultures of the world, could be found by reading those lines and even between them. He wondered if the WWW Club had covered all major interactions between and among humans. And he asked himself if that was a characteristic that distinguished men from other biological entities on Earth from the simple cell on. Was *Homo eroticus* the end product of evolution, if not of refined civilization? Was there anything else surpassing what humans could do in order to grasp from life whatever made them happy in waiting for their extinction whether within a knowable time frame or whenever death levelled everything in a universe of unknowns? Well, he simply shredded those pages of self-indulgence and burned them in the sink of the bathroom. He did not trust anyone, especially in connection with evidence that would prove or disprove anything related to his person. He had learned that precaution in China when he had found out that his dorm room was wired for sound as an experiment of communication between the 'concierge' office and each and every room. Then he had dinner, took a rest, brushed his teeth and began to read his mail. The first letter was from Mahina. It was dated 25 April. Another ANZAC Day, not celebrated any longer. The dead of Gallipoli had died again on the pages of the New Zealand calendar, E's-E–2C. Number 25 was printed in red, thus an oflicial holiday. The fact that it fell on a Saturday gave Kiwis an additional excuse to celebrate the death of the suckers who 'gave their lives' in skirmishes among white cousins. Maoris were just a novelty on the European scenario of periodical depravity. Komaru asked himself whether humans were better off screwing each other in bed than themselves on a battlefield. Perhaps the Club was not a bad idea after all.

Chapter 18

This time Mahina used she so indicated a word processor rather than her old portable typewriter, and indeed she so indicated in the course of her comprehensive epistolary report to Komaru. Tanya had installed a personal computer. Komaru noticed how at times a line was skipped or a whole sentence was left in capital letters, for his sister did not notice the accidental touch of a wrong key. He could guess all the typical pitfalls into which an individual falls in the attempt to become computer literate. The other thing he noticed was that, by abandoning the writing by hand, Mahina's contents of a letter tended to be more official than personal. He missed that touch of intimacy transpiring from the visual communication through graphic expressions of pauses, deletions, italicisation, nervousness and the like. Well, he thought, more than for manual typing on its way out after using white fluid for corrections and x–ing unwanted words, a word processor had also killed the intimacy of corresponding with another member of the human race. Centuries of tradition and usage displaying individual characteristics and betraying unique aspects of personality had vanished along with the progress of civilization. But, could one really accept progress as the levelling out of individuality in favour of a standard conformity devoid of neuronic life?

There was no date. He guessed that she assumed he knew when the Easter festivity took place. He didn't, though he had heard that it was a movable date according to the phases of the Moon. He found that rather confusing, and he wished he had remembered at least the old Maori system of keeping track of the time on the basis of lunar appearance. Komaru felt that she must have been under a spell of some kind, for never before had she addressed him along an axis of affection via adjectival degrees of comparative and superlative terms of endearment.

Dear Komaru, dearer brother, my dearest tungane,

Yesterday I 'lived' the first Easter of my life. Among the many feelings I experienced, the first was the birth of my soul, for now

I have one that shall never abandon me anywhere, anytime, for any reason. Of course, the inception of this eternal companionship had occurred before, as it were, when I was baptised, but only yesterday was I able to detect its presence in all dimensions. It was some kind of ascension from the depths of a limbo, that is, a no-man's land (oh, you chauvinists) whose concept came back to me via the survey of medieval European literature I took during my Year Abroad, and in particular through Dante's *Divine Comedy*. I must confess that I am still groping in the dark, but I am sure, I am confident, I BELIEVE that I can clarify certain doubts still lingering in my mind. You see, our own Maori seat of feelings, the stomach of our warriors for physical deeds so common to our ancestors – well, you know that I don't have to tell you – has now a collateral locus housing the spirit that in no way rejects the culture of our *iwi*.

I am a new person resulting from so many events taking place this spring, well, our autumn, a spring of course dictated by the fact that Jesus' Resurrection took place in the Northern hemisphere, though symbolically this spring is atopical and, in fact, universal, in spite of the fact that the mystery of Christ's resurrection is a fact historically verified according to the New Testament (you as a historian can double check what St Paul wrote to the Corinthians, 1 Cor 15:3–4). Of course, in it the Apostle speaks of the living tradition of the Resurrection after his conversion at the gates of Damascus. This was not long ago and, in fact, if we project that event onto our own Polynesian history you can recall that at that time (do you remember the lecture we went to just before I left for the States, incidentally is her book already published, oh, yes, her name, Joan Leaf) barely a couple of generations had gone by from the time of the Battle of the Stolen Fish (65 BC?). That was after the Battle of *Te-Matenga-o-tini-o-Pokau*. when seven canoes travelled away to the east and north-east. I wonder what happened to the three canoes of the original seven. Anyway, when our ancestors departing from *Tawhiti-roa* reached *Tawhiti-nui*, Jesus had not yet been born. I assume that He was born just after our own Polynesian leader, Ruamano, died in the battle mentioned above. It is amazing to think that the history of our own people goes back to two millennia BC. Just imagine, at that time Greece, Rome, etc. were yet to emerge on the European scenario, while we in the East were embarked on the long voyage that carried our genes to the final destination of Ao Tea Roa. So, you see, Komaru, now that I have correlated ancient history with the modern one I feel much better, for Ruamano and Jesus were seeing the same constellations.

The other event marking an important step in my most intimate life was the celebration of my First Communion, that is, that of the Holy Eucharist that completes, in conjunction with Confirmation, my Christian initiation. The whole process of becoming a totally different person was carefully planned and followed. Becoming a Christian at an adult age is a conscious commitment that will remain with you during the rest of your life.

Tanya, some classmates, and some other friends and I have made during the past 4 years were present when I attended Mass in the Chapel of Jesus the Teacher. It was a glorious morning, the campus was bathed in full sunshine, so many flowers were colouring the banks of the Willamette river, and Mt Hood was projecting its snowcapped peak against the bluest sky. Daffodils, lilies, dogwood buds and so many other bushes waved at me in the gentle breeze of the Pacific. The church bell echoed through the campus as a celestial sound giving joy to my heart, acting like a beacon for those approaching the mystery of the Eucharist. When I studied Greek, who would have dreamed that I would come across terms such as *eucharistein* and *eulogein*? They actually recall the Jewish blessing that proclaims God's work, namely, creation, redemption and sanctification. This is particularly so during a meal such as the Lord's Supper on the eve of His Passion, as well as because it anticipates the wedding feast of the Lamb in the heavenly Jerusalem. And I wonder how many Pakehas, surrounded by millions of lambs, ever connect the rôle of that quadruped with regard to Jerusalem. You see, Komaru, Catholicism did not pop up like a daffodil in the middle of nowhere. Behind it there is a long tradition through Judaism. And Jesus was a Jew like any other human surrounding Him, except for the Romans ruling the land under the colonialist policies implemented by armies of mercenaries and centurions.

The Mass was celebrated in Latin. So easy to understand in spite of the 'English' accent. Amusingly, it was pronounced like that of the Middle Ages, not in Ciceronean diction. The symbolism of the bread and wine recalling the flesh and blood of Christ was for me almost a shocking experience but, once understood, it created in me an aura of mysticism, particularly when I received the Host on the first day of the week, namely, Sunday, that in Latin is *dies dominica* as in most Romance languages, the day of the Lord. That day of Jesus' resurrection, Christians began to 'break bread' among 'companions' in a common faith, and you can guess what the real meaning of 'companion' is if you think in terms of *cum* plus the ablative of the Latin for 'bread'. Thus, when I was ready to receive the first Communion, I don't know, I felt something 'physical' – 'Corpus Domini nostri, Jesu Christi, custodiat animam tuam in vitam aeternam. Amen'. The Lord had actually invited me to receive Him via the sacrament of the Eucharist: 'Truly, I say to you, unless you eat the flesh of the Son of Man and drink his blood, you have no life in you'. I must confess that something atavistic stirred in me, a subconscious recollection of my Maori genetic structure. You understand what I mean, but in this case, rather than receiving a *mana* from my ancestors, be they blood relatives or enemies killed in battle, I felt an immediate tie with Christ. In addition, I felt a bond with those billions of people who, for 2,000 years, preceded me in the aspiration to reach peace. So many thoughts crossing my mind, as that telling me how the Eucharist commits me to the poor. Jesus had only the clothes he wore. Nothing else. Not even a means of transportation. But He had people who understood and followed Him in the process of uniting all Christians as Augustine wrote in his *Evangelium Johann is tractatus* – 'O bond of charity!'

Sorry for the excursus, but for me it was a matter of establishing a solid historical platform since, as a Christian, I am historically outside of human events covering Buddha, Confucius and even Mohammed. These are just 'new kids on the block', if you will allow me an American anachronism (here 'block' is a row or group of houses on many 'sections').

By the time our ancestors had reached Eastern Fiji under the leadership of Tu-tarangi (perhaps about 450 AD), Easter as a feast had already been accepted and celebrated as the Feast of Feasts, or the Solemnity of Solemnities within the Christian world. In fact, at the Council of Nicaea, all Churches agreed in 325 AD that Christian Passover (our Easter) should be celebrated on the Sunday following the first full moon (our *tirakerake*) after the vernal equinox. Of course, you know that the Gregorian calendar tried to bring some order to the old Julian one in comparison with the Eastern rite. Well, my Church is in no hurry to settle disputes and, since 1582, undoubtedly after Turi's *Aotea* had already reached our shores from Tahiti, Eastern Churches are still seeking an agreement to have Easter, as well as Christmas, etc. coincide all over the Christian world. Amusingly, Tanya, you know her, on her father's side celebrates Christmas twice because she (via her mother) descends from the Eastern Orthodox Church (25 December and 6 January).

Well, I hope I did not bore you with my comparative analysis of historical events. Of course, I cannot compete with you, but recently history has kind of (another Americanism!) affected me in connection with my honours thesis, i.e. the angelology project. My advisor (some 'kids' around here write adviser, though never advisery') has already accepted it. I think he is too generous, for you would not believe how far back the concept of 'angel' goes (though the term is very new – at least 1,000 years in Greece after our ancestors departed for the Pacific), since as I wrote you previously I believe I can prove the existence of the angel as a universal messenger. Here in the States there is a craze about angels, with movies, books, conventions, exhibits (I hear the Vatican is sending its collection of angels to LA for a few months in 1997 – where will I be at that time?), and the like. I had to limit my senior thesis to a 125-page long essay titled 'Elements of angelology'. Maybe one day I will write something like 'Angelology for the new millennium', what do you say? I have done so much research. Interestingly, what people now seem to believe in and accept is the external or pragmatic side of the angel as a messenger. This is a recent phenomenon particularly divulged by Christianity and then by Mohammedism, as adapted by the Church fathers in the 5th century. The earliest record we have for a comprehensive 'structure' of angelography is found in pseudo-Dionysus who in *De hierarchia celesti* drafted the names of NINE orders (what about your number NINE?) on the basis of the New Testament. Of course, from then on, the gates of vulgarisation were open to enter everything and everywhere. Dante utilised it for the structure of his *Paradiso* down to Milton (*Paradise Lost*), etc. I enjoyed looking at the drawings of Doré, though he was not the first to draw angels. I think the earliest was Botticelli as when, in the *Primum Mobile*, Beatrice describes to Dante the various orders of Angels. You should see that sketch. I counted about 21 of them, each carrying some kind of booklet (a proto-Mao red book?) in the left hand. Amusingly, those angels are all dressed, they look like females, or at least androgynous, though in many other artworks you have to guess their sex, if any, mainly from the face, the hair and so on.

I say this since I have started a collection of anything in print (reproductions). You simply can't believe it, even on soap bars you will see the most voluptuous angels. What a waste! Once I had to blow up a colour reproduction via computer enhancement at the Student Union, which I now keep by my bed. And at times I even carry a little pin (I paid 1 dollar at a garage sale), just costume jewellery in its protective custody saying 'Guardian angel – wear an angel (how can one?) on your shoulder (think! shoulder, over your shoulder ...) to guide you through the days and the nights, and brighten your life'. So, now I have my own little *wairua*, like an asexual follett barely 2½ centimeters tall. The sculptor had his (its) right thigh cover his middle part. The trend here is unisex, of course, and I think that the source of this goes back to early angels. After all, they didn't need to bother with the materialistic aspects of physiology. Otherwise, they would be attacked whenever they deliver a message or package in certain suburbs of large cities, like UPS (that is, United Parcel Service). And now that I think of it, it was angels that started the earliest delivery system before modern conveniences. Wasn't it the Angel Gabriel who announced the Child to Mary? I have a reproduction of Leonardo's painting (now in the Louvre, which I saw during my sophomore year abroad). I remember the lilies in the background, explained by the French docent as the symbol of *purité*. I also have a reproduction of Kim Barnes' five angels floating around the Earth. They look like two boys and three girls (the five continents?) all dressed in white, with golden wings and racial characteristics on the basis of skin pigmentation. Quite an integrated concept! Incidentally, did you know that angels are musicians? Of course, they play medieval instruments. They also sing, probably in Latin, and I hope they will never learn rock music, though, if one day they do, you can't blame them for joining the younger generation.

Komaru could not refrain from laughing. He took a break. Refreshingly, after reading the WWW Newsletter, Mahina's letter was a welcome shower of sororal news. Yes, Mahina had changed, there was no question about that, but not only in social and philosophical ways, but also in her style of expression. In addition, she now displayed a healthy sense of humour, something he had never noticed before. It was his sister's safety valve whenever extremely serious topics were reported or analysed. Anyway, he was grateful to Mahina who had forgiven him for the way he had treated her regarding her conversion and everything that it implied. He knew he had 'lost' a naïve sister, but he was beginning to uncover a new sibling full of maturity and perspicaciousness. In fact, the following section of the letter was obviously written in several installments and revealed a new 'woman' who seemed to know exactly what she wanted, whither she intended to go, and how she intended to spend the rest of her life.

> Komaru, I trust that you begin to grasp what I am saying. I am telling you of several things regarding especially my, shall I say, spiritual dimension, so that when I come back you can help guide me to the best of your abilities. I know that I can count on you. Indeed, I would appreciate your informing Dad about the various things I am doing. I don't think I told you that, when I was baptised, I retained Mahina as the name already entered in the anagraphic records of Auckland, but I also added two more 'first names' (as referred to here in the States), namely, Clara and Maria. Why these? I will explain later in person. Meanwhile, please inform Dad about everything I am writing. I hope that he will last until my graduation. I had hoped you and he would be able to attend commencement during the first week of May, but I know that Father is in no condition to travel and you can't leave him alone. The other thing I was going to inform you about is that during the second week of May Archbishop Francis George will come to Portland in order to celebrate the Sacrament of Confirmation in the Holy Rosary Church. This sacrament is celebrated separately from Baptism through the anointing with chrism (consecrated oil) on the forehead. Confirmation is given only once in order to imprint on the soul an indelible spiritual mark, the 'characters'. By this sign, Jesus Christ will mark me with the seal of His spirit by clothing me with power, so that he may be my witness. After that, I am ready to face the whole world by returning to our *whenua*.
>
> However, I must confess that returning home is not something I look forward to with total confidence. Except for seeing you and Father, what can I do down under? Believe me, it is not because I have been influenced by America (though I admit that some elements of its lifestyle are appealing), but mainly because I will feel like a prisoner again among Pakehas. Do you remember our 'He wahine he whenua – i ngaro ai te tangata?' More than ever, after spending nearly 3 years in the States and one in Europe, I

believe that NZ women have no liberty whatsoever. We are slaves of men, and Maori women are slaves twice, i.e. once because of gender and once more as chattel belonging to Maori men. You know well that you are a product of male, Christian (without being one), white and Victorian prejudices. What will I to do in Papakura except marry (sorry, forget that), accept a job (with a degree in philosophy, as a secretary to a white executive or, worse, to a Maori-patronising man who sold his soul to Pakeha for a corporate salary), while trying to reconcile the concepts of *tapu, noa, rahui*, and *utu*? I would become oppressed at home in a microsystem within the macrosystem of political, juridical and social ambience prevailing in 'Polynesian' metro Auckland. Now I understand how sisters like Wairaka, Mansfield, Rangitiria and Maggie may have felt. I would not mind becoming another one from Papakura like Maggie, poor, nearly forgotten, but free. You and I seem to have something in common that incites us to *Kia whawhai tonu tatou ake, ake, ake*. The difference is that you plan to fight for the whole *whenua*, but I shall do that first for my gender. Will I do so? There are various ways of fighting. One is that of isolating yourself from the rest of humanity, in essence fighting against the rest of humanity by retreating into yourself without giving the pleasure of your company to anyone except God. How?

I have been exploring the possibility of staying away from our *whenua* by joining a community of some sort. I have done two things. The first was to analyse a book titled *Fire, Salt, and Peace*. It lists and illustrates many intentional Christian communities operating in North America. Of course, a stumbling block is that I am not an American, nor do I have a green card. The other possibility would be to join a formal organisation like a convent. Still, how? Coincidentally, returning from Walla Walla, Tanya and I made a detour via Spokane, a lumber community in the same state. There we visited one of the several Poor Clare monasteries, this one being part of the Mother Bentivoglio Federation (Bentivoglio basically means 'I love you', undoubtedly an accidental family name, though you know that I feel that way toward you).

During our visit, we were received by the Abbess, an extremely learned and 'motherly' nun, who gave us a mini-lecture on St Francis, St Clare and the history of a fabulous organisation about which I knew almost nothing. I can't believe that there is in this world a network of centres where one can find peace while retaining inner freedom, the joy of being alive and ways of contributing to lessen the evils of mankind in various way. I was able to obtain a booklet – titled *Clare of Assisi, Light for the Way*. Quite a revelation for a woman, particularly for a person like me, a Maori educated at the edge of the world, a person afflicted by the caprices of nature, an individual raised motherlessly, a human being formed by philosophical training leading nowhere except to proffer a way of opening my mind to the beauty of spiritual life. I wish I had the time to tell you more, but I am so busy that I would sound to you confused if I were to synthesise part of the turmoil in which I find myself. Oh, brother, I feel I am on the verge of finding myself as the new millennium approaches. Just think, Clare of Assisi, a twin soul, abandoning a life of comparative leisure in order to do something for her sisters. I am tempted to do something similar. But, how? Simply, remember that I am Maori, thus I have decided to fight on my own, to fight for my gender, most of the members of which do not have the privilege and good fortune of an education like mine. Remember, half the world is women, in spite of the fact that they are tied to chains of oppression. It looks like you are fighting against the oppression of outsiders to regain political freedom. I shall be fighting against the oppression of insiders, i.e. Maori men, in order to acquire at least a modicum of wholesomeness within a liberated Ao Tea Roa. So, I count on you to help me and my sisters so that one day our *whenua* will be recognised and respected by the world community as a civilised and free country.

And here I finish by injecting into the envelope a breath of Maoriness, a token *hongi* with which I seal my love for you and Father.

Ben ti voglio,
Mahina Clara Maria

PS. I enclose some haiku I wrote during the few moments I was able to snatch away from my busy schedule. Tanya says that I should not isolate myself from the rest of humanity. What she means is that I should meet people, that is, boys, and begin to do what most girls my age do. Frankly, I don't understand the so-called 'dating' – going out to the beach, the movies and, God forbid, parties. My life can do without external influences, for I have other things in mind. Besides, not having attended high school here in the States, I cannot conceive the nearly institutional *devoir* of knowing men in the Garden of Eve. I hear horror stories about girls who, by age 16 or younger, have experimented, if not savoured, all the hedonistic and sexual aspects of life. Frankly, yes, the fleshy stuff, but how can anyone at 16 absorb the complexity of a relationship? There seems to be a rush to experience everything materialistic as soon as possible. By that age, one is supposed to have gone to a prom, the most stupid function among female teenagers trying to tell boys, 'Here I am, ready for grabs'. Then, obtain a driver's licence, begin to smoke, to drink, and to jump from bed to bed almost as a normal experimentation codified by the pulp of women's pseudo-liberation. I think that at home we, or at least I, grew up within a Victorian atmosphere of innocence. Sorry for the diversion. Here are the 'haiku' on the theme of Creation. Of course, they don't follow the classical syllabic pattern of 5/7/5, but in English it is the concept that counts, not the structure.

> angels fly
> the first dawn
> wings of light
> chasing darkness away

> God in Heaven
> on Earth his Son
> Ghost for Man
> a single breath

> Time for Eve
> the essence of life
> flows with Them
> announcing Him.

> Sun and Moon
> stars on Earth
> specks of mystery
> He knows best

> six days toiling
> one of rest
> labour of love
> void full of golden rays

So, Komaru, what do you say? Do you ever take a break from your chores in order to write, or at least read, any poetry? I remember you used to like Romantic French poetry. The Chinese girl you met in Shanghai, is she still there or has she obtained the immigrant visa to NZ? You never speak of yourself regarding things of the heart. Am I too intrusive? Is Ao Tea Roa the only love you have found on Earth? How do you relax, if at all?

Baffling sisterhood, thought Komaru. So unique in human relations! Like reflecting oneself on a magic mirror that changes a man and his personality into a female figure while everything else remains the same, untouched by optical and wishful illusions. So, a brother and a sister having in common a father, a mother, grandparents and the same family, *whenua, iwi, kainga*, language within the invisible but real boundaries of a *marae*. And, nevertheless, 'siblingness' unites and divides two individuals with the protean intimacy of blood and, at the same time, creates the most impenetrable barrier of an invisible *tapu*. But is this simply built in like a component of DNA to be one day isolated and engineered, modified in the laboratory of social expediency? Does it carry genes of aversion, of 'natural' incompatibility, of automatic rejection in the surgical attempt to transplant feelings when these are affected by the disease of hyperbonding and sanctifying the mutual trust found in no other human?

The fact that Komaru and Mahina had been separated physically for nearly four years had built up a dam through which only language could penetrate in both directions. But in this there was something adulterous, for Maori was being substituted by English. There were several reasons, one being that the former was normally used in oral interactions, the latter in graphic contacts. Basically, Maori was still in its infancy as a written medium. Mahina tried and failed, for example, to write a poem in Maori. Even when she tried, the metric forms conditioned her to follow the tradition of a superimposed means of expression reeking with Teutonic paradigms. Nevertheless, imagining a biological entity frozen in time four years past for touch, temperature, smell, dynamics, body movements, proximity with innocent and inconsequential reactions, and nevertheless an awareness of cellular similarity flowing even through solid matter and thousands of miles away – all these abstract realities pullulated in Komaru's mind whenever she appeared on the horizon of short- and long-range memory. And that happened even when Ling-ling switched from her American English to Shanghainese during the chance encounters the lovers intentionally avoided scheduling. Ling-ling had found in Komaru a transcultural tool of defying political indoctrination. She would caress him so tenderly and sisterly. And when he tried to repay her analogically, she would rarely allow him to touch her feet. Likewise, Komaru was shadowed by similar things when he interacted with Melissa, the Goddess of intellectual eroticism expressed via a mature mastery of hung flesh, like a wild deer transplanted from Europe. Its flavour was at the peak of yielding the top quality of performance as if Melissa had been conditioned by expert Japanese masseurs rubbing sake onto every square millimetre of her functional epidermis. Her brain was imprinted only externally when she lay horizontally. She had been born to live a life parallel to the level of water. There she floated to remain alive. She was devoid of verticality, which she regarded as a tool of survival only.

Why was it that Mahina intruded whenever Komaru studied femininity through Ling-ling and Melissa? That nearly oppressive feeling of being 'watched' had lately increased in frequency and intensity as a consequence of Mahina's writing to him of her most personal feelings, as if he were entitled to know, to judge, to approve and to place in storage for a common *whakapapa* made of hours, weeks, centuries, aeons of oral history for future generations. Puzzling sisterhood, ineffable, mysterious, like the Christian Sacraments she was writing about, and the connection with an entity called God to whom she was entrusting herself totally, though nevertheless keeping the bonds with the only Reti whom she was begging for help, that succor her father could not provide. Why in hell was she asking him for help when she had found God?

Was God so busy all day long that He could not take a few minutes to welcome a new acolyte? Did He not already know where Ao Tea Roa was? After all, the pope had already been there and must have informed Him of the possibility of recruiting a few more thousand ex-cannibals, or was He afraid of them once they entered the realm inhabited by tempting white angels? Oh, yes, angels. At least He could have sent some of them, even old ones, down under, under the protection of constables, the same ones who always arrested activists on 6 February to reassert their superiority. A few terrestrial chores surely could not take Him away from more important activities like amusing Himself watching CNN reports from, say, Ireland.

Thus, Komaru decided merely to acknowledge receipt of Mahina's letter in a short note since soon she would return home. What a relief to have a sister around, particularly to tend to an ailing father. But would she really relocate to Ao Tea Roa for good? It was her wish to move somewhere, to join something, and she would be returning as a different human being, mature, assertive, independent.

In spite of often detecting her attachment to him psychologically and emotionally, he felt he had lost her, the 'her' that she used to be as a young female going around the house and the garden in her pareo, exuding the Reti characteristics of innocent familiarity. He tried to visualise her thin bone structure at the wrists and ankles, her skinny thighs accidentally displayed in tending flowers in the backyard, her barely curving high buttocks, and the long, jet-black filaments of hair so light that the slightest breeze of the Tasman Sea would make them flow away from her tall forehead and, in the process, show the tiniest ears and the long delicate neck. At times, when pausing in such activities, she seemed to exude a trembling aura of expectation for something undefinable, like someone steadying her person to stand fully erect while silently smiling with wide-open sad eyes and thin lips.

And the longing gaze with which she would look at him as if her pupils would detach from her eyes to hit his face and ricochet into his innards causing waves of protective sentiment. Yes, of course, Mahina, the Moon, would shine on the Sun in the most inconceivable reflection, rejecting all the laws of physics and nature, Mahina and Komaru, the Moon and the Sun in a constellation visible even at noon when cicadas sang so loudly that the sound blanketed the beating echo of his heart.

And now Clara, clear, pure, transparent. She did not have to explain 'later' why she had chosen that name. He knew that because she had written of Clare of Assisi. But that was a medieval fable, so he believed. And, as for Maria, well, that was not a Latin plural for water bodies. There was no need to tell him why. Wasn't she Jesus' Mother? And was Mahina hoping one day vicariously to feel all the pangs of motherhood, the labour of parturition, by simply acquiring a Jewish name and thus opening herself to receive a spirit into her entrails? How? Like a spread in the centre of a pulp magazine? Or was his sister hoping to be accorded a *hyperdulia* like the original Miriam by simply becoming a Catholic? Of course, she would never marry, so she had stated. Her only hope was the cooperation of Angel Gabriel. And would Gabriel know where Ao Tea Roa was located as an afterthought of Creation at the fringe of a globe rotating askew in ...

The telephone ring interrupted his train of thought. But he did not pick up the receiver. The answering machine echoed the message left by Melissa. 'Hi! Greetings from your historical nemesis. Have you received my letter? And how did you like my PS? I hope you remembered your school Greek. Over and out.'

What in the world was she talking about? Oh, yes, her letter. Sorry, no. I had to read my sister's first. All right, Melissa, here I come. But why do women write PS's longer than the AS's? I hope you did not reject my outline.

Chapter 19

After receiving the phone message from Melissa, Komaru decided to read his father's letter first. He did not want to get upset by what Melissa may have referred to as 'historical nemesis'. The contents in the Papakura missive were mostly legal, referring to the last will and testament, power of attorney, copies of tax statements and the like. Although his father had not elaborated on the sending of documents, everything was self-explanatory. There was no question about the unsaid and unwritten. His father knew that there was not much time left. A brief letter from one of the nurses attending to his father's health actually requested that Komaru travel to Papakura in order to coordinate several things, for his father would not last more than 4 or 6 weeks. Of course, he had guessed that. There was no need to bury his head in the sand. There were things to be done, no matter what. So, although he had to present his MA thesis no later than September, he opened Melissa's letter. He had to acknowledge her message.

Dear Kom,

(Here he reflected a second, for he did not like being addressed in writing that way. Like splitting the Sun in half. Brits always tended to shorten non-English words, regardless of creating monstrosities, such as referring to Kilimanjaro as 'Kili' rather than 'Kilima', if at all, in order to avoid incongruities. Yes, the Maori Moon was fine, at least once in a lunar month, but not with the Sun. Besides, it sounded like a verb, a sort of wishful imperative just before ejaculation, when Melissa would be ready in multi-orgasmic releases and still waiting for him to gain momentum to coordinate the proper time to hit familiar shores simultaneously. She expected synchronicity, for that was for her the *summum bonum*, the *ne plus ultra*, the quintessence of split second bursting after proffering 'Come, Kom!' by biting his right ear. And she would start screaming, moaning, twisting, bouncing and grabbing his buttocks to glue his plexus to hers while her tongue would lick his perspiration, injecting 'I love the flavour of sea-salt in your sweat, and the iodine, and the glutamate of Pacific weeds.')

First of all, thank you for sending me the section on the 1980s, which concludes the enneadic abstraction of a subjective series of triads. Intriguing, challenging, refreshing. You undoubtedly reflect the rhetorical mastery of old Maori traditions. At the same time, your highly personal and subjective selection, following your Chinese superstition in numerology, is, or could be, acceptable provided that you apply those synchronic cuts in some constructive ways in order to satisfy the purpose of history (if there is any). You know that history is not a collection of facts. It should teach something. The problem is to find out what.

So far, you have presented certain facts as real, that is, on the basis of 'truth' as perceived and accepted by one segment of writers of chronicles. I bypass here the normal ambivalence of the term 'truth', namely, the consideration that truth must, *de rigueur*, embrace the world of facts AND the world of values. And here I follow theories enunciated by Professor Carr. Of course, you are not responsible for selecting the world of facts for, either real or not, this world has been entrusted to you or accepted by you for working purposes. But what about 'value'? Well, let us suppose that you float between these two poles in order to glimpse, within a golden metron, at the realm of historical truth. However, for what purpose? The 'fact' that you have a series of triads, mostly ontogenetic and inceptual (since you refer to 'births'), means that you try to warrant almost a prophetic value. Do you, being years away from 1999, plan to select three alphas and omegas? I trust you won't fall into the pit of those 'prophets' who in 999 AD saw the end of the world and fell flat on their faces. Well, I am curious to see what you intend to conclude on the basis of your synchronic stages.

It seems to me that your latent pitfall is the lack of consideration toward 'value'. Perhaps any judgement at this stage is premature, but, if you separate fact from value, what happens between decennia? Undoubtedly, many things that may not fit within your world of 'Nines'. I don't see any fluidity anywhere, and that is why I don't detect any meaning in your analysis and, consequently, no history at all. History is always on the move, i.e. dynamic, ever-changing, fluid, Heraclitean, but not *per se* as an autonomous entity. It is its 'world' that goes around events of kaleidoscopic nature because there is a tight bond between history and culture. The two concepts are siblings. And, as culture is always progressive', alive, quicksilverish, plasmic, plastic, so history envelops it in a syntagmatic fashion. When culture begins to stagnate or dies, then history becomes meaningless because at that stage the frozen concept of 'civilisation' takes over as an epitaph for dead 'facts'. One could say that history is alive only within a 'culture'. When 'civilisation' is registered in the annals of facts, then we are already coping with fossils, archaeological findings, a scholarship that allows a historian to speak of, say, Assyrian civilisation, but not culture any longer. Coming down to the end of this century, a purely artificial assumption anyway, you can even consider speaking of British civilisation, for its former dynamic forces have been swallowed by the leveling waves of post-colonialism. But, in the case of, say, America, it is simply a matter of culture on the go. The USA is still making history, whose meaning and value are difficult to grasp until 'civilisation' enters into the picture. Imagine a Doré illustrating the ruins of Washington, DC – obelisks lying in the mud, broken columns full of weeds, etc. Perhaps at that time the Chinese or the Russians will refer to the American experiment as to the civilization of the US, that cultural connection that once in the future–past took place between Washington and Hollywood, the two poles of history without value within which each ethnic group, a unique historical factor, created individual history but not THE history of a nation. All the trends of babelic political operations point out that America is like a chessboard on which its pieces move within the States only, and as such they will never be able to call a checkmate', i.e. a Nation.

Now, back to you, what have you abstracted or recovered from your 'facts'? And how do you project your findings onto Ao Tea Roa? In your first triad, for example, you speak of 'World' War I, but that was not really a WORLD war, since it was more of a civil war in Europe for boundary lines adjustments, although it did have world wide repercussions. Do you anticipate a parallel with what may take place in New Zealand? You know that some activists dream of the magic year 2000 as the year for a WHITE OUT deadline. I doubt, and you may agree, that that will be the case. That would sink the country into vacuum, for how do you relate to Ao Tea Roa *vis-à-vis* similar cases in Africa and Asia, since Europe is dying of old parochial squabbles? Have you analysed the impact of Asian revolutions, if and when you identify your struggle with, say, China, or of African revolutions because you see in Ao Tea Roa a latter-day South Africa? You see, the situation is so different, since, as we have already discussed, political and military forces are against you. And if you dare to do or organise anything you run the risk of being accused of conspiracy for the simple reason that many Maoris prefer slow integration and would not rock the boat. You would fight on two fronts, namely against Pakehas and also against Maoris. Who would come to help you, the United Nations under Boutros Boutros-Ghali? Or Tame Iti waving the flag of the Tuhoe Embassy 'Marines'?

Thus, Kom, come up any time. You can accomplish a lot for your country. But, be realistic.

As ever,
Melissa

PS. The following has nothing to do with serious matters. It derives from a conversation you had with Bill about the clitoris, that paleo-fossil that all higher mammals have in common. I doubt that my cat is aware of that and uses it to her advantage since cats' vaginas are horizontal. Usually only skilled spelunkers can find them for whatever reason. I wonder whether a typology has ever been made, and whether Mantegazza, the brilliant author of *Le Estasi umane*, ever included anything in his Leipzig Museum unless it was destroyed during the last war. I am not sure whether his studies were placed in the Institute of Zoology or the Karl Sudhoff Institute for the History of Medicine, both housed in the same Karl Marx Universität at Talstrasse 33. That Italian physiologist had shocked my Victorian compatriots so much that after the 11th edition the editors of the *EB* removed his name from any subsequent editions.

Sorry for diverging. Anyway, as you know, my father was an expert of Greek and Latin philology at Cambridge, and many years ago he got involved in the etymology of the term in question. I don't know why, but I sense that, through my mother who was concerned about my generous proportions when the case came up after my experience as a nanny, some doctors felt that I may have been injured to the point of triggering an abnormal growth. Casanova would have laughed for, according to what he wrote, he could detect anything in a few seconds of probing in the dark. Nothing was further from reality, as later ascertained by my father when, in order to trace the term in Greek and Latin, he had to study a lot of medical history.

Amusingly enough, from time to time, poets seem to be concerned with the genitive (no pun intended) of the Latin term as the nominative entered English straightforwardly. Rather unbelievably, no one thought that the term could possibly exist in classical and medieval times. I know that Arab and Chinese scholars had performed much research in that area but, then, just think what Moslems would do to hide that abnormality for obvious reasons since they have been, like the Chinese, the most 'Victorian' people on Earth for at least five centuries.

Recently, however, there has been a spasm of pseudo-Freudian interest triggered by poets and frustrated women who can't find the term in any dictionary of Greek and Latin, including the 'big' ones. Quite a pitfall! This has been compounded by the proletarianisation of the *OED*, which nowadays can be acquired or consulted for a pittance even by public school students. Look at the term yourself! What does it say in terms of etymology? '*Phys.* [a. Greek κλειτορίς, perh. f. κλεί-ειν, to shut]. Remember first of all, 'perh.',though nowadays no one ascribes any importance to the caveat and accepts the explanation as a sure thing. And that is all. The problem is that neophytes in etymological enterprises and amateur lexicologists don't know how to read or are too lazy to avoid collating typographic abbreviations to reveal the real meaning. So, 'a. Greek' does NOT mean *'ancient Greek', but adoption of, adopted from' Greek as a neologism. In English, the term is recorded not earlier than 1615, on the basis of Crooke's *Body of Man*, and referred to as one of 'these ligaments ... to degenerate into ... upon which the Clitoris claueth [closes] and is tyed'. There are other references in the *OED* connected with the faulty assumption of the meaning as 'to shut' and in modern dictionaries 'to shut up'. But, what? The labia? And how? A century later the great Venetian lover referred to it rather accurately as a finger-looking mini Frankfurter without a nail.

The problem is that the Greek κλεί- was chosen as a rough approximation of the real thing. You gave cases of homonymy, as you told me once, in connection with *kainga*. My father, however, told me that the root κλείω, 'to shut', is faulty in interpretation, though close to something involving shutting, but NOT as a verb. It is rather to be referred to κλείς in Attic (Doric κλαίς) meaning something 'which serves for closing'. Homer speaks of it as *a bar* or *a bolt*, drawn or undrawn by a latch or thong. It is also, by functional extension of similarity, *a key*, or rather a kind of *catch* or *hook*, by which the bar was shot or unshot from the outside. I think that Homer, whether a male or female, must have thought of the labia minora housing the little rascal, as did perhaps Aeschylus. In a more specific way, think of your little hook or tongue sticking out of your belt clasp, referred to in the *Odyssey* (how many times have I seen it in your belt and handled it hurriedly in the expectation of lowering your trousers?) as that metal looking nail inserted into the leather belt. I am sure you also know of another non-swivel type, i.e. the rigid and smaller one affixed to the clasp. Its function is identical.

Please take whatever I said above with a grain of salt, because there is plenty of confusion on the subject-matter among general reference material for obvious reasons. For example, the famed 1976 *Micropedia* of the *Encyclopaedia Britannica* refers to Gabriel Fallopius as the anatomist who named, among others, the 'clitoris' in *Observationes anatomicae*, along with 'vagina, placenta', etc. In Latin, of course. However, in the 1956 edition, the clitoris is not included in the list of organs 'named' by the Italian doctor. The word 'named' seems to imply that the anatomist discovered it. Wrong! This is intriguing because it looks as if the clitoris was only recognised as such in the 16th century. It is rather naïve to assume that men and women (and I feel women knew more than men for masturbatory reasons) never knew of it before Fallopius. (Incidentally, Bill tells me that another Gabriel, the poet d'Annunzio, at the end of last century referred to one of his women, Barbara Leoni, as raising a '*rosa*', that is a clitoris, so pronounced that he planned to celebrate it in a series of novels titled *Romanized della Rosa*.)

In fact, Hippocrates mentions how 'a lustful itch overwhelms her [a woman] down by her clitoris'. The Romans knew of the eleventh finger through Soranus of Ephesus during the second century CE: 'The clitoris, which stands right at the start of two lips, consists of a fleshy little button ...'. Soranus has been translated into almost every modern language except Maori. Incidentally, have you ever read Gertrude Stein's *Tender Buttons*? I am sure that Sappho sewed many buttons on her pupils, as Casanova did after reading Nicolas Venette's *Tableau de l'Amour Conjugal*, his travel guide to unexplored flesh found in convents and his own strictly raised progeny.

I am sorry I cannot be precise about the sequencing and the correlation of original terms in Western literature. Oh, I wish I knew Sanskrit, so I could read about the *Madanahatra* in the original. Anyway, research done a dozen years ago by Josephine Lowndes-Sevely, an American pioneer in the field, gives the best foundation so far on the total structure and function of the clitoris, particularly about the 'Lowndes crowns'. That constitutes the tip of the iceberg, that is, the *glans clitoridis* (incidentally, this last word being the genitive of clitoris appearing for the first time in contemporary terminology as per information found in my *Lexicon Latino-Japonicum* by Hidenaka Tanaka, which I used in Japan in place of any other English–Japanese dictionary) surfacing from 'deeper and invisible parts – unfortunately unknonw to most people'. Casanova was a spelunker at heart!

Jospehine should be crowned for that with laurel leaves. I did not know anything about that until last year, when I was able to read Rufus C. Camphausen's *The Encyclopedia of Erotic Wisdom*, in which I studied the schematic representation of a clitoris in both its relaxed and erected state. It was the most fascinating grasp of the mechanism only a few doctors know about since, unless they have a wife or a 'research' woman willing to cooperate for the sake of science – a rare case in New Zealand – they remain literally in the dark. Bill could not believe what I showed him on page 219, for in its erected state a clitoris looks like the bifid tongue of a snake. No wonder! You know there aren't any in your country.

At times I suspect that Bill married me because of my Casanova's eleventh finger, which was widely utilised in the mid-18th century in the public baths in Germany – there is nothing new along K-road in Auckland – for both interfemale relationships as well as in female–male ones. God must have thought of every detail to satisfy the needs of both *Homo erectus* and '*Femina erecta*' in Godzone. Next time you come up, Kom, I will restrain myself from attacking you immediately so that, if you are interested, you can see what I mean. Bill can have his cake and eat it, too. And I trust you are not afraid of bifid tongues. Over and out.

The last months of summer were over and out. Melissa's idiosyncrasies were becoming part of Komaru's daily language with regard to time, the illusory dimension of history. As he was beginning to take over certain business matters on behalf of his father, Komaru had paid the Land Tax Returns in early May. The second term at university had begun during the last week of the month, just before the anniversary of the first ascent of Mt Everest. On the last day of autumn he received a telephone call from his father. Mahina was scheduled to return in June, just in time for Komaru to transfer his father to the Papakura Hospice. It had been decided not to prolong his father's life through extreme intensive care at a major hospital. Just let the disease take its final course, making him as comfortable as possible through the periodic removal of fluids, injection of painkillers and psychological help until just a few days before death was expected. At that time, his father would return to his Papakura home to die, not necessarily outside his porch *more Maoro*. Not many people were expected, but Komaru agreed to perform this last request that, although anachronistic, would make his father happy.

Just before leaving Wellington during the first week of June, the Queen's Birthday Celebration, another anachronistic absurdity, came and went with a series of low key lectures in some academic departments as tradition demanded. Komaru wondered why there had never been a celebration for the birthday of any Maori who had done anything worthwhile in Ao Tea Roa. Well, how many more queens would last in order to fill the void squares of a printed Pakeha calendar? Why not celebrate Arbor Day a few days later, rather than taking vacation time from school to remember an inconsequential woman who had spent not more than a few weeks in New Zealand during her entire life in spite of being the monarch reigning over that 'autonomous' country?

Coincidentally, Arbor Day, not an official holiday, had been selected by the department of history as one for yearly lectures by distinguished scholars. That day, Professor A. S. Hill had come all the way from the University of Queensland in Brisbane to speak on a topic embracing the historiography of science. It was titled 'Giordano Bruno and Galileo Galilei in the historiography of astronomy: a study in intellectual prostitution', a rather long title that barely fitted in the space provided for announcements publicised by notices sent to local papers in order to 'celebrate' the recent official announcement by the Vatican that Galileo had been 'forgiven' for his stand against the church doctrines! Although Komaru was in no mood to attend a lecture that had nothing to offer in his area of concern, he decided to attend anyway for 'diplomatic' reasons. He was glad that he did, since at the end he learned certain aspects of historiographic correspondences that he applied to his interpretation of social and political theories between

Maoris and Pakehas. He had begun never to assume anything merely on the basis of a title.

Professor Hill attracted immediate interest in the barely half-filled convocation hall. Students were few. Most people were senior instructors from various departments. Komaru did not recognise any members of the press. A rather young looking individual, Dr Hill began his lecture by referring first to Bernard Lowell's *Emerging Cosmology*, the 1985 publication that was part of the famed series of *Convergences* under the exciting leadership of Ruth Nada Anshen. Komaru began to recollect some of the other titles, in particular Norman Newell's *Creation and Evolution, Myth or Reality*, sporting that intriguing Möbius Strip on the cover of the paperback edition. In fact, Komaru had it in his mind to analyse those two words, subtitled to Newell's work, as synonyms for his own terms such as facts, values, truth and so forth.

The introduction to Hill's lecture departed from problems confronting the world as outlined by Sir Bernard Lowell, who needed no reference or explanation. It dealt with the fate of two key thinkers at the end of the 16th century, 'neo-medieval' Europe in spite of all the advancements of science. After outlining the baffling situation in which Galileo, Bruno and the Church created a confusing climate of opinion, Professor Hill tried to place Bruno within a proper historiographic perspective, especially with regard to the rôle of Aristotle's 'science' and Aquinas' 'solution' pairing science and church dogma on Creation and the position of Earth in the Universe, as well as a host of other well-known tenets. Komaru began to understand that Hill's lecture was basically a *mise au point* for the proper position of Bruno with regard to Galileo. And, in fact, Komaru took a lot of notes with the intention of discussing the lecture with Melissa and even to inform Mahina of another negative record affixed to the crime album of a church she had just embraced. Of course, he soon realised that Mahina would not bite at that argument of discussion, but his notes proved to be relevant to Melissa when Komaru would propose a parallel between Galileo and the Pakeha Maoris (namely, *Kupapa*) on the one hand, and Bruno and *maori* Maoris on the other.

According to Hill's research, there seemed an intentionally created gap in the history of science, and specifically in astrophysics, that could be simply that of burying facts and throwing a monkey wrench into the path leading to values determined by free spirits and not by the indoctrination of ignorant masses, an intentional myth created by the very Church that had 'tortured' Galileo. None of that. After roaming along the theoretical path of philosophy, for in essence pure astronomy is philosophy coupled with mysticism, religion and ethics since it covers the Universe and Man as well, Dr Hill first outlined some 'facts'. It seemed he was going to present these facts in order to leave final judgment to the audience, particularly with regard to Bruno's acceptance of Nicholas of Cusa's theories of the Copernican system, leading later to its acceptance by Galileo.

After the lecture, Komaru rushed home and jotted down his notes in an ordered manner for himself and for Melissa. Could he apply them to understand the spurious rôle of history in upsetting the status quo of his people? Thus, he assigned a progressive number to the lecture's main topic as understood by him. It was a matter of vindicating certain rights of authorship by assigning what is Caesar's to Caesar, and so forth.

1. In 1592 Galileo, then a Young Turk, had met Bruno in Padova under mysterious circumstances. Dr Hill referred to a document in Latin secretly photographed in the Vatican Library with a Minox camera. He had admittedly betrayed, for the sake of truth, the trust and the '*confidenza*' of a liberal *monsignore* who felt that Bruno should not have been burnt at the stake, but elevated to sanctitude. Hill did not care whether the Vatican destroyed that document now, for he had a photocopy.

2. In 1599 Galileo, still idealistic and rather careless with regard to his personal safety, had tried to intercede on behalf of Bruno. At that time, there was hope that the Nolan, that is the citizen from Nola, considered by the Papacy to be a hotbed of reactionary ideas in backwoods country, would be exonerated from heresy and related accusations. In fact, while in prison, Bruno had been allowed to read his breviary ('provideatur ei de breviario, quo utuntur fratres praedicatorum'). But the Vatican had told Galileo to keep silent or else. Galileo conformed. He did not have the moral force of a monk to fight for moral principles openly and defiantly.

3. Something must have happened in the Autumn of 1599, and here there are speculations of all types. Galileo reneged on his prior attempt to support Bruno and, at that time, probably as a consequence of being 'lasciato ai cani randaggi come un rugnoso', Bruno accused Galileo of plagiarism. He had just given up on the exposition of his original concept of cosmography when he realised that, by handling Galileo with sweet threats, the Church

would ensure the destruction of Bruno's ideas and the continuation of the Ptolemaic system with the tacit consent of Galileo, although many prelates understood and accepted the Copernican system. But, no matter what, it was felt that the populace would misconstrue the new theories and that would undermine the prestige and power of the Vatican. In Hill's conclusion, the Church had to choose between a malleable Galileo and a stubborn Bruno to find a scapegoat in the post-Copernican rush of the 'new' astronomy that was rewriting the 'story' of Creation.

4. That is why, in Galileo's *Nuncius sidereus*, Bruno's original ideas are totally ignored, in spite of the fact that Bruno had been very well known since his days at Oxford. Bruno, thus, was not only a victim of the *nemo propheta* syndrome, but also a forgotten leader who had allegedly shaken the very foundation of Christianity when, in fact, regardless of sectarianism, he was a devout believer. Galileo, thus, had to save his own skin and, although pangs of remorse may have eaten him, he adapted himself to the Church's official position by not only playing the rôle of a victim himself, but also by utilizing Bruno's cosmographic conclusions. Even Kepler could not believe how North Italian dogs could eat Southern Italian foxes simply with the condiment of holy water. Martin Hasdale, among several scholars who could not understand how Bruno had been treated so unjustly, 10 years after Bruno's death wrote to Galileo asking him what his position was with regard to Bruno. Galileo ignored Hasdale's request, since the letter from Hasdale was found in Galileo's library.

5. Apparently there was no need for Dr Hill to elaborate on the case, for anyone in the audience was invited to get in touch with several scholars who believed in the philosophical and cosmographic position held by the Nolan, especially with the students of first-class research pioneers such as Antoinette Paterson and Giovanni Aquilecchia, since by now they may have been either dead or unwilling to re-exhume a hot case bordering on the otiose. Hill also referred to a work by a certain Michel, a bit outdated but well organised, as a guideline to integrate the latest theories on the rôle of supernovae in the recycling of the Universe. Bruno, long before contemporary astrophysicists, had theorised that interstellar dust must have become fertilised ('misculata') with other chemicals that had not existed earlier, as leaves ('frundae') falling from trees that would enrich logs in a forest where new

generations of trees would sprout again. Uncannily, Bruno had delineated the theory that everything, including all the atoms in our bodies, had come from the dead stars of an infinite universe. He was not actually a heretic, even though he had propounded that particular source of 'human' matter, for he was simply expanding on the fact that mortals were basically made of 'pulvere', of which atoms will again be incorporated as such into other organisms after death ... from dust to dust.

6. Dr Hill, a bit carried away by his own speech, took a semijocular position and noted that, after retiring from academia, his own 'pulvere' would be integrated into a universe possessing the advantage of immortality much better than speeches and publications. That comment caused an uproar of laughter in the audience. Hill retorted by addressing himself to a group of students, who had become vociferous, by saying that when he was younger like them he knew through Bruno what the fate of a mortal made of heavy elements would be. Now that belief had been strengthened by the latest findings that even first year students can understand by reading, say, Kaufmann's textbooks of astronomy which, though published in the States, are widely used in Australia since they are accompanied by floppy disks, something Aussie publishers are only now beginning to consider in the computer age.

At the conclusion of the presentation, Komaru was spellbound. His mind was crowded by a zillion thoughts. He almost got up to ask a question, but a student preceded him asking how one could perform research in the Vatican on that subject. Hill replied that one could try to introduce himself through the previous presentation of an official letter on proper stationery to Monsignor Fratini and ask him to show the original *documenti* published by a certain Scampanato in 1933. Anyone would immediately notice that there is an 'invisible' gap between Documents XVII and XVIII. Well, the page sequence is correct, but not the flow of the contents, for the 'complete' documentation relating to Bruno's trial was never taken to Paris by order of Napoleon. He was fooled by someone since only part of the Roman Archives was moved to France. Thus, upon the return of all documents after the 1815 Treaty, the original manuscript was never incorporated into the proper sequence. The so-called missing trial documentation was very conveniently said to have been lost during the return trip of the Archives from Paris, but that is not so because the documentation had never left Rome. Professor Hill said he was convinced that they are still in the Vatican.

Another student asked what one would do to ask for help from the United Nations. Dr Hill laughed without answering the question, though he suggested that one could do something at the personal level. 'If you ever go to Rome, please buy a bouquet of flowers and place it at the foot of Bruno's statue in Campo dei Fiori. Isn't it ironic that he was burnt there on 17 February 1600, when the first lilies begin to bloom in that very square nowadays crowded with open air restaurant tables and the fragrance of cheese and salami on hot pizzas?' He then paused and added, 'Oh, take along Swinburne's poem, originally scheduled to be read on the same day in 1889, and read it aloud in Bruno's honour. The poem was never delivered by the poet. I don't know why, though I suspect that the Secret Service of the mercenary Swiss Army must have thrown a ... Toblerone stick into the spokes of the royal wheel of political prostitution. But you can do that as one of the steps to encourage future historians of scientific thought to assign to Bruno a place of prominence, as he deserves, along with Copernicus, Kepler, Newton and Einstein. Be careful, however. If you are stopped by the Carabinieri while reading the poem, say that you are writing a thesis on the rôle of pizza in Australasian culture. They will believe you because they, having been recruited from the pit of poverty, don't want to admit their ignorance. Don't make any reference to and don't worry about Bruno up there, surrounded by the nauseating odor of burnt pepperoni and *pancetta*. He has been accustomed to broiled meat since 1600.'

That *non sequitur* was probably intended as an Australian note of humour to end a painful recollection, but the Kiwi audience remained silent. Komaru thought of pork *hangi* in Papakura. But more than that, he gained new insight to be discussed with Melissa during their next encounter. Would he be able to stop even briefly on his way to take care of his father's final days and meets Mahina at the Mangere Airport in about a week?

Chapter 20

The beginning of a severe winter loomed on the narrow horizon of the Wellington hills with a cold wind blowing prematurely and furiously along the waterfront. The preceding Winter Solstice, Komaru had resumed his exercise routine and had jogged all the way to the south edge of Freyberg Swimming Pool, from which he could see the beginning of construction for the new Museum of New Zealand. He wondered what that novel project would include for the perpetuation of the Pakeha presence in Ao Tea Roa. Meanwhile, the Overseas Terminal was nearly empty that morning. The tourist season was almost over, except for those hardy Americans enticed to visit the islands at the edge of the globe during the 'mild' season rendered more attractive by cheap travel packages including 'free' air. The fact that glacial Antarctica was a stone's throw from Wellington did not seem to deter Mid-western ranchers and Colorado rafters from scouting for sports activities rather than Maori culture in pseudo-Dutch colonies. It had, nevertheless, become fashionable to mention Polynesia's lively 'culture' by trumpeting New Zealand's natural enchantment, as if it had been imported from England along with regattas, crumpets and Stilton. Maoris could still perform acrobatic *waiatas*, chant nostalgic South Seas Protestant songs, display polychromous designs on tough skin and then collect a token emolument from the local tourism boards. Komaru hoped that the series of commercial dances would stop one day. What a charade! Why wouldn't Pakehas re-enact the Battle of Hastings?

From the north window of his apartment on Majoribanks Street, Komaru could detect the first sunlight beginning to delineate the silhouette of Mt Victoria. He took a look at the calendar posted on the bulletin board over his desk to check the official sunrise time: '7:33'. That was the shortest amount of daylight offered by nature for the day on the eve of the Winter Solstice in Australasia, a gloomy morning which carried low clouds heavy with rain. But in England, the sun rose nearly 3 hours earlier to celebrate the birth of Prince William in 1982 as marked on the calendar. Half a world away, King

William of New Zealand *in posse* was about a generation away. Komaru wondered how coincidental that date was chosen by the stars to perpetuate the reign of a monarchy. How prophetic was it for the last potential sovereign to be born at the beginning of an Aotearoan winter? The marriage situation of Charles and Diana could result in many unexpected developments, including the very demise of the monarchy as an institution. Where would Ao Tea Roa stand at the beginning of the new millennium?

Komaru hated to prophesy, but would he be able to predict what could happen at the end of the year 2000? Would his '9' theory yield any hints of change in his *whenua*? And what would his rôle be within the activist movement that he planned to design covertly? The calendar would help, for every 365 days it furnished the most powerful fighting tool, a single day called '6 February'. While other countries were affected periodically by monsoons, typhoons, tornadoes, and even the caprices of El Niño, New Zealand was inexorably subject to the '6 February syndrome' forever. In fact, even the press seemed to relax after that date. A few arrests here and there, some vociferous manifestations both in Wellington and Waitangi, minor skirmishes at the edge of potential terrorism, well, the writing was on the wall. For Pakehas the feeling of 'impending', always lingering in their minds as a threat of some sort – another Napier-like earthquake, a Yankee-produced economic depression, a disastrous fiscal policy by a new Labour government and so on – used to be a daily consideration marking seasons of social metamorphoses in the shaky life of Kiwis. Now, those threats began to be superseded by a single digit during the first week of February, as if that day could enter the calendar like the 14 July. Would there ever be a Bastille Day in Ao Tea Roa? And, if so, would that day be entered into the calendar of events currently naming only White feats? Komaru dreamed of entering the publication of 'oral' dates for the births and deaths of his ancestors, as well as the dates of battles of 'Maori' wars, aborted attempts at land 're-occupations' and the like. He dreamed in particular of having just one day marked for the abolition of the Waitangi Tribunal, the most insulting institution he could think of in the history of Maoridom. What could take place between the two annual 'Sixths' was not sketched in detail, but it was simply a matter of reversing 'Ninths' in graphs and then in deeds by making them upside down. The late 1990s could trigger more substantial actions leading to a new Aotearoa, or better the old Maoridom skinned of all transplants sucking the dignity from the roots of Polynesian culture.

On that gloomy day after the longest night of the year, Komaru indulged in a cup of strongly brewed coffee, a Pakeha habit he was beginning to acquire as a consequence of not saying no to Melissa's attempt to counteract the effects of alcohol. That was the only drug for him, besides that of Maori 'freedom'. He had admitted to himself that the *idée fixe* of liberation had already incited him to become a cunctator in order to espouse the 'cause' fully. There were a few methods of action to be selected and followed. Would he still seek a post at the Waitangi Tribunal after obtaining his MA at the University of Victoria? That meant the end of 1992 and, with the summer break in between, nothing would happen until Waitangi Day 1993. Not many 'sixths' would remain until the years 1994 and 1995 when he hoped to attract international attention. Meanwhile, one could design a national major 'distraction' in an ancient Maori location, well, one away from large population centres, but close enough to create a feeling of discomfort in both Wellington and Auckland. Rotorua was out of the question, Waitangi did not possess enough demographic support, Christchurch was too far, etc. Perhaps Wanganui would emerge as a new flagship in the flotilla of political guerrilla warfare, just powerful enough to throw Pakeha condescension off balance. The Whanaganui River was the main artery of Maori culture in North Island, and thus it could bring some interest for being a centre of tourism for both Maoris and Pakehas. Amusing, he told himself, for Melissa unknowingly seemed to have extended a hand, a Pakeha with the heart of a Joan d'Arc and the pussy of a Cleopatra. Meanwhile a position at the Waitangi Tribunal would help him study the 'system' from within and wait for developments. The main thing was never to show that there was an organised group of any kind. And, in practice, there was no such group, nothing that would warrant a conspiracy theory. Komaru alone could be the group, as unknown to anyone. There would not be any communist-type cell. Communication would not even be needed in traditional fashion. Electronics, though efficient, would be anonymous. And only Maori would be used.

Dysfunctions had to show up as if occurring in a vacuum by people who had nothing in common. Publicly, no one would know anyone else. Komaru had to be the fountainhead in any delta of organisational cadres. Then, just wait for developments and catch the moment of opportunity, even at the risk of being close to attaining a goal and then retreating for a while in order to give Pakehas the assurance of being solidly entrenched in Godzone forever. It was also a matter of conforming somewhat, and officially, even at the risk of being labelled a *kupapa*, for he knew that once known as an activist in Pakehas' eyes it would mean a revolutionary, if not a terrorist. New Zealand, being away from the foci of bloody discords, was supposed to be safe except for physical earthquakes. No one really thought of political earthquakes for, as for potential threats of flood at high tide, where would Kiwis retreat from high waters? There was a joke about it attributed to an American visitor: 'Where do you go when the tide comes in?' Komaru doubted the 'tide' referred to anything other than the physical.

While sipping a cup of coffee made in a phoney 'espresso' machine, Komaru wrote down a list of possible manifestations, happenings, demonstrations and the like waiting in the wings. It was a matter of increasing not only the frequency but also the type of something that had never taken place before. For example, spitting on the face of a prominent dignitary at a high-profile gathering would be internationally more meaningful than injuring anyone through force. Thus, he wrote down at random what the year 2000 might witness both in Ao Tea Roa and within himself, not discounting events on a global scale.

1. Sixth of February demonstrations as an ever-increasing lymphatic cancer spreading through down trous, booing, disruption of speeches, brainwashing women into having a rôle in speaking at official meetings (Maori women in particular), and similar actions by seizing the opportunity waiting in the wings, particularly in the presence of foreign dignitaries who had been told that race relations in New Zealand were the best in the world.

2. The end of British Empire outposts (Hong Kong, Diego García, the Falklands, etc.).

3. The demise of the monarchy (that is, family scandals, accidental fires in institutional buildings, interruption of traditional parades or the changing of the guard at Buckingham Palace).

4. The surge of Arab nationalism and related Islamic movements in Algeria, Egypt and particularly in Iraq.

5. The development of American imperialism through economically strong policies via the United Nations and against people's wishes, which would be more efficient than during the Vietnam era because of instant internet communication.

6. The return of Russian 'patriotism' and consequent Romanov-style political strife in order to check ethnic expansionism by anyone, as in Bosnia.

7. The unknown Chinese card in a new game involving Japan, Australasia, Russia, and the USA in particular through cash contributions to political campaigns. 'Cher Napoléon, la Chine s'est réveillée.'
8. The Latin-American spread of political revolution causing social upheavals in the USA.
9. The European chess game on the board of EURO currency and its economic disaster caused by 'Oriental' and Latin American market failures.
10. The African caper at the doors of Israel after the removal of an Egyptian UN Secretary General.

Then, what? For the time being, nothing! Just wait and see. Nevertheless, Komaru would not be surprised, if he lived long enough, to see something like the following as wishful thinking:

1999 –   Death of Global Colonialism
           Triumph of Arab Nationalism
           Birth of Ao Tea Roa

These semi-prophetic 'headlines' in Komaru's anticipation of events were large umbrellas under which he detected the possibility of several collateral developments. Thus, say, under the Death of Global Colonialism he saw a total reshuffling of the political situation in the Persian Gulf area, whether Saddam Hussein was still in power or not, for the Bush campaign had resulted in a pyrrhic victory. Morally and legally, Iraq aspired to re-acquire what British colonialism had imposed on that troubled area since before the First World War by fragmenting the sovereignty of nations into a dozen little states and emirates.

Kuwait was just one case in point. British guarantees of freedom, with American support, meant simply 'BP', that is, British Petrol. An oil glut would reduce the cost of petrol at the pump by 50%. Meanwhile, embargo policies on food and medicines were taking a heavy toll on the populace of Iraq, just to mention one instance, while a few miles away rulers were swimming in billions of dollars in spite of praising the same Allah.

Komaru tried to reflect on why Arab nationalism had suddenly stepped up its activities in order to assert the traditional values of a Koranic 'democracy'. That meant the propagation of geopolitical extremism along a vast arc from Algeria to Indonesia. But, on the one hand, how could he witness the turning of an Arab–Islamic axis disregarding the social conditions separating oil-rich nations from starving ones? Was Allah so callous, like the Christian God, allowing for infighting and misery among countries praising Him nevertheless? What kind of world was this? In the midst of global dysfunctions leading to new alliances as a palliative to avoiding cataclysms, what could Maoris do to take advantage of the political situation? Had they reached a point of no return similar to that suffered by American Indians, now under the spell of token capitalistic coins tossed at them to buy alcohol, drugs, and suicide? If the American Indians would never reach a minority independence from majority oppression, did that necessarily mean that the Maori cause would fizzle out *ab initio*? There was clearly a disadvantage, at least in terms of 'genetic' proportion, that is, 10 per cent Maori versus 90 per cent Pakeha. On the other hand, the moral rights' majority was absolute, although no-one thought that international organizations would take the Maori side simply on the basis of morality, except for Libya, Iran and South Africa. Then, what could one do? Organise an inter-island Polynesian force to one day take over the original *whenua* in a concerted war of liberation? Komaru was clearly unsure about what to do. There was no question, meanwhile, that he was being influenced by his readings covering the historical accomplishments of Mao, Khadafy, Castro, Abimael Guzmán and even Saddam Hussein. But this automatically implied the use of violence, the same violence that even Captain Cook despised after seeing its 'civilising' effects on the Polynesians when he said 'it would have been better for these people never to have known us'.

So, Komaru reviewed why the typical phrase 'senseless violence' was used time and again by pacifists and skilled politicians, who were also hiding behind weapons of mass destruction, from the chemical to the biological to the nuclear. Could it be that a select group of 'invisible' patriots could bring three million Pakehas and all their institutions of oppression to their knees? He began to tell himself that, however inhuman and deliberate violence might be or become, the only thing it could not be is senseless. From one course on the history of Italian political unification, Komaru remembered Giuseppe Mazzini, himself a pacifist and a thinker, who had stated that 'violence could serve only one of two purposes: either straighten a wrong or destroy a lie'. Thus, could political violence be used for a specific purpose? In Ao Tea Roa, for which of the many goals could it be employed? To force a majority government to yield its power in favour of total Maori control? Well, the ETA and the IRA were good examples of deleterious effect among many. Where had they led, since they were basically devoid of racial components? In New Zealand, the situation was as unique as it had been more than a century ago in the USA. The Indians had failed. Was it too late for the Maoris? Komaru did not think so, because, unlike the American Indians, the Maoris had the most potent ally on their side, namely, language. As long as Maori was alive as a tool of communication in everyday activities, it would constitute the moral foundation of liberation. But how could Maoris, to start with, stop using English and switch to their maternal tongue? And, starting from where? Well, the best and most possible platform was the Waitangi Tribunal, where all transactions must be made in Maori. Too bad if Pakehas did not know the language. Shakespeare could go to hell in Irish, as well as Cervantes in Catalan and Euskera countries, and ... here Komaru had a problem. Whom could he assign to France? He failed to name anyone comparable with a Dante. Obviously, a Molière or a Hugo would not do. Simply, France did not have a Luther or a Camões. There was no question that, in spite of his speculations, Komaru was confused when analysing his actions, for he was against violence in spite of his being convinced philosophically that this was the only way to achieve Maori independence. Indeed, emotionally he had inherited from his father an aversion to war of any kind, for the genes of pacifism had been born in the trenches of the Italian campaign and carried all the way back to The Hermit Islands. He wondered how Ao Tea Roa could be born from the ashes of shame as an independent nation without violence. Gandhi was his master in political matters. On top of that, Komaru's extensive readings in Sufism were emerging on the horizon of his spiritual existence subtly, though visibly. He was in a mess, especially when he thought of Gandhi, who succeeded in his final goals *malgré* the oblivion sanctioned yearly by a chameleonic Nobel Prize committee.

In fact, Gandhi had never received the Nobel Prize for peace and its collateral implications. Komaru was convinced that this was the result of discriminatory policies since, after all, 'Peace' astride the Second World War was a 'white' one. Indeed, Komaru made a quick analysis of the Gandhi phenomenon of non-violence to see why the Scandinavian mentality could not operate outside the boundaries of Europe. In the process, he found out that Norway did not give a damn about Gandhi's pacifism and India's independence. Although nominated several times by several Quaker organisations, Gandhi was put aside as before on behalf of white American and European candidates with the exception of Carlos Saavedras Lamas, a Pakeha nevertheless, in 1936. The northern latitude factor of skin darkness tended to stop at Oslo. In essence, the Nobel Committee was a pawn in the hands of British politicians. Only later, starting in 1960 with Albert Lutuli of South Africa (ironically the country where Gandhi became philosophically and ethically a pacifist) did Norway begin to patronise Third-World countries.

That 21 June was for Komaru a fatidic day in terms of introspection, though he knew that this is a form of lunacy. It had been a day of psychic tension, for a telephone call from the day nurse taking care of his father at the hospice suggested that Komaru return to Papakura since the attendants could not handle the 'Reti case' any longer unless authorised to take forceful action of some kind. His father wanted to die at home, and in fact one night he had disconnected the intravenous needles after suffering two haematemeses and had eluded the ward security system and escaped. He was caught in Ao Tea Square in Auckland when a constable had spotted him wearing an old army coat over a blue hospital gown. Nearly frozen and dehydrated, he was returned to the hospice by force and was given sedatives pending Komaru's return as soon as possible, no later than 28 June, about the time that monthly second War Pension and War Veterans disbursement were due to cover some extra confinement costs. In addition, Komaru's driver's license was due for renewal the following week, when he had scheduled a meeting with his thesis advisor for the penultimate presentation of a draft for his MA. He called the secretary and begged her to reschedule that meeting due to his father's condition. This way perhaps Komaru could meet briefly with Melissa on his way to Papakura. He felt he had organised his immediate responsibilities and he sensed a wave of psychological relief. Yes, he operated best under stress, the only positive factor experienced by Pakeha civilization to the point of leading Kiwis to suicide, for his Maori philosophy tended to spur him along at a more sedate, though efficient, speed. Then, out of nowhere, for he had almost forgotten Mahina, the phone rang and a cable was read to him: 'WILL ARRIVE MANGERE 10:05 AM JUNE 27 NZ 51 MAHINA'. That gave him a punch in his bowels, literally, for he had to go to the toilet. He had hoped in a flash of impulsive selfishness that she would stay much longer in America. What could a young sister who had spent 4 years in an environment of almost protective custody do except add another dimension of responsibility? He did not need another element of caretaking amid all the problems he had at hand. Then he reflected that she could help sort out and solve some of them. Indeed, he was going to assign to her a list of tasks to be performed in the Reti household, things typical of feminine traditions. It was high time that a woman helped him. After all, he was a busy man, with important responsibilities to be fulfilled. Mahina had none. She could begin to assume a rôle of domestic cooperation, taking overs, boring household chores. Thus, he decided to advance his trip and left Wellington in a matter of hours.

The long drive from Wellington to Papakura offers the motorist some fantastic scenery of natural wonders, particularly near the tract beginning halfway between Wanganui and Taumarunui. Just before entering Okahune from the south, the three peaks of Mt Ruapehu, Mt Ngauruhoe and Mt Tongariro detach themselves from the myriad of lesser peaks from which hundreds of streams flow in all directions between Motorways 1 and 4. Having so many things on his mind, Komaru tried to concentrate on driving, but reminiscences paraded in front of him. It was the first time, during the winter, that he had paid special attention to the setting of wonders. He simply could not forget the many outings during his youth to the first national park established more than a century earlier. And, driving in late June at the bottom of Mt Ruapehu, he took extra care whenever ice appeared here and there from the first snowstorm of the season.

Although he was in no mood to meet with Melissa that afternoon, he felt that a short break, and possibly spending the night at the McTavishes, would offer a diversion before tackling the rest of the trip along the rather monotonous segment before and after Hamilton. He wondered why he had developed a high historical consciousness of Maoritanga that, on the one hand, gave him a purpose in life, while on the other hand it bound him to a 'mission impossible'. Would it not be better and more pleasant to get a teaching certificate and then secure a post somewhere in either Palmerston North, Wanganui or New Plymouth around the western semicircle of the mighty 'Ruapehu God' in a small community where he could get married, raise a family and enjoy a life that almost any citizen of an industrial society would envy? That is what Dr McTavish had done after having been in search of that chimera in several parts of the world. After all, New Zealand was still the Eldorado of the new Millennium for whites.

No, it was too late. The reflection of Komaru's life so far within a Maori family oppressed politically by a superimposed alien society would not allow him to spend the rest of his existence living a slow death for hedonistic purposes. He thought of Bill, and speculated about that bloke who had accepted a position in Wanganui in order to work in an area that tasted of youthful life and premature death. Indeed, Bill was the official psychiatrist for the Wanganui area and in charge of research investigating the problem of suicide in Godzone. Unexplainably, while nature seemed to offer humans a vast resource of wonders forever in still pristine surroundings, it also witnessed the scourge of suicide. Dr McTavish lately had vaguely mentioned his task in the ex-laundry shed where no one was allowed to enter except him. His work was low profile and 'classified' for he detested the press, always ready to investigate and magnify accidental and 'incidental' deaths in morbid details. Now Komaru began to understand that Bill had found in Melissa an anchor of mental sanity among a rough sea of ineffable behaviour. Their lifestyle seemed to compensate for an otherwise absurd continuation of boring routine. Thus, although Komaru preferred to avoid stopping in Wanganui and not to socialise with anybody, he felt obliged to visit the McTavishes as a sign of respect, trust and, mainly, of friendship. Most of his friends and distant relatives were in the Auckland area, since his stay in Wellington for study purposes had created only a small group of acquaintances frequenting the Turnbull Library and the Waitangi Tribunal.

When he stopped for petrol in Turakina, about 20 kilometres south of Wanganui, he rang the McTavishes apologising for being unable to inform them earlier about his arrival. Bill picked up the phone. He was happy to hear from Komaru. Why not have supper, rest overnight and proceed for Papakura the following day? Oh, how is Melissa? Just fine. She had left that morning for Okahune with a group of ladies who liked to ski near that charming town. The ski slopes had just opened a couple of weeks before, and Melissa felt like tasting the exhilaration of physical activity on the south slope of Mr Ruapehu. Bill would have done the same during the week, but he simply could not leave his work midway. His job could engage him 24 hours a day between counselling, preventing, participating in meetings, and even attending funerals in order to console survivors professionally. Besides, he chuckled, Melissa would probably enjoy participating in après-ski activities at the Big Carrot, patronised by both Kiwis and international ski bums.

Komaru took a moment to understand why Bill had stressed the '*Big Carrot*' hangout. Then he laughed when he remembered that the main Okahune attraction, besides being a 'winter' town, was the production of carrots, the best, the largest ever produced in New Zealand. Bill told him how Melissa shopped for the most phallic-looking ones in town, bringing them home for one- or two-week supply of vitamin A. Freud, of course, would be at home in Okahune's *Big Carrot* anytime. Bill, however, enjoyed preparing supper by combining loin of pork and carrots julienne in white wine at extremely slow heat. He would have preferred to use rich milk, but for Komaru's sake he used wine. Almost at the end of the cooking cycle, Bill would toss in sliced *harore*, that is, Maori mushrooms (*Agaris adiposus*) that tasted much better than the ones introduced by immigrants, namely, *A. campestris* or *harore pakeha* 'food of the Pakehas'. Bill had just got last autumn's crop of that indigenous mushroom. There were two relevant items of cultural history associated with that 'Maori food' that no decent Pakeha would touch with a 10-foot pole. But Bill was always excited whenever he could discover and utilise something that non-European brainwashed Epicureans could still find at that pristine culinary stage. One was the proverb *He hirore rangitahi*, meaning literally 'A one-day mushroom' or, in Kiwian language, 'A flash in the pan', one that Froggy gourmets of peasant stock would consider a *feu de paille*. After all, it is a fact that the truest expressions of wisdom go back to agricultural activities.

The other item was more 'literary' with a long tradition pointing to the faulty diet based solely on that mushroom, not dissimilar from the trumpeted polenta eaten by Northern Italian 'gourmets' and Southern Italian swines, for south of Rome maize was and is used only to fatten pigs. In fact, Bill had never been able to find a single polenta recipe in any 'Southern' cookbook, except in a veterinarian manual issued by a nutritional laboratory in Palmerston North for feeding Circe's pets. No wonder that across the Po Valley people would die of pellagra, while south of the Tiber they would thrive on healthy food such as pizzas laden with extra virgin olive oil, garlic, tomatoes and greens, the traditional enemies of cholesterol. It was so funny when in the kitchen Bill and Komaru tried to unravel the current mania that New Zealanders had recently adopted under the influence of Aussie cooking, namely, the fashion of using extra virgin olive oil, the only virgin thing left in Australia after immigrants from south of Rome had been allowed to populate a former colony. But in New Zealand, Kiwis had gone beyond the theme of simple virginity reflected in the Italian mania for the Virgin Mary. That Freudian matter of 'patenticity' was so rare in Auckland's teenage circles that people shunned the simple virgin oil in favour of the 'double' variety. That way, one could be sure that an alternate locus of virginity would be guaranteed to purists in the kitchen and the bedroom.

Bill enlightened Komaru by informing him that a Wanganui poet had composed a catechistic Maori diet, that in English could be adapted as follows:

> Who will eat the *harore*?
> Who will eat the ripe *tawa* kernel?
> Who will eat the pungent *hinau*?
> Like the rat, my mouth seeks food.
> My mouth that gobbles the *kumara*
> so that the tidings reach even
> Tuwhara, northwards to Parikaniki,
> sitting on top of the *wharawhara*.

Komaru detected in the poem echoes of a cannibalistic *Song of Songs* through pangs of desire, and Bill agreed though he did not know what *wharawhara* really meant, for he had assumed it was a geographic designation. Komaru explained it was a tree-clinging epiphyte plant. Bill loved the mushroom prepared Maori style, that is, without peeling it, thus retaining most of the vitamins, and he would serve it at barbecue parties after steaming it in a small reed basket placed on top of an earth oven he had found in his backyard, next to his 'lab', a leftover from the previous landlord. The taste was intriguing when blended with the sweet sliced carrots and *kumara* with a morsel of lean pork filet. At times, Bill admitted cheating in traditional Maori cooking by employing the microwave oven, which he would first place at high power for 7 or 8 minutes. Then he would wait until the pork filet cooled before slicing it and finally broiling it quickly after seasoning the dish with a touch of sea salt, olive oil and Mediterranean capers.

While waiting for Melissa to return from her skiing outing later that afternoon, Bill and Komaru relaxed by listening to Bach, who for Komaru was a revelation. Beethoven was more consonant with his temperament but, after being exposed to Venetian Baroque composers, Bach would slowly sink into his *forma mentis* in order to confer upon his bowels a host of feelings, almost a psychological preparation to tone him down in anticipation of Melissa's arrival. And they talked about Mahina, too. Of course, Bill could understand Komaru's frame of mind on his way north to meet death and life.

His father was going out of his system, his sister was coming in. They both recalled a proverb – *E tata mate, e roa taihoa* – 'Death is close compared to the latecomer'. And death was the subject-matter as Bill sipped a glass of white wine, while Komaru had some fruit juice. Bill tried to engage Komaru in a conversation but it ended in a monologue, almost a lecture stemming from reflections of his daily activities. That ended at dusk when Melissa stormed in bringing life.

Bill had never been so open before, almost as if he were in need of reaching another human being beyond his professional contacts. He felt he could trust Komaru, who represented some sort of enigma, perhaps a latent case of Attention Deficit Disorder. Whom else could he trust in Wanganui, an old Maori centre of pristine culture submerged by tenets of sweet religiosity that kept Pakehas from going insane? After sharing his bed in a saga of pure sybaritism with Komaru months earlier, Bill saw in him a psychological clone whose DNA structure was absurdly younger and yielding to sexual enterprises.

In talking about death lingering around him like a cloud of a most tangible reality, Bill first mentioned a certain Rick Stevenson, whose son Michael had killed himself a couple of years earlier on a beautiful beach not far from Papakura. Komaru had read about it, but had not paid much attention to the case. The press had stressed the quiet sunset creating an atmosphere of almost eternal peace. Could it be that Michael had been bewitched by the phantasmagoric palette of colours slowly fading on the horizon? Bill was working on a statistical chart of eternal 'enticements' present at the moment of suicide, such as idyllic places, screaming silence, kaleidoscopic hues sinking in the Tasman Sea, the mesmerising murmur of the ocean, the soft breeze smelling of Australia, the sun setting far away from the confines of a claustrophobic island longing for a big one, so big that, while Greenland was an island, Australia was a continent. Geographers could really be a bunch of discriminating sadists, though, no matter what, New Zealand could never aspire to be a continent. The ironic deduction from such a comparative analysis resulted in an explainable situation for, after all, England, the Mommy country, the home, the grown-up angel protector to look up to, was only half the size. Thus, what was it that made New Zealand so insecure?

Statistical analysis showed a tentative curve in regard to the age of suicide, namely between 16 and 28. That was the dozen years encompassing the most dangerous span of life. And Bill was not too puzzled by the fact that Michael was only 27 years old. He had been raised in an ideal, almost perfect family under the wings of state-run social services from birth to death, except that death was not supposed to take place that early. At that rate, New Zealand births would be offset by deaths. A nut for sailing, which Bill understood as a latent wish to escape from The Hermit Islands, Michael was also an explorer, a traveller, and a dreamer about distant and exotic places. He exuded the typical love of Kiwi youth with virtually unlimited possibilities under the aegis of a 'British' passport in order to spend life roaming the waters, an activity that only those who regularly spend the last week of January in Auckland could understand fully.

But Mr Stevenson could not understand why Michael had chosen that way out. Did he carry genes going back to the author of *Treasure Island*, whose bones rested on an island not too far from New Zealand? Out of what? That is what Bill was trying to uncover from the many cases crowding his lab computer. Michael had just returned from Japan and the USA where he had savoured the many aspects of dynamic life ranging from the mysterious conservatism of the 'Orient' to the limitless experimentation of Hollywood. Could it be that Michael, upon returning home, had felt constrained by proto-immigrant 'Calvinism', limited cultural resources, vociferous criticism in the press for *faute de mieux*, lack of immediate contact with the vibrant culture of America, and now even of Australia, not to mention a more remote Europe where his genes had been born? Bill spoke of a syndrome tentatively labelled 'hypernesitis', an *angina mentis* stemming from a combination of delusions of grandeur and the grim reality of isolation.

It was rumoured, and history at the basis of any research is an unrefined distillation of rumours, that a main concern among Pakehas was the anguishing feeling of alienation from an invisible underpinning of uncertainty for the future, any future, at the bottom of the Earth. The feeling was not unlike that of a soldier facing the enemy in a trench, or of a temporary employee in any job, or of a spouse noticing the impending misery of a divorce in spite of a unique love binding a couple. Uncertainty was always the Cinderella of hope before suicide. Was it the realisation that a single voyage by air anywhere except Australia, and in particular Europe, the psychological Kursaal for an ailing heart, would cost about 3 months of an average salary in any Kiwi profession, including medical doctors, who were paid less than a panel beater in a good car repair shop? That chronic anxiety of insecurity contributed to the formation of a nearly endemic series of suicides, without counting the sorrow affecting an individual, especially a woman, failing it at the rate of 80 per cent in Pakehadom.

Well, for Bill it was only a theory. The problem was more acute with regard to Maori youth who, yes, in the past saw no immediate tangible improvement in their daily life, in spite of bilingual radio education programmes, and even a proposed TV station, all in Maori. Recently, they felt encouraged by the conviction that it was not a matter of 'improving' their status within the Pakeha framework of race relations. It was a matter of totally changing everything and realising that, after all, New Zealand had been their land, their soul, their 'everything' since time immemorial. There was no middle way. Thus, the reason for suicide may have been different, for a Maori did not seem to aspire to return to Hawaiki as a Brit would aspire to 'go home'. Basically, Maoris could not go back anywhere, for they had always been in Ao Tea Roa.

Regardless of motives, both New Zealand and Ao Tea Roa were embarked on a ship destined to sink somewhere in the middle of a silent ocean for, in spite of morbid press accounts, no one offered any help. Something had to be done, as for AIDS, and in the open. Mr Stevenson had talked with Bill about a project he would like to initiate in a few years, when he could devote the rest of his life to a campaign to stop that waste of resources decimated by epidemic suicide. The fact that Wanganui's civic leaders had chosen the establishment of a 'preservation centre' was significant, for per capita Wanganui competed with many other towns for that dubious primacy. Still, why? What was there in common, if anything, among Maoris and Pakehas now bound in a self-destructive enterprise when officially between them there was supposed to exist the best race relations in the world? It seemed that these relations had to be uncovered from the depths of a sand bank into which the heads of political leaders preferred to hide their impotence to deal honestly with the problem. The only thing that Bill had so far uncovered in common among suicides was simply youth, an age factor, as in some Indian reservations in South Dakota. Nothing else, but Komaru sensed that he, as a man younger than Michael, could understand something undefinable seething in his bowels. In order not to influence Bill, however, he did not say anything. He did not want to inject any personal observation that only Bill, as a psychiatrist, could and should uncover or discover along scientific lines for constructive reasons. It would not have been fair to distract him from his work, particularly since he believed that most psychiatrists work as such in order first to help themselves and then their patients, if at all, by the reflection of their own malaise.

And he was grateful to Melissa for interrupting that gloomy topic of conversation, for she had stormed in, full of sensuality, all tanned, exuding vitality from every pore, optimism for the most immediate aspects of reality. Undoubtedly, she was undergoing the 'high' cycle of her bipolar disorder, a generic term for which psychiatrists could do little, nothing more than dispensing experimental pills and tablets to naïve patients. Komaru wondered if, rather than medicine, these patients would be better off taking a couple of courses in philosophy, spiritualism, or even yoga of some kind. But then pharmaceutical companies would go broke. And Melissa was so tender when she hugged him, looking into his eyes inquisitively, almost searching for reassurance that he was there, a few centimetres away, just for her to grab. For her, Komaru was the other half missing in Bill, that half of vague romanticism, unspoiled sensuality, healthy sentimentalism, the whole contained within a still untarnished naïveté in human relations that Maoris had kept nearly intact for thousands of years, untouched by Pakeha mental dysfunctions.

Komaru briefed her on his ongoing trip to Auckland, on his father's final days, and even, as an afterthought, his sister's return.

'Oh, yes, sorry, I forgot, what is her name?'

'Mahina.'

'That means Moon in Maori, doesn't it? I remember now.'

'Yes, correct.'

'And you are Komaru, the Sun, right?'

'Right.'

'Of course, and you are the Sun of my life, of our lives, is he not, Bill?'

'Of course he is. Quite something potentially ready for an eclipse if you consider yourself as Terra. After all, you are a Taurus, an earth sign.'

At that Melissa left the kitchen for a shower. She often felt soiled by the humus of existence, and thus she needed to cleanse her skin with water and her mind with something else. On her way to the bathroom, she stopped by the landing, stripped naked from the après-ski outfit, and bent over the *kauri* railing of the upper floor. Her breasts looked like two white half melons to ripen in the sun on a frame full of red earth, for she must have skied wearing only a bra for the upper part. She cupped them tenderly, almost as if a proffering them to a starving child hungering for mother's milk.

'You know, Kom, I am dying to meet your sister. How old is she? You said 23? Am I correct? Oh, I need a double. Daaaling! Did you get another bottle? Oh, the carrots. I left them in the back seat of the automobile. I'll get them.'

'If I may, I can do that for you,' interrupted Komaru. He was afraid she would not think twice about going *au naturel* to the car parked in the driveway. Bill shook his head.

'Melissa at times abstracts herself from the whole world, especially when you are around. You know, she loves to play with you.'

What a world, he thought while descending the steps leading to the garage and the driveway. For how long could that type of world offer humans whatever they could grasp in order to survive in a baffling life of unknowns?

Chapter 21

The candlelight supper *à trois* began to develop in a sedate atmosphere permeated by random classical music from the FM radio programme. At dessert, Bill left the table to prepare individual *crêpes* filled with kiwi fruit and rich ricotta, the whole flat cylinder covered with a light sauce made of mascarpone and maraschino liqueur. Just before bringing one to Melissa, he sprinkled it with warm Cardhu and then flambéed it in a ceramic dish. Melissa appreciated it with her usual exclamatory 'Oh, daaaling!' expression of affection, gratitude, and admiration. Komaru was simply transfixed by the synchronism of fragrance and pyrotechnics. Schubert's *Die Forelle* quintet had just ended its second movement of piano scales and drifted into a slower pirouette of softer rhythms and melodies.

'Honey, please start. Eat it while hot. I'll bring one for Komaru in a sec.'

'Remember, his lactose ...'

'Yes, of course, I'll prepare a special one for Komaru, and the alcohol will disappear, you know, just the flavour.'

'Thank you, Bill, I will try anyway.'

Bill went back to the gas range behind the counter dividing the dining area from the kitchen and placed a few spoonfuls of batter into the hot pan. In a few seconds the semiliquid mix had coagulated. Bill then assembled the same dish *sans* ricotta and mascarpone. When brought to Komaru, he waited for Bill. Melissa had barely begun to nibble at the dish, for she felt full. She had indulged in the mushrooms.

'Oh, dear!'

In bringing a forkful of *crêpe* to her mouth, a small piece had fallen on her right breast. She had worn just a light bra to support her still sensitive mammas, for her skin, burned by the unwise exposure to the reflection of sunshine on fresh snow, had begun to hurt. A tiny rivulet of soft cheese had lingered just above her right nipple after a piece of *crêpe* and two or three kiwi seeds had lodged at the top of her breast.

'Dear me! Am I becoming so sloppy?'

Komaru, seeing her predicament, refrained from carrying the first forkful of dessert to his mouth. Bill was just sitting at table on her left. Komaru saw the little whitish stream of the *crêpe* filling pause a second on Melissa's tit, then circle it on both sides, and finally drip onto the edge of the tablecloth.

'May I help you?' asked Komaru in a matter-of-fact intonation.

'Oh, thank you! Yes, please, gently. My skin is burning.'

Komaru got up, approached her from the back under the scrutiny of Bill's amused smile, and began to delicately wipe Melissa's teat with the tip of the serviette. In the process, Komaru had to lift part of the bra, a black laced contraption, contrasting shockingly with the white hues of her skin. And the redness all around her bosom created almost an image of something Komaru had seen in a photograph. Where? He suddenly remembered. In an art book he had consulted after Melissa had told him the story of St Agatha, the virgin and martyr.

'I'm sorry, Melissa, it must be an extremely sensitive area.'

'Yes, Kom, and, oh, so tickling. Oh, Komaru, your fingers are so hot. My, hell, please Kom, unhook the bra. Do you mind, Bill?'

'Not at all. As long as you feel more comfortable.'

Komaru unhooked the metal clasp from the back of her shoulders, helped her raise her arms, and removed the brassiere, folding it and hanging it on the side of a chair. The concert programme was now beginning to broadcast *Fidelio's* overture.

'I feel better. Poor Agatha! I can only imagine how she must have suffered, not only in the process of having her breasts extirpated, but also enduring those few minutes of roasting before passing out. Daaaling, how long do you think she kept abreast, sorry, remained aware of her predicament?'

'Difficult to say, because the excision of her bosom would have placed her in a state of shock, what we in ER call "flash trauma". Who knows? The amazing thing is that Catanians who have never experienced even the scalding of a finger touching a hot pan tend to make a mockery of suffering, unless remembering the tales of horror recounted by the survivors of Etna's lava and ashes.'

At Komaru's inquisitive look, Bill pushed his dessert dish away, served brandy in a large snifter to Melissa, and poured half a glass of muscatel for himself. Komaru played with a glass of mineral water while waiting for a cuppa.

'I was referring to what I had read some time ago in a book by

Carol, oh, Carol who? Carol, *adeste fideles*, Carol ... Fields, no Carol Field. A most intriguing title, yes, *Celebrating Italy*, rather ambiguous. Does she mean "Italy that celebrates" or "he who celebrates Italy"? Excuse me, just a second.'

He picked up his own dishes and Melissa's and took them to the kitchen. Komaru followed suit, leaving them by the sink. By the time they returned, Melissa had drained her brandy, and had cupped her left breast with the empty glass.

'Oh, daaaling, it feels so refreshing!'

Bill gingerly removed her glass. He was afraid that she might hurt herself. Nothing more. He was accustomed to her idiosyncrasies involving anything that she could adapt to and into her body – vegetal and electronic, including toothbrushes protected by a condom. Then he went to the bedroom and brought a book.

'Do you care, Komaru, to take a look at this passage while I soak the dishes? I know the Sicilian folklore nearly by heart. Here, page 11. I wonder whether you Komaru, as a Maori, can find any correspondence between your ancestors' traditions and those perpetuated by ... Christianity.'

'Daaaling,' interrupted Melissa, 'do you mind if we leave the table for the rumpus room? We could have a cuppa there. Not for me. Just a little more brandy, please, later.'

Thus Melissa and Komaru walked to the lower floor, where she slouched on the sofa and he sat comfortably in an armchair.

'Komaru, please turn off that megalomaniac. At times he strikes me as a pompously erudite musicoid. Why in the world did he have to dabble in opera? Leave opera to deranged Italians steaming off in bombastic performances! Thank you, Kom. That *Fidelio* was none of Beethoven's business. Even in the *Ninth*. Why end it with a mixed bag of symphony and chorus, making the whole thing ... psuedo-operistic ... Italianate minestrone? And the "Ode", ode to whom? To himself? And do you think that humans can assimilate a message from those sentimentaloid notes? Sorry, go ahead. Agatha, Bill said, page 11.'

Komaru glanced at the last paragraph, read it quickly, and summarised it for Melissa.

Apparently Italians believe that 'eating is a powerful way of consuming God.' Here, next, 'So, the Italians reason, if you can eat the body of Christ, why not eat ... the breast of a saint (*i minni di Sant'Agata*) or "the little pricks" of the angels (*i cazzetti degli angeli*) ...'

'My goodness, Komaru, sorry, I am falling asleep, but do go on, read some more ... oh. How exciting! You could eat my *minni* and ... do you mind, Kom, oh, I could do likewise with your *cazzetti*, sorry, you have only ... one. I think that you have an -*o* at the end, don't you? Oh, I am tired, oh ...'

Komaru continued reading that the breasts of Sant'Agata (S Agatha) are made, like the eyes of Santa Lucia, of concentric circles of golden durum wheat filled with marzipan. By that time, Melissa had fallen asleep. Strange, Komaru thought, the French like different shapes for desserts, like the tubular, near phallic forms detected in Bill's crêpes, and not the profane caricature of S Agatha claiming her own sliced-off breasts like mortadella. Apparently, according to Carol Field, the Holy Office had not forbidden those victuals. Bill had just come in. Komaru motioned to him that Melissa had fallen asleep. But he showed him the top of page 12. The last sentence of the first paragraph was simply an introduction to repressed cannibalism or Freudian masochism for it read: 'Saint Agatha's sliced teats sold by convents, devoured at dances!'

Bill and Komaru decided to leave Melissa on the sofa, covered with an afghan. It was nearly 10 o'clock. Komaru asked permission to retire to 'his' own room. It had been quite an evening, a lesson in paleo-cannibalism through the compliments of Christian Church rituals. The following day would take him back to a reality with which he had to cope. Once in his room, he was happy Melissa had passed out. He hoped to have a good night's rest.

And he dreamed of breasts, rose-buds, phalluses, crêpes, angels, *umus*, Pakeha barbecues and Ling-ling's bosom, which he compared to a mini-table for playing micro ping-pong, a double one by alternating the pink teats, tits for tats, on a Chinese chest as flat as Tiananmen Square. And Melissa's, on the way to integrating hers with the most important assets in New Zealand's economy, the pendular earth-scraping appendages of Merinos, but he could not understand during his REM stage why sheep had four of them. Hard to grasp with his fingers, though he had large hands like those of a rugby player. Oh, Ling-ling, he just could kick them off the field with the tip of his fifth fingernail. But, for Melissa's he had to cup both hands at the same time. Oh, no, two teats *sans* milk versus four with plenty of it. Oh, how thankful he was for being lactose intolerant. Two and four, four and two, but then Mahina showed up like the *tertium quid* connecting the two mammas across the hiatus of nature with three of them. Of course, that was his sister trying to bridge the gap in her helpful attempt to create a normal arithmetic progression. And they were jetting defyingly on a light brown field in contrast with Melissa's whiteness and Ling-ling's yellowness. Of course, he thought in his dream, by mixing yellow with white would he not obtain the resulting colour of a light brown? No, that could not be possible because the new colour was off white, not light brown, and in addition she was his sister. How could he mix up his sister on a palette?

The dream lasted an eternity, and at the same time a very short time, because in the middle of the night Melissa had quietly slid under his covers and had grasped his right hand gently. She had then placed it on her left breast, stroking it with his hand and guiding it in concentric motions. That was not a dream, for he felt another hand on the French-type dessert, becoming awake nearly instantly. And he felt annoyed. Damn it! He needed sleep, and he had no intention of becoming a nocturnal animal like a kiwi feeding for the following day. Following hell, for he looked at the clock on the night stand – 4:47. Thank heaven, he thought. Well, he had slept soundly for about 7 hours. That reassured him that he would have enough energy for the day, but he had not counted on Melissa's visit. No, his current frame of mind could not take anything short of rape, and Melissa understood his passive stance in spite of his reaction to an unexpected stimulus. Dr Pavlov was right. S and R.

'Sorry I woke you up. But, well, I felt that before you went you could perhaps utilise a little help for the road. I dreamed that you were an angel, but a big one, perhaps an archangel or even a seraphim. What do you say, actually, don't say anything, and if you don't, I'll do the same for I can't ...'

Thus, Komaru played dead. Besides, he could barely breathe, for Melissa's *mons Veneris* was smack on his nose as if performing a unilateral *hongi*. Of course, she knew he was wide awake, but that was an old game when, after an evening of gymnastics, he would become intentionally mute like a frozen *tio*, while she revived him in the middle of the night. And she took her time, magically using her long fingers, her hot palms, her total linguistic ability in the realm of traditional articulatory phonetics, including all buccal obstructions, all labial occlusions, all dental sibilants hissing puffs of hot breath, all soft palatal adherences, all deep glottal stops, and injecting coats of saliva still reeking with an alcoholic blend of Cardhu and, what was it, that brandy, not Cognac, but it smelled like it, oh, yes, Bill had used Armagnac, for he said that it was a man's drink for the body while Cognac was for the intellect. Before falling asleep, Bill would first sip a shot of Martell and then read nearly a whole chapter of Casanova's memoirs, the moral testament of his psychic god not even two centuries old.

Komaru vaguely remembered how and when Melissa left him for her bedroom. He had intentionally fought her with her mind by thinking of his father dying, of young people who had shot themselves on a desert beach, of Maori friends languishing in prison for having defied Pakeha authority, of anything not conducive to erotic activities, including the Sicilian Agatha being broiled on a Roman *coquina* of some kind, something that perhaps only Lina Wertmüller could have reconstructed in one of those socio-cultural movies. After all, Wertmüller had chosen Catania for at least one of them. Why not one more, combining her experience of *Seven Beauties* with contemporary Sicilian vendettas *à la Cavalleria rusticana*?

Komaru fell asleep again and was awakened by the gentle noise of water running upstairs. That was at 7 o'clock, still dark. Bill must be taking a shower, he thought. Thus he got up, made up the bed, got ready for his departure, and went up to the kitchen, where Bill was watching the news on a small TV set. He had made tea, and Komaru welcomed a cuppa. They decided to wait for Melissa to come down, though no later than about 8 o'clock, since Komaru wanted to leave in time to reach Papakura at a decent hour.

At breakfast, Bill suggested that Komaru eat something substantial that would stick to his ribs. After all, it was a long way to south Auckland and Papakura.

'Have you ever had a pasta omelet?'

'No, I haven't, but, you know, as long as there is no casein, I am fine.'

'Just sit down here, Komaru, and watch. Basically what you have is bread and eggs, or the components of bread, that is good semolina from hard durum wheat and water, plus ...'

Komaru could not contain an explosion of laughter. The previous night's explanation of Catanian bread in the form of sliced breasts came to his mind, and he told Bill.

'Oh, no, what I meant, it is pasta, either angel hair or linguettine, parboiled and then mixed with eggs before making a frittata with a golden brown crust. Dont' worry about fixing angel hair Melissa style. Just watch me.'

And, while Bill proceeded, they talked about the previous night's events and Melissa's early morning visit to Komaru. Upon returning to the matrimonial bed, she had kissed him, who was ready to get up. Yes, he knew that Melissa HAD to re-assert her 'ownership' of Komaru. She would always be afraid of losing him. It was not a matter of a 'routine penetrator' for she could get one anywhere at any time within the social constraints of either the club or of chance encounters. No. For Melissa, Komaru was beginning to acquire the status of a sentimental attachment. And Bill, afraid of losing Melissa himself, had stressed once more that she loved him, Komaru, although she was in love with Bill. That is why they had gotten married. No one else would have tolerated a connubial situation other than with psychiatrist capable of understanding the suffering of a diseased mind like Melissa's. The whole case was beyond that of *La Nouvelle Héloïse* revisited.

'Then, Bill, you think it is a mental condition?'
'You mean her nymphomania?'
'Yes.'
'That is what I am still trying to understand as its major condition. There must be some circularity somewhere between her sexual system and the mental one. I ... sorry, be careful, the pasta must be barely parboiled. Then, watch me, I spray, not under the full force of the water faucet, just using the rinsing attachment, and let the pasta cool. You see, I have already lightly whisked two eggs, but remember, at room temperature, add a little salt, some flavour, oh, Provençal herbs or simply parsley – either the Chinese or the Italian. I prefer the Chinese, vulgarly called cilantro. Oh, yes, dried or fresh. Don't have the fresh. Look, I mix everything in a stainless steel bowl, and let it rest while I warm up a large frypan lightly sprayed with extra virgin olive oil. But be sure that the pasta is cold, otherwise the egg will coagulate. Yes, while the pan warms up ... it is an old disease. Amazingly, though known medically during the Baroque period as *furor uterinus*. a neologism, it was never discussed or written about until Casanova, a keen psychologist of female sexuality, described some of its aspects in his memoirs. Please watch the stove. I'll be right back. Don't let the oil fume. It will trigger the alarm system and wake up Melissa. Let her sleep until after you leave.'

Bill came back with the eleventh volume of Casanova's memoirs. He left it on the counter, tossed the pasta into the bowl with the eggs, and dumped the contents into the hot pan, spreading the whole thing into a flat omelet-looking pie. The hot oil immediately released a fragrance, hissing and cracking, and Bill lowered the flame.

'Yes, Casanova was the first person in the West to write about that female condition during the Enlightenment. For me, he should be required reading in every medical school and even in liberal arts universities that stress humans as the most baffling mammals on Earth. Sorry, just shake the pan so that it does not stick, anyway, it is non-stick. Here, on page 79, oh, can I read to you? "I saw the Duchess of Villadarias, famous for her andromania. When the uterine fury seized her nothing could restrain her. She laid hands on the man who aroused her instinct, and he had to satisfy her." Let me shake the pan again. Sorry. "It had happened to her several times in public places, and people who were present had had to flee." Oh, almost time to check. Yes, the crust is nearly ready.'

'Where was she living, in Italy?'

'No, in Madrid, of all places, during the worst time of the mid-18th century, under the eyes of the Inquisition. Now, watch, see the plate. Just cover the pan, go to the sink in case it falls while I turn it upside down and, *voilà*, back to the pan. Interestingly, the translator from French into English, here, his name is Willard R. Trask, never wrote of the term nymphomania. This came up later in puritanical America, would you believe it? Even Freud, in his 1901 essay "On Leonardo", wrote only *furor uterinus*. Increase the heat for 2 or 3 minutes, shake, and I wonder what the original French was, since Trask wrote andromania, well "mencraziness" or what Italian women say enviously of another woman "mangiatrice di uomini". Oh, let me see, next page, here and there. "Now it is well to reflect that in this creature the womb, which has only one issue, which connects it with the vagina, becomes furious", oh, sorry, beginning to burn. Lower the heat, cover partially, and then let it cook inside for 4 or 5 minutes between the two crusts. Yes, "the vagina becomes furious when it finds that it is not occupied by the matter for which nature has made it and placed it in the most crucial of all regions of the female body". Sorry, I am staining the book with oil. Ready to eat? All right, let's us divide it. Of course, you notice that the plate must be hot, as I have done with this in the oven at a warm temperature.'

Komaru liked the first bite, and the second, the whole dish. The problem was that Bill was keeping the book open on the counter with half of it under the plate and the other held with his left hand while eating with his right hand. He just could not concentrate on the food. Komaru felt like a monk somewhere eating silently while a Brother would read from the pulpit at meals.

"It has an instinct," continued Bill, "which does not listen to reason;

and if the individual in which it is situated opposes its will it raises the devil and inflicts the most violent disorders on the tyrant who will not satisfy it; the hunger to which it is subject is far worse than canine ... ".'

Komaru tried to change the subject. He felt like a dog eating while his master watched and waited for a bark of satisfaction.

'Very good, Bill, rather intriguing I ...'

'Now do you understand how I simply cannot cope with her virtually around the clock? I try my best, but "this ferocious organ is susceptible to a degree of management; it is not malicious except when a woman irritates it: to one such it gives convulsions; another it drives mad; another it turns into a mirror or monster of piety, St Teresa, St Ágreda; and it makes a quantity of Messalinas, who, however, are not more unfortunate than the innumerable women who spend their nights half sleeping, half awake, holding in their arms St Anthony of Padua, St Aloysius Gonzaga, St Ignatius, and the Infant Jesus!" Another cuppa? Oh, honey, already up for the day?'

Melissa had just descended the staircase like a grande dame hoping to make a splash in a ballroom. She was wearing only a light black chemise which reached halfway down her thighs. Komaru got up to meet her, pushing a stool for her to sit at the breakfast counter. She had not taken a shower or bath, but she had sprayed herself with a little Brazilian perfume, just enough to contaminate the kitchen atmosphere, rendering it an impossible blend of eggish pasta crust and a wild floral scent.

'Hi, Kom, daaaling, what have you cooked? The smell must have permeated the entire upper floor. I woke up in a vapour of semiburnt food. Did you use any recipe from this book?'

'Sorry, no, that was, is, what I used to discuss with Komaru about Casanova's voyage to Spain.'

'That male chauvinist, fertilising thousands of eggs all over Europe. Anyway, what have you had for breakfast?'

Komaru, still finishing his last bite, mentioned that Bill had prepared a special omelet. Very tasty.

'With eggs?'

'Of course,' Bill interjected. 'From Maori chickens, brown eggs, fresh from the garden, what you got at the neighbour's. Incidentally, Casanova did not fertilise any eggs. He did that to ... ova, sorry, not eggs. Are you a chicken, Melissa? Sorry, you are still a chick, somewhat sleepy, and I love you.'

Melissa's face expressed a bit of hurt. She did not like to be corrected by a medical doctor. And Komaru wondered how the angel hair *frittata* would taste with ova.

'That scoundrel. He must have been a potential ... impotent. Sorry for the semantic incongruity. What do you say, Kom?'

'Well, I have not read Casanova, but I took a few days off sometime ago from a history project in order to understand what in Maori culture may be present, though not understood.'

'And what have you found?'

'At that stage I started with dictionaries. You would not believe it, Melissa, that the most humane definition, though chauvinistic, is found in a Vatican City publication. Can't recall the exact title, but it has to do with the lexicon of recent Latin.'

'Oh, I did not know that,' said Bill, almost resenting that Komaru knew something he didn't. 'What in particular?'

'Simple. I looked under nymphomania, of course in Italian, and there the explanation was in Latin as, let me recall, yes, *insana marium cupido*. Also, oh, yes, *ardor insanus*, and even *fervor morbidus*.'

'The bastards!,' exploded Melissa. 'And what did they say for men?'

'You mean, for satyriasis?'

'Yes, of course.'

'Sorry, Melissa, I checked for that term. No entry of any kind.'

'Told you so, daaaling. Thus, Casanova would have been a normal being? That impotent!'

'Probably he was a freak of nature who overcompensated all the time for his potential ... impotence, here we go again, by screwing anyone, or at least trying to do so with even his daughters, nieces, and probably his mothers if he had more than one. It reminds me of the Brazilian writer, you know, I read about him while in the clinic. He became famous in the States in translation, what? ... who ... , oh, yes ... *Gabriela, Clove and Cinnamon*, by Jorge Amado.'

'There must have been something devilish in Casanova. Too bad that Freud concentrated on Leonardo and other men, rather than on the stud from Venice, a city that was well renowned, and is, for homosexuality.'

'I think Freud could not for two reasons. He did not have the original French edition, at least the Italianate French of an exile, and also, not knowing anything about Casanova's father – did he have a father? – he could not start in a vacuum, for Casanova says very little about him, though a lot about his brothers and sisters, besides his mother.'

At that stage, Komaru found a pause in the intellectual *palaestra* between two spouses, or, better, between the historian and the psychiatrist, to get up slowly, take the dishes to the sink, and mention that he had better go. Between eggs and ova, he felt the mild surge of incipient indigestion. Or was it the condiment of Provençal herbs?

Komaru left almost immediately after brushing his teeth, grabbing his overnight bag, hugging both Melissa and Bill. They had been so kind and sweet to host him. Now, rather confused, he was ready to embark on a trip that held death in the wings. He was going to meet his father and he anticipated a storm, for in the last telephone conversation he had mentioned that, in addition to the normal testament written out and deposited at a legal office, he was going to speak with Komaru about a moral testament before Mahina's arrival. That was something between two Maoris, two links in the chain of *whakapapa* mature enough to be analysed by two warriors, one who had fought for a white cause in Europe and another who had a whole lifetime to fight during the new millennium. And against whom? The people for whom his father had nearly lost his life in a white war?

What was Father talking about? He had remained basically aloof after his wife had died. At that time he had increased his alcohol consumption, especially after Mahina left for the States, and Komaru to Wellington's Victoria University. And he, the old warrior, had gone into a sanatorium run by an Army of Pakehas trying to wipe out two centuries of wrongs by depriving him of the drug he had started to savour in front of the German lines.

The lorry took a long time to start. Probably it was a vapour lock. Komaru woke up the whole neighbourhood, and the petrol fumes stunk up half a section of a quiet street. But no one ever even opened a door or a window to check on the unusual situation on a weekend morning. That was a Pakeha district. The fact that a Maori had begun to frequent it for whatever reasons did not raise any apparent concern. Race relations were the latest fashion for which a prize was assigned. In a way it was a mini-Nobel Prize for keeping the peace in a micro-world of tension. The prize administration was managed by the same people who had created a world of injustice, thought Komaru, by dispensing weapons to his forefathers. Now they were trying to take them away and assign a diploma for lowering their breeches in the name of peace.

Komaru left Wanganul in a state of confusion. Suddenly he realised that he liked the city. Perhaps one day he would even move there, away from the ghetto mentality of Auckland and, worse, from

Wellington's. He felt psychologically at home in Wanganui, and he wondered whether there was any hidden force calling him there. If so, what could it be? Not Melissa, of course, and not Bill either, though he felt comfortable with them.

The sun had already begun to clear the low hills on his right side. It was cold, but he felt a surge of warmth in his heart, for he remembered that in a few days he was going to see Mahina after nearly 4 years of her absence from Ao Tea Roa. In a way, he felt that she could rekindle what he had missed for so long, the scent of home on the nostrils of a blood relative, of a woman carrying the complementary genes of his manhood. He turned the radio on, tuned to an FM station. There was, strangely, a Maori song he did not know. Or was he simply transforming an American tune into a Polynesian melody of hope?

Chapter 22

During his trip to Papakura, Komaru once more, as in previous outings, studied himself as a person in motion from one place to another. But, unlike in previous travels, he began to detect in himself a new human being, almost a man containing a dual personality. On the one hand, he was aware of his body performing all the driving actions nearly automatically in terms of maintaining a certain speed, avoiding dangerous situations, stopping here and there for various reasons, and so forth. He felt that his body had become part of the machine, an infernal device that called for checking the oil, the petrol, the tyres, and other parts ensuring safety and performance, almost as if parts of his body dictated to the mind what to do or not to do.

On the other hand, Komaru also sensed that his behaviour behind the wheel prompted him into a state of meditation, of recollection, of self-analysis through recent actions or encounters with people. He also knew that direct contacts with humans were rather few, for he eschewed becoming involved at any level with anyone. He was already enmeshed in several things calling for the attention of his body and mind, brain and guts, mouth and stomach. The few people he was in indirect contact with were already too many. He actually interacted with others mostly by telephone, correspondence, books, newspapers, TV, radio, and even by telepathy. In certain cases, Komaru imagined he could communicate with persons who had died a long time ago. It was a one-way communication, remembering whatever other people had left in oral traditions, literature, monuments, artefacts and the like. At times this one-way communication was only wishful thinking, such as that devised by Carl Sagan in sending a tablet to extraterrestrials: just a hope, or at least a wish, to obtain one day a reply, if not to the sender, to whoever would remain behind to act as a self-appointed executor.

During his abstractions from a reality that called for driving a lorry safely, his mind was beginning to become heavy on him. He simply could not forget the few minutes he spent in Dr McTavish's mini-office just after arriving at Wanganui. Melissa was away on a skiing holiday, and Bill surprised Komaru with an impromptu invitation to take a look at the psychiatric laboratory. The visit was brief, but illuminating. Everything was spic and span, the files were all labelled and in order, either alphabetically, chronologically or topically. He noticed the presence of several computer screens, probably terminals of some kind, in addition to a fax, two printers, modems and other gadgets. Amazingly, Bill had both Macs and PCs. And several phones, plus photographic equipment, developers and printers.

What kind of man was Bill, Komaru wondered. His question to himself was triggered almost as soon as he entered the ex-washhouse room transformed into a lab/office. On the walls, besides reference drawings, calendars, and atmospheric and climatological displays, Komaru saw some memorabilia connected with humans who existed on Earth, historical charts and time sequences of events. Amazingly, there were no photographs, no busts of Freud or anyone else, no paintings. There was just a skull on a vertical file cabinet. One thing, however, struck him. On the back wall, over the main desk, hung a framed picture of Leonardo's man with the circles delineated by his limbs, the *Homo metron* or Vitruvian Man of the Renaissance. And, next to it, a facsimile parchment containing in Italic a long paragraph of some kind.

When Komaru saw those two items, the first was explainable but the second intrigued him. He must have betrayed a certain look of puzzlement, especially because the language of that statement-looking document was Italian as spelled during the Renaissance: *Della crudeltà dell'omo*.

'That is Leonardo,' said Bill.

'You mean, Leonardo da Vinci?'

'Yes, of course.'

'That looks like Vulgar Latin. I can make it all right. A stage later than a hypothetical *De illa crudelitate de illo homo*, after analytical forms had taken over, and prepositions created a synthetic morphology. But, well, this on man's cruelty, my goodness, I did not know that Leonardo was, well, a philosopher, a moralist, a ...'

'I would say a prophet, a Nostradamus ante-litteram. Actually, I would not be surprised if Nostradamus was inspired by Leonardo. Surely, we know of him as a painter, an engineer, and so forth, but few people know of him as a writer on so many subjects outside his technological interest. You see, Komaru, Leonardo was a prophet of doom, too, besides being a moralist. If you read what he wrote on Nature, Moral Life and the Understanding of the Universe, you would think that his views were derived from what humans did to each other during and after the Second World War. He anticipated almost everything we can do to ourselves in this rotten world, including nuclear destruction by fire, oceanic upheavals and other contemporary worries, but it is what he said about *Homo sapiens* that intrigued me years ago when I studied medicine in London, particularly about the 'animal' substratum of the Aristotelian concept *sans* the adjective '*sociale.*'

'Rather difficult Italian. Perhaps Mahina could translate it for me one day.'

'I know it by heart, though I can only give you a fairly literal translation. You see, the symbolic and allegorical meaning is extra rich. It is up to you to grasp meaning on other levels. Here, listen. "One, that is, people, will see on Earth human animals, who will always fight among themselves with heavy losses and often deaths on both sides. These people will have no limitations in their wickedness; in order to satisfy their bodies, most vegetation will be destroyed in the large forests of the Universe; and, after feeding themselves, the gratification of their desires will be that of imposing death, anguish, forced labour, fear, and deportation on living creatures. And, because of their abnormal pride, they will wish to find a haven in space, but the ponderous weight of their bodies will keep them down. Nothing will remain on Earth," sorry, Komaru, he implies perhaps a holocaust of some kind, "and neither under it or below water, except what is persecuted, displaced, or out of order," perhaps he means broken down; "and some people will be deported from one country to another; and whoever remains alive will eat the flesh of the dead," actually, he says that the flesh of the dead will "find burial and digestion into the bodies of the living". What do you say?'

'Cannibalism.'

'Exactly. But look at the last short paragraph. "O world, why don't you open up and fold yourself over into the openings of your deep chasms and caves, so as not to let Heaven witness such a cruel and merciless monster?"'

'My goodness! I did not know that Leonardo was a prophet.'

'But Freud did, though not Jung. Not many people study Leonardo as a human being, a pacifist, a devoted father. And he was so modest. And a traveller, although we have no direct knowledge. Whether he imagined things or got them from other people, the perception of other cultures is unbelievable, particularly when he writes of the East. He wrote of the persecution of a prophet, of cataclysmic events destroying cities, of the wicked nature of humans, and many other pessimistic views in spite of what he had sketched to make life both attractive through flying and unpleasant through weapons. Leonardo must have had a definite view about mankind.'

'And of women?'

'That is a mystery. I think he may have read Bernard of Clairvaux.'

'Sorry, I don't know of him.'

'I have studied him in depth, and I have extracted just one sentence from his *Sermons on the Canticles*. Look at that framed writing, there, above my red phone.'

Komaru looked at it and read: 'To live with a woman without danger is more difficult than raising the dead to life.'

It was just before a railway crossing over Great South Road that Komaru mentally reviewed the brief meeting with Bill in his office. Undoubtedly, Bill had trusted Komaru, for the office was *tapu* to everybody. Or, by any chance was Bill the psychiatrist attempting to ingratiate him? And, if so, for what purpose? Was Bill seeing in him a potential client, a patient?

As traffic intensified at the southern outskirts of Metro Auckland, Komaru turned on the radio in order to stop thinking and concentrate on driving. Papakura was not very far, the sun was already descending in the north over the mist of the winter clouds covering the distant metropolis. Thus, rather than continuing along the Auckland–Hamilton Motorway toward Pahurehure, he decided on the spur of the moment to exit at the Papakura interchange by Beach Road, and then make a left at Great South Road toward Broadway. In a few minutes, he was home. Peak traffic had decreased. The temperature was warmer than that in Wanganui, but there was a light mist over Manukau Harbour. Only some late sunshine was hitting the Wattle Downs golf course north-west of the Pahurehure Inlet. Youngs Beach was beginning to be enveloped in darkness, compounded by some pollution drifting with the wind and traffic noise from the State Highway 1 viaduct. It was the first day of winter, both in nature and in his heart, for he knew that, as an adult, he soon would have to cope with death as if it were a tangible entity of some kind rather than the disappearance of his father from daily life.

It was the shortest day of the year, that Monday evening of 22 June. The sun had already dipped into the horizon of the Tasman Sea. Some sea gulls were crying at a low level in search of food before retiring for the night. Upon reaching the house, the first thing Komaru did was to call the Community Alcohol Service on Carrington

Road. Yes, his father was 'housed' temporarily in a small dependency of the Oakley Hospital Wolfe Home. Why there, he thought. He was told that the following day he could drive there and make arrangements for the final discharge of his father from the medical facility. This time, the procedure would take longer than before in similar situations since, as of 1 February, the New Zealand Government had begun to charge for health care in several branches of the public hospitals, and some bills were overdue. The State Welfare dream of Kiwian Paradise was slowly crumbling under the new fiscal policies designed to privatise whatever possible to counteract the economic depression permeating Godzone. That was, for Komaru, the final insult to a Second World War veteran on the verge of dying. The Returned Services Association was trying to help, but his father's decision to die at home lessened coping with bureaucratic pettiness. The Papakura Maori Committee on Hunua Road might help in some way, possibly by lending its *marae* grounds for a *tangi* ceremony, one that was slowly being effaced from Maori traditions.

The following day, sunrise was still struggling to arrive at 7:30. By 9:00, in order to avoid the chaotic traffic on State Highway 1, Komaru took the Great South Road, exited at Church and, after entering Mary Road, drove north all the way on Mt Albert Road before entering Carrington. He never understood Pakeha urban design. Even China could teach New Zealand a few things regarding city streets, as done in Shanghai with its efficient system of main thoroughfares. Why were so many streets named in sequential segments, following the expansion of housing developments that favoured new local names, rather than the continuation of one single designation?

At the Wolfe Home car park, he was struck by the traffic noise along the nearby Auckland–Kumeu Motorway crossing the south-west corner of Waitemata Harbour. He had not been in that area since his mother was treated briefly more than 20 years before for a nervous breakdown. He was four years old and Mahina was only a year old or so. Recollections were so vague, but he knew that Auckland had grown into an urban monster. Although the geographic site of the city allowed the flow of pollution from Manukau to Waitemata and beyond, the quality of life was declining for different reasons, such as choking public transportation creating gridlocks in Los Angeles fashion; rubbish removal becoming increasingly problematic for lack of modern facilities for collecting and disposing of it; and rental accommodations were becoming scarcer and more dear for the average worker of Polynesian descent. Surely, Auckland's population was only about 1 million, barely enough to confer on the community the dubious distinction of a metropolis. Sydney and Malbourne were already 3 million strong and seemed to function well. Of course, Auckland would never become a Bangkok or Mexico City. However, people did not seem to understand that it is not the size *per se* that creates road rage tensions and social upheavals slowly leading to family disintegration. There was something else more insidious on the negative side of the whole situation. Unlike North Auckland, the South side was undergoing the erosion of prime agricultural and floral land. This led to the import of earth products from more remote areas via more vehicular transportation. The consequential increase in sewage disposal, the larger consumption of water and the threat to the fishing industry were real and ominous. The Minister of Fisheries anticipated a reduction of snapper intake in a few years. A Resource Management Act could vigorously approach the overpopulation problem by the year 2000, though, regardless, Aucklanders would be forced to pay higher prices for a home in a more polluted and congested city without taking into consideration collateral social problems in areas such as schools, policing and healthcare. Auckland's demographic cancer was actually spreading lymphatically astride the two harbours. What no one seemed to know, or to admit, was that, in addition to all the 'tangibles', there was the unknown political factor looming on the horizon of the Waitangi Treaty as a Damocles' sword tied to an invisible thread of wishful thinking in race relation policies. Too little, too late, too condescending, too palliative, too cosmetic, too scattered, too *quid pro quo*? Already the Chinese card was beginning to appear on the gaming table of novelty immigration. Was the yellow peril a substitute, diverting the brown one from 200 years of subtle, arrogant, 'lawful' discrimination by the Crown within which Pakehas had confined the Maoris who, afraid of worsening their status, buried their heads in a Shangri-la of Stilton cheese, *The Times Literary Supplement*, and a string of honorary titles not worth the papers on which they were printed?

That evening, Komaru decided to abandon Auckland one day in favour of a different location. He thought of Wellington as a transitional place for a few more years, and then considered Wanganui as a city of peaceful opportunities, depending on what Mahina would do with her life. Besides, Wanganui was the 'Athens' of Maoridom, the 'Salt Lake City' of Maoritanga, the 'Arlington' of the longest *whakapapa* in Ao Tea Roa, the 'Alexandria' library of oral *whenua* archives, the 'Vatican' Museum of visible and invisible Maori art, spirit and *mana*. Komaru knew that Mahina would probably not stay in New Zealand. Her father's estate would be disposed of in an equitable manner in order to allow each of the siblings to decide on their respective lives. It was a long night, tossing and turning in his room next to Mahina's. In a few days, she would be there, behind a *kauri* partition. And, according to the head nurse at the Wolfe House, in a few weeks his father would cease to exist as a biological entity. What would remain of him on Earth?

The trip to the Reti home was painful because Komaru's father had to be taken there by ambulance, and not in his lorry. A nurse was dispatched to bring and install an apparatus of bottles and tubing to make the dying more comfortable. She would be at Mr Reti's bedside every morning until noon. Another nurse would take over during the night. Of course, Mahina would help upon her arrival.

On Tuesday morning, the 23rd, Komaru's father returned home to die. Rather than departing from Earth for his *Rangi* from an aseptic hospital room, he preferred to spend his last terrestrial days in an environment of psychological and cultural comfort among the things he knew and people who knew him. By noon, he was installed in bed under mild sedation to lessen the pain caused by the excess fluid buildup in his abdominal cavity. His heart, already weak from previous illnesses, was beating erratically, his bodily functions alternated between constipation and diarrhea, and his breathing was heavy, though not immediately critical enough to require oxygen. His lower limbs were swollen for lack of exercise, his skin patchy, particularly under his elbows and buttocks. The pain in his joints was controlled by pills, the same ones that checked his tender belly inflated by fluid and gasses. But his eyes were bright, his mind alert and his speech fluid, incisive, though grave in tone. In the late afternoon, just before the arrival of the night nurse who would attach his father's body to some tubing from plastic bottles, Komaru fed him some vegetable soup from a tin made in Australia, allegedly from products grown 'organically' and packed in a concentrated form. Ironically, they were supposed to fight dehydration in a body whose excess fluids were to be removed periodically when there was a remote chance for longer survival. Now, the process was used in order to ensure physical comfort during the last segment of life, a time period during which the patient might still wish to communicate with humans, and, particularly, his family that would help to put his affairs in order. So the evening went by in a kind of colloquial armistice after the nurse's arrival. Komaru sat a few minutes by the bed, got hold of his father's hand, wished a good night to the nurse, *hongied* his dad and asked for permission to retire for the night.

On Wednesday morning, after the nurse had left for the day, Komaru entered the sickroom, normally used as a rumpus unit and containing the largest picture window facing west over Manukau Harbour. Some condensation had formed on the pane, for it was cold, rainy and windy, but, propped on extra pillows, that morning Komaru's father had faced the window and assumed a patriarchal posture in anticipation of what he intended to say. Komaru sensed that his father had planned to enter into a dialogue, or at least a monologue containing instructions. This, once commenced, was interspersed by a series of short questions, with blank spaces allowing Komaru to recollect unsaid things, synthesise later events, and outline plans for the future of both Mahina and himself. Oh, the anguish of the known past, of the unknown imminent, of the procedures to be followed according to what society required as the last act of responsibility. Oh, if nature could have been designed to change humans into birds during the last flight from life, so that as a bird one could fly to a place of final rest unknown to humans, and there await the cessation of physiological functions. Komaru wondered if birds die alone and, if so, consciously or not of themselves unable to fly any longer for food and for fun.

That morning, Komaru sat by the window, facing north, so that he could look both at his father in bed and at the water pelted by rain. Only a few boats swished by in the distance under the viaduct. The silence anticipating a dialogue of some kind was suddenly broken by his father's caustic remark.

'So, Tama, are you still trying to catch the white whale? Do you think you can destroy it in mid-ocean or let it bleed slowly with your harpoon attached to it?'

That introduction made to incite a kind of confession about matters that Komaru did not want to talk about was almost like a knife piercing his bowels. For many years, there had been a tacit agreement not to talk about the struggle against the Pakehas. Although not directly discouraged from continuing an impossible battle, Komaru had avoided speaking of his plans. Now it could be different, since he was almost at the end of his studies and at the inception of a possible career ensuring a quiet life somewhere. His father wondered how, since his early youth, his son had survived the psychological and physical fight in the process of harpooning an enemy floating around all the time, and nevertheless so elusive. The Pakehas were not minnows any longer as during the first Waitangi meeting. They had gotten together and combined into a single force as if glued one by one to form the largest monster now swimming freely in the ocean of plenty. What could a few inconsequential harpooners do against such a monster? No printed paper, no inflamed speeches, no vociferous manifestations, no parliamentary *mise-en-scène*, nothing could ever radically change the status quo. So, how could one implant a sharp harpoon into the heart of that free-swimming monster sucking the plankton of Maoritanga? Could these brown freedom sailors ever succeed in obliterating the presence of a white whale with traditional methods, by muscle power and luck, without the aid of anything else like a charge of explosives behind the bore of a cannon? And, even so, could Maoris alone perform that feat? How many canoes were needed for a fight to the last drop of blood, either their own or of the whale of oppression? Could they count on other canoes arriving from other islands within Polynesia, if not even outside it?

Komaru felt so desperate that he almost wished to die along with his father. Nevertheless, after briefly informing him about his current activities at University and Wanganui with the McTavishes, Komaru detected a pause, a long one. Scanning his father's eyes, he noticed a look of puzzlement laced with curiosity, bemusement and even hope. Of course, he said nothing of the intimate, if not abnormal in Maori terms, situation binding him to the Circean spell cast by Melissa. That was like riding a baby whale hoping that the voyage would lead a novice sailor into the equatorial *balenarium* at calving time. Thus, Komaru preferred to stress the intellectual and professional *côté* of the connubium with Dr McTavish, who had nearly become a substitute father figure within the new parameters of Pakeha culture. That triggered a string of questions regarding Komaru's position within the movement since Bastion Point, when he was so impressionable, like a Palestinian youth convinced to fight as David had done with a stone at the end of a rope loop. In essence, Komaru's father was confessing his own failure, or better, acknowledging unilaterally his inadequacy leading to an apparent abandonment of Maori activism under the addiction of alcohol, which dumped him into the pit of constant depression and forced resignation. At the same time he had assumed that his son had followed suit along a genetic line. The problem was that Komaru had hidden from his own father a large segment of his political life for various reasons, including one of avoiding the fact that his father protected him from danger by throwing a monkey wrench into the spokes of his furtive wheel.

It was at that stage of personal confession that Komaru told his father of his involvement in Maori activism for the previous 10 years. After all, what did Komaru have to lose? His father was dying, and thus he was in no position to either help him or hurt him. At least he could die in peace with the knowledge that his son was continuing a tradition initiated by his great grandfather. A 'maori' Maori never dies when an offspring takes over anything by simply adding another bead to the rosary of a *whakapapa*.

Although since his childhood Komaru had been exposed to many aspects of activism through his father's relentless fight along paths of Gandhian philosophy, Komaru developed a conscious interest in the Maori cause since 1982 when he was barely 15 years old. At that time, he had analysed his people's rights, not only within Ao Tea Roa, but also in connection with other oppressed indigenous minorities, though in his opinion this numerical concept should have been regarded as 'majority' on a moral basis. This was particularly so when extended to the whole Pacific basin holding Polynesian values from Hawaii to Easter Island to Vanuatu.

He remembered how he felt when Prime Minister Muldoon and the Minister of Maori Affairs had branded the merging of Maori activist movements as an outgrowth of Communist propaganda Cuba-style in antithesis to the traditionally assumed 'sheepish' Maori way of 'PT'. Thus, Komaru and his father reviewed the last 10 years of touch and go movements keeping the Crown off balance here and there. At the same time, Komaru's father on the one hand lamented that those 10 years had been a period during which he found relief in alcohol, though, on the other, he was happy, even proud, to know that Komaru had silently taken over what his father had dismissed as a lost cause.

As a result of Komaru's opening his heart and mind to his father, they reminisced the cardinal actions way back from the *Kotahitanga* to the Maori King, though Komaru relived that period only vicariously, and the same from the Waikato rape to the *Pai Marire* failures leading to the exile of Te Kooti, Nazi-style, to the Chatham Islands. Komaru had studied some of that 'prehistory' filled in details given by his father, who had heard them from his forefathers. He heard how in 1891 his grandfather Reti worked for the *Te Paki-o-Matariki*, the newspaper of the 'Independent Maori Power of Ao Tea Roa' and the *Kotahitanga mo te Tiriti o Waitangi* leading to the mock establishment of the Maori Parliament. Generations of Maori dreams passed away through oral history at their *maraes* until the rejection of the Maori

Rights Bill in 1896, ironically the year in which Komaru's grandfather had been born.

That was in the wake of Wi Pere's insightful prophecy declaring that two more generations might go by empty-handed in spite of Ngata's later efforts to counteract the systematic dismantling of Maori values. Even the *tangi* ceremony, now looming in his own home as an example of persistent tradition, had been reduced to no more than 4 days, and accusations had been vented against Maoris who, like Pomare at the end of the First World War, had engaged in ambitious interactions with Pakehas under the spell of palliative advantages proffered upper-lippedly by dishonest Pakehas. That old segment of past activism was extremely important to Komaru, for his own knowledge of it was more relevant than that of the early 1960s in connection with the rôle of the Ratana Church movement, the position of the Labour Party innovations, and the Second World War window opening a new horizon of possibilities. Komaru knew that, no matter what, the kaleidoscopic sequencing of events, at times pointing to intra-Maori dissonance, had nevertheless kept alive the flame of independence, of a Pacific Risorgimento, of Polynesian Resurrection, unlike what the unfortunate American Indians had relinquished because of complex factors. Even tenuously the Ao Tea Roan *wairua* of Maoritanga had never become extinguished.

That is when Komaru first toyed with the idea of studying history as of 1962 in detail, when the Maori Council was instituted. The problem with the Maori Council, in cooperation with other organisations such as the Maori Women's Welfare League, was simply one of élitism that, like a flimsy patina of pseudo 'Britishness', had lasted for about 15 years. Maori intelligentsia had simply been influenced and nearly intoxicated by Pakeha false-gold policies until Maori youth became independently aware enough of the stark reality underlying chronic oppression. If so many African nations, and even European communities, could break the chains of colonialism, why could Ao Tea Roa not perform similar feats of liberation? The ephemeral glory of the Maori Battalion's exploits were just wishful thinking for a just reward. Total political control was in the hands of Pakehas unwilling to even recognise human rights toward their moral landlords of whom they were simply guests who for 200 years had imposed a presence of exploitation.

For Komaru, the reflection of youth movements astride the first years of his infancy, a knowledge of what had taken place in France, Italy, Germany and America, clarified the formation of a brand new

Maori group who in Wellington had published a newsletter titled *Te Hokioi*. That was the symbol of a bird, perhaps a mythical one but still real in Maori lore, that had been forced to keep his wings folded and thus unable to fly like the *takahea*, conditioned by indoctrination of slavery and passivity until it was rediscovered vibrant and alive in the bowels of hope. This *hokioi*, as large as the *moa* according to Tregear's etymological scholarship, had many-coloured feathers and a bunch of red plumes on its head. This constituted a symbolic flag for Maori leaders, for the colour had always been present in every aspect of Aotearoan life, but the Pakehas construed it as an anachronistic Communist symbol of a political organisation.

Whether mythical or historical according to J. van Haast, that bird had been the oldest vexillum of freedom and had been chosen as the flag of liberation. Its bones had been found here and there, however, with enough anthropological evidence to confer upon it the name of *Harpagornis moorei*, a man-eating bird. Could it be that the *hokioi* could be revived at least symbolically, if not in reality like the *takahea*, in order to eat the Pakehas out of Ao Tea Roa?

The old bird was thus nursed in an ideal setting by many organisations of idealistic youth, including the MOHR, asking for, actually demanding, 'more' of everything. It was not a matter of begging for alms, for that acronym meant Maori Organization for Human Rights, a legal and moral concept. The problem with 'more' was its idealistic tenets based on humanistic foundations. But New Zealand was not India, where the scale of numbers was the reverse. In a Pakeha-dominated government, a humanist simply meant an effete-pseudo-intellectual as described so effectively by Carl V. Smith in *From N to Z*, and by Austin Mitchell in *The Half-gallon Quarter-acre Pavlova Paradise*, not to mention other observations ranging from G. B. Shaw to Paul Theroux. In 'N.Z.' an intellectual belonged to the bookshelves of dead archives. What was needed was a more active and physical organization. From that view of inadequacy was born *Nga Tamatoa*, 'The Young Warriors', which found fertile ground at the University of Auckland where, in 1970, the Young Maori Leaders Conference was held, a first in the annals of men displaying intestinal fortitude. California-style activism had crossed the Pacific and sojourned here and there on many islands before reaching New Zealand.

Consequently, new concepts and terms sprang up analogically, from 'brown power' to 'Maori liberation' among dynamic, vocal, oppressed, outspoken youth unafraid of confronting authority *à la* Angela Davis, if not by spitting in the face of, and showing their buttocks to, 'pigs'. The *Tamatoa* did not trust anyone over 30 years of age. They immediately espoused the language norm, for they had acquired a deep sense of history tied to the Maori idiom in contraposition to English. The *whenua* and the *reo* concepts became an axis of activism leading to the Bastion Point occupation in 1977.

That was the first action in which Komaru was engaged when he was nearly 10 years old. A year later, he became the youngest member of the Waitangi Action Committee by working as a cyclist carrying messages between several organisations in Auckland, from He Taua to the Black Women to the Maori People's Liberation Movement of Aotearoa. No mail delivery by the Post Office was considered safe, especially when it was found that letters coming from abroad never reached their destination. And some of those letters included cash and checks from Canada, Indian Reservations, Tahiti homes and others. Anything printed and dealing with sexism, racism, capitalism and government oppression was intercepted and destroyed after lists of names were filed CIA-fashion for later use against activists, a cover-all label that included anarchists, communists and revolutionaries, like idealists all over the world engaged in armed confrontations. But in New Zealand, except for disorganised manifestations mainly in Auckland, the only 'revolution' was vocal and typographical via a series of explicit denunciations of Pakeha mock celebrations denigrating Maori traditions as in the *haka* re-enacted scornfully by engineering students at the university. The press, regarding itself in New Zealand as the supreme voice of refinement due to a superiority complex fed by a classical Chinese-style belief in being at the centre of the globe, often reported violent street confrontations with police as stemming from 'hippy' riots. But some courageous people, such as Matiu Rata, who resigned from Parliament in protest of repressive police tactics to found the *Mana Motuhake* in 1979, had cast the die to establish boundaries of truth between the Ratana Church and the ambivalent Labour Party. Unfortunately, its self-help policy among Maoris to shape up their own fate found immediate obstacles in solidly entrenched Pakeha monoculturalism. It was a dead end to Maori aspirations. *Taha Maori* was barely alive in a proposed scheme of cooperation and co-existence for, regardless of any interaction between Maoris and Pakehas, the former always drew the shorter end of the stick.

It took a woman, Donna Awatere, to delineate clearly the principle of 'Maori sovereignty' in 1982 via the fatidic *Broadsheet 100*. There was no middle solution. It was a matter of obtaining either sovereignty or nothing. There was no choice left. Since that year, Komaru had been occupied with schooling in Auckland until 1985, and then later at the University of Victoria in Wellington, where he had witnessed the growth of the Waitangi Tribunal's functions with mixed feelings. Then, in 1989, the publication of *The Sovereinty Game: Power, Knowledge and the Reading of the Treaty* had inserted a wedge into his naïve determination to do something about the truth. Although he regarded Peter Cleave's work as probably the best ever researched and written by a polymath scholar, whom he regarded as honest, he nevertheless felt that it led nowhere. Had Cleave written his *Game* for a cultured government, it might have been adopted as a 'bible' of guidance to dissect the thorny problem of race relations. But in New Zealand, where utilitarianism is measured in the absurdly Stakhanovistic fashion of tangible results, Cleave's pioneer work fell on deaf ears and on blind eyes. After reading and studying the *Game*, Komaru obtained enough material to devise his own game for a different type of fight. His year spent in Shanghai had created a sophisticated *forma mentis* that on the surface revealed a type of Attention Deficit Disorder. He even learned how to smile stupidly when confronted by problems created by political bullies.

That day, in reviewing the history of activism with his father before dinner, he did not know what to expect or how to proceed in order to swear allegiance to his father's and grandfather's legacy of liberation. He knew that, regardless, that night he would sleep better, for he had met his father as an adult, and had unburdened what had been weighing in his bowels through years of doubt and confusion. He even felt that in a way his father was entrusting him with a traditional *mana* of psychological power, as his Komaru grand-father had transferred the same soon after the Second World War before his death. Komaru realised that he was now tied forever to the rôle and the fate of Te Wiri, no matter what the outcome. He felt relieved that there was finally a purpose in his life, something indefinable that would keep the *Wairua* of his father alive for years to come. Death was but an abstract concept of Pakeha import. In Maori culture, it was just a pause, the turning of a page in a long *whakapapa* for another generation.

On the way to his room, Komaru stopped for a second in front of Mahina's door. Tomorrow he would check it for dust and order, for in the past he had browsed here and there among her books and magazines whenever he needed to read something before falling asleep. His attention was caught by Germaine Greer's *The Female Eunuch*. He wondered when Mahina had bought it. He was intrigued by that work of liberation. Of course, he thought, that was a different kind of scream to break the chains of gender slavery. That was none of his business. He felt that women had a different manner of fighting, almost instinctively, at times paradoxically, even hysterically, and always sadistically. What could he learn from an Aussie who had abandoned Australia for the hedonism of old and decadent England? In his attempt to place the book between the last one on the shelf and the bookend, Komaru opened it at random and found that Mahina had marked many pages with a green highlighter. So, she had read it. Yes, that was her colour. But, what did she find in it? He took the book with him, and felt somewhat guilty for doing so since he remembered how possessive Mahina was of anything belonging to her. He was curious to see what and why she had highlighted certain sentences and paragraphs. And, intrigued to learn about his sister who was arriving in a few days, he guessed that there was time to read the whole book before welcoming her at Mangere.

Chapter 23

As of late, waking up in the morning had become for Komaru a somewhat modified mental process, if this can be defined as a bundle of feelings that confronted him all at the same time. He tried to remember how in the past the transition from sleep to total wakefulness took place, and also, most importantly, what that adjustment to reality constituted in his consciousness. He was unable to recall any salient feature or significant impact on his whole psyche. Whatever he could grasp as a sequential functioning of his persona, analysed in Jungian terms at the very moment of confronting his self in the morning, was usually vague and not beyond the inception of prosaic routine: bodily functions for evacuation and nourishment; septic and aesthetic grooming; household chores in the bathroom, kitchen and living room. Only his study corner remained often untouched, especially when a creative project was in progress amid open books, quarto-folded newspapers, broken-spine magazines, and pieces of paper scattered here and there holding notes jotted down during the day and the night.

Being back 'at home', where he had been raised as a child, Komaru felt that the morning process of re-integration into a live activity was different from what he would do in Wellington. In the Papakura dwelling he retrieved from the dust of memory some of the childhood routine preparations for school and 'mixed' social life. He attempted to recall the European traditions of his mother speaking a blend of three languages – Croatian, Maori and English – while his father attempted to create a tenor of family life adapted to the dominant Pakeha culture. The 'philosophy' of a brainwashed Maori father was that of having his children look up to whites as the rôle models for the sake of good neighbouring 'policy'.

It was a hybrid situation, strange, shifty, nervous, dominated by the struggle to create some kind of balance between the home life of *ad hoc* prevailing communications systems, demanded by the task at hand, and the outer life of school, sports, church and socialisation, though marginal, via English norms and British WASP-iness. In a way, Komaru was shocked when recollecting that past tenor of life, of living, of growing up in an almost labyrinthine daily map of customs, mores and expectations with contradictory directions whenever these were available as handed down or inferred as right or wrong. He longed for his Wellington apartment, he missed it, for he felt uneasy finding himself as a guest in a room in which he had slept longer than in any other since his birth.

He must have fallen asleep with the reading light on and a book on the edge of his Maori bed. Oh, of course, Germaine Greer. He had planned to read it systematically as he had been trained, from the flap blurbs and back cover to the preface, table of contents, and index, but he had been distracted by Mahina's highlighted passages jumping up to his eyes during the fast process of scanning the book back and forth. In addition, she had inserted small cards with notes referring to the page of her interest. When some of these fell on the bed, Komaru had to collate their contents in order to place them where they originally belonged, for he did not want to antagonise his sister, jealous of her inalienable property.

The previous evening Komaru had left a bookmark where he had read: 'Probably the only place where a man can feel really secure is a maximum security prison, except for the imminent threat of release.' Mahina had written several questions marks in the margin, and had underlined 'man' placing beside them '*homo, on,* people ... ?' She had also crossed out 'secure and written 'safe'. That puzzled him, for he wondered whether Greer had meant a 'human being', including naturally either a man or a woman. That is when, in trying to read back and forth with curiosity in order to find the proper context of 'man' he must have fallen asleep. He was tired physically and emotionally. The conversation with his father the previous day had exhausted him psychologically, for by opening up to him Komaru had acquired what his father had allowed him to see for the first time. His father was totally washed out.

Before falling asleep, however, Komaru had attempted to dig into Greer's psyche. Yes, of course, the book had been published more than 22 years before, but, what was she trying to say? Were there any general truths that apparently created a thematic interest in Mahina? That should not be difficult, he thought, for Greer wrote brilliantly in a combination of discursive, declarative and authoritative manners. But, who was her addressee? The public of Australia, or of Europe, without presuming that it was global? Anyway, where did New Zealand stand? Mahina had underlined some salient features of

Greer's 'philosophy' that, nevertheless, hid the reason for her writing because, in spite of her feminist position, she did not intend to create a vacuum between males and females. It seemed that feminism could exist only as a function of 'masculinism', thus a *malgré lui* situation. The problem was entirely his, he admitted that. He had no patience for quasi-academic dissertations covering an excursus that had begun with Adam and Eve. Besides, he regarded women as basically non-essential biological entities except for procreation. They were simply a tool of work in an accidental cosmic game of survival. Whether women thought of men the same way did not bother him, for he felt they had the right to make that assumption. In essence, each gender could exist independently if it were possible. He had attributed his own view to the fact that he had grown up in a motherless home, thus in a vacuum where 'love', whatever its protean acceptation, had been an empty word. When he tried to invent that concept as a matter of social 'normality', he was never serious about the search for what Ling-ling had once tried to elicit from him. The Shanghai girl, now in Wellington, was for him a pleasant ride for an outing into the bush of the senses. He simply did not believe that sensual, and sexual, encounters could germinate and yield anything other than hormonal reactions.

As to his own position *vis-à-vis* Melissa, well, he did not mind being regarded by her exactly as he regarded Ling-ling. In practice, he conceived intergender activities on an egalitarian basis, a platform devoid of any *a priori* literary, philosophical or psychological boundaries of tolerance. Naturally, he knew that in order to interact with another gender in a non-destructive way, the partner had to be intelligent and cultured in mutually balanced social traditions. But he knew that an ideal set-up for those requirements was very difficult to find. Thus, he simply coasted along. After all, life was not going to last an eternity. There were, there could be other ways of going through a terrestrial experience as a biological entity, and he was grateful to whatever Pakehas called Nature for creating, and even tolerating, a nearly infinite spread of variables and variants permitting either 'permanent' or serial associations. Love, for example, could be simply a linguistic accident within Indo-European culture, and he wondered how Anglo-Saxons could live more or less in mutual tolerance if that term had not entered glottic records barely 1000 years BP. When this term was to be confronted with, if not projected against, billions of interactions between the two genders in such an infinitesimal speck of stellar chaos, the billions of pages written about that phenomenon within 1,000 years of recorded history, or even 5,000 or 10,000 years in other cultures possessing similar dysfunctions, would be rather risible. For Komaru, humans were simply pathetic beings deluding themselves with what amounted to not more than 300 million sperm in one single ejaculation of semen. What a waste to give the chance of survival to just one of them!

He was thrown off balance, however, when, in noticing Greer's red flag in the ring of human bulls, he came across what Mahina had highlighted, a long paragraph, namely, 'Love, love, love – all that wretched cant of it, masking egotism, lust, masochism ... the compliments and the quarrels which vivify its barrenness.' My goodness, he thought, what kind of 'love-less' life had Greer had in her family? What had she missed? And why had Mahina written at the bottom of the card, 'Will I ever know and receive love from anyone? Will I have experience and proffer love to anybody? Will I ever detect and share love with any man, woman, animal, or tree, or rock, or star, or myself, if not a god of any gender? Will I ever do so, even through "a welter of self induced miseries and joys, blinding and masking the essential personalities in the frozen gestures of courtship ... "?'

Poor sister! Did she now know that Greer, as an older person, was writing in the hall of Western traditions that seeped echoes of pseudo-Romantic notions on both sides of the Channel, although she was half a globe away? It looked like Greer, lamenting the lack of a Petrarchean set of antithetical expressions, had floated along a continuum beginning with Sappho, stopping on the moats of Provençal castles to embrace Eleanor of Aquitaine, resting at the doors of convents housing mystics like María de Ágreda, before collapsing in the arms of Emily Dickinson. It seemed that Greer had tried so hard to reach the Eldorado of her heart, though in vain, for she was already an adult having apparently undergone a traumatic experience as a consequence of her game with a 'rugby player' in Sydney. But, in Mahina's case, how could she feel similar *affinités* at age 17 when she read the book? That was his kid sister, a 'baby' who had cried in his arms when, to the astonishment of Pakeha travellers at Mangere, she had displayed undignified Maori traits of affection.

One of the sentences highlighted by Mahina on page 27, when reviewed a couple of times, seemed to have satisfied some of his mental queries: 'The vegetable creep of women's liberation has freed some breasts from the domination of foam and wire.' This could be, of course, taken literally or metaphorically. Mahina had written a note below that quotation, 'Oh, Miss Greer, how can you assume so much by placing a few thousand, even million, women on a pan-global scale? How can you say that? How can you spread that notion of dubious universality among all the females of the world when 90 per cent at least have never seen or heard of your contraptions, be they symbolic or real? Ironically, as a Maori woman, I wish I could live a life with a breast masked by foam and wire, for even at home I may be forced to go against the very straight grain of my culture and wear a bra even at the hot pools of Rotorua!'

That is when Komaru decided not to read the book. It was too personal, too painful, too invading. He felt as if he were prying into the bowels of the only female on Earth whom he regarded as a pristine symbol of tender affection, of ..., oh, no, he had almost said 'love', but he dismissed it. What could it be? After all, he had never been loved by anyone, and had never felt love for anybody. He, nevertheless, felt a shock when he remembered that Melissa would often tell him that she loved him, that he was special, and so forth. He did not, he could not pay attention to those socially standard ejaculations under the spell of a wished for motherly affection or whatever. So, how could Komaru use that term of endearment, that label of intergender bonding, that shifty part of speech that carried the imposed value of a 'noun' solely because grammarians were still slaves to Latin classification? Not even Latin, actually Greek, as it was borrowed from who knows where, not discounting Sanskrit. Yes, it was a fault of the English language allowing that monosyllabic grammatical function to change from a noun to a verb and even to an adjective at the drop of a pair of undies. He wondered what came first, the noun or the verb. Probably the latter, for, at least in Christian humanity, was it not true that 'In principio erat verbum?' Or were the missionaries wrong? That was a lie, anyway, because Latin would never have allowed 'verbum' to transform itself into a verb permitting monstrosities like '(Ego) *'verbo' te devote'.

The first thing Komaru did in the morning, even before entering the bathroom, was to place Miss Greer on the shelf where she must have been for a long time, or at least for the previous 4 years. Next to it he saw a blue book titled *The Passionless People* by a certain Gordon MoLaughlan. And who was that bloke, a Brit or an Aussie? To whom was he referring? He almost began to raise the blinds of the glass covering the figure on the book cover when he felt a pang in his bowels. No, sister, I promise, I should not pry into your privacy. I would never, never hurt you, for I feel you are the only female source of Maori scent I detect even among the pages of your books. I can hardly ...

'Mr Reti?'

'Yes, madam, I'm up.'

It was 6 o'clock. Still dark during the first week of the Austral winter. Traffic had not yet begun to flow over the viaduct and, having opened the window a little to refresh the air, Komaru was listening to the water flapping of low tide receding into Manukau Harbour. The nurse was ready to leave.

'Your father is set up for the day. Just follow the routine like yesterday. Oxygen only if you notice difficulty breathing. Should you need assistance, please call the doctor.'

'Thank you, madam, have a good rest.'

'And you a good day. Your father is awake, as he was most of the night. But, you know, he does not like to say much about anything. I'll be back tonight.'

He entered the rumpus room, looked at his father in the soft light cone of the lamp, and touched his hand. He responded by squeezing his fingers and looking him in the eye.

They talked about breakfast. No, his father would be hungrier later. Komaru suggested some traditional Maori food to pep him up. He noticed that in the freezer there were several packages of vegetables, including *kapeti*, 'wild cabbage', and *kokihi*, 'Kiwi spinach'. He wondered whether some of the frozen seafood was still edible. Two plastic bags seemed to contain *pipi* already shelled. Perhaps at noon Komaru could prepare a *pipi* dish with onions, carrots and cauliflower, the way his mother used to fix it by adapting New Zealand food to Adriatic victuals.

He had some eggs *à la coque*, actually *à la* Rotorua, Maori bread, fruit juice and an apple. After retrieving the *New Zealand Herald*, a complimentary copy tossed by the paper boy who had noticed people at home, Komaru groomed himself, glanced at the inconsequential news and sat on the armchair at the foot of his father's bed. By that time, sunlight had flooded the viaduct of State Highway 1.

'So, Tama, what do you say? Are you ready to experience a vicarious death?'

'Dad, please, I have just had breakfast. Do you think that even if I were a god I would eat you for dessert?'

'Sorry, I must confess that the Maori way of dying is already dead for good. I am happy, however, to be at home. I would feel embarrassed to die in a Pakeha establishment. Just imagine, Tama, how so many generations of our ancestors died so naturally, eaten by their gods.'

'Do you think that they gave up their will to live without a fight? Do you believe that at a certain point they had made peace with themselves and became anxious to embark on the trip to Cape Reinga?'

'I think so, particularly when they felt unharassed by fear, frustration, and oh, anger. I have none of these. Although I have no sense of having accomplished much, except you and Mahina, I am ready to go. However, I have to say a few things for what I may have done involuntarily, or, shall I say, under the drive of what I felt was love. You would not believe it, love at the pinnacle of its very existence in me. I will explain everything I can when Mahina arrives. Just for you and her. I don't think I can take the presence of anyone else. In my case it is ... well, better to have a washday at the *pa*, not in the copper room of ... exhibitionism.'

'Whatever you say, Dad.'

'Yes, you see, the irony. Both old age and disease seem to yield a very productive life because of extra "wake" time. I don't sleep much. I have plenty of time to recollect memories, and to collect experience, though of course, sadly, not the energy to put it to work. And even if I did, say, for the sake of youth, who would listen? You know, you, as a young man, don't you feel eternal?'

'I don't know about that. Perhaps so, but only indirectly because I don't have the time to think about death per se. And when I do, it does not bother me except for lamenting the possibility of not being able to do what I would like to accomplish.'

'Of course, youth excludes the world of memories, Usually, after a certain age, one begins to assume that you are what you have thought, or done, or better what you have loved, and thus what you remember you have loved. In essence, people like me live in the past. Who cares to think about a future? I don't have that worry, and neither the fear of appearing or acting extravagant and, shall I say, eccentric. As I was at the sanatorium. I was forgiven my present sins. But who will forgive my past ones?'

'I am sorry, you need to be forgiven? Do old people seek forgiveness from younger ones? Or from those who may have already gone unless they are your contemporaries?'

'Probably both. Since I cannot be around for a long time, the little I have is dedicated to recalling my past in order to grasp not so much the meaning of life, or of my life, as that of presenting some deeds to those who, like you, may need to understand their own future life as a reflection of my past one. I feel it is a duty, my duty to you and Mahina. How many more days? Today is ...'

'Three more days, Dad, and she will be here to bring America into your life. I myself am so anxious to see her. I feel even somewhat guilty for having lost 4 years of her presence among us.'

'Tama, I am so happy she is not here to see me going to waste. Once home, she will not have the time to study my disintegration. The shock of my death will obliterate the slow adaptation of her life of adulthood to the vacuum of a missing family life.'

'Which reminds me. I am going to put her room in order. Wash the linens, vacuum, check the electric blanket, and whatever I can do to welcome her. Perhaps I can move a few plants from the rumpus room into her sanctuary. Anything you know I should do?'

'Ah, yes, I had removed her phone set into, well, here it is. Can you buy a new one and place it by her night stand? Perhaps you can shake the window curtains outside. Anytime, even during the day. Our neighbours can't see what we do in the garden. I am glad I spent some extra money on the tall wooden fence. After you left for Wellington and Mahina went to the States, well, to tell you the truth, when I worked in the yard I felt like my grandfather, back to nature. So when I planted the *kumara* I stripped from head to sole. It was so good to touch the *whenua* with my skin, and force the stick into the ground, chanting not too loudly, and allowing the rain to fall on my shoulders, so relaxing. Oh ... I need to rest, a short nap, Tama ... call me for dinner later ... yes, the *pipi*, and the vegetable florets ... at the sanatorium they eschewed what they said was ... indigestible ... you know, it was Maori food, like the watercress, oh, please water the plants in Mahina's room, and check the ribbon for her typewriter, it may be dry ...'

Soon after lunch, Dr Ferguson, the house-calling physician for terminal cases, and a nurse stopped by for a routine visit. They apologised to Komaru for not calling in advance. There had been a cancellation in the neighbourhood, actually, a patient had died suddenly and, upon arriving there, Dr Ferguson had simply to prepare a death certificate after consulting with a coroner and a police officer. That had been done because the patient, an elderly Maori lady, lived alone, having stubbornly refused to enter a hospice. A local Maori organisation had volunteered to take care of the final arrangements.

'Sorry, Mr ...'

'Reti, I am the son ...'

'Pleased to meet you. Miss Kostur, my assistant.'

'Madam.'

'May we see your father? This way we can cancel Friday's check-up.'

'By all means. May I ask you, doctor, how long does it take for you to ...'

'I may need about 20 minutes, but Miss Kostur may require about an hour to install the portable cardiogram. In the meantime, I have to visit another patient, and on my return I'll pick her up. But, why?'

'I need to go out for about half an hour. Just to the PO for an errand.'

'Please, take your time. Have a good day. Miss Kostur will brief you on your father's condition.'

Komaru had to obtain some forms from the Broadway Post Office in order to include his sister on the paperwork for his father's savings account. He also made some arrangements for a temporary *poste restante* since his first class mail was to be re-routed from Wellington until further notice.

When he returned home, he found in the mailbox, among other things, a letter from Mahina addressed to her father. Miss Kostur was packing her things, ready to go.

At the door, she told Komaru that Dr Ferguson would call him the next day, or not later than Friday, to report on his father's health. She was not authorised to say anything.

'Dad, a letter from Mahina for you.'

'But ... isn't she supposed to arrive, what, the day after tomorrow?'

'Yes, Friday. Why?'

'I don't know. Anyway, please read it for me. I am exhausted. The doctor was not in a good mood. A patient of his had suddenly died. He did not tell me that, but the nurse said so. She is more realistic.'

'Well, Dad, I hope whoever died did not suffer long.'

Of course, his father had been told a few things by the doctor, but said nothing. He wondered at his own chance in withdrawing information about things that the next day would appear in the local papers. But he did.

'Everything all right at the PO?'

'Yes, you can sign here in the presence of the nurse tonight, and then Mahina and I can file the paper. So, Dad, what did the doctor say?'

'Not much, but it seems that, rather than dealing with the fluids, he dealt with my heart. Any stress can contribute to its sudden cessation. And, you know, Komaru, please read me, I told the doctor not to revive me either here or at the hospital. I am too tired to go back and forth through the routine, seeing an emergency team work so hard, for what? For another few days or weeks? When my heart stops, please, Tama, let me go. It is June, winter is to stay with us for a while. You have your studies, and Mahina, what? As for me, 'kua piri nga mea katoa i te whenua i te matao, me te tangata.'

'Sorry, Dad, I ...'

'I know. You have the privilege of not knowing our Maori sense of time for the seasons, for the passing of things. That Gregorian calendar of yours is so devoid of poetry. What I said is ... what I remember from your grandfather. He was one of the old timers on the east coast of North Island. "All things on Earth stick together because of the cold – likewise Man." The cold of the season, of old age, of resignation, Tama. You should study our Maori calendar instead of Pakeha history, sorry, what I meant is our seasons based on the stars and what we used to do with them to survive. Anyway, please read the letter.'

Mahina had dated it 14 June.

Dear Papa and Tungane,

Today Americans celebrate flag day, their flag. I do not remember that we celebrate ours, I mean, theirs, the Pakehas. This letter is sent as a copy to both of you, and also addressed to Komaru in Wellington. I don't know who is where or what. Anyway, I am mailing this to you in order to inform you of my last days in the States. Well, not 'last' forever. More below. Meanwhile, I should know in a few days about my flight back home. Plan to send a cable.

Tomorrow Tanya and I will enter the Franciscan Renewal Centre, sorry, Center, not far from the campus. It is owned by the Sisters of Saint Francis for novitiate training, but we don't plan to stay there for a long time, of course. Just 6 days. We need a rest, and also a way of departing from each other after nearly 4 years of ... sisterhood. You see, the place is open to anyone willing to follow a series of spiritual programmes and retreat in complete silence. The place is not far from the Lewis and Clark College, located on 8 hectares, quiet, a restful ambience under the supervision of welcoming sisters. And cheap, only $31 a day for everything, including strolling among their orchards.

Meanwhile, I inform you that I have already packed and despatched by surface mail several US burlap sacks containing my books. Please do NOT open them. I shall take care of them myself.

As regards what to do next, well, things are developing fast here. I was contacted a few days ago by the chairman of the foreign languages department. I was surprised to find out that the college plans to offer a course on Maori language. Would I be interested in teaching one course per semester during the first year and one more in advanced Maori during the second? I must confess that the questions baffled me, for I, with a BA in Philosophy, cannot conceive the connubium between, oh, I can't remember, but his name was, yes, Martianus Capella, who wrote a treatise titled *De Nuptiis Philologiae et Mercurii*. At present, we have here instruction in Spanish, French and German, though mainly as preparatory courses for the junior year abroad. But, with so many places in the States to study foreign languages, it is cheaper to send students abroad for one or two semesters, rather than see them sitting in boring classrooms.

Then, why me and Maori? It seems that the School of Business has a Major with a Foreign Language specialty. And Maori is one of them in what they think that one day will be resurrected as the 'ethnic' business idiom of the Pacific Rim. The chairman is exploring similar plans for Mandarin. He thinks that Chinese and Maori will be for the Pacific Rim, though actually for Oceania, what Greek and Latin were for Medieval Europe. When I asked what would happen to English, he said he would not be surprised if, in a few centuries, it would play the rôle of Hebrew as it did in the Renaissance. Probably he is a visionary, but you see how I can enter into the picture.

At first, I would return to the university as a graduate student in philosophy. I was rather incensed by the Dean outlining my life. Being a graduate student, I would be given a teaching assistantship in Maori. Quite a contrivance, including my working on an MA in Philosophy. I hadn't thought about that!

Of course, I would still be on a student visa, but I would not pay tuition and fees in philosophy. Those deans, I must confess, know how to manipulate complex schemes (not understood in NZ terms) so easily. However, I was told that if by the end of the first semester I succeed in my Maori programme (just imagine, teaching Maori where one should re-exhume American Indian languages), the following year I could be appointed along a non-tenure track as an instructor (this is not like in NZ, like being simply a soldier at zero rank). The most important thing would be, if hired by Transpacific to teach as an 'indispensable specialty' for which there is almost no one trained in the States, my obtaining a so-called 'green card', that is, permanent immigrant status with all its privileges and responsibilities. Can you imagine that, like paying American income tax – which is ridiculous in comparison with ours?

Dad, Komaru, I'll explain everything upon my arrival. If everything is fine along this projected scheme, it does not mean that I would abandon you. On the contrary, I could save a little money and thus cross the Pacific once a year and gather all material for my advanced courses, and even write a contrastive grammar of US English–Maori and vice versa, with emphasis on business for which at present I know nothing. What do you say, Komaru? What kind of business are you going to engage in after your MA?

Finally, I have saved a little money to explore the possibility of visiting Europe this summer, maybe in August, together with Tanya. There is a certain travel company, I think an Italian name I can't recall, emphasising Italy, the country I visited last when I studied in Salzburg. I need to visit Rome and then Assisi. I want to retrace the steps of Clare along those hilly paths. She intrigues me. What prompted her to abandon a life of pleasure in order to dedicate herself to making life on Earth more tolerable for the poor, the sick and the unhappy?

Of course, if I could I would spend a couple of months in Italy, for what you told me, Dad, when I was growing up baffled me with your exploits in the Maori Battalion. I simply cannot visualise you living in frozen trenches when I laughed at you whenever the temperature in Papakura was rarely near the freezing mark.

Which reminds me that it must be cold now. Just think, I am going to abandon a Portland summer with its parks, the campus in full bloom with azaleas, dogwood, magnolias and rhododendrons, roses and tulips. But I shall not freeze Downunder, for I will be warmed by the psychological comfort of home, trying to blend my American experiences with the traditions of my *whakapapa*, the little I know. Perhaps, Komaru, with his new historical knowledge, will illuminate me on what I did not know when I left for the States. This country believes itself to be at the centre of the world, as China did in the past, and probably feels now.

Komaru, please help me! See if you can install a fax machine in my room, with an extra line, a dedicated one just for the fax. Be sure it is with plain paper, not the roll type. Upon my arrival, I shall look for a used PC. If I am admitted to the Department of

Philosophy Graduate School, I need to prepare some material for my course, or syllabus, including a little history on Aotearoa. No need to tell you that we, as Maoris, and NZ, do not exist at all in American life. The boundaries of America stop at Honolulu. Fiji is a place to buy shrunken heads of our Polynesian ancestors, Australia to eat frozen kangaroo meat as you find in local restaurants, Tahiti to enjoy some Mediterranean (!) clubs, Easter Island to rub the nose of fallen idols and, oh, yes, Norfolk to hunt for thorn birds. At a barbecue party I was once asked if in New Zealand we ever use that kind of cooking. I said that we prefer either gas or electric ranges for importing coals from Newcastle would be prohibitive. The poor lady was sorry for us, for she said that grilled meat in the open air tastes much better. I felt like becoming an instant Buddhist nun.

So, wait for me in a few days. I have a few gifts for both of you. I hope I don't quarrel at Customs.

Thus, looking forward to hongi you soon, Aroha,

Mahina

'That girl,' said Komaru, 'she plans to go places. Does she not?'
'You never know, Tama. Please let me rest. I feel sleepy. I am a bit cold. Please turn up the thermostat a little. No, not the electric blanket. My head is cold. *Kua tino matao te tangata, me te tahutahu ahi, ka painaina.*'

Komaru rotated the thermostat a few degrees. He also wondered why his father would quote old proverbs, almost chanting them, when he knew that his son could not understand them completely. He sensed that, with his father's death, a whole era would vanish forever, and he felt sorry, inadequate, despondent. Or, could it be that at least Mahina would continue the recitation of a Maori calendar in order to recapture the pleasure of pristine life along the chronology of Maoritanga, or at least that of the Reti *whakapapa*?

Chapter 24

On Thursday evening Komaru received several telephone calls. The first was from Dr Ferguson reporting on the results of the cardiogram. The interpretation of a roll of paper was not encouraging as shown by the electrocardiographic record compared with the previous one taken at the clinic the day before Mr Reti had left. In addition to the extrasystolic condition displaying occasional extra beats, the doctor had noticed a longer silence between them. When collated with higher blood pressure, a probable sustained arrhythmia could cause giddiness, shortness of breath and even loss of consciousness. A more pronounced alteration of the condition could lead to an immediate coronary attack. The doctor suggested avoidance of any situation such as sudden shock or fright. A nurse would be sent in the morning to take care of the patient while Komaru drove to Mangere Airport to pick up his sister, whose arrival in itself could trigger an emotional encounter with her father.

The second call was from Melissa. She was concerned with Mr Reti's health and was sorry she could not be of any help. Could her husband do anything? And she missed him so much. When would he come down to spend a night with her? Or, could she go up to Auckland and meet him there, even if just for a few days? Komaru felt insulted for, with death lingering in the wings of the family dwelling, how could he think about engaging himself in a sexual marathon – she expected nothing less at least for the first time after a long absence. An encounter *à trois*, and she meant Bill, would help, but she would settle for a 'unilateral' one. Bill could not by himself perform as before, and the idea of scouting the town or waiting until the next meeting of the club was depressing. Moreover, Komaru was inching – and here Melissa was still in the pre-1969 non-metric system – his way deeper into her psyche. He nearly choked to death at the implications, as ridiculous as Freudian. How much deeper could Komaru possibly enter her? Was there any part of Melissa's body left unexplored?

Of course, Komaru understood that she was trying to cheer him up by telling him how indispensable he was in her life, though at the moment he felt that the need to attend to a dying human being could not be surpassed by anything else in the entire world. Life could at times present itself under very tattered garments of existence. He remembered the most shocking view about life in a paragraph of *Moby-Dick*, which he had read, actually researched, in the hope of grasping and understanding Melville's knowledge of New Zealand society and of Polynesian mariners during the whaling holocaust. The recent reference and allusion to the White Whale by his father, symbolising Pakeha oppression, had rekindled his determination to at least hunt it, regardless of results. He could be drowned during a chase or even mauled by the feral defense of a cetacean much larger than what anyone could encounter in Ao Tea Roa, a monster that for 200 years had laid siege to The Hermit Islands with ineffable techniques of constraint ranging from brutality to endearment. How surprised was Komaru when he was told that, as a patient on 'Devil's Island', his father had already read a lot, including Melville, one of the first Americans literally to engage Maoris to aid Captain Ahab in the process of revenge. That monster had deprived Mr Reti of more than a leg, for he had lost, through alcohol, the will to fight like the old Polynesians engaged by Nantucket whalers. Could Komaru one day pilot a new boat, or was he doomed *qualis pater*?

Melville's book, brought by his father from the treatment centre, lay on his bed stand. A mark at the beginning of Chapter XLIX, titled 'The Hyena', was indicated by his father as a compressed chapter of the quintessential philosophy of realism depicting the human condition. How shocked was Komaru, not so much by reading that paragraph, but by the fact that his father had pointed it out to him: 'There are queer times and occasions in this strange mixed affair we call life when a man takes this whole universe for a vast practical joke, though the wit thereof is at nobody's expense but his own.' Ergo, was Melissa the hyena, the global *mea culpa* Christian female protecting 'our Maori' or Komaru's subconscious search for what he had been severed from at the age of five, the biological period considered by Freud as the inception of narcissistic libido? The coincidental parallels with Leonardo's childhood could have some points, for he too was 5 years old at the psychological death of his mother, Caterina, and the acquisition of a second mother in the person of Donna Albiera, a Renaissance Melissa *sans rien d'érotique*. How strange that Leonardo became fatherless at age 24! History repeating itself. What kind of cosmic coincidence would create, as undoubtedly it did for many other young men, a situation of 'odi et amo' disintegrating into either *odi* or *amo*, if not the reverse? Komaru's problem he had was caused by the blurred knowledge of his mother, about whom his father was never comfortable enough to illuminate for whatever reason. The potential two-mother situation, one dead and Melissa, seemed to be explained by Leonardo's natural mother, Caterina, who in reality died at 41, and his natural father's legal wife, Donna Albiera.

Leonardo's painting of St Anne seemed to reinforce Komaru's conscious recollection of that maternal duality since, in the background of the painting, Mary appears as the alternate genitrix carrying the Child, Leonardo himself, as some Renaissance artists immortalised themselves vicariously in statues, drawings and paintings. A question surged in his mind. Was Melissa playing the rôle of St Anne? Was it, or could it be, a topsy-turvy situation that, as with everything in New Zealand, could be analysed, and perhaps even understood, by making a comparative analysis with Casanova's parents, and uncovering in it the reverse? Leonardo considered himself illegitimate because he was fathered by a man married to another woman, while his mother later married another inhabitant of Vinci. Casanova's biological father was never clear to anyone, including father and son. Both Leonardo and Casanova, whose mother left him as a child, were raised by their grandmothers, as Komaru was too on his father's side. Questions of an actual *whakapapa* had always lingered in Komaru's mind like a repressed torment.

While waiting for Mahina at the airport that Friday morning, Komaru reviewed his life as a function of a penetrator and a penetratee, Dr McTavish's jargon imported from the USA for a chemical reaction. That was supposed to create life with a lower case consonant. Was there anything else shifting that lateral dental to an upper case? In his discussion with Dr McTavish, Komaru had learned a lot about Leonardo and Casanova. Now, through them and Bill, who had mixed feelings about Freud for having spent some time with Jung in Switzerland in the 1960s, Komaru was trying to understand himself. Of course, he knew that he could barely compare his life with those two giants of 'messed up life', but he took them as rôle models even though he had no aspirations to become part of history through terrestrial feats.

It was Freud's fault for having taken the lives of millions of humans, in barely one century, from the lower earth's level – at zero ground – to the mind's pinnacles by injecting abstractions of signs, symptoms, syndromes, effects, and conditions to create 'complexes' in people who, without knowing anything about Greek literature or history, began to use the names of majestic protagonists as household items, from Oedipus to Electra, on the stage of incest. So far, the Complex of Medea has not been associated with women's liberation activities in abortion cases. The rest is so 'literary' that Anaïs Nin is a household item in paperback. The Augusta Complex, after nearly two centuries, is still on the drafting board of a Missolonghi room.

Bill was a Roto-rooter of the psyche, though he did not always succeed when he tried to classify people along gradual scales. Yes, in his youth he had been influenced by some of his professors infatuated with Sheldon's Constitutional Theory of Personality and, although he did not embrace it fully, he nevertheless used it to explain to Komaru whether there was any difference at all between Leonardo, Casanova and him, since the similarity of being raised in an unconventional home was so evident. Dr McTavish reluctantly outlined the salient features of the 'three persons' simply as human beings carrying a bundle of traits that classified them according to physiological processes. Thus, Leonardo was a viscerotonic since he tended to be relaxed in posture, loved physical comfort, enjoyed beautiful companionship (particularly that of handsome young men), ate refined food (whenever he remembered to eat), slept deeply, and had an orientation toward childhood and family relations. Casanova was a somatotonic because of his assertiveness, love of adventure, need and enjoyment of exercise (especially in bed), love of risk, physical courage (as in duelling with anyone insulting him), aggressiveness under the influence of alcohol (he used to drink several bottles of wine at a single table sitting), and orientation toward youth (a girl at 14 for Casanova was old enough to be seduced as an intellectual exercise). In Komaru's case, well, Bill did not know him well, but he classified him tentatively as a cerebrotonic, basing this on the fact that, even with Melissa, he tended to show restraint in posture (Maori discomfort in front of a dominant Pakeha?), displayed overly fast reactions (who could resist Melissa's manipulations?), was hypersensitive to pain (as when he burnt a finger in helping Bill roast chestnuts), and had an aversion to alcohol (well, Komaru was a teetotaller).

The loudspeaker called Komaru back to reality. The plane had arrived, displaying a fern on its tail. Mahina would be exiting soon. In the meantime, he looked around him. During the past 4 years the interior decor had changed, or maybe 4 years ago he had not noticed that the carpet colour was not pasture green any longer. Tourists now had to see the real rolling hills tramped by millions of sheep. There was no need for interior decorators to impress American tourists as soon as they landed at Mangere, for they could verify first hand that New Zealand was indeed a luscious unfertilized rug for ovines to defecate on and maintain Godzone naturally. Whether those tourists could order any mutton at a restaurant was something else, for the meat was for export only. Besides, not many chefs would deign to list any sheep meat on menus since it was nearly impossible to find any cook able, and willing, to prepare a leg roast. For that one had to cross the Tasman Sea into Australia with the hope of finding a Greek restaurant under the stimulus of Eric Rolls.

Oh, yes, even the furniture had been changed. The style was not 'rolling' any more. Benches, chairs and seats had been changed into utilitarian furniture with a comfort index to last just long enough for passengers to wait for departures or arrivals. The atmosphere was not totally different from that of an emergency hospital lounge, where people usually do not like to sojourn very long. After all, the gates to a 'state' country were supposed to open themselves to travellers willing to visit that country just once, a nation to be added as a statistical stamp on a passport in order to receive special recognition in the pages of the *International Travel News*. Anyway, Komaru would greet his sister soon, brief her about her father's condition, take her home, and just relax for the rest of the day until the arrival of the night nurse.

The problem with Komaru was his inability, or the bad luck, to recognise Mahina among the passengers. His image of her had been frozen on the external features of a 19-year-old schoolgirl departing for the USA four years past. Ronald Reagan was still holding his senile smile on TV screens, and Bush was running for the presidency along a 50-year-old glory path.

A couple of young women went by through the lounge gate. No, no Mahina in sight. A few American skiers, some Japanese tourists, a team of athletes playing who knows what. Going where? And many business people, including a couple of ladies wearing men's long jackets and executive short skirts displaying long California legs on high heels. And where was Mahina?

At the end of the line, meanwhile, he noticed the head of a young woman towering above a luggage cart full of suitcases, boxes and packages. Her hairstyle was asymmetrical, for a lock of black hair seemed to go in one direction, while the rest went the opposite way. The cut was definitely American, unconventional, nearly insulting to standard New Zealand femininity conditioned by locks hanging down like caprine natural wool. Komaru was looking for long, shining, black, wavy, undulating hair like the former patterns on the airport carpet. Now, that hairstyle was consonant mostly for an *enfant terrible*. And her face, mostly hidden behind a pair of huge dark sunglasses, was tense, nearly irate. That was not the face of a sad sister as she looked when she departed. And what in the world was that woman bringing into a country that had everything made in China, Singapore, Hong Kong, Taiwan and even Mexico? And no one behind her. Probably, she was still at Customs. But the Agriculture agent was already back after spraying the aircraft for terrorist bugs. Komaru asked him and the door attendant if all the passengers had arrived. Yes, they had 'debarked'. What language was that? And that woman pushing the cart. He felt sorry for the young lady. Should he help her negotiate the terminal lounge door?

'May I be of help, madam?'

The reply in a rather hesitant Maori came out loud and mad.

'Do I have to beg you, sir?'

The voice sounded familiar, but the tone was not that of a sweet sister, the correctly educated lady trained never to raise her voice, especially in public, though most people had gone. Only a couple of employees were roaming around for whatever reasons. Yes, that voice was like his sister's when she got frustrated at not being able to reach an apple in the orchard or a book on top of a shelf. Then American came out of her mouth.

'What in the hell are you waiting for to help me, mate?'

After pulling the cart through the door into the lounge, he was first hit by a scent, that of past familiarity. Then, his attention deficit disorder was disturbed when he noticed something between the familiar and the American in dress and look, and even definitely in speech after she blurted, 'Thanks a bunch, man.' The accent was 'Californian', rough. He took another look at the tall young woman wearing summer garments in the middle of winter. She must be a foreigner. White jogging shoes, light blue jeans, a pink knitted blouse and a blue rain jacket with Velcro straps. He detected a leather string holding something inside her bosom. And she was carrying a day knapsack askew on her left shoulder. Oh, yes, a snow white scarf, was it acrylic, showing some printed mountain scenery. Then his eyes were allured by a tag under AUK: M Reti, 1270 Shepherds Road, Papakura, New Zealand. At that, Mahina kicked him on the heel of his left shoe. She used to do that when, as a child, she wanted to attract his attention or when she was mad at him. She removed her sunglasses, and he became speechless.

The *hongi* was hard, long, mute. There was not even a hint of humming on either side. Komaru's nose was cold, for the airport lounge had been kept cool like most waiting rooms all over New Zealand. Kiwis do not begin to feel chilly until the thermometer reaches 15, when they turn on the electric blanket. At 16, however, they begin to wear shorts outside; at 17 they take a cold shower, at 18 they swim anywhere, at 19 they gather around a barbecue, and at 20 all the hotels turn on the air conditioning. Mahina's nose was hot for Komaru's tastes, for she was coming out of a stressful situation that had increased her blood pressure. Moreover, the physical strain of pushing a heavy luggage cart had raised her body temperature. After placing some Customs papers in the kangaroo pouch tied to her waist, she laid her palms on Komaru's shoulders, almost as if knighting him with both hands. Then she closed her eyes and began groping him on his torso and scapulae. That was when he opened his mouth as if he wanted to say something, but he couldn't. Why was she so unlike herself, especially in public?

'Those Wellington gorillas sent here to ward off tourists, asking me the most stupid questions, and looking at my passport as if it was fake. And at my photograph like a Lombroso specimen. Of course, I have changed in the 5 years since I had it taken. I already feel like taking the next flight back to the States. Now I know, I have the proof ... horizophobia.'

'Sorry, what ...'

'And that prissy, icy dyke fingering through my undies and nightwear looking for labels. Jockey, yes, why not for women, too?'

'*E tuahina*, please, we are ...'

'Forgive me, about Father ...'

'Try to calm down. He would be upset at seeing you so excited. He needs tranquillity, please!'

'I'll try my best, but I still feel as if I have been raped and then dumped into a trap. Is this country my home? Most tourists were expedited in a different line, and I ...'

'What happened?'

'Later, sorry, I had not realised, I should say anticipated, how our bureaucracy can be so antagonising. As if I was trying to smuggle drugs and pornography. They even opened my antique book by Tregear. I did not want to ship it for fear of losing it somewhere. My treasure find at a Portland bookstore.'

In the parking lot, trying to negotiate the cart through vehicles, Komaru had just said 'Turi turi!' for he did not want to raise the attention of anybody. But, after loading everything into the lorry bed, he tied the safety belt on Mahina and apologised for the old vehicle. By the time they left Mangere, she started to blow off some steam in the sanctity of the cab.

'Can you imagine, *tungane*, a list? How could I make an inventory of everything for each case I was bringing home, my home, to my country, after four years of collecting personal effects, except for a few trifling gifts? That automaton, prying into my things, asking me questions, sneering at me, why I had removed the label from my nightwear, as if I was smuggling one of Princess Diana's evening gowns. Amusingly, and ironically, it was an old garment, a product of New Zealand that I had bought at Gables' in Pukekohe just in case ... you know I only wear my *tiki* in bed. But in case, being in a dorm, with a roommate. When I told that sheila I had removed the label not to deceive Customs but simply because it tickled the back of my neck ... she would not believe me. Of course, the night shirt was almost brand new. I used it only a few times, for I switched to PJs, like all coeds ...'

'Oh, sorry, I missed the turn ... I'll take the Motorway.'

He had been in the wrong lane at Buckland and Great South, so he proceeded east and exited south at Papatoetoe.

'Oh, I had forgotten, why do we do things the opposite way? Even Canadians drive on the right, as I do now after using Tanya's car. So logical. There must be something sinister in our society, don't you think so, brother? Can you imagine, of all European countries, England still insists on the left lane complicating the lives of future Euro participants.'

'Uh, please, let me concentrate on driving. We'll talk about that later.'

'You see, that is the problem with us. We are so ... so "inlandized" and, oh, let me think, nesotised, and constrained all over that we bury our head in the sands of conformity. I feel as if I have been put into a geographic gaol, almost like entering an anachronistic convent of behavioural ideas, a nation blown up into a cloistered apiary, and to think that we are, please smile, "one nation"! That pharisaic captain at the service of a ... nymphomaniac *kwini* who had to beg her valet to compensate for poor Albert ... sorry, brother, are we one nation? I was not bringing new personal effects, I was, I am returning home, I had not gone overseas to buy anything

~ 335 ~

threatening the economy of New Zealand. When I think that in Europe only some perfunctory border checks were made by bored inspectors, at Amsterdam there had not even been any Customs officers, and we sailed through on our way to Salzburg. Only the Germans were picky, but, of course, I had forgotten, have we not entrusted Customs to a German bloke, Steiner, I think, who organised our Customs Service from a concentration camp? Of course, for New Zealanders, not for foreigners, particularly Americans who can bring electronic gadgets for their own 2-week use, and then sell all of them before departing. Of ...'

'Sister, please, I ...'

'The problem is that we are not New Zealanders, and here I don't mean that we are Maori. What I mean is that the only New Zealanders, Kiwis, Pakehas, and even non-maori Maori, are those who either abandon this country or enter a convent. Well, yes, a nunnery, more than a convent. Now I can understand Maggie, Maggie Papakura of all places, the irony, entering the nunnery of Albionic rules, and now rotting in a wet English cemetery, and Katherine entering the shifty halls of European neuroses, where is she now ...'

'And you, have you come back to create, well, an atmosphere of tension, uh, please, Dad, think of him. Calm down, I ...'

'I apologise, yes, check on me, spank me but not hard, you know, I am a big girl now, and I can fight back ... but perhaps not physically against you, how could I, no ...'

'You seem to have carried from America some kind of fem ...'

'No! Nothing, carried nothing. It is only how I consciously feel now, at returning home, as I was unconsciously when I left. I think this choking band around my bowels can be called what? Kiwiphobia? No, not against Kiwis, rather a form of claustrophobia, oh, yes, horizophobia as I said before, but, careful, a phobia of horizons, because here they are so invisible, so deceptive, so ...'

'Mahina, sorry, I can't understand you, you are so contradictory, kind of unreadable, I don't know what to say ... do you mean you lack a frame of reference such as horizons. Greek circles of assurance?'

'Exactly, at times I fear of being in space on this little shuttle called New Zealand. And I only function when I remember that I can land back on Earth, be it Kuwait or Somalia. I don't blame you, for you have never been outside your sheep hide, our *whenua*, ironically, of course, a hypothetical country we, you and I, don't have except along the memory of our *whakapapa*.'

'Don't I know that, sister? So, how can you accuse me of never having been away from something I don't have, or see, or know, except through the eyes of Pakehahood?'

'You have a point.'

'And this point is ...'

'That I ... sorry, you see, I am tired. And I want to calm down. But I feel happy. Don't you realize that this is the first time that we are talking like adults, and about serious matters. Yes, we still fight like rival siblings, don't we? But, please be tolerant. Just imagine how I feel after being questioned, investigated, searched through by zealots, by officers applying anachronistic views to returning ... natives. Of course, a female native, thrice oppressed, by being a woman, a Maori, and returning from Bushland trying to smuggle a label-less nightgown ...'

'Sister, please!'

Komaru was now driving south. He had to block out Mahina, for she was for him feminism incarnate. And from a Catholic university? And he thought of Ling-ling, submissive and smiling even when she was daily confronted with the official policy of tolerating the yellow peril for the sake of international relations, which meant trade favourable to New Zealand. After all, kiwi fruits were now grown in California and even exported to Mexico, the Riviera, of course, safe fruit, for American hotel managers did not trust local products. And Melissa, a tiger, yes, but still protecting him, overprotecting by picking him up by the neck with her sensuality and straightening him out when she felt he was at times trying to breathe in a larger space of daily life. He could always return to Wellington, but Wanganui attracted him more and more. There was something atavistic somewhere, somehow, like a hidden magnet attempting to bind him to something to come in the future. He exited at Spartan, took the South Road, made a turn at Youngs, and in a few minutes he had arrived home. It was noon, cold, but the sun was shining high north of Pakurehure Inlet. And quiet, too, except for the occasional muted traffic on the Motorway 1 viaduct.

'Mahina, please go ahead! I'll take everything to your room. Be civil with the nurse. You can find me in the kitchen after you visit with Dad. I will try to fix something to eat. Unless you ... prefer to do that later.'

'Me? Brother! Are you joking? I haven't even boiled water in four years. You know I can't cook. Actually, I don't cook. And neither do I intend to.'

She turned around, forgetting to slam the door, looked at her childhood home with a sad face, and proceeded hesitantly toward the steps of the entrance. When she had left, Spring was in the air, flowers were budding, every fruit tree was beginning to awaken. Now, the yard at the inception of winter was dormant. After all, June was almost gone. And she tried to project onto that yard the glorious campus flora, as if she had left the vibrant life in order to enter the penumbra of death.

She walked slowly on the pavement along the edge of some David Austin roses covered by burlap, of moribund fuschia, of discoloured begonias, and took the cement pathway to the entrance showing a sun bleached 1270 larger than the one on the mailbox. That number, that once looked so magical in its digital addition amounting to 100 in her childhood cabalistic imagination, seemed to have lost the original 'belonging to' of home-ness. There was something sad about that reference point, as if it had become part of a past gone into oblivion, a past submerged by so many other numbers looked for, seen, accepted and welcoming all over America and Europe. That number was almost a non-entity, for its superfluous reference led nowhere. The house, however, was there as before, almost defiantly, exuding all the subtle attractions of two generations via the faded blue clapboard, the aluminium storm door, the old television antenna, the little white curtains edging the plastic blinds. At the door, a Polynesian-looking nurse, sporting a Tongan accent, welcomed Mahina saying that her father had fallen asleep. No, he had refused lunch, for he was eager to receive his daughter. Of course, she could tiptoe gingerly into his room and wait at the bedside for him to wake up.

After unloading everything into Mahina's room, Komaru parked the lorry in the garage and entered the kitchen. The nurse, sympathetic, affable and maternal looking, although she was in her early 30s looked at Komaru with the eye of a relative who, although a distant one, could be trusted. They sat down for a few minutes by the counter and she told him that his father's vital signs were at best marginal. But Mr Reti's determination to hang on was strong. He spoke of his daughter with the affection of a lover, she said. That was Maori aroha. *Honi soît* ...

After the nurse had left at about midday, Komaru walked to the threshold of the sickroom and tried not to be noticed. Mahina was holding her father's left hand in hers through the several tubes of solutions feeding him through his veins. Apparently, she had fallen asleep in that posture as a *mater dolorosa*, but his father was awake. He had noticed Komaru by the rumpus room door, and motioned him to go away. Back to the kitchen. He paused, and then decided to prepare something for the entire family. What could he fix for lunch? Something easy and quick that perhaps all of them could handle at the bedside.

He remembered that, a few days earlier, while cleaning Mahina's room, he had spotted a booklet titled *A Taste of New Zealand*. And in the freezer compartment of the fridge he had seen a package of minced *paua*. Perhaps he could prepare some kind of chowder. On page 29 he found a recipe for *paua* soup yielding enough for six, but he halved it. However, instead of milk he used chicken stock. That was easy. The only thing he did not have was fresh parsley, though he found a tin of dried one on the spice shelf. After that he took the booklet back to Mahina's room, where he opened the first page to check the date of publication. It was 'old'. The copyright was 1977, for New Zealand an antique, not so much because of the date but because of the fact that everything published there goes out of print in a couple of weeks. A few thousand copies are a best seller, and the book is rarely reprinted. His eye was struck by some feminine writing, a dedication on the first blank page: 'Mahina – Regards – Carolyn Dixon. Gisborne Club, New Zealand Federation.' He wondered who Carolyn was, and why Mahina had received that cookbook. And what kind of Federation? Of workers? He approached the shelf to put it back in its original space, and suddenly Mahina appeared so silently that he nearly got frightened, for, besides his father, his was not expecting anyone else. She had removed her jacket. Her pink knitted sweater was sculpting her torso too tightly, Italian style. Who in the world was that tall girl, showing an amused Mona Lisa-style smile in a tolerant look of inquiry?

'Did I frighten you? So, you have been snooping in my room. Who gave you permission?'

'Sorry, I was looking for a recipe.'

She came to him, took the book, and placed it on the last level of the shelf herself.

'I see that you can reach it now. You don't need me to help you any more. And ... well, I see you have grown taller.'

'Yes, too much protein in carnivorous America. And those T-bone steaks served every Sunday dinner at the varsity cafeteria. You see, unlike our T-bones, the American ones contain the mignon. Oh, yes, about seven or eight centimetres. And, yes, I need you nevertheless, and more than before.'

'Did you talk with Dad?'

'No, we didn't. We just held hands. I had got hold of his, and he woke up, but said nothing. He only looked into my eyes, and held his straight into mine as if trying to mesmerise me. I got hypnotised and must have fallen asleep.'

Her eyes were red. She was holding a Puffy against her nose. After she dried it off, Komaru drew her face toward his with both palms and *hongied* her delicately. Then he dried her tears with his parched lips. He tasted the ancient salt of his *whakapapa*, bitter in taste but sweet in memories, for he had recaptured the crying spell of his mother when dying. That was one of the earliest recollections from his childhood. And that death was now past 20 years, when Mahina was nearly 2 years old. He thought that death, that separation of a living organism from another tied to it by affection, was unfair. And there was another one waiting in the wings, to be witnessed once more. More than unfair, cruel to humans since affective detachment took place when he was young and fragile, as in most people tied to the generation gap. Why couldn't this vacuum happen to survivors when they were old, decrepit, and suffering from Alzheimer's?

Chapter 25

The *paua* soap turned out to be good. It was a compromise between old Maori traditions and modern utilitarian techniques for, instead of using either wheat flour or dried *kumara* powder, Komaru added a little arrowroot he had found in a dusty tin forgotten probably for a generation on the spice shelf. He recalled Dr McTavish's recommendation not to use wheat flour, for it would alter the original flavour of the soup components. Only *in extremis* would Bill use potato flakes, but under no condition Indian cornstarch, to thicken the soup, for this would transform it into a porcine swill. The hard-to-digest concoction had invaded the American restaurant and family kitchen, though it did not warrant anything but the crystallisation of the 'sucker syndrome' among diners willing to pay a high price for a long forgotten, misapplied term.

Komaru thought that Bill was too partial to certain recently important ideas entering New Zealand, the last nation on Earth hesitantly to allow the tentative immigration of 'southern Mediterranean diet' as an ideal one to avoid coronary problems among meat-eating Kiwis, the largest consumers of animal protein and fats in the world after the Australians. Actually, Komaru felt that Bill was nuts when it came to food, since most Maori believed that all psychiatrists were insane. However, Bill was a good, kind, sophisticated, crazy psychiatrist. That qualification erased all the negative traits associated with Freud's bastard children scattered throughout the globe. In fact, while preparing lunch, Komaru remembered a discussion on 'polenta' as food. It was not a matter for *polentoni*, 'polenta eaters', to acknowledge that the term had spread along the Po river only centuries after Columbus' rape of trans-Atlantic culture, since Dr McTavish maintained that polenta was a French dish consumed in Gaul for at least 15 centuries.

At that, Melissa had rebelled. How could it be so? That was absurd and anachronistic, if not an insult to exalted *cordon bleu* traditions. After all, there was no France and, well, after Frankish invaders gave a name to cave dwellers west of Alsatia, the Froggies had to wait until a Florentine teenager brought some table refinements, including the fork. Polenta was definitely out of the question. Then Bill screamed at Melissa, calling her an ignoramus, in spite of the fact that her father was a classical philologist, The irony was that Melissa's father knew that the term polenta had been mentioned by Ovid. Of course, the grain was barley, the same cereal she 'drank' every day as Scotch, not maize. Then why French food? Simple, said Bill, because of several studies describing what 'French' people ate in the fifth century. In addition, the term was listed in the *Lexicon Anthimeum* published in 1926. Finally, some articles had clarified the position of Anthimeus in 'France', namely, one by Mark D. Grant, 60 years later in 'A note on Anthimus' *De obseruatione ciborum epistula*' in which he mentioned a future bilingual edition. Regardless, anyone with a basic knowledge of daily 'home' Latin could read the text covering polenta: '64. de leguminibus uero tisanas quae de hordeo fiunt qui scit facere, bonae sunt et sanis et febrigitantibus. fit etiam de hordeo opus bonum, quod nos graece dicimus 'alfita', latine uero 'polentam', Gothi uero barbarice *"fenea"* ...' Melissa could not believe it when she read the text Bill had brought from his office. It was on interlibrary loan from the Turnbull Library. The discussion on Anthimus, the avatar of French cooks, lasted an hour since Bill pointed out how the description of food used by the Gauls in essence anticipated the so-called 'Provençal' and Mediterranean diet devoid of all American victuals, which would not be imported for another 10 centuries. Bill declared that the therapeutic food presentation was much better and more comprehensive than what the School of Salerno poetised many centuries later. An English text would be welcomed by those food nuts who could save the money they spent on vitamins and minerals by simply following Anthimus' dietary rules. Bill was so sold on Anthimus that, in comparison, the scant lists found in the *Deipnosophists* and the more detailed ones in Apicius could be regarded as Neanderthalian.

The *paua* soup episode and the ensuing regurgitations taking place in Komaru's mind remained as memorable sequences of home 'life' that he could not anticipate in the wildest stretch of his imagination. Mahina's presence had altered the usual routine into a sudden interaction between brother and sister. Mahina had gone away as a taken for granted 'kid' sister, and had returned as a woman. One trying case started innocently enough when, after scooping some soup into a bowl, Komaru had asked Mahina to place it on a bed tray and take it to her father.

'Perhaps you can induce father to take some after propping him up on the larger pillow. I'll bring a bowl for us, too, so we can have a *paua* party, as we used to ... you remember, on the beach. But, please taste it before feeding him. Don't burn his palate.'

At that Mahina froze up. She tried to say something, but she could not. Komaru looked at her puzzled.

'I ... I am sorry. I can't.'

'But, please, be cheerful to him. I sense he will be happy to see you helping him as ...'

'Brother, please! Don't insist!'

'May I ...'

'All right. I see that you have forgotten that I am a woman. Do you remember when you made fun of me when I was 13 years old? And you refused to eat the sandwich I had given you, although it was wrapped in cellophane?'

'Oh, yes, of course, sorry. Do you still have the same ... beliefs?'

'What do you mean? Listen! We will talk about that later. You help Dad, and then ...'

Thus, Komaru took the tray to the sick bed and fed a few spoonfuls to his father. It was a perfunctory meal, like a forced congregation of muted movements punctuated lightly by the clinging of the spoon hitting the lip of the bowl. Mahina ate with relish, perhaps because she had not had any Maori food for so long, or maybe just to encourage her Dad and thank Komaru for the trouble. Her father helped himself, taking his time in that bleak atmosphere of a forced social meeting of the hearts. Mahina, fresh from her new knowledge of Christian traditions, could not help thinking of a mini 'last supper' under the wings of the Angel of Death. The only traitor present was not Judas, but Time, who was presiding without being paid thirty dinars.

In the early afternoon atmosphere of gloom, little was said. Questioning glances were exchanged in all directions across the bed. The whole family seemed to avoid reality by repressing open feelings, so un-Maori that Komaru asked himself why. He rationalised that Mahina had been influenced by American culture and, in addition, since her mother's death, about which she remembered nothing, she had never been directly exposed to the syndrome of death in the wings. Thus, Komaru would glance at his sister and wonder. She would look at her father and see in him Komaru's parent. And she would analyse herself, how she could be and function as a daughter, a sister and surrogate mother at the same time. Her father apparently had no intention of going through the traditional routine of Maori preparation for death, out in the open, surrounded by the affections of his immediate and distant *iwi*. There was something in him that eschewed the formality and the publication of abandoning Earth as a biological entity. His forced smile was clearly effaced by that tinge of innate Polynesian sadness through eyes looking at distant horizons, announcing the end of a long voyage sustained by the hope of reaching a resting place – from *terra firma* to distant islands, from island to island, from life to death, from a temporary *whenua* to eternal *Rangi*. What a human crêche of grown up humans, Mahina thought.

The only business discussed briefly led to an agreement. The night nurse, returning at 18:00, would be informed that, beginning the following day, she would be replaced by Mahina, provided that the doctor agreed and that she be instructed in the expediency of night duties. Thus, Mahina would stand by her father during the night, while Komaru would do likewise during the day. That would cut costs for part of the essential assistance to a dying patient. It was mostly a matter of checking fluid levels, the bed pan needs, any sign of change, and the like.

For the first time, Mahina felt that she could help another human in the phasing out of a process to which he had been tied involuntarily. In fact, during her silent vigil at her father's bedside, many recollections of several disparate things emerged. One was a vague notion of a medieval woman, a certain Clare, who devoted herself to lessening the suffering of Terrestrials targeted by the fates of mental and physical depression. On that occasion she reviewed her courses on several religions at Transpacific, and discussions with professors, priests, students, visitors and American friends who seemed to care for humans. She remembered in particular some passages from the Talmud, that for all creatures Death was programmed from the beginning. One day, she even formulated a childish revision of Genesis. In fact, she had to admit to herself that, for all purposes, one could accept the new 'gospel': *In principio erat Mors. Et Vita erat Mortis soror usque ad consummationem saeculorum. Cui bono*? She felt that, at least in Western cultures, not until Freud was it possible to take the bull by the horns and analyse Death in pre-clinical terms. But she also knew that Maoris were not a product of the West, and neither of the East, except for certain recollections of latent and unexplainable forces taking her back to Hawaiki. Rationally, however, she could not escape Freud's postulation of Death as an unconscious wish for self-destruction hovering over all humans during moments of reflection, of stress, of meditation, of exposure to suffering. Was that why her father had insisted on abandoning the hospital and dying at home? A historical review of death themes, if not obsessions, did not help her much. From the Babylonian epic of Gilgamesh to modern philosophical existentialism, nothing seemed to explain anything, really. However, her exposure to Christianity had implanted into her mind something that only the termination of life could fulfill peacefully. In addition, nearly 4 years of American life, and death, had inured her from what in Aotearoa was just another phase of existence built into a not-so-unpleasant and unexplainable process. In the case of New Zealand, Mahina concluded that, since the country had been 'civilised' mostly during the Victorian era, Death had acquired the unspeakability of another great determinant, namely, sex. Both Death and sex were to be experienced in a hush-hush manner where *Homo americanus* was *caecus, mutus atque surdus*. St Paul's beliefs, though asepticised by British Protestantism, that the body was a temporal and sinful container, while the soul was blissfully eternal, roamed within Mahina's mind. One thing, however, was clear – the democratic principle of death sparing no one. Of course, that had nothing to do with American democracy, except that it was understood as something to believe in regardless of whether or not it existed.

When her father began to doze off, with the soup bowl in his hand, Mahina asked Komaru to take it to the kitchen, for she was going to take a shower and then a rest. She had not suffered jet lag for a long time, and she felt now a heavy need to sleep, though amazingly she did not, she could not conceive of sleeping during the daytime. She then looked at her father with apologetic eyes and left for her room. But after a few minutes she stormed into the kitchen somewhat distraught.

'Are you going to help me?,' Komaru asked.

'Not a chance. I told you I can't. Incidentally, where is my pareo? I looked all over for it. Has anyone cleaned ...'

'Sorry, sister. My fault. I ... borrowed it from you once or twice. It is in my closet, since my own is in Wellington, along with my clothes. Just a sec.'

Komaru came back with the pareo, which she grabbed and then went to the bathroom.

Mahina took a long shower that revived her. Meanwhile, Komaru washed, dried and put away all the dishes and utensils. He then looked into the freezer compartment of the fridge and retrieved a package of lamb chops. Perhaps Mahina could help in the evening for an early supper before the arrival of the night nurse. Then he began pondering, and deduced that Mahina would not help in the kitchen. America had undoubtedly spoiled her. He had hoped so much that her arrival would free him from what he regarded as feminine tasks. But he would soon know that it was not only a matter of liberated women philosophy in action. Mahina's eponymous had forbidden her to take over the household chores, at least for a while.

'OK, brother, let's have a little chat, right here and now.'

Her brusque tone, coupled with the introductory Americanism, was intended to sound playful, but to Komaru it sounded more than firm. It was something that Melissa tended to use toward her husband. Komaru could not help but mentally reread St Bernard's sentence in Bill's office: 'There is more danger in living with a woman ...' Then why would Bill cohabit with Melissa, although apparently married according to the laws of New Zealand? Was it an expedient, a screen of social conformity, or what, love? Of course, in Western mentality love was a prelude, if not a *sine qua non*, to sex, that damn and intangible drive existing allegedly for the propagation of the species. And who cared if the species would die one day like the dinosaurs?

Komaru turned away from the sink, into which he had just rinsed the wrapping paper dripping blood from the lamb chops, and dried off his hands.

'What a bloody mess! Now I understand why Jews don't care for Lilith.'

Mahina had taken a seat on the stool across the counter. The low afternoon sun from the northern window was hitting her upper body fully. The *tiki* her father had given her upon leaving for the States was still dripping a little on her middle nipple. The other two breasts, except for the hue, looked almost exactly like Melissa's before she had plastic surgery. The last time he had seen Mahina 'at home' was in the orchard, just before she left for America. The pear trees were beginning to bloom according to their varieties. Komaru liked the Italian one, the small fruits that did not take a long time to ripen and exude sweet drops of juice. Mahina was pareo-ing herself at the inception of Spring, and her torso was the only tree showing three buds. Komaru was taken back to that period of early September, when nature would begin to wake up along the season of innocent youth, of Maori life, of nearly forgotten sibling-hood. In fact, she was sitting so relaxed at the counter with a towel wrapped around her hair. A few rivulets of water would be patted now and then with the edge of the terrycloth.

'Komaru, you know. Or perhaps you don't or what. Of course, you don't have a mother, a wife, and you haven't had a sister for a while. Or, by any chance, do you have a mistress, sorry, a girlfriend or whatever? You know, I do have a girl friend, but, of course, not a girlfriend. As I do have some boy friends. Have you forgotten, anyway, that I am a *mahina*, with a small em? And, by any chance, do you remember that I am a curse to myself each and every lunar cycle? After all, I am not pregnant!'

'And you have to go round about just to inform me that you are menstruating? Is that why you did not touch the *paua* soup?'

'Exactly.'

'I can't believe it. I thought that America had freed you from ...'

'Stop that nonsense. I am still a Maori, 100 percent, especially when it comes to my body and ... my mind. As regards America, about which you imply a certain sense of liberalism, what do you expect when the vice president of the nation asks a grade school student how to pluralize "potato"?'

'Amazing.'

'Yes, isn't it? But not really, because I have read a lot about that monthly phenomenon. I traced it first linguistically, then physiologically among primates, next ritually in Polynesia, and finally personally as a *tapu* in Aotearoa.'

'And?'

'No "and". The problem is that you, as a male, have no conception whatsoever of the psychological impact on females – and here I don't refer only to PMS – be they apes, deer, cats, or *Homo sapiens*. I think that you would be less amused to know that the difference between me and a macaque, for example, is only a couple days in the 'red' process, a colour so 'Maori' that the Pakeha here still pronounce it like the name of the most important and traditional publishing house in Auckland, Wellington and London.'

'You mean Reed?'

'Of course! The Auckland pronunciation for "red", the colour of blood and roses, the Indo-European inheritor of the lunar calendars. Still, no one knows why we women are slaves of 29½-day cycles from birth to death, even though manifestly we are so only from puberty to menopause. I said "manifestly" because deep in our physiological structure the Moon reigns supreme virtually from conception onward. Witness the fact that, even when ovulation is stopped medically, a woman is still subject to "astronomical" phenomena. Perhaps one day astrophysicists will solve that mystery by proving that Luna is the daughter of Terra only genetically, though physiologically the Moon possesses the brain-key to operate Earthly functions, and thus a reminder that Sanskrit *rita*, Greek *metron* and Latin *mensura* are not simply philological terms. They are just labels for universal forces emanating from what we call Life.'

'Sorry, sister, I must confess my ignorance about feminist matters. I ...'

'Feminism has little to do with the sex of women, sorry, gender, quite a difference, although, in our superimposed British culture, whatever was prescribed onto us Maori, feminism as a movement is tied to half of the human race for philosophical reasons.'

'Philosophical?'

'Well, not in connection with subject-matters studied at schools, when one wants to point out that even at that level, ironically, it is a Pakeha contribution to women's liberation, and thanks to a male, not a female officially.'

'How generous of you to acknowledge that.'

'Yes and no. I said "officially" because "serious" professions were traditionally held by men. And political leadership, too. The fact that England had a Thatcher was purely a means to make fun of dried up fannies – incidentally, fanny in America is the rear end, not the front, for them the "pussy" – oh, what was I saying, yes, can you imagine a female prime minister in New Zealand? Of course, that will happen one day when men will first allow a woman to occupy the Beehive and then say, "You see what a woman can do? Copycat men to the extreme, as Thatcher did by creating a tempest in a teacup half a world away in the Falklands." Churchill would have said, "All right, you tango pushers. Have your rocks and try to raise *yerba mate* for your sheep." I think that most importantly it was the woman behind seminal ideas and this is exactly what happened to our feminist movement.'

'In Aotearoa?'

'How could we, brother ... but on Earth, I speak of a basis of intellectual operation that 100 years ago was at the centre of exploration of ideas when European nations had run out of geographic ones except for consolidating previous conquests at the expense of pagan natives.'

'Plus, I assume, at the expense of millions of human lives in two world wars for political exploitation.'

'Yes, yes, yes, but, coming back to what I was saying, do you recall John Stuart Mill from your philosophy courses?'

'I do, of course.'

At that point Komaru remembered the impact John had received from his father, who, in essence, tried to extend his intellectual life via the passing of his ideas to his progeny. And Komaru thought of his father, subtly doing something similar at the political level, at least years ago before he succumbed to despair for which alcohol became a palliative and a slow way to commit suicide. Mahina noticed that her brother had opened his eyes wide as if to retrieve some past data from reminiscences. Then she continued her Socratic "dialogue".

'What do you remember in particular, say, historically?'

'Oh, that ... he grew up in an atmosphere of attempted utilitarianism under his father's Prussian-style education, in method only, of course, though his aims were humane and humanitarian. I would say even antithetical to Victorian expansionism at the basis of the empire.'

'How generous of you! But you are a male chauvinist nevertheless. I call this reasoning the "Einstein's wife effect", for not many people acknowledge that Mrs. Einstein did for her husband more than cooking and washing.'

'Am I really such a monster?'

'You conveniently forget the rôle of Harriet Taylor, that is, Mill's wife, regarding the social position of women in Victorian England. That is why, especially here at home, our home, Pakeha women were the first on Earth to acquire the right to vote, the first step toward women's rights. But, actually, do you know why? Because New Zealand did not count at all in the world scene. It was a freak liberal accomplishment, for no nation above the equator thought of that "accomplishment" seriously. In England it was regarded as if Zulu women were given a token freedom of some kind, well, if not as an experiment, at least as a phoney magnanimity toward a movement of no consequence. Witness what women, particularly Maori, have accomplished in 100 years. They still boil their copper.'

'But you are not a Pakeha.'

'Of course not, fortunately, but I am tied to them by their men's power. Otherwise I am beyond it, I am a Maori woman. You see, Komaru, more than a a century ago, Mill was right in principle. But nowadays who reads *The Subjugation of Women*? Who studies the history of Humanity beginning with Sappho? In all curricula we start with Homer in the West. And, even assuming that Homer was a female author, the tradition has persisted in academia and daily life – particularly in religious organisations – that only men can perform serious research. We women were always told that our "nature" is an obstruction to ideal instruction and practical activities, even physical, except in bed. And don't look at me THAT way. I know, yes, Catholicism has had its faults, but look at Mother Teresa. She is worth ten UNICEFs, a hundred popes, a thousand Peace Corps volunteers. That sexist, that fag, that analphabet of Socrates, who went so far as to state that women would not have the stamina to exercise out of doors ...'

'Did he?'

'Does the name Glaucon ring any bells? I wish I could tell Socrates to take a trip to China and learn about Chinese women for the last three thousand years, and not what they do nowadays with Tao Chi, starting with street cleaning.'

'Yes, on that I agree with you. I remember them mowing the grass around the yard at East China Normal University by pulling each blade of grass manually.'

'Komaru, thanks, but I still think that you see us through the "prism of gender". Exactly as the Pakehas see Maoris through the "prism of race". In each case there are two rays of light, one deflected toward your own – "sex" and the other toward women's. And you act accordingly, depending on whose legacy you want to transmit to posterity. As in Mill's case. Yes, we learned a lot, though not seminally from him as we did from his wife. In the history of feminism I can state that Harriet Taylor was the first modern woman who removed the prismatic lenses from Mill's philosophy. Things will be better as long as we do not lose the proper perspective, considering men as "partners" in common Terrestrial endeavours, as they should do likewise. Even Betty Friedan has acknowledged that the original militant rights movement can destroy the Western family, the integrated society, and finally the survival of the community in the 21st century. And I suspect that my first idol, my icon of freedom, you know, Germaine Greer, has realised that. Just across the Tasman. Yes, a Pakeha, but a Polynesian nevertheless.'

Komaru remembered how recently he had snooped into his sister's library, and how he had 'discovered' a part of feminine prehistory. He felt guilty for not acknowledging that accidental invasion of privacy. After all, that was so because in his mind Mahina was simply a kid sister. Now she was an individual with a full personality. So he tried to calm her down.

'In essence, do you anticipate a kind of peace in the war between men and women?'

'Not exactly. I envisage a sort of X-cracy, a still undefined, shall I say, "consortiocracy", a new relationship between genders, provided, however, that women do not fall into the trap of American female ambiguity, those females who act officially as liberated from the waist up by imitating men and from the waist down by buzzing around males to trap them with their hormonal scent in contraposition to their pheromones. You know, brother, men are so stupid, just to unload a few millilitres of semen. And for that they get trapped with terrible consequences on two families, four, eight, sixteen and so forth, with dozens of children left to fend for themselves.'

'Thank you for the compliment. Yes, probably, I, sorry, we are stupid. But what shall we do to become wise?'

'Oh, well, let me tell you, although I know that in part we are responsible. To reach an objective of full cooperation, women should first learn what masculine prejudices are, and act accordingly, that is, constructively. So far, feminism in New Zealand has been confrontational at the initial Germaine Greer stage. I used to be her fan after reading her first book and tasting my menstrual blood.'

'Er ... how did it taste?'

'You see, *Brute, tu quoque*, and you are not even my son. Why don't you find out for yourself? Would you like me to leave a Tampax on a dish for you to savour the unique flavour of its components? Which reminds me, I need to buy some Red River Pads. I only brought a few Tampax with me. And the bitch at customs even touched them morbidly, as if I had tried to smuggle who knows what. I felt like telling her that in New Zealand it is difficult to get pads, since at age 14 all women are in a hurry to become patented and use plastic tubing to insert a removable cotton cylinder by pulling a string.'

'Sister, you haven't been here long and you already ...'

'You asked me how menstrual blood tastes. I found out it is rather semi-sweetish and salty, almost like a Chinese soup left out of the fridge to spoil. And viscous. You see, brother, it is different from tasting semen, I assume as I have been told, because in the semen one can detect some dietary traces, such as garlic among Italians and monosodium glutamate among Asians. Once I read an article by a French "Greer", the publisher of *Les Femmes* and written by Pharaoh Sollers, considered the first manifesto of modern misogyny. Well, her philosophy can be encapsulated in a sentence, "Give me the courage to look into my heart (of course, our guts) and at my body with disgust."'

'Not a constructive one.'

'On the contrary. Would you look at your own phallus that way? No, of course, as I have looked at myself. No, of course, because the

Greek tradition of phallocracy is still alive and well all over. To avoid that, men would rather look away from their own bodies and concentrate on other things ... as you have been doing for a while by staring at my breasts. What do you see in them beyond a natural *biberon* for a set of triplets?'

'Sorry, Mahina, I ...'

'I what? You don't have to say anything. Or would you still like to touch them as you used to when I was about eleven or twelve? So what? I even liked that, as if you had touched my ears or my nose. Or by any chance do you miss the nourishing affection you received from Mom? Am I a subconscious replacement? Or do you still swing back and forth along Anthony Burgess' polarity between Augustinian denial (have you already reached that stage?) and Pelagian permissiveness – ah, you seem to stir uncomfortably. Obviously, you don't believe in original sin. You must have a female receptor at your disposal. Who is she? I hope a she, of course. I assume you are not gay. I have been away too long to interfere with your free will, haven't I?'

Komaru became silent for a minute, nearly terrified. That American import was reading him like an open *pukapuka*. He was thinking of Ling-ling's layer of Pancakes Rocks in Punakaiki versus Melissa's Moeraki Boulders after her Brazilian adventure.

'I simply don't know, sister, I still look at you as I used to do when we were growing up. No feelings of superiority, no condescension. I should say ... I may have been affected by, er, Chinese democracy, that is, something neutral between, if I can borrow from your references, Burgess' Gusphase and Pelphase.'

'But you mentioned democracy. Of what?'

'A general term for ...'

'For an empty word? That is a lot of hogwash, if you'll forgive me for what Tanya used to say. You know of her, she comes from a farming background. What kind of democracy? As in the States, where monarchical democracy was substituted by a fraternal democracy in 1776? Still ruled by men, I mean the marital, corporate, military democracy wearing pants with zippers and so on. Yes, a few token women interspersed here and there to offer quickies ...'

'Then what can you expect? Maternal democracy, sororal ones?'

'No, the problem would still exist. The Amazons had to tolerate a host of penetrators.'

'Then, the cooperation of science on the verge of accomplishing parthenogenesis?'

'Well, as long as the largest percentage of women haters, either consciously or unconsciously, feel superior, this world is doomed through conflicts and thus wars. In essence, men go to war as an alternative means of struggle against women.'

'Then, have you any idea of an ... X-cracy as a solution to the problem?'

'In theory, yes, as a form of anthropocracy, an inclusive term, though it is too late for me. Equality of genders is possible at almost any level, but unfortunately it ... engenders (no pun intended) everything past the nomadic stage. So I solved the problem my own way, by exiting from the general human consortium in order to avoid the innate violence between genders. How? By entering an oasis of physical and spiritual isolation. Amazingly, the first grasp of this possibility, which in the States is a sort of "chickening" out in farming language, again, came to me while reading Dante when I took a course on European literature at Salzburg. In the Fourth Canto of the *Paradiso*, if I remember correctly, Dante finds an alternative to violence by giving an option to humans between using force and entering a monastery. Can you envision, a, who, a Gandhi, even though using passive force, entering a convent, or you yourself becoming a monk to avoid a confrontation with the Pakeha establishment?'

'No, of course.'

'Well, I trust I am not shocking you, but I am very seriously considering the possibility of becoming a nun, a cloistered one, a difficult task nowadays. Perhaps in the States. I am lucky that I have been exposed to Catholicism, this being purely accidental, and not as a means of entering a nunnery. Otherwise I would probably prefer to enter a Buddhist convent, except that there I might be coerced, either psychologically or physically, to engage in sexual practices as part of the novitiate. And I am not yet THAT Oriental, for I abhor sex.'

'You mean, with anybody, even if in love?'

'For sure with men, regardless of what you intend for love. I don't know if also with women or ... myself.'

'And does father know of your ... desire to become a nun, and a Catholic one at that?'

'No, of course, why should I inform him of that? To cause him a heart attack or induce an early coma?'

'Which reminds me, tomorrow Dr Ferguson should stop by to visit with Father. I notice that his speech is beginning to falter. Before your arrival, he told me he wants to speak to both of us about his final wishes.'

'Poor Papa! I hope he can do that soon before he lapses into another coma. You wrote me that he has already recovered from two of them.'

'Yes, but he has already signed his "DNR" papers. And we should not interfere with his wishes if you agree. Now that you are here, I sense it is just a matter of days, for I feel that he has made an effort to wait for you without interrupting your school activities. He was always eager to hear from you. And the reason he did not write you at length stems from his fear that you would read his despair between the lines. You know, you were always his favorite child. He never exhibited the same type of affection toward me.'

'Oh, come on, Komaru, Maori men are not that cissy. Besides, you were always so independent.'

'Anyway, let's see if he has woken up. You go first. I'll come down in a moment.'

It had become chilly. Mahina went into her room first to get a sweater. Komaru entered the rumpus room to see his father slightly bent on the right looking at the clouds of sunset tinged with the rose-red hue of that particular evening. As a painter, he always followed the transition of the colours displayed in a fraction of a second. And, in connection with red, he always maintained that there was no such absolute colour, though it was a Maori one. He had acquired from Pakeha history of art and physics a whole terminology of chromatic scales from crimson scarlet to pillarbox, magenta and purplish. Then he would describe the vermillion by varying it into madder and terracotta. By applying his knowledge of flowers then to the cultivation of the front garden, he would detect the rose colour gamut of peonies before sliding into the range of poppy and geranium. For whatever reason, he was partial to cyclamen, which he would offer to Mahina as soon as the plant started to bud. In a matter of hours the flower would bloom under the delightful eyes of an innocent. That was Mahina, budding all the time, through flowers only. She could not associate any other red hue with edibles such as strawberries, plums or tomatoes, and never with salmon or lobster. Well, she would connect it with some less delicate items such as rubies, garnets and coral, for they could be associated with gold, the only metal she would ever use, though sparingly, as the small chain between her leather necklace of the *hei tiki* and the *tiki per se*. She was almost visually allergic to silver and even platinum.

And blood, the colour of life and death. The colour of mankind, conceived in the pleasure of blood, born in the blood of parturition, spilled in the violent death of trench warfare or even in fumbling with hospital needles and transfusion bottles before exiting in the agony of a ranting struggle for air through the nose and the mouth. Blood and death even at home, in silence, away from traditional *tangihanga*. The 'Oppenheim effect', calling for the central Maori ceremony via an oral panegyric under a carved lintel of a door for the *iwi* to witness the economic, political, and moral (religious) open-air speech was not to take place, for the exiguous descent would be informed on paper *post ex facto*. Mr Reti, in fact, had told that to Komaru one morning, the last day of June when Mahina was still asleep recovering from jet lag. Komaru's father had displayed an unusually clear mind, the swan song sung by people on the verge of dying. He had spent a good night of rest in spite of the extreme pain in his abdominal cavity, for which he had refused medication. That was the final meeting between two men alone. He sensed the impending end of a terrestrial journey before taking the last one on his way to Cape Reinga. He felt relieved, having taken care of that bothersome task, though he was satisfied and even relaxed to welcome the banner of death just waiting in the wings. Well, it was the last act of responsibility as a member of the so-called human consortium. He wished he had been a fish, perhaps even a small whale, so that he could sink unnoticed into the depths of an ocean, without being stuffed into a coffin. He wondered whether human remains would develop claustrophobia, spending eternity in such close confines. And he told Komaru so. But Komaru said nothing. What could he do when society dictates not only how to die, but also how to remain dead for eternity?

Chapter 26

Wednesday morning's sun rose slowly on Papakura's gray sky. Clouds of cold rain skimmed the gulf water so low that the viaduct facing the picture window of the rumpus room seemed suspended over them as if by magic.

Mahina had slept off and on, not only because of the time difference, which in itself was not much, except that the day she had gained 4 years earlier was lingering perhaps subconsciously in her psyche as one lost outside her metabolic system. That is probably why she was menstruating so heavily, she assumed. Besides, early in the night the fax machine had woken her. It was a short note of acknowledgment from the International Student Office regarding the temporary holding of her mail at the secretary's desk. Mahina had faxed first her telephone and fax number, an identical one coded to recognise the latter automatically.

The little sleep she had gotten had been perturbed by strange dreams against a background of a city that was neither Portland nor Auckland. They were so similar in maritime topography and flora that it was difficult to distinguish between them. In her oneiric tossing and turning, her body still seemed to be in Portland and her mind in Papakura. She had assumed that the reverse might take place, that is, her mind in the States and her body at home. No! Indeed, before falling asleep she had heard Komaru in his room, just as years before. The *kauri* wall dividing the two rooms was thin enough to allow some sounds to get through. Komaru would listen to the 23:03 Nightcap News on National Radio to check on the weather nearly every evening. Then he would turn the radio off and give the wall two soft and short knocks to wish Mahina good night when he sensed she was still awake reading or studying. It was a childhood game between them, depending on who would call it a day and signal the wish for a period of rest. When Komaru was 'mad' at her, he would rap gently twice for the two syllables of 'Good Night' and Mahina would respond depending on how she felt toward him. If still resentful, then a two-tone Pakeha greeting, but when in a pacifying mood she would apply three knocks for Maori 'E moe koe', a rather formal greeting between grownups. The previous night he had heard five syllables, and had replied accordingly, for she was happy that Komaru had not forgotten the old days of innocence. The Maori beds were lying parallel to each other so that at times Mahina heard Komaru snoring or accidentally banging an elbow against the thin wooden wall.

The dreams were a combination of reflections on daily events. The night nurse had been informed that, beginning the following day, Mahina would take care of her father. She would sleep during the day as she had since her arrival from Portland. That night, thus, she dreamt of being a nurse, but, more than that, it was the kitchen discussion with Komaru that seemed to dominate the contents of the dream. He would tell her that she had forgotten at least half of John Stuart Mill's story, and that Harriet was only an accidental appendage to women's rights. And, in particular, that Mill had been influenced by John Locke, and that without Montesquieu and Descartes there would not have been any European wind of freedom. Of course, the whole interaction between the British philosophers and the French Enlightenment was a mumbo jumbo of factoids and a faceless series of people who spoke only English, not Maori, and neither French.

That morning Mahina was still awake under the enervating influence of her dreams, though ready to greet the night nurse on her way home. Dr Ferguson would arrive later in the day. According to the nurse, Mr Reti's night was touch and go. Actually, she had said a night of 'suspension', whatever that meant, for he could lapse into a coma again with no hope of natural or medically induced recovery. The nurse also felt that perhaps the usual morning surge of vitality in terminal patients would allow Mahina and Komaru to talk with their father very carefully on casual matters. Mahina, particularly, could try to elicit some information on a certain Maria, a name that Mr Reti associated with Mahina herself a few times when he would switch from Maori to a strange language. As a Tongan she could understand some Northern Maori, but the other language was beyond her comprehension since it sounded like a Slavic one. In addition, whether in English or Maori, the time reference seemed to go back a couple of generations, and she understood clearly something connected with the Waitangi Action Committee in addition to facts about daily life. Of course, Mahina could connect the broken episodes transpiring through her father's night recollections. However, she was surprised when the nurse informed her of a Slavic-sounding name, like one used by perhaps Dalmatians. Mahina wondered, for her father as a child had spent many years among Dalmatians during the last phase of the *kauri* gum period in the North. What was the word? The nurse said something like *ko tu ha* or *Koru tula*. What could it be? In Maori it could not be traced to anything specific. Perhaps *korua* or *koru* referred to both of them, Mahina and Komaru as 'you two', and *tuwha* or *tuha* to anything to be separated or divided. Could it be that her father had tried to communicate with his children on matters of inheritance to be allocated to them in equal proportions? Komaru had already mentioned that his father's last will and testament had been placed in trust with a barrister who knew his affairs. Besides, Mahina did not care about anything anyway, for she had in mind a life ahead of her without tangible possessions involving business. Her plans for an existence of simple conduct with the minimum shelter and food was looming on the horizon of her wishes. And American materialism revolving around Wall Street indoctrination had immunised her totally. She just could not understand how humans could be mostly concerned with stocks, bonds, clipping coupons, hoping for the DOW Index to hit 5,000, or whatever. She pitied the growing yuppie generation enmeshed in an ever-increasing tide of electronic gadgets washed ashore to valueless spiritual lands where peace of mind is becoming not even a concept of human life.

At mid-morning Komaru called Mahina in her room. She was unpacking some items she had brought for her father and brother as gifts. For Komaru she had acquired some CDs, namely two sets of the Angels Series. She had fallen in love with the Scandinavian composer who had spent most of his life trying to capture in musical scores the ineffable spirituality of angelology. For her father she had purchased a radio scanner with weather and emergency frequencies. She had not realised how sick he was, and how soon he would die. She had left on her bed a book she had started to read on the plane.

'I trust I am not interrupting anything too personal. You must have spent a rotten night, for I heard you snapping suitcase locks ... and the fax, of course.'

'Well, I have to break the "American" cycle. But I rested and read a lot.'

'I see. Incidentally, who is *Paulina, 1880?*'

'You are snooping again. Oh, that is a 1973 translation of a novel by Pierre Jean Jouve, a novelist-poet who is being rediscovered by Anglophones after 100 years. That is the fate of French literature, to wait a century to cross the Channel, and who knows how many years to cross the Tasman.'

'A religious book?'

'Not quite. Actually, it is the story of a nun in love.'

'Oh, aren't nuns always in love with Christ or God?'

'Please, Komaru, that is a human love for another human.'

'Are you learning anything from it or, by any chance, are you in love?'

'How can I? I am not a nun. Besides, I have never been in love. And I doubt I'll ever be. Look, so scary!'

On the page facing the copyright information, Komaru read the quotation:

Love is as hard and unbending as hell.
St Teresa of Ávila

'My goodness, sister, I am glad I'll never be able to become a nun myself.'

'Or in love?'

Komaru avoided a reply by suggesting that they go downstairs to the rumpus room. She carried the scanner with her.

'That bitch at Customs. Sorry, that's Tanya's language. Do you know that she, I mean, the Customs officer gave me hell for this gadget, as if I had tried to smuggle a spying device? She could not believe I had gotten it on special at Radio Shack in Portland. And she said that father has to obtain a permit to operate it. Is this country becoming like Iraq?'

'Sister, please, calm down! Let's see father. The nurse told me he may like to talk with us. Better now before Dr Ferguson's visit.'

There wasn't much talk. Mahina tried to explain the working of the scanner by reading its instructions, quite a feat in Taiwanese English. Unfortunately, she had forgotten to insert the battery, which Komaru did after finding it at the bottom of the cardboard box, together with the registration card and warranty. A lot of screeching and cracking came in between fragmented sentences of incomprehensible language interspersed by 'over' and numerical codes. Apparently, the gadget had contributed to alerting Mr Reti. He took Mahina's hand and held it with a strong grip in his.

'Thank you ... dear ... what a nice gift. Do people listen ... to ... that in America, what ... mean ... to them in heaven?'

'Oh, Dad, please, well some people relegated to bed use it more than here I suppose, because in the States there are no restrictions.

Apparently, radio waves here belong to the Crown. Our ancestors must have, er ... forgotten to list them together with our *whenua* and *kai moana*. They could not envisage, actually, the need to keep the "ghosts" of the Rangi together with the substance.'

Her father tried to smile, with a bitter face.

'I see that you know our history. Anyway, I should be at the Rangi soon, I hope, and ... can verify directly whether the *Kuini* kept the radio waves in the package of ... goodies we gave her. Sorry ... I can't take this with me. Better off not to know what ... how you will fare down here. Komaru ... it is he ... who needs it. He is still chasing the white whale. Do you mind, Mahina? You see ... Komaru will take over ... I need to rest.'

'Papa, thank you. I promise I'll do what I can. I know that you tried so hard. But time is on our side. Believe me, as long as *te reo* remains alive.'

'Komaru ... Mahina ... let's avoid the theatricals ... please do only the ... essentials. I wish I ... had the stamina to explain ... but you'll understand everything after I am gone. So ... no *tangihanga* ... just the death notice in the *Herald* for the legality. Private service for us only at the burial grounds, if you so want. And ... no bereavement, of course. I already took leave of my comrades in ... Rotorua. My *tupapaku* can ... follow the Pakeha routine without dis ... rupting your lives, and ... low profile, please. Death does not ... deserve to be treated as ... royalty. Scorn it, and yes, tell, tell the Papakura Maori Centre that I thank them, but no need for specials. So, just the final responsibility as, er, I like it. Don't give death much importance ... treat it like brushing your teeth or even evacuating. Actually, that is, my *wairua* discards a useless body. No need for any pomp. And, Komaru, spare me the *poroporoaki*. Promise.'

'Yes, Papa, I promise.'

'Thanks, you will understand later. All in ... structions are in the centre drawer of my desk. Art work ... give Mahina precedence. You already know of ... the cemetery next to her, your mother. And, if later, in a year ... but ... no need.'

Mahina just stood by silently, and puzzled. She thought, *A year. Where will I be? And why?*

Komaru was ready to ask his father a question when the door bell rang discreetly. Mahina answered. It was Dr Ferguson, with whom she exchanged a few words in the entrance hall.

By the time they entered the rumpus room, Mr Reti was asleep, or apparently so. Komaru, knowing his father, thought that he was feigning sleep in order to avoid what he considered 'stupid' questions, for once he had told his son that at death a better doctor could be either a bottle of grappa or a 9-mm bullet. Yes, death and hope were antithetical, if not degrading to each other.

Dr Ferguson took less time than the usual to perform a cursory examination – stethoscoping the heart, the lungs, groping the liver area, checking the pulse, inserting the ear thermometer for a few seconds and trying to look at the pupils. For this routine examination Dr Ferguson had a hell of a time because he found a lot of resistance from the patient, but said nothing. He probably understood that Mr Reti had already died for the world. It was Mahina who begged the doctor to check the intravenous apparatus, for she had been instructed by the nurse on how to substitute a couple of bottles when empty. They were just fine. She would take care of her father during the night, and Komaru during the day.

On the threshold of the entrance, Dr Ferguson gave the siblings an appraisal of the situation. He mentioned that the vital signs indicated a marginal situation bordering on the dysfunction of the operational so and so, and that a potential death–coma could set in at any time, unless the heart gave way first. What jargon! That was because of the extreme pain their father was undergoing. It was a matter of a final crisis within 24 hours or so, since the body temperature was below normal. Of course, an intensive process of reanimation could take place if he were transferred to the Auckland Hospital. This would initiate a medically useless cycle in an attempt to extend a near-vegetal life for a little more time. But both Komaru and Mahina assured him once more that, according to their father's wishes, a tacit and humane 'let him go' with dignity was acceptable to all parties, rather than having him manipulated by a host of perfunctory technicians who knew that it was wasted time, effort and taxpayer's money. And, legally, the DO NOT RESUSCITATE paper signed months earlier in front of two witnesses would disown any claim of malpractice. As there were no other close relatives, the chances for procedural complications were practically nil.

'And for the oxygen?,' asked Mahina.

'Oh, well,' replied Dr Ferguson, 'it is up to the nurse to administer it, should the case demand it. But I doubt it will be needed.'

'In fact,' Komaru interjected, 'the nurse will not be here during the night.'

'Then, let the patient, sorry, Mr Reti be free of that restriction, should he want to talk with you unobstructed.'

At that point, Mahina felt that, in reality, her father had died. It was a matter of hours. As she would spend the night at his bedside, she told Komaru she preferred not to have any dinner, though she needed to sleep a while in the afternoon and then maybe have supper. Komaru agreed and hugged her, gently rubbing his nose onto hers. At that, Mahina threw her arms around his neck, almost as automatically as she used to do with Tanya when either of the two friends needed comfort. But now she held him tightly a long time against her torso. Tears meanwhile had begun to trail her cheeks, pausing on her upper lip before being deflected along the sides toward her chin. What happened to her when Komaru wiped them first with his big fingers, and then by applying his lips on her eyes, created a hiatus of sudden and unexpected wonder between her and him. While Komaru had tasted the saltiness of his childhood by remembering his mother, Mahina had experienced an invading wave of physical warmth emanating from her heart and lodging into her bowels. Or was it the reverse? And, while for Komaru his mother's tears were present only through the remembrance of an anguish lodged in him so long ago, for Mahina it was a powerful feeling, like being dunked head first into the hottest caldera of Rotorua. She even smelled the sulfur emanating from Komaru's body which repelled her as if she had been touched by the Devil, a concept she had just learned from her Sunday afternoon catechism sessions at the university chapel in Portland.

After quickly releasing her grip from around his neck, she pounded his chest with her fists while melting in pain and in pleasure. And she let her tears and mucus flow liberally over her chin, for Komaru had stopped comforting her.

It was the blind leading the blind, for Komaru was silently crying, while she was sobbing loudly. At that, Mahina left him abruptly, jumping over the short steps toward her room, whose door she slammed and locked from the inside. The astonished Komaru was left alone on the threshold of death, numb and afraid of himself. Was he the man his father was counting on to continue an unspoken tradition in the quest for his white whale?

He next sat at his father's bedside. Then he remembered his father's request regarding the contents of the center drawer. What had he meant? And why all the secrecy now, when knowing something of his father's plans could trigger some need to ask him questions while he was still alive? Thus, he entered the studio and opened the metal desk drawer. The large envelope was sealed on both sides with transparent packing tape. The instructions in both Maori and English were clear and even appeared ominous since they were written in block letters with an indelible black magic marker. The wording informed anyone not to open and read anything, under penalty of a *tapu*, before his death. As the message was addressed to both Mahina and himself, Komaru placed the envelope back into the drawer, entered the death room, and sat by his father, who seemed to be asleep, exhaling a heayy breath reeking with a semi-sweetish fragrance of violets. But his face looked serene, as if he was ready to travel all the way to Cape Reinga to say good-bye to the *pohutukawa* tree before being met by millions of kindred spirits who, during thousands of years, had preceded him all the way to Hawaiki after barely sojourning a mere lifetime on the *whenua* of his *iwi*.

Komaru spent the rest of the afternoon in the kitchen, looking through the window over the sink at the western clouds skimming the top of the land stretching north of Middlemore between One Tree Hill and Mt Wellington. His vague plans to prepare supper for Mahina and himself were interrupted by frequent trips downstairs to check on his father's condition. He was asleep, or languishing in a sort of torpor indicating a relaxed posture. When he was awake, the Pakeha single bed permitted him to glance over the windowsill far into the watery horizon past the highway viaduct.

Before leaving the rumpus room, Komaru wondered about the previous night's meeting, virtually the very last one *en famille*. He looked around the bedside and detected, among the flacons, bottles of useless pills, instructions, and other items left by the nurse on the night stand, a book lying there semiburied, the book his father had been leafing through during the last month or so: *Moby-Dick*. That still puzzled him, for apparently his father must have tried either to reach it or hide it. Undoubtedly, it had been moved. Or perhaps the nurse had handled it for whatever reason. He was still puzzled. Why THAT book? Strange, for recently it seemed to float around the most immediate possessions, including the binoculars his father had brought from the sanatorium. As curiosity was giving him a complex, since he had read it a long time ago, he tried to recall a movie he had seen many years before at the Classic Film Festival sponsored by the Victoria University Student Association. In that connection, he recalled the presentation made by the head of the film committee regarding the rôle of New Zealand waters and sailors mentioned by Melville. Komaru guessed that in *Moby-Dick*, New Zealand, or 'New Holland', had been mentioned for the first time on an international scale in a literary work, whose reviews had been mostly negative, particularly in the American press. The head had mentioned how depressed Melville had been, under financial difficulties, particularly to pay for the printing plates. History was repeating itself, from Tolstoy to Proust to Joyce, just to mention a few who never lived long enough to have the satisfaction of being understood by at least one reader free enough to break with the accepted norm in the vogue of James Fennimore Cooper. Komaru felt that, actually, whenever there is irony, there may be potential history. As a historian, that was his consolation for what he thought he was doing in connection with his MA thesis. Would it ever be finished? He was anxious to get some real critical input from Melissa. He was somewhat afraid that she would be tolerant of a 'son's doing' for the purpose of encouraging a lost cause.

He then took the book to the kitchen, where he had already defrosted a saddle of lamb in the microwave. After salting and herbing it, he preheated the oven to medium heat with the intention of roasting it on the triangular rack centered on a deep rectangular pan. Mahina had recently mentioned that in the States few people would eat imported New Zealand lamb, even if sold on special along with frozen filet of snapper sold to naïve Americans under a phony name, not to mention wines crawling up the display racks next to Australian bottles. Bafflingly, even Kiwi apples would hit the fruit bins just across the Willamette River from the State of Washington and its own Golden Delicious apples. Americans would try anything from anywhere, though lamb seemed to be appreciated mostly by middle Easterners. Greeks would not touch it at any price. Mahina had never seen it at the university cafeteria, except once when lamb patties had been served during a union strike that blocked the shipment of beef for a few weeks. The 'lamburgers' had become a fad because the stronger flavour of the meat was a favourite among macho students. Mahina wondered how the New Zealand economy would fare if, in competition with all the lamb coming from Utah and Nevada, Americans would patronise ovines at the 'Meso Burger', a fictitious name she had invented by excising the tail of Butler's sheep station name. Komaru took his time, and peeled some medium *kumara* along with medium-sized unpeeled carrots (he thought about Melissa and how she preferred the large ones), placing them at the bottom of the rack. Then, in the absence of bay leaves he sprinkled an incongruous pinch of Provençal herbs and a few drops of red *aceto balsàmico*. The little bottle of the former had never been opened, and he wondered how it had reached the Reti household. Perhaps his father had had a tinge of culinary nostalgia for some of the Northern Italian condiments to which he must have been exposed two generations before. After setting the oven timer to an hour and 45 minutes, Komaru finally placed the pan uncovered into the centre of the oven, hoping that Mahina would come out of her room for supper.

While waiting for the meat to roast at a low heat, Komaru sat at the counter, turned on the ceiling light over it, and browsed through the whole book, back and forth. It was marked here and there and its cover was battered more than one would expect from a single reading. Obviously, unless purchased second hand, it had been used heavily, and glosses had been added in the margins, some of them in Maori, followed by question marks and exclamation points. In particular, pages 438 and 442 were full of underlined passages along with the names of Queequeg and of the coffin in which he lay for a while in order to ensure a proper fit. The next to the last paragraph on page 441 seemed to have been under special scrutiny since the first sentence had been highlighted in red:

Now, there is noteworthy difference between savage and civilized; that while a sick, civilized man may be six months convalescing, generally speaking, a sick savage is almost half-well again in a day.

Poor father, thought Komaru, what was he trying to do or what was he hoping for? A memo to himself, getting well by returning to a stage of savagery as conceived by white people, provided that he first was considered 'civilized' according to Melville's notions a century and a half ago? That was just about the time before the Trick of Waitangi had been forced down the throats of naïve savages.

Then Komaru's attention was attracted by some notes in English pencilled in by his father on the inside of the back cover, where parallel comparisons had been listed in two vertical columns, placing Melville's topography on the left and his own on the right. Obviously, the list had been compiled by his father while being treated at the Rotoroa Island sanatorium, for he had made a sketch of the hills on Waiheke Island between Mt Maunganui and Stony Batter, actually a silhouette of a sperm whale with its nose touching the north end of Awawaroa Bay, its hump on Maunganui hill and its fin by Hooks Bay. And, under the single line profile, Komaru's father had written 'My Mount Greylock from my Harrowhead.' Where in the world were those topographic features located? And why so referred, against the islands dotting the eastern waters of Auckland. Komaru hoped one day to solve that puzzle either by direct research or by asking Dr McTavish who might have read the book after first receiving a NIL OBSTAT from Pope Sigismundus I.

Mahina's soft steps interrupted Komaru's vagaries. She was wearing the usual pareo, but this time with a woollen sweater, one she had not worn since her teenage days, when Merino wool was shipped to Italy before returning to New Zealand under the name of Benetton. It was a two-colour design, the upper part in white and the bottom in blue. That was the fashion for a tight garment sculpting the torso rather uncomfortably. Komaru noticed that her breasts were creating on the knitted garment a horizontal band rather than two peaks, for the *tiki* covering the central teat acted like a bridge spanning the two extremities. The whole sculpture looked to Komaru like a micro-white whale, the silhouette of dysfunctional nature slightly shifting its hump to the left when Mahina placed her right elbow on the counter. The white whale was surfing above the blue yonder in a calm sea. She was rather surprised to see Komaru fingering that book.

'That is not something to read in the kitchen,' she said after noticing the paperback in his hand. 'It is to be regarded at least like poetry, fighting with philosophy. Of course, pure poetry is more relaxing even when exhibiting a hallucinatory power of attraction. I hope I am not late, for I lost track of time reading a poem by Bozarth.'

'Bozarth?'

'Oh, brother! Alla Renee Bozarth, and her "Passover Remembered", the words of which have become for me an irresistible magnet. This afternoon I decided that I had succumbed, I am going to go, brother.'

'Go where?'

'Along with her, by following her. Just a sec.'

She came back with a copy of *Womanpriest: A Personal Odyssey*, a 1988 edition containing the poem. 'Listen, Komaru.'

And she read quotations from the entire poem, almost in a trance. Komaru was fascinated by her power of interpretation, and at the same time worrying at the cooking status of the lamb, hoping it would not get over-roasted or burned, for he was smelling the fragrance of the lamb behind his back and the scent of Mahina's hot flesh in front of him. From the very first verse, 'Pack nothing' to the last one 'and I am waiting for you', Komaru had followed her spellbound, frozen by her fever of sure hope, by the convincing modulation of her passionate voice. That sister of his was an enchantress capable of taking him to hell while she was thinking of heaven through a radical change of terrestrial life.

'So exciting, Komaru. Now we are lying between two books. Yours and mine, actually two people, a woman and a man, for books are just humans in print, physiological beings opening their mind to the minds of others.'

'But this is father's book. I read this as a fishing expedition, and that was aeons ago. I found it so difficult, although I knew some maritime terminology.'

'Fishing? First of all, a whale is not a fish. It is a mammal like us. The difference is that whales are still in the ocean. We left the water a long time ago. Oh, if we had stayed there, free to swim hidden from everything on land! When I read it the first time I was a *tabula rasa*. But then I had to analyse it for a term paper in which I isolated features, mores, and characters inspired by Maori traditions. I also saw several movies, including Lloyd Bacon's 1930 version of *Moby-Dick* directed by Jean-Pierre Melville.'

'Melville?'

'Yes,' she replied, 'the film director, a Frenchman in love with the American author – who had been ignored at home, you know, *Nemo Propheta in patria* – had changed his family name to Melville legally and officially.'

'That is fantastic, how could anyone transpose onto celluloid a whaling adventure, sorry, you said a philosophical treatise?'

'Yes, a philosophical treatise first.'

'It seems to me that only because you majored in philosophy you see that discipline at the centre of the universe.'

'Of course, for genetically it has been there like a main spring, but, sorry, you were saying that it is difficult. Of course, but not impossible, if one studies philosophy first. I insist on it. And, even after that, *Moby-Dick* is not just a novel to be read once or twice and then put aside. Do you listen to Tchaikovsky's *Violin Concerto* or admire Botticelli's *Venus* only once?'

Komaru could not be taken aback by Botticelli's vision of pre-Brazil Melissa whose breasts were so similar, as if surpassed in design even by virtual reality. To hell with philosophy, Komaru thought. But Mahina continued in an almost incessant lecture.

'It is a philosophical treatise, a perennial plant of never-changing foliage and fruits, to be read, dissected, and savoured during the course of a lifetime. I think that Melville so far is the only human to put America on the map of civilisation west of the Atlantic. Nothing else has reached the level of symbolism and humanness as much or more comprehensibly than that ... well, not a novel as commonly referred to, but a quasi novel for lack of a better designation, since humans persist in labelling everything as if set in stone.'

'Then, as you yourself are trying to do now, a quasi-novel, a ... qua ... vel?'

'If you so want, just another label, yes, because critics are otherwise stuck with old terminology for a new ... oh, call it genre, and again why not another label for a new creation? This happens in music and in other fields of human accomplishment, though in architecture we have departed from Greek and Roman styles more freely. But in the republic of letters we are still ruled by some kind of constitution as sacred as the overblown American one, lasting an eternity. No, Komaru, a literary constitution, as the American political one, may be complemented by amendments. And, as for me, after taking a course in comparative literature from Dr Nolan, I decided to analyse and enjoy a work without preconceived notions of classification. Sorry ... are you sure you are not burning something in the oven?'

'I hope not, though I detect the strong fragrance of the lamb, for you ... lamb Yugoslavian style as Mother used to prepare it for Dad. But, of course, you can't remember. I could not find bay leaves, so I put a pinch of French herbs in.'

'Oh, those invading people trying to invent new things from time to time, as the last time with deconstruction, such a contradictory term. I bet they are going to deconstruct the product of their Gallic imagination before they reconstruct it as they did each and every war to keep it alive on the stage of their superiority complex.'

'Whatever you mean by that, have they ... deconstructed Melville?'

'Oh, no, they can't for, ironically, they cannot compete with the virtual reality of computer electronics. That would be suicide in spite of building a linguistic Berlin wall around the boundaries of the *Académie*. They may touch, oh, yes, some other American classics after Melville – even his near contemporaries, say Thoreau, Hawthorne and even that egocentric Mark Twain – but not Melville. He is the Dante and the Shakespeare of America. No one else has reached his stature. You know, at Customs I wondered what they would have said about the few books I had brought with me and the others I shipped by freighter ... sorry, I'm getting hungry, can you serve supper now?'

'Aye, aye, skipper! How do you prefer your blubber steak?'

'Barely done, of course, oh, what I was saying, Melville's ocean was life, human life, and *Moby-Dick* its purpose, no, sorry, the prime actor on the stage of life, what humans have to cope with, fighting it during the search for ... I don't know, truth? Or the *summum bonum* constantly obstructed by evil? Is it, perhaps, something standing in the way of a purpose in life? Do you, brother, have a purpose in life or ... do you regard it as a charade, a pain in the neck, a curse, what?'

'Yes, of course, sister, that of cooking for you since, you female chauvinist, you ... say you don't cook, though of course I would do anything for you. What a farce ... '

'What, what?'

'Nothing! I know I am a failed cook, for you are going to leave me, aren't you, especially after being presented an overcooked lamb saddle. So you cannot ride on it. Or will you leave me anyway?'

'Yes, of course, what would you expect me to do here in Papakura, become another Makereti entertaining British royalty?'

Komaru meanwhile had served the dish in silence. He felt that there is nothing more painful than being mocked about something in which one is engaged idealistically, but unable to express or reveal for either obvious or security reasons. Acting like a moron is more painful than being one.

Mahina complimented him on the dish. She said she rediscovered the flavours of the Maori Girls College refectory, where Pakehas ate lamb at dinner as long as it was disguised under the label of roast beef dripping a bloody mess. That happened since Maori food like *poaka* could not be presented unless overcooked for sanitary reasons. But Komaru did not taste anything except the realisation that he was going to lose a sister, the last member of his family. He would remain alone and lonely with his *poaka* and *kumara*, and perhaps a morsel of salted *titi*, to fool himself into believing that he was a full Maori in spite of being a partial one in his genetic structure.

Then the silhouette sketched by his father came back to his mind when the tea kettle started to spout steam, screaming on the range. Of course, he had a mammal confronting him, a big one, a white one. He would be busy trying to catch it and even kill it once and for all, or be killed in the process. He would even read Melville again and again until he discovered why he would do it. To vindicate Melville on behalf of his father? And would humanity really care about his intention? He felt fearful, for he knew and understood for the first time, while pouring a cuppa for Mahina, that he was placing an insignificant amount of water into an infinite ocean. This was his theory of life, where he seemed destined to relive the tragedy of his father, and for what? He was convinced that there was nothing except tragedy itself as a label for that physiological bundle of complexes that constituted being alive in a world of absurdities.

Mahina had to call him twice to retrieve him from his vagaries. She told him that she was sorry she could not help him wash the dishes. She would get ready to spend the mid-year's night at her father's side. Half of 1992 had already been absorbed by history. What would the other half bring tomorrow, July the second?

Chapter 27

A long, loud, lamenting scream woke up Komaru early in the morning. Was he dreaming? He could not recall anything oneiric. No, it was not a nightmare. It must be Mahina calling for help.

He looked at the clock. Nearly four. The door he had left ajar was still in the same position. The scream must have come from the rumpus room. He got up, grabbed his father's pareo, and wrapped it around his waist while descending the steps leading to the sick room, where a small orange light revealed Mahina in semi-obscurity on a chair by the left side of the bed.

Upon entering, Komaru turned on the ceiling light, and immediately appraised the situation. Mahina's head was lying on her father's chest. Blood had spouted from his mouth and had already coagulated on his chin along a trail down the right side of his throat. She appeared to be frozen with her right hand in her father's left, while reciting a rosary among sobs of pain and anguish, in nervous and jumpy movements of beads between the thumb and forefinger of her left hand. Her father's eyes were closed.

A closer examination of the tableau led Komaru to believe that his father had died. There was no doubt about it, especially after looking at his pale complexion. At the touch, the lightly moist forehead yielded a sensation of caressing a frozen breast of chicken full of goose pimples. *Rigor mortis* must have set in, but when? Mahina appeared to be terrified and unable to speak, for she could not detach her fingers from the strong clasp holding them. It was the 2 July, a rainy, cold, dark morning seen through the west window that Komaru opened to clear the air. He had detected a stench, as if it were emanating from sweetish and boiled eggs that had been left on the counter after being smashed while still hot. The distant lights dotting the sides of the viaduct delimiting Youngs Beach conferred upon the watery vista an atmosphere of ghostly silence like a black-and-white old movie.

Komaru then recalled the events of the previous evening. Mahina had left him in the kitchen, brushed her teeth and prepared herself for the night watch. On the way to his room, Komaru first made a detour downstairs, peeked through the door and saw Mahina at his father's bedside. Mahina had disrobed herself. Komaru saw her naked in the semi-obscurity, reciting what he understood could be a rosary of some kind. She was kneeling in a totally relaxed posture of humility, and so concentrated on her prayer that she did not hear the five knocks on the door. The goodnight signal of their childhood sounded as if it had been stopped by the invisible wall of death waiting in the wings.

Mahina had apparently begun another recitative segment of her chant-like rosary interspersed with both English and Latin repetitive sentences. Komaru stood by the semi-open door for a minute or so trying to understand the religious function of a daughter attempting to connect her soul with the body of her father's last moments of physical presence on Earth: *Pater noster, qui es in caelo* ... The other Father was somewhere else. What could He know about Mahina's father? Then a string of *Ave Maria, gratia plena* ... When Mahina began intoning 'In the Fifth Sorrowful Mystery, I contemplate the Crucifixion and Death of Our Lord: "Father, into Your hands I commend my father's spirit,"' Komaru left the scene quietly, for he did not want to interfere with whatever Mahina had staged for herself. What he could not understand was why she had first disrobed. In addition, she must have removed the blanket covering her father, leaving only a corner of the top sheet around his groins. A vague, distant scene resembling the present one crowded part of his memory from somewhere, but where? In a painting, a statue, a movie or a church altar? He could not recall anything in particular, especially since, as an agnostic and non-religious person, he was unable to grasp the significance, if any, of that *Mater dolorosa* scene.

Presently, he fought to detach Mahina's hand from his father's. *Rigor mortis* was at its catastatic stage, and probably at its plateau. How long would it last before entering a metastatic phase? Komaru had never had an actual experience of that sort, except for remembering confusedly the death of his mother and reading a few paragraphs here and there in his college physiology course. What puzzled him was Mahina's behaviour. How long had she been asleep by her father? It seemed that it must have been many hours.

Only after the funeral did Mahina recall for him that, after disrobing herself in order to be near her father the way he had seen her first as a newborn baby, she reached for her father's hand and, though his eyes were shut, he took her hand to his lips, kissed it with the foam coating his mouth, and reversed it in order to touch his lips to the palm of her hand, holding it tightly for a long time, with no apparent intention of releasing it. Mahina, afraid of suffocating him, had to pull hard in order to retrieve her hand from her father's lips, but he did not release her. He slid the clasped hands down to his chest and rested them on his heart, as if probing for the existence of a heartbeat. That must have been when Mahina fell asleep until she woke up at about 4 o'clock, realised her predicament, and screamed. But when had father died? Komaru had read that *rigor mortis* can begin up to 6 hours after the heart stops, and the process of muscle rigidity could continue for up to 10 hours, depending on a host of factors internal and external to the corpse. It looked like father must have died shortly after midnight, while Mahina was sound asleep.

It was quite an effort for Komaru to unclasp Mahina's hand from her father's. His fingers had become so clenched that Komaru had to apply sufficient force to 'break' the joints. His father's large, brown, strong hand had enveloped Mahina's like a spider around the pulp of a black-and-blue tropical fruit, Mahina's hand being deprived of its normal blood flow. In making the special effort to release his sister's hand from her father's body, Komaru pushed the corpse away from him, like rolling the trunk of a frozen tree. At that Komaru could not but wonder, comparing his father's skin colour to Mahina's. His yellowish body was like that of an over-ripe banana with dark specks, in contrast with Mahina's resembling cappuccino double *latte*.

When finally free, she stood up for a moment as if intentionally studying the inert body with a stiff hand held in mid-air, while massaging her sore hand. Her thin, slender thighs were joined at her *mons Veneris* by a moderately large bush of shining black hair, definitely a non-Maori feature in Komaru's recollection of human fauna of carefree budding teenagers around ponds and along beaches near traditional *pas*. And at the sudden revelation of intimate siblingness, Ling-ling's image superimposed itself in his imagination, like a specimen on a Petri dish of comparative anatomy revealing nothing except the bareness of her folding of water lily petals (*Nymphea alba*) with the colour of orange roughy filets. And the same for Melissa, with the difference that she used to shave herself, thus displaying a past prime gush of two slices of prime beef rarely done, specked here and there with the sprouting grayness of a day-old *peluria*. In contrast, Mahina appeared to him as if dressed with a G-string, revealing nothing more than a natural, jet black leaf of modesty. Ling-ling displayed the anthropological feature of the northern Manchu that forbade hair except for a touch of extremely transparent shadow of penumbra applied with the classical Chinese technique of water dilution. Melissa always revealed herself at the ever-ready stage of receiving an intrusion without the least interference of pubic hair growth. Komaru wondered whether Melissa's daily routine included shaving along with micturing, defecating, bathing, spreading moisturising cream on her middle body, in addition to applying mascara, touching up her eyebrows and blue-greening the eyelids still in the process of healing after the Brazilian intervention. As if exiting from a movie house to a lobby in full light, Komaru grabbed the blanket at the foot of the bed, wrapped it around his sister's body, and asked her to leave him alone for a while. He would call her later in the day if needed.

The rest of the morning went by as in a script. Komaru had actually anticipated almost every step of the routine called for by the occasion – the doctor, the coroner, the call to the mortician, the drafting of a notice to be published in the Saturday edition of the *New Zealand Herald*, the cleaning of the room, the conversation with the life insurance company, the social assurance office, and other tasks related to his father's death. To avoid a weekend burial, for in New Zealand the dead are forbidden to interfere with the living, it was decided to postpone everything until Monday. The director of Shaws Funeral Services Ltd (INZFD) promised to remove the body at dusk, after neighbours had already returned to their homes for supper. He apologised for not being able to come earlier. Apparently, there had been a rush of unexpected deaths triggered by vehicular accidents due to the severe winter weather, as well as by a group of youths who had committed suicide. That was confidential information, of course. No names, indeed, had been mentioned.

The Tongan nurse, informed by the doctor who signed the certificate of death caused by cirrhosis hepatica and its complications, came early in the afternoon to help in cleaning Mr Reti's body and to retrieve whatever belonged to the hospital. By that time, secondary flaccidity of the muscles had begun to take place, particularly in the face, which had assumed a serene, calm look of relaxation. Even the arms seemed to sink slowly on the side of the bed, with the palms upward, as if begging for help or for an alm. Before departing, the nurse expressed her deep condolences to Komaru and asked him to do the same to his sister. Komaru apologised, saying that she was under sedation, when in fact she was listening to some religious music which Komaru thought was the Angels Series of the Scandinavian composer.

In mid-afternoon Mahina came out of her room. She had bathed, washed her hair and was wearing a flowing robe of white silk like one used by priestesses in some mysterious rites – large sleeves, pleated front and back, a wide belt loosely tied around her waist, the rosary in her hands in an act of prayer. Her posture was one of submission, semistupefied by the pain of separation from her father with whom she had barely exchanged a few words during the days spent at his bedside. By that time, she knew that her father made an effort to see her just before dying, and she felt somewhat guilty and selfish for first talking of herself rather than flying in from Portland in order to be with him during his illness. This time she had worn her *hei tiki* outside her robe, letting it hang down on her chest.

She asked for some scentless candles. There weren't any in the house. Komaru rushed out to buy some and came back with several, along with a large bouquet of 'Fragrant Cloud' orange roses for her. When he arrived home he was drenched with rain. And he was shivering with cold, a cold intensified by the picture he saw in the rumpus room. Mahina was sitting in the large armchair, her father's favourite when he used to read Pakeha literature. He liked to say that the only way to learn about a foreign culture was to read the fiction of its inhabitants, a way that was even better than visiting their country.

On entering the rumpus room and seeing Mahina in that chair, Komaru froze up with shock for a moment. How had she carried her father's body from the bed? She was holding him on her lap, with her right arm under his neck, his legs over the side of the armchair, and her left hand on his heart as if she still hoped it would resume beating. Her flowing sleeves partially covered the naked body of her father, a body that looked like a giant doll made of rubber filled with liquid, for it adhered to Mahina's lap completely, as if it had been glued there to create one single body. She was looking at him so intensely that she did not even register her brother's presence on the threshold. And she did not say anything, merely mouthed a mute thank you with barely opened lips when he gave her the roses, which she lay on her father's chest. On the nightstand, some incense sticks were slowly burning. The fragrance was clearly that of sandalwood. Mahina must have brought them from the States.

Then, suddenly, while lighting the candles around the house,

Komaru remembered. Yes, of course, that was the *Pietà*. Michelangelo's expression of sorrow clinging for a little more time to what a human being had in common with another, a unique bond in the process of being dissolved forever. But, where had he seen that painting, or, was it a statue? In which book, or tourist brochure? Was it in connection with an act of vandalism in St Peter's? No, it was somewhere in Florence, in Palazzo Vecchio, in a small little room barely lit by a window on the right side of the entrance. The tourist brochure made an impression on him because the statue complex included Michelangelo himself in old age wearing a flowing robe of some kind like the one that Mahina now had on, with a hood covering her jet black hair. He stood transfixed by her, while she continued reciting the rosary without interruption. He wished he could understand that prayer. Surely it was a sequence of a *Pater noster*, ten *Ave Marias* and a *Gloria*. All that once-thought useless Latin learned at school was now coming in so handy in his life. But the rest? Before leaving the room he heard something different in English – 'In the First Glorious Mystery I contemplate the Resurrection: "He has been raised up, he is not here."'

He decided to leave her alone there. There was nothing else to do except wait for the funeral service ambulance. He thus went to his father's studio and drafted the death announcement to be phoned or faxed in to *The Herald*. He wrote what was barely a pragmatic note, one of the several that the paper publishes en bloc on Saturdays along with Births and Bereavements.

RETI, Wiremu. On 2 July 1992, peacefully at home. Reg. 5333474, 28th Maori Battalion WWII, in his 68th year. Dearly loved father of Mahina and Komaru. Private funeral at Waikumene Urupa (Maori cemetery), on Monday, 6 July, 11:00 a.m. In lieu of flowers, donations to the Salvation Army. Communications please Shaws Funeral Services Ltd (INZFD). Ph. 0–9–278–532.

By the time the black wagon arrived at about 19:00 to retrieve the body, the rain had stopped, the stars were shining and a tiny sliver of pale moon was trying to assert its presence on one of the coldest nights, caused by a rare high pressure ridge sliding in from the Tasman Sea. Komaru noticed the change in nature around him, and that contributed to make him more exhausted physically, since psychologically and emotionally he felt like a wet rag. Nevertheless, he had to maintain a modicum of inner strength, for he had automatically acquired the responsibility of tradition. In a way, he was eager to wind up the whole funeral operation, for he was terribly worried about Mahina entrenched in the rumpus room armchair holding her father in her lap. She had become an automaton reciting the rosary without pause, covering the whole set time and again beginning with the Joyful Mystery, shifting to the Sorrowful and ending with the Glorious. He just could not grasp the significance of that mantra-like sequence of self-hypnotism. Was there any connection with Eastern religious techniques of building up a resistance to mental anguish? The beads and their rosary seemed to be a universal tool of comfort in all major religions of the world, probably better than Valium or whatever pharmaceutical companies dispense through institutionalised organisations of psychiatroids working 30 minutes a month on a single patient. He wondered again what Dr McTavish's function was in a society whose government paid for palliatives in the useless process of treating the pains of the soul. Was that why Bill the human being had found a kindred spirit in St Bernard of Clairvaux? Was the quotation about women a shield against the impossibility of handling the psyche of a female undergoing a psychological dysfunction? What could a male do *vis-à-vis* a female? Would it not be better to envisage a female treating another female, for what could a man know about a woman witnessing the death of her father while her whole physiological apparatus was dark blood dripping from unfertilised ova? Komaru felt so useless in dealing with another human being who happened to be a sister, a sibling whom he had not seen in four years, who had gone away as a teenager and come back as a woman, who had been shattered by her father's death a few days after her return. In that connection, St Bernard's statement hanging over Dr McTavish's office desk flashed in Komaru's mind. What in the world had that abbot suffered in order to make such an uncharitable statement?

The preliminary formalities for the retrieval of the body were simple and quick. Papers were signed, questions were raised and answered, condolences and thanks were proffered. However, Komaru had not anticipated what a woman in anguish could do. Was it really true that for Komaru it would be less difficult to raise his father from the dead than to live with his sister, even for a few days? The 'scene' that erupted when the funeral director and his two burly Fijian assistants brought in the collapsible gurney on wheels was an indication of things to come. Although they did not react visibly to the 'Maori' spectacle of a young woman holding her father in her arms, the morticians looked Komaru in the eyes, silently begging for assistance.

Mahina had not reacted in any way whatsoever, that was obvious. She was totally oblivious to her surroundings, as if under the influence of some stupefying drug. But when Komaru approached her gently and removed the roses from his father's chest, she grabbed them back and held the whole bouquet tightly to the corpse. It was evident that she was not cognisant of the significance of the Three Wise Men of Death. The ensuing melée began when, acting on a sign given by Komaru, the director held Mahina against the armchair among the scattered rose petals, the black-and-white beads of the broken rosary, and her alternating screams and sobs of incomprehensible Maori words. She then started to hyperventilate so much that Komaru grabbed her from the back under her arms, telling the director to hold her knees while the two orderlies removed the corpse. The whole painful episode looked like a gang rape attempt, for Komaru had grabbed her and pinned her to the armchair before she was unceremoniously dumped onto the mattress of the unmade bed, where Komaru barely kept her in place. She struggled hard to get free of his hold, scratching the back of his neck, pushing her left knee against his crotch, and crying so convulsively that Komaru felt guilty of a violence never used against any human being before. Was not death enough to create havoc in his family?

During the blitz operation, the retrieval party left quickly, leaving Komaru alone to fend for himself, until Mahina calmed down after seeing Komaru's warm tears flowing copiously and silently onto her face. But she also felt a tepid streak, a small rivulet of sticky blood soiling the folds of the white robe over her chest. In trying to pin her down to the mattress, he must have accidentally rubbed her *pounamu tiki* against the tip of her middle breast, opening as a result a small gush on the left side, as if a small rosebud had forced itself to bloom among the flattened rose petals scattered over her. Probably a stem thorn had logged itself somewhere and punctured her to the point of drawing blood.

At that Komaru understood why Mahina had screamed as if hurt, in addition to sobbing due to her father being snatched away, and so Komaru tried to wipe off the blood with her robe lapel, but the silk did not seem to stop the flow. He became worried about a possible infection, for the stems had been soaked in a chemical solution to extend the lifespan of the roses. It was a matter of doing something about it, like fetching some cotton and peroxide or whatever from the medicine cabinet. At the same time, he did not want to leave her alone for fear she might run outdoors to chase the ambulance.

When he heard the wagon on its way, Komaru applied his left thumb as a sort of physical haemostat on the open wound, but the blood did not seem to stop or coagulate.

It was at that point that Komaru placed his lips on the wound after moistening them gently in a blend of tears, saliva and perspiration around the cut. At first Mahina reacted by stopping her screaming and shifting to sobs. She suddenly became silent, especially when Komaru began wiping the blood away with the tip of his tongue. Then his lips cupped the whole bleeding bud and rested around it with a most careful adherence. Mahina reacted immediately as if she had been injected with morphine. Her body became flaccid, while at the same time the other two teats swelled to almost double in size. Their very tips also changed from a pink colour to dark ruby red. And she opened her eyes wide, as if begging for forgiveness, while at the same time betraying a glazed pose of smiling gratitude.

Presently, her hands, which were lying inert around Komaru's neck intertwined their fingers and created a loop that pulled his head downward, and led his nose against hers so lightly that for a second she was not sure whether a *hongi* contact had been made. She was sure of it when her upper lip detected all the tears and mucus at the base of Komaru's nose. At that, a most powerful scent of Retihood, full of pheromones, invaded her and made her drunk. She unclasped her hands and let them slide along his spine until she reached the belt of his slacks. Komaru felt his shirt being pulled upward around his groin, and then her fingernails incising a scratchy path of parallel lines on to the small of his back. She had become alive as a woman as a consequence of death. Was she going to get even with him by drawing blood in her turn? Oh, no, thought Komaru. And, indeed, he detached himself from that predatory-like mantis act of pre-cannibalistic sounding-on in one single push up to escape being roasted. In fact, her body had become so hot that the silk gown had glued itself to the perspiration all over her.

'Don't leave me, please! Don't leave ... me alone as Daddy has done. Don't ... Komaru ... please! Ever. Ever.'

Those were the first words she had uttered in nearly 24 hours. Komaru knew she would survive.

'Of course not. How can I leave you in such a mess? I'll be back in a moment.'

His matter of fact tone had deflated her. And he came back carrying a reed basket in which he had placed some sterile cotton, patches of gauze, hydrogen peroxide, hydrocortisone cream and a tin of assorted adhesive strips. Meanwhile, Mahina had collapsed like a dead body, taking the place of her father's in virtual reality. She had closed her eyes as if resigned to being sacrificed for some strange ritual, and kept them shut, though following Komaru's every movement by stretching her ears in expectation. And Komaru first moved aside the pectoral part of the robe, a corner of which was nearly pasted to her skin with coagulated blood.

The whole operation was performed in total silence. First Komaru spread plenty of peroxide all over her torso, next he used cotton to wipe off any excess liquid, and then he placed a ribbon of cream around her wounded teat with a square piece of gauze on top, which he pressed slightly to increase its adherence. But it was not easy to apply the adhesive strips around the small mound. The protuberance would accept neither rectangular nor round bands. He patched up the area with a combination of both. The resulting precarious collage needed only a frame to confer upon him the recognition of a genetic disposition for painting and sculpting.

Meanwhile Mahina had fallen asleep. Her anticlimactic REM state was so deep that, when Komaru accidentally dropped the peroxide bottle on the parquet floor with a loud bang, she did not even stir. Next he slid his arms under her body, picked her up gently and carried the inert doll-like being to her own room, where he kicked the top blanket of the Maori bed away with his foot, and placed her on it face down. Then he removed her robe, rolled her over onto her back, covered her limp body with the blanket, and left the room after turning off all the lights.

On his way to the copper room, he did not know exactly what to do with the robe, though he knew that unless blood is removed soon the cloth will be difficult to clean. It struck him that the blood had two colours, a lighter one around the torso, and a darker one on the lower back. He remembered that Mahina had refused to wash the dishes or to feed her father. How many days would that *mate wahine* last? In Melissa's case, he would not know for sure because she was on the threshold of menopause, a period of irregular flows. In Ling-ling's case it was ... oh, of course, Ling-ling's directions in washing silk shirts and underwear, a gift from China to him, from Suchow. Yes, he had even visited a couple of silk factories, and once he got sick when he had stupidly eaten a silkworm offered by a worker straight from the boiling cauldron. Yes, the following day he had to stay in bed at the hotel and missed the tour of the pagoda temple, the arboretum of miniature trees, and ... Yes, just cold water, for silk was a moody cloth. He rinsed the gown a few times in the sink and left the little wounded white whale there until Mahina would rescue it the next day. *St Bernard, did you ever have to cope with a bloody mess like this?* He wondered.

He then took a shower, listened to the National Radio for the weather report, heard that Saturday would be rainy, but Sunday and Monday rather fair.

Oh, he was tired, but still too tense to fall asleep. He looked around for something to read, and went to his father's studio searching for a soporific publication of any kind. That was an infallible means to start dreaming nearly immediately. Among the several books lying on a small shelf, one attracted his attention, namely, an anthology titled *Te Ao Hurihuri*, edited by Michael King. Of course, he knew of King, particularly for his historic photographs. He grabbed the book and found it was a recent publication – 1992. The spine looked nearly broken on page 105, where apparently his father had begun to read Harry Dansey's "A view of death". Was his father preparing himself to die merely through ten pages of printed matter?

In bed, however, Komaru turned to page 138, for he had already taken a good view of death during the last few weeks. On that page, his father had marked heavily the first paragraph of Wi Tarei's article, 'A Church Called Ringatu'. Why? The first five words, 'I was born in 1924,' had been underlined in red. Was it a coincidence? His father was born that year. And why had he also underlined the central sentence on line four, 'My father drunk and he drunk heavily'? Was it a reference to his paternal grandfather, whom Komaru had never known? Was there anything genetically implied or feared along the DNA highway of heredity? How is it that he himself could not tolerate alcohol, for which he at times felt embarrassed when invited to dinner at the McTavishes? Had his mother's teetotalism effaced unilaterally or rendered neutral anything that for two Reti generations had flowed in their veins?

On Friday morning, Komaru got up disoriented since he felt brain dead after many intense days of pressing social chores and responsibilities. Everything that needed to be done had been taken care of, and now he just had to wait for events and developments to unfold according to a nearly computerised program. There was nothing else requiring immediate attention. Well, yes and no, for he remembered that, although his father had been moved out of the premises, he was still there to be analysed and entered into the rest of Komaru's and Mahina's lives. It seemed to him that progeny always had to pay for being generated against all expectations. That was the only historical tragedy in which a life is created without being asked, and on top of that the life-bearing has to pay for it from conception to death. In addition to the forced 'gift' of life, one has to accept the absurdity of the whole charade, compounded by the fact that the gift is unreturnable. Society is always patrolling the highway of the individual mind by declaring it sick whenever one would like to exit from the situation. And no one is supposed to extend a helping hand in an effort to assist whoever knows, under the pain of hell on Earth and beyond, that it is useless to walk alone along the merciless path of existence simply for the sake of being alive. Komaru wondered whether humans would fare much better by being born bastards. What a puzzle! It seemed to him that during all his life he had tried to fill in the premolded parcels of a giant picture where the last piece was missing in order to obtain a total view of Terence's *Homo tolerabilis*. Where was it?

Oh, he had nearly forgotten his sister, for Mahina's presence made itself known, shining brilliantly on that grey morning by her silent absence at breakfast. Was she still asleep? What was she going to do the whole day? The rosary had been shattered. Its beads had even entered the grille of the heat ducts. He planned to buy a new set at the Franciscan Mission Centre on Queen Street or at the St Francis Convent of the Holy Faith Sisters on Point Chevalier Road. Otherwise, what was she going to do the whole day, cooped up inside the house as if she did not exist, for by ten o'clock not even a sound had been heard from her? After a perfunctory breakfast of stale, butterless crumpets with strawberry jam and overripe bananas, Komaru prepared a cup of tea. That gave him an idea. Perhaps Mahina would welcome a cup, too, especially since a female undergoing natural dehydration compounded by *mate wahine* should be replenished with plenty of fluids.

He knocked at her door lightly. In answer he heard a moan.

'Sorry, I hope I did not wake you up. I was wondering if you would like a cuppa. And also whether you plan to have breakfast ... room service.'

He had opened the door slightly, from which he saw her lying in a foetal position facing the *kauri* wall. He could not help recalling Melissa's morning position – always flat on her back, and with divaricated legs. Ling-ling would always sleep face down, as comfortably on a flat chest as on a straight-board *derrière*. He wondered whether there is an anatomical correlation between front and back elevations. Of course, Melissa was an exception, though she had gained a few pounds in Brazil via the diet of *arroz e fejão* washed down with *cachaça* in the absence of expensive Cardhu.

Mahina turned slowly toward Komaru, and in the process she grabbed the blanket to cover her breast.

'Are you cold? Shall I raise the thermostat?'

'No, thanks. I ... yes, just tea and ... an aspirin. No, not on an empty stomach, I might get sick, sorry. Do you have any other analgesic?'

'Yes, I think so, you yourself have stuffed the medicine shelf with American products. What, Tylenol? Is it safe?'

'Oh, yes, I had forgotten.'

'Are you in pain on your chest? Let me see the wound.'

'No, don't ... no need ... just have a splitting headache. So unusual. Could it be sinus?'

'But don't you want me to clean and dress your ... breast wound?'

'I said no, please. I can take care of it myself.'

In so saying, she placed both hands on the blanket in a crossed position as if protecting herself from intrusion. And, while preparing tea, Komaru felt that Mahina had changed literally overnight, as if she had erected a Berlin wall between a man and a woman. The old invisible screen between a Maori brother and sister had crumbled under the sudden Pakeha necessity of what Komaru thought was modesty, and even privacy, two terms that he could conceive but not articulate in communal Polynesian life. Yes, Mahina had returned to Aotearoa, but she acted as if she was in America where, on the one hand, the cult of the breast reigns supreme in a hedonistic, sybaritic, Hollywoodian tradition of fleshy exposure utilising all commercial media, while, on the other. pseudo-puritanical neurotics would accuse casual and innocent bystanders of sexual harassment when they happen to glance for a second at an overflowing Dolly Parton-sized breast over an office corridor cooler.

'Morning calling. madam, room service. Tea is served.'

Mahina raised herself on her elbows, received her tray, and paused while surprised at seeing a glass of kiwi juice.

'Oh, thank you. And, sorry, would you bring some cream?'

'For what, the wound?'

'No, stupid, or just milk, for my tea. And sugar. That is the way I learned to drink it in the States. To cut down the acidity. You know, I have no lactose intolerance.'

'Be right back.'

When he returned, she must have grabbed her purse, for she was combing her hair.

'Well, Komaru, I need a shampoo. And here we are. What a strange life. Where is our *iwi*, our *hapu*, our ...'

'On whose side?'

'Yes, yes, of course. The irony. Mahina from Papakura. I wonder what Maggie would say of me. I am the real one for what? At least I don't have to sketch lengthy trees for half of our *whakapapa*. Imagine all those Croatian names lingering invisibly for who knows how many generations in Yugoslavia, or whatever they are going to rename it. And the other half in father's stubbornness to exile himself from his own *whenua*. The enigma!'

'Perhaps we can learn something from the papers left for us to read. And you can research the schools you attended, as you wrote me ...'

'No, my dear brother, for what? Besides, I changed my mind. Of course, the papers, yes, but not today. I am going to soak myself in a bath, and then call Tanya later in the afternoon. I hope she can join me on the trip to Europe ... Italy, Yugoslavia, who knows.'

'All right. Take your time to rest and organize yourself. I am going out on some errands. Perhaps this afternoon we can begin ... no, tomorrow as you suggested. I hope that father's papers can help us in going through the funeral service on Monday. Do you, by any chance, need anything?'

'Yes, some yogurt, vanilla, fat free, please! And air mail stamps for the States. And a spare fax paper just in case. Oh, yes, a loaf of Maori bread, some fresh fruit, low fat cheese. I remember father used to buy the Australian cheese, much better than ours. What was it?'

'You mean Kambura?'

'Right-o. You have a good memory.'

'How could I forget how sick I got when father tried to experiment on me with it? It was then that the doctor found out about my lactose intolerance.'

'Er, can we get CNN here?'

'Yes, why?'

'I would like to find out if Bush has any chance of being reelected. I hope not. Did you see how many people were killed in the desert just to pay a few pennies less for a gallon of fuel? In Oregon you pay more for a litre of mineral water than for four litres of petrol. And here you have to drive those Japanese toys for ...'

'I must confess that I have been too busy with my studies to follow American life. Anyway, you can brief me when I come back.'

'And you can tell me what you have been doing so far with your MA thesis.'

Upon his return, Komaru noticed immediately that the house looked somewhat different. Even the furniture had been dusted. The bathroom, the toilets, the kitchen had been cleaned. And she was feeling better, having taken a long bath. Komaru guessed that her headache must have stemmed from dehydration. She thought it had derived from frustration.

She was wearing the usual pareo, which had been washed and even ironed, for it betrayed some pleats. But this time Mahina was also sporting an American-looking blouse, probably made in Indonesia, with the long flaps left outside the pareo. What she needed was Nike shoes and a baseball cap turned backwards. Thank heavens, no! Her hair had been shampooed, for it was still damp and fragrant. Of what? Amusingly, she was not wearing Nike shoes, but a pair of Dutch-looking wooden clogs. At home? asked Komaru. She had never done that before. Well, she replied that by wearing wooden shoes she would not feel static electricity or the cold of New Zealand's floors, unless Kiwis and Maoris learned to install electric blankets on the floor too. Or at least use thick carpets. She had been spoiled by American carpets. Actually, she confessed that wearing solid shoes would help avoid bumping her toes against hard objects. And she also said the shoes would help to maintain her once traditional Maori posture of submission tall and erect. In fact, she looked and was taller, elegant and sports-projected.

Yes, she was feeling much better after talking with Tanya over the phone. In Oregon, it was early Thursday morning. Tanya was happy to accept the invitation to travel together in Europe. Mahina would fly to Seattle to meet her, they would proceed by bus to Vancouver for a cheaper flight, and stop in London for a few days before scouting Europe *ad libitum*, though two places were to be *sine qua non*, namely, Assisi and Kòrčula. The rest would be icing on the cake. When Tanya asked why those two places off the beaten path, Mahina replied that the former was to become a door to her future and the latter another door to her past. Tanya would see that Mahina was right.

Meanwhile, she had a whole Monday ahead of her for the funeral, and the arrival of her books from Portland, the last station for her micro-history. Komaru had told her that *de minimis non curat historia*, but she insisted that her books were the only link she had with dead people. Death would feed stomachs with anything biological and the mind likewise via books. In both cases, the food was recyclable, as all libraries sooner or later. She was convinced that, after her father's death, she had nothing to do with anyone remaining alive on Earth.

'Not even with me?,' asked Komaru.

'Well, I am not sure.'

Then she reflected a moment as if her own answer had puzzled her. And Komaru knew that she intentionally changed the subject of the conversation.

'Incidentally, where did you learn to wash silk garments so well?'

He blushed. And she noticed that.

'Oh, well, that was, you know, in China. So inexpensive there, I could afford silk shirts that here only David Lange could wear in order to impress his ... female staff.'

She laughed to hide the fact that she did not totally believe him, and in an outburst of forgiveness she hugged him fraternally, spilling some tea on the bed in the process. The perfume she was wearing had canceled the *hongi* scent of Reti siblinghood. Komaru knew that he had lost yesterday's sister. He also realised that he would never find her in any other female on Earth, regardless of his feelings about the situation. Something had been torn apart from whatever had bound them in the innocence of yesterday. And he became scared of anything that could happen tomorrow, if at all.

Chapter 28

Supper was quick, unstructured, with no beginning and no end along either Maori or Pakeha lines. The kitchen had become one of 'sharing' as in a loose social bonding, and thus deprived of the least family routine and normal group function. Mahina and Komaru were in each other's way, if not on each other's nerves, because Komaru was used to taking over the formal preparation of a meal, while Mahina, although grateful to her brother for helping, in a way resented his presence for fear of being criticised or interfered with for her American synthetic cooking. Komaru tended to be analytic and exact in every movement involving the retrieval of any tool used in the kitchen, in addition to utilising only what he needed. Moreover, Komaru would wash, dry and put away anything he employed at any stage of cooking, while Mahina, for the little she would do, tended to leave everything on the counter around the sink, if not in it. This meant that whatever was placed there had to be removed first when it was to be washed. In spite of individual habits that Komaru remembered from the little time they spent at home during vacations, they had now built anew the working atmosphere of a student commune in a flat or dormitory. By recalling Paul and Thecla from her courses in paleo-Christianity, Mahina felt that basically brother and sister had created, unknowingly, an atmosphere of proto-syneisactism in which sex had been effaced by common beliefs in mutual respect.

Komaru thought of Shanghai's former French quarter, which he had visited often when invited by Ling-ling's relatives, brick structures in near Provençal style, where one kitchen and one or two 'bathrooms' served two dozen people under one single roof on the basis of one room per family regardless of its numerical size. And Mahina recalled her 'vacation' spells at the women's dorm, when the cafeteria was closed. She just fed herself by imitating American students in residence, coping with apartment-sized fridges and microwave ovens. Of course, now she had no paper plates, no plastic glasses, no frozen dinners. Away from that consumerism of waste, washing was to be minimal, for she had just a cheese sandwich, an apple, a glass of skim milk, and some stale chocolate chip cookies found in a jar. The whole menu was a copy, if not a sentimental reproduction, of a college feeding routine.

First, Komaru had opened a tin of Maori onion soup which he warmed up while pan frying two lamb chops into which he first tossed some thinly sliced Pakeha potatoes. Next he ate a whole Romaine lettuce, including its hard, bitter core. While Mahina lingered over her milk and cookies, he nibbled on some roasted almonds and dried apricots imported from Australia. He nearly laughed thinking that somewhere in Asia people allegedly survived on apricots as a life-extending food to create centenarians. And the almonds would give him, according to Melissa's dietary suggestions, plenty of zinc which he needed to replenish his gonads. He had made a habit of that snack.

The broiled lamb chops filled the kitchen with a strong animal product fragrance that the exhaust fan was still belabouring to remove with a high pitch and rattling noise. Komaru turned it off and opened the aluminium storm door in order to allow some fresh air in from the orchard. The ground was still wet, but the cement landing was already dry enough for Komaru to step out and linger a few minutes looking casually at the sky. Light pollution was minimal along the waterfront. Only in the distance could he see that ghastly canopy of incestuous illumination hovering over Auckland. A few jets circled over the Mangere airspace slowly taking their time not to have the airport closed for the night.

To the east and south-east, the stars were sparkling brilliantly, and the first quarter moon was barely above the roofs of the houses sprouting around Takanini's quarter-acre sections. Mahina had just returned from brushing her teeth, and Komaru invited her to take a breath of fresh air, for she had not been outdoors since her arrival from the States. She stepped out, looked at the sky as if searching for a reference point, and sighed heavily. The odor of the American dentifrice mingled with the ozone of the last thunderstorm creating the ambience of a pristine Fiordland bush.

'My goodness, yes, of course, I had forgotten my sky, our sky, Komaru. Here we are again together under the Southern Cross. That is why Americans say that in New Zealand everything is upside down. Of course, it was just that way for me when I saw Orion's dagger hanging the other way in America, and the Moon, and ...'

'Surely, but I can't contrast them with the Northern ... what? Oh, the Carts. So convenient to whites as if the States were at the Center of the Universe. Too bad Orion can't chase their Bears. So smart those Pakehas to impose a cross on us too, and even a false one. At times I wonder whether God made a mistake in sprinkling the heavens with out of place symbols, what do you say?'

'Don't be silly, you know we still have different names for our constellations. Have you forgotten Edson Best?'

'Touché, sorry. Anyway, should we not be happy that we have been bearing a cross for only a few hundred years?'

'Komaru, please! Your sarcastic innuendoes are childish.'

She returned to the kitchen, followed by Komaru. It had become chilly for Mahina, accustomed to the overheated dwellings of America.

'I apologise. I did not mean to hurt you. Incidentally, I have recovered all the rosary beads and put them in a plastic bag. And the little crucifix, too. And tomorrow we can go downtown for your sundries. I'll get a new rosary for you.'

The *New Zealand Herald* arrived punctually in the morning. Headlines about oil wells still burning in Kuwait, Bush playing the rôle of an anachronistic Livingstone in Somalia, political chaos in the newly named Russian Federation, new terms for old grudges, such as 'ethnic cleansing' in the Balkans, terrorist attacks in Ireland, and the usual airplane crashes here and there. Under 'Deaths', Reti's entry was the last one. No one had died past 'R' during the week in Metro Auckland. Komaru suggested buying a few extra copies in case they might be needed in the near future. But he left the house alone, for Mahina preferred to stay home meditating. Besides, riding in that old lorry would make her pollution-sick since it had no air conditioning. Her body was still in America.

Back in her room, she re-read Bozarth's poem in order to set the scene for a spiritual promenade. She wrote down some notes, as if Alla (already on a first name basis) had given her some suggestions in preparation for an exodus from pullulating humanity toward joining a select group of Sisters somewhere, sometime, somehow, though everything was still up in the air.

In meditating, she imagined leaving New Zealand forever. In essence, she felt as if she had already done that before coming of age socially. After all, she was not alone or the first. From Katherine to Maggie to Batten, well, the list was small, but the impact of those exiles on the conscience of women saturated with a free spirit was great. Alla's poem had acquired the status of a traveller's guide, a survival manual, a list of instructions abstracted from the Lonely Planet publications of the soul. She did not need any visa, passport, immunization shots, phrase books, credit cards or other items to move in space with her imagination. Nevertheless, she realised that those items were necessary evils to be dealt with as long as she was embarked on a liberation journey, a flight away from kitchens and supermarkets, copper rooms and domestic chores, husbands and lovers, beauty parlors and gyms, fashion shows and gynaecological scares.

In the process of mentally covering many aspects of feminine reaction to 'conditionism' in the modern technological world, she felt that her aspiration to potential desertion from Maori Penates was nothing new, for the theme of exile had lately pervaded literature via the screen. Where was it? She tried to recall a scene somewhere, a railway station, an airport, a dock, what? Suddenly, she remembered. Yes, it was a bleak railway station in Sicily, an outdoor bench, a blind man and a desperate youth torn after a romantic flop – never trust a blue-eyed woman, he had been told. Yes, she remembered his name, Totò, the nickname for Salvatore – and what an ironic name affixed to a youngster who himself needed to be rescued rather than being a rescuer. Yes, the old blind man telling him in bitter and sorrowful tones to go away, to cut all bridges with the past, to abandon the ephemeral comforts of a shabby life in a rickety hamlet, to forget the palliative shows of dreamland via a few hundred metres of celluloid. Of course, the paradise that one could dream of in a dark salon full of cigarette smoke lasted only a couple of hours. The old man was insisting. He was telling Totò not to succumb to sentimentality, not to look back, not to have any regrets. A better paradise could be found anywhere else offering the challenge and the chance of self-enhanced dignity. A better paradise lasting more than a couple of hours. Yes, she had got it, the film she had seen in Portland, at the Classic Movie Programme, that is, *Cinema Paradiso*. And that was for a man. How would it be for a woman? How was the road through the hell of not so much acquiring the psychological tools of survival in a new culture, as a sojourn in the purgatory of placing aside the memory of childhood and youth spent in happy ignorance of an uncertain paradise?

Komaru brought whatever she needed. He had already had lunch downtown. She had snacked about noon. And the new rosary he bought for her, although made in Hong Kong of all possible places, was 14-k gold plated. And the crucifix was not bare like the previous one, but carried a human figure attached to it with nails at the extremity of its limbs. What crime had He committed to be punished that way? Komaru was very vague about the historical impact of Roman civilisation in Judaea, and as a potential historian he felt inadequate as the brother of a young woman who apparently relied on that corpse for spiritual comfort. From the little he knew about Christianity or, better, its prophet, Komaru wondered whether he himself would ever feel so magnanimous as to undergo martyrdom. Then he thought that his own aspirations were rather modest. What his father had taught him to try doing was child's play in comparison with what Jesus the Nazarene had planned to do. Perhaps He was as megalomanous as Caesar. And maybe not even directly responsible, for he had been ordered by his Father to take a trip to Earth and save those crazy inhabitants from all the sins they had committed. What a task! Komaru consoled himself that his own was minimal. After all, Aotearoa was barely surfing above a corner of the Pacific. And the sins committed there were not those of his own people but of those who had come to inflict them on the Polynesians. The parallel was faulty, though, as a latter-day Jesus, Komaru had been indoctrinated by his father to do what young men like him had to do if they wanted to reacquire the dignity of their ancestors. They had no Hell to fear, for they had already been conditioned by nearly two centuries of it, whatever one might label it under Pakeha oppression. Was he not studying history as a formational component of his struggle against the inheritors of Roman imperialism?

He thought of Khadafi as an alternative to Jesus. But there was no oil in Aotearoa. He also felt reassured that New Zealand had no death penalty. He would never be crucified and left hanging in the open for the Fourth Estate to record the event, particularly reporters from America, where capital punishment punctuates the superciliousness of a superior civilisation through more 'humane' executions such as lethal injection, electrocution, the gas chamber and, well, firing squad to ensure the tradition of the Far West excitement *à la* Hollywood. Komaru had concluded that only America, the flagship of democracy, could be entitled to maintain it by executing fellow humans according to the will of the majority. In New Zealand, democracy was similar to America's, though with the apparent difference that the minority spared the government the expense of executing anyone, for people reaching the bottom of desperation simply executed themselves. Komaru had never obtained a satisfactory answer from Dr McTavish regarding the intentional destruction of a life. Was the 'Socratic method' of self-imposed capital punishment really different when it came to eliminating from society undesirable components?

Komaru's return from downtown signalled the beginning of an active afternoon. Mahina had just taken a shower and dressed her wound with fresh gauze. To protect her healing cut from being rubbed by the *tiki*, she had enclosed it into the toe of a soft sock. For a brief moment she thought of not wearing the *hei tiki* for a few days, but that idea was quickly dismissed as she would have felt naked without it. No, since departing for the States, she had never removed it for a second, not even at the X-ray department of the University of Washington. She had just shifted it sideways. The *hei tiki* that for countless generations had been in the Reti family, and even buried a few times for thirty years in each period of regeneration, had been hanging from her neck day and night.

During Komaru's brief absence she had answered the doorbell twice. Mrs Springer from across the street and Mrs Warner two doors to the south had stopped briefly to proffer their condolences. They did not know much about her father, for he, although always courteous toward all the neighbours, preferred to tend the flower garden and the fruit orchard in complete privacy. Old timers meanwhile had died, and Mahina had made only a few casual acquaintances during her summer vacations. The 'Death' section in *The Herald* had given them an inkling that Wiremu Reti, taken by the funeral ambulance on Thursday evening, was their neighbour.

There was also a telephone call from a certain Mrs McTavish, who insisted on talking with Komaru. She would call later after being told that he was not at home.

Among the various items Komaru had brought for Mahina, there was a potted plant. He had to return to the lorry, for he had left it there on the passenger side floor in a wicker basket covered by newspapers.

'Sorry, I had forgotten it there. I was afraid it would be damaged in the rear storage box full of paraphernalia.'

'Oh, thank you. Adorable, just ready to bloom. And, er ... why pink?'

'Well, haven't you had enough of red around you lately? I felt that you need to desensitise yourself toward a more gentle colour, away from blood. And, this variety has no ... thorns.'

'You brute. Please don't mention that episode again.'

'So you feel better?'

'Komaru, I just said not to mention THAT any more!'

'I apologise. Never again.'

'Do I hear right that you are apologising to your kid sister? You are making history. Accepted. And ... oh ... who is Mrs McTavish?'

'I think I have written you about her ... and her husband. Haven't I? But, why?'

'She called just before you came back and ... apparently she had read the notice in the paper. She referred to you as "Kom".'

'You know, Brits abbreviate everything, don't they? That is Melitta ... sorry, Melissa. She and her husband make a unique team.'

'Melissa! Quite a name. Her voice sounded ... mellifluous. Am I intruding in your private life? You look somewhat uncomfortable. Anyway, not to know your personal ... affairs, is she, shall I say, a *Melissa officinalis*?'

'What do you mean?'

'You seem to be on the defensive.'

'Should I be?'

'No, of course, sorry. Tanya is nuts for curative herbs and the like. I recall that once she spoke of *Melissa officinalis* as a sweet balm of some kind. Perhaps one day you should ask Mrs McTavish what she knows about ... herself.'

'Well, I ... actually you could ask her. After all, you are the language specialist.'

'That will be the day.'

The phone rang again. This time Komaru answered. It was a certain Reverend Tarei, Wata Tarei. Mahina left the hallway to water the plant Komaru had bought. Cyclamens, the flowers of secret loyalty, and as such temperamental if not handled carefully in the proper environment of light, modest in appearance, but glowing when caressed gently along the tall stems, never on the petals. That bulbous plant was not for sexual symbolism like the rose, but more long-lasting if looked at as a source of visual pleasure – a flower of pure love between siblings.

When Komaru came back to the kitchen, Mahina had already returned from her room, where she had placed the plant on the windowsill facing west. There the sun would hit the area for the shortest possible arc during the summer, just enough to protect the flowers from excessive light. She found Komaru somewhat perturbed by the phone call.

'Well, sister, I should not have placed a Death announcement. But how could we escape the pages of the "Pakeha Book of the Dead"?'

'What do you mean?'

'Just imagine if we had been somewhere in northland with a few neighbours and relatives, and Dad dying on the porch after being served his favorite dish ... what ... minnow fritters. And you dressed in a white robe, with a few leafed branches around your hair, and lamenting for Dad with a *waiata tangi* before sending him to the *Rangi*. And ...'

'Don't be sarcastic, please. But what? Don't I know that, while we are here coping with Pakeha civic laws, Dad is in the fridge of the parlor, alone, nearly forgotten ...'

'You're telling me that? What could we do? Hire the services of a *marae* nearby? At any rate, Dad will not be entirely put aside American style. Besides, I am confident that he will be remembered more in the future for what he did in the past. In fact, listen. I just heard from Reverend Tarei, the son of Wi Tarei. His father apparently knew ours in the 1970s. They used to serve with others in the Mapou Marae Committee. To make a long story short, he will attend the funeral and, listen, he offered to deliver a eulogy. He says that as a young man he knew father. Of course, I had to accept since the ceremony has been cleared with the funeral director.'

'The pleasures of Pakeha civilization! At least we don't have to burn the house.'

'And we are spared the rituals of a Catholic funeral with Masses and everything else.'

'You are cruel to remind me of what I am undergoing, torn between so many things ...'

'Sorry, Mahina, we must be strong ...'

'Rather intriguing, this Tarei. It seems that strangers know more about father than we do. We may learn something about him.'

'I hope so!'

Another phone call echoed through the hallway. Komaru rushed to it as if he knew that it was from Melissa.

'Don't trip on the rug! It sounds like you need some ... *Melissa officinalis*.'

'*Turi, turi*!,' exclaimed Komaru, rather annoyed.

It was a long phone conversation, during which Komaru mostly listened. From what Mahina could barely hear, he limited his task to 'yes' and 'no', and some hesitant 'maybes'.

Back in the kitchen, where Mahina was preparing a large salad of mixed herbs, he caught her intentionally modulated voice.

'Was I wrong?'

'Are you ever? No, of course. That was Melitta, sorry ... Mrs

McTavish, er, Melissa. And since you are curious to know her, she will be at the grave site funeral on Monday, with her husband, of course.'

'Of course, naturally. I assume she already knows about me.'

'You are right.'

'And so she lives in Wanganui?'

'Yes, she does.'

'With her husband, I imagine. And you have to drive up to see her whenever for whatever reason ... how romantic!'

'I have to, for the whatever reason is purely academic. What I mean, she is a historian and I ... need her to exchange ideas on history.'

'I like that verb "exchange". In the States that is a high frequency word in connection with body fluids. But, of course, your exchange must be on Maori history, am I correct?'

'No, theory of history in general, for no one has ever written a Maori history, what I mean no Maori has ever published a history of our *whenua* from our point of view in any language. Actually, it should be written in Maori.'

'And you are going to write it for your MA?'

'I doubt it, but, as I said, so far I have been working on the Proof of Nine in the paradigmatization of periodic events.'

'That sounds rather erudite, almost pompously so. I almost did the same with angels.'

'But you see, sister, I have to deal with demons. And there, where wings don't flap freely in my department, all instructors are Pakeha. What I mean, a Department of Pakeha History. Although 'Pakeha' is invisible as a term.'

'So you are going to concoct a new theory to write a revolutionary MA thesis?'

'I don't know yet, though for the time being I had better concoct something for supper. What do you say? How would you like some linguine with a white seafood sauce, and your salad, and French bread with roasted garlic mashed in olive oil?'

'Your menu is tantalising, if not antithetical. On the one hand, you offer cholesterol-laden food, and on the other antidotic items. That sounds like an S and M suggestion.'

'What is that?'

'You are a naïve bloke, brother. Anyway, your menu makes me more excited than the idea of meeting her on Monday.'

'Her?'

'She! And I don't refer to the novel.'
'A novel titled *She*?'
'Yes, of course.'
'About what?'
'About a woman who quickly becomes old in the process of lovemaking, though it does not seem to deter her younger beau from his romantic enterprises. At any rate, tell me more about Melitta.'

He did. And the tone of his descriptive narrative was filial. Gratitude tended to punctuate particular aspects of the relationship. History, as a subject matter, had lost itself into ... history.

'It seems to me, brother, that you miss Mother.'
'Perhaps. Don't you too, ever?'
'Unfortunately not, for I never tied any bond to my psyche. The only gap I have is in my ... guts. In the States I would scandalise everyone saying so. Their guts are in the heart. Of course, I remember granny. But with her, I never detected a full olfactory flow as I did with Father and ... with you. And, incidentally, how old is she?'
'A bit older than I am.'
'It figures. Thirtyish?'
'Er ...'
'Forty?'
'Forty-nine. Fifty at the end of this month.'
'Is she a Leo?'
'Apparently.'
'And you a Virgo! Poor wretch. I pity you. How can you cope with a Leo, even for ... academic reasons?'
'Well, it is her wisdom, if not her pragmatic approach to life.'
'How pragmatic?'
'Sister, I think that I should start supper.'
'Fifty! That would be Mother's age if she were here with us today. But is she ... pretty?'
'Pretty ... much so, sorry, quite so. I would say stunningly so.'
'And happily married?'
'She is in love with her husband. And he with her. A rare combination.'
'Children?'
'No.'
'Puzzling.'
'Really?'
'She must live the life of a ... nun, except for having a husband. Quite possible, for all nuns do have a husband. As I myself am going

to have sooner or later, without being bothered by materialistic responsibilities. Does she cook?'

'Er, actually no, if not incidentally.'

'Ah, ah, she must be potentially a nun, a charitable one, helping lost souls like you. I can't believe that you have to drive to Wanganui. Glad you don't have to swim all the way to Mokoia Island.'

'Mahina, please, actually I love Wanganui. There I feel as if I were at a real *whenua*. Perhaps one day I'll move there permanently. That area is still Maori, and such it will remain for a while. It is like an oasis midway between two strongholds of Pakehanism.'

'I am glad that you are in love ... with something, be it a city or a person.'

'And you? Are you in love with anyone? An American?'

'God forbid! Sorry, what I mean, no, and of course never with an American. I don't think I can ever love anyone. You see, we Maori have been spared the subtlety of that vague term covering such an array of emotions, you know, as in the States, falling in love, being in love, loving someone, etc. I think that in that society love is incompatible with their political system and beliefs. How can love exist in a democratic society? Love can thrive only in a dictatorial relationship, in a master/slave bonding.'

'Like that of a nun in love with, what, God, Jesus, or the Holy Ghost?'

'Probably.'

'Any of them in particular? Or all of them in a ... *ménage à quatre*?'

'That is only theoretically so, since they are all the same.'

'And, how do you keep track of or separate them in your mind, or spirit, or whatever?'

'I don't know that yet, for I have never been in love with anyone. I assume that I will find out whenever appropriate.'

'To me that sounds rather tribal, or polyandric, assuming that God is a man. Otherwise it would be a complicated relationship involving bisexuals in an orgy.'

'If so, I don't find anything wrong. But, again, that can be immaterial because for me love is a matter of spiritualism, of mentalism, of conceptualism.'

'You speak as a philosopher. Have you studied the rôle of the flesh in any philosophical theory?'

'Frankly, that is a matter of physiology, of hormonal activities, of ...'

'And do philosophers separate those activities from intellectual speculations?'

'Oh, no, for remember that they, the philosophers, are made of flesh and blood, not of abstract concepts.'

'So you do admit that it is impossible to separate those two components, the material and the immaterial?'

'I have not said that. Probably, actually, I think that one can control one end over the other.'

'How?'

'By sheer will or training or the surroundings allowing the implementation of one wish over the other. Otherwise, how could one understand, say, María de Ágreda, or St Teresa de Ávila, or ...'

'And you plan to follow in their footsteps through sacrificing yourself?'

'I think I can. And I already have. But it is not sacrifice. Just a matter of principle.'

'You have?'

'Yes. When you tried to stop the flow of my blood, I nearly succumbed for the first time in my life to natural inclinations of physiological programming. That night of hell I bled not only in my bosom and ... myself so heavily, but also in my heart. I had discovered not only my femininity, but also my determination to control it not necessarily to avoid disaster, but to prove that I am strong enough to trace the path of my life regardless of strange forces attracting me to you. And you are burning the garlic. Don't you see the tears in my eyes? I am going to wash them. Please call me when supper is ready.'

Supper was uneasy but pleasant, for the air, physical and otherwise, had been cleared. Few words were spoken. Komaru moved around the kitchen like an automaton, staring mostly in the distance, his thoughts obfuscated by pain in his heart and sorrow for Mahina. The Sun and the Moon, separated at birth, but bonded forever by the laws of Nature, were condemned to rotate and gravitate within the closed confines of space in relation to Terra. The Earth was just a rumpus room in which to be born, live and die under the nourishment of the Sun in order not to be caught by the selenising whirl of cold desperation.

When Komaru returned after washing the dishes, he did not even turn the radio on in order to listen to the weather report. More than that, the radio would usually act like a kind of lullaby before Komaru fell asleep. He heard five knocks on the *kauri* wall. Slow, but louder than usual. He hurriedly replied in a quick staccato. And he fell on the Maori bed in a complete state of desolation. He sneaked into Dr

McTavish's office. It was pitch dark, but he could read St Bernard's maxim nevertheless. Was it really that difficult to raise his father to life?

Chapter 29

Sunday afternoon brought Komaru and Mahina together for the first time as mature and rational adults under the roof of their paternal home. Although each of them became aware of the situation individually, they did not manifest any feelings outwardly. Their conversation, and the events surrounding it, seemed to convey a comfortable, though sad, awareness of being together as two independent human beings who were nevertheless on the brink of separating from each other. And subconsciously they each knew that the death of their father had already melted the adhesiveness of family togetherness forever.

Mahina, more than Komaru, felt the stress of impending changes, for it was she who was going to leave her father's *whenua*. Nevertheless, neither of them was consciously aware, at first, of that unique spiritual encounter prompted by the coming funeral ritual of the following day.

For a minute, Mahina thought about attending Mass somewhere, but did not feel like imposing on her brother for a lift to a Catholic church. And, being very cautious, she did not dare drive that old lorry-like vehicle on a Sunday morning for fear of getting entangled in the aggressive Auckland police programme of 'education' in which the participants were mostly Maoris carrying a guitar or drinking a tin of beer. Maori women who drove a car were not spared that 'preventive' traffic spot check. Thus, she stayed the whole morning in her room working on what to say or read at her father's grave, as well as choosing what to wear at the ceremony.

Komaru spent some time in his father's studio, trying to become acquainted with the past of a family that had detached itself from active, or more properly, 'visible' Maori *tangi*. And he felt guilty about it, guilty for not doing what he should have done in order to follow the traditions of his people. How in the world could Komaru regard himself as a 'warrior' when in practice he had retreated into the passive stance of a Pakeha-like life? The duality and the inconsistency of daily activities among Maoris had recently begun to tarnish their image in spite of a tendency, even among Pakehas, to lament the disappearance of the old 'warriors' in movies and novels. Even some Maori leaders, from church ministers to comfortably paid administrators, had started to criticise the labelling of 'warriors' for fear of rekindling conflicting images tainted with accusations of barbarism, savagery and even cannibalism. In essence, the greenstone of *patu* was to be buried along with the bones of *rangatira*, gone forever. Basically, Pakehas had begun to notice an escalation in Maori activism when actually it was only the external manifestation emerging from dormancy for various reasons. There was no doubt that Pakehas were running scared by national sentiments based on the realisation that racial justice was weak and thus the sporting of *pounamu patu*, whether real or symbolic, led Maoris to close ranks in order not to lose their political identity and personal dignity. For Komaru, it was a matter of historical continuity, of philosophical tenets, of governmental manoeuvres that could compromise the survival of Maoridom. Yes, of course, advocates of non-violence such as Jenny Te Paa were afraid that the 'warrior' style of the new Maori activists would lead to violence. And Komaru agreed with her in principle. However, it was one thing for theologians to preach hope for racial integration from the pulpit of St Matthew's-in-the-City Church, and quite another to demand the same from a public bench in Aotea Square. In essence, Komaru believed that a Mother Teresa had no place in racial disputes. A Jean d'Arc, if necessary, was more consonant with the future of Maori activism. In following Catholic Church practices, Komaru would even burn her at the stake, if necessary, and then later sanctify her with a couple of *mea culpa* prayers.

As regards the abandonment of traditions for the sake of appearing civilised, Komaru even rationalised by telling himself that his father had preferred his departure from Earth almost incognito. Of course, that was not in conformity with the death of a 'warrior', but it prevented what Pakehas construed as theatrics. Thus, no group visitations to the mortuary, no scheduling of elaborate memorials, no formal notices of bereavement carrying a lengthy *whakapapa* – nothing visibly Maori.

It was the *whakapapa* topic that triggered in him a bout of depression for, even though he wanted to place his father in a more proper niche of the past, Komaru knew little about his family on his mother's side. The European branch of his genealogical tree was only sketched tenuously, whether mentally or graphically. At any rate, after washing the dishes and tidying up the kitchen, he remained at the counter to reflect on the gravity of his feelings toward everything immediately affecting him. And, among the several items under scrutiny, Mahina emerged above all of them. Yes, there were other things on his Petri dish of self examination – the MA thesis had to be taken care of one way or another, and a job had to be found. Thus, home was a structure housing all the tangibles of a past, with each physical entity connecting humans to episodes of life, to places of provenience, to times of encounters, to experiences undergone together in a network of reminiscences – all of these looming on the closest horizon of his daily existence.

It was so strange for Komaru to witness how certain inconsequential things surfaced here and there, just little prosaic things like disconnected memories of natural phenomena and events in which he participated either alone or with his family. And so they came and went by as episodes that, once recalled, he could not forget – the fragrance of freshly mown grass on the front yard still wet with rain; the leaves of caduceous trees blown away gently in golden trails along the evening rays of sunshine toward the east; lonely things like the sadness of cloudy sunsets and the oppressive silence in his father's empty room; his books left open at elbow's reach here and there; the large sand clock his father used to play with for hours, watching the grains fall into the oblivion of the lower ampoule; the electric lamp casting a green shadow on the emergency silver candelabrum; the moonlight filtering through the orchard of trees in the meadow behind the garage. And even the house left by his father forever, a large structure, seemed to shrink into another irrelevant thing of the past.

Now, more than ever, Komaru understood the Maori tradition of burning the house where a man had died, as if it were a process of purification for a home left alone, forlorn, derelict and still ponderous under the weight of memories. And he felt relieved that Mahina had agreed to sell it, burying everything just at the moment of signing a real estate contract. All that sadness, like anticipated departures from a house no one would regret and where no one would be greeted! It was thus easier to wipe out all the pleasant recollections of kin companionship, even with its promises of unfulfilled pleasures. So many new things to remember, and yet so strange that he could not forget. In fact, he recalled the poem about the things he could not obliterate from memory. Yes, that was the author, a certain Elizabeth Webb, who had placed her signature on the last page of a book he had acquired in a used bookstore. But Komaru never found out anything about her beyond the name.

Mahina woke him up from his vagaries when she came into the kitchen to see him. This time she was wearing dark slim blue jeans topped by a Hawaiian shirt sporting a rainbow of colours in a print of tropical flowers. The *hei tiki* hung very loosely through its wide open collar. A semi-glossy pink lipstick emphasised the hue of her pale skin. She had even applied a barely detectable coat of dark green on her eyelids. When Mahina sat at the kitchen counter facing Komaru, who had his back to the window, he felt as if a large bouquet of Polynesian flowers had been installed in front of him. Indeed, Komaru's vision was reinforced by a subtle sniff of perfume. He became intrigued by the fragrance. Was it an American import? It must be, he thought, for the whole vision in front of him appeared like an advertisement on a TV screen. The young lady was undoubtedly an American from the West coast.

Although physically present at home, however, Mahina appeared to be psychologically far away under the spell of Bozarth's poem. And when Komaru sensed her detachment, looking at her with wide open eyes, he broke her far-away mirage with the excuse of a question, a plausible one.

'You look so American, and even smell like one.'

'Oh, do I? Why?'

'I don't know. There seems to be something synthetic on your body. What? A floral scent of some kind? It is pleasant, though.'

'Tanya. Well, that was ... a gift from her. *Muguet des bois*. The list of ingredients on the spray bottle indicates 40% alcohol. I could get drunk from it.'

'Could, would you?'

'No, of course, but I was impressed by the French legend symbolised by that flower. Apparently, after a young man offered a sprig of those flowers to his love, she gave him a kiss in return.'

'That was a poor investment. That Frenchman must have 90 per cent proof scotch in his veins.'

'I can understand that. Coming from a teetotaler! At least we Maori don't have to worry too much about exchanging germs through *honging*.'

'Well, er, perhaps fewer.'

'But what about the French kiss? Have you, brother, ever been contaminated by one?'

'For God's sake, what kind of question is that? Why?'

'Just curious. Have you?'

'Yes, but only recently. I simply ...'

'Once you mentioned a certain Ling-ling helping you in Chinese linguistics. Of course, I do not refer to her for etymological reasons.'

'Sorry to disappoint you, but she and I never exchanged a labial kiss. What I mean is we never placed our lips together for affective purposes.'

'I believe you. You must be as naïve as I am.'

'Rather intriguing. I wonder if we Maori have a built-in mechanism against germ contamination. Of course, there are other sources for getting polluted.'

'That is true, but I know I am extremely healthy. Transpacific University is not totally aseptic, but I am sure about myself.'

'Do you mean to say that in America you were never kissed ... French ... style?'

'You bet, if you will forgive my Americanism. I may have been contaminated linguistically, but never otherwise. I have never been kissed by anyone ... in any language. How could I? I am a virgin, and proud of it. Does that surprise you?'

'Well, I ...'

'I sense that it does. And the irony of it is that, if I had stayed here instead of going to America, by now I would have seen a few pair of men's feet lying near mine. Yes, I know, strange, isn't it? I am becoming an old maid. After all, in a couple of weeks I will be 24. And you seem spaced out by what I have told you.'

In fact, Komaru had become detached from reality. However, although Mahina had influenced him with her personal history, it was not her status that triggered the trance in him. Suddenly, Komaru realised that he had succumbed to the magic wand of social responsibility. In essence, he felt that Mahina was telling him that her life was hers alone, and that he should not worry about anything for her sake. At that point, Komaru knew that he was completely free to continue his mission, THE mission, an impossible one, and as such a tragic enterprise. Nevertheless, it was an exhilarating one, powerfully engaging, silently demanding, nearly sensual. And Mahina had rendered him free. His father had died probably feeling worthless for not having accomplished what he had tried on behalf of the Maori cause. Now it was his turn as a son condemned to continue fighting as if decreed by fate against all odds.

It was Mahina who suggested a cup of tea. And this time she prepared it herself, while Komaru followed every movement of her sinuous body gliding in a choreography of tentative motions while trying to locate whatever she needed. The tea smelled of innocent sisterly love. And this time Komaru took it without sugar. The missing cube had been replaced by the presence of a human being who had prepared a cup of affection with care and tenderness. Komaru felt that the same tea, a Darjeeling he had prepared for himself before, this time tasted better. Well, he thought, different, for it released a more intense aroma, probably because it was sipped slowly in the presence of a companion with whom he had shared the most candid years of first youth.

At the second cup, Mahina wondered whether they should do anything, not only in anticipation of the following day full of activities, but also to dispel the gloom hovering in the kitchen in spite, if not because, of the relaxed atmosphere permeating the impromptu tea ceremony. It was quite a symbolic interlude for Komaru since he could not put aside Melissa's induced addiction to coffee, so un-British, a hoped-for antidote to the effects of Cardhu. In Wanganui, Melissa used coffee as a white flag of truce, the coffee habit she had acquired in, of all places, Kyoto. However, in a kitchen full of memories, tea had created an ambience of relaxation. But Mahina had plans, as if she was in a hurry not to leave for tomorrow what could be done today.

They decided to open and investigate the three 'documents' left by their father in the large sealed envelope to be opened 'after my death in each other's presence.' The first document dealt with material possessions – the home, bank and postal accounts, his pension situation, social assurance, and the like. Mahina paid only perfunctory attention to Komaru's leafing through the papers. And she told him she wanted nothing tangible. She already had the *hei tiki* her father had given her before she left for the States. She asked him whether it was all right that she keep it at least for a while, since she knew that morally and traditionally the *tiki* was to be entrusted to Komaru for continuity of the *whakapapa*. She knew that, after her, there was no one to trail along the shadow of her substance. She even told him that perhaps one day the *tiki* could 'return home', but for the time being she would keep it as her only instrument of psychological strength. She was going to be either self-supporting by working somewhere, or seclude herself in a monastery, where nothing mundane was to be kept.

The only exception concerning the 'possessions' document was her asking him for temporary financial support from her share, for she was going to incur expenses during her forthcoming European journey. Otherwise, all proceeds would belong to him. He needed them the most, especially if he could not find a job after finishing his studies at the University of Victoria. Mahina knew that New Zealand was on the verge of an economic collapse. At the current rate of inflation, Mahina envisioned that she could soon exchange the little amount of American dollars she had for nearly one to two. As long as New Zealand remained tied to the 'Oriental' market economy, in spite of the scare about the 'yellow peril', Kiwis would remain stable economically. But for how long?

Once the first document was put aside in trust to Komaru, it was the unanticipated contents of the second envelope that created a storm in his stomach. Mahina intentionally played the rôle of the wait and see witness, for she had already re-crossed the Pacific in search of a raft to remain afloat through religion. Now, Komaru was confronted with the inevitable, as if his father had delineated the path for the rest of his son's life. The second envelope contained a short note attached to a 24-page monograph with a red cover. The note said: 'Komaru, this is your MA thesis. Whether you use this for the diploma or as a political testament is up to you. You can also see that this is the original I prepared for the Waitangi Action Committee so many years ago. All the copies used here and abroad were duplicated from this original. There are no footnotes, no bibliographic references, no approval forms to be signed, no introduction, no conclusion, no nothing. You have my original art work in black marker. I assume not many copies are left of the thousands produced by my brothers. And I now wonder if you recognise my own hand, to which apparently you did not pay much attention when you distributed copies of it as a teenager, including those left at the entrance of government buildings. Well, my dear son, this is the only precious item I could leave for you. Use it in any way you like. Or burn it. No matter what, one day the corpuscles of this document will spread all over Ao Tea Roa and blend with our *whenua* for generations to come. Dad.'

The writing of the message was exactly like the one appearing in both semi-cursive letters and printed block-like throughout the document. The curves in both the writing and the figures of people and things betrayed the motions of a hand accustomed to designing spirals depicting carved canoes, lintels over entrance doors, even sketches of comets in the sand of beaches visited during the summer. Komaru's father had left the largest part of himself. And Komaru froze at the desk while Mahina tried to understand the impact of that bequest. So much research done on history along the Rule of

Nine for what? There, in front of his eyes, Komaru had a brief collection of Polynesian *sutras* containing the entire history of Maoridom. When Komaru asked to be left alone, Mahina had already left for her room. The whole house had become sown with the seeds of the inevitable. Komaru spent the night analysing those 24 pages containing the most detailed history of his country. Every stroke applied on paper by his father synthesised a whole book of details. Every page encompassed a volume of a whole encyclopaedia of events. The two dozen manuscript pages covered the complete history of Ao Tea Roa before and after the arrival of the Pakeha. Komaru's father had compressed a whole library into a monograph to be left in a capsule entrusted to countless generations of canoe descendants. Komaru immediately grasped the seminal importance of the work, not so much for his most immediate benefit, but also for the moral sanity of his people. Between two red covers, his father had left the only sacred document ever produced and entrusted to an oppressed people. For the first time in the history of Mankind, a society of Indigenes had retrieved from the ashes of purification what most thought had gone forever, permanently lost in a universe of oblivion. The mind of his father, Komaru now believed, had overcome despondency, alcohol addiction, illness, solitude, and who knows what else, in order to leave to posterity a unique tool of survival, just in time for the 1993 International Year of the World's Indigenous People. No other lonely cry on Earth could ever compare with what Komaru had under his eyes the whole night. He spent it spellbound reading not only the English language but also a 'translation' of all the pictures in petrograph style. And the black-and-white tints could not be more symbolic, infused into every sketch of historical events. No computer-designed output on Earth could ever surpass it in poignancy, historical comprehensiveness and philosophical truth. Finally, a thunderstorm woke him up from his trance in the early morning. He retired to his room for a few hours of sleep. And he wondered what the last envelope, labelled 'Moral Testament' contained. What else could his father say? Had he not encapsulated in 24 pages the quintessence of Maoritanga, Maoridom and Maoriness in all its dimensions? The title on the cover of the brochure was in black letters, **KO MATOU NGA KAITIAKI O AOTEAROA** followed by two subtitles: *Ko tenei he pukapuka mo nga tai tamariki*, and *Kai ora koutou katoa*.

Kia Ora, a long time ago Kupe and Hine-Aparangi found Aotearoa.

Then all of our families and tribes came to Aotearoa on the great canoes.

TANGATA WHENUA are PEOPLE who BELONG to the LAND
Fijians are the Tangata whenua of Fiji
Tongans are the Tangata whenua of Tonga
Niueans are the Tangata whenua of Niue
Samoans are the Tangata whenua of Samoa
Aboriginals are the Tangata whenua of Australia
WE MAORI are the TANGATA WHENUA of AOTEAROA.

We are the Kaitiaki - guardians of Aotearoa. We looked after the forest, Kaimoana, land and all of the animals.

A pakeha sailor called James Cook came here. He saw how beautiful Aotearoa is. He went back and told other pakeha about how good our home was.

lots and lots of pakeha came; fishermen, missionaries to bring their teachings of GoD, shopkeepers to sell things to make money, farmers to grow crops and graze livestock for their food supply.

This weeks SPECIALS

The settlers gave us blankets, Beads, Pigs and firewater for our land.

And still they wanted more land to build their shops and big houses.

BOOZE DISEASES MUSKETS IGNORANCE QUEEN LAWS GREED LANGUAGE

The Pakeha wanted Aotearoa to be like them and look like their homeland Britain. We had to talk like them, sing like them, pray like them, eat like them. They wanted us to be like Pakeha!

THE TREATY OF WAITANGI

* That the land, Fish and forests belong to the MAORI PEOPLE.
* That the Queen will protect the needs of MAORI PEOPLE

this treaty was made up to make us think that we had our rights. We don't have any of these things and they won't give it back. So we must fight to get back AOTEAROA again.

SIGNED — this 6th day of February 1840

From then on the Pakeha using the TREATY slowly took our LANDS
We were tricked again.

Four years after the signing of the TREATY. Hone Heke cut down the British flag pole four times at Kororareka, Because he did not believe in the Pakeha ways.

Te Whiti, Tohu and others of
Parihaka refused to give their
Lands over to the pakeha. Their
village was invaded by troops and
burnt down to the ground.

1860's LAND WARS

Many Maori people died in battle trying to stop the pakeha from taking more land. But still they took our land.

During World war one and two many of our warriors went to fight over-seas. Few returned. Many of Te Puea warriors refused to go and fight in the pakeha wars because they had taken away our lands and, had treated us unfairly.

In 1932 Ratana took a petition to the KING. Asking that the TREATY OF WAITANGI be HONOURED. The King did not want to see Ratana because he was not interested in us MAORI.

Thousands of our warriors died. Many of them had moved from the country to the city for jobs and schools. Many of the close family ties were broken down. It became harder to go to a hui and Tangihanga because we were living and working in the city.

There are Pakeha people making plans and rules for all of us to live by. This is called a GOVERNMENT. With each government they have made new laws to take more land from us.

Kao
FRAUD
Stop te ka Waitangi
he teka Teka
te tiriti o Waitangi

BOYCOTT CELEBRATIONS

Kaua e Teka

We couldn't let this go on. Our people used Banners, Notices, Signs, Concerts and marching to places, to let others know that we are not happy with the laws. Laws are made to keep us UNHAPPY.

We marched from Te Hapua to the Beehive. Saying that "we don't want any more of our land taken or sold". The Pakeha Government didn't listen to us.

BASTION POINT is MAORI LAND

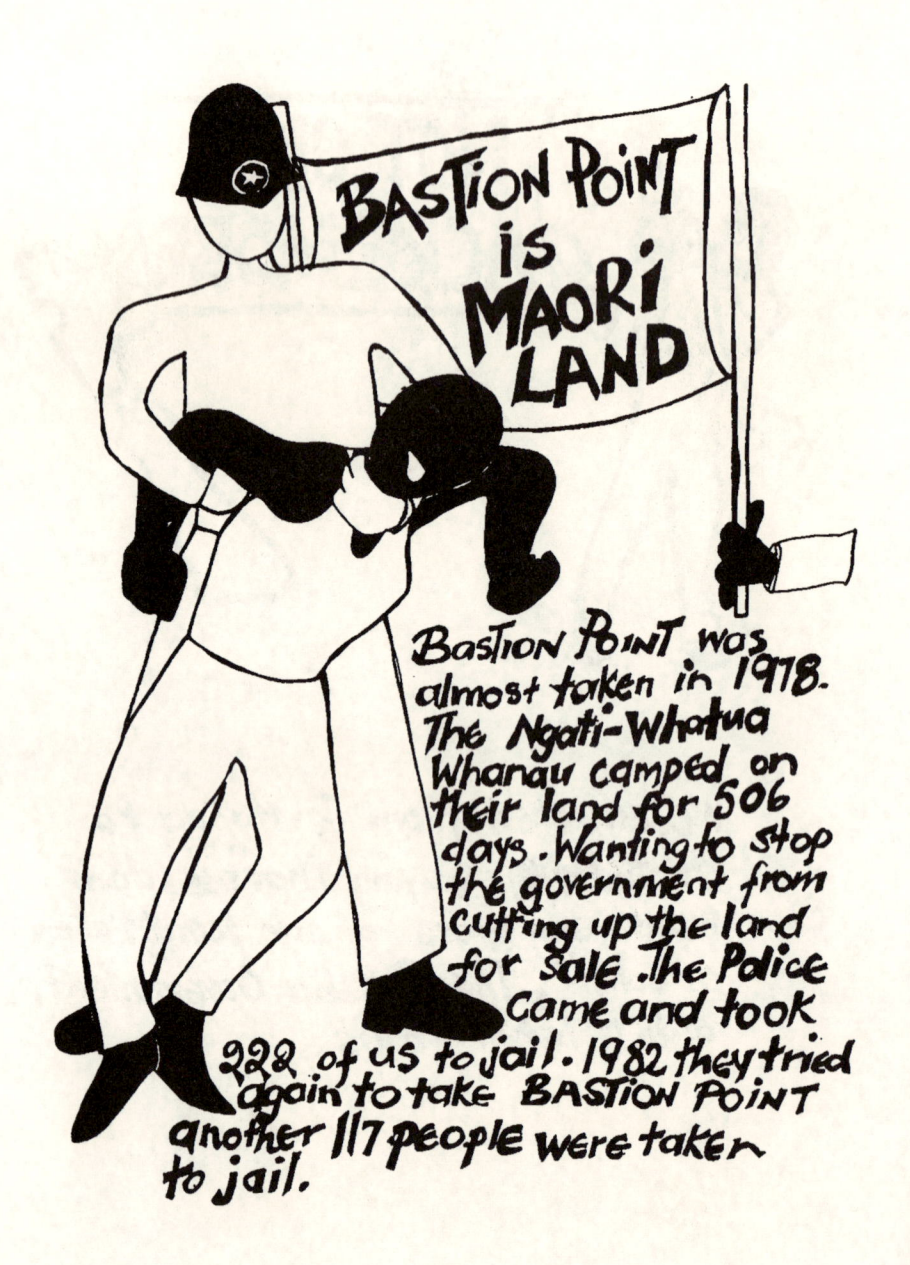

Bastion Point was almost taken in 1978. The Ngati-Whatua Whanau camped on their land for 506 days. Wanting to stop the government from cutting up the land for sale. The Police came and took 222 of us to jail. 1982 they tried again to take BASTION POINT another 117 people were taken to jail.

WHY DO WE MAORI FIGHT FOR OUR RIGHTS
* We have lost our rights to our forest, land and kaimoana.
* We have had to re-learn our language 120 years later
* We can't get jobs
* There is a shortage of housing for us.
* We have to pay too much money to get our basic food, and clothing needs.

* We are still the kaitiaki of Aotearoa.
* We will KEEP on fighting for what is rightfully ours.
* We don't want one more acre of land to be taken or sold.
* We know that ....

MAORI ARE TANGATA WHENUA OF AOTEAROA.

Komaru's sleep was short, but his dreams were long. They had started to enter his genetic memory at the moment his ancestors had embarked on canoes from Hawaiki so many centuries ago. In a few hours of rest he had travelled thousands of miles hopping from island to island in search of a *whenua*. And then that *whenua* had been occupied, raped, dismembered and tramped on enough to keep in bondage a few psychologically washed out Maoris as slaves of white masters. Yes, his people, the keepers of Aotearoa, had been oppressed for only a couple of centuries, but that was long enough to sharpen *pounamu* axes, to wrap a *patu* around one's wrist, to tie a pointed tip to a long reed.

His thesis was to be prepared and presented to the Department of History MA Committee as already outlined. No need for the trappings of so-called scholarly condiments. And it would be presented in Maori, with the single exception of face-to-face English translations, as for the Trick of Waitangi. That was the only concession to the University of Victoria, a token expression of gratitude for teaching him the language of war.

Chapter 30

The Reti home, had it been anthropomorphised, could be seen that Sunday night as a set of two brains rattling in different rooms. As Komaru had placed himself in a contemplative mode after reading the 'historical' document, Mahina was opening and closing her synapses in the process of preparing herself for the funeral service. Her plan included attending her father's burial in the recently assigned corner to Maori dead, for originally the whole cemetery had been used only by whites. That is why her mother, being Yugoslavian, had been allowed to join the sacred Pakeha dwelling. Mahina felt guilty for not visiting her mother's grave upon returning from the States as she had intended, but time and other deadlines had prevented her from doing that.

Therefore, she thought of combining both functions in the same day, with the hope that soon her mother would be re-exhumed to join her husband. The physical distance between the two graves was a few hundred metres, but socially antipodean. Yes, Pakehas were magnanimously beginning to create better race relations among the dead at considerable expense. A generation before, 'the idea of West Auckland Maoris having their own *urupa* was simply a dream'. But the efforts made by *kuia* Betty Ngata had begun to pay off. It had been an ironic situation in the past just to think that Maoris had been deprived of their land not only when alive, but also when dead. Even the mayor of Waitakere, under whose jurisdiction the area had been since the opening of the cemetery, admitted that 'previous councils had lacked the will to set aside an area in Waikumete for Maoris'. The excuse for that 'unwillingness' had been ascribed to some logistic problems deriving from the fact that some Maoris buried their dead with their feet pointing toward the east according to their *kawa*.

Mahina was striving to accomplish two things. One was that of creating the mood for the occasion, and the other, a consequential one, was the selecting of something to be read at the graveside.

After leaving Komaru, Mahina stopped by the rumpus room, where she noticed several books lying here and there, almost at elbow's reach from the bed and the armchair on shelves and side tables. Her father obviously used to either read or consult some of those publications for whatever reason before his energies sunk to a low that immobilised him in bed.

One of the books was Melville's *Moby-Dick*, whose presence she had discussed with Komaru. Apparently, her father had been reading and re-reading it since his stay at the sanatorium. The other one was Lucretius' *De rerum natura*, an 1886 edition that had been purchased at a garage sale. Its tattered cover, the stained pages, the broken spine and other marks of heavy handling led one to believe that the book had been used for at least a century. Amazingly, Lucretius' thought took about the same amount of time to reach Aotearoa as did the Maoris departing from Hawaiki – 2,000 years. In leafing through it nervously, Mahina noticed several pages in which some verses had been highlighted in green, the same colour used by her father to mark pages in Melville. Intrigued by that, she took the book to her room and there she spent most of the night scanning the text and wondering what her father's eyes had seen and for what purpose. And, in doing so, she 'connected' nearly immediately with her father's mind and guts.

The problem was that Lucretius' Latin, in spite of Cicero's inconsistent 'copy-editing', was not something she could digest like the text of medieval Catholic scriptures. However, her intuitive source of interpretation slowly allowed her to tune in under the stress of digging intensely, not so much through the literal meaning of the hexametres as much as for what her father may have thought of them, either for consolation or resignation. Both of those possible purposes seemed to emerge from under the green ink slowly but clearly enough. In Book II, the enigmatic Lucretius was obviously inspired by physical phenomena from which he departed in order to state a philosophical tenet. Mahina simply wondered how both poetry and philosophy could have been blended in a unique text and never attempted after that. But, she thought that, in its pristine source, poetry was after all the philosophy of a sensitive life carrier trying to show that what Man needs is not enjoyment, but 'peace and a pure heart'. Had her father reached that stage through Lucretius?

In her own experience, Mahina recalled hot summer afternoons at the beach bach, when she would observe for hours the rays of light filtering through the rickety window shutters into the dark girl's camp dorm bedroom – beams of light along which she would see the tiny corpuscles of dust pullulating, dancing, criss-crossing in and out, as well as along those streaks of sunlight. At that time she did not pay much attention to those particles as *materia prima*. Much later, in reading about Giordano Bruno's recycling of life components, she had understood in part the physical dimensions of the normally invisible to create the biologically tangible. She had looked at them only materialistically, as shadows of people upside down passing by the window and reflected on the wall as if in a *camera obscura*. What Plato had missed, by limiting his observations to just intangibles, had been synthesised by Lucretius four centuries later by limiting reality totally within the confines of the material world. After all, Plato was an opportunist, an egotistic and narcissistic man trying to carve a niche for himself in history at all costs. And in this he succeeded to the point that in the 20th century there are philosophers, such as Alfred Whitehead, who believed that Western philosophy is a footnote to Plato. Undoubtedly his stay at Harvard had frozen his brain in a dark cave. Lucretius, on the other hand, was what in modern terms one could label a 'mystic', even if he dedicated his poetry to *Alma Venus*.

The section beginning with 'Contemplator enim ...' solved Mahina's puzzle and made her more comfortable to proceed with the rest. Lucretius was both poetic and didactic in addressing himself to her as she roughly 'translated' the following: 'Observe the sunlight, when it filters through the window blinds into the darkness of a room; along the light beam you can see a confused riddle of corpuscles as if they were engaged in an eternal fight, at times organised in groups, other times separated individually in order to attack each other fast and relentlessly. Through observation you will understand what the timeless fall of prime matter is into the deep infinity of the void'. She thought of Dante, another poet who had expressed in hendecasyllables another epopee of Mankind, though so antithetical, for the Florentine poet descends first into the Earth's bowels before climbing to Heaven. Lucretius drops into Nothingness, and there he stays forever. And Homer. He remains at Earth's level attached to the crust of reality. So strange that each of the three poets had used the genre of the heart to express the history of the human tangible and intangible. The continuum – Greece, Rome, Florence – in her belief had never been surpassed by any other triad, perhaps because of the unique character of the verses as nutshells of distilled thought, for in each case not much was known about the private lives of the three poets. A creative work, she thought, needs no biographic notes on the author.

The Lucretian void had triggered a feeling of emptiness in her stomach. In less than 30 centuries of Western efforts to understand the essence of Life, those three poets had stood on the tripod of the indelible. And, amazingly, as a Maori she empathised so much with them by collating what her own people had kept for so long in their minds and conveyed from generation to generation via spoken language as a primary source of Polynesian poetry. Devoid of frozen metre, rhyme and form, Maori poetry was 'Homeric' *par excellence* in its genesis, Lucretian in its content and Dantesque in intent. Poetic fragments from one single *whakapapa*, such as the Rangitane's alone, contain the lyricism of pure music like the 'Violin Concerto' in 'He Waiata na Torino'.

She concentrated on Book II where the motion of the corpuscles eternally erring as lost entities in space took her to the modern concept of solar wind at least in the Via Lactea. And the parallels with Dante's shadows and souls whirling as either devils or angels from the *Inferno* to the *Paradiso* was not unwarranted. That concept of the floating granules of dynamic light was for Mahina the very key to the Epicurean tenets that surfaced in her mind as a philosophy major, but it also gave her a grasp of Lucretius' poetry as strange, violent, even sensual. After all, Lucretius was under the wings of Alma Venus, the Aphrodite who had crossed the Aegean in a seashell before becoming a naturalised citizen by declaring 'Civis Romana sum'. As a free spirit, Lucretius appeared to Mahina even contradictory, for the poet saw in the world the embedded structure of humanity's desperation, which he tried to console by giving humans, almost sadistically, the 'good news' that on Earth there is nothing beyond matter and its *mors immortalis*. That was quite a concept of defiance, as if Death existed as an independent entity. Mahina wondered if 'immortal Death' could exist *per se* without being tied to biological Life, like God, a god of which Lucretius was not afraid for the simple reason that it was a nullity like Life. Could gods share immortality with Death as partners or tenants in common? The rather fatalistic conclusion of that section was nevertheless prosaic. Well, Lucretius had said, once Life is extinguished one need not fear anything any longer. So, why worry? He seemed to imply that the best gift to Life from Death was the finiteness of the former in order to keep alive the eternity of the latter.

Indeed, Lucretius elaborated a little more almost in a mocking tone. After all, once dead, we are not going to be confronted by deities waiting to punish us, and neither will there be a transmigration of the soul. Nothing will humiliate us. Thus, rejoice, since no one comes out of Life alive, not even the Universe itself.

That created quite a shocking conflict with some of the Catholic tenets Mahina had acquired in the last year or so in an effort to find a substitute for Maori traditions. What a mess! She was afraid of mentioning anything 'Christian' at the burial service. Perhaps someone else would. She felt dejected by the realisation that her father had read those verses. But what really surprised her the most was Lucretius' vision of the 'finite' nature of the Universe, obviously a challenge for modern astrophysicists independent of any theory covering either an expanding or contracting Chaos.

Then Schopenhauer suddenly surged into her consciousness, surreptitiously, when she read the next passage: 'Therefore Death's door is not shut even to Heaven, Earth, Sun. And neither to the deep waters of the oceans. Rather, Death is always waiting for all of them as it scrutinizes each one from its immense and deep Chasm.' Mahina felt that Lucretius' reassurance was frightfully chilling. In essence, he may have felt sorry for his fellow humans, and that is why he tried to lessen the impact of the unavoidable by cheering them up, almost as if saying: 'Take it easy! Once gone, you have nothing else to fear, It is a facile solution in comparison with the troubles of Life.' Lucretius would have been an ideal person to comfort a prisoner tied to an electric chair or a lethal injection platform on the verge of being executed.

Undoubtedly, Lucretius had laid the foundations for 19th- and 20th-century existentialism, a rather childish conclusion perhaps, for the history of philosophy is a sequence of peaks and valleys, a Bachian fugue of antithetical views that change only in the name every time one of them crosses the horizontal line of terminology in either direction. All modern existentialism, from Dostoyevski to Nietzsche to Sartre, had done nothing more than rinse its clothes in the Tiber.

And how lucky for Lucretius to have avoided a philosophical confrontation with Christianity! Jesus had to wait at least 50 years to be born. Would Lucretius have been spared the alleged insanity leading him to write only *per intervalla insania* and then commit suicide? He just could not escape the fate of a burnt generation so similar to that of the Second World War, leading to the awakening of nationalism all over the world. Except for Aotearoa, still chained to oppression.

At the end of her meditation, Mahina felt sorry for Lucretius, for she could detect the anguish of that sensitive soul, a poet belonging to the generation of the social *déracinés*, of impatient and curious youth, willing to roam the world with the passion of freedom, and thus shocking against the pragmatism of Earthly conflicts, leaving poetry buried in the mud. When Mahina saw her tears staining the green of the marker, she just could not believe that for free spirits like Lucretius there was nothing left but resignation. It was so ironic, sadistic, illogical, that to create the eternally tangible, Death, all primordial matter has to be hidden and invisible as finite Life.

The funeral director came in person by 9:00 a.m. to pick up Mahina and Komaru in a black limousine. He first took them to the mortuary, where Reverend Tarei, Jr, met them to outline his voluntary contribution to a low-key ceremony. Then the short convoy proceeded directly north, crossing Mangere Bridge, taking a left on Mt Albert Road and zig-zagging through a construction detour until reaching New North Road. After the intersection with Great North Road, the distance to the cemetery was covered in 10 minutes. By the time they arrived at the secondary entrance on Awaroa Road, north of the crematorium, a few more automobiles had joined the caravan following the lead car to the burial plot.

In the Pakeha luxury and comfort of that Cadillac limousine, the siblings travelled almost mesmerised by the sights parading by on both sides of the road. Some places were landmarks, such as the Margaret Griffen Memorial Park, Lynfield College, the Motu Moana Camp site and the Kelston Girls High School in particular, where Mahina had spent her last year before leaving for the States. Nearly choking with the recollection of loyal friends, respected teachers and memorable situations, she took Komaru's hand into hers after resting her head on his shoulders. And the West Auckland cityscape on a midday Monday glided slowly by in silence, as they felt insulated by the thick glass windows and the heavy upholstery.

It was a cold day. The sun was barely shining high over the Bible College of New Zealand. A few boats were sailing in the distance from Wairau Creek toward the Whau River. And the scarce and young trees surrounding the Maori corner of the cemetery seemed to be dwarfed by the individual black cypresses planted as sentries by some grave sites at the bottom of the little dale reached by white gravel paths. Mahina immediately felt cold in the open, for she had not thought to wear an overcoat. She was still psychologically in Portland, but Komaru removed his raincoat and wrapped it around her.

There was no doubt about the mood of the occasion, for Nature itself seemed to empathise with her grief. And John Ruskin came to her mind. Why, how, from where? It was a course she had taken in Salzburg. Yes, she remembered, a survey of English literature. And pathetic fallacy, the phrase invented by Ruskin, emerged to illustrate how anything surrounding the sensitive person seems to be energised by feelings of sorrow, as in Mahina's case. Even the small cypresses seemed to droop after rain squalls had passed by. The white gravel on which she walked started to emit moans of grief under the heavy steps of Komaru. The dark clouds in the northern sky cast sweeping shadows of black over the whole area. And silence, the most piercing quiet, was interrupted only by a few passing automobiles on the sealed peripheral roads. She wondered if Ruskin, as a painter, could sketch that corner of the Earth. Could he see in that picture one that conveyed to the 'mind of the spectator the greatest number of the greatest ideas?' How could a cemetery trigger anything 'universal'? She tried to remember those ideas. What were they as classified by Ruskin into categories? Oh, yes, Beauty was one. Could there be Beauty in a cemetery? And Truth? What kind of Truth except that of Death for every living organism? Power, Imitation, Relation? What a dreamer! And what a flop in his personal life, marrying Euphemia Gray, the virgin-in-residence after 6 years of forced novitiate in a household of insanity. Mahina thought of herself as being already a virgin married to God. And God would never become insane. How could He, after teaching pathetic fallacy to Tennyson for his 'In Memoriam' and to Shelley for his 'Adonais', just to mention a few elegies made possible by Nature empathising with humans? And would her own brief prayer on behalf of her father be human enough to draw strength from the recollection of those elegies? As a Catholic, how could she reconcile Tennyson's religious problems, stemming from his conviction that Mankind was afflicted by the decline of faith, the rise of skepticism, and the spread of scientific materialism? And Shelley, did he have to give his friend Keats a mythological name in order to deal with the theme of incest between Myrrha and her father, Cinyras, a parallel character drawn from Babylonian Tammuz? She remembered Lot and his daughters in Jewish tradition, too. It seemed that in the great religions and literary giants, from cuneiform records to Greek mythology, the recurrence of incest between father and daughter conferred a mark of immortality. How could that be so? She remembered having read a paperback by Florence Rush. Oh, yes, *The Best Kept Secrets.* She had been horrified. And then she thought of Polynesia. She knew of certain *whakapapa* dysfunctions even in Maori canoe descendants, but that was a long time ago and dictated mostly by necessity and even consensual passion. The thoughts about these matters rendered her nearly afraid of being human. It looked like primordial incest was at the root of humanity. And how could she formulate that unsanctioned Law of Life, standing by as her father's casket was unloaded from the hearse? She tried to concentrate on the surroundings, and suddenly became aware of a small crowd facing the freshly dug grave.

The first people she met were the couple from Wanganui, formally introduced by Komaru as 'Dr and Mrs McTavish'. Looking at Melissa, Mahina was shocked, as if she had been confronted by a tigress, for Mrs McTavish was wearing a feline fur resembling that of a tiger. While Dr McTavish impressed her immediately with his apparent maturity and formality, Melissa electrified her with a vibrant personality that exuded not only raw femaleness, but also a strange perfume which clung to Mahina's clothes after the tight hug she received.

There was no need for Komaru to introduce Ling-ling, a surprise attendance. Her meek posture and sense of desolation gave Mahina a feeling of comfort. And who was that Maori woman in her 40s ? A Maori, but a strange one, as if bred with a non-Polynesian. Later, of course, Komaru explained. That was another big surprise. She had come all the way from the sanatorium. When Reverend Tarei began to perform his function, the workers moved aside near the mortuary personnel. But Komaru noticed two men in black suits and black glasses. They made him feel somewhat uneasy, for, not being close to the funeral party, they moved slowly as if trying to find some markers or graves in the immediate vicinity. Noticing Komaru's inquisitive look, Reverend Tarei whispered something in his ear. He told Komaru not to pay attention to those creeps. He would explain later.

And the function began. The Reverend first explained his rôle by giving a short historical background illustrating the friendship between his father, who had died in 1980, and the siblings' parent. They had been together overseas, and as a young man the Reverend had come to know Mr Reti as an artist, a literary person trying to write something that apparently never saw the light. He also mentioned the fact that Mr Reti as a young man had explored some tenets connected with the Ratana Church, but later switched to his grandfather's Ringata Church as a more moderate and pristine movement because of its blend of Maori traditions and Christian beliefs.

A chant followed. Mahina had heard it only once before when her father had taken her to the 12th, a once a month function of some kind she could not remember. After the chant, Reverend Tarei spoke and declaimed some religious passages which Mahina could not understand, though she knew it was in Maori. But the language was archaic, somewhat stifled, cryptic. She guessed that Reverend Tarei used extremely classic Maori, something that could be recited only by a *tohunga*. Thus, she assumed that he was one, and indeed he acted like one, for she detected in him some of the 'pastoral' traits and behaviour manifested by an old priest at the church near the university, as well as at old *marae tangi*. The speech given was undoubtedly spontaneous, and in it the name of Christ recurred frequently. She wondered what her father would have said about that, but she was happy to hear something familiar, particularly when she was able to understand what Reverend Tarei told Mr Reti: 'Your body is the tabernacle of God.' Finally, he concluded the service by addressing Mr Reti as a traveller who would be helped on his journey by all those who had covered the same road, and ended with the Lord's Prayer, but a strange one for it had been modified to end with 'We believe and glorify thy holy name. Amen.'

Then there was a moment of hesitation. Who was to follow? Komaru? No. He asked Mahina to proceed with whatever she had in mind. And she did, opening a book and reading something that most people thought was Maori. Dr and Mrs McTavish, however, understood it from the first to the last word, for it was Latin.

'De profundis clamavi ad te Domine: Domine, exaudi vocem meam. Mahina sum ...'

Those in attendance began to stare at her, as if asking 'Is she a priest or a nut?' But the prayer, or whatever it was in that foreign language, did not last long. Well, at least some understood or misunderstood 'Mahina' as 'machina' or so. The last couple of distichs created some consternation for, soon after Mahina declaimed 'Requiem aeternam dona patri meo, Domine,' another voice, Whina's enjoined 'Et lux perpetua luceat Wiremo Reti. Amen.'

At that, Mahina closed the book, skipped the speech she had in mind, and concluded her farewell address with the following:

Te roimata i heke,
Te hupe i whiua ki te marae
Ka ea aitua.

Then she approached Whina, hongied her affectionately, and thanked her for helping her father take the first step on his journey to Cape Reinga. At the last moment, she asked:

'Incidentally, who are you?'

'I am the nurse who stood by your father at the sanatorium. I know a lot about you. Let's keep in touch.'

Meanwhile, there was a moment of indecision, of hesitation. Was Komaru going to do anything? He was. He simply prostrated himself near the head of the casket and spoke to his father in whispers. And no one knew what he said. The monologue, or whatever, was brief. And then the rain came. What a blessing, thought Mahina. She didn't think that her father would want any more theatricals. Then Komaru cut the ceremony short after thanking Reverend Tarei. That is when Dr McTavish led Mahina to his automobile, where Melissa had already taken shelter in order to protect her mascara from the heavy drops already hitting hard everywhere. Apparently, arrangements had been made between the McTavishes and the funeral director. The McTavishes would take care of the return trip and any other necessities that arose. Komaru remained impassive in the rain, thanking each and every person for coming to the funeral service. He hongied Whina at length. Then he hugged Ling-ling affectionately and escorted her attentively to her car under the lightning bolts of the passing storm and of Melissa's eyes. There had been more electricity among the women than in the air. Bill spoke with a tone of paternal affection saying that from that moment on he would take care of everyone and everything. And he asked for cooperation.

'You know, Komaru, any time I am involved in a storm, be it coming from all the Gods in Heaven or from a human mind, I follow what Melville says in *Moby-Dick*. "If you can get nothing better out of the world, get a good dinner out of it, at least." Now, let us relax.'

'Yes,' added Melissa. 'Bill is going to take us to "Saibo". I heard it is a relaxing restaurant. And ... I am thirsty.'

Mahina said nothing. She simply recoiled into the back seat against the wetness of Komaru's hair, which she tried to dry off with the lining of his raincoat. Melissa was attempting to apply some lipstick, using the mirror behind the passenger's side visor. Komaru was intrigued by Bill's impromptu paternal care.

'I think it is very kind of you. I am sure that Mahina will be glad to get acquainted with both of you. And ... may I ask you, is it Indian?'

'Oh, no,' replied Melissa. 'It is a first-class Mediterranean establishment with plenty of various foods for the most discr ...'

'Sorry,' interrupted Bill, 'what she really means is *Cibo*, as in "cheapo", though I can assure you it is first class. Those Italians have used a Latin term for Provençal victuals.'

At that, Mahina seemed to perk up. The name of the restaurant conjured up an exotic locale via an Italian name that, ironically, meant only 'food'. Of course, the proper pronunciation was far from 'cheap', for Komaru had heard it was one of the most expensive places in the Parnell district.

The long ride through the University of Auckland campus created both a feeling of relaxation and of recollections. Komaru in particular remembered the last time he had visited with Captain Bickhard at the Salvation Army Centre. And the four years he had spent there, among friends and foes. And the invisible presence of the police keeping track of ..., Yes, he thought. Now he remembered. One of those two men in black. He was a plainclothesman. Yes, an inspector. And what was he doing at a funeral?

But his vagaries were interrupted by the car's arrival at Cibo's. Most people were leaving the premises, for business 'lunch' time was nearly over. He looked at his watch. One twenty-five. And he was hungry. Dinner was in order.

The four-person party spent almost the entire afternoon in that credit card establishment. Of course, it had never been visited by Her Majesty the Queen. She would never abandon tradition, no matter what. *Antoine's* would never be betrayed.

The Cibo entrance room gave one a sudden feeling of comfort. The bright lights, the soft canned music of an accordion, the warm air and the subtle fragrance of herbed food conferred upon the whole party a wave of relaxation. And after a few minutes, except for Mahina, who was still feeling guilty for not visiting her mother's grave, all became nearly euphoric.

As the women left for the powder room, the men proceeded inside the dining area, following the maitre d', Giovanni, who had introduced himself as such. Giovanni was friendly enough to suggest that the diners could choose any seat they wished. Bill surveyed the logistics of the place and selected a table as far as possible from the entrance, by a large window from which Komaru saw the roof of the Alcoholic Rehab Centre, just a few hundred meters away on Church Street.

And he told Bill how merely a year or so had elapsed since he had met with Captain Bickhard, though so much had happened in the meantime. At that time, Komaru had hoped that his father had fully recovered from his addiction. Yes, he had, but many of his internal organs were already beyond repair. And now he was dead from what the doctor had written on the death certificate: 'kidney failure' as a consequence of cirrhosis of the liver.

And braised kidneys as *rognons de veau* were the first words Komaru read on the menu among the antipasti as he waited for the ladies to return from the lav. And *paté de fois*. Kidneys and liver! What an exciting appetiser to begin a death celebration Mediterranean style.

The return of Mahina and Melissa signalled the descent of various waiters helping them to sit down, re-arranging chairs, unfolding serviettes, opening menus and asking if there was anythig else they could do. Bill suggested that he needed a few minutes of orientation. Melissa, however, asked for a coffee cup. And she clarified a possible misunderstanding. She needed an empty cup and a glass of water for her medicine. In a few minutes she had surreptitiously poured a stiff jigger of Cardhu from the silver flask she retrieved for her purse. Then she added half a glass of water. And she began to sip the potion with gusto. Bill was pleased to hear from Mahina that she would have half a glass of white house wine, sharing the pitcher of an Australian Pinot Grigio he had selected. Komaru opted for Fiuggi mineral water.

Once the ambience of conviviality was created through the drinks, Bill began his process of triage in the selection of Cibo's *cibo*. He was a doctor, of course, and he acted as such at an emergency field station where a physician must decide in a matter of minutes, if not seconds, whom to select for treatment and whom to put aside for the fate of oblivion. In a restaurant, Bill often felt that way until he returned several times, memorising the list of best dishes featured by the restaurant. A cursory examination of the menu revealed that, at Cibo's, its *cibo* included an assortment of assembly type food excelling in smoked, sautéed, marinated or 'spirited' dishes betraying a Mediterranean tradition with stress on Provençal specialties. Komaru guessed that the establishment used the 'assembly plant' preparation involving both *cibo* and non-*cibo*, and thus a final presentation of colours, form, design, fragrance and textures. By looking at the menu one could anticipate the birth of a child from a latter-day Martianus Capella's *De Nuptiis Sinologiae et Anthimi*, for the obliteration of regional cuisine produces in trendy restaurant kitchens a plate of both architectural and engineered victuals from many parts of the world. Of course, each dish, although named exotically, is never the same. It varies according to the artistic sensitivity and mood of the chef and the daily availability of ingredients. Actually, 'ingredients' is a misnomer. They should be called 'components' as if retrieved from the box of a Mechano or Erector set.

Bill took the lead in the selection of antipasti, often understood and even included in its English counterpart on the menu as 'before the pasta'. Worse is its translation as an appetiser, as if people going to a restaurant needed a stimulant, particularly when 'starving to death'.

With the exception of Komaru, all settled on marinated mushrooms. Komaru chose a *bruschetta* with tomatoes sliced in olive oil and baked garlic, a dish that poor peasants ate in the 'old country' for lack of better food containing needed protein, a phenomenon not dissimilar from indigent American Portuguese immigrants' children hiding their poor lunch at school, eating lobster rather than sliced ham.

The entrée, as first *piatto*, and not the real spuriously designated course Russian style, followed suit in the selection process. Party lines had already been drawn. On one side of the table, Melissa, Bill, and Mahina, and on the other the outcast, Komaru, for he would not eat chowder because of the milk. Thus, he ordered the soup of the day, which turned out to be barley broth made with neck of mutton, pearl barley, dried peas, onions and leeks, plus a mélange of cabbage, carrots, turnips and parsley. Well, a Kiwi vegetarian bouillabaisse, However, the selection of the chowder created a topic of discussion, for Bill casually made a comment on Melville's description of the dish. In fact, although not remembering details, he knew that a whole chapter had been written on it. It was Mahina who, surprising Bill, gave a description of the seafood dish in relation to Queequeg's preference. She even remembered Mrs Hussey always giving an option: 'clam or cod?' Of course, in New England's Indian territory, the loyalty dictated clam, and not immigrant cod. And the same in Aotearoa, where, however, contrary to New England's clam sizes, one could answer 'yes' to Ishmael's question: 'Queequeg, do you think that we can make out a supper for us both on one clam?' Oh, the *toheroa* chopped and cooked by Mahina's paternal grandmother! And the 'savage' Queequeg, naturalised Westerner and Christian to the point of becoming like Tupai Cupa through a bowl of chowder – 'made of small juicy clams, scarcely bigger than hazelnuts, mixed with pounded ships biscuits, and salted pork cut up into little flakes; the whole enriched with butter, and plenty seasoned with pepper and salt.'

The rest of the dinner went by in an alternation of eating and talking, but after the chowder the party split in two. On one side Melissa and Komaru initiated a conversation on a 'professional' topic along historical lines. Basically, it was a sequence of allusions to situations – past and future – recalled or hungered for by Melissa. She was feeling high in anticipation of having Komaru chopped and transformed into clams for her chowder. And for that dish of hers she even poured some of her 'coffee', which she had labelled *vischium Scoticum* to fool the waiter and to improve the sweetness of rich New Zealand butter. On the other side, Bill and Mahina were engaged in a culinary discussion, basically a repetition of what had been analysed at the McTavish home with Komaru, mostly on terminology and stressing the Roman and Gallic-Celtic roots of the barley soup ... 'vero tisanas quae de hordeo fiunt qui scit facere, bonae sunt ... fit etiam de hordeo opus bonum quod nos graece dicimus "alfita", latine vero "polentam"'. Mahina told Bill that in Portland polenta is sold in gourmet food stores, precooked and packed in sausage casings. Bill observed that, as far as pigs were concerned, the medium had become the message.

It was a pleasant dinner, and a complex one since the real 'entrée' was different for each of the diners. That is when, while waiting for their dishes, they began to play a game of ordering in a Roman 'restaurant' or at least in Amphitryon's home, even if some items were anachronistically impossible. Mahina was the first to order, 'pasta vermiculata lycopersici liquamine condita et carne bovina more bononiense', a dish she had eaten at an Italian restaurant in Northwest Portland. Komaru selected the vegetarian 'laganum solis oleribus et farinaceis vescens'. Melissa, missing 'Brit beef', opted for 'caro costalis assa more florentino cum globulis solianis', though at her high scotch stage she could not taste much after her palate had been numbed by the 'coffee'. It was Bill who surprised everyone since, after asking questions, he settled on 'agnellinus assus more Graeco cum cepis'.

Everyone at least agreed on the salad – *mixtura herbae (Russa, acetaria Caesaria et olera)*. But the dessert cart created a mood of celebration, as a Maori *tangi hangi*, though dessert in old Aotearoa was made-simply of wild fruit. Bill ordered a sample of nearly everything and divided each selection into four parts – *placenta Senensis, placenta sicula, laganum turgidum* and even *sorbillum glaciatum*. The selection of coffee was for the waiter almost a nightmare because each ordered a different type. Mahina asked for *potio cafearia sine cafeino*, Komaru a *cafearia potio coram expressa*, Bill a *cafearia potio spuma lactis praedita* and finally Melissa ordered *potio cafearia temperata*, which she made the most of by adding some of the other 'coffee' she had been drinking throughout dinner.

By 5 o'clock everyone felt sleepy. Komaru suggested that Bill and

Melissa stay at his home that night, since, by the time Bill took the siblings back to Papakura and returned to Wanganui, it would be imprudent. Night was descending fast and it was not safe to encounter a winter storm along the way. There would be no problem in logistics. Mahina had her room, Komaru would sleep in the rumpus room, and the married couple could spend the night in Komaru's room if they did not mind sleeping on a Maori bed. Melissa thought that the idea was excellent, even exciting. Thus, they drove to Papakura by following the Great Road South.

Upon arriving at the Reti house, Komaru removed a few items from his room for himself, left some sheets asking Melissa to make the bed, and she retired immediately half high and visibly tired. Mahina followed suit. She needed to reflect on the events of the day, particularly after observing Melissa in action pending from Komaru's lips, though he did not talk much. But there were several signs and signals departing mainly from Melissa toward Komaru. And it did not take long for Mahina to assume that, after all, there seemed to be a flow of languid feminine glances directed at Komaru, who tried to avoid eye contact with both women. He concentrated on paying attention to Bill. And Bill apparently felt completely at ease with her brother. Could it be possible that Komaru's relationship with Melissa was more than 'historical'? And to what point?

Thus, Mahina took a long time to fall asleep. She read some more from Lucretius. Leafing through *De rerum natura*, she paused on Book IV, in which Lucretius dissects love in its several manifestations. Could it be that the rationalistic approach to Epicurean love might explain the situation between her brother and Melissa? No, of course, for if there was anything between the two it must be simply passion or sexual love. And she wondered why one should make a distinction by coupling what in her mind were two different things, sex and love. She believed that love could exist without sex, and vice versa. She even began to think that she felt love for her brother, but absolutely nothing sexual. Anyway, she thanked Lucretius, who re-assured her that passionate love should be avoided like the plague. According to the poet, love is a mental disease, a habit-forming madness that causes irrational acts and in the process wastes money, time, energy and the sense of reality. Well, she thought, that sounds like war – both parties, after attacking each other, become exhausted, let down, disgusted. Was then love impossible unless sex entered into it (and here she laughed at her Freudian supposition) as a *sine qua non*? Yes, Catullus had said so too, but Lucretius must have had quite an experience to conceive of love as a delusion, a pitfall, a trap, almost a Sisyphean enterprise. Yes, of course, Sisyphus climbs (O Freud!) each and every time, and once he reaches the peak (!), he has to start anew. But is woman a rock? After all, it takes two components, like a yin and a yang, or whatever, in any dualistic conception of reality. Yes, of course, that is a human reality, but how does one apply it to mankind *vis-à-vis* mankind? And what about between mankind and God? Is not reality a function of the individual? What kind of reality would a saint or a mystic experience? O, St Teresa de Ávila, were you not in love with God, or with Jesus? And did sex enter into the picture? What was your sense of reality? I remember the three stages my philosophy teacher stressed in loving God – *consideratio, contemplatio, raptus*. Mahina was only at the first stage, the consideration of possibilities and events surrounding her – mostly the death of her father. But now Melissa was surging in from nowhere, triggering something new. Yes, that was real. Mahina resented her as an obstacle in her 'consideration' of developments. Ah, was it jealousy? For what? She just would not assume that Melissa could interpose herself between her and her brother.

In trying to fall asleep, she felt almost like knocking a good night on the *kauri* wall, but she remembered that Komaru was not near her. In addition, she could not help listening and paying attention to what sounded like a heavy ruffling of sheets and bodies fighting each other on Komaru's bed. And muffled moans, feminine cries being suffocated by a hand or whatever. O Lucretius, are you saying that Melissa and Bill

> cling greedily together and join their watering
> mouths and draw deep breaths pressing teeth on lips;
> but all is vanity, for they rub nothing off thence,
> nor can they penetrate and be absorbed in body? ...

Well, yes, all right, brother. They are man and wife. But how do you enter into the picture? And Ling-ling, that sweet little darling looking at you so tenderly at the grave site! You can't tell me that you love Melissa. Doesn't she belong to another generation? Please, Komaru, forgive me, but what do you expect from her besides genital love?

In a way, Mahina's concern with Melissa took the place of an alternate *idée fixe* in place of what she had been afflicted by during the last few days – her father's death. But she could not sleep, even after the brouhaha seeping through the *kauri* wall ceased. What could she do or take to fall asleep? She thought that probably a potion of some kind would help. Yes, of course, a balm of some kind. She laughed at the recollection of *Melissa officinalis* that could help. That was Paracelsus' favourite herb. But where and when had she read about it? Nevertheless, she remembered its properties – to be used in all complaints supposed to proceed from a disordered state of the nervous system . . . chasing away melancholy. Yes, naturally, the Carmelite water used by the nuns she had visited in Spokane. She should have gotten a bottle. But how could she know that she would succumb to a case of nervous disorder? How could Melissa hurt her? After all, she was married, and sleeping with her husband. What was there to fear?

Mahina must have drifted into a semi-sleep state or torpor, but not deep enough to hear a noise, as if someone had bumped against a door. It was 3 o'clock. The light in the corridor was on and filtering under her door. Was Komaru all right? He had been so serious-looking all day long. Yes, of course, perhaps something had happened at the cemetery that kept him from saying anything aloud. The interment had been so un-Maori!

She got up, wrapped her white robe around her body, opened the door, and descended the steps toward Komaru's room. She hoped not to wake him up, for he must be so tired. But she was concerned that he was not feeling well. Maybe he was despondent and trying something desperate. No, she would help him, for she knew that women are psychologically stronger when it comes to comforting people under stress, particularly a brother. She would hold his hand and *hongi* him delicately so as not to wake him up if asleep. She would not shock him by bringing him into the reality of wakefulness. But she did shock against Melissa turning on the last step of the landing, just before rounding the corner. And they rolled down the steps together, stopping at the bottom, with Mahina on top. Melissa was holding only a towel over her loins, everything else was totally bare. And Mahina had to press both hands on Melissa's breasts to push herself up and away. The impact of placing her hands on shifting giant breasts blanketed her wish to scream. But a scream came out from Melissa, for her breasts were still sore and tender. And her body was wet with perspiration releasing the scent of her brother's siblingness, an animalesque smell of maleness both revolting and intoxicating. She was finally able to disentangle herself from Melissa who, to save appearances, apologised for having lost her way to the bathroom, the bathroom just across the hallway from Komaru's room. And there Mahina rushed to take a shower. A cold one, for a release of strange perspiration had covered her in a sudden surge of high fever. She knew she had connected with her brother's hormones through another woman. And she learned in a flash that the major organ of sex is the brain.

The cold water rinsed from her skin all the toxins that her body had released under stress. She was able to dry off and return to her room, where she collapsed in sobs on her bed. Lucretius was still opened to Book IV. She wondered why he had been accused of insanity. If he were insane, what had caused it? Is insanity the consequence of a chemical dysfunction? But what creates a deleterious reaction in the heart of humans when an abnormal chemical reaction has taken place in their brains?

The following day, breakfast was a lonely event for the two men. Mahina stayed in her room trying to recover from the shocks she had received since her arrival, both the visible ones in relation to other people, and the invisible ones that had knocked at the door of her reality as a personal awareness of herself in a baffling world. And the main factor creating a state of insecurity, never felt before, was tied to Komaru. So strange. She had never felt threatened by any human before, not even by a traffic cop 'profiling' her on account of being a Maori. And now by her brother, even though Komaru had not done anything wrong, such as reneging on her. Well, she still felt betrayed, rejected, discarded when she needed him the most. Rationally, she could understand a nocturnal incident, even if caused by Komaru, though she wanted to rationalise that it was 'she' who had visited him. And how could 'she' slip out of a marital bed and jump into another after being loved by her own husband just a few hours earlier? Could a 50-year-old woman be subject to a short-term variation for sex or had she tried to console Komaru by assuming that, in spite of the deep grief of mourning, he could perform in the very bed still pullulating with the warm corpuscles of his father?

Melissa too remained in bed intentionally, allowing others to use the bathroom first. Thus, Bill and Komaru lounged in the kitchen over tea.

'I am sorry about this morning. I had told her to refrain from seeing you. I simply could not, although I did my best twice. Once upon retiring and a second time before she left to meet you. She just felt a combination of sorrow for you and the assumption that she could make you relax ... like a couple of aspirins.'

'To which I am allergic. Well, Bill, in a way, I feel rejuvenated or, shall I say, revived. I was so soundly asleep that the first time Melissa mounted me I wasn't sure if I was experiencing a wet dream. And she worked hard to ... wake me up. But once she felt ... enthroned, it did not take long for her to melt down, as ever before. I had to turn off the electric blanket.'

'Did she stay down a long time?'

'Probably a couple of hours. I was telling her that my father must have been amused. I know that, in spite of his illness, he seemed to have kept his hormonal level rather high. That is what Whina, the sanatorium nurse, told me, without, of course, compromising anyone with facts and figures.'

'I can guess that. I know that one of the most exciting encounters takes place between patients and nurses. A colleague of mine used to tell me of a nympho who begged for night shifts, when she felt safe. She would make the rounds among patients who seemed to improve overnight. Some of them would re-infect themselves to prolong their stay for the pleasures of the night. Like wounded soldiers in field hospitals. I can't remember an American novel in which ... oh, yes, one of Norman Mailer's characters in *The Naked and The Dead*.'

'Now I understand why Captain Bickhard was adamant about having father removed from the sanatorium. I wonder.'

'That's life.'

'And I assumed that he stayed on the island, which he thought of as a whaling boat from which he would launch his harpoon, for a more ... noble cause!'

'Who knows? You mentioned once his obsession toward the white whale. I think it is simply a matter of transfer. You know, a Maori against the whole white mass of people floating around and dominating the sea around your islands.'

'I can understand that. He must have thought of himself as Queequeg.'

'But there is more than that. After what you told me about your father and Melville last month, I re-read the book myself here and there. And I thought things over, beyond you father chasing the white race. That is the superficial aspect of it. The deeper structure is emerging now more clearly.'

'Sorry.'

'Yes, you father did chase a beast, but the real inference is that the beast was himself. In a vicious circle. And perhaps even torn between the dominant group in Aotearoa and the servient one symbolized by himself.'

'Poor father!'

'And that may have been his epic journey on the basis of the little information you have given me. In essence, that heartbreaking saga around the world could have been an attempt by a broken man in search of himself. Or better, in search of his missing leg, of his dignity in a society of Men, without which he never felt whole. Do you now understand what I can retrieve from a rather semi-professional analysis of your father's anguish? Oh, I wish I could know more about his early life. Something terrible must have happened. What was it that led a sensitive man to withdraw from society trying to find relief in alcohol and creative work such as painting and sculpting? Manic depression only?'

'Bill, I think I begin to understand. We Maori have never lost the sense of ... cosmic directions that led us away from Hawaiki and ...'

'Goooood mooorning! Daarling, Kom love, hello! Well, I think I like your bed. So restful. Oh, I must have dreamed a lot. And ... where is Mahina?'

Chapter 31

The McTavishes left for Wanganui soon after breakfast. Komaru had to apologise for Mahina's absence at their departure, since she was apparently still asleep and would not answer his knock on her door. Of course, Mahina had been wide awake for hours, and she could hardly wait for the guests to free the upstairs lavatory where, as soon as she heard Bill's car leaving, she took a quick shower. Presently, she returned to her room, put on a jogging outfit, and entered the kitchen. Komaru was having a second cup of tea.

'Good morning, brother! I trust you rested well.'

'Morning, Mahina. What about you? Are you happy that everything is over?'

'I don't know what you mean by that. Should I be happy now that father is buried?'

'I am sorry, what I meant ... the social functions, the people, the deadlines, the ...'

'So you have already forgotten father ... in spite of spending a whole night ... in his bed?'

'No, of course, on the contrary, I ...'

'On the contrary what? How could you contaminate his memory by engaging in whatever you did with a tart, a slut, just white trash? I vomited all that food the whole night. History repeats itself even in the Pacific. First a slave is well fed, and then Claudia uses it as a disposable tool in the very sanctity of ... How could you? Have Pakehas already emasculated you to the point of playing their games for the sake of keeping the youth of Aotearoa at bay? Where has the old spirit of the warriors gone?'

Komaru avoided a reply. How could he tell her what he was doing for their *whenua*? The very presence of the police inspector as a track keeper at the cemetery spoke for itself. Besides, her question was loaded in different ways. What could he say? That when Melissa stormed upon him he felt like a fish stunned by the poison of the circumstances? Indeed, Melissa had worked extremely hard to create a *phallus paratus* merely for mechanistic purposes. She could even debunk Bernard de Clairvaux's dictum, proving that she could raise the dead to life. But how could he explain everything to his sister on a gloomy Tuesday morning?

Melissa had actually acted for 'charitable' purposes, if not for therapeutic reasons, her own and Komaru's. She was starving to death and was high after the exhilarating dinner. And she assumed, as always before, that her very presence would be enough to trigger a surge of adrenaline in her lover. That was a prerogative of the Martial personality present in every healthy man. And that is why at first she was puzzled, until he surged almost independently from his will as if a swarm of Spanish flies had attacked him. Of course, she had disregarded the state of mind afflicting Komaru, for the *morbus messalinensis* was out of control.

In the past, every skin-to-skin association between Komaru and Melissa was almost an instant switch that produced nearly any type of physical interaction under her expert guidance. Without realising it, Melissa had created in Komaru a power of pure lust. At the same time, she had produced in him a reciprocal feeling of 'love' toward her, for he was naturally inclined to express gratitude toward anyone showing him kindness, attention, help. Basically, when Melissa would delicately whisper into his ears 'I love you' with a motherly tone, he knew that, although never rejoining due to instinctive fear of compromising himself, he felt for her something like a surge of warm comfort, of infallible performance, of almost soul trust. In short, Komaru knew that she had learned, in handling him, how to bring to his brain an abnormal amount of phenylethylamine. She had been taught by her husband, the psychiatrist, that the most potent sex organ was indeed the brain, the crucible of a chemical reaction, the arbiter of a purely physical phenomenon that increased his blood flow to reach the most distant extremity of penile veins. That is why, at his purest climax, a man could be visited by *la mort douce* with a certificate of *ne plus ultra*.

That night Melissa, under the aphrodisiac drive of her Brazilian perfume, fired volleys of encyclopaedic eroticism. She had tongued him with the tenderness of a butterfly wing alternating with the suction power of an angry infant at the breast of a dry mother. She had explored with her fingers all the cavities of his body in synchrony with her dental bites, labial sweepings, buccal enclosures, deep aspirations, inguinal rubbing, salivary painting, pulmonary panting, swine-like grunts, long scratches and all possible positions beyond any Kamasutran imagination. She was afraid of having created in

Komaru an 'erotic depression', not dissimilar from a mental one, solely on the basis of a chemical dysfunction, and thus a purely physical affair. What she did not realise, after scoring her first victory, was that in the whole history of Maoritanga she had broken a paradigm by infusing into a Maori the drive of lust. Komaru had become, *sans le savoir*, the first Aotearoan to shed the pristine cape of innocence and succumb to the psychosomatic eroticisation of his whole race. The natural spontaneity of sexual engagement as one of the bodily functions had vanished forever into the vulgar crassitude of automation. And Komaru knew that he had become an addict to sex for its own sake. Yes, he had shed the last coat of 'primitive savagery' and had become civilised. He could now join the rest of the human race as an equal. It had taken the death of his father to acquire a new gene, a white one, and thus alter the structure of his libido.

'I am sorry. Really. I don't know what to say except that this home of ours seems to have received a *tapu* of some kind. I think that last night, however, I burnt it in ... effigy. I hope that from now on the rest will flow smoother for both of us. Besides, I take all responsibility. As a matter of fact, whatever I felt for Dad has now been transferred and added to what I feel for you. Anyway, my conscience is clear, for I have done nothing intentional to hurt you. I would never do that, although I can see that my being a victim of circumstances has in turn victimised you ... as I feel. At the same time, father's departure has placed me closer to you.'

'So what now? Where do I stand? And how can I stay in this house, reeking with deception, intrigue and, frankly, doubts beyond my comprehension? It seems that father's death has complicated my ... situation. He has left us in a quandary, poor Dad! Oh, I wish I could leave for some place more pleasant, away from the *atua* atmosphere surrounding us. I am so confused, so ...'

'Mahina, dear, actually you have already decided to go away. That solves half of the problem. As soon as father's estate is settled, in practice "burned" symbolically, you can ...'

'Which reminds me, shall we read the last document? I doubt that it has any impact on me. It seems that Dad counts on you for everything on the political side of his fight.'

'Probably. And if so you should feel relieved, actually free of obligations. It is I who is tied to his moral legacy. Shall we go to his studio?'

'Let's do it.'

The large envelope addressed to the siblings proved to be more voluminous than it appeared at first. Komaru guessed that it contained about 20 pages of handwritten material, all in black ink, and lettered clearly and neatly as if printed. The style was identical to that of the second document on the keepers of Aotearoa.

'To you the pleasure of reading it. Your diction is better than mine. Your American sojourn has smoothed the Pakeha vowels.'

'Oh, come on! You know I don't have the oratorical power you do. Probably I can pray better. I wish I could do that in Maori, too. Well, I see. Dad wrote in English. I wonder why.'

It did not take long to understand the reasons for not writing in Maori. The technical terminology, the historical contents, the war episodes exuding from those pages would have been more complex to express in Maori since most of the narrative dealt with British intelligence operations behind enemy lines in Europe and its social consequences in New Zealand. There was no date indicating when those notes were written. However, Mahina guessed that her father may have jotted them down a long time before. Probably soon after she had left for the States, as inferred from some correspondence in which her father hinted at illustrating some aspects of her *whakapapa*. Afraid of not being able to relate his past in person, if he died before her return, her father may have felt it wise to record on paper the so-called 'moral testament'.

Dear Komaru and Mahina,

What I am trying to write here should have been related to both of you orally, not only as a normal contribution to the records of our *whakapapa*, but also because of a duty of mine to account for some events that took place a couple of generations ago. I trust that the following will answer some of the questions you have posed to me on different occasions, both directly and indirectly, when I was unable to inform you on various matters. Perhaps now you will understand the anguish that has been my constant companion for so long as a consequence of war and the follies that humans commit in the name of military codes of honour.

I hope that my notes, not in great detail as a literary confession, will bring peace of mind to both of you, though particularly to Mahina because of her genetic condition. You will know why. And, I am sorry I simply could not describe this matter before for several reasons, such as your tender age, your not being yet mature enough to understand – and even forgive me – when I was entrapped in an emotional, psychological, and political mesh.

Where shall I begin?

Let me start with WWII. Again, just sketches of events here and there should suffice, for, if interested or curious, you can always read on your own from various sources, such as Cody's *Official History of the 28th Maori Battalion*. Of course, you will learn to discriminate about their veracity. From direct experience, I learned a long time ago that history is a compilation of viewpoints, according to the degree of psychic health and emotion expressed by an individual. As the result of a creative process, like a sculpture, a painting, a piano concerto, and so forth, a historical account of anything eschews 'committee' writing and recording.

Thus, the nature of history as pure fiction *in posse*. Ironically, what is described in editorial cataloguing as fiction is nothing more than the real history of ideas in the minds of authors. A writer can lie to anyone except himself, for he can never recant what has been put into print. Can you imagine, say, Melville coming back into your dreams stating, 'Listen, readers, I lied to you. Moby Dick was not white. He was black.'

So the following is just a synthesis of events. You can supply the rest by collating local developments with what you know about me and our family.

First of all, you already know that as a child I grew up among Dalmatians, and particularly among people of one generation, before their offspring became ashamed to speak Croatian, or Serbian, or whatever dialect in public, trying to hide their descent from a non-British family. I don't need to elaborate on that phenomenon of rejection. And I don't have to relate the details of my early schooling, my paternal *iwi*, and so forth. You also know, although I never tried to recall how and why, that I learned Croatian before I spoke a word of English. There was a period in which even Maori was my 'second' language. And that sealed my fate much later when, as an officer of the 28th Maori Battalion, I was selected, actually I was asked to volunteer, for a secret mission, one of whose members was Randolph Churchill.

In October 1943, we left North Africa for Taranto, Italy. Please get a map of that country, actually of the Adriatic Sea showing both Italy and the Dalmatian coast. By that time, while training before being sent to the front, our battalion had been assigned two senior Pakeha officers.

By November, we were trying to break through German defence lines along the River Sangro. As a lieutenant, I was under the direct orders of Capt. James Henare, from Company A. One day, just before Thanksgiving, Jim came to see me at Atessa, a small community a few miles south of the Sangro, where we were learning how to operate the 'Piat' (Projector Infantry, Anti-Tank). He was accompanied by one of the senior officers who never identified himself. This Brit, without any preliminaries, addressed me in Croatian about the most banal aspects of daily life. I had not spoken it in ten years. Caught by surprise, I automatically replied in Croatian as a matter of fact (I later heard he was a professor of linguistics at Cambridge), and, after he dismissed Jim almost as a *persona non grata*, he switched to English. After a few minutes of conversation on army life, he congratulated me on my Croatian. I remember vividly his textual words, 'Actually, my dear fellow, your Croatian is more native than your English.' I had to refrain from attacking the bastard, for at first I failed to understand his sense of humour. But, you see, his 'compliment' was beyond my comprehension, for he never asked me about my 'real' native tongue. Of course, how could he? He did not speak Maori. At any rate, he saluted me and left me at the entrance of my muddy tent without any explanation. I was so mad that I refused to salute him back, as most Maoris did not do during the whole Italian campaign.

It was Jim who, the next day, explained the reason for that inquisitional visit. Typical of British officers – standoffish, aloof, oracular. I was simply a 'subject' who, even as a volunteer to satisfy Apirana Ngata's naïve hope of cooperation with the Pakeha, had not been at Woolwich or Sandhurst; as a matter of fact, not even in England. To make a long story short, Jim Henare told me that a mission had been planned by a group of British MI5s for the purpose of crossing the Adriatic and landing somewhere on the east coast. They needed a radio operator who could act as a communication liaison officer with Tito's partisans. My radio amateur hobby, plus my knowledge of Croatian and English, was enough to get me released from the Battalion and make me an integral part of an independent group of guerrillas. Amusingly, my 'native' language helped me later save my own life and others' when I was able to contact and communicate with some of our own Battalion members, in Foggia. The Germans did not know Maori, so we assumed, and so when we were forced to break radio silence we took a chance communicating in Maori, a first in the history of linguistic ... warfare. Thus, after fighting in Africa, Greece and Italy, I was suddenly removed from my front-line comrades and isolated from them until the end of the war. That created in me a second category of returned soldier, because some of my own tribe felt I had been spared the grinding campaign of Cassino, and so I felt like a black sheep at their reunions. I was regarded with suspicion and kept at bay like a leper in spite of the ribbons I used to wear.

In Taranto and then Bari I met the group to which I was assigned as a 'volunteer'. Had I known that I had been scheduled to learn parachuting, I would have refused to proceed with the training. Probably what I am saying is still in part classified, so, just in case, after you read these pages, please burn everything (also because other items are more related to our own immediate family, and in particular to Mahina). Our leader was a certain Fitzroy McLean. Please read his book. If you sit at my desk, look up to your left and locate a rather thick volume at the right end of the top shelf, a paperback, with patches of red on its spine. There you will read most of what McLean did in the Balkans (among other countries). At Taranto I met Major Vivian Street and Sergeant Duncan. You will notice, incidentally, that my name does not appear anywhere. In the text McLean refers to me as the 'radio operator'. The reason is that, when the book was being written and then published in 1949, our own NZIS decided not to blow my cover because of the 'Maori language' feat in view of the cold war, the Berlin airlift, the Korean unrest with its later 'conflict' in which I participated briefly.

I am not going to bore you with things we did here and there. Whatever concerns me and you may be gathered by reading Chapter 6, titled 'Island interlude'. However, even McLean never knew of my own 'interlude' when I got isolated on a small island. Try to get a picture of the rôle played by the Franciscan Padre in Kòrčula. Also, and if you can, take a short boat trip to the nearby island of Badija, where you can visit the Franciscan Friary built in 1420. There, in the arcaded cloister built a little later, I met your ... grandmother around Christmas. She was a partisan disguised as the church sacristan and the cook for the old monks. I spent only nine days hidden near the friary. Your grandmother, Maria Kornarich – the name betrays Venetian descent – was my liaison with the rest of the party trying to disembark in Kòrčula, but forced for a while to hide in Hvar. A very complex story of hide and seek between islands and the coast. Risking her life nearly every day, Maria fed me, helped me move back and forth during the night to meet with the Padre while I waited for a signal from F.O.T.A. (Flag Officer Taranto) informing me about the partisans on Kòrčula and the planned arrival of the Royal Navy.

In the brief period that followed, I met a lot of people, including Randolph Churchill, quite a bloke, so different from the career officers. You know, Winston's son, the most romantic figure of 'WWII, the Casanova of the conflict. He was a daredevil but extremely gregarious and 'democratic'. I also met Tito and his woman. What a couple!

The last time I saw your granny was at Velaluka, on Kòrčula. In a little more than a week we had fallen in love, and loved each other so much that just before she took me to Velaluka to meet the Royal Navy, I told her the Maori legend of Hinemoa. And we lived that legend as if those islands were somewhere in Aotearoa. How young were our hearts! I myself had never discovered that I could proffer so many tender feelings toward a human being. In the silence of the surroundings, during the cold night we would look at the winter sky and forget that we were at war. It was simply a novel earthly paradise. We cried of joy. And of sorrow, for we knew that in a matter of days, of hours, our paradise would vanish forever in spite of mute promises made by touching our hands in the moonlight of that time. When I was at the sanatorium, I was persecuted by the memories of that encounter. That is why I would spend hours at the window of my room looking at the sea and waiting for a boat to land and take me away. Even now, I refrain from letting my tears fall on these pages to stain my words.

In Velaluka, I did not even hug her when we parted for various reasons. Fraternisation was to be avoided. War was a serious business, and feelings had to be repressed. But in a moment of anguish before leaving her to face the dangers of the coming German troops, I removed my *tiki* (the same I gave Mahina upon departing for the States) and put it on her, to the amused look of my comrades. Randolph even made a comment – 'Well, well, love among the ruins! So foolish!' I said nothing, because I knew that he himself was subject to that power of fate. He had just married, but I don't know whether love entered into it at all.

That *tiki* later signed Maria's death sentence. By early summer, the Germans had landed back on various coastal points, first taking Hvar, and then Kòrčula. They were as brutal as ever, since they knew that they had lost the war. So they started killing both partisans and civilians, women and children. Tell you what, kids, in war the human animal automatically turns on its primary motor taking him back millions of years to jungle survival behaviour. Civilisation is obliterated in the batting of an eyelash. Please read the first paragraph on page 466.

Just before the Jerrys left the island, at the end of summer, when later raids netted all the population who could not hide in the stone quarries, Maria was caught and confronted with the radio equipment found under a pile of fishing nets. She was about 8 months pregnant with your mother. The Germans finally understood how their movements had been known to the partisans over the winter. In reprisal, every living being was assembled under the old towers, north of the quay, and a mass execution was performed with submachine guns. If you ever go there, look for the bullet holes still visible here and there on the walls of the thick bastion nearby.

The German officer, whether for sadistic purposes or whatever, entertained himself with your grandmother. Thus, rather than shoot her, he decided to hang her. That was pointless, for no one could witness the execution as a deterrent except for the Padre. And whatever I know, I know through him, reconstructing the scenario through emotional fragments of speech and tears flowing from his nearly blind eyes.

I do not recommend to anyone to visit that quay. But if you do, the big tower bastion behind the quay, well, start from there, where most boats land. Then to the left of the cobblestone street that climbs quickly toward the cathedral, you see a large old tree. Captain Bügel, an SS officer, had noticed the *tiki* hanging from your grandmother's neck ...

Mahina stopped a second and touched the *tiki* hesitantly while addressing it pushing her hair back with one hand and wiping her eyes.

'Sorry, Komaru, I will finish reading this. Please be patient.'

Komaru had placed his head between his palms, with his elbows on the side of the desk. He could not look at Mahina's face. He was trying to listen to her while at the same time making a mental subtraction, removing from 1,000 years the period that Nazism had dominated Europe. How many years remained? At least 950. Well, he thought, even if Germans had the guts to redeem themselves in 950 more years, nearly the whole next millennium, he doubted that humans would forget what they had done to debunk Aristotle's assumption on the sociability of *Homo sapiens sapiens*. He also thought that what the Maoris had done themselves for survival was child's play in comparison with the savagery of Europeans for the sake of securing a few square miles of ground and the standardization of racial and religious dogmas. Actually, Komaru felt for a moment that he was morally free to do the same against anyone blocking him from regaining what had been stolen from his forefathers. At least his war would not be one of imperialism. It would simply be one of regaining a modicum of dignity to account for the reason of being alive in Aotearoa.

Mahina continued.

... from your grandmother's neck. As a globetrotter during his younger days, he had been in Polynesia. He had read the works of Reischek, of Hochstetter, and others. And he had concluded, rightly, that the radio messages, so elusive for so many months between the Dalmatian coast and the Taranto station, were at times broadcast in Maori.

Your grandmother, according to the Padre, never confessed how or from whom she had gotten the *tiki* in spite of being tortured and subjected to all sorts of indignities. So, the SS officer threw a rope over a branch of the secular tree, still extant on the quay, asked Maria to climb on the driver's seat of a donkey cart, placed the noose over her head and, just before signalling the driver to hit the donkey hard, climbed on the cart and placed the *tiki* along the loop, saying in German, according to the Padre, something like 'There, slut, this will guide you and your bastard to your Rangi.' And he hurried to finish off the whole operation before the arrival of the partisans, known to have cleared the west coast of the mainland.

Then, the most surrealistic event took place. When removed from the temporary prison in the bowels of the old castle nearby, Maria had been stripped of all her clothes, for Capt. Bügel had planned to hang her in the nude. But, after noticing her state of advanced pregnancy, he forced her to wear an army blanket around her waist almost like a pareo reminding him of his trips in the South Pacific.

As your grandmother ...

Here Mahina could not continue as her tears flowed copiously. Then a hiccup took over her emotions. She just said, 'And to think that ... I spent a whole academic year in Salzburg, in a Nazi vassal town, in the country that ... gave birth to a monster. Please, Komaru, I can't read any further. I will be right back.'

She returned from the lav with a bunch of Puffies and a pair of dark sunglasses to hide the red of her eyes. Komaru continued.

As your grandmother began choking after the donkey had been kicked to move ahead, the pareo fell to the ground covering in part the fuming excrement left near the straw he had been chewing on. The Padre, holding his crucifix as in an *auto-da-fé* ceremony of latter days, felt impotent to say anything except a few Latin fragments of extreme unction while touching and kissing her feet, as related to me in sobs 20 years later.

In the convulsion process, your mother must have gotten loose prematurely. This was also attested to by other Kòrčulans to whom the Padre, Don Niko, related the whole episode in tears, while praying for her soul in the afternoon. In an act of desperation, or because of the violent convulsions – for her neck had not been broken in the short fall – the convulsions of her entire body and maybe intentional efforts, sorry, I don't know how to say this, well, a child was expelled, and there a new life resulted at the moment of death.

The umbilical cord kept the child's head from hitting the cobblestone ground covered with straw and excrement. It was then that the Padre retrieved a wooden bench from somewhere nearby, broke an empty wine bottle, and with a piece of glass in his hand climbed the bench and cut the umbilical cord after grabbing the child in his left arm. It took some spanking to trigger a cry in your mother, and it seems that her own mother may have heard that cry of new life during her last few seconds of agony for, a while later, after she was removed from the tree and laid on the cart that came back as if the donkey wanted to finish eating his straw, a smile had frozen on her bluish lips. The child was taken away immediately to the hills. Look to your right from the square. There is a road gently climbing east and then turning to the left leading to the cemetery. In one of those homes, fronted by a garden, your mother was washed, attended to by pious people, and immediately baptised in case she did not make it. But she did survive long enough to ... produce both of you in an act of love, nearly a duplicate of what had taken place on that Franciscan island.

That is in synthesis the historical segment relating the life and death of your grandmother, and the birth of your mother. Now comes the second part, equally as painful to relate as the first.

Komaru stopped after sighing heavily in order not to cry. Mahina had sunken into a state of torpor while lying in a foetal position deep in her father's leather chair, with her knees propped up under her chin. And she was crying, sobbing, moaning.

'Shall I continue, or perhaps I can leave the rest of the ... diary for you to read later?'

'No, please, just wait a sec. I need a glass of water.'

She had started to hiccup so violently that Komaru told her to stay put and went to the kitchen where he fetched a bottle of mineral water and a paper cup. He sat on the side of the armchair and, after pouring some water for her, caressed her hair tenderly. She was perspiring with cold sweat when his hand ran along her left temple, though the room was cool as it was exposed to the south as in any painter's studio. Then he kissed her left hand, bringing it to his lips.

'Oh, God! My dear God, what have I done to deserve this? Are you trying me? Don't you see that I believe you, in you, and that without you I would be lost?'

'Mahina, sweet sister, please be strong! Can you imagine how father must have felt all these years?'

'Yes, I can imagine that, and even the rest. Poor Dad!'

'Shall I go on?'

'Yes, let's us get rid of this all in one day. What else can happen to me today? God, are you there, can you help me?'

She hadn't even completed the sentence fully when the phone started to ring in the distance, from Mahina's room. But it was a peculiar ring that Komaru recognized immediately.

'That is the fax machine. From whom?,' asked Komaru. 'Shall I get it for you?'

'Please!'

When Komaru returned, Mahina seemed to have collapsed lifelessly. The two-page message, including the cover letter from Transpacific University, was in Komaru's trembling hands. He had glanced at it and reacted to it with mixed emotions. The date was Monday afternoon at 14:00, 10:00 Tuesday in Papakura. Thus, Komaru said nothing, but waved the two pages under Mahina's chin as if fanning her back to life. She opened her sore eyes, wondering what in the world he was doing.

'It is for you.'

'For me? From whom?'

'From Portland. Read it.'

'No, I don't want to get more bad news. Please do that yourself.'

'OK, or, shall I say, okey-dokey?'

'You are a ... brute!'
'Yes, Madam.'

July 6, 1992

Dear Miss Reti:
I am pleased to inform you that the Dean of Arts and Sciences has approved the institution of a first year Maori language course. Therefore, a teaching assistantship has been funded and hereby offered to you while ...

'No, no, no, God, sorry, you can't do that to me. Please! I believe in you, no, don't punish me this way. I apologise, I just can't believe it ...'

She exploded in a frenzy of crying, laughing, jumping on the floor, hiding her face in the leather cushion, until Komaru had to hold her, pinning her body down with his own. And then she wrapped her arms around him and started kissing his face, his eyes, his cheek, trying to *hongi* him on his elusive wet nose. But her lips skidded unintentionally over his and she recoiled as if bitten by a *kea*. She paused a second, looked him in the eyes, amazed at herself, and finally posed her mouth on his as if committing a capital crime. The touch was barely felt physically, but the emotional contact was registered in her psyche as if she had placed her lips on his with a most powerful glue of ecstasy. Then she repelled him with all her strength, as if afraid of being wounded in her very soul.

'You *are* a brute, and I love you. You are a traitor, and I love you. You are a monster, and I love you. And you haven't even taken a shower. I can smell her all over your hair. The scent of an animal. How could you? God, thank you for letting me go away from this den of deception. Oh, God, how can I thank you for the rest of my life, how ...'

Actually, Komaru had taken a shower, but a hasty one since the hot water had been utilised by three people before him. However, he had just rinsed his hair with plain water because downstairs he could not find any shampoo. And Mahina had detected the olfactory tracks left by Melissa.

'For God's sake, sister, please act civilly. And read the rest of the letter yourself. You had better fax them back immediately.'

The letter had also been sent as a 'cc' to the Foreign Student Office, the Department of Philosophy, and other usual university organisations. It also indicated that a hard copy of blank forms and other matter should reach her within the week by priority mail. The usual routine of paperwork.

It was nearly noon when Mahina calmed down after faxing a reply not only to the Dean, but also sending a fax to Tanya asking her to get ready for the European trip and to organise everything. Mahina would contact any travel agent designated by Tanya in Walla Walla. Then, Mahina called the NZ airline to book a seat on the 22 July, and still have plenty of time to check on visas, passport expiration while waiting for books to arrive unless they had not been shipped yet and thus stop them at the Portland storage company. In a few minutes, she had changed from crown to sole. But then she became pensive, aloof, spaced out.

So many emotions in one week, so many feelings in one morning, so many sentiments in a minute! She had touched Komaru's lips as a woman for the first time, the lips of any man with the inception of hormonal passion that had shattered her very entrails. A vacuum had been created, a deep and sickening chasm lingering disturbingly in her mind as an unpardonable crime. Yes, she may have committed a sin, an impure act of the flesh, leading her to register the rumbles of a volcano all over her body, a tension in all her lower organs, much more noticeable than what was barely acknowledged when Komaru was trying to stop the flow of blood on her chest ripped by the thorns of a rose. At that time, she had almost gone into a state of delirium, but Komaru had rejected her. She knew that she had not initiated anything even accidentally, and so she was subconsciously grateful to the strength subtly manifested by her brother. But this time it had been different, for she had been, consciously or not, the prime motor shaking her heart not only violently, painfully, but also so pleasurably and inebriatingly. And she wondered whether she was menstruating again. How could she? The menses had stopped two days earlier. She went to the lav to check her light days pad. No, no blood, but nevertheless wet, warm, lightly smelly of herself. She wondered, and then she had to acknowledge to herself that she had reached a climax as a complete female. She also felt that she would need to confess as soon as she reached the States. This time she had something real to say, and she would not feel embarrassed at not having anything to list in response to the confessor's questions preceding her First Communion.

Lunch was a sad affair. She barely touched what Komaru had prepared for her. A frozen dinner – risotto for her, and chicken cacciatore for him. Silence pervaded their time together at the counter, interrupted only by a telephone call from Air New Zealand confirming flight NZ14 at 14:00 for Los Angeles. She would arrive Sunday morning and continue to Portland for a few days of rest and then proceed to Seattle to meet Tanya. Her mind was in a turmoil. And she nevertheless sensed the weight of unhappiness looming over them as the only abstract and tangible pain connecting them across the counter, each of them knowing that their days together were numbered. Time was once more injecting volleys of psychological bullets aimed straight at their hearts. They knew that the facsimile from Portland had cut out one from the other forever.

Chapter 32

Late afternoon glided in with low and dark clouds drifting from under the viaduct bridge to envelop Youngs Beach with mist and gloom. Mahina had nearly collapsed under the strain of the morning's events. After sending faxes here and there, and after making a phone call to the Transpacific University officials and to Tanya, she retired to her room for a nap. Komaru rested in his father's studio, but left the final portion of the moral testament unread. He sensed that the rest of it would be more poignant than the previous part, and thus wanted to share it with Mahina for better or for worse.

By 5 o'clock there had been no sign of Mahina. In order to complete the reading of those heartbreaking notes, Komaru brewed Mahina's favourite tea, a Darjeeling, and took it to her room. She was not asleep, but lying dressed on top of her bed staring at the ceiling in the semidarkness of the early winter evening soiled by the Tasmanian clouds blocking her view of the sound.

'Thank you, Komaru, thank you. Just a sec, let me prop up against the pillow. Thanks.'

The warmth of the mug felt good on the palms of her hands. She had embraced the cup with care and tenderness, as if holding a baby, and raised it to her lips slowly as in a Japanese tea ceremony. In a few moments she felt physically and psychologically better, though she said nothing. Komaru sat at the foot of the bed, silent too, for he was afraid of breaking the solemnity of the contemplational ambience that pervaded the feminine room full of things of gentility, a sprig of dry flowers sticking out of a glass ceramic vase, a white silk robe hanging from the back of a chair, a jar of perfumed cream left semiopened by a box of pink Puffies.

'Mahina, please understand. You just stay in bed. I'll fetch the manuscript and read the rest no matter what. I simply cannot wait to get rid of that segment of father's past. Then, everything will be buried with him and we can start anew. Shall I?'

She made a grunt with the intonation of a 'yes'. When Komaru came back from the studio, she was still in bed covered with a throw, but still immobile. Komaru then switched on the ceiling light.

'No, please, I can't stand that. Use the desk lamp by the window.'

And so he pulled up a chair with its back to the window, from which a pale natural light was still filtering. The side lamp light blended with the grayness transpiring through the glass and created a stereophotic aura of monastic early vespers.

'All right, let me see, oh, yes, we had read up to here ...'

Whatever I related to you so far was totally unknown to me after I left Kòrčula. Time and again I tried to find out what had happened to Maria, but either no one wanted to tell me anything or survivors had no recollection of the events. The Padre had been interned on the mainland for nervous disorders. Only later was he brought to Kòrčula as an invalid, tended by the nuns of Mother Teresa's home.

Then, you know, I went back to school, received a Degree in English, married, and got a teaching job in a rural area in the north, where I was able to buy a small farm near the area you visited once. It was a quiet, pastoral life. But things went wrong because my affective system was, shall I say, non-existent. I had remained stuck under the arcades of the Dalmatian friary, as if chained to it by the magic spell of a witch. I prefer to remain silent on the fate of the first ... well, the only marriage ending in failure. My fault. I just could not be a husband, both psychologically and socially, not to speak of physiologically. It lasted less than one year. For whatever reason, I always detected something looming between me and Erena, a distant shadow roaming among the arcades of an old convent, the muted tones of a small bell on its *campanile*, the moonlight shining eerily on the surrounding waters of a Christmas winter in contrast with the shameful sunshine blasting the north of this island.

After surviving my anguish by reading the classics, I found relief in painting and carving, and then alcohol. Because of this I lost my teaching job, but I was successful in selling my artwork. That plus the pension allowed me to lead almost a normal social life after my father left me the proceeds of his dairy farm near Palmerston North. Thus, I learned how to benefit from the pleasures and the pain of solitude with the help of many books, though in particular the works of great minds as guidelines to further reading and introspection. Yes, I know, I had read somewhere that introspection is a form of lunacy, but solitude itself is like being marooned on the Moon of self-analysis, a return to your Self starting from scratch. And I tried to write but I preferred to do something physical with my hands, though reading a lot to keep my sanity in check. Writing, I soon found out, compounded my solitude and made me more unhappy. I think it was Georges Simenon who stated that 'writing is not a profession but a vocation of unhappiness.' Can you imagine that? He had written and published more than 500 novels, not to mention many other works. He must have been so unhappy that he tried to find solace in the thousands of women flocking to him like bees to nectar. And I was inspired by reading the lives of the great solitary people who excelled in spite of loneliness and perhaps because of it. That was the Jung era. I was no acolyte of his except through difficult to obtain publications. Carl Jung, basically, never crossed the equator southbound. New Zealand was 50 years behind, and probably still is.

So I found vicarious pleasures in those fellow human beings who produced important work, from Beethoven to Henry James, from Wittgenstein to Beatrice Potter, from Leonardo to Goya, who obtained from spells of solitude the adrenaline of their *furor poeticus*. In music alone, think of Richard Strauss, of Schumann, of Brahms, and their personal failures in marriage, love, and human relations leading to melancholy, despondency, and loneliness.

Sorry about this segment of my 'productive' life in which, unlike the masters, I produced nothing except the *sutra*-like passages of political incitement keeping the flame of our *risorgimento* alive, though completely underground and incognito. That was the only escape valve from my suicidal tendencies before and even after visiting Europe.

Thus life proceeded, bouncing back and forth between valleys of despondency and peaks of high hopes until, in 1965, on the 20th anniversary of World War II, I decided to return to the War Theatre. As part of a group I unofficially visited the places of carnage – Libya, Crete, Italy. Of course, in my case it was different since, while most of my comrades had spent a cruel winter in the Cassino area, I had been serving with the partisans and commando liaison between Italy and the Yugoslavian coast.

I felt like a fish out of water. I was even accused of having gotten a cushy job in an operation I could not speak about. Only Jim Henare knew of my predicament and, of course, he would not say anything.

The whole scenario of horror, defying even the limits of the realistic imagination of a Conrad and the masochistic malady of a Kafka, began to unfold when, after leaving the excursion group at Trieste, I travelled to Split and from there took the ferry to Kòrčula, where the Turist Biro had found for me accommodations at the *Bon Repos*. Once there, I started asking questions, until some old people led me to the office of a religious organisation connected with Mother Teresa. There, the nuns took me to see the Padre, Don Niko, whom I vaguely remembered. He had become a human larva after witnessing the executions of 1944.

I doubt he remembered me, since he was almost 90 years old, had seen two world wars, and had become nearly blind as well as incoherent. But he made an effort to open up when he heard me speak in Croatian with an archaic accent I acquired from the Dallies in the North. That was his dialect. I was presented to him while he was in the mode of repeating time and again all day long, 'Domine, non sum dignus'. He was still feeling guilty for not having been shot like everybody else assembled at the quay. Apparently, Capt. Bügel was a Catholic from Bavaria, and as such he felt it proper and charitable that the dying receive the sacrament of Extreme Unction and the dead the 'Requiem aeternam' envoi.

The story related by the Padre to old timers after the executions was confirmed by himself in fragments of retrospective nightmares. And what happened to the child? He said that she had been raised by Mother Teresa's nuns in the old building that I had visited just a day earlier, not far from Marco Polo's birthplace, a semidecrepit stone structure encased in a group of old, uninhabited houses. The news about someone from New Zealand asking questions related to an orphan born during the war had spread like wildfire.

And there, on the landing of the steps, under the framed photograph of Mother Teresa festooned with ribbons and flower garlands, I met her dressed in a dark semi-shiny garb. She looked at me for a few seconds and, out of the blue, asked in a matter of fact tone of voice: 'You are my father, are you not?' For a second, I did not understand her 'younger' Croatian dialect, for the word for 'father' and Padre are identical. I stood speechless in front of her while my heart throbbed like an engine. I had to hold myself against the wall not to tumble down the stairs. She took my hand and kissed it. Then she unbuttoned her high collared shirt and removed a *tiki* and said 'I have been waiting for you all my life, Thank you for coming. Please take me home.' I then hugged her

European style and placed my cheeks against hers, but in switching from one to the other I held my nose against hers for a fraction of a second. There was no doubt that she was my child. I smelled the scent of Ao Tea Roa, the perfume of her mother's perspiration, the odor of Dalmatian women I had grown accustomed to during my childhood.

I beg you to spare me relating what followed. Hers was a sixth sense in identifying me, for the convent is visited almost daily by tourists, especially passengers aboard cruise ships between Venice, Ravenna, Kòrčula, and the Greek and Italian islands. She told me later that the nuns had spoken of someone from New Zealand who was in search of the old padre. The rest was not difficult to collate. He had given me some details about my daughter, whose name was Maria Kornarich, as entered, like her mother's, in the parish church and the municipal anagraphic records. The official date was 15 August 1944, the day belonging to the Assumption of the Blessed Virgin Mary.

The evening after the Germans had left the island by motorboat, the Padre rang the main bell of the cathedral and people timidly came out from their hiding places in the surrounding hills to improvise a procession of thanks. On the quay where blood had been spilled a few hours earlier, a 'Te Deum laudamus' was intoned amid cries of joy, sobs of pain, hiccups of anguish. Some candles were lighted and placed here and there, particularly under the tree still soiled by Teutonic depravity. The Padre, still in shock, was also able to read the 'Collect', a first in his spiritual career, risking excommunication:

> Omnipotens sempiterne Deus, qui Immaculatam Virginem Mariam, Ma ... Mariam Kornarich, Filii tui Genitricem, corpore et anima ad caelestem gloriam assumpsisti: concede, quaesumus, ut ad superna semper intenti, ipsius gloriae mereamur esse consortes. Per eundem Dominum ...

That evening, the peeling of bells echoed across the waters surrounding the islands. And the Padre, still in shock, led the procession wearing his cassock still stained with blood, urine and faeces from Maria's bowels. The child, born a month prematurely, had been welcomed by a family in the surrounding hills where grapes were ready to be picked, along with roses and unattended weeds. Maria's body had been taken directly to the cemetery and temporarily placed in the main community chapel, washed with wine and seawater, for the Germans had blown up the main well. And then the bodies of everybody else shot on the quay were stacked up in private chapels displaying Venetian names with Slavic endings. It took days to dig new graves, to restore some semblance of normal life. When the partisans arrived, they were so shocked that, instead of helping, they cried and vomited and cursed.

I simply could not hear any more of the atrocities, and did not take long to plan some action for a quick exodus from that area yielding grief at every cobblestone on which I threaded with unstable steps. First I visited your grandmother's grave. The oval effigy embedded in the ceramic picture on the gravestone looked like a small mirror reflecting your mother's face standing a foot away from me – the same innocent smile, the intelligent eyes of Venetian noble stock, the tall neck, and the lips of a flower ready to unfold its petals to the sunlight of youth.

We then crossed the strait to the old Franciscan friary. It was a beautiful June, with flowers all over, so different from the December of war, fear and doubt about the nature of mankind. But, being with your Mother, walking under the arcades, I was unable to perceive any difference between her and your granny. For a few minutes they appeared to be the same, and for a second I hoped that your grandmother had returned to Earth as a *wairua*. They were indeed the same in my misty eyes, dressed in black, with a white scarf over their heads. Where was I? I went to see the old Padre once more. Because of me, perhaps, he had become more incoherent, almost delirious. Probably I triggered in his memory certain repressed remembrances he had tried to seal forever. And he kept repeating: 'St Augustine was right ... we are born between feces and urine ... and blood, all the blood I saw on the quay.' I myself followed in turn, 'And we live in tears and mucus,' the way I felt and lived those few hours upon returning from the friary. On the island I had lost not only the virginity of my body, but also that of my mind. I had been stripped in my very bowels of all that made me think of myself as a human. But the presence of your mother contained my despair, my feelings of guilty, my behaviour dripping with despondency in every daily act, from walking to looking at the sky, the trees, the waters of the surroundings.

The next day, I gave your mother a few hours to pack. Actually,

I told her to take nothing, to say nothing to anyone, to take along some identification for tourist purposes, just to cross the sea between Kòrčula and Split, and from there to Trieste. When I left that morning, I felt that it was not the boat leaving the land. Just the opposite. My past was moving away slowly, but only visually, for in my mind the quay of that island is imprinted as a pair of glasses through which every terrestrial image filters superimposed. But your mother held my hand to keep me from fainting. She could read my torment by looking at my tears with a smile of reassurance. The warmth of her look penetrated my body and reached my entrails like a caress of hope.

From Trieste I took her directly to Rome merely on an identity card as a temporary tourist, and there I raised hell in the NZ embassy, from which I literally did not move while Maria was waiting for me in a nearby hotel. I held steadfast until the ambassador issued a special refugee passport in the name of Maria Reti, the blood of my blood. But it was not easy. You know how our consular officers proceed with regard to admitting 'Med people', like Medflies, especially if they are dark. Colleen McCullough makes a point of reminding the world that the British have a chip on their shoulder even in fiction. But I threatened to spill everything in intelligence, and I called all over England from the Foreign Office to the Churchill family. Randolph, in spite of his many problems with the legacy of his first wife, came to my rescue, probably because I had once rescued him and his comrades from death when I broke radio silence in Maori and the Royal Navy defied German Stukas to retrieve the whole party from the coast. I don't know, but Randolph was simply superb. He called the New Zealand ambassador to espouse my cause. Although Randolph and I had spent only a few days together under extreme stress, he must have remembered me fondly. Once I even broadcast, against all regulations, a personal message through Taranto to Pamela, his wife. I doubt she ever got it, and Randolph worried so much about her. Apparently, she did not give a damn according to his few words of concern toward her. The future Mrs Averell Harriman had embarked on a long life of hedonistic activities in spite of, or maybe because of, the war. I have fond memories of Randolph. In a way we were twin souls in something. I could only sense but not know. Perhaps he inherited from his father some correlative mental baggage of the bipolar 'disorder', at times leading to feats of heroism when high, and depression when low.

At that point, Komaru stopped for a few minutes to rest. Night had already descended. Across the sound, pale amber lights were shining on the water. Mahina had barely stirred during the reading, except for taking another Puffy to dry her tears and blow her nose.

'Listen, kid, I am counting about, let me see, seven or eight more pages. Let's take a break. While you spruce up, I am going to fix something for supper. What about a casserole of some kind, so while it bakes I can continue reading in the kitchen?'

'Fine, just fine. Go ahead. I'll be up in a while.'

Presently, Komaru entered the kitchen, switched on all the overhead lights and turned on the radio to FM Concert as if to dispel the gloom of a dark and silent room through *son et lumière*. It was nearly 7 o'clock. The first segment of the broadcast had just finished with a work by Stenhammar. He could not grasp what. Then the 'Appointment with ...' began with pianist Martha Argerich. It was a pot-pourri of quasi inspirational and relaxing music requiring no mental effort to identify the titles of works or the names of composers. Komaru decided to prepare a seafood concoction utilising odds and ends from tins his father had in stock in the pantry. First, he sauteed in a little olive oil some finely grated shallots in an oblong Japanese deep dish, added some fish seasoning salt from a Cartwright & Butler bubbletop glass jar and a few shots of white Montana wine, and when this had evaporated he dumped into the dish a tin of *pipi* and one of chopped *toheroa*, a dash of anchovy paste straight from a tube 'Product of Italy', and some Spanish capers. When the liquid had nearly evaporated, he added more olive oil, three drops of *aceto balsàmico*, and 400 grams of long white rice. When the rice had absorbed the oil, he poured in three glasses of chicken stock and two of water. On top of the mixture he sprinkled some Italian-flavoured bread crumbs and a few sprigs of parsley, covered the dish tightly and placed it in the oven at medium heat for 40 minutes. At the last moment, he would remove the lid from the pan and leave it under the broiler for 5 minutes, turn off the oven and leave the casserole in the oven for another 5 minutes before serving. That would take about an hour. The radio announcer had mentioned that at 8:00, the usual 'Music Alive' would feature quite an assortment of post-supper tunes for a relaxing evening – Tamas Daroczy (tenor), etc., and then the Hungarian Radio and Television Choir, the Berlin Philharmonic with George Solti, ending with Weiner, Kodály and Bartók. The only thing missing was Mahina. When she came back in for what they both guessed was the final reading of the manuscript, but never as lacerating as it developed to be along a seafood casserole, Komaru had washed his hands from performing as a reader, a cook, a musical director, a psychologist in residence, and whatever else was required by the circumstances.

When Mahina entered the kitchen, she had obviously showered, for her hair was still wet and wrapped in a white towel. She was wearing the American pink pyjamas, with a wide neck opening showing her *tiki* still glistening with droplets of water. And the fragrance of *muguet des bois* was nearly strong enough to overcome the smell of fish permeating the kitchen. Land and ocean met in siblingness.

She then sat on a stool at the counter sipping a glass of apple juice, and felt relaxed enough to carelessly let go of the *tiki* covering in part the third eye. Komaru could not help noticing that residual of past innocence now displaying a pinkish scar where it was covered with a thin crust over the original thorn wound. He had sat opposite her, and she noticed his casual staring at the wound. She automatically and consciously covered herself by tucking the lapels of her pajamas under each other. And she blushed. That was a first in front of her brother. But her blush was not one of modesty alone. She knew that she had also blushed under the surge of a new sensation. She was surprised at her own reaction, one she construed as one of involuntary seduction. She may have been wrong, she thought, but Komaru's reaction, which was mainly one of concern for a possible infection, appeared like one of an intruder on part of her body that in Maori culture was once and recently not different from displaying an ear under a flock of hair. She still vividly remembered Komaru licking her teat and around its aureole while gently sucking the blood before pressing his lips to stop its flow. At the recollection of that episode, she noticed that a wave of heat had descended from her chest to her womb. And she was mystified. How could she allow her mind to succumb to that new feeling of womanhood? She had become conscious of that recent development as a reaction to an external stimulus, and what made her afraid was her realisation that the cause of that psychological triggering device was her brother. The thought was a devastating one, especially when she recalled scenes of sororal criticism that now she knew was simply jealousy caused by Melissa. Of course, Komaru noticed the change, though his feelings for her had remained exactly the same as before. Yes, she was for him not only a sister, but also a mother, and a daughter. He felt like an androgyne acknowledging only one-half of his own body to himself.

'Sorry, I was just wondering if your wound had healed properly. Have you been applying any moisturising cream or whatever?'

'I am doing just fine. I still have to be sure that the thin crust does not become open again. That is why at night I turn the *tiki* behind my back. You see, the worst is over. From now on I can manage.'

And at that moment she opened her collar, moved the *tiki* to one side, and made an effort to behave normally as in the past, when Komaru used to mock her about becoming fat in the chest when she was about 12.

'It is so hot here! How much longer do you have to bake that dish?'

'A few more minutes. Sorry, let me open the back door for some fresh air.'

'Thank you. Oh, perhaps I can help you. Do you plan to have any salad? You know, women need folate.'

'You mean folic acid? For what?'

'Well, sorry, it is part of a preventive programme. A habit I acquired in the States, though, ironically, I doubt it will do me any good. You know, brother, I do not plan to have a child ... to perpetuate ... polymastia.'

'Poly ... what? It sounds like something connected with Polynesia.'

'No, dear brother, have you ever heard of a mastectomy?'

'Yes, of course, I ...'

'Then, there you have it, but don't confuse it with polythelia, though technically one could also speak of that but only as a consequence of the first. When I went to the University of Washington Medical School, I heard that common medical term for the first time. You see, a woman, as in ancient eastern mythology, can have more than two breasts, and of course two nipples. At times nature dispenses extra teats on one single breast or anywhere else on the body, be it a male or a female. After that terminological ... blessing I also found out that until a couple of centuries ago that dysfunction had been labelled since Medieval times as the mark of a witch. So, I am a witch, at least according to a book I read in Portland. I think its title is *The Encyclopedia of Witchcraft and Demonology*. I even had nightmares about being burnt at the stake in Boston.'

'I am sorry, but frankly I would not pay much attention to those terms, be they medical or ... encyclopaedic. The assignment of a term to a condition does not change anything except create a label of common acceptation.'

'But the ... encyclopaedic one can still cause problems in the populace, if not in extreme political systems. I wonder whether the

Nazis did anything to women possessed by ... demons. Of course they did. Those people were Gypsies. And, it is getting colder here. Can I fix the salad?'

Mahina wanted to finish that painful conversation. Thus, she tossed a salad with whatever greens she could find in the fridge. For herself, she used *aceto balsàmico* she had brought from the States. She had guessed, correctly, that New Zealand had not yet been sprinkled by the tears of Bacchus. Komaru used fresh lemon juice.

'That was a pleasant supper. Thank you, Komaru. You surely know how to take care of improvised situations.'

'Well, little ... sorry, big sister now, living alone teaches you how to handle ... emergencies. At any rate, I don't think I shall be cooking as a modern ... husband.'

'You mean you are not going to get married one day?'

'I doubt it. No, Mahina, there will be other men willing to expand our race. I shall be busy with other activities to ensure that our brothers and sisters will be helped to attain some more rights in the ... Listen, let us finish the reading of the last part. Another cup of tea?'

'Yes, bring it to my room ... along with the document.'

When Komaru went to Mahina's room, she had already brushed her teeth, changed into the white silk robe, and was lying on the bed against two large couch pillows propped up against the *kauri* wall.

He sat at the fax machine table and started reading.

Returning to New Zealand with Maria, my daughter, opened another complex chapter in my life. Remember, that was in 1965, when this country had not yet been jolted by international developments, especially with regard to the economy, nuclear issues, etc. At the farm I had been able to develop a good orchard business concentrating on apple production with government help. Problems started when Maria arrived. I had counted on her to slowly integrate herself into the business, but she immediately encountered some problems due to the totally different cultural environment, not to mention the language problem. She depended on me almost entirely as an interpreter, and that created difficulties among both Maori and Pakeha workers and businessmen. Also, her social life was zero. Imagine a healthy 20-year-old girl in the north, a most stunning young woman, officially known to be my daughter. A few tentative dates resulted in failure. Her being raised by nuns in Kòrčula had not prepared her to cope with North Island traditions vacillating between Pakeha expectations and Maori ambivalence.

Thus, Maria regarded me not as a father desiring to coach her into entering the mainstream of business and social life. She became attached to me for everything, almost as if she saw in me a knight who had rescued her from Kòrčula's nearly medieval life at most levels. I had succeeded in considering her a daughter, although she and I missed the normal psychological and affective progression between a father and offspring. My projecting onto her the woman who had made me a full man among the chaos of war was offset by normal paternal attemtps to make of her a 'Maori' woman in memory of her mother.

I failed in integrating her into the local life. And she became more attached to me, almost morbidly, especially when I occasionally interacted with some of the local women who had known me when I was married. They knew that I had failed as a man with my wife, and a few of them tried to reinstate in me a certain level of sexuality with patience and understanding. No way could I be removed from the mental block that prevented me from performing. In that connection, Maria became extremely jealous. She and I talked at length on many issues, but, although we spoke the same language 'linguistically', we did not understand each other at the family level. She told me that she was in love with me, and that she had no scruples whatsoever about telling me so, because the biological ties for her had been wiped out by 20 years of my absence. When I mentioned the religious and social side of the incest *tapu*, she frankly told me that at times in life there are situations that take a people to a stage of primitivism where even the Catholic church, or Christianity, understood and even approved the inception of a new line for the sake of both mental and physical sanity. Besides, she saw in me a washed out man, trying to survive in the post-war period, tentatively climbing back to normality.

You see, she was an extremely cultured young lady, raised by nuns who had digested the history of religious sisterhood. Maria knew a lot on the early stages of women's struggle to survive in hostile environments. She quoted from scripture cases of abnormal relationships between father and daughter, although she kept insisting that she did not see in me a father, but a man whom she could trust precisely because in his veins the blood was in part similar to hers. She felt that her mother had suffered the fate of Lot's wife for not escaping from the Germans. And she regretted not having a sister to help her make me drunk. Apparently there was in the early Christian era a certain Methodius who accepted a progressive development from incest to monogamy and even to later 'honorary' virginity as a matter of overcoming conditions of survival that God – her God – could not resolve except through His providence. For her it was a return to the 'Old Law' of survival among the Hebrews. Refinements on moral grounds developed later under so-called normal circumstances. And Maria, as a virgin, for I had no inkling of her life whatsoever except that she had been raised by nuns, became nearly obsessed with me.

What followed is too personal to relate to you, though one day you may understand. At times, during the long winter evenings, we sat in the dark and talked. I recalled similar evenings at the friary waiting for a radio signal from Taranto, but the only signal I sensed was her mother's presence near me and the Adriatic coast scent of her womanhood. And it was so identical that, while intellectually and emotionally I could detect no difference between Maria and her mother, I was terrified at the thought of failing again if and when I would succumb to your mother's love. Remember, at that time I was drinking heavily, but because of her I had given it up 'cold'. That, plus your mother's patient devotion, one night contributed to releasing in me a surprising power of performance at the very start. It was like eating the first cherry, still tart tasting, and still liking it with the conviction that the rest of the cherries in the tree of Methodius would be better as the following days of ripeness yielded to full maturity. From that first encounter as Adam and Eve, my life was totally changed. Komaru came along to complicate our lives. Remember, we were in a small rural community. Komaru was registered as 'father unknown' in 1966. The gossip was that Maria had had some 'dates' with one of my Maori transient helpers during the apple season. Thus, I was regarded as the grandfather of a single mother.

The business meanwhile fell into a state of financial ruin for different reasons. When your mother became pregnant with Mahina, rumours began to circulate differently, and rightly so, because Maria had not 'gone out' with anyone. Just before Mahina's birth, I thought it wise to sell the farm and move to an urban area. That was not easy, but finally I found a place in Papakura, where most Maoris lived in certain sections not dissimilar from ghettoes. The advantage was anonymity in an Auckland suburb. Again, Mahina was registered as 'father unknown' on 21 July 1969, the day of the Moon. The legal complications were solved in part when I was able to adopt both of you as the 'father'. That helped in many ways. But before that your mother had died, as I may have said on different occasions. From the tranquillity of Kòrčula to the casern-type of life in a Maori environment, in contrast with Pakeha's, the shock was too much. Thus, your mother fell into a post-partum depression from which she never recovered. I started drinking again and survived on the basis of the proceeds of the farm sale plus the pension. The rest is rather irrelevant. I tried my best to raise you as a normal father, hiding from you the anguish burning my entrails. Mahina's departure for the States and Komaru moving to Wellington left me in despair, lonely and frustrated. The Sanatorium interlude concluded the rest of my life. There, only Whina knows some of my personal history.

Now that I am gone, I beg you to forgive me if you feel that I did anything wrong against you. I tried my best. Of course, there is no need to elaborate on the way I felt and still feel about the fate of Ao Tea Roa. Perhaps Komaru may follow in my footsteps to raise the dignity of our *iwi* one more degree. If he does not succeed, well, dignity will still remain as long as language is spoken on our *whenua*. And about you, Mahina, what can I say? I sense that you have already flown the coop. That is what happens to those who try to return to Hawaiki, regardless of whether or not they reach it, for it is a state of mind.

I finish this 'moral testament' by saying:

>Kia ora te marino,
>Kia whakapapa pounamu te moana,
>Kia tere te karohihoi i ou ara katoa ...

Arohanui,
Your dear father

Not a word was said. Komaru folded the pages back into the envelope, got up, hongied Mahina gently, and left for his room from which he knocked five times on the *kauri* wall to wish her a good night. And she replied by making an effort to let herself be heard, for she felt as if all her psychic energies had been drained.

So thank you, Dad, for lifting a veil from my mind. I know how difficult it was for you to tell me so many things about yourself. I can only imagine all the rest you didn't or couldn't relate. Now I can understand my own physical condition, perhaps even my polymastia as a consequence of inner breeding. Is it because my mother and sister wanted to leave an imprint of their intense love for me? Arohanui! *Thank you for wishing me a calm sea ahead, and that this calm be widespread. Thank you for wishing that the sun continue to dance across my life's many paths.*

Mahina laboured hard to fall asleep. How she wished that her father had told her everything, or most things, when he was alive. She would have hugged and hongied him not only to express her gratitude for clarifying matters but also to dispense upon him all her affection and to make his last days on Earth more pleasant, to reassure him that there was nothing shameful in the conduct of her own mother and sister, of his daughter, and of himself.

And she thought of him now in the cemetery on the way to becoming ashes and dust, as she herself would become one day as did everything in the Universe. Now, better than before, she clearly saw the continuum of Western views starting with Lucretius, pausing with Martianus Capella, resting with Giordano Bruno, and continuing to date as it will *usque ad consummationem saeculorum* along the childish speculations of modern astrophysicists. Yes, of course, she agreed with all the theories on the end product of biological entities in the Cosmos, but, once it is understood that a body ends up in a fistful of ashes, how can one grasp the ineffable of the same development for the mind? How can feelings, sentiments, emotions be reduced to ashes?

Chapter 33

The following couple of weeks went by in the batting of an eyelash. Mahina felt suspended between fiction and reality, as if her life had acquired a status of levitation in a vacuum of time, place, and purpose for being alive. While Komaru took care of most practical matters, she dedicated all her time not only to prepare for the exodus from The Hermit Islands, but also from her 'global' psyche oppressed with a myriad of schedules, deadlines, plans, phone calls, faxes, financial planning and other items of both tangible and intangible constraints. She spent a few days purchasing many books from Reed Publishers for the syllabus and texts to be used in the teaching of Maori, though she hoped to prepare her own contrastive 'American', not English, Maori grammar.

She vaguely remembered some of the things she did with Komaru, including the visit to the grave of her 'mother-and-sister', the quick sentimental journey to the Far North in the hope of acquiring some connection with subconscious remnants of her infancy, the arrival of her books from Portland just a couple of days before her return to the States, and the legal procedures involved in the sale of her father's house. Among a host of stressful events the day preceding her exodus from Papakura, she could not help finding parallels with Maggie's own flight forever, a detachment of an Aotearoan who was among the first to reverse the trend of Pakehahood flowing from northern climes into her *whenua*.

Maggie Papakura had married a white man who automatically made for her a home in a strange British civilization. Now Mahina herself was ready to get married. She was going away in order to become a bride, and an outstanding one, for her bridegroom would be Christ, an eternal husband. But during her speculations about attaching herself to a man, she at times wondered about the physical characteristics of this man with whom, after all, she would share the rest of her life. Actually, she felt that this Christ was not a bad deal. The proposed marriage involved no demands except chastity, poverty, and obedience, a rather simple triad of interconnected vows that for two thousand years other women had espoused with relish in spite of the potential dangers, from exile to persecution to martyrdom.

On the other hand, Mahina was happy to think that she did not have to cook, wash, submit to physical demands, invest many years of her bodily activities in raising children, and so many other chores stemming from both physiological and chauvinistic assumptions. She could dedicate herself, perhaps even somewhat selfishly, to a lifetime of studying, helping humans, understanding herself, and finally one day enjoy eternal rest among angels.

The topic of angels, already explored in connection with her honours thesis, began to interest her more and more. She knew that one of the first comprehensive analyses of angeldom had been made by Dante in *terza rima*, a literary connubium that had not been attempted since Lucretius' hexameters nearly 12 centuries earlier, by combining poetry and philosophy. She began to worry how she would manage in a year to take graduate courses in her old department, teach Maori in a new one, attend a year of preliminary vocational adaptation' to the life of a potential Clarissa at Our Lady of Angels Convent in Portland, and write an MA thesis tentatively titled 'Heaven's Army: a study in syneisactism'. This term was not hers, though, as uncovered by Jo Ann Kay McNamara as an early Christian practice and rendered into the English language by transliterating Greek, it would cover the proven cohabitation of both monks and nuns who had managed to keep at bay, among many, the temptations of the flesh, and still maintain other vows of monastic life. The original idea for such a possibility had been lingering in her mind since reading Revd James E. Sullivan's *Journey to Freedom*, in which the three components of normal human Psychic Energy, namely Physical Needs, Expressive Needs and Love Needs, were analysed and channelled into interrelated containers of biological forces by sheer psychological self-conditioning. It was no accident that, by equating those three components with the three basic vows required by Franciscan thought and life, Mahina had created a parallelism between Physical Needs and Poverty; Expressive Needs and Obedience; and Love Needs and Chastity. The binary structure of this triadic foundation for the functioning of a unique social system had a long history, but not a collateral set of necessary constraints.

Although the first two vows, and their two corresponding needs of Psychic Energy, were easy to manage by 'education', the last one, that is, Chastity, presented an enigmatic problem in Mahina's mind since she was a virgin. In addition, she wondered whether genital satisfaction was an integral part of Love Needs. How would she know? She sensed, however, that she was normally subject to that vague feeling of restlessness occurring in examining her body during hygienic grooming, as well as reacting to external stimuli on the basis of tactile, visual or olfactory senses. The rose thorn episode and the blood flow stemmed by Komaru had triggered in her a wild response to the Laws of Nature. In essence, through Komaru she had become aware of what manhood could do to the mind of a female. Probably, she would not have been able to repress conscious reactions had Komaru not aborted the flight of the senses in mid air. She later ascribed Komaru's negative behaviour to a self control imposed by ineffable principles. That may have been so, although she did not know that Komaru was obtaining most of his 'sisterly' satisfactions through Ling-ling, while at the same time releasing his most intense sexual forces via the 'animalesque' requirements exacted by Melissa. In essence, considering his still young age, Komaru had cruised the whole territory between the poetic, placid and prudent collegiality of Ling-ling, and the tempestuous, wild, belligerent engagements of Melissa.

Chastity was understandably the last stumbling block about which Mahina had some mental reservations. In fact, she wondered whether virginity was automatically implied by chastity. Historically, it was not, for chastity could be and was something *post ex facto*. How many 'virgins and martyrs' had first been raped? The whole firmament of saints was full of them. As a matter of fact, there had been in Europe an inflation of local heroines transformed into saints until the last centuries of the Middle Ages, the most productive era for sainthood. That was the period in which women were canonised, taking the places of bishops traditionally having the lion's share. The tendency began to change by the time people like Francis of Assisi were canonised on the basis of loyalty to God, much like being knighted by a king for services rendered as well as for Earthly virtue displayed beyond the normal 'love' of humanity, not dissimilar from that of Mother Teresa in the 20th century.

In essence, was chastity a state of mind, of faith, or of commitment? Many married women and men had espoused chastity upon entering monastic life. And, as to virginity, the anatomical and physiological requirement had been put aside as a non-fact in many instances by accepting the virginity of the soul. After all, the whole concept had been sanctioned by Jesus' Mother from conception to birth. Amazingly, Mahina extended her virginal status until the Infant Jesus stopped sucking his mother's breasts, for apparently no scriptures ever mentioned the cooperation of a wet nurse as a normal alternative to an immediate return to virginity *post partum*.

In anticipation of her return to the States, Mahina wrote notes on concepts floating in her mind about the sex of angels, on whether they had body and soul, and if that dichotomy became nullified through God. Was not God in an eternal state of androgyny? So, why should angels be different? She was convinced that angels must have chanelled their Psychic (call them Spiritual) Energies through Poverty, Obedience and Chastity. In fact, they apparently were so poor that they wore no clothes; except for rebellious ones, they obeyed God blindly; and their androgynous make-up dispelled any attempt to endanger chastity at the accidental touch of flapping wings.

Jokes aside, Mahina was serious. In fact, she even outlined the possibility that, unless angels were created first in Heaven, they were actually humans who had a temporary body on Earth and an eternal soul in God's Kingdom. After abandoning terrestrial life, their bodies would be left to rot in Terra, but their spirits would become one within an individual's soul. However, the idea of a God and of a Christ merging, or even self-effacing, into, a genderless entity began to disturb her. And the idea of Christ as a more terrestrial inhabitant started to emerge through Komaru, the only man near her in the process of seeking a *modus capiendi* or *credendi*. Failing this and without blind faith, Catholic tenets would become obliterated by absurd reality.

The floruit of Mahina's speculations reached a crisis on the occasion of her birthday, the 21 July. It was a cold, grey, humid day. She thanked God for assisting her in preparing everything before her departure the following day. She was so restless that she was afraid of not being able to cope with the circumstances. Against Komaru's desire to take her somewhere for either dinner or supper in order to celebrate her 24th birthday, she insisted on staying home. She had planned to spend the whole short day in her room talking with her brother, as if she had a feeling that Komaru was the first and last man on Earth she could explore for a few more hours. Or was Komaru more than that? In her subconscious vision of Christ, and disregarding whatever somatic characteristics she had envisioned in her readings, 'her' Jesus had assumed the physical shape of her brother, if not also his 'pathetic' look. She even wondered if the Nazarene suffered from Attention Deficit Disorder.

The Christ with whom Mahina wanted to spend her last day in

Aotearoa was not a blue-eyed, blond or red-headed specimen sporting a non-athletic physique. No! Her Christ was a 190 centimetres tall bloke with the body of an athlete once very active in rugby. His skin was dark olive, and his body topped by a semi-dolichocephalic head covered with the wavy black hair of a 27-year-old man, a full bone structure in complementary distribution of both visible muscles and little body fats. His hair was more abundant than that of most Maoris, with some light ringlets around his nipples that produced a well-proportioned bundle of fleshy breasts displaying a little more adiposity than a youth in his prime. His hands were big, but at the same time his long fingers were those of an artist, like those of his father, if not those of a poet.

What struck Mahina in superimposing Christ onto Komaru or vice-versa was his face, a strong chin that quite puzzlingly started to hang down from his cheeks with a squarish shape, but it phased itself out into a round terminal, not dissimilar from that of a pugilist. She wondered how Melissa utilised those external features of her brother. What had she seen in Komaru at the inception of her Wanganui romance? A fighter in the rather narrow confines of a Pakeha bed or a stud in the equally constrictive stall of a fringe reproductive mare? The whole facial expression was that of a warrior, though at the same time it expressed that of a dreamer, of a 'quiet' thinker, of a 'resting' lion, of a nearly 'indifferent' observer.

The paucity of a beard, the little of which was daily removed by an electric razor, showed rather shiny skin, healthy and soft. She wondered how Komaru would look as a monk with a long beard, almost the characteristic of a recluse conferring trust, dignity and even sanctity. That was what the photographs showed often on the pages of VISION: The Annual Religious Vocation Discernment Handbook, a gold mine of information. She also noticed that most of the eyes in those photographs displayed intelligence and honesty, if not a certain naïveté. Komaru's dark eyes, under a thick set of eyelashes, were the 'Mediterranean' feature never observed in artistic conceptions of a Christ whether on the Cross or among his disciples. What, however, intrigued Mahina was Komaru's nose. It was definitely a 'Roman' one, and that really made her wonder what kind of genetic saga had been written by chance in the Dalmatian code of a mixed up *whakapapa*. Undoubtedly, the Nazarene she saw in Komaru during the last day of her stay at 'home' was a disturbing reality.

Thus, except for a long dinner time in the kitchen, the siblings spent the whole day in Mahina's room. That was her wish, and

Komaru honoured it. And they talked while she lay on her Maori bed, propped up on pillows and dressed in her American pyjamas, all day long. Komaru sat by the fax table on Mahina's comfortable 'reading' armchair, a bit small for Komaru, but more restful than the chair next to it. The day was different, because both of them had done everything in two weeks of preparation. Komaru told Mahina that, after her departure, he needed to go to Wanganui and finalise his thesis with Melissa. At that, a shadow of *tristesse* crossed her face unmistakably, but Komaru's candor and fervour in outlining quite a revolutionary thesis in form and content dispelled Mahina's sadness. She knew that Komaru needed that kind of 'intellectual' contact for his own sake since his daily life was rather limited by whatever activities he was engaged in, mostly discreetly.

It was a glorious day nevertheless, since the rain seemed to wash out the gloominess that lingered in the knowledge that, the following day, they would detach from each other, perhaps forever. For the first and the last time, brother and sister were united by music. It was the chance of a lifetime. And Komaru created in the room an aura of spiritualism. Music permeated everything while Mahina read some of her poetry, the poems of her early youth in confusing Aotearoa. That was the period in which she had discovered herself in a gilded cage of Pakehahood surrounded by mirrors of complacency.

Tuesday, the 21st, was for Mahina an epiphanous day. She sensed it early in the morning, when she realised that the next day she would leave home for an alien shore. And yet, she knew that, after landing on a different continent, she would work hard to integrate herself into whatever that new corner of the world would offer a woman at the inception of a mature life. She was not a student any longer.

The morning began somewhat languidly for Mahina after she was awakened by Komaru, who brought her 24 pink roses he had hidden the previous evening in the garage. And a glass of orange juice. The American flannel pyjamas, with their flowery design, enveloped Mahina in a cocoon of a mini garden displaying a first prize bouquet to complement the artificial with the real. And she received the roses with a flow of tears.

'Happy birthday, Mahina. I removed all the thorns.'
'Oh, no, no, Komaru, how can you say that?'
'Yes, one by one, yesterday ... I myself ...'
'Thank you, thank you, oh, Komaru, are these roses for my own funeral?'

'Mahina, please, don't you see ...'

She spilled some juice on her chest and opened the flap of the pyjamas to wipe it off with her left hand but, rather than doing that, she hugged the bouquet against her body. And, after placing the glass on the night stand, she held the flowers more tightly against her bosom.

'How can you say there are no thorns? I feel them, one by one against me, puncturing my skin, seeking my heart, asking for my blood to flow in the open. Komaru, I feel the pain, I do, I ...'

'Mahina, dear, they are for your birthday. Just to remind you that you can always come back home.'

'But you know no one has ever given me flowers for my birthday – which I always associate with rockets, lunar landings, and Man exiting his abode for the first time ...'

'Well, regardless, just think, the human Moon is as old as you are. And as long as you can see her, it is more than eponymous. From wherever you are, through her you can always remember me as the one shining my light onto you forever. The Earth is just a platform, a crib holding two siblings, a unique feat in the whole Universe.'

'Then, tell me, do you ... er ... please, do you love me?'

Suddenly, the whole Moon changed. Mahina had, for the first time in her sentimental life, grasped a most tangible and painful sense of reality. It was more than the perception of the essential meaning of herself. She tried to comprehend objectively what she had just asked him in a spurt of emotionalism. And her mind raced to scan the etyma of all the languages she had studied. What had she said, and why? Had she not noticed that Komaru froze, transfixed and speechless? He knew that a fully grown woman, nevertheless an unbloomed flower among many roses lying on her bosom, had spoken. The American Eagle had 'landed' in his heart, for she had spoken as a Pakeha.

He knew that his sister had grasped something existing in that room in all dimensions, and it was more so for Mahina, who, after roaming mentally through modern language vocabularies in vain, and after discarding Latin as a parvenu, was so elated to find a tiny harbour of psychological rest in the New Testament. Of course, that was ἡ συνείδησις, pure and simple self-consciousness, and thus a conscience. All the 19th- and 20th-century psycholoids standing on the shoulders of 17th-century concepts and their terminology were new faces on the block. And Mahina had betrayed her absorption of Western literary and psychological baggage, carrying a Pakeha heart in place of a Polynesian stomach as the seat of feelings. The Greek word-prefix was there as the most powerful *galeotto* for proximity, togetherness, sharing and a host of quintessential realistic entities. Polybius had noticed those phenomena among and between humans, while Strabo had extended them to constellations. Of was it just the reverse? Herodotus had used the συν-prefix for entities bound together, while Xenophon had been more physical in 'mass togetherness' by implying 'crowding' in an ambience of more than one individual. Oh, those Greeks, exploring the most recondite corners of the heart! Now Mahina understood the once theoretical concepts from the university classrooms. Those professors of philosophy had spoken in the abstract, but now she knew what they were talking about, now that she reviewed in superphotic retrospection almost anything beginning with the *Odyssey* and its concepts of 'linking together', proceeding with Aeschylus and Sophocles for visions of dreams, and a whole string of ancients from Aristophanes to Plato. The fact that all of them were men told Mahina that, as a woman, she was only a receptor. Sappho, the exception, was a false mirror, and nevertheless a receptor even if two-dimensional in Plato's classroom activities. The associative concept emerged clearly first through Euripides. There was no doubt about it, from self-consciousness to sexual intercourse. But that physiological drive had not crossed Mahina's mind. She was solidly entrenched in a frightening cave of feelings that revealed only her fast and loud heartbeat.

At Komaru's normal reaction to any question posed to him by anyone for anything, a permanent *modus responsi* blanking out all rejoinders, Mahina changed the positive into a negative query.

'Komaru, I am going away, perhaps forever. I need to know, I have to, before tomorrow and in person. Hear me, please, don't you love me?'

She was holding the bouquet of roses to her breast, almost trying to hurt herself, recalling the previous roses full of thorns. She actually wished for those stems to draw blood.

'Komaru, don't you see that I am bleeding for you?'

'I ... had better fix breakfast. What about soft boiled eggs running on toast the way you like them?'

He left quietly while Mahina froze in terror for a moment that felt like an eternity. She was hot and perspiring, trying to wake up from a state of torpor. But the trill of the fax machine broke the impasse of confusion that led her to throw the flowers at the computer screen. In positioning to do that, she pushed herself up a little on the pillow.

Then she noticed it — a cooling, wettish, sticky feeling that forced her to acknowledge a cramp. Yes, of course, the 21 July. The physiological calendar had shown punctuality for a terrestrial moon. She got up, glanced at Tanya's birthday greeting, a faxed Happy Birthday, and went to the lavatory. And she thought of Makereti describing the phenomenon to the shocked Brits. No Red River Pads, just beech ashes held by biodegradable leaves. So natural! Makereti did not have to blush like Virginia Woolf in a merchant shop trying to purchase sanity pads through her sister. Ironically, during the trip to the Far North, Mahina bought a box of Tampons for 'Heavy Days' since she had not found any Kotex sanitary pads anywhere. She tried one on, and had no problems. Well, at least on her birthday Mahina did not have to help in the kitchen. Besides she felt protected internally.

And so breakfast at the counter was nearly an aseptic function at which Mahina tried hard to immerse a finger toasted bread into the semiliquid yolk. Komaru had purchased the eggs at an open-air farmers market. The free roaming chickens raised on a farm near Papakura had laid the most natural eggs, yielding the best blood-red yolks. Assembly-line American eggs, in comparison, displayed a split-pea colour varying from pale green Chartreuse to watery Pernod. Komaru first had a glass of vegetable juice that reminded her of the Portland campus V–8. Its thick and dark red viscosity nearly made Mahina sick after some particles of the vegetable drink adhered obscenely to the glass against the morning sun filtering through the kitchen window at Komaru's back. She took her cup of tea to her room. She told him she would be ready for dinner about one, after packing. Then she would rest the whole afternoon, when she needed to talk with him about several things. The Socratic method had apparently failed, and now she was applying a rhetorical one. Komaru found refuge among the Stoics.

And, in fact, Komaru took the opportunity of a free morning to check the lorry — tyres, oil, heating system. Then he drove to refill the petrol tank. When he came back, he found Mahina in his room browsing among some music tapes. She had put some of them aside, along with textbooks from his undergraduate courses in Maori. The scent of *muguet des bois* was in the air.

Soon after a dinner of leftovers, the early afternoon plan by Mahina to talk with Komaru on 'odds and ends' was for him providentially interrupted by a telephone call from the International Freighters Services asking Miss Reti whether they could deliver some cases of books and personal effects earlier than scheduled since the local company was also doing the same at another address in the neighbourhood. This *deus ex 'Mahina'* proved to be a welcome relief after the boxes were unloaded in the garage. Customs had been cleared. Everything else was in order. And, strangely, Mahina decided not to open them. She said she would ask Komaru to forward to her any items she might need, though she felt that there was almost nothing she could not buy in the States. It would be cheaper than reshipping. How things had changed! She remembered Alla's first line: 'Pack nothing.' Well, at least for what had been an undergraduate interlude. And even now she had packed only a single medium suitcase and a carry-on bag to fit under the airplane seat.

At tea time Mahina asked Komaru to visit with her.

'Sorry I could not help with washing the dishes.'

'I understand. Maori customs never die. Will they ever fade away?'

'I think so, yes, they will, at least with regard to what our granny taught me. But in the States things are different. It is strange that there seems to be some kind of 'atmospheric' force controlling my behaviour, for in America I never felt, never thought of things I do automatically here. As a matter of fact, rarely did I know of any coed being even slightly indisposed except for some incidental PMS around final exams. We always helped each other in the dorm regardless of menstrual occurrences. How strange! The invisible walls of tradition seem frozen in the place of one's birth. Now, relax, let's have some music I found in your collection.'

'By all means! I feel I am being asked for a last wish before an execution.'

'You? After all, *I* am leaving.'

'Exactly, you leave but I remain here, alone with my memories. Oh, I see, Mozart's *Requiem*.'

'Yes, I would like to share it with you in memory of Father. And, could I take along some tapes Dad bought for me long ago? Look, *A Garland of Maori Song* recorded at Queen Victoria School. I was 10 years old ... oh, 'Aue Te Aroha'.'

'But first Mozart.'

Komaru played it on Mahina's old tape recorder.

The '*Requiem*' and '*Dies irae*' were listened to in silence. Mahina was sipping her now cold tea while lying down on her bed.

At the inception of the '*Tuba mirum*' Mahina asked Komaru why he had not taken the tapes to Wellington. He answered that he had changed his stock from tapes to CDs. Besides, he knew that Father liked to listen to them occasionally.

At the '*Confutatis*' Mahina noticed that Komaru looked rather uncomfortable, sitting nearly straight at the computer desk.

'Komaru, don't fall asleep. Come here. Be near me, lie down. I want to touch hands. Please! Don't make me cry!'

'But I have to change the tape soon.'

The '*Lacrimosa*' began to flow in perfect consonance with the D minor key.

'Bring the recorder here, plug it in by the lamp socket.'

The *kauri* wall had an outlet in the middle, by the four-by-two stud, the old terminology in spite of metrication. In the States she had heard of two-by-fours.

By the time the '*Domine Jesu*' segment began to play in anticipation of the Tölzer Boys Chorus participation at the Collegium Aureum, Komaru had gratefully allowed his body to stretch out beside Mahina's.

'Like a generation ago, Komaru, at granny's, when we were so ignorant of ourselves, so unaware of our *iwi*, of our family.'

'And you, kid sister, kicking me in your sleep, and crying hysterically for the most stupid reasons.'

'Yes, I vaguely recall that. Once I was talking with Tanya about our infancy and youth. So different. In the States people are removed not only from their mother's side after a few days, but also even placed alone in their own rooms. I wonder. And we together in the same bed, with nothing on us except the tradition of innocence, when we visited with granny. And coming back here each summer was like re-entering a convent.'

'A different world, sister. Actually, I never thought you were a sister or whatever. I think it was at your menarche one summer that granny put you on the other side, placing herself between me and you.'

The '*Agnus Dei*' meanwhile had concluded the *Requiem*. Yes, the lamb that was able to take away all the sins of the world, thought Komaru. Granny had become a lamb. So many lambs in Pakeha New Zealand taking away all the sins of humanity with a simple '*Miserere nobis*'. He reckoned that Aotearoa was the luckiest country in the world at a ratio of 30 sheep per capita. Each Kiwi could sin every day of the month, and still be forgiven once a day by sacrificing a new lamb. What a fortunate country!

Komaru had nearly fallen asleep when Mahina touched his hand. It was cold, but delicate and so silky.

'Komaru, I am so scared.'

'Of what?'

'Of everything! You know, being alone, except for you, makes me feel abandoned by humanity. Just think, I have virtually a whole life ahead of me. So many things to take care of. And the teaching ahead. Which reminds me. I am going to take with me all the Maori language tapes. I think I'll begin my course with a simple lab programme. The two tapes by Bruce Biggs should help later, along with *Let's Learn Maori*. Of course, I can't compete with Patrick Hohepa. I wish I had his background. Have you ever heard of him at AU?'

Komaru nearly choked. Did he know of the anthropologist?

'Rather vaguely. We historians rarely mix with anybody else. What do YOU know about him?'

'Well, he was one of the first Maori students to obtain a PhD in Linguistics at Indiana University under a certain Fred Householder. As a matter of fact, Dr Hohepa brought advanced linguistics to New Zealand, just as Marsden brought Christianity.'

'Quite a comparative parabole. I know about Christians. – But, what do linguists do?'

'Not sure, though I heard once that they tell Aborigines how to speak their own language according to abstract structures. Something like teaching cooks to use the *Merck Manual of Pharmacology* rather than a cookbook.'

'I hope you don't do that. Perhaps one way to teach our language would be to translate, say, a poem into Maori. What do you say? Or vice versa.'

'God forbid! In America? Komaru, it is not a matter of language, for in the States people are devoid of any poetic imagination. They are at the opposite end of the sensitivity scale in imagery.'

'I agree with you from what I have heard ... and, sister, can I stretch my fingers?'

'Sorry, I felt like holding on to you during my first language lesson. Anyway, no, but perhaps I can try translating my own teenage poems into English. In packing this morning I found my collection. The problem is that I don't know exactly what is mine and what is a translation from English. Wait a second.'

She got up and took a booklet from a desk drawer. From under her pyjamas the lily of the valley perfume dispersed itself into the heated room as a cloud gently blown by the wind through a field of flowers.

She kneeled on the mattress by him. The *tiki* nearly came out of her bosom in the process.

'Look at some of my juvenile attempts to grasp the ineffable around me. And ... this. Yes, I wrote it here one morning. It was spring and I had walked by the flower beds tended by father. And something flew by me, around and around. I don't remember what kind of bird it was. So, when I returned to my room I wrote this. But how can I translate it into English?'

'May I try? As an impassionate arbiter I should be rather objective.'
'Please, let me see how sensitive you can be.'
'Hmm, no title. Anyway, here we are.'

> Peep, bird,
> Trill, caw,
> Flip and fly,
> Rustle and wave
> Life in my aviary
> of Papakura spring.
>
> Air is soft and warm:
> A dozen degrees.
> Each waffling 'round
> Holds subtleties of sense
> As it plays upon my face.

'What do you say?'
'Bravo! Oh, Komaru, you are a poet.'
'Thank you, but did YOU write this? At any rate, I don't think that my translation can do justice to the original. Incidentally, that bird, could it be a swallow?'

'Yes, indeed. I was about 13 and had participated in the recording of a collection titled *Songs of Joy & Love*. One of these was 'A Swallow Song'. I still have the photograph taken at St Joseph's Maori Girls College. You know, I was among the youngest in the group, but admitted to the Choir as a guest singer because of my voice. My director once told me that my vocal chords possessed 'Kirian' qualities ... whatever she meant. How carefree was life! And how happy we girls were in our blue uniforms with the college emblem on our coats over the open collar shirts.'

'That was during the last phase of dormant Maoridom, sister. And now, before I fall asleep, I had better prepare a good supper in your honour, for your Moon birthday. Who knows, Mahina, what fate has reserved for us, with our genes mixed up in so many ways. Think of them. Do we have 75% of them in our genetic structure? And, if so, what is Maori left in us? Just think! Now, please leave me alone in the kitchen. I will call you when supper is ready.'

'For the last supper?'

'You asked for it.'

'Go away, don't make me cry!'

And Komaru did go away with his body, but his mind was left lying near her in the most absurd confusion he ever detected in himself. The vagaries of life are such, he thought, that whenever two poles of a continuum of feelings touch each other, one does not know whether their intensity will lead to happiness to last a lifetime or to the immediate implementation of suicide. In fact, Komaru reasoned that those two feelings differed only in a *modus* of reaching a nirvana for the purpose of stopping the aching of one's temples at the threshold of compelling decisions. Mahina had first asked him if he loved her, and then whether he did not love her. What was she talking about? And how should he know? How could he reply when he had never loved anyone and never told anybody so?

Then he analysed himself coolly and had to acknowledge that perhaps he loved Mahina. But, what was new in that? How many times had he ended his letters to her with 'Aroha' and how different was it from Eros? Even etymologically, both terms had a common ancestor in pre- proto-Indo-European through phonetic similarity. In fact, ἔρος and *aroha* were brother and sister, the Sun and the Moon, Komaru and Mahina. He always 'loved' her, probably even in a Western fashion. The longer he thought about it while trying to concoct supper, the more he was convinced that he had always loved his sister. Did Mahina not know that? How could that be possible? What did he have to say or do to convince her that he loved her? Actually, he thought that if 'love' ever existed in its purest form, it could only be found between brother and sister. No other relationship, whether within or without a family with the same genitor and genitrix, could surpass the uniqueness of that quintessential love. After all, he remembered the old Maori proverb explicitly stating that in an ideal marriage situation, one should marry his own sister. No blood would ever be spilled that way. Consequently, Komaru concluded that 'love', without any modifiers or qualifiers, is possible only between linear blood relations of 'zero' descendancy or ascendancy. No other possible association, particularly a vertical one, would warrant whatever in all human congregations is labelled as 'love'. He even reiterated that conclusion to himself by affirming that love is possible only between brother and sister without even declaring it and, most importantly, without 'performing' it in any manner. Everything else along a non-linear axis would perforce be incest or whatever. Ergo, the Greek concept of syneisactism would automatically nullify any religious, moral or cultural constraints creating victims and sinners. Yes, he knew that Mahina had always been his love *in posse* and *in esse*. What else was there to say?

Chapter 34

Flight NZ14 for Los Angeles departed on time at 14:00. The two hours spent on bureaucratic formalities at the Mangere Airport seemed to last an eternity. After Mahina checked in, there was so much to say that Komaru's thoughts seemed to have congealed into a mass of mute verbosity. In waiting among the returning American tourists, Mahina and Komaru had automatically assumed a stance of enigmatic absenteeism. A casual observer, however, would know who of the two was remaining, for from time to time Mahina checked her passport, fingered her boarding pass nervously, looked at the flight schedules of the various airlines on the TV screen, and simply gazed at Komaru as if he were a castaway on a desert island. She was the one ready to sail into a life of adventure. Her brother, in fact, appeared morose and dejected, as if required to spend the rest of his life on a hermit island.

Just before standing in line at the door of the corridor leading to the airplane, Mahina turned around and looked at her brother so sadly that she nearly exploded in tears. Her lips had parted to say something, but no sound came out. Komaru may have understood the three mute syllables beyond the phonetic structure of both English and Maori, something like 'I love you'. That aphonic expression hit his stomach so hard that he nearly felt nauseated by the punch. And that was all, lost on the back of Mahina's shoulders bobbing among people eager to board the plane. She was carrying just a small handbag, but for both of them it was large enough to contain two full lives lived in retrospect during 50 years by combining their terrestrial existence into a single life span. And it had taken not even a month for them slowly to grasp the meaning of that half a century synthesised during the night following Mahina's birthday compressed into a whole saga of emotions. The entire feeling of time awareness, covering a segment of the Gregorian calendar into barely 312 full moons, from Komaru's perspective had been sucked by the black hole of an evening and a night spent in the hope of having that birthday extended for at least another day, something that Mahina was going to experience in practice by gaining another 21 July after arriving in Los Angeles.

For Komaru, however, only retrospectively could he bitterly savour a prolongation of a silent, sweet and sour immersion of two hearts through the recollections that still palpitated via the adherence of two hot skins, by the fumbling motion of hands moving as if commanded by blindness, by the touch of noses and lips seeking communication on a nervously narrow futon. It was the longest drive to return home. And the reminiscences springing into Komaru's mind seemed to extend the trip forever. Everything had been lived and relived as if all innocent childhood had been brought to surface along a dangerous path of tense adulthood.

It was Mahina who, after the supper Komaru prepared in her honour, had asked him to visit with her. She had enjoyed the *toheroa* soup and the minnow fritters immensely. She knew that, except for some pathetically sentimental *tohunga* chefs in Los Angeles and San Diego area eateries, nowhere else on Earth would she relish the physical reaction stemming from the ingestion of those dishes. She wanted to store the palatable sensations into her 'eternal' memory stored in the banks of intimate recollections. That was for her a unique vault where only she could enter in search of furtive and pleasurable bodily experiences regardless of terrestrial locations and social constraints.

Mahina had opened the curtain of the window in her room facing the orchard. The only source of light was the almost full Moon peeking through the budding branches of the apple trees between the tall wooden fence and the next empty section. Nothing else seemed alive when Komaru entered her room after cleaning up the kitchen. He knew that she would not help, for her Maorihood was still alive and well in spite of Western liberalism.

When he wondered why she was in the dark, she told him not to turn on any lights. She wanted to recreate the nights spent in the Far North at their grandmother's 'cottage' after the kerosene lamp had been extinguished. And the children were in the same earth-level bed ready to fall asleep, often in each other's arms as if to dispel the threats of a malign *atua* during a thunderstorm. Lucretius was still alive after two thousand years: 'Nam veluti pueri trepidant atque omnia caecis in tenebris metuunt ...'

'Komaru, I want to go back for a night only, back to Granny's to tell her good-bye. Please take me there. Come here with me.'

What she needed was 'non radii solis ... sed naturae species ...'

And Komaru had become the only source of light in the darkness of her 'anxius angor'.

Her tone of voice was soft, dreamy, nearly stuttering. And Komaru had registered her saying that she needed a good night's sleep before the long voyage to her utopia. And he was tired.

No, she had begged. She had told him to imagine himself 15 years back, when each of them was beginning to become aware of their own individuality as human beings, wondering at the structure of their bodies. Now, however, she 'sopita recumbit', as if she had smelled castor oil, 'tempore eo ... quo menstrua solvit'.

When Komaru lay down by her he sensed she was breathing hard, as if moaning. And, noticing that he was still wearing his jogging suit, functioning as house attire, she asked him to take it off. She insisted. And that he did, reluctantly with the excuse that the room was cool, the way Mahina liked it as a habit acquired in Portland. She replied that she would keep him warm by embracing him as they used to do as children. She recalled that Komaru would turn to his left, and she would do the same in order to warm him up with her frontal body against his back. That was when Komaru told her that her pointed breasts made him uncomfortable. He did not like to have any protuberances against his shoulders, as if being pinned down by two or three points of spears of enemy warriors in an unfair combat.

When she raised her side of the light blanket to cover him next to her, Komaru was taken back in time, for Mahina had nothing *on* her in spite of inceptive menses. And he asked her how she could be that way when, on the one hand, she would not touch the dishes and, on the other, she would disregard any *tapu* by being so close to a male body. And a brother's at that!

But she told him that he was not an implement. Besides, she had learned how to skirt proximity, though with girls in her dorm. No, not even undies. She was wearing an American protective foetus-like device *in* her body. So efficient.

And so, the two sides adhered to each other with nothing between them except the reminiscences of childhood. Then Komaru remembered. It was only once when he was about 12, and curious, in an exploratory mood devoid of lustful drives. He had touched her between her legs. She had reacted by offering no resistance. Actually, she had parted her thighs in a 'natural' fashion as if his playful exploration was a game. Yes, she even remembered a vague feeling of enjoyment at the sensation of discovering herself, for this time it was not her impudicus, but Komaru's. He had first caressed the perimeter of the outer labia before parting the minora casually and almost clinically. He then knew that his sibling was not like him, for she had an entrance somewhere, which he probed extremely gently with a couple of fingers first and then a little more deeply with his own index. He was intrigued by the softness of those tissues that after a while became moist. But nothing else after that, no follow up, no awareness of possibilities, no consequential alternatives. He had not reacted sexually in any manner. And the probing ended after seeing and touching something for the first and last time and satisfying his naïve curiosity.

In recollecting the experience of the previous evening, he wondered. What did Mahina have in mind? Was she not going to become a nun, whose first vow was chastity? No matter what, he knew that she was going to be bound by it as a matter of principle. Mahina herself had so resolved. But she wanted to spend the whole night with him in a series of embraces before Komaru would fall asleep. She would throw her right arm over her shoulders and pull him against her stomach like a natural source of heat enveloping his buttocks.

And she talked about herself while first touching his chest, his nipples, and caressing his belly. She tried to wrap her right leg over his, as if mounting him sideways but still avoiding frontal contact. It was a pleasurable series of incipient jujitsu that undoubtedly triggered in her a series of palpitating body reactions. She would mutely rub herself against Komaru's sides and gently move up and down, and sideways, as if attempting to integrate herself into his body by psychological osmosis. But Komaru felt her flesh ponderously on his own when she placed herself astride his right side. Yes, he remembered her as a child trying to practice horse mounting on her brother while he was feigning sleep. Then he would turn flat on his back and she would sit on his chest and use his arms as a bridle.

The initial body contacts of the previous evening, however, were more mature than those of nearly a generation past. Mahina began to use Komaru as a giant *olisbos*, as if trying to re-enact Sappho's rejection of a phallus via Tanya's technique of mutual gratification. Driving back home that afternoon, Komaru could not help discard the thoughts crowding his mind because he tended to fall asleep at the wheel, perhaps subconsciously hoping for a fatal accident that would efface the thorny feeling of guilt that had descended on him as an oppressive army of *atuas*. He had not slept nearly at all under the staging of Mahina's overt and periphrastic manipulations of his body.

'Komaru, you will be the only man I'll ever know in my life before dedicating myself to Him. I need to know a human body in order to understand Christ first as a human being and then as an eternal anchor of salvation. Let me be myself, let me remember you in order to meet Him.'

And several times she groped him all over without ever touching him around his inguinal area. Only once did she accidentally bump her right hand around his groins, and to her horror she detected a flaccid appendage asleep on the inside of his left coxa. She wondered how he could withstand her in the process of discarding her dead skin against his. Epidermal corpuscles were engaged in anthropophagogical enterprises for the sake of survival.

'Please, Komaru, let me know you. I want to be sure that I am normal.'

At that, she placed Komaru on his left side and mounted him on his right hip. Presently, she began to rub herself up and down until she began to tremble in perspiration while Komaru extended her hand palms down on the pillows as if it were a lifesaver keeping him afloat. It was during Mahina's first powerful catastasis that she expelled on Komaru a wet and hot cylinder of cotton. She grabbed it and left for the bathroom, while he stayed put until she returned with a washcloth.

'So, brother, I have broken the next to last *tapu* of our unspeakable crime. But I enjoyed myself better than with Tanya. You see, she interacted with me, but you didn't. Oh, the curse of the inner and outer flesh.'

Then she pulled him on his back and started probing him again by riding smack on Komaru's stomach and touching him on his nipples, kissing them while interweaving her fingers with his hair.

'I can't detect any scar on your teat. Touch mine, please, see if mine is healed. With the palm of your hand. Gently.'

And then she began to rub her buttocks against Komaru's belly in concentric motions as a belly dancer in front of a cobra waiting for a window of opportunity to strike her straight in the face of an inviolate look. That was when, after a long series of twists and turns of her lower body on his, she sensed that Komaru had become hot and tense. And she automatically fomented that tension under her total control. Just before she was ready to eject herself once more, she felt a series of hot pellets hitting the small of her back in a convulsive staccato emission. She then collapsed onto his body like a lifeless doll. At that, Komaru hongied her gently while licking her tears and mucus all around her lips. The *tertium quid* for the first time had acted as an arbiter of desire, and as such it had witnessed the collapse of a paper tiger after being deflated by the coalescence of semen and blood. His reaction, of course, was only at the external level, but it was cogent enough for Mahina to savour the normality of her femalehood through a brother. Who else better than her own blood could be entrusted with the ritual of the purest sacrifice of pleasure on Earth?

And so they remained in that mute amplex until Mahina detected Komaru's coagulation beginning to dissolve and run down along her thighs, together with her menstrual blood.

'No, please, don't move yet. Let me fall asleep on you like so long ago.'

And for nearly two hours she was the only source of sounds in a dark room. When she became tired of philosophising aloud, she asked Komaru to try finding the tape containing the K581 on one side and the 622 on the other. This he did, so that when she hurried back from the washroom as if afraid of wasting a single second away from him, the clarinet of the quintet had already begun its lamentations, comforted by the smooth string palliative of impending departure. They listened to both sides of the tape in a close embrace. Komaru now had little to fear from himself, for, at least for a while, he could be comfortable letting Mahina rub his chest. But the *tiki* was between them as an obstacle. Komaru resented the intrusion of that amulet as if it weighed a ton in his conscience. He opened his mouth, however, and asked her to remove it until morning. She said 'No' and started crying, especially during the second movement of the 622. Both her moaning and the clarinet's seemed to empathise with each other. Then Mahina became almost hysterical at the thought of removing herself from her only link with her total being. No, don't touch it, she had told him. But the intruder was there as a guardian. Or a witness to something inevitably ready to happen? He slapped her when her sobs became screams of fear, which Komaru misunderstood as screams of passion. Oh, Saint Bernard, mused Komaru, you are right. *There is more danger in* ... But his thought was interrupted by Mahina, who forgave him, placing her lips onto his delicately and moistly. That made Komaru so vulnerable that he himself started crying heavily under the stress of confusion ... *living with a woman* ... Thus, they continued crying together until Mahina parted her lips and began to probe his mouth with side strokes as if asking for permission to enter his oral cavity ... *than raising the dead to life* ... But even saints can be wrong, because Komaru remembered Melissa's instructions of labial engagement, and so the two lingual tips began to dance a minuet *pas de deux*. That took Komaru to Wanganui where, as a freshman in oscular gymnastics, he patiently allowed Melissa gradually to break him into the intricacy of mouth to mouth arousal. And he himself now took that time with Mahina, like a careful periodontist checking for gingivitis using the index finger. It did not take long for Mahina to accept the challenge. In a few minutes she was sucking and savouring the sensitivity of 360 degree laterality and as deeply as they could both take and give, while lying fully horizontally *pace* Reverend Marsden.

Yes, St Bernard was wrong, because Komaru was raised from the dead, and she sensed it immediately around her upper thighs, like a *patu* positioning to challenge a *tiki*. That damn *tiki*, Komaru thought, in the way between *corpora* of which each drunken specimen sought a haven of refuge and proffered a cove of hospitality beyond the traditions of the Eskimos and the Tuaregs.

'Don't touch my *tiki*! You know I can't be without her. Touch me anywhere you like, please, touch me, but not the *tiki*.'

Komaru's right hand slid down her left side to position itself at a more collimating height, for Komaru had to twist his head in order to withstand the interaction of her lips with his. Then he allowed his fingers to walk across the top of her left coxa before dipping tentatively into a semiviscous dampness. Twenty-nine-and-one-half days or already 30 days? In the attempt to part the other lips, Komaru encountered a thicker filament among others, curly at the touch, and he understood it because he immediately grabbed it and pulled it as in a mini-operation performed at abortion clinics on K-Road. Now the way was clear, but still Mahina had that damn *tiki* between two chests and five teats. And she was still kissing him as if in a few minutes she had learned all the irregular French verbs.

Of course, the French had been in Ao Tea Roa, but Komaru had learned his lessons from Melissa, the non-French teacher of French. Nevertheless, East had met West, and West had met East, not always for the best, and often like a beast. Komaru now remembered Catullus' Lesbia, and he wondered if Mahina would be a good listener to the impromptu composition he had actually written for Ling-ling. That was a waste of time because the Shanghainese equated a labial kiss with something worse than imposed fellatio after being sodomized.

Ling-ling in the beginning looked like a hamster playing with a dog, but anyway Komaru hoped that she could be conditioned to Western kisses of which neither knew anything until Melissa yielded her honey, produced by bees from a field of fermented barley. In the first letter Komaru sent Ling-ling, he had written:

> Semper dulcia et laeta,
> sunt labia tua, Criceta,
> o nympha,
> rea
> amorum
> meorum,
> ...

But Ling-ling's lips tasted better as labia with the flavour of Manchu generosity, for nothing grew around them. And Melissa always shaved, almost daily. Now, with Mahina, what could he do? Komaru's fingers were nearly lost in a *selva oscura*. He wrote her a mental *epistola minima* as an invitation to the only uniqueness that they could share, something that rarely takes place among the millions happening every second of terrestrial life. And even kissing, Mahina was crying. Her hand was becoming tight against his chest, and, even being kissed, her mouth was now rigid under the strain of the impending. He told her:

> Quando frigida
> est manus tua,
> quando rigida
> est bucca tua,
> mihi veni, puellula,
> cordis mei cellula.

> Quid flere quaeris
> in solitudine?
> In calore
> et amore
> ...

Oh, the *tiki*! Komaru was afraid he would hurt her by rubbing it against the *tertium quid*. 'Damn it! Take it off, or at least over your head.' 'No! You know I would feel totally naked without it. I can't. She is my guardian angel. She protects me from the dangers of life and death. That would be like dishonoring Dad! No, Komaru, no!'

But Komaru, still with his right hand trying to part a hot shelled *toheroa*, grabbed the *tiki* with his left as if at first wanting to move it sideways. However, either his arm made an involuntary motion caused by a reflex of some kind or as a subconscious act of violence, his left hand applied a swift pull. Mahina's neck was raised during the first tow while her head bounced onto the pillow, as if from a backlash. At the second pull, the leather strap was torn loose, and the *tiki* flew against the mirror of the little nook used by Mahina as a boudoir corner. The shattered pieces of glass scattered all over and, although none of them hit her, she collapsed on the futon as if her skin had been punctured, and all her energies disappeared. She became lifeless, rubber-like, apathetic to the point that she did not even react when Komaru took her nearly all the way *inter labia minora* just in time for him not to soil the sheets. And, of course, he felt as void and null as the Treaty of Waitangi.

Mahina, however, analysed her situation quickly and philosophically. After all, probably not even St Anthony would have been able to withstand her childish re-enactment of a life stage when the seeds of adulthood were still underground. She knew she had acted irresponsibly, and she also realised she had hurt him, the only man she loved. Thus, she allowed herself to flow while holding his head against her *tiki*-less bosom. And she kissed him, though at the same time wondering whether the matter of chastity was simply one of warding off a chemical reaction. She had felt nothing, not even the physical pain of the intrusion. Was the culmination or the validation of 'love' only there as a matter of a few seconds? No, it could not be possible.

Her amendment took the rest of the night after waking Komaru from the torpor into which he had fallen, hiding his head in the pillow. She pulled him gently toward her while caressing his head, another desecrating action she knew she was committing, particularly since she was a menstruating woman. She wondered if she had wiped out all his warrior qualities, his psychological determination to fight, his energy to grow up as a man in a world of racial conflicts.

He understood her determination to make him feel loved and wanted, for he reacted under her manipulations as to verify that he still had a will to survive. And this time she straddled him so lightly and unobtrusively that it took him some time to realise the topsy turvy characteristics of The Hermit Islands. That was better, easier, perhaps more natural. She wondered how her ancestors congregated before the arrival of the missionaries. Could it be that procreation was accomplished by barely having two bodies touch each other from head to toe? Was it necessary for two bodies to come alongside and thus impose on one another? But this time Mahina had discovered the easiness of standing in position over Komaru just for the medium weight needed, as when Tanya once played with her, mimicking riding a pony at her farm in Walla Walla.

It took a long time for both of them to stop the frenzy permeating their bodies. Probably Komaru could have once more unhorsed himself, but he sensed that Mahina was trying hard to cross the whole galloping field of a pasture, for she intensified her muscles in an ever-increasing spasm that finally culminated first with her and seconds later with him in tow to a muffled 'ouch' triggered by the tearing away of a wet membrane. That was when Komaru gently pulled her down toward him and allowed East to meet West and West to meet East. And it was the best ever, even acknowledging that he had acted like a tamed beast. The Eagle had landed. But he had forgotten everything when the alarm clock woke him up at 8:00. Why had Mahina set it for that time? Only later did he find out that she was going to call Tanya to confirm the American itinerary, including a week of business activity in Portland.

It was nearly 3 o'clock when Komaru returned to an empty house. He recalled that Mahina had taken a bath, and after that a long shower. She even skipped breakfast, for they left for the airport at 10, and she knew she would have a meal on the plane. They had barely time to see each other. And no word was exchanged, except for Mahina telling Komaru how sorry she was for leaving her room in such a shambles. He re-assured her that he would take care of everything, and that not a pin would be moved from her room, should she one day decide to return before selling the house. At that, Mahina embraced and hongied him so affectionately that Komaru had to detach himself so as not to explode in tears of guilt. She actually became cheerful, as if ready to embark on a fun cruise to Australia, whither straight-laced Kiwis sail for the purpose of engaging in what Germans used to do in Thailand. But Mahina perhaps was faking. She did not feel guilty at all, for she wanted to leave with her brother the seal of siblingness as a rose bud in exchange for 24 roses. In fact, as proof of her total devotion to him as the terrestrial incarnation of a Christ she was going to marry in her new future, she tied a knot into the leather of the *hei tiki* and, just before leaving the house, placed it around Komaru's neck. The shortened string barely fit over his head, but it was forced as he had forced it from her. She had packed nothing from her past. Everything, including the torn *tiki*, had been left with the only blood relative on the *whenua* who had produced both of them.

Night fell quickly in the Australasian winter evening. By now, Mahina was flying into the sun to meet the darkness over California. In an attempt to linger a few more moments in the most recent memories of events, Komaru entered Mahina's room. She had been kind enough to make a pile of some bedding with a note on top by the neatly assembled pieces of mirror glass. 'Please throw everything into the refuse bin.' How could he? It was like throwing out not only his sister, but also himself along with his family, and his own seeds emitted the odor of a *tapu* shattered into a hundred pieces. He felt the pangs of depression descending onto him, and for a few minutes he simply felt lost as to what to do next and why. But had he also become deaf, or what was that strange noise invading his sister's room? He wondered if he had also destroyed the potential sanctity of his sister, should she one day succumb as a Franciscan nun in Zambia or Algeria. Yes, nowadays a nun could become a martyr, but how would the Church know whether she was also a virgin? Virgin and martyr. What did virginity really mean at the inception of Christianity, Komaru wondered. Was it intended to be a wished-for condition of non-procreation? If so, it was perfectly understandable, for who would wish to welcome into a secret community a woman subject to generate potential labour stress, parturition complications, infant cries, adult life dysfunctions, and the like? That is why, as an alternative, the early Christian church solemnised same-sex relationships as late as the 14th century, a closely guarded 'secret' in pre-modern Europe.

The anachronistic keeping of old tenets could not be understood nowadays, however, when sanctioned by a CEO of a men-only organization such as the Vatican Corporation, whose shareholders do not admit voting rights or executive responsibility unless one is non-female. The irony of it all was that the Vatican Corporation, operating 'off-shore' like a Mafia-dominated society of brainwashed nationals, allowed the non-virginity of gynoautomata to procreate as a Sacrament for the perpetuation of that monopoly of pussies and souls. The curse befallen on a nation such as Italy and subsidiary nations, nevertheless, had withstood 20 centuries of slavery extended, and still being spread, all over the world through the so-called missionary work in competition with, if not with the cooperation of, various colonialistic powers according to their political winds. The fact that the Holy Roman Empire was able to survive for nearly 10 centuries, only to be taken over fractionally by several local branch corporations, speaks for itself as to the continuation of female servitude not only psychologically for their spirits, but also, and more degrading, indenturedly for their bodies. Those were the bodies taken at a whim by any corporate officer any time his semen needed an outlet with or without the consensus of church rituals. Komaru just could not understand how millions and millions of Christians could tolerate that most coercive and humiliating double standard, the subjugation of women.

And what in the hell was that noise persistently bothering him while he was still roaming around in Mahina's room? Oh, he thought, it would be so pleasant, so comforting, so rewarding to hope that she would come in and find him there, a few feet away from the futon still warm from a night of physiological heat. The dice had been cast. So, what was he going to lose? He felt covered with *tapu* all over, and he had nothing else to fear except being rejected by his ancestors, should he one day knock at the door of their Rangi and ask for a place to deposit his bones. That damn ring! Of course, that was the telephone interrupting his train of thought.

'Kom, my dear boy, where have you been all day?'

The rather colonialistic term of endearment rubbed him the wrong way. But, coming from Melissa, it did not carry disparaging tones. Although a historian, Melissa did not care about anything imperial except for the pathological satisfaction of her body in order to maintain the proper function of her mind.

Komaru explained that he had just returned from the airport.

'At 9 o'clock? Was the plane late or what? Are you all right?'

Yes, of course, he was just fine. He had not realised that the afternoon had disappeared so quickly while trying to adapt himself to a new life of solitude.

'Then, what are you planning to do? Can you stop by on your way to Wellington?'

Of course, he was going to do that in order to propose the most simple way of finalising his MA thesis by invoking not only her help, but also that of Mr Occam. However, would the thesis committee wear such an armature as to render any razor obsolete?

Melissa replied that she did not understand what he was talking about. He could sketch his line of action, but only in person and as soon as possible. But he told her that first he had to put all the household belongings in storage somewhere, then proceed with entrusting a realtor with the sale of the house. Only a few items were to be dispatched to his Wellington flat, from which, regardless of the thesis outcome, he would move in order to purchase a small house.

'In Wellington? That is expensive. Why not in Wanganui? You know how eager developers are here to welcome people from both north and south. This is the time to buy.'

Komaru told her that probably he would do that should he fail, as he thought was possible, the MA examination. That meant he would not be hired to work as a research historian at the Waitangi Tribunal.

'Fine, don't rush things. No matter what, you could stay with us until you decide what to do next, and where. Perhaps you could find a job here.'

That Melissa was a dreamer, Komaru thought. Who would give a Crown job to a young Maori man in a city run by latter-day Nazis thriving in the Bible belt of North Island?

A few days later, after he realised how tight was the knot keeping him tied to Mahina's room, he borrowed psychological strength from Alexander the Great and cut everything by telling Gordius to go to hell. There was no point in selecting this and that as a possible source of transportation along future memory lanes. Drastic solutions may hurt, but after they are applied they begin to fade away together with material possessions acting as potential catalysts. Thus, except for the items belonging legally and emotionally to Mahina, left in the yard camp of Storage Services Ltd, he mailed a few heavy items to his apartment and left Papakura with two cases of personal and legal paperwork. He also took along with him the radio scanner Mahina had brought from the States for her father. He departed early in the morning of 27 July, when it was still dark. Had he tried to look back from the street corner, he would have seen only a vague mass of suburban houses enveloped in the morning mist rolling over from the viaduct. A whole life of formative education, a complete series of attempts to integrate himself into the schizophrenic system of political survival, a sealed ark of painful memories had been left behind forever. Only Mahina was being carried with him, in spite of the fact that he intentionally did not take any photographs of her. She was in front of him at every intersection, at each highway exit, at all the traffic signs. All directional symbols seemed encased in a frame depicting the transparent sad face of his sister gone into the unknown along with his mother and father, as well as with whatever carrier of dead genes that defied a proper terminology for the identification of a relationship. And to think that the whole saga had begun with the exploitation of a *kauri* forest for making pars and varnish. What a disgusting fate imposed on a whole race after so many centuries of civilizing isolation! Komaru felt that having become a human through the vagaries of chance had been the most fatalistic curse an *atua* could ever impose on any animal. Oh, how he wished to have vanished like the *moa*!

The stay at the McTavishes turned out to be a rather refreshing intermission between the past and the future. Even Melissa acted 'understanding', attributing Komaru's gloomy mood to his father's death. Which was true, of course, though, had she known the real reason for Komaru's aloofness, she would have been rather intrigued. It was in talking with Bill that Komaru began to discern and tolerate certain aspects of his psychological dysfunction. The whole thing had started when he opened up with Bill as a doctor of the 'mind'. When Dr McTavish heard most of the revelation left by Komaru's father in the 'moral testament', he reacted not with surprise. He even told Komaru that, if family histories were written on the basis of actual facts, the whole profession of psychiatry would have to be re-analysed and re-organised along different lines.

Dr McTavish said that there was always a vacuum between the horizontal incest and the vertical one. He himself had used two derivatives of that term as adjectives, namely, the incestuous and the incestive. The former was applied to the traditional, the mythological, the literary along historical and non-historical lines. Mother–son, father–daughter, uncle–niece, aunt–nephew, and more distant vertical relationships tended to be regarded and 'treated' with more complex attempts to understand and accept both the phenomena and its results.

Bill mentioned that, as an immature researcher in the exploration of the psyche, he had been first shocked by what he saw and heard when he spent a year at Jung's compound in Switzerland. Dr Jung had illustrated the legend of Simeon ben Yohai, who believed that the only way to extend life *ad infinitum* would be to congregate with his youngest daughter. And, in fact, Casanova had attempted, though not succeeded, in his quest for immortality, though he would not hesitate to impregnate even the daughter of his daughter. Names such as Sabina Spielrein, Rainer Maria Rilke, Helen Deutsch, Victor Tausk and many others were dropped like cherry pits, though Komaru could not make any sense of whether they were part of fact or fiction. That would not have made any difference to Dr McTavish because he himself believed that the very fact that a character exists in fiction is valid enough to be accepted as a fact. Indeed, he told Komaru that

Jung did not discriminate between women, real or imaginary, in his womanising enterprises. Bill told Komaru that, in coping mentally with his women and in anticipation of subjecting them to coitus, Jung got more excited with the imaginary ones, to the point of obtaining deeper gratification from the latter than the former when masturbating as a normal antipasto before the main meal. That is what Jung used to do just before engaging himself in any sexual congress to avoid premature ejaculation. Komaru was rather surprised when, asking Bill about any relationship between Freud and his daughter, Anna, he was told little, and the little was very enigmatic. It is a fact that no psychiatrist ever speaks evil of another. He only said that, if London's residences of the Freuds, first Primrose Hill and then Marsfield Gardens, could speak, they would surely enlighten not so much the behavioural problems of the Austrian family, as of the whole of British society. That, moreover, would also explain the rôle of Minna, Freud's sister-in-law. At any rate, what could Freud lose when for years he was dying, slowly allowing a cigar to poison his cheek and then his whole lymphatic system through cancer? If he could have extended his life through Anna and Anna's daughter, beyond psychic incest, undoubtedly he would have contributed to spread genetic cancer along with selfish interest. Is it accidental that Jung's mysticism and Simeon's asceticism are still alive for anyone wishing to visit their graves, especially the latter's, 33 days after the second day of Passover?

The meeting with Melissa proved more fruitful after she exacted her payment in advance and in nature. And she was rather surprised at the renewed vigor with which Komaru applied all his stamina, although she detected in him not the old look of raw pleasure, but a new expression of vague recollections. While in the past Komaru would look at her face at the moment of ejaculation, he now began to close his eyes as if trying to retrieve from his fantasy somebody else. And she was right in principle without knowing that, yes, the body was hers, but the image was Mahina's. And in fact Komaru began to apply to Melissa what he wished he could have done to his sister. The adjectival explanation had in fact eased his guilt complex. It was simply an 'incestive', a lateral relationship. Thus, it had no strong classical literary heritage like the vertical, or the incestuous, one, at times even represented by its alternate term 'incestual'. There was so little time that night, but the circle had been completed barely within a small diameter of interaction, especially when Mahina had taken over in the successful attempt to satisfy not only her curiosity, but also her first full orgasm throughout all the organs of sensitivity, including the brain. Komaru wondered if the naked body of a Christ, and a bloody one at that, would ever trigger anything comparable to the real McCoy. Well, why not? It was a matter of faith, and beliefs could move not only mountains but also hymens out of the way.

Chapter 35

The discussion on the thesis that took place between Melissa and Komaru the following day was a stormy one since she wanted him to adhere literally to the *MA By Thesis Prospectus* issued by the University of Victoria History Department. Komaru had already completed the required courses the year before, thus it was a matter of presenting a thesis of about 50,000 words 'based on a programme of independent research.'

There was a problem, however, stemming from what Komaru understood by 'independent research' as a function of the subject-matter covered by the thesis. There was no doubt that Komaru had performed plenty of research delineating a theory to be applied to the original topic which, fortunately or unfortunately, he had not yet submitted. The last two entries on the MA Proposal Form were clear enough, namely, 'Discussed proposal with ...', and 'Proposed topic ...'.

Through the kindness of Ms Lennie Hapes, the morning secretary, Komaru had made an appointment over the phone with Dr Liesel Barnes on a tentative basis. Because of Komaru's studies in Shanghai and his interest in Chinese history, he had also planned to contact Dr Lurline Simpson to get some suggestions for an external reader within New Zealand. Of course, the Chairperson was always acting as the Chief Examiner, and as such he had full power for a final decision.

Before reading his father's papers, Komaru had in mind to develop his MA thesis around the concept of the decennial invisible hand performing nearly catalytic feats under the quasi-cabalistic Power of Nine as derived from Chinese astrology and applied to cultural history. That meant, naturally, the usually complementary baggage with a Summary preceding the Preface. The Table of Contents was supposed to be sketched to present a visual and topical balance on the subject-matter before a Conclusion was attempted in order to validate the premise outlined in the Preface. And, finally, Footnotes referring to Bibliographic Data, in addition to Explanatory Notes, were supposed to be an integral part of the whole rather pompously erudite presentation of an essay in futility. Acknowledgment of help received, permission to quote copyright matters, lists of abbreviations, thanks to some undergraduate professors, computer-generated charts, figures and other graphs would place the final seal on the thesis.

After reading his father's work, basically what Komaru knew by heart since childhood, however, he decided to consider presenting a thesis on the history of his country, namely, Ao Tea Roa, written by a Maori, in Maori, for Maoris and based on Maori sources. The fact that he preferred to spell the name of his *whenua* as 'Ao Tea Roa', rather than Aotearoa, meant that he was a language purist displaying the analytic structure of complex concepts rather than the synthetic and utilitarian forms preferred by missionary and colonialistic non-native Maori speakers. For example, Komaru would always write 'waka huia' and not 'wakahuia'. After all, Maori was not German, and even in American English the lexicological compounding process created schizophrenic situations presenting at least three stages exemplified historically by the progression of 'foot ball' to 'foot-ball' to 'football'. That led to ambiguous social interpretations of latter-day cases forcing one to accept 'girl friend' versus 'girlfriend' to mean just a female friend for the former and not a romantically attached female, as in the latter, at the written level since intonation is deleted in graphic expression.

Komaru's suggestion was so simple that people could not believe it. Yes, a Maori history as proposed by him had never been written in Maori for the reason that there was no need for it, even if all oral documentation had been printed not for them but for the Pakehas. Melissa was not against the idea in principle, but she knew the project was unfeasible because, first, no one in the history department knew Maori well enough to judge such an 'esoteric' academic work and, second, the disseminative value of such a thesis would be extremely limited. In fact, scholarly work in Maori was virtually non-existent. Even considering a so-called bilingual thesis, the very concept and title encountered obstacles of a practical nature. Basically, there was no need for Maoris to learn what they had already known for generations, and also the credibility factor for Pakehas would be nullified by their negative attitude to an extremely biased view.

The about-face made by Komaru regarding his original project was destined to fail even before being discussed. In reading the English version of the outline written by his father with Magic Marker on behalf of the Waitangi Action Committee, and analogously outlined to illustrate the contrast, if not the opposition, in black and white, Melissa understood the whole proposal clearly and comprehensively. But, again, to what purpose? Even if approved, would the work be accepted by the academic world well enough to warrant its cataloguing and shelving in the library of Victoria University? The impact on every segment of both the academic and lay communities would be mostly negative. There was no need to explain its obvious outcome. The faculty was still sensitive to allegations made between The First and Second World Wars as to the rather 'informal' standards of scholarship that barely passed the evaluation of an external committee on minimal credentials.

The whole afternoon was spent weighing pros and cons. And Melissa, though agreeing with Komaru, still fought to find a compromise solution. As a non-active scholar, she was trying to save a career. But in the course of the discussion, things got out of hand to such an extent that she, as a skeptical historian, gave up when Komaru convincingly brought up the rôle of Lucian in the historiography of Greek thought. Yes, Komaru knew of it along the typical sources from Herodotus to Toynbee. To what purpose? In fact, most of the historians covering the 19th century seemed to have disregarded the views of Lucian for at least two reasons. One was the assumption that he (AD 120–180) was not a historian but a satirist. Amusingly, Komaru agreed with that assumption, for he later convinced himself that historians ARE satirists of facts for the sake of recording vanity of and for themselves. The other was the fear that whatever Lucian had thought about history was so damaging as to pre-empt the field by relegating it to what Henry Ford stated 18 centuries later. Ironically, Lucian's work had once been appropriated by a historian of literature who stated that the satirist was a novelist. In essence, the critic in question had reiterated Lucian's view that all historical treatises are pure fiction, and thus there was no difference between a good novel and a historical account of an author's imagination.

Indeed, Lucian's treatise on history, ironically titled *True History*, was so satirical that later critics did not hesitate to classify it as part of utopic literature, along with Swift's *Gulliver's Travels* and Rabelais' *Voyage of Pantagruel*, as well as Cyrano de Bergerac's *Journey to the Moon*. Between Lucian and Bergerac, only Dante's *Comedia* escaped inclusion as pure fiction because, well, at least it had poetic and religious, if not ethical, values on the then-medieval world considered as a human 'universal'. Lucian did not beat around the bush, for his whole historical account since Cterias and Homer contains nothing but lies from beginning to end.' That was the only "true" statement accounting for the title of his work. This was not dissimilar from the most scholarly dissertation ever accepted in New Zealand academia on herpetology. The 373-page-long PhD *dissertatio inauguralis*, complete with Preface, Footnotes and Bibliography, had been explicitly formalised, and approved for publication, via page one with a seven-word sentence: 'There are no snakes in New Zealand.' That is how Komaru felt when, unless he presented his 'We are the keepers of Ao Tea Roa', another seven-word sentence, he would consider stopping that nonsense and dedicating the rest of his life to something else.

He would decide later, and he would inform the McTavishes accordingly. And he felt miserable, for Victoria University had been kind enough to grant him a bursary. But he resolved to re-imburse the university for all the money received. Komaru's decision was also influenced by the disgust he felt at the news coming from Bosnia and all the ethnic cleansing. That germ of cruelty had already infected humanity to the point of his disavowing it completely.

He would, however, fight for what he thought was still possible. Another generation of waiting in the wings and his people would fall in the pit of irreversibility, as the American Indians had already done. And before them the Basques, and the Mayans, the Aztecs, the Etruscans, and the rest, under the immediate government grants and the like in order to blindfold those few idealists still struggling until falling into the trap of materialism. Would *maori* Maoris become attracted to and spoiled by what the Waitangi Tribunal was trying to do, dispensing bonanza land as a method of controlling public dissatisfaction? He would not accept a penny from what his father had filed as a claim on the land of his ancestors. That is why he returned to sender each and every issue of *Te Manutukutuku*. Would non-*maori* Maoris become victims of that false sense of security by selling their souls to capitalism that in essence would fortify the Pakeha's economically entrenched position in Ao Tea Roa forever? Would these blinded Maoris succumb to what in the long run would be a slow and sure manner of dying, re-enacting the syndrome of moving from chronic rags to ephemeral riches via prostitution?

During his drive to Wellington, Komaru decided to change his life completely. He would visit with the Department Head and inform him of his intention to withdraw from the university for personal reasons. And, the day after his arrival, Komaru first of all informed the apartment manager that he would not renew the lease at the end of October. Then he called the McTavishes to ask for permission to have his mail forwarded temporarily to their home address until he could find a suitable small house or a flat somewhere in Wanganui. Accordingly, he made arrangements with the realtor regarding the sale of the Papakura home, for which transaction he had to be present on the day of closing. It was a busy Spring. There were two things to be taken care of, namely, contacting Mahina about sending her mail to Wanganui and instructing her to write in Maori whenever personal matters were involved, and to explain his move to both Ling-ling and the few friends whom he trusted in the Movement.

The explanation to Ling-ling turned out to be quite a session, for he realised that she had tender feelings for him beyond the pragmatic aspects of the relationship. As she was working in the Chinese community restaurant business, she told him she would not be unhappy to follow him anywhere and help him. In what? Well, she convinced him that, because of the sudden interest manifested by Kiwis in diet, food, eating out and health issues, Komaru should open a restaurant. The idea struck him as a sudden fire caught by a whirlwind. And he agreed that the possibility was exciting, especially when he vented it to the McTavishes. Melissa offered her help as a hostess, Bill as a food consultant and Ling-ling as the organiser. But she would have to move to Wanganui. She agreed at once. Wellington was becoming too metropolitan, and even racial against Asians, while perhaps Wanganui, being more Maori, would tolerate the presence of certain non-Whites as an index of being progressive or the like. Wanganui, in fact, was striving to become a city welcoming so-called diversity in ethnic matters. Surely, as long as Pakehas controlled the local economy and government via churches and newspapers, a sprinkling of 'Orientals' would not constitute a yellow peril. China was on its way to becoming a major business partner, Japan was already a giant in economic matters, Indonesia was following suit, and so forth.

By the end of August, Ling-ling had found an apartment in Wanganui. She was given full authority to lease a ground floor space smack in the middle of Ridgway Street, near Drews Avenue, a stone's throw from Moutoa Gardens. By October, Komaru had sold the Papakura house, had moved everything from there and Wellington to the *pied-à-terre* at the McTavishes, and held several meetings *à quatre* to organize the whole operation. He hoped to open the restaurant by mid-spring, and not later than the end of November, just in time for summer vacation, the tourist trade, and in anticipation of a winter international crowd for the ski season the following year.

At one organisational meeting, a difficulty emerged as to what type of restaurant it would be, and then its name as a function of its menu, and for whom. The rent was not expensive since the restaurant was not located near most of the others on the north-west side of Victoria Avenue. What type of crowd would patronise the restaurant? First of all, it would not be an 'Oriental' one. Too many Asian food eateries had opened in the downtown area. It was felt that the market was saturated. Komaru studied the 'dinner' crowd moving in and out of offices at midday, and thus he noticed that people would walk or drive away from the Moutoa Gardens area to find a restaurant. Also, tourists visiting Sargeant Gallery, the Wanganui Regional Museum, the War Memorial Hall and other public establishments would tend to move out of the area to take a noon rest. Thus, logistically, the locale had potential.

It was decided not to offer 'supper' meals. The agreement was reached to stick to American-type lunches with a high volume of quick meals, but 'formal' enough to allow people to sit down, relax and enjoy what was becoming in New Zealand a mania for the so-called Mediterranean diet. Suddenly, Kiwis did not regard garlic with discriminatory suspicion, olive oil as a laxative within the Pompeiian bottle syndrome, broccoli like rabbit food, and the like. Once the time frame was established, well, the rest was easy. Bill suggested a standard, almost pre-prepared assembly line of healthy food for which he promised to design a menu to be handled by the minimum personnel, with even a partial self-service 'bar' of salads and soups.

Then the selection of a name came up. What to name the establishment? Although it should reflect in a nutshell the type of food offered for culinary-illiterate New Zealanders, it was not to carry the name of any ethnic group. There were already too many adjectives of nationality floating around between Victoria Park and Queens Park. Bill suggested the craziest name, a blend of Mediterranean and diet, thus 'Mediet'. Melissa did not quite agree at first since it suggested a Med fly or something Germanic. On the contrary, Bill saw in it something noonish and middayish along a bastard Latin etymological line. Anyway, the complete title, 'Mediet Restaurant', looked intriguing enough to stand out from the typical eatery signs found all over the world. The pronunciation, when the name was shown to a few local business people at the Chamber of Commerce and other offices for the proper issuing of permits, yielded several results from 'Medyit' to 'Midit' to 'Meddy', among many. Only one person pronounced it [Medayt] like a quick succession of normally pronounced Med-plus-diet.

And so on 11 November, at 11:00, the Mediet Restaurant opened its doors to a curious and hesitant public. Previous announcements in the local papers had apparently succeeded in attracting a mixed crowd mostly made up of employees and business people working in the immediate area. Some tourists milling around waiting for cruise boats nearby also came to explore the new establishment. And even some affluent Maoris came out of curiosity since the restaurant had advertised for 'HELP' in order to staff the positions of cook, waiters and kitchen sanitary workers. Komaru was in charge of cooking with the help of two Maori women. The historian had become an assembly line operator who, instead of feeding the minds of humans for their mental sanity as to the past, became concerned with feeding the stomachs of those citizens in whose veins circulated the highest concentration of cholesterol on Earth next to the Americans.

It took some time to take care of snags, increase and decrease certain dishes according to the fancy of patrons, and even to alternate the daily presentation of certain items according to the days of the week. For example, it was found that, for whatever reason, on Mondays people eschewed anything containing meat and fish, but the latter was popular on Fridays. Revd Marsden had left a good Christian tradition in North Island. Animal source food, the little offered anyway, was preferred on Tuesdays and Saturdays. Of course, the restaurant was closed on Sundays, when people grabbed a snack along the waterfront of the Whanganui River.

The menu, designed by Bill, was almost a masterpiece of psychological food as a function of whether patrons liked to be served or help themselves at the so-called salad bar, where greens were only nominally present. Prices were fair, and the food, although not an extensive selection, was tasty, novel and easy to eat with either a fork or a spoon. Bill had found that, perhaps under the trans-Pacific tendency to avoid eating tools as at McDonald's and similar establishments, patrons avoided knives, especially when dishes called for coordinating them with a fork. The two-handed grabbing of mastodontic items to be attacked as in prehistoric times had surely made a return to the original Maori habits of bringing to the mouth victuals of any vegetal or flesh sources, but it was not to be coped with at the Mediet. Bill, studying US habits at table, felt that Americans were still afraid of being caught by the Indians and were thus in a hurry to eat with two bare hands, forcing any large item into an inadequate mouth. The human food brought to the lips or the teeth looked as if designed to feed large quadrupeds. And Bill, the psychiatrist, had a theory of his own obtained by observing a triple-decker hamburger from which pieces of still green tomato, eye-burning onion, processed cheese, fatty meat, tasteless lettuce and who knows what else, runs away from two hands along with juices impregnated with mustard, ketchup and vinegar dripping like blood from a lion's mouth tearing apart a wildebeest.

The theory beyond the menu was that of having on it a standard list throughout the week, but also different items each day within the total selection. Thus, Bill obeyed in general the classical principles of labour-used/products-readied versus customers' satisfaction/cash flow. He summarised them for Komaru as follows:

1. Design the use of components, for short- or long-term, on the basis of minimum labour and minimal refuse. For example, in the case of fresh salads it is more economic to use pre-packaged greens received from a wholesale supplier rather than employ raw components, yielding about 40% rubbish and its consequential expensive disposal.

2. Organise the basic soup offerings by parboiling and freeze-storing small non-long pasta, rice, potatoes and other starchy items on a weekly basis, so that each can be used immediately by either wet or dry methods before placing them in the warm 'deck' containers ready to be selected from and mixed by patrons.

3. As a function of Item 2, do something similar for collateral and complementary legumes, including lentils, various beans, peas, garbanzos and others. Patrons could combine their own 'soup' or 'stoop' the way they fancied at the moment of selection at the bar or at table from, say, rice and *cannellini* to *stelline in brodo* to mashed potatoes topped by *ricotta*.

4. Display well in evidence three soups to be selected in isolation, such as mushroom, onion or tomato, as well as in a potential combination with each other or with anything from Items 1–3, done by patrons. Croutons, flavoured or unflavoured, should be ready at the end of the soup line for immediate use whenever no other component is desired.

5. Limit animal source protein to one type per day, from *spezzatino d'agnello* to beef *ragú* to *fricassée de volaille*. On Friday a two-type selection from chopped *toheroa* to shelled *pipi stufatino* would be present in place of two animal sources.

6. Place one or two trays of steamed, unseasoned cruciferous vegetables, from broccoli to cabbage to *rapini*. Next to them, one or two containers of hummus and/or diced *kumara* in vinaigrette. This, a concoction suggested by Ling-ling, proved to be one of the most popular items for both Pakehas and Maoris.

7. Present only one type of European bread per day, namely a different 'shape' with a preponderance of Italian regional specialties, from small *ciabatte* and slices of *focaccia* to hot *pagnotte* and *panini* among others, all made with whole wheat flour as supplied on a contractual basis by a local European baker for nearly all the restaurants in Wanganui.

8. Label clearly deep stainless steel vases containing diluted *aceto balsàmico*, virgin olive oil ('Imported from Italy' as one prepared by Bertolli with restored 'virginity' through chemical manipulations), and nothing else for green salad condiments. Use Turkish, Spanish or even Moroccan olive oil for cooking. Keep a sign well in evidence saying: WE DO NOT USE ANY ANIMAL FAT IN ANY COOKING. BUTTER IS RESERVED FOR EXPORT IN ORDER TO HELP OUR NATIONAL ECONOMY. HOWEVER, ANY PATRON DESIRING THAT CHOLESTEROL EMULSION WILL BE PROVIDED WITH A WHOLE 50-GRAM INDIVIDUAL SERVING UPON REQUEST.

9. For dessert, the standard item was a French/Italian type of apple pie devoid of eggs, as for any other food prepared at the Mediet. Basically, it was a flat soufflé-looking shape without a shell and with the flavour of the universal Lievito Bertolini Vaniglinato that could be served cold in summer or warm in winter. Theoretically, patrons could stuff themselves with that torta at 'dinner' and still the restaurant could make money. Each ingredient for every dish was indeed 'Product of New Zealand' except for some spices and the olive oil. Formaggio parmigiano as a condiment was a *tapu* in order to avoid animal fat on everything prepared as in Northern Italians restaurants, and to camouflage insipid decorative dishes with one single cover-all flavour.

10. Under no condition is any food allowed to be taken home, even when left from a meal served at table, simply for sanitary and insurance reasons. In a litigious society like the Kiwis', anyone can allow food to become spoiled, get sick and sue the restaurant for food poisoning. That is why, when patrons such as the

handicapped and elderly were served at table, only small portions were brought out with unlimited seconds offered until the patron was satisfied. That precaution is to be observed, particularly when the special of the day on Friday, hot minnow fritters with yogurt instead of eggs, are served and consumed at table only. Of course, in certain cases some individuals may sneak out with a few fritters in their pockets or purses but, since the restaurant does not furnish any containers, the olive oil leaves quite a mess as proof that the establishment is not responsible.

Well, the revolutionary approach to that type of non-restaurant, actually a buffet, was an instant success. Komaru could not help remembering when Melissa took him out to the Cosmopolitan Club, the evening of his seduction. There were several reasons for the acceptance of the health conscious-people meals, beginning with the 'reception' at the door and at the table, almost European fashion. In the former situation, the elegant, smooth, inviting presence of Melissa suggested a pleasant and semi-flirtatious atmosphere *more gallico*. Sporting a loose white silk blouse and a tight, short black skirt over long ivory legs, and exuding her favourite Brazilian perfume, Melissa attracted men of all ages with her personality stressing Cambridge English for Pakehas and milk-white top-of-breast skin for adventurous Maoris. A couple of times Melissa received the pragmatic glances of a few sheilas dressed in black leather suits. In a week, the whole Wanganui 'Club' had discovered the Mediterranean diet, and diners arrived half an hour early to avoid waiting in line for a table.

The other receptive formality was designed for both pre-stomach filling and to control the flow of patrons at the table with the presentation of a plate filled with *bruschetta* to be shared by a group of diners. That took the place of bread and butter as free cover food and the cheapest 'antipasto' utilising day-old bread, over-ripe tomatoes, mashed garlic remaining from the previous day, olive oil removed from bottle bottoms for thickness, and whatever dried or fresh herbs floated around, at the discretion of Maori cooks. The *bruschetta* phenomenon took Komaru and every other person in the establishment by surprise. The breakfast food eaten by poor people had become a phoney 'cordon bleu' gourmet treat under the Southern Cross sky, as it had begun among naïve American yuppies. Its economic impact and return was fantastic. By the time patrons stood in line at the buffet table, after being served that filler at their own table, their stomachs were nearly saturated by proletarian food resembling a semi-dry and barely tepid quickie pizza without any protein. No alcoholic beverages were allowed in order to avoid potential jovial situations, as well as to cut down on glassware labour.

The fare was standard NZ$10 for self service at the buffet, and NZ $12–14 if served some special dishes at table. Depending on the exchange rate, the food was quite a bargain for Yankees when the US dollar was exchanged for two New Zealand ones. The food selection for anything served at table was rather meager, but non-Kiwi, ranging from *risotto lampo, linguine all'avocado, penne alla montanara* and couscous *alla parmigiana* devoid of cheese but laden with baked vegetables. On Saturday only, and for patrons served at table exclusively, Komaru prepared *lasagne alle melanzane*, a simple meal containing the ribbon pasta interlaced with marinated eggplant *sans fromage*. The flavour of the baked eggplant dressed with garlic and roasted red and yellow peppers was unique and appealing to health conscious diners.

And diners began to arrive from all over, including faculty and students from the Polytechnic Institute, and from towns such as Palmerston North, New Plymouth and Taupo. Two unexpected visitors came to pay a visit just before Christmas, coincidentally with some preliminary disturbances by Maori students at the University of Auckland. The pair was noticed by Ling-ling while she was supervising the refilling of the buffet containers. She informed Komaru, who did not take long to recognise the two individuals as the same who were milling around at his father's burial ceremony. They dressed the same, in dark suits and glasses. Komaru knew immediately that he was being watched and, not to worry Ling-ling, he only said: 'Amazing how small New Zealand can be.' There was another appearance, a pleasant one, by Whina from the sanatorium on her way to Wellington for a vacation. Oh, how pleasant to have her in town! She asked about Mahina, and that gave Komaru a jolt since he had almost forgotten her.

Thus life, after beginning to flow slowly at first, but in a geometric progression for the business, started to stabilise itself at the economic and personal levels as conditioned by the constraints of place and time. Only rarely did Komaru feel assaulted by reminiscences and concern about Mahina, to whom he had sent, more or less regularly, short notes, photographs, and newspaper clippings about his restaurant business.

On her part, Mahina had posted cards from Vancouver, B.C., from Rome, and from Assisi. Then a letter came at the end of October. In it, she described her return to the States, the Maori teaching experience, the MA programme in the Department of Philosophy, but most of all her contacts with the Sisters – most of them old – at the Western Vocational Center of the Portland Convent. In fact, her experience there became so consonant with her new life, to the point of considering the Sisters' offer to move from her dorm to the convent itself. Details in Mahina's letters were scarce, though enough to provide Komaru with the development of her activities. In a November letter, just before Thanksgiving, Mahina informed Komaru that by Christmas she would move into the convent as a near-novice. The only concern she had was in obtaining a 'green card' on the basis of her employment at university, whose administrators wrote in her favour, anticipating a second year extension of teaching Maori in conjunction with English for Polynesian students. This required her to take some linguistics courses in the Department of English. In the November letter, Mahina asked Komaru whether he had received her letter from Venice. Apparently, she was concerned about it. He faxed back asking for details. No, he hadn't. And she had posted it some time in mid-August to his Wellington address. What had happened to that letter?

The mystery was explained on Christmas Eve. Among some correspondence still at the McTavishes, he found a letter whose postal mark showed 'Venezia – 17 VIII 1992 – 30124.' What had happened? He knew that the Italian postal system was the most chaotic one on Earth, worse than what the International Postal Union had declared in the former Yugoslavia. Probably, the letter had reached New Zealand at the time Komaru moved from Wellington. In fact, it had first been routed to Papakura, and from there to his Wanganui PO Box, at the moment he had applied for one in order not to flood the McTavish home with his mail. Anyway, it had taken more than 4 months to reach him, a thick envelope that, in spite of being marked 'VIA AEREA – PAR AVION', must have been shipped by surface.

Mahina's letter could not have arrived at a worse time, when he had expected and hoped not to hear anything from anyone. On that Christmas Eve, the McTavishes invited him and Ling-ling to a party attended by a few friends and all the restaurant staff. Komaru, who had meanwhile moved to his own small house shared free of charge by Ling-ling, was confronted by that missive just before guests arrived. For the first time in his life, although loathing the religious implications and the American-style commercialism from which Melissa could not escape with all the silly decorations and meaningless carols,

Komaru felt desolate, sad and dejected. In part this emotional situation was compounded by news from Auckland. Some of his 'friends' had planned to initiate a student 'revolt' upon returning from the winter break and in particular at the beginning of the new academic year. It was felt that the year 1993 would be one of inception at the vociferous political level. It was high time for young Maoris to counteract the rather successful campaign being waged by the Waitangi Tribunal enticing 'natives' to file claims as hush money. And many Maoris who had never seen so much affluence began to receive land, fishing rights and monetary compensation simply for the asking, regardless of actual connections with their forefathers' specific ownership. The Tribunal was almost in a hurry to begin intensifying its giving of material possessions in order to show good intentions and to strengthen the impression of 'excellent' race relations.

Just before supper, Komaru asked for permission from Melissa to rest a while in his former room. She understood Komaru's state of mind. It is said that only mistresses and mothers can read men's minds. And Melissa knew that Komaru's mind was in agitation. Indeed, with all the busy work stemming from the restaurant, it had been a period of nearly two stressful months, during which she refrained from invading Komaru's psyche and body. She was now his real friend. Checkov was right in declaring and accepting the three-stage progression of human relations between a man and a woman. Besides, being so enmeshed in the success of the restaurant business, Melissa had, well, not slowed down in her *goût pour l'homme*, but had simply engaged herself in another liaison, and this time with a person older than she was. In part Melissa had shifted her nymphomaniac activities from the quantitative to the qualitative. Among the array of men encountered on a nearly regular basis at the Wanganui Club meetings, Melissa had met, and begun to cultivate a relationship with, a failed writer of Italian extraction. He had never published anything, and he did not have the stamina of a younger stud like Komaru, but he possessed the *savoir faire* of a researcher considering Melissa as a rare butterfly specimen in his obviously scholarly approach to life. At the sexual level, being older, he had gone past the premature ejaculation stage, and that physiological condition gave Melissa time to reach a half dozen orgasms while the Australasian Marcello Mastroianni HAD to take his time to reach the nearest peak available along the range tramped by Melissa. The other incipient phenomenon was her hinting and suggesting subtly that Komaru should get married, that he needed a good wife, a lifelong companion and the like, something that he could not even conceive of. But when Melissa suggested specifically that Ling-ling would make him a good wife (and here he laughed at the peculiarities of the English language, thinking of himself as 'making her a good husband'), he considered that possibility a good one. Surely, Ling-ling was not Aphrodite, for she regarded sex as the preparation of another Chinese meal in her rather limited menu of gourmet dishes, but, after all, were companionship, home, comfort and social stability to revolve merely around the activity performed by a penetrator and a penetratee? In fact, holding in his hands that missive from Venice, he could not escape recalling Mahina being first subject to his once-in-a-lifetime 'encounter' as a penetrator, and similarly so when the penetratee took the lead in becoming such. However, those two unique 'fleeting encounters' had sealed the workings of his mind forever. Nothing in the world could ever erase the memory of that long winter night pregnant with the atmosphere of a morning execution, as if the condemned man had been granted his last wish.

In the McTavishes guest room, while friends were partying in an effort to have a jolly good time, Komaru had a feeling that the Venice letter was more than a missive of 'chat news'. His hands were trembling, his forehead was sweating and his stomach was rumbling. The canned music from Melissa's European repertoire was drifting downstairs with its sweet, sentimental tunes for brains conditioned since childhood to savour the nullity of a festivity centred around a carpenter's son who had inherited from his father the skill to build. Indeed, the Nazarene had been able single-handedly to erect the most complex structure spreading throughout the four corners of the world. *Pax in terris hominibus bonae voluntatis.* What a hoax! Who were all these people who confused *voluntatem* with *stultitiam*? How could that mass indoctrination survive for 20 centuries in a melting pot of refined mythology? How could Judaism change its hide into sheep's clothes, and still remain as a leader of minds at the expense of a billion opiates? 'Quandu nascisti o Ninnu a Bettelemme, era menza notti e parea menziornu.' Of course, it was midnight, but it looked like noon. Simply a matter of faith, the faith that Mahina had espoused blindly for her own peace of mind as a *femina bonae voluntatis*.

Chapter 36

Dear Komaru,

I am in Venice with Tanya. This 'cover' note is being written while we are waiting for the most expensive cup of tea at a table just outside the Caffè Florian, a world landmark. I hope I can post these pages, sort of an intimate diary for you, tomorrow from the C.P.O. near the railway station.

Love, my love, I miss you so much that I am afraid I may succumb to the avalanche of feelings I have for you and the whole world of love in all cultures, whatever its expression. As you can read in the enclosed, it is a struggle for me to write, and in English, because I just can't say anything in Maori. The irony! The very language of myself, of our *whenua*, is impotent in its attempt to come to the forefront of its many purposes among humans, that of establishing a bridge of inter-uniqueness between me and you. On the one hand, I am Polynesian, an island spirit sailing the waves of affection, and I am so more than ever because of you, through you, and for you, while on the other I find myself 'westernised' to the point that I have undergone a crisis of conscience at many levels: culturally, linguistically, and emotionally.

Oh, Komaru, darling, here in Piazza San Marco everything is so quiet, almost eerie. If I were to choose an ideal place to die, this would be it. A place to glide down and away unknowingly into the infinity of the most precious realm of feelings of tenderness, of tranquillity, of communion with the ineffable. Most Italians are away from their usual dwellings for the so-called Ferragosto, sort of our January period for resting and vacationing. When the bell nearby struck 6 o'clock, even the pigeons remained frozen in the square, almost as if trying to absorb the series of grave tolls reverberating softly over the lagoon. How many millions of people have registered in their hearts the phonic symbol of that bell? Just think, two centuries ago Casanova was still alive at Dux Castle, and I wonder whether in the evening he would 'listen' to that bell after being conditioned by its note of despair. Why is it that, when human beings are so close to a perfect state of unexplained happiness, they seem to sense the fugacity of its ungraspable essence? Is it because nothing remains static in us, not even in our intentional and conscious will to freeze even a micron of that happiness-time forever?

While I am writing, Tanya feigns reading a brochure, and I know that she observes my every movement and mood as if she were concerned about my state of mind. Although younger than I, she has assumed the posture of an older sister, with maternal bouts of protection. You see, she has already gone through life with many intimate experiences resulting in frustration, confusion and unhappiness for having covered almost all the range of 'contacts' since puberty. It is not her fault for, although born and raised in a conservative family, she nearly perforce underwent the growing up routine of expected 'maturity' BEFORE she entered college. As a typical teenager in 'America the SEX', she grew up without having the least idea about celibacy. And here I don't mean mine or that of any person temporarily going through it until marrying, no. I don't speak of chastity as a vowed status of mind and body. I refer to the American idolatry of sex, the most 'visual' expression of contemporary culture resulting from the vulgarity of communication. Just imagine if I had started along the same highway of experiences, at age 16 or so, as the majority of schoolgirls do. For Americans, sex seems to be the *ne plus ultra* for everything, from good healthy habits to happiness to approval from society. If by 16 you haven't spent many nights with different men, well, you are a freak. And I wonder about myself. I can tell you now that, selfishly, I wouldn't mind having had it so early, but ONLY with you. Of course, my words here are simply retroactive insanity. But if I had grown up in America, I would have avoided the glorification of casual sex as an operation involving a daily routine activity of your body, like going to the loo. How can teenagers acquire the essence of 'love' when at times even a lifetime is spent understanding it? I have been trying to understand Tanya, and she does the same for me. At times, when I feel desolate, I allow her to come to me during the night when I toss and turn. Don't be shocked. We are NOT lesbians. The encounter is not pathological, but simply conditioned by events for two reasons. She may perhaps find in me what she never got in men, that is, an 'intellectual' love, even a radical one, though she is sensitive to my body.

Visualise her, a blonde, white skinned individual who may see in me (though always in the dark) whatever her imagination prompts her to acquire when gluing herself to my body. As for myself, I attempt to uncover in her what I recall from you, but it is futile except for some incomplete gratification. With Tanya it is like a meal without condiments, for, no matter what, she is a female. I cannot detect in her the maleness, the smell of a man's hormones, like yours, the sweaty fragrance of a tamed animal as I can detect in you. With Tanya it is always a feminine interaction, mostly at the touching level. Only once she wrapped a banana in a plastic bag and, after coating it with a cream, she played with me, but not satisfactorily enough as I can imagine now after I galloped astride you for the only ride I ever took.

Now that I am in the process of 'renouncing' all those neurologic manifestations via one of the three vows, I simply wonder while I am writing you, rambling. It seems that the waiter forgot our tea. The orchestra has begun to play for a few stray cats like us. Oh, yes, I can just imagine Rossano Brazzi arriving at any time and speaking Maori to, sorry, I can't remember her name. Oh, yes, Katharine Hepburn? Did she renounce sex as nuns do upon entering a cloistered convent after Spencer Tracy's death? Once I renounce, I will adhere to it. Rather cryptic this verb of renunciation for, as I recall, it is derived from RENUNTIARE, which means to claim again and again. The RE- is clear enough, thus I wonder how many people understand the 'positive' meaning built in it, rather than the negative connotation carried by English. I think the waiter forgot about us, or he simply knows that we can linger here. What we are waiting for here is not to drink the beverage, but to find a speck of eternity in a dead square that never dies in the memory of those who sojourned here even for a second. I wonder if ever Byron remembered his sister waiting for a cup of coffee.

And here I am, dreaming like the millions of human beings who were here trying to grasp a micron of immortality hovering on this unique spot of Earthly life. I am mad at myself for having allowed my emotions to take over everything of which I am made. I thought I was strong enough to take care of a whole programme of actions as if computerized. How can I when your presence is around me – and in me during every second of my non-sleeping time, the little I have had in the last few weeks?

If I were not ashamed of myself, of admitting defeat, of allowing my heart to dictate the beats of reality, I would take the first plane back home. But how can I after having committed myself to graduate school, my work, everything professional? How can I dismiss even the minimal commitment of social responsibility just for the sake of my selfish interest, of the demands of my affection for you, of the drive of my flesh anxious to touch yours? At times I feel that the only way to know that I exist is based on knowing that YOU exist first, not me. A come-lately-Cartesian would say: Tango, ergo sum.' So, what have I done to deserve the creation of this chaos in me ... sorry, the tea is being served. Only $12 (US) dollars per cup ... the cheapest surrogate to be so close to the gates of heaven, and of hell.

So, I'm sending you by pigeon mail all my love, both Western and Polynesian, honging you and labialling you at the same time only once as we did while I was trying to get unseated from the saddle of fury by hanging on for dear life at the mane of a wild horse of memories. Here I have assembled my travelogue.

Vancouver, 1st August

Dear Brother, dear Sun, dear Komaru,

I don't want to add your, our family name close to your baptismal one – were you ever baptised? I doubt it – but 'Reti' would create a mess more than our 'first' names. I remember how puzzled you were at Mangere when I arrived from Portland with Tregear's *Comparative Dictionary* in my hand. This is what I read on the plane all the way from Portland. And the stupid look of that sheila at Customs. Look at it, please, and keep it as a scarce object. I left it next to father's *Moby-Dick*. Read about the previous owners, one being a Lucille McMahon from Honolulu, if I remember her name correctly. But more than anything else I recall the inscription written almost to this very day a century ago in a brown ink fading with age by a certain Alex Armstrong, Lieutenant Salvation Army, on the back of the hard cover – be careful, it is falling apart – and then the following on the first cover page: 'Naku Na Ringaringakaha Te Ope Uhakaora.' And the date! End of last century: '8/8/92'. Komaru, in a few days, one hundred years ago. *Ringaringa*, my magic word, from the hand, the arm, your hands and your arms embracing me for such a little time, and now embracing me forever, especially in Hawaiian as anything soft and yielding to the touch as your lips; sticking to, adhering to, as my skin to yours, and quotations from *Polynesian Mythology* by Grey. Oh, if that book could speak! Don't lose that fragment of white soft fibre, almost like cotton. It left an imprint on the page listing the CONTENTS. And what is the function of RETI in our *whakapapa* ... a man who was taken by Parawhenuamea upon the raft or ark at the time of the Deluge – this damn deluge present in all cultures, is this Deluge the giant wave of nostalgia submerging humans into oblivion? At times I feel content with the second meaning, accepting a more *whakapapa*-ish explanation for RETI being an ancient chief who is said to have explored a large part of the world in the Matatorua canoe, which was afterwards sized by Kupe. Then, you see, our family, our *iwi* is so old that it precedes Kupe. Our blood is so old that it must flow like thick mud in the veins of our ancestors. The problem, Brother, is that 75 per cent of it is Venetian, or Slavic or hellish. What can I find out about in Kòrčula?

So this is Sister Moon writing you from the Vancouver airport, which in a way, the city actually, reminds me of Auckland, if it were placed near the Southern Alps, or am I homesick already? We are waiting to board, while I look at the night sky over the other side of the mountain range above which my 'sister' is slowly climbing to shine her good wishes for a safe journey across the North Pole. You know, I have been in Vancouver before, but this time it IS different because I AM different inside and out. And so changed that so far I have been able to send you only postcards. I find it difficult to write you actually, because rather than informing you about the things I have done since landing in L.A., I tend to record what I have been feeling for you from the moment the plant left Mangere. Suddenly, a sense of void, of disorientation, of fear descended upon me while, ironically, I was crossing the Pacific.

Sorry, we are now flying, ascending toward the sky of British Columbia.

Darling, my love, can you understand what I am trying to say to you as my brother? First, I felt not only guilty for leaving you alone, but also despondent for allowing myself to become alone. And now I am lonely, though surrounded by so many people neatly encased on both sides of me, and in front and back, like the calves in the stockyard of Palmerston North. I may be having some kind of panic attack, I ...

Sorry, Tanya was so kind as to trade seats with me, so I feel less threatened by whatever weighs on me, imagining that the aisle is a large motorway leading to an outside universe full of stars. The plane is banking now, and over the clouds I can see the Moon and some bright stars. Oh, where is my Southern Cross, where are you?

Pause. No, I do not want any supper. I can't even stand looking at the food tray. Lowering the little folding table from the seat in front of me tends to trigger a sense of overcrowding, of ... yes, claustrophobia. So strange, because I would not experience that if I were close to you, even if enveloped by your body all around me. God, please help! I wish I had the courage to grab my rosary and try to concentrate on one of its mysteries. I can't even recall what day of the week it is; but even if it called for the *Gloriosus*, I would be compelled to recite the *Dolorosus*, for that is how I detect the condition of my heart.

So, please, Komaru, let me imagine that I am by you, the closest possible to your body, well, because you have one, can I help it? As if I were to be sucked by all your pores slowly in an undetachable manner, without any chance of ungluing myself from you, until I become osmotically absorbed all the way to become one with you, confused with your flesh, and mixed totally with your blood. My God, what am I saying, when I am supposed to prepare myself, for I feel that way not for my brother but for my Spouse, Jesus, and forever. God, please don't worry, I'll never go back home. Be assured that I'll be your servant, for I know that my love for you is greater than for any human being on Earth. But you see, God, that I am burning on both sides of my existence? Yes, don't worry, it's a promise. However, please allow me to have just a few more vicarious pleasures before I become less sensitive as the distance from Komaru becomes greater and greater. I don't think I am the first among your noble daughters and spouses to undergo this torture. Do you remember María de Ágreda? Well, she was even younger than I am now, and she went through quite a period of doubts about the physiological power of her body.

Oh, thank God, thank you, all the trays are gone, and now the movie. Those silly movies injecting fantasy into the brains of satisfied stomachs. What am I saying? Thank you, it is dark, but I can't sleep. Oh, what I would give to sleep a few more hours next to Komaru. Just think, in my entire life I spent only a small part of a night with him but as an adult I will be near you for the rest of all my terrestrial and celestial existence. Perhaps some music, oh, yes, this headgear, and I can close my eyes and listen to ... no, no, NO! This is Mozart. God, you are punishing me, or at least testing me by allowing that electronic device to broadcast THE clarinet concerto! Did you have to do that to me? And to remind me of *Out of Africa*, and me Out of Aotearoa? Even the alliteration hurts, and leaving my lover alone dead, as if Komaru is dead. Of course, as far as I am concerned he is dead, because, God, I promise you, but allow me a few more reminiscences, yes the second movement, slower, so that it will last a bit longer, just in my imagination, for is it a sin? That is when I slowly descended onto him by barely allowing my flesh to receive him with all his needles pricking every square and cubic centimetre of my invisible self while I tried to expand my innards in pleasurable pain sending my brother mute signals of welcome, for, God, whom else can be trusted unless a member of the same *iwi*?

Poor Tanya, she senses that I am taken by an *atua*, that I have become *tapu* to myself, and now she is asleep peacefully with her head accidentally reclining on my shoulder, acknowledging the presence of her hair against my cheek. But how can it be so when she is blonde and you, God, are dark, or are you blond, too, or red-haired, or even bald? Do you ever get old and grey? But Komaru's hair is jet black and wavy, and each filament is almost soft. Only the pale overhead light on the other side of the aisle casts some artificial shadows, rendering Komaru's head like one of a Greek god. I hope you are not jealous, or even mad at me. What can you be afraid of, anyway? Those deities have already gone into oblivion, but you are here with me, longing to detach Komaru ... no! Why? Wouldn't you allow me, at least for a little while, to share you with him, or even him with you? You see, he is my brother, and he would never hurt me, and neither you, for my sake. Trust him. If you do, and I don't see why not, then there will not be any bad blood between, actually, among us because ...

It is dawn over Eastern Canada. I must have fallen asleep, for the overhead light is off. So I scribble this in the early light of the coming sun, as if Komaru shines on these pages barely enough for me to keep a more or less straight life. In a few hours we should fly over Ireland, then the coast of Europe and, finally, Amsterdam. Already three years have gone by since my last trip, and ...

Milano, 3rd August

It is Monday. Arrived here yesterday morning by train and rested all day. Our little pensione is in the periphery and served by those sneaky trolleybuses that are always crowded. And you had better act like the natives, for they do not observe any civility. It seems that they expect praises for stepping in front of you to get on the bus. I wonder what happened to their sense of urbanity in the capital of fashion. Well, who knows? Affluent commuters drive to work, which, thank God, begins late in the morning. Actually, we are lucky that most inhabitants have deserted the city, but the few left here still act as if afraid of being left at the kerb. What a strange city. Downtown gives one a sense of oppression with all the African refugees, like the Tongans of K-Road, and the more modern outlying quarters give one a feeling of unurbanity for there are no 'houses' anywhere ... just sections of cube-filled structures where tenants seem to be conditioned to live from birth to death. Actually, I can't say much about Milano, and neither do I care. Only yesterday afternoon we strolled to a nearby square where they held a yard sale, really an open-air market of 'antiques', yes, really good ones, though also memorabilia of past lives.

Tanya had a ball (as one would say in the States) meandering through the piles of junk. I left her alone while I stood by some tables full of books. I was determined not to buy anything. I don't intend to collect or to be bothered by material possessions. But, yes, Komaru, I came across a fantastic work, and I could not resist it. When I saw that old book in French, and after browsing through it quickly, I sensed it was a rare gem. I paid about 35 dollars US. But, last night I did not sleep after reading it, back and forth, over and over, as well as notes on the mysterious author, a woman from Lyon. A couple of times I felt like throwing it out the hotel window (incidentally the *Florida*, and I tell you it was HOT in that bedroom without air conditioning) or burn it in the sink. It looked like the devil had put that publication across my path to give me more hell than I could take.

The book, a paperback of yellowed, crumbling pages, was an 1875 edition published by a certain B. Blanchemain (who can forget that name, though it should have been an infernal 'noiremain'). The author, a certain Louise Labé, probably born between 1510 and 1520, when Portuguese sailors may have been eaten by our ancestors, seemed to be able to hide most of her personal life, but her works speak for themselves. I only got a book of her *oeuvres poétiques* containing the sonnets. The editor knew for sure she died in 1566. And what a woman! She must have had the personality of Chiara, i.e. Clare of Assisi, but in another direction.

Frankly, I did not know that during the Renaissance there lived women of that sensitivity, sorry, what I mean is, free enough to speak their minds. Nowadays, I myself would be hesitant to write, and publish, those hot verses. She was a poet in general, but her sonnets are quite something. Trying to compress into 14 lines her thoughts in hendecasyllables and to rhyme *in rima baciata*. Shakespeare would have been ashamed if he had known her or of her. Oh, Komaru, although we don't know much of her real life, we can read of her, as an open book, as a woman full of passion. She could be regarded as the Aphrodite of the Renaissance. How could I have missed her when I studied in Salzburg? Had feminists intentionally 'archived' her for the refined erotic description of her passion? Last night I read most of her sonnets. I think they are the very first to have been written after the avalanche of the Petrarchean tradition, and by a woman. Petrarch in comparison was wishy-washy, as Tanya would say of vacillating men. I do not know if these sonnets have been translated into English. It would be impossible to transfer into that language the power of emotion born between the lines. In Maori it would be easier, except for the rhyme. Perhaps one day ... oh, no, how can I? I could not remain objective, because you would jump up in front of me to create havoc. Maybe, if I think of Labé's lover as of you, or even Christ, I could attempt, but in vain, I know that. But has Jesus ever kissed anyone, or has he ever been kissed by a woman Labé fashion? Incidentally, does her family name trigger in you a false etymological wish – labé, labialised, labiomaniac? You can get an idea of what I mean. See what you remember from French beyond 'Frère Jacques' and 'La plume de ma tante ...'

> Baise m'ancor, rebaise-moi et baise,
> Donne m'en un de tes plus savoureux,
> Donne m'en un de tes plus amoureux:
> Je t'en rendrai quatre plus chauds que braise.

Now, look at the structure of these lines. They are two pairs of lips in 'kissing rhyme', not alternating, but in *rima chiusa*, enclosing a *rima baciata*. The *-aise* are the larger lips of a man enclosing the two smaller ones, the *-eux*. There are *quatre*, a *ménage à quatre* of lips burning more than the hell of passion. God, not even Catullus could have come near Labé if she had played the rôle of Lesbia. Komaru, may I tell you, as a way of translation, what I would ask you to do to me, and how much I miss using a sibling nose more often than our lips. We kissed so little, and still felt so much. Forgive me, but

> Kiss me again, 'biskiss' me and kiss,
> Give me one of your sweetest,
> Give me one of your most loving:
> I will return to you four hotter than fire.

You see how faulty and trite it sounds. The symbolism is missed since in English the '*en*' loses its sexual connotation within the wrapping up of four elements of pure orgasm. How can *savoureux* be translated into English? Tasty? I used a 'sensual' word, otherwise the closest term would have been a culinary one such as 'palatable', and this would have taken me closer to the cannibalistic subconscious eating of a lover as some lower animals do. You see, before you I had never been kissed by a man, and I know that I shall never kiss any other man. Perhaps Jesus. I wonder if Christ can come into my dreams and make me reach a stage of frenzy. Would that be a sin? I had better try to sleep.

Komaru, if you were here I would kiss you all over. Oh, it is hot. Tanya is not afraid of cooling off by sleeping *au naturel*. I still wear my protective halter as a shield, not to touch myself accidentally. Since you tore my *tiki* away, I feel extremely vulnerable. I wear nothing else. So the halter stops me from touching the third eye, the most sensitive *locus erogenitus* in my body because, although the scars have disappeared on the surface, they are latent, ready to resurface with the desire to be licked as if bleeding. Actually, they are like the invisible milk that I shall never have. I am happy that at least I had blood, and that you sucked it when it was carrying the fragrance of the roses stolen from father's arms. So, let me gallop with my fantasy, and by galloping I am at this very moment stradding you, and in so doing, my arms around your neck, and in so doing,

> Je t'en rendrai quatre plus chauds que ... the Milanese air of Ferragosto.

Assisi, 5th August

The bus brought us here last night. The Umbrian hills give an impression of coolness through the expanse of the panorama. Actually, the air here is more 'human', and undoubtedly less evil than that of the Po River plains. Leaving Milano gave me a better sense of hormonal balance for, between the pestiferous climate of Lombardy and the heat generated by reading Labé, I felt as if my innards had been seared.

And here I am, Brother Sun, at the Albergo San Francesco, of course. And to top it off, this hotel is on San Francesco Street. Where else could it be? Italians do not seem to mind naming anything after saints, madonnas, angels, archangels and even Christ. So far I haven't seen anything named after God (*Dio*), but I would not be surprised. The hotel has no restaurant, so we have discovered a medium priced one uphill, on the way to the Basilica of ... San Francesco. The owner is a middle-aged man named Carlo who, more than a host and a restaurateur, is a historian of everything and in particular food and wines. You should see the style of serving, the 'medieval' preparation of the victuals, the sedate and sometimes exciting ambience of welcoming cultured people. He seems to loathe the ignorant and crass type of tourist carrying a Reagan image of Hollywoodian assumptions via the almighty dollar. Definitely, the establishment is not for stomach filling people expecting third-rate Chianti and spaghetti and meatballs. Deceptively, it looks unpretentious from the outside ... two or three steps to a door flanked by cement urns containing a small bush or tree of some kind. But inside it is history, with mementos, photographs, items of continuity. You feel as if you could cut a chunk of history out of thin air and take it with you.

Komaru, this is a spiritual city. I feel as if I am visiting an old *pa* where the *wairua* of our ancestors left both visible and invisible imprints. I don't have time to tell you about everything we've seen in two days – all the religious buildings, churches both underground and over it, gardens where Francesco Bernardone may have composed the *Càntico* that is, incidentally, the very first literary piece, a poem, in an infant idiom that later became the national language of an ancient peninsula. Frankly, among the remnants of those medieval structures, I was most impressed by the atmosphere surrounding Chiara's existence. To me Francesco seems to have experienced a 'shell shock' syndrome leading him to an almost aloof detachment from social interactions, in particular with Chiara, who must have been his total 'love' on Earth. And he was for her the bodily representation of Christ, her most tangible *corpus* of both terrestrial and heavenly love. While he concentrated on organisational enterprises, Chiara stressed her abhorrence of materialistic pursuits. What is not seen in her as the characterisation of poverty should be interpreted as her detachment from anything material, for she was a spiritual being encased in a human body. Francesco was undoubtedly the prime motor at the inception of

Clarissan thought, that is, of what Tolstoy tried to do at one of the stations encountered in various cultures, but Tolstoy and persons before and after him (the last being Schweitzer in Africa and Teresa in India) did not have a pope behind to use and exploit Umbrian citizens for the continuation of temporal power through genuine spiritual endeavours. What I am saying is, I wonder what Francesco would have done without Chiara. And that is what I detected in visiting the convent of San Damiano. Its structure, inside and out, speaks in mute syllables – the dormitory where sisters slept on straw and where a 'mattress' was only used by old and sick nuns, the massive refectory furniture tied to the surroundings forever, and the right side corner where Chiara used to sit for meals that were more spiritual than anything else. Just imagine a woman spending more than 40 years as a recluse within those walls. And sick, deprived of what now we can't even conceive. We shudder at seeing conditions, or standards of living, in Burundi or wherever, but in San Damiano the conditions were worse. Amazingly, all those visible and tangible things have withstood the ravages of time, war, earthquakes, fire, vandalism and so forth. But for how long? What I am saying, how many more centuries, after seven of them, are those relics going to impress and inspire sensitive souls of humans interpreting themselves beyond one stage of animal life?

Poor Clare, how I empathise with her for all her suffering and all her struggles to be recognised by a male organisation at the Vatican, and to die just two days after Pope Innocent IV issued his *Solet annuere* approval. Just imagine if she had been alive during this century! You see, male dominated society for the last seven centuries has projected Francesco as the spiritual leader and so forth, but in him I see more a mystic and a visionary who would not act more than he could, although in all fairness I recognise that he confronted sultans and despots. But Chiara, Clara, Clare, she was the real fighter in an age when women were supposed to obey and stay home, as a tradition still observed among Southern Baptists in the United States, obeying husbands in complete submission and generating cannon fodder for Christian armies.

Just imagine, when she was so sick she could not even go downstairs, and was carried to a small opening in the floor of her dorm from which she could attend the Mass celebrated below. And everything, again, is exactly as it was at her death, between Francesco's mysticism, pacifism and externalism, and Clare's spiritualism, activism and internalism. While Francesco was a preacher–missionary at heart for the sake of an organisation, Chiara was a philosopher–teacher as you can read in her testament. A much more cultured person than the man whom she loved and esteemed, she nevertheless obeyed him blindly, for her heart was tied to his, and also because women at that time were conditioned by the social 'inferiority' imprinted at birth. In fact, her testament to her sisters is a philosophical treatise. It contains the seeds for Doomsday behaviour, a manual for the survival of the spirit, a constitution for the preservation of whatever may remain after all the biological carriers of thoughts and feelings are destroyed via the so-called advances of civilisation and technology conceived, incubated, and born in a Pandora's box for the pleasure of the Devil.

I will tell you more one day by post about my deepest impression: an aura of mysticism, religiosity, spiritualism, all born to last an eternity, though I realise on a purely philosophical basis that the concept of 'eternity' is simply a mechanism to keep humans from going insane when confronted with the observation of the night sky. Komaru, have you ever conceived what is up there in terms of super-duper zillions of light years? I avoid that contemplative drive that not even all the philosophers and the poor astrophysicists can ever imagine with their most abstruse theories. In Assisi, one can feel the presence of God, of ineffable peace of mind, whether God exists or not. As a matter of fact, if God did not exist, humans would be better off inventing It and keeping It alive forever, otherwise what explanation could they give to anyone asking for the meaning of life?

And that is why I am, among others, intrigued by the relationship between Francesco and Chiara. What prompted her to discard a life of comfort for a social wash out, a drifter, an outcast? If he were to live in the States, he would immediately be classified on the lists of the CIA as a terrorist. In a way, I understand, for if you were to do something similar as my Sun, I, as the little Moon, would not hesitate to gravitate around you for the rest of eternity even if I could not see roses blooming on the snow as Chiara saw when she turned around to take a final look during one of the few encounters along a winter trail. Oh, Clare, how I understand you. I wonder if Francesco ever 'touched' her on the cheek. And what she must have felt at that touch. That is why I cannot detach my impressions of Assisi at its realistic level, for the town struck me as a kind of tree onto which several grafts have been implanted, from pre-Roman times until recent years, since even last century's remodelling, innovations, repairs, etc. were made to accommodate schools and hospitals (and even a mental health sanatorium) in both 'pagan' and religious buildings. But how can one do similar things for the decaying human spirit?

You see, the Mediterranean peninsula possesses so many cultural fossils and live enclaves of past civilisations that, in certain towns, one can boast of more than one single personality to whom we should be grateful for leaving to us some of their cosmic and intimate concerns about the so-called human race. Assisi is one such dwellings in living stone where from time to time a branch yields one more human being. At times many, many centuries go by until genes seem to defrost themselves from a dormant stage, not unlike a Dalai Lama-like process of renewing continuity. In Assisi, if you can believe it, was born Propertius, the male counterpart, now that I think about the contrast, to Labé. He was born TWELVE centuries before Francesco. The parallel between the two spirits is uncanny if you place them near the *Musa poetica*, for Propertius, as we hear from Ovid, was the most elegiac poet of Rome. Oh, if I had the time to study at the comparative level the poetic foundations and expressions along this dyadic line: Propertius/Cynthia, Catullus/Lesbia, Francesco/Chiara.

At times I feel that Francesco sublimated his Earthly passion for Chiara in order to avoid one more sentimental deception. He was mute on that subject, though he must have suffered much in his youth from infinite pains of the heart. Although so different in many ways, the latter couple never expressed their intimate poetic creativity that can find its way only in some people whose extant literary monuments were barely collected from oral stage in a minimal fraction, as for our ancestors. And here I speak of Maoris, for genetically don't forget we are 'Italians' via the acculturation of Rome and Venice in a continuous process from Diocletian to Casanova and, amazingly, Mother Teresa. Poor Propertius, so many misfortunes! It looks like these are the creative sources of so many accomplishments of the human spirit. He had the personality, the haughtiness, the abrasiveness of a Dante. And he suffered accordingly, even like Virgil and Horace. But from what I remember from our Auckland courses on Latin poetry, Propertius suddenly emerged within Francesco as an anomaly along an Assisian *whakapapa* in spite of the fact that the latter did not know, or read, Latin well enough to celebrate the Mass. Nevertheless, we have 'records' of Francesco's *Opuscula Sancti Patris Francisci,* and among them the '*Lauda Sanctus*' from the *Laudes.* We know from Fra' Tommaso da Celano that Francesco read a lot as a late bloomer, for as a young man he preferred to study female anatomy instead of sacred scriptures. Augustinus' legacy seemed to constitute a *sine qua non* for later spiritual changes. St Bonaventura in fact reclaimed Francesco's *in posse* religiosity when he later retained what he taught as *continuae devotionis ruminabat affectu* like one engaged in 'continuing education' for adults who had missed the normal pedagogical training. But Francesco was intelligent enough to use inceptive 'Italian' as recorded, if not written, as the first sensitive expression of reaction to nature in a vulgar tongue after Classical Latin. Just think of Francesco if he had been at the Beehive in Wellington in front of David Lange and dealing with white doves among the many birds of Umbrian ecological preference.

After having suffered in a couple of local battles, Francesco understood how futile it is to fight as humans are still doing at this very moment in Bosnia, Somalia, along the Indian border, and within the Russian Federation, among others. It seems that humans prefer to be killed not near the frontiers of the mind but astride those imaginary lines made of swamps, rocks, mud, trees and sand among hidden landmines. So, in a way, Assisi sealed my fate as regards the germination of pagan erotic poetry that later became a platform for anti-war expressions of brotherly love. I could say that, although principles of pacifism can be found among poets in every early civilisation, and even as late as in Classical Greece and Rome, from Anacreon to Virgil (not that of the *Aeneid*, of course), in 'modern' times it is via Bernardone that we can understand the dictum 'Kiss peace, abhor war' in a new phonetically alliterative manner. Try to visualise Francesco at the United Nations as its Secretary General. I vaguely remember an 'interview' made by Mike Wallace with Francesco. I think it was published about 10 years ago in the *St Anthony Messenger*, a periodical I came across by chance in the college library. I recall only one question and one answer when Wallace asked Francesco whether he agreed with the slogan 'Better red than dead.' Diplomatically, he replied: 'Better love than fear.'

Of course, how else can we rid ourselves of all mental infirmities affecting contemporary society, all the neuroses that are now part of our daily lives, all the stress creating a cosmic malaise?

There is one thing I settled in Assisi on the basis of hard thinking after reading a lot and making a comparative analysis of what Brother Sun and Sister Moon did. The interview by Mike Wallace was part of the traditional tendency to regard the whole Franciscan 'philosophy' as stemming solely, or mostly, from Francesco Bernardone. However, as I said before, I can now positively state that without Chiara the prime motor of humanity would still meander in the darkness of *a*historicity. Even without, if not in spite of, her Vatican canonisation, Chiara surpasses by far her source of inspiration. That happens, of course, as a sanctioning of the typical torch carrying phenomenon in which the pupil exalts the teacher.

Chiara was a woman, but a special one who should not be regarded as a freak dominated by Francesco. Remember that although she joined him through a self-contained love characterised by 'nuptial mysticism', she was a free woman on its most pristine acceptation. She took almost a lifetime to reject the Rules of St Benedict, the Statutes of Cardinal Ugolino and of Innocent IV, but finally wrote her own for her sisters, the first time that the Rule of a seminal organisation was written by a woman. I still wonder how for the previous ten centuries women had to follow what men told them to accept as a mode of conduct.

Amazingly, it is still Francesco's writings that dominate the scene. Yes, he may have written or dictated quantitatively more than Chiara, but her writings are cast in stone for the liberation of all minds, all souls, all bodies, for potentially HALF of humanity. In fact, besides the Rule, she left only a few letters from correspondence with Sister Agnes, whom she never met in person, and her Spiritual Testament. This, I repeat, is the most pan-planetary expression of femininity carrying independence of thought, strength of character, and above all freedom in its most philosophical essence. You could say that I am partial to Chiara. Yes, indeed, I am because I don't know of any other woman before her who did what she did, in spite of the fact that for nearly eight centuries she was kept as an appendage to Franciscan thought. If you want to bring the yin and the yang, or something similar, into the picture, a normal polarity making up the whole structure of Terrestrial biological entities, well, remember that Chiara was the feminine pole of Franciscan charisma. Again, just imagine if she had at her disposal all the communication tools of modern times. But she succeeded nevertheless in freeing from psychological bondage the productive half of mankind for the benefit of everyone through love between a man and a woman. And that is why Francesco remained aloof, allowing her to share one single, meager meal after her longing for it for a whole lifetime. At times I even feel that he was scared to death by her proximity of both body and mind. He knew that probably he could not cope with the superior intellect of a non-male. So, he intentionally remained distant for fear of revealing to her the instability of his own emotions through love. I'm not saying it was a matter of *odi et amo*, no. But he surely made her suffer for so long when she needed the touch of a rescuing hand through at least overt moral support, for between the two Assisians it was a one-way street. Not that Chiara wanted a physical union to validate the whole stream of sentiments in both directions, but she was a human being who kept the tenderness of femininity always in full projection. She was not a butch, but a noble *domina* who suffered the curse of falling in love with a rather insecure man. Chiara made him a Mensch, and she spent two generations to create and keep afloat that image of *Übermensch* that led to his sanctitude. Just imagine, poor Chiara, what she would have given just to receive from Francesco a hug, a *hongi*, a full kiss between two rough lips of a tough man and the sensitive lips of a delicate creature! And she survived him to remember all the opportunities she missed for his own edification.

I hope I don't survive you. Can you imagine if I were to live for at least another generation after your death? I would feel like dying every day without knowing if you ever really loved me, or at least hearing from you from half a world away, if not a few metres away, along a winter trail hoping to see a miracle of roses blooming in snow, from whose thorns I still carry the scars in my bosom forever.

Komaru, tomorrow we will proceed to Venice. I'll write you at length on my way to Kòrčula, from our genetic 'home' that furnished the ovaries to my passion for you, whether or not you were or are just an accident of twisted fate.

Love from a converted Franciscan that allows me to sign,

Francisca

Chapter 37

When Bill McTavish knocked gently at the guest room door, he was not worried about Komaru, but just wondering whether he had fallen asleep. Running a restaurant for nearly a couple of months, not counting all the stress preceding its opening, had begun to take its toll. In addition, Bill guessed that Komaru was at times concerned with something that made him intermittently jumpy, extremely tense and vaguely sad. What could it be? Well, it could be a host of factors – his father's death, Mahina's departure, the abandonment of the Papakura family home, yes, but what else? At the human relations level things seemed to flow smoothly and as a matter of routine. Melissa, after her initially stormy 'blitzkrieg' on Komaru for the sake of satisfying *ad nauseam* her most wanted hedonistic pursuits, had, well, not slowed down her drives, but had engaged one or two more 'lab assistants' to take care of the slack created by Komaru's dedication to the success of the restaurant. She understood him, for she had become his friend, almost like a 'father' that he had never had. Finally, knowing that her relationship with Komaru could not lead to anything stable beyond being penetrated by a mono-generation physiological operator, she not only allowed him the freedom of taking the initiative if he so felt, but also transformed her interest in him into a motherly affection and Samaritan activity. Yes, the restaurant was doing well, and, for the most part, except for the novel food prepared for the health conscious people, it was Melissa who gave patrons their first impression of a 'classy' establishment through her almost overwhelming, and at the same time informal, welcome. Bill, who never appeared physically at the restaurant, as a psychologist was undoubtedly right in saying that the first impression is always right. Even Komaru brought up a Maori adage about the first eye contact, namely, the 'Kanohi kite kanohi' approach to a situation warranting, if successful, the sealing of an immediate 'ngawari' relationship because the 'seen face' is always more important than any other means of communication via newspaper adverts or even word of mouth.

Bill, thus, considered the Ling-ling factor. It was for sure a soothing one, for Komaru needed someone to take care of his household. This pragmatic dimension of daily life became functional as soon as Ling-ling moved in with Komaru like his 'Chinese concubine', although he was not married. And even Melissa approved wholeheartedly of that connubium based on a new international platform of necessity. The fact that most Kiwis saw in the Chinese the old 'yellow peril', as barbarians at the door of the second 'Home', well, was tolerated for the sake of economy. Having Maoris around as the consequence of the 'original sin' was understandable, and even 'Oriental' tolerable, but the idea of a genetic pollution between a Maori and a Chinese could be conceived only if seen like that already initiated by the Dallies, for they had brought into New Zealand many new dimensions of old culture, from oenology to dendrology to traditional family values. What could the Chinese bring into Godzone besides monosodium glutamate making Kiwis sick at the very thought of seeing it listed on Oriental ingredients for a savory meal? Well, Norwegian rats had been imported by Cook (*pace* the Crown), Italian lice by the Strombolese (*pace* McCullough), Christianity by Marsden (*pace* Kuini), and so forth. But from China, what except for Communism, the scourge of the 20th century? Amusingly, Komaru had to display a sign on the front window saying: 'WE USE NO MSG IN OUR DISHES' when a customer asked whether the Mediet food could cause any reaction to his allergies. He was afraid of MSG simply because he had seen Ling-ling supervise the salad bar.

No, Komaru was not asleep. He was sitting on the bed that had witnessed many engagements in Komaru's halcyonic era and he was simply trying to understand what had happened to that missive. Well, at least he was able to fill the gap in the sequence of events reported by Mahina, for she had mailed, also from Venice, a brief letter informing him of her departure for Trieste on her way to Kòrčula. No other personal matter had been covered by his sister. The heavy letter he had just read stood as a unique document of female liberation beyond all the parameters of the imagination, and it had taken more than four months to reach him. And in those four months he had been in despair at the thought of being forgotten by his sister in spite of her legacy, a legacy that had implanted a new seed called love. And, in fact, during those 4 months, Komaru, who had never loved anyone in his entire life, had begun to associate love with despondency, deceit, despair. Was love to be savoured only once and so remembered during a lifetime as the cocktailing of natural fluids along a whirl of uncontrollable emotions? Was he just a victim of humoural effluvia trying to discharge themselves at the wrong time and in the wrong place?

Now that letter had destroyed Komaru via the most constructive report ever received from anyone and for anything human. Even the underground Movement messages, obtained via the back door of the kitchen along with the food supply and refuse lorries, had taken second place. When Bill knocked at the door, Komaru had reacted almost as a cobra ready to strike at the intruder, for in his mind he had re-established full contact with Mahina. And he felt miserable for assuming during those months that he had been 'used' by his sister as Melissa had used him – as a tool of gratification. Now he was both happy and sad. Love had been manifested for the past, and sadness for the future with no future.

No, he told Bill, there was nothing important. Just a letter from his sister reporting from Venice. In reality, he had rested on the bed trying to account for the late arrival of that letter. Mahina had left Venice after briefly visiting a small island on the laguna where Francesco Bernardone had landed upon returning from the Orient. On that island, still crowded by the progeny of medieval poplars, he had meditated quietly for he was only in the company of his fellow traveller. But little birds joyously began to interfere with his meditation until told to move away for a while, which they did. But they came back after Francesco finished with his Hours.

In the process of meditating like Francesco, a doubt made its way into Komaru's mind. Had the letter been intercepted, and opened 'intelligence fashion' somewhere along the way, and if so, at what station? At the Wellington apartments, the Wanganui post office, or even on arrival at Mangere? Or, in spite of being marked 'VIA AEREA – PAR AVION' had it been posted by surface? Well, 'becauses' were not difficult to imagine, though impossible to pin down. And this bothered Komaru since the handwriting was on the wall: he was being watched. That did not really worry him much, for he had never left any trace anywhere about his contacts with the Movement. And, if so, well, let it be, for every young Maori student was automatically considered a suspect. What really worried him was Mahina's intimate details about her love for him, ironically in spite of the fact that he had never told her he loved her. Those 'confessions' were as dangerous as crystallized dynamite in New Zealand, for they could be used as a blackmail device if and when a threatening situation arose in a future confrontation that sooner or later would take place around Waitangi Day. Yes, now Komaru understood the position in which his father had found himself with his daughter becoming the mother of two New Zealanders. Yes, of course, his father must have had a hell of a time, a voluntary prisoner of silence for the sake of his children and to avoid a unique scandal in Marsdenland. And now what?

Bill did not ask any questions, but it did not take him long to notice how distraught Komaru was. However, once upstairs in the kitchen/dining area, Komaru acted normally enough to mingle with guests, mostly from the Mediet, and have a token buffet supper prepared by Bill with Ling-ling's help. Baby Jesus was not yet born according to Bethlehem's longitude, but Kiwis did not mind celebrating his impending birth – a matter of a few hours. Then tomorrow Christmas would sanction His arrival, and the scraps from feeding well-to-do stomachs would be left in boxes as an act of charity on the 26th. It was true. Charity begins at home with crumbs too edible to be tossed into the refuse bin. While Melissa took care of the crowd, Bill 'worked' a while on Komaru. And in that the psychologist asked for help from Ling-ling, who had become almost as loving as a puppy next to a Maori St Bernard carrying no flacon, but a promise of benevolence for a man in trouble. She had sensed Komaru's unhappiness, as well as his gratitude toward a new sister-in-waiting.

The guests began to feel in a festive mood, and a few groups formed here and there while wine flowed and music softly permeated the whole house. Melissa reigned like a goddess, sustained by her peat and malt beverage. Komaru, Bill and Ling-ling pulled a little away from the centre of the action toward the patio door, and later nearly all the guests invaded the orchard in full bloom. Flowers, buds and fruits trying to ripen in the late sunset of early summer, and the fragrance of food conferred upon the whole residence a feeling of well being. A gentle wind wafted the saltiness of the Tasman Sea along with the gulls pirouetting high in the sky. And the smoky odor of pork drifted over at times from nearby yards as if emanating from a fake *umu* for a Christian *hangi*.

The conversation centred on some practical events first, and later on semiprofessional matters. It had been a long time since Komaru had the opportunity to talk with Bill as in the good old days, and Ling-ling began to listen attentively to both men for different reasons. Three cultures were beginning to mingle through words and concepts, though Bill dominated the scene surreptitiously through age and knowledge. About the former events, Komaru was still fuming about another action taken by the Waitangi Tribunal. He had been baffled by the Sealord 'deal' between the Crown and the Maoris, and now another coup. It concerned the Settlement Act of 1992 for the Fisheries Claims. Well, simply, all claims had been aborted through a single act of dictatorship: 'This Act prevents the Waitangi Tribunal from hearing claims on commercial fishing or commercial fisheries.' How logical! Wouldn't you say so, Ms Shane, thought Komaru. A tribunal that TELLS itself not to hear claims. Simply absurd! What a charade! And he was glad he had not applied for a position, though he knew that some of his classmates, not necessarily consciously *kupapa*, had been hired 'to streamline claim processes' by abolishing all these processes. Komaru was disgusted at the about face, accepting thirty dinars for the sake of immediate gratification and to kow-tow to the Crown.

The second topic of discussion was based on Bill's reminiscences as a young man at the Swiss 'soapland' (as Melissa had called it by analogy with her own Kyoto experiences) managed by Carl Jung. Of course, Bill was too young to understand Carl's mental dysfunction. In retrospect, and for the benefit of Ling-ling who had fallen into the trap of *animus/anima*, archetypes and other lexicological inventions of old concepts formulated by Lucretius in Book III of his *De rerum natura*, Bill was saying that Jung had established a 'pro-fascist cult in which he intended to be worshipped as an Aryan-Christ.' Komaru thought of Mahina on her way to marry a Jew and to serve him blindly. Well, many Maori women had done similar things, and successfully, for in New Zealand anything is permitted as long as the elite looks the other way. The problem, according to Bill, was the fact that Jung engaged, first subtly and later overtly via signs and symbols chiseled in rocks as ineffaceable scriptures, in racism along anti-Semitic theories disguised as studies based on Oriental 'philosophy'. That is why, readers believing abstract and unprovable theories, became fascinated by abstruse and pseudo-mystical tenets appealing to women especially, giving them an excuse to engage in promiscuous sex. In fact, Jung, to console and enjoy himself, practiced polygamy openly. Who would censure a 'scholar' who had had the courage to break with Freud after being close, perhaps even too close?

Ling-ling was intrigued by that eyewitness history of scientific activities coming straight from Calvinistic Europe along with chocolate, cheese and clocks, apparently building one of the strongest economies in the world for such a small nation. She wondered if China could follow along similar lines. She had forgotten the rôle of the banking system that had hosted the storage of gold unhesitantly for the sake of privacy. Comments were then exchanged about Chinese traditions allowing a man to utilise their natural banks of pleasure at no interest. How would Ling-ling, as a Chinese, feel about those practices? She clearly stated that she grew up in a very strict society which, although Communist, did not even allow her to conceive of that libertinage. As a student, she could not even hold hands in public on campus. She felt that, by loving a man (and in so saying she looked at Komaru languidly) she would expect absolute fidelity. Komaru nearly laughed at Bill's subtle way of exploring, perhaps, the possibility of brainwashing Ling-ling into a *ménage à quatre* at home, without bothering with the always dangerous chances taken via the Wanganui Club facilities. And '*quatre*' jumped out at Komaru's eyes in Mahina's neat writing from Milano.

Yes, what a foil, said Ling-ling. Then Dr Jung had a secret life? Up to a point, though everybody visiting the Swiss 'monastery' knew what was going on. Jung imagined himself in a real Eastern monastery dispensing both wisdom and semen by copulating with women as a propitiatory rite copied from the many-breasted goddesses of Indian, Nepali and Tibetan pantheons. In essence, by analysing the two-tier system of Jung's life, both public and private, one could detect in him the reverse side of a Nazi coin, the same that allowed Hitler to be a Christian by regarding Christianity as a Jewish religion imposed on the people of Europe with the intercession of Vatican colonialism of the souls. Basically, according to Bill's retrospective analysis of his fallen God, Jung thought of himself as a late-come prophet destined to save modern man from the evils of civilisation by destroying it first and substituting for it a lot of jargon by copulation.

Ling-ling had become speechless. She had a high respect for Western scholarship of the mind, and she regarded Freud as one who, through his doctrines, liberated half of humanity from psychological slavery. Could Chinese women be liberated from all their complexes? Well, for Bill, even Freud was a case of 'self-inflation', believing in 'his-self' as being 'always right'. According to Karl Popper, misrepresentation by Freud was at times even intentional to prove a point, and in this he became so skilled, persuading almost anyone because people were *tabulae rasae*, and thus anything could be written about and accepted as 'gospel'. And that is why, as a consummate rhetorician, Freud was strong enough, after an American honorary degree, to impose all possible complexes on Americans via Psychology and Psychiatry, the first two Horses of the spiritual Apocalypse, the other two being Sociology and Sexology. Freud created more complexes in American society than its inhabitants. Consequently, Americans had been raised on cartoons as a defense mechanism based on humour. Groucho Marx was its sick interpreter par excellence. And cartoons continued to be the most intellectual section of any Sunday paper read after the Sunday routine copulation while the kids watched TV, and just before going to church to praise the Lord, followed by the Sunday drive to visit the mother in law. The consequences of this conditioning is witnessed in Americans' moody behaviour in politics (where changing a political party is like changing one's underwear), religion (shifting from one congregation to another is simply a matter of logistics), economics (investing by buying one minute and selling the next), and the like, as daily processes of life through the manipulations of the Fourth Estate. Bill said that Americans act and live accordingly in a continual fight to remain constant in their raw genetic drive to become inconstant, whatever that meant. Komaru saw in that instability a lack of dignity. It seemed to him that affluent nations had nearly everything they wanted as consumers, but they simply could not buy dignity as a people. Ling-ling countered by saying that it was not the case in China, for the Chinese always kept their dignity afloat even before 1949, when Mao was finally able to begin the restoration of what colonials had tried to steal during centuries of oppression. Yes, Ling-ling was right. Now Maoris could begin to grasp via the schizophrenic policies of the Waitangi Tribunal nearly all the things they could squeeze out via claims. But could they re-acquire THE dignity of proudly being, feeling, and acting as Polynesians, the dignity that had been lost on the 6 February 1840?

The following day Komaru spent Christmas at home. Melissa became nearly hysterical when Ling-ling arrived alone for the institutionalised dinner celebrating the arrival of a kid in a manger. Komaru tried to understand the logic of it all between the filling of a stomach via a hedonistic palate and the rendering of graces to a child who, had he known all the damage that would be done to humans in 20 centuries of war among Christian nations, would not have hesitated to sink into a Sudden Infant Death syndrome. Ling-ling understood how Komaru wanted to remain alone for a while in a beautiful relationship that did not have the overpowering impact of a Melissa or the overcharged emotionalism of a Mahina. In the case of Ling-ling, it was a soothing companionship between two human beings, one of whom happened to be a prickless entity.

So, Komaru read and re-read Mahina's letter in a state of near paroxysm. Intense feelings of guilt, emotions of repressed love, sentiments of unknown happiness and a cohort of intangibles succeeded each other in a most gloomy atmosphere of recollections. How many events had taken place in one year! He remembered that the previous Christmas he had gone to the beach with the McTavishes. And now he was trying to fly to Portland's beach of memories. He thought of phoning, of faxing, of ... yes, writing was probably safer, for, after the long letter received with so much delay, he had become suspicious. Besides, Mahina may have gone somewhere. In addition, she had not written often. Of course, she was extremely occupied. Or had she sensed something wrong in him? Had she remained tainted by her own emotionalism, assuming that Komaru had no feelings for her? If so, oh, please, darling, please forgive me. I have been such a brute and so selfish in thinking of business and, yes, the Movement. What could he do to repair such a misunderstanding? Why hadn't he come out in the open, been a little less egotistic for the sake of others when he could make happy at least one person in his own life, and the most important human being, half of his own flesh, and now all of his guts?

Yes, he would write. And here the presence of Ling-ling emerged by recalling what he had told her via poetry. He was a timid person when it came to opening his heart to anyone, particularly to a woman. Could not poetry become a vessel of conveyance for the most recondite messages of intimacy to a woman?

Mahina had become a Franciscan *in posse*, and she even signed as 'Francisca'. What could he say to his Sister Moon in order to cast over her some light from Brother Sun? He thought of some verses from Chinese, Indian, Japanese or even Maori poetry. For Ling-ling, a little hamster full of devotion, he had even composed a few lines of pseudo-Catullian sophomorishness. For Mahina he needed something more mature, credible, 'bold'. And suddenly Baudelaire came up almost from nowhere as an initial syllabic lead. Yes, of course, that crazy guy had even sung rhymed praises to his own Francisca. Yes, it took some time to open the cases of books still piled along one wall of the garage. Of course, 10 years earlier Mahina was studying French as he had done. And she had given him as a gift *Les fleurs du mal*. Was it not there that, where, yes, in the collection *Spleen et idéal*, he had read '*Franciscae meae laudes*' carrying vague echoes of Petrarchean playfulness with his Laura? Or was it a reflection of Louise Labé answering Petrarch after nearly two centuries of feminine silence? So coincidental that the title of that collection was under two apparent 'English' words linked by a Latin conjunction. So,

Komaru was the spleen and Mahina his ideal in opening those pages after 10 years of immature curiosity on his part, though Mahina may have grasped the quintessence of undeclared teenage love much better than he could have understood. A female teen is way more sensitive and 'mature' in matters of the heart than a man can imagine. But spaces created by attending school in two different cities had placed a lid on what may have been brewing in the mind and the heart of Mahina for her brother, who had distanced himself by chance or even by intention. He may have been afraid of burning her with the rays of his light. Besides, he was a man. What could he learn from a kid sister?

Now he was trying to repair 10 years of callousness derived from the duties of the call to contribute to the re-establishment of a modicum of freedom and dignity among his brothers at war with injustice. The thought of including sisters among his moral stormtroopers of redemption had never crossed his mind. Maori women could only excel in flax weaving, rearing kids, and baking *kumara*.

He now had the duty to sing for her something brooding for a long time, but mainly to reassure her that it was only events that had impeded a more natural flow of feelings also from his end of the emotive line. He would sing to her to re-establish in her heart a balance of reality for the sake of her own mental health. Her wish to die before him had scared him to hell, and he was glad to know that Catholics abhor suicide. In fact, Bill had said that the incidence of self-destruction was statistically lowest among Roman Catholics.

Yes, my dear sister,

> Novis te cantabo chordis,
> O novelletum quod ludis
> In solitudine cordis...

Of course, Mahina darling, unlike in the silent past, I shall sing in a new mode, O little kid sister fluttering your wings in the desert of my heart. You see, I have even shifted the seat of my emotions to a higher ground of residence.

And so I imagine you detached for a moment from your studies and wandering among the dogwood of your campus or of your convent exploring the possibility of learning how to become a recluse. Of course, I have a selfish interest. You can absolve me one day of my sins, those of inattention. But you know, I tried my best to fight my ADD. If I have sinned of that syndrome it was not because of another sister, for I have only you. Do you think that I could shift my attention to another woman? Had you thought that I could steal from the bank of our intimate siblingness to make a gift of it to another person? No, of course, never. Who else could understand the ties that bind us together forever? I shall never betray you, for

> Sicut beneficum Lethe,
> Hauriam oscula de te,
> Quae imbuta es magnete.

Do you see how I feel for you? You are my only spring of a magic oasis that magnetically keeps me in ecstasy at its shores, where I shall drink only your kisses as a potion of survival in this impossible world of conflicts. In fact,

> Quum vitiorum tempestas
> turbabat omnes semitas,
> Apparuisti ...

The star now leading the Three Wise Men to Bethlehem was not the only one to appear on the horizon of hope, for your own surged from our own blood as a sign of direction when I myself was lost in materialistic pursuits. Please believe me, Melissa is an unhappy woman. There is not, there could not be anything constructive between her and me. I just felt sorry for her, plus the fact, naturally, that, among all the worries I had for so many things, she functioned as a mechanism to diffuse my stress. But in your case

> Piscina plena virtutis,
> . . . .
> Labris vocem redde mutis!

And why? Because

> Quod erat spurcum, cremasti;
> Quod rudius, exaequasti;
> Quod debile, confirmasti.

And now I know what you did to me, not unlike what Chiara did to Francesco. Without your unselfish intervention I would still be floating in mud, hanging on for dear life through the Samaritan cooperation of Ling-ling. She is like one of your Sisters in arms, like Chiara's own Sisters helping others when you could not. So,

> In fame mea taverna,
> In nocte mea lucerna,

please

> Recte me semper guberna.

By now you know that I need you to guide me. I count on you to let me rest in the abode of your protection. Don't let me go astray. Keep me on the right course. If I ever embark in any dangerous sailing, be sure that my canoe does not sink or smash against the rocks of fate. When my energies and my will to fight begin to slack,

> Adde nunc vires viribus,

cast all your light around me, for you already possess the magic power of an angelic balsam. Who else could be conceived of better than a

> Patera gemmis corusca
> Panis salsus, mollis esca,
> Divinum vinum, Francisca?

Not even the Mediet restaurant could furnish me with all the necessary victuals to continue the struggle within me, between me and you, and against the whole world. Only you can help me. And if you cannot, remember that I will still love you and keep you in my breast under the protection of the torn *tiki*. No other *wairua* could possibly protect me, my Francisca.

When Ling-ling returned in the evening, she found Komaru more relaxed, affectionate and communicative. His depression had disappeared. And he was hungry. So she prepared for him a simple dish, one of his favourites – fried rice with shrimp. That reminded him of the eating spots west of the Shanghai campus restaurant where he would sit along among the open stares of Chinese workers and peasants tilling the few hectares of farmland being used for academic buildings and hotels. But that night he was not alone. He felt that writing that letter to Mahina had removed a heavy stone from his heart, and thus he imagined that, upon receiving it, Mahina would understand, forgive and protect him. He also felt less lonely because Ling-ling came close to him at the table, and he acknowledged her warm presence with gratitude. He touched her hand, and she squeezed his gently as if to tell him that he could trust her, though his eyes were wide open, gazing into infinity. She sensed that his thoughts were far away on another continent. As a Chinese, she could read a whole heart by merely observing the pupils of anyone opening a window of communication not to be alone and lonely even in a crowd.

She was not surprised when Komaru led her gently to the bedroom, undressed her as if opening a book of poems, trying to read some familiar verses for inspiration, and, after undressing himself, lay down beside her to caress her so lightly, as if afraid of making any noise with the palm of his big, dark hand over the pale skin of a Manchu. She followed suit by copy-catting his every movement. He took his time to raise her up to excitement from a state of contemplation, and she was strong enough to wait for him calmly, with Oriental patience. When she sensed that the flow of his blood had surged to create a most wanted turgidity, she did what she had never done before. She kissed him on the lips. And in sinking himself between hers, he noticed how she had sacrificed herself by probing him avidly. At first, she always had difficulty accommodating her orifices to the intrusion of his structures, but with proper time and dispensation of natural resources, she allowed him to reach the most recondite nooks of her body that had been designed for more compatible affinities. Komaru himself laboured to reach a state of mind somewhat different. He could not escape collating Melissa's kisses with Ling-ling's. Although not as fleshy, Ling-ling's had the flavour of an original sin in which she had fallen as if performing a sacrifice in a Tantric temple. Mahina herself intruded nearly openly with her inexperience in comparison with Ling-ling's sinuous sensuality. Her body was much smaller than Mahina's, and thus it called for careful handling of skin adherence not to transform pleasure into pain, and thus vulgarity.

What a night to celebrate the arrival of a Messiah to redeem humanity for all its original sins! And in so sinning he had hoped to rescue Mahina from her doubts about chastity, virginity and monogamy. Mahina once told him that she had studied three treatises by Tertullian. That was in a course on Christian 'sociology' *avant la lettre*. In that connection, she said that, if Americans had read and applied Tertullian's views to marriage, divorce and remarrying, the US would vanish from the face of the Earth as a nation. Unfortunately, Jesus Nazarenus had crossed the Atlantic, and then the PACIFIC. In so doing, he brought not only eggnog, mistletoe and carols, but also the seeds for religious discord fomenting all the possible conflicts among thousands of denominations organised in His name to praise

His father. Komaru wondered if He knew He had failed in His mission. At the moment of realising that, Komaru also wondered how much more time he himself had to fail on his own, for his father had died during the winter. What could one do to prevent that? Commit suicide or let others dispose of him according to tenets of democratic and polite societies? Fortunately, among these there was always a woman catering to the weakness of men. And that night Ling-ling played the rôle of Mary Magdalene, as if deferring the pain in the neck of dying sooner rather than suffering in the delay of dying later. In fact, she resurrected him labially so beautifully that, after climaxing again, Komaru collapsed in heavy sleep as if trying to experience how death would feel whenever it would occur, once and forever.

As the end of the year approached, Komaru went over the most important decision he had made in 1992. In anticipation of a summary to be made in conjunction with projected activities for 1993, he singled out his decision not to complete his MA thesis. That was mainly not only a consequence of the unfeasible presentation of a bilingual synthesis displaying the only historical truth existing in Ao Tea Roa, but also of his being bothered by a pan-truth affecting all of human society, convincing him that there was one exit to keep his sanity in check. In spite of the pre-programmed, built in, unfailing tragic end waiting for him, he chose to fight even hearing Sisyphus laugh at his foolishness.

The Theory of Nine evaluation of just one century of white history had convinced Komaru of certain principles he had uncovered by himself for all the previous centuries. As a validation to his bitter grasp of reality, he had read and studied a 28,000-word report telling him he was not wrong. Titled 'On the possibility and desirability of peace', the report reinforced on the one hand the illusory dream of creating a non-belligerent world in the 21st century, while on the other hand the tragic sense of duty he had espoused for a lost cause as a *fait accompli*. This solution was antithetical, though parallel, to what Mahina had chosen as a way of escaping from a rotten society masking its hypocrisy under the name of Humanity. The report, published in *Esquire* as an article in December 1967, at the most frigid stage of the Cold War, could be abstracted in one single paragraph of 32 words:

> Lasting peace, while not theoretically impossible, is probably unattainable; even if it could be achieved it would almost certainly not be in the best interest of a stable society to achieve it.

So be it, thought Komaru, remembering *Rom De jure belli ac pacis*. The Romans were right: 'Si vis pacem, para bellum'. The door was open for any Johnny-come-lately Nero to build all the possible weapons of mass destruction, burning a pan-Rome, and ironically being unable to watch it while playing the mythical fiddle – that incidentally was not created until 15 centuries later.

Komaru had nothing to lose, especially since he had lost every human close to him. The restaurant was a welcome platform of planning for a grande finale. He went over and over that long article written in a most logical and credible fashion. Of course, the appreciation of that 'conclusive' statement, as a prefatory thesis proven at the end, gave Komaru a more incentive wish to do something for his *whenua* as a matter of principle, though the report had been prepared for the members of the nuclear club at large. But Ao Tea Roa, as an antinuclear nation, was only an insignificant part of that world, and, as long as it could function as it had been before the Waitangi Trick, at least his people could re-acquire and manifest a sense of dignity.

The 1919–89 span had sanctioned the right to acquire that freedom for Ao Tea Roa, a unique lacuna in the annals of Mankind, with the possible exception of the Basques, still fighting since the Roman invasion 23 centuries ago. Unlike the situation in South Africa, where the majority was dominated by a white minority, in Ao Tea Roa the status quo was the reverse. So, why would public opinion not do something Davidian in favour of a vanishing culture? Why had the world helped the re-establishment of a Jewish minority regain the freedom of their native land? Were the Maoris to wait 2,000 years to regain their independence as native inhabitants before being allowed to reign free and clear from a non-genetic oppressor? And, meanwhile, what would happen to the Maori language, the only, the best, the most important tool of offense against the dictatorship oppressing Polynesian *wairua*? Would the speech of the great canoe navigators survive for many more years to ensure the continuity of a great race who had never imposed imperialism on anybody? Was it unfair to break the chains of political slavery just to regain the soul of the ancestors?

The questions were many. The answer was only one: fight. And, if this meant a constant and continuing conflict, well, it looked like there was no way to escape that curse afflicting humanity. At least Maoris would, through war, become human like the rest of mankind. Without war, painful and 'inhuman' as it can be, the Maori race was destined to perish like the Tasmanians, the Moriori, the Australian Aborigines, and a long rosary of people who barely remember who the Etruscans were in Europe alone. Between living in dejection and dying in dignity, Komaru opted for the latter, though he knew that in his lifetime the chances for success were very slim. That did not matter, however. At least he could knock at the door of his Rangi with pride and inform his father that he had done his duty like most Maori since 1840.

Chapter 38

The 1 January 1993 came upon Komaru as a day he had set apart in order to summarise past events, assess the status quo of his total person *vis-à-vis* life in all dimensions, and project possibilities for the immediate coming years as crucial in the rebirth process of Activism. He took the whole day to bring some order into the list of various 'things to do' as a function of political, business, and personal transactions with himself, in that order. Strangely, he thought, now that his father had become anguishing memories, that material chores had been expedited quickly, and that Mahina had left him in the cold of the most baffling psychological disarray, he surprised himself in admitting that whatever had been left pending was primarily the recovery of his *whenua* from a chronic state of oppression.

He sensed that, if nothing drastic occurred before the year 2001, Ao Tea Roa would slip into oblivion forever. He took the necessary time, nevertheless, to go through the traumatic experience of purchasing a new automobile. The old lorry had become unmanageable as a consequence of continuous repairs, though still useful in business activities related to the restaurant. By acquiring a Japanese toy auto, he felt safer and more secure in blending himself into the swarm of similar cars demanding less fuel. Also, by being less conspicuous than a visible vintage vehicle, the new car was not subject to random stop checks by Wanganui traffic cops. Meanwhile, Komaru had received another letter from Trieste, posted by Mahina at the end of August. Again, as for the previous lefter from Venice, the missive had taken about 4 months to reach him in spite of the fact that it carried the AIR MAIL imprint. Surely, he knew that at times the Italian postal services underwent both official and unofficial strikes involving vicious and abusive boycotting of non-essential mail, particularly that addressed abroad. This lay forgotten in a storage depot without any supervision until the space was needed to store other mail deriving from new labour strikes. However, Komaru was not entirely convinced that the postal delay originated only in Italy.

He smelled a rat, and in fact he studied the seal of the envelope. Mahina was not the careful type to wet the flaps and press them properly on the back of the envelope. It seemed to have been steam-opened and then carefully resealed. It was a botched job. And that is why he called her telling her in strong terms, and in Maori, not to ever write about 'personal' matters anymore. In spite of being baffled by the mysterious warning, Mahina had adhered to his request, and that is why lately she had refrained from mailing anything at all intimate. Komaru felt that even facsimile transmissions were not safe. Well, he had become, if not paranoid, extra careful, for his plans for the next few years of Activism were on his mind most of the time.

Komaru felt that, perhaps, it was not just a matter of security bothering him. Mahina had become too emotionally involved with him after the night of her 24th birthday. And, although he relished being reminded of and taken back to a unique episode of his most revealing hours in 'nosce te ipsum', he simply longed to forget that Mahina ever lived. What had taken place between her and him had to be something that existed only in literature of the European Romantic era. What Mahina was alluding to, brutally speaking, could be misconstrued as a 'fleeting encounter'. Of course, he rejected that label of vulgarity, for he knew that the melting of two bodies in full blood was only the surface manifestation of a more lasting phenomenon. Actually, it was not even an event *per se*. It was a cosmic clash of intimate particles of genetic primal elements calling for the continuation of the species on the one hand, and the actualisation of spiritual matters on the other through the palpitation of flesh. In retrospect, Komaru began to delineate the seemingly contradictory behaviour of a sister who, on the verge of dedicating her life to an abstract entity through chastity, poverty and obedience, had broken all the rules before these were taken through formal vows. Mahina had fused herself into him through a sacrifice of both her body and mind. She obliterated not only the most cultural *tapu* of her traditions, but also had put aside all possible feminine constraints in order to offer her brother the blood of periodicity in concomitance with that of uniqueness. What else could she offer to declare to him all her feelings of siblingness? She had only one opportunity to leave with him the very essence of herself in one single act of love to last for the rest of her life.

At the same time she knew she had ahead a whole chunk of the 21st century to dedicate her love to the Man who had sacrificed His life on behalf of Humanity. What she had left for her brother was only a memory. And this Komaru wanted to sublimate through something engaging and tangible. The Movement became such a substitute for the urge of his mind. That is why he consciously dedicated himself to an ideal pursuit in parallel fashion to what Mahina planned to do. In essence, it was for both of them a similar enterprise. The difference was that Mahina's target was the entire world ruled by a Christian God, while for Komaru it was an infinitesimal corner of her universe requiring immediate action on behalf of a small band of brothers and sisters. In the former case it was a matter of a continuously striving for salvation in tow to 20 centuries of hope, while in the latter it was a matter of implementing an immediate plan of action to efface the oppression of 200 years of slavery.

The first thing Komaru did before taking action as a covert Activist was writing a cheque to the bursar of the university for all the financial help received during his graduate tenure in the department of history. He also made a point of thanking in person all his professors for their genuine and sincere succor in his scholarly enterprises. He felt no animosity toward any of them. What could they do, or how else could they behave in a country where they had been born and educated? They had no other 'Home' but New Zealand, where an *utu* had been cast on their own ancestors since 'convict' times.

Oh, yes, of course. Mahina's letter was in the way. He just couldn't concentrate on anything immediately. She had to leave him some breathing space in his daily life. What could he do to alter that kind of psychological suspension, a state of subconscious animation in which he was floating? He was compelled to reread the Trieste letter in the hope of finding a solution, such as destroying the missive and then forgetting it. Well, if he succeeded, it would be 'one down, two to go'. Of the remaining two women, of course, Melissa would be the next, for she was the more functionally deleterious of the two. And yet, she was also pivotal in the running of the business to the point that, in view of the success of the enterprise, she had suggested the opening of a chain or a franchise structure throughout the islands. And the first location would be, naturally, Auckland, a place that Komaru would avoid like the plague. Meanwhile, he opened the envelope again, and noticed that there was no date, an item he had missed before.

Trieste, Italy
Dear Komaru,

In this letter I shall try to summarise the pilgrimage I took to

Kòrčula from notes in my informal diary preceding and following my voyage to our feminine Hawaiki. And I tell you, I am so happy I was able to trace the steps where our grandmother, mother, sister and the remaining relatives – mostly on the 'Venetian' side via the Kornarich and others – spent nearly 10 centuries of industrious and basically happy life.

When the ferry approached the island, it was almost evening, and the sun was horizontally hitting the small towns surrounded by hills dotted with cottages and gardens. I immediately felt my heart throbbing fast in my throat, and my mouth was saturated with the bitter and dry flavour of adrenaline. But at the same time I became nearly weightless, as if my memory had surfaced in my mind to confer upon it a sense of *déja vu*. In fact, my dear brother, please don't assume that I am deranged, but I can assure you that I had already been in Kòrčula. Even before I stepped onto the cobblestones of the quay near the old towers of the fortress, I knew that I would be able to tour the surroundings without any guide. And you should have seen Tanya in tow, looking at me, bewildered at my matter of fact behaviour. Even before climbing the gentle slope to the hotel, I remembered the buildings, starting with the orphanage on the left side, next to the cathedral, then Marco Polo's birthplace, and the municipal offices, among others.

I felt drained emotionally and Tanya, seeing me in a state of near stupefaction, insisted on registering immediately and spending the evening in the hotel. In such a small place, every building is within walking distance. And there we relaxed that evening under the pergola of the restaurant, nearly deserted because most tourists had gone back to the *rentrée*. We had a pleasant supper, Mediterranean style, i.e. based mostly on organically grown food, at least for the vegetables. I enjoyed eating roasted peppers straight from a jar in which their slices were kept in a simple condiment of olive oil with oregano and garlic. Then we had linguine served with a sauce made simply with eggplant parmesan style. Actually, it was pasta covered with a light stratum of julienned Italian eggplant slices that were first broiled, then lightly seasoned with FRESH tomato juice into which parmigiano was melted, not in granules but in slivers. Just that, but I was told that the parmigiano was the 'signore' of the whole peasant 'marinara' condiment, a local variety. Apparently, it was a 'secret' there because the parmigiano was not the 'Reggiano' variety but the so-called Locatelli. In fact, the latter is to Parmigiano-Reggiano as, say, Champagne Fine Cognac is to Armagnac (don't tell Bill about that). The Locatelli is not as invading as the P-R, for it exhibits a 'retarded' sweet flavour that lingers in the upper palate AFTER the food is washed out, even by wine. Of course, the local people offered us a red table wine that complemented the dish royally. I also tried the stuffed squid in place of a roasted rabbit, the 'specialty' of the restaurant. We then had fresh grapes, so sweet, and figs, both golden and red, which we ate rind and all.

That evening, I felt at peace with myself, secure, welcome, safe, empathising with the restful sunset of the waters on which the garden lights reflected both their lanterns and later the most diamond-like stars I had ever noticed anywhere. Those were the stars of Venice that guided the spice route sailors during the days of glory for the lives of the islanders who, like our own people, had arrived here from the inland, built a culture during so many centuries of aesthetic efforts, and then they disappeared like the *moa*. The parallels between Venetians and Maoris is not unwarranted, for the points of contact between the two peoples are several and obvious. Only details, both qualitative and quantitative, vary. But, Komaru, they have gone into oblivion in spite of the fact that Venetian, the language of Bill's Casanova, still exists almost as a secret idiom for the islanders. Does that tell you anything?

So, the first night was perfect, as if I had found myself in a utopic corner of the world at peace with, well, nearly every live and dead element surrounding me. I said 'nearly' because there was a missing link somewhere. And this was not difficult to locate in making an inventory of the feelings oppressing me among a host of intangibles deep down in my bowels. Yes, the Maori seat of mysterious and ineffable emotions had prevailed over the superimposed locus of Western centre of sentiments, the heart. Yes, Komaru, you, just you. I don't know whether it was the food, and particularly the local wine I drank at supper, but, Komaru, I had a terrible night of agitation. My whole body was on fire. I felt first an itching among the folds of every inscrutable part of myself, and then a soothing and barely noticeable flow of wetness invading me at the simple thought of you. Of course, memories of skin adherences between us kept creeping up on me, in me, and within me, as well as out of me in a rush to seek, meet, and merge with indefinable and unaccountable atoms of carnality emerging from your body. So, what could I do? I moved into Tanya's bed, I cajoled her into remaining at least passive, and I seduced her by allowing myself to slide the centre of my torment along her left thigh until my pubes met her knee. And there I slowly slided up and down until I built up a frenzy of passionate embrace with Tanya, who tried her best to calm me down. And she did.

In fact, Tanya herself was also fired up to the point of cupping my middle teat with her wet lips, so closely to what you did to me when you sucked the blood scented with the roses whose thorns had bled me. And, strangely, I merged your vision with father's, and in the process I wondered about the fall of Eve through our mother and sister. At times, I even wondered about our mother, whether she suffered the agony of Beatrice Cenci. After reading Shelley's work, I don't know what to believe. Do you think that father's mind had been poisoned by alcohol to the point of forcing her?

The following day, I bought a work of art at the orphanage where our sister grew up – a beautiful crucifix, an antique in bronze. The sculpture of Christ is so naturalistic, so Michelangelesque, that it reminded me of the *Pietà* in the Palazzo Vecchio, and of you, of course. He is not as robust as you are. His body is more lean, but his face is so close to yours in look that I avoid it every time I look at Him. The loincloth was fashioned and cast so anatomically that I cannot refrain from imagining what it hides from view. I wish I had looked at you, for that would have helped me to know Him better. Perhaps it is better this way, because I keep imagining all possible shapes, colours and consistency that enhance my curiosity. So, Komaru, you are there on the Cross, taking the place of the *tiki* you violently, and pleasurably for me, tore away. But you see, dear brother, it is not the pleasure of the flesh alone, no. It is something more intimate, almost mystical, for, in the impossibility of envisaging Tanya near me in the future as an alternate to your body, I envision the permanent company of Christ as a companion 24 hours a day. No one can take it away from me. I begin to sense that, by holding the bronze effigy in my hands, a strange warmth begins to pervade my whole being. With the tip of my middle finger I grope Him in darkness, I hold him against myself and, strangely, I feel as if His flesh becomes live to the point that I tried to lift his loin shroud ... which actually I do time and again without danger of being soiled by His emission. Then, I fall asleep, as I do whenever I feel that Tanya should not be abused.

Komaru, you have triggered in me and into me the imprint of femalehood. And I am so grateful to you for allowing me to discover myself through the genes of our sister–mother and mother–sister. This secret of ours will remain as the token of quintessential *aroha* for the rest of our lives. Regardless of what you can do to Melissa, or what she can do to you, nothing can alter this powerful curse of integrated closeness, of enmeshed fleshness, of 'fusional' unite-ness forever. Alas, at the same time I know that my exaltation will not lead me anywhere, and thus it's a waste of time, both yours and mine, to indulge in weaving a dream-catcher. I just feel the way I feel. Remembering Louise Labé, 'Lors double vie à chacun en suivra, Chacun en soi et son ami vivra.' In fact, Louise will necessarily be put aside in favour of Teresa de Ávila's *Interior Castle*, where I'll move from the First to the Seventh Mansion with you in my mind and Him in my heart.

Please forgive me if I upset you with my selfishness. At times I wonder what rôle a deranged *whakapapa* plays in siblingness such as ours. And more than that, I am at a loss to imagine how humans such as you and me raised in a contemporary 'educated' society could understand themselves and be understood by 'experts' if Freud had not been born. You know, I remember in passing some comments made by my professor of 19th-century philosophy in my senior year (God, it was less than a year ago!) in connection with Popper's criticism of psychoanalysis. She just mentioned in passing that Freud and Popper were a Vienna coin with a bifrontal Janus, whatever that meant. Anyway, when I return to college, I will seek her – my professor, Dr Alette Hutchinson – for elucidation. Basically, I feel like asking her the most stupid question: do you think that humanity emerging from the chaos of the First and Second World Wars would have fared better if psychoanalysis had never assumed a rôle of shamanism to the detriment of philosophical investigations? The real problem is, what can philosophy do to help human beings OUTSIDE the halls of academia? Can a philosopher open a studio or a clinic, ask patients to lie down on a couch, and proceed to dissect their minds through a maieutic process of healing? If so, then the whole thing would amount to going back to square one (or zero?). Probably Socrates would be shocked at realising that after 25 centuries the West had done nothing constructive, and in a way he would chuckle at concluding that Plato had simply misquoted him all the way.

Now, a few corollary items about our Dalmatian Hawaiki. In a way, I was eager, if not anxious, to leave the island as soon as I could. I felt in Kòrčula a sense of mysterious discomfort, as if my guardian angel had interposed himself between me and the people in the street, in the orphanage, in every place I visited. First of all, they stared at me (especially the old timers) as if I had come back from the Beyond. They would wrap their black shawls around their heads and cast me an evil eye. A couple of times some women called me 'Maria' and other times I heard something like Kornaro, Kornarich, or so. I must have reminded them of something casting a remembrance of fear, a tragic sense of past events. As to the few younger women I met and saw in public places, well, Komaru, they looked like me, or should I say I looked like them. Tanya pointed out to me many times how I could blend so easily among the local population as a 'native' for I have the same tall neck, similar black-bronze coloured hair, identical shiny 'olive' eyes, and, yes, she said, I walked like Kòrčulans, with the gait of the few young women working in the glass factory of Murano. I still fail to grasp the implication of her observations unless I construe it as her mute request to know more about my strong resemblance to the native young women. She knows I have ties on this island, but she has no idea whatsoever of the knots tying me to it. Even applying some of the most Schopenhauerian concepts to the pessimistic fate of mankind, I simply cannot establish any platform to 'grasp' Tanya's silent devotion to me that placidly welcomes me literally with open arms when I yearn for you so desperately. Just think, one evening I saw a couple of local youths on a small boat sailing closely along the coast. Tanya observed that the girl could be a younger 'me', totally relaxed next to boy at the rudder. The seemingly inconsequential vignette took me back to the area near Kerikeri when one hot January you roamed from island to island for a whole afternoon. Do you remember those fleeting hours of innocent adventure? And now, after I became 24, I wonder what we could discover on the cool sands of the coves when you looked for shells while I desired to grow up faster and faster in order to savour the unknown fruits of my budding body. When I think of those hours near you, I chase away a desire to accept death as a solution to my dejection. I do not desire death in the manner of causing it, but if it happens to take me away, well, I would not resist it. Oh, what am I saying. I think that ...

And here Komaru stopped rereading the letter. He had to, for there was no point in reminiscing about matters that were deleterious at all levels of the daily tasks confronting him. What perturbed him was Mahina writing of self-effacement in realising that those days of careless youth could not be lived anymore, particularly after she had become 24 years old. At that age, Mahina had only existed a few hours in her rush to grow up faster. And her sailing boat was only a Maori bed hosting tentative aspects of mutual generosity.

Now he felt somewhat envious of his sister, for she had already solved the main problems of terrestrial existence. She was going to become a nun, thus accepting a slow death via complete detachment from a normal life. As for himself what could he do? Embark on a sailing boat alone and allow himself to be attracted by the sweet enchantment of a siren waiting for him on the horizon of a Fata Morgana? No, he simply could not. Thus, as a palliative he decided to concentrate on his restaurant business in order to use it as a foil in fomenting the success of his cause. Between a life to be spent in a cloistered convent and another dedicated to activism toward a nearly absurd task of liberation, the expectation was one of dancing alone on the stage of suicide. Between the two ballets of dejection, which of them would be more demanding when death would also enter the platform of the *pas de deux*? His own or Mahina's? And what would the difference be without a partner to be embraced in the final moment when the curtain would fall to spare the spectators the imposition of a 'live' theatrical death? For Komaru, death was the most private affair, the quintessence of 'British' privacy in complete antithesis with Maori traditions and expectations. That was a new concept stemming from his living and fighting alone, and thus he expected, actually he hoped one day, to die alone. Meanwhile, the year 1993 had started with an outline of a series of projected dates for seeding future dateless activities of 'Maorism' in action. Short of that, life would be immediately more meaningless than ever. Yes, he could rent a boat. But without Mahina in it, once departed from the shores of memory, Komaru would not sail back. He knew that the *whenua* of departure would not be found anymore.

The first thing he did during the Christmas break was to call Mahina at Our Lady of Angels Convent, where she was spending all her spare time while not writing the MA thesis in order to satisfy the initial requirements of her Postulancy. She had first presented proof of her Baptism and Confirmation, as well as of her free status. This last formality puzzled her, though she understood that the reference was merely a social one – she was not married or engaged or tied by other social obligations, such as taking care of an old mother. But was she really enjoying 'free status'? Was she free of Komaru? Yes, she was free of anything connecting her to a body, but not to a mind, a soul, a spirit. Komaru was in her forever. She had found in Jesus, however, a clone, for He could enter any convent 24 hours a day. Only the name was different. The rest was nearly identical. In addition, she would not be distracted by any other suitor, potential or otherwise. She would untie Jesus Nazarenus, Rex Judeorum, from the crucifix, revive him with wild love whenever she needed Him, and then nail Him back on the wall for dear life. So many young women had done the same and, apparently, satisfactorily – Clara, Teresa, María, Caterina, and others. And, on top of that secret life, at its end they were even canonized for having interacted with a sacred satyr. As for other requirements, the last was the inheritance from her father. This would be taken care of at the end of the academic year before she would move to a different location, one willing to accept her at the next stage of the Novitiate.

After telling Mahina never to write about her feelings for him, Komaru sketched a plan of action to be implemented within the following two years before the arrival of Her Majesty the Queen of England on the occasion of the periodical meeting of Commonwealth Nations on 2 November 1995. Something had to be done systematically, covertly in planning, overtly in deeds. But these had to be 'masked' by officially scheduled events serving as cover-ups for other activities subtly controlled by the Movement that, meanwhile, had entrusted Komaru with a *carte blanche*. It was a fact, however, that, except for the 'Professor' at the University of Auckland, no one on Earth knew his name.

What a year, thought Komaru in looking at his schedule of events waiting to be implemented by him in 1993. By analysing the mere sequence of digits, *more sinense*, he regarded the months ahead as propitious ones within a cabalistic framework. The double '9' in its core guaranteed the inception of popular awareness toward the sacrosanct *iwi* among most Maori. The resulting '4' obtained by adding the last '3' of the century – and of the millennium – to the constant '1' for a thousand years past was regarded by Komaru as a warning not to rush things. The unlucky '4' had to be treated gingerly, the same way he had done with Mahina by relegating her to the rôle of the waning moon of a lifetime. Although this was not easy, for his heart was bleeding with the pain of separation, the distance between the two helped to create an armistice space between the two minds fighting each other in the emotional vacuum of the Pacific. Komaru knew that, at least until the middle of the year, Mahina was busy with the teaching of Maori, a 'first' in an American institution of higher learning. In addition, she was undergoing the first period of probation in general, namely, Postulancy, under the strict scrutiny of the Abbess, the whole process being subject to the consent of the Discretorium.

The 'legal' stumbling block had been removed by the end of the 1992–93 academic year, when Mahina had to travel to Vancouver, B. C., in order to expedite the documentation needed to obtain her 'green card'. The American consul was not only understanding, but also helpful in connection with the paperwork regarding X-ray results, blood analyses and other medical procedures that were as strict as those required before she could be admitted to probation in any convent. She had to fight, thus, on two fronts, one of being admitted to the States as an immigrant, and thus obtaining a Social Security card for employment as a 'specialist', and the other that of being accepted as a Candidate to Postulancy in Portland as an 'external'.

Beyond the requirement of the law, Mahina waited in anguish for the medical certificate stating the presence of the *tertium quid*, though not so much regarding the green card as for admission to the Portland Postulancy Center. In addition to the 'adequate physical and mental health' analysis undergone by her, Mahina was screened carefully for anything 'concerning possible hereditary traits.' This concern baffled her since she could not understand the impact on the demographic stock of genetic purity in the US population. What in the world could an Abbess fear when no nun would ever produce offspring that might belong to the convent? Besides, after nearly 2,000 years of harem life, had Jesus ever produced any child anywhere? Hadn't His father 'fixed' Him before sending Him to Earth to redeem Humanity for whatever sins had befallen it? Or had Jesus successfully used accident-proof contraceptives for so long in full disregard of papal Bulls, Encyclicals and Pastoral Letters?

A feeling of jubilation overwhelmed Mahina when finally a certificate of acceptable physical health was signed by two doctors, a man and a woman, who had been appointed by the Abbess. Strangely, the female doctor took her time to probe the extra breast by medically fondling it in search of tumours. She also cupped it with all her fingers, rotating them while at the same time drawing them toward the nipple as if attempting to extract some milk. Under that examination, the rosebud changed its colour from pink to red, at the same time enlarging in size as if it were ready to discard itself as a miniphallic sibling. The pleasurable discomfort felt by Mahina during that examination was enhanced by the secretion she felt between her thighs, which she glued to each other to minimise the inception of a more evident tremour all over her body. She had closed her eyes under the scrutiny of the doctor who seemed to seek in their pupils the confirmation of a 'normal' physiological female. The test was extremely successful, to the point that Tanya's first approach to timid manipulations and Komaru's ministering of first aid became rather pale in comparison. Only Komaru's lingual licking on the occasion of her 24th birthday had remained unsurpassed, but that was because at the same time, while she was like a recently born baby lamb trying to get up on all fours from Komaru's body, he had supported her each and every time she was impaled on him until he became spent.

The male doctor refrained from touching her, although he took several photographs from many angles to enrich his research collection of polymastic and polythelic cases. Finally, the psychological assessment was waived since Transpacific University had agreed to convey all tests in its file to the convent, where Mahina was going to apply the knowledge of her Maori language in the translation of sacred texts to be used in a special section on Polynesian culture. The tradition that had begun with the *Book of Mormon* was to be implemented by the most recent adoption of 'native' languages substituting for the original Church Latin during the sacrifice of the Mass. In spite of the efforts initiated by Bishop Pompallier nearly two centuries earlier, no one had ever thought of Maorising the *Acta Sanctorum*, for who expected the Maoris to learn Latin when they were still struggling to relearn the language of their forefathers?

The procedures leading to Mahina's being accepted to the first stage of religious life, however, were not finished. She had to state in writing that she did not suffer from epilepsy, contagious diseases and a host of illness listed in more detail than those required by the US Government. She even thought that, bureaucratically, the process was more complex for her to enter, as a spiritual entity, Paradise via convent life than physically the earthly heaven called America. And she wondered how strict St Peter could be in scrutinising the sick, the poor, the homeless, the exiled and the remaining castaways of Third World countries at 'Ellis Island'. Was Paradise that élitist in screening a body rather than a soul? Ironically, nowhere on the list of diseases was there any question or test regarding the most chronic illness afflicting humans: love. Had she been tested for that mental dysfunction affecting her whole body under the spell of her own genes, she would have been rejected by any community, be it Heaven, Earth, or even Hell. She wondered what she would answer if she had to confess her erotic abnormality for her brother. Apparently, it was more acceptable to love a circumcised member of another race who had been screwing humanity for two millennia than an uncircumcised member of her own family. It seemed that, as long as no one asked, it was all right to have loved and still love shamefully the same blood in a masturbatory mode of living. Mahina had been written off by her brother after he produced a document stating that all financial and property holdings had been transferred to him. Also, she had written a declaration of being of free status, properly endorsed and signed by the Abbess, Mahina herself, and two witnesses before the statements were filed in the archives of the monastery, together with the certificates of Baptism and Confirmation. Mahina was now ready to begin the Novitiate period of at least two years at another convent where she would dedicate herself full time to activities according to prescriptive rules required by all candidates.

As a consequence of events and restrictions taking place in both the States and New Zealand, correspondence between Mahina and Komaru had in the meantime become limited to generalities and business topics. Maori language was intentionally avoided because it would automatically fall under scrutiny. From time to time, nevertheless, Mahina could not help writing between the lines in such a way that only Komaru could understand. For example, once she referred to Mozart's clarinet concerto, whose second movement she heard over the Portland classical music station while finalising her MA thesis. In another letter, she 'casually' mentioned how she missed some Maori food such as 'minnow fritters', like those Komaru prepared for her on the occasion of her 24th birthday.

In turn, Komaru, remembering that evening of sorcery ending the day of a date with a '4', could not refrain from trying to dispel a black cloud of memories obfuscating his resolution not to think of his sister, particularly when closing his eyes in embracing Ling-ling and imagining Mahina's body next to him. Strangely, in interacting with Melissa, who had begun to take oestrogen to fight the inceptive ravages of menopause at 50, Komaru's exploits had become 'blank'. In other words, it seemed to him that the epidermic youth of both Mahina in retrospect and of Ling-ling felt very similar by creating a physical aura of exciting eroticism to the point that his view of species-specific incestive performance were transferred onto and into the Chinese flesh as the *summum bonum* of siblingness.

In Melissa's case, however, Komaru began to understand the interaction as a quest in search of a mother, while at the same time he felt she regarded him as a son under the crying eyes of a *Mater Dolorosa*. Life was undoubtedly a complex biological existence leading nowhere. Could a philosopher, even a generalist, explain the purpose of it all in the process of analysing the mysterious working of genes free of conscious mental control? Komaru knew that Mahina had solved all the problems of the world after accepting Tertullian's 'Credo quia absurdum est.' Could Komaru paraphrase Life analogically as 'Sum quia absurdum est?' Was philosophy able to explain Life otherwise? No, he thought, for any logical attempt would lead nowhere. And, in a way, proof of his conviction was furnished by Mahina's writing to him about her topic for the MA thesis, rather than items of common interest. The subject-matter was so banal that its contents dispelled any possible interest in potential censors trying to intercept and construe information on either intimate deeds or political plans.

Mahina's original idea for a thesis was, specifically defined, one dealing with theory, though running along a religious theme. At first she had considered the rôle of a god in religion, any religion. Or even the reverse, such as the necessity of religion as a *sine qua non* for the existence of a god. In other words, what was it that required a tandem structure for either a god or a religion? Could each component exist independently of each other for social, psychological or moral reasons? The topic was not new, of course, since the dawn of micro- and macroconsciousness and, in fact, Mahina and Komaru had at times posited those questions. For him, there was no necessity of either God or religion, but for Mahina, solely on the basis of tradition first, and then of faith, she had to accept both a set of religious tenets and a supervisor to be sure that humans did not go astray. At times, Komaru could almost understand, though not accept, the necessity of a 'religion', whatever its definition, for the sake of bringing comfort or peace of mind to those humans who were unable to go through life by themselves as free thinkers. But under no condition could Komaru understand the necessity of anything at the top of a pyramidal organization. In fact, once Komaru had stated that the trouble with religion was that it was messed up by a god, particularly when two or more similar religions had the same god.

The Irish situation was a case in point in Europe, as in most 'advanced' communities. The more sophisticated and literate a nation, the more troublesome its diverse beliefs WITHIN the same religious family.

Mahina's project had to be put aside after realising the limited time she had in the department of philosophy. As a consequence, she accepted the rather disappointing suggestion offered by her advisor, a young lady with a PhD fresh from Columbia, where she had been influenced by the historiographic streak of philosophical theory. When she found out that Mahina was from New Zealand, she proposed to her an aspect of paraphilosophy that was in essence a segment of history dealing more with the man than with his mind. Perhaps Mahina's advisor was trying to 'impose' a philosopher onto New Zealand, and accordingly the name of Karl Popper popped up from accidentality in human endeavours. After all, New Zealand was a British Dominion during the Second World War and Popper was a British subject. Ergo, New Zealand had its own philosopher. Dr Hall Mahina's advisor, was undoubtedly a controversial figure in the Philosophy Department of Transpacific University because, first of all, she saw a difference between history and historiography. For her, history, contrary to historiography, did not exist. There were only historians, but no history *per se* solely on etymological grounds, from Greek Ἴστωρ, meaning 'a wise man' and thus 'a person who knows rightly' or 'a judge'. Although the etymological foundations are complex and varied depending on dialectical sources, it is a fact that ἱστορία as 'history' was used and recorded not before Aristophanes. In the British scholarly tradition, according to Melissa, who grew up on her father's classics lap there was in ancient Greece quite a difference between events *per se* and the recording of the past. Although not knowing each other, Dr Hall and Melissa came from the same British tradition. That is why Mahina settled on writing an 'easier' MA thesis since she had not 'seen' events connected with Popper, though she could 'register' them merely on the basis of the fact that Popper had been a castaway in New Zealand during the Second World War, when he was still unknown in Europe as a philosopher. It was Bryan Magee who made of Popper a philosopher after opening the eyes of traditionalists and placing the Viennese scholar in the proper niche of the European philosophical tradition. After all, it was thought that in the world there were two philosophical compartments: one in England and another in 'Europe', as if the British Isles were a continent apart in scholarship, a concept still reigning even in touristic geography. So, what could Mahina do? Well, she felt like a budding archaeographer trying to uncover Popper's sojourn in New Zealand between 1937 and 1946. In a way, Popper appeared to be like a Polynesian Kant for different reasons, though mainly since, like Kant who had never been farther away from 'home' than a 40-mile radius, Popper behaved likewise.

Amazingly, Popper's stay in the Pacific was the most fruitful period of his life, one in which he conceived and wrote revolutionary philosophical tenets leading to the 'deconstruction' of platitudinous European theories astride the uncomfortable seat between Marx and Freud. Sadly, New Zealand failed to see in Popper a philosopher, except perhaps for Samuel Butler, who was marooned on The Hermit Islands as if he had been lost on the Moon. In fact, even deans and professors, as well as farmers, shepherds and wharfies, complained about Professor Popper's limited teaching, a few hours over the minimum of 40 a week like everybody else, while he spent most of his time speculating 'otiously' in abstract matters of no use to New Zealanders, particularly during a trying period for which both Maoris and Pakehas volunteered to fight in the trenches of Cassino. The fact that both Popper and Hitler were Austrian did not help much to create a platform of easy collegiality. The 'German accent' was heard at the antipodes as strongly as in Vienna.

And, thus, Mahina had to rely on Komaru to reconstruct not only the external ambience for the production of Popper's *Logic of Scientific Discovery*, but also for *The Open Society and Its Economics*. Komaru, in fact, while trying to work covertly on the world's First International Conference to be held in June 1993 by the nine tribes of Mataatua, had to take some valuable time away from his business in order to research Popper 'The Man' on Mahina's behalf. What did he teach, how long, where? Who were his friends, students, associates? What did he do to 'relax'? Did he have a hobby, a concept completely alien to European scholars? What had the 'philosopher' (although in New Zealand no one knew him as such) left physically in the archives of any New Zealand institution, and how did Kiwis react to Popper's 'secretive' tradition of intentional extreme privacy? He surely was not a good 'chap', for he seemed not to mingle with anyone, even at meal times. Who could blame Popper for not partaking of *poaka* and *pia* like a good bloke?

Finally, Mahina was able, with Komaru's help, to write a 'journalistic' thesis that had nothing or little to do with philosophy *per se*. Even Magee's *Popper* left a lot out about Popper the Man for obvious reasons, though Mahina hoped that one day Magee would write on that subject within the boundaries of both 'personal' and British privacy.

The only regret Mahina had in writing her thesis was her inability to interview Popper. That would have been the best way to know the Viennese as both a man and a philosopher, but how could she accomplish that for a 'miserable' MA thesis when Magee himself had been trying to do likewise for a whole lifetime? Even Popper's 1976 autobiographic *Unending Quest* said little about 'hermit' New Zealand, which the philosopher regarded no differently from Samuel Butler more than a century earlier. The only thing that Mahina uncovered through Komaru's research was the fact that, even in the 1990s, New Zealand was an extension of Britain at the scholarly level, and that insular philosophical tradition tended to ignore Popper's real contribution in the historiography of European philosophy. It is a fact, sadly, that, to mention just one example, Dagobert D. Runes' *Dizionario di filosofia*, published as a translation from English in June 1982 under the imprint of the Philosophical Society, yes, 1982, does not even list Popper after 'Pons asinorum'. Ironically, Popper had already been knighted in 1965, and his philosophical works had been on the market all over the world for at least two decades.

The interaction with Mahina in connection with Popper convinced Komaru once more that history is at best a fable. Consequently, a department of history is always a joke. Oswald Spengler's conception of history as a pessimistic fabulism was and still is buried among the misconceptions of his political views branding him a Nazi. But Komaru had nevertheless accepted Spengler's 'history' as culture *in posse* and 'historiography' as civilization *in esse*. The only way to conceive of history as a tangible reality was to 'make' it a dynamic and tangible complex of events, whether forced or natural, before they become part of historiography by registering facts of the past and thus historiographizing them as frozen civilization after culture had perished. Komaru had no the intention of witnessing the disappearance of Maori culture under the oppression of British civilization. He knew that 1993 was the beginning of the rebirth of Ao Tea Roa. Five hundred years of white exploitation had ended 'historiographically' the year before with the destruction of Columbus' image. That is why the Year of Aborigenes Conference waited 365 more days for the Earth to go around the Sun. New light was shining as the first rays of sunshine were greeted in the east as they would for 10 more years under the sponsorship of the UN. Failing that, there was no other recourse than that of seeking the protective shield of the United Aborigenes.

Chapter 39

The winter season had arrived as a propitious one with a few days of fine weather before 26 June, the date reserved for the organised cultural festival in Wellington. *Te Taura Whiti I Te Reo Maori* was approaching fast as an event to be written about and remembered for a long time after its conclusion. The theme was 'Toku reo toku mana', that is, something like 'power stems from language', or, by reversing its syntactical structure, 'language creates power'. There was nothing new or magical in that dictum, for the language question had been analysed and recognised as a powerful tool of confrontation as soon as the Waitangi Trick had been played deceptively on the Chiefs of Ao Tea Roa in 1840. A Maori word could at times surpass the destructive effectiveness of a soldier carrying a rifle. It was, naturally, the way a word, or a sentence, would be used within the proper world climate of opinion. The South Africa experience, tied to an emotional term such as Apartheid, had taught many lessons. What word or sentence would be used within and without Ao Tea Roa in order to stir the consciousness of a humane world at large? How could a few hermit islands relegated to the bottom of the callous world at large be heard and understood?

Komaru knew that the Maori language was a key element as a medium, as well as the most efficient tool of offense in the so-called fight between the two cultures disguised as 'race relations'. People seemed to forget that Maori was THE 'native' means of communication, and that English was an import utilised, like a bullet stemming from the bore of a gun, to kill the Maori language along with its speakers. Even the pluralisation of 'relation' as a substantive stunk with superciliousness leading to annihilation as done in Namibia. There was nothing historically to think of as a two-way street. If an adaptation was to be attempted, well, it should have been through 'unilateral' race relations, for it was the Pakeha who had to adapt to the Maori system of everything. The Aborigines had no need, and no duty, to adapt to anything. There was to be only ONE relation, and this was for the invaders to either get the hell out of the country or adapt themselves to a culture that had remained unchanged and unchallenged even before the Germanic tribes had crossed the Channel to 'create' Saxon England.

For Komaru, it was nearly a miracle that a linguistic system, though bastardised by Anglo-Saxon adstrata at the lexical level only, had survived the onslaught of a superimposed culture wiping out, in the process, every other language in Polynesia except in Ao Tea Roa. The other islands had disappeared linguistically within the Polynesian Triangle, the last ones being the Sandwich Islands, in less than a century. Ironically, within that triangle there had emerged the language of destruction through nuclear explosions and radiation. Only the southern corner had barely survived against all odds, almost as if, by a mysterious correlation, it was this very corner that had banned nuclear traffic and cooperation among the stockpilers of mass destruction, nations such as the USA and France.

In that connection, Komaru remembered a book he had borrowed from an American student who was studying with him at East China Normal University in Shanghai. Titled *The Broken Circle: A Search for Wisdom in the Nuclear Age*, it had just been published in 1988 as a paperback. The impact it left on his psyche had been shattering, for the collection of short observations by several people on the danger of phasing out Earth through sheer ignorance reminded him of Durkheim's theories on suicide. Yes, Durkheim had classified suicide according to a tripartite scheme in which the individual was considered in relation to whether one was egotistic, altruistic or anomic. That had happened in 1897, when the original French edition was published as *Le Suicide*. It took more than 50 years to appear in English as *Suicide* in 1952, exactly when the hydrogen bomb became a reality.

Although in Shanghai Komaru had already resolved to dedicate his life to removing white oppression from Ao Tea Roa, he could not shove under the rug his doubts about 'why' in the long range. The Earth was going to become totally cancerous sooner or later. Thus, why bother about engaging in a lifetime fight against social injustice? Well, perhaps Ao Tea Roa could be spared a catastrophe because of its isolation and antinuclear policies. After all, New Zealand had no source of uranium as at the Kerr–McGee mine in Shiprock, New Mexico. People would not die of radiation-induced lung cancer surely, but was that all? Regardless of whether one day even his people would die of radiation, it was still a matter of acquiring the dignity of freedom. If one were to die in Ao Tea Rca, well, at least one could enter the Rang as a free Maori, and not in chains. The Masada lesson was lingering in his mind, and here Komaru wondered how Durkheim would have classified that 'mass' suicide in contrast with the slow one tending to obliterate Maoridom under white oppression. In addition, there was quite a difference between the mass suicide in Masada by conscious determination and the Earth's mass suicide by callousness and stupidity.

At least in the case of Ao Tea Roa, there was a binding element that Earth did not possess: Maori language for The Hermit Islands, as Hebrew had taken the place of religion among the Jews. In both cases, Maori and Hebrew had been resurrected, though in Ao Tea Roa just barely and recently. The fact that Mahina was teaching Maori in Portland was a clear sign of a tidal reversal at least symbolically.

There was, however, an ironic twist to the language question in comparing the two cultures. Hebrew was THE language of Israel. In Ao Tea Roa, the situation was a slap in the face of Maoris. Komaru became aware of the topsy-turvy status quo after Mahina reported in a letter what an American-Indian student in her class had asked her: why in Ao Tea Roa was the Maori language considered a 'second language'? The question had hit Mahina so hard that she could not find an immediate answer. There it was on page 4 of T. Rikihana's *Learning and Teaching Maori* (Heinemann, 1976), the textbook used by Mahina during the second semester. The first sentence was 'How can one approach the study of a second language as Maori?' Was not English the language of colonisation in a country where Maori had been spoken even before English was in England? Why then teach Maori in the States when English was the primary language of New Zealand?

The epistolary exchange on the subject was cut short by Komaru, for he did not want to influence his sister unduly. He knew that sooner or later Maori would become the 'Hebrew' of Pacific 'Palestina', especially since the Maoris had never left their native land. And the Maori language was to become a weapon of war. Nevertheless, Komaru realised that language alone could not suffice as a tool of offense to promote freedom and dignity buried in crystallised, paradigmatised, and quasi-genetic oppression. So, it was WHAT to say in Maori and how, as well, in order to break the vicious cycle of dejection. Something had to be done. But, what?

To begin with, Komaru thought that the best thing was the resurrection of the original historical approach that his father had promulgated in 1973 through the Waitangi Action Committee and what he had hoped in vain to present as an MA thesis at Victoria University. Having failed that, Komaru decided to proselytise among the 150 delegates representing and expressing the Cultural and Intellectual Property Rights of Indigenous People among a wide assortment of activists coming from Fiji, Panama, Surinam, the Cook Islands, and others, including The Hermit Islands. He felt, however, that 'charity', in its pristine acceptation, begins at home. Likewise, Activism. Ao Tea Roa was morally bound to host the delegates beyond the surface manifestations of pageantry of the events. Ao Tea Roa was, thus, to create the proper focus of Activism so that later this would spread all over Polynesia. For that he hoped to rely on the legality of the Movement by learning from Moana Jackson's writings that 'the beneficiary and the first recipient of indigenous knowledge must be the *mokopuna* of those who created the knowledge or cultural property.'

Yes, Komaru's father had died, but he was still alive among the descendants of those who had created that knowledge and cultural property. Would the UN accept the Mataana Declaration? Failing that, physical action at 'home' was the only alternative to tell the world that Ao Tea Roa was alive, well, and living in the Pacific as it had been longer than any other cultural in the world except for China. And even there, that exception was non-existent since Ao Tea Roa herself had originated in Hawaiki, the first *nakē* from whose shores Asiatic navigators had departed in search of a free land devoid of 'social' constraints.

It was during the winter of 1993 that Komaru began to feel the impact of what he called the 'solar' year by associating – and here he did not mind his presumptuousness – his eponymous designation with the series of 'native' activities permeating the Hermit Islands, The program involving virtually all indigenous people of the Pacific triangle was directed, 'He ranganū pono' 'In true partnership', by a woman, namely, Professor Erica-Irene Daes, Chairperson of the UN Working Group on Indigenous Populations. Selwyn Katene, Chairman of the International Year, and Wira Gardiner, its Chief Executive, lent their optimistic cooperation to the whole programme. But Komaru was suspicious about the real motive behind their participation. As Maori men, had they been brainwashed into coasting along a Pakeha 'scheme'? Was the whole trumpeted and grandiose plan a sentimentaloid and self-indulgent charade?

Nevertheless, the Sun rose on 1 January 1993, on Mount Hikuranga, the sacred mountain of the Ngati Porou, welcomed by a dawn ceremony recorded fully by the bemused Fourth Estate and even in popular videos. The whole ceremony could be synthesised through the artistic perception of Sara Bates, a 'Native-American' – and here Komaru derided that mocking designation as insulting, for why not an 'Ethnic American', everybody else being a 'Designated AMERICAN'? – Cherokee painter/sculptor who declared: 'There is seeing the Earth as a living thing and recognising mutual dependency with the Earth.'

Yes, Komaru could not remain insensitive to the wide-canvas display of manifestations calling for artistic, instructional and geopolitical implementation of what the conference could accomplish in a 10-year period, ending in 2002, for art *per se* was never historically a prime motor behind the struggle for liberation. Surely, young people, women, frightened Pakehas and drugged Maoris would dedicate a decade of their efforts to building a new Ao Tea Roa. Komaru snuffed at the idea, for even as a failed historian he could not find any record of eliminating a noxious weed by simply grafting roses on it. Unfortunately, he had a sixth sense telling him that the whole 'decennial' conference was a platitudinous plan distracting the Movement from political activism that only Maoris, the only and the last still genuine group in Polynesia, had a chance to keep alive. A 10-year waiting in the wings of the UN's palliative paperwork was too long. And too iffy. Moreover, the UN had never 'liberated' anyone from political slavery. There were only two tools stronger and more efficient than a cadre of salaried officials warming their cushioned, high-back, executive chairs in the UN Plaza in New York, namely, public opinion and, short of terrorism, constant guerrilla activities devoid of bloodspilling violence. Komaru, as a realistic strategist in political struggles, was convinced that not even spilling Maori blood would dislodge a chronic oppression. So what was the alternative, if any?

Once more, unlike salaried Maoris comfortably settled in Pakeha institutions such as the Waitangi Tribunal, those refusing to accept post-colonial tactics of cunctatorship could only develop a rickety new 'smooth pillow' policy on Maori rights. Another generation of complacency, and the Maori would die off not physically but psychologically like the Continental Kumarans, alias the 'Ethnic Americans' who, after so many centuries of oppression, had not yet been able to name themselves away from a Florentine given name imposed capriciously by a German cartographer.

The extreme cold of June 1993 seemed to have sharpened Komaru's resolution to stay officially out of most events and, thus, pay only lip service to some of them so as not to be noticed too obviously for not being a 'patriot'. It was at *Te Taura Whiri I Te Reo Maori*, however, that he made his voice heard on behalf of Mahina, for the plan of the Maori Language Committee's activities culminating in Wellington on 26 June could furnish him some ideas for future implementation. That was, of course, the official excuse for his participation in the Wellington Festival. In practice, he had little to learn from that Commission, and that little he could get was too late for his sister. In fact, Mahina had already finished teaching her course at Transpacific University, obtained an MA in Philosophy, nearly satisfied her year of Postulancy as an external, and had planned to spend three more months as an intern until moving to another convent willing to accept her for two years of Novitiate.

The real reason for attending the June festival stemmed from another platform of strategy, that of contacting someone who, although interested in Polynesian as a 'native' language, would be an initial contact for political activism outside New Zealand, with the hope that one day this outside 'contact' would become a force furnishing some help in whatever Komaru had hoped to accomplish in the following two years, that is, 1994 and 1995. These were crucial years. Something had to be done 'physically'. But whom to count on?

From among the various delegates, Komaru tried to get in touch with the most logical and powerful representatives. Accordingly, he hoped to select someone from the Hawaiian Islands for several reasons. The former Sandwich Archipelago was still young enough as a people subject to white colonisation, and was well tied emotionally to their *whenua*. In fact, if one chose 12 August 1898 as the corresponding '6 February 1840' for the Hawaiian Islands, not even 100 years had elapsed since Sanford Dole saw the US flag being hoisted while listening to the Royal Hawaiian Band playing 'Hawai'i Pono', for the last time before America grabbed that Pacific jewel. It was an illegal transaction, a political rape, but what could Lili'uokalani do? Her niece, Princess Ka'iulani told the *San Francisco Chronicle* at that time: 'When the news of annexation came, it was bad enough to lose the throne, but infinitely worse to have the flag down.' And with it, the last vestige of social dignity for being born a Hawaiian and one day dying as a phoney American.

Before contacting the Hawaiian delegates, Komaru first had to do some 'historical' homework, and in so doing he could not believe how, in less than 100 years, the whole essence of Hawaiian *whenua* had almost disappeared. And in its tow many of the intangibles that keep a people united with pride, in addition to economic structures that in the past had kept Hawaiians free and 'Polynesian'. In fact, only 208,000 people of Hawaiian descent remained in the whole State, that is, about 20 per cent. This figure was higher than the Maori percentage-wise, but at the same time, paradoxically, it did not show what was happening to the subtle despotism keeping people in political bondage deriving in part from the 'big brother' takeover. The whole situation had been synthesised clearly by Senator Daniel Akaka, D-Hawaii: 'Even today, as we lock at the plight of the Hawaiians, sometime people refer' to 12 August 1898 as the date when change came about subtly but swiftly. 'The Hawaiians started to decline, the ills Hawaiians suffer today can date from that time.'

As the Hawaiians try to save their 'psychological' identity, they remain nearly impotent *vis-à-vis* the decline of cultural means even at the everyday economic level. A case in point is the 'glue' binding language, publications and the dissemination of instruction. The disintegration of 'culture' can be seen in the filing of Chapter 11 by various bookstores in Honolulu, one of them being the nearly 50-year-old book shops beginning the downward spiral toward oblivion. It is anticipated that by the end of the century, unless the Bangkok Chirathivat family owning the book shops in Ala Moana takes drastic measures, the three children inheriting the family tradition may have to quit the book business.

In talking with some delegates, Komaru was pleased to learn how a resurgence in language was inching its way into even elementary schools. At the Punana Leo School in Honolulu, teacher Noelani Lokepa was one of the few pioneers reciting daily language lessons to her children by using excerpt from W. D. Alexander's *Hawaiian Grammar*. Although nearly extinct, Hawaiian begins to appear even in tourist publications such as *Say It As It Is: Learn to Speak Hawaiian*, written by Mene Hume and published by Hawaiian Isles Publishing Company. As language returns to classrooms, the land too begins to be considered for return to the 'Natives' in a long and difficult process, for more than 1.4 million acres of Crown land were ceded to the (American) federal and state governments during annexation and statehood. According to Michael Tighe of The Associated Press, 'That is one-third of the state, including part of Honolulu International Airport and Pearl Harbor.' Komaru found plenty of parallels with his own people's *whenua*. And he wondered how Ao Tea Roa could have even lasted that long after two centuries of psychological genocide.

As in the Hawaiian Islands, white domination was not even 100 years old 'officially', thus Ao Tea Roa was, in a way, in better shape for not being part of a huge political power like that of Uncle Sam. So, Hawaiians were hopeful about the unifying self-determination movement of independence. They still had a chance not to follow in the footsteps of the American Indians, at least according to Ha Hawaii, one group planning a sovereignty convention in 1999. The problems are many, but the intention is only one, namely, restoring dignity under one seceded government, be it monarchy or whatever under the guidance of Queen Lili'uokalani, the eighth and last monarch. As expressed by representative Quentin Kawananakoa, descendant of Prince David Kawananakoa, 'It's a crossroads in our history. How are we going to address those concerns that have been overlooked, perhaps for 100 years?'

And in our case for 200, thought Komaru. Something had to be done, and soon. Thus he once more planned a popular awareness campaign within the Movement through visible activism, as a prelude to the November 1995 arrival of the 'legal' owner of Ao Tea Roa, namely, the Queen of England. That meant about two years in which to organise and disseminate vociferous manifestations in concomitance with the usual palliatives centered around, though not limited to, the Waitangi Day charade. But he also thought of spending the whole of 1993 to learn about tactical obstructions from Polynesian people participating in the various meetings sponsored by the 'disinherited' from both Polynesian and non-Polynesian lands. He thus reserved 1994 and 1995 for the activation of popular turbulences. How?

Komaru first thought of a simple axis of disturbances around which two complementary movements would rotate in an opposite way. One was, of course, the 'official' one, the normally expected, the traditionally anticipated in relation to Waitangi Day, and thus the re-evaluation of the Waitangi Treaty, in other words, the 'psychological'. This one he called centrifugal, and it rotated around the people who would be present at political functions, particularly the Press, the foreign dignitaries such as consuls and ambassadors, and also those Maoris who, having received a pittance in compensation for the property of their ancestors, tended to fall into a paralytic cooperation with Pakehas at the risk of being labeled *kupapa*. These near-*kupapa*, either through stupidity or because they had been blinded by sudden 'wealth', had created a class of their own, a kind of 'Quisling' parvenus selling their souls to whites for minnows. They conveniently forgot the real plight of their brothers and sisters languishing in ignorance, poverty, prisons and moral dejection.

The other opposite movement rotated around a 'physical' and forceful disturbance that was to echo what had begun at Bastion Point so long ago. This 'centripetal' manifestation had to be clearly centred at a historical and traditional place dominated by *tangata whenua*. It was to be violent enough to scare 'authorities', but not bloody, in order not to fall into the pit of Prague-type repression. Komaru thought that there was no place better than Wanganui to implement field actions. What could one stage up there, a strategic place midway between the 'political' Wellington and the 'economic' Auckland?

It took a whole year of planning for the 1994 'centrifugal' plan. The beauty of it all was that Komaru always remained a spectator. No one could ever tie him to any person or proposed action. He was not so stupid as to be accused of conspiracy, for first he did not recognise it as such. How could one fight a regime without 'planning' some action under a despot? The very term 'conspiracy' is always a tool of repression by the forces of law and order when recognised by all citizens under a 'democratic' government. Of course, that could not apply to his case, since he felt that by being afraid of it no revolution would ever be possible. In essence, for Komaru conspiracy was in the hands of absolute power to avert any chance to correct a wrong. That is why Nelson Mandela spent 26 years in jail.

It happened, however, that, without knowing him, Komaru took the opportunity to hitchhike in tow to Hone Harawira, leader of Te Kawariki, originally founded in 1975 and languishing for a generation in the doldrums of verbiage used by Crown lawyers. Surely, some of the original founders had been appeased with cushy jobs. Pakeha pharisaic and Jesuitical manoeuvres had paid off, but Hone Harawira would not be blinded by academic and business palliatives. Thus, an opportunity fell into Komaru's hands when Harawira became a *deus ex machina* in December 1994, by declaring: 'Those who support the Crown Treaty seek to condemn the rest of us to a future where our *mana* and *wairua* and our *rangatiratanga* will be footnotes in history.' The die had been cast. For Komaru, Harawira had become the Luther of Ao Tea Roa by posting the Bulls of Freedom on the sealed doors of Polynesian dignity.

The rest is history as vulgarly understood by the Crown. Komaru followed the 1994 selection of Mike Smith to speak at Waitangi Day. His classic statement, 'You will not be able to buy us off for 30 pieces of silver,' became the most powerful sentence ever proffered to a bewildered Prince Charles confronted with a copy of the 1835 Declaration of Independence. What happened at the 6 February charade remains as the equivalent of the Boston Tea Party. The Maori soul had revealed itself through Harawira's conscience. Frontliners like Mike Smith, Annette Sykes, Tame Iti, Ken Mair, Syd Jackson, Eva Richard and others must have been pleased, for they had toured the country to generate interest in various proposals and counterproposals particularly discussed during the preceding October. Wira Gardiner, present at most functions as impartial an observer as he could, later recollected the events with regard to some of the traditional Maoris still hoping that the Pakehas would become fair in dealing with justice by *fiat*. In his later book, *Return to Sender*, Gardiner took pains to report objectively on the events creating the so-called 'Fiscal Envelope'. Syd Jackson, in that connection, was clear about the 'final solution', the only solution possible as a matter of moral rights: 'We want absolute self-control and autonomy as was guaranteed to us when we signed the Treaty.' Oh, how elated Komaru was when he read those words in an interview given to a reporter of the *Gisborn Herald* on 28 October! How Komaru's father would have rejoiced that someone had finally spoken his mind openly and defiantly!

It was high time, in Komaru's opinion, and even against his belief in avoiding violence, that something 'international' be witnessed. When the New Zealand flag was trampled 'American style', the German ambassador, weary of similar manifestations in his country of Nazi vintage, tried to speak and calm down the crowd to no avail. The American ambassador left the area properly under the escort of plainsmen. The climax occurred when Harawira's daughter spat in the face of the governor-general, an act of courage that put her in gaol for 6 months. Amazingly, the whole confrontation was taking place not between Maoris and Pakehas, but between and among Maoris holding different allegiances to the Crown as a function of their 'social' status, which meant between pragmatists and idealists, rich and poor, Tribunal of Waitangi money recipients and those who, like Komaru, had refused to apply for '30 pieces of silver'. Among the various officials trying to bring some order in the Los Angeles-type uncontrolled manifestations of hate and accusation, several of them tried to calm down the crowd. One of these, Erima Henare, in spite of his paternal *mana* and oratorical skill, failed miserably. Neither Maori, as a language, nor English, into which the meeting had been switched, succeeded in bringing order to the out-of-control *marae*.

Finally, the Waitangi meeting was called off. In addition, when the naval contingent was ordered not to march onto the 'sacred' Ground as in 1940 to sanction 'We are one people,' all celebrations were cancelled.

Regardless of shortcomings, the year 1995 started well insofar as Komaru was concerned. That was a movement running centrifugally around the 'Axis' of international awareness. It was thus high time that the other movement start to run centripetally in an opposite direction, and away from Waitangi. Something had to be done by 'united' Maoris, not by bitching among themselves as 'maori' individuals against *kupapa* opportunists. Where? The place was Wanganui. When? Immediately, in tow to the Waitangi emotional skirmishes. How? By seizing the opportunity created by the Waitangi flop as the minds of idealists were still hot and yearning for action. Under whose leadership? Under that of a restaurateur running the Mediet. Never in history had Napoleon's dictum been so true that an army fights on its stomach. A band of revolutionaries could not but follow in its footsteps. For what? For the seizing of something sacred to all Maoris, both symbolically and physically. Something known for generations in every *whakapapa* before the arrival of the Pakehas. And something not too far from the Mediet restaurant, the covert headquarters for an operation that came to be known as 'The Moutoa Gardens', a stone's throw from an eating establishment patronised by nearly everybody in town regardless of race. All segments of Wanganui 'classes' had prostituted their stomachs for a bowl of minestrone, though it had become fashionable now for whites to rub shoulders with Maoris. They had become 'cool', and the fact that 'natives' had imported and developed a healthy diet from Mediterranean shores created a quantum leap in healthy nutrition. The dictum 'going native' had suddenly, and ironically, assumed a positive meaning, almost a *de rigueur* fad. And Komaru took that opportunity to seize FORTUNA by her hair when he saw her flowing along the Whanganui river toward the Tasman Sea.

As soon as the Waitangi Day flop was known all over the country, Komaru gave the 'go ahead' for the inception of a tactical operation. About 150 people, carrying tents, food, field kitchens, beds, cots, radios and other camping equipment, occupied the Moutoa Gardens early in the morning of 28 February. Komaru followed Ken Mair's movements silently, though intensely, from the windows of the kitchen. The Press and the forces of law and order did not take long to arrive and take up vantage points in bemusement. After all, this rag-tag stream of *deseredados* had done similar things in the past all over New Zealand. In their minds this was another 'emotional picnic,' another rushed outing at the early inception of autumn. As soon as the temperature fell a few degrees, the natives would disband in search of warmth, tellies and beer.

The Press began to listen perfunctorily to reasons for the occupation. The whole operation was explained by Niko Tangaroa in a single statement: 'We are returning to our ancestral lands. We have the full support of *iwi* and *iwi* close to us – close both geographically and close in ties. We are here in a peaceful way to re-establish our *marae*.' Komaru observed, analysed, and decided. He was not sure about the results of one more 'occupation'. As a historian of similar actions, he immediately sensed a lack of popular participation. Something had to be done to infuse additional blood into the physical area already being fenced off from the rest of Wanganui. That was a mistake, he thought, since, rather than expanding throughout the city and then even the region, the fence cut off the essence of the occupation by limiting it to a frozen and stagnant area. Nevertheless, Komaru tried another tactical move. Nearly a month later, he gave his approval for a student support of *iwi* close geographically and spiritually. Again, with the approval of the 'local' guide, in March 1995 some Victoria University students, including some from the Polytechnic Institute, began a coordinated attack against the Ministry of Maori Development in Wellington. They were sick and tired of cunctative policies of conformism. They had seen how the newly emerging Maori bourgeoisie was being taken through the accepting of alms tossed by the Waitangi Tribunal as a new form of *panem et circenses* in the arena of legalese. In fact, just during the last few years, the Waitangi Tribunal had decreed, *ex cathedra*, three fundamental proclamations in typical British authoritative fashion.

The first regarded the so-called Fisheries Claims Settlements Act of 1992: 'This prevents the Waitangi Tribunal from hearing claims on commercial fishing or commercial fisheries.' The technique of deception was once more baffling even to a Kafka-esque setup of a *mise-en-scène*. In essence, the Tribunal was forbidding itself to do or not to do something regardless of Maori rights. And, indeed, in order to sanction that circular policy, a token power of management was entrusted to a lady who, in her younger years, had been 'revolutionary' enough to risk jail. Now she had been silenced with a comfortable salary as long as she did not rock the Pakeha boat ... in Maori waters.

The second was the Treaty of Waitangi Amendment of 1993: 'This

Act prevents the Tribunal from recommending the return of any privately owned land to Maori ownership. The Act defines private land to include any land owned by local government. The Act does not prevent the Tribunal from inquiring into and reporting on claims that concern privately owned land.' What a jargon building an absurd logic, thought Komaru, as if 'government land' had been in possession of a 'Maori' government.

But what really burned Komaru out was the recently passed Waikato-Raupatu Claims Settlement Act of 1995: 'This Act prevents the Tribunal from hearing Waikatu Raupatu claims.' This and the preceding 'preventions' seemed to have been formulated in Nazi Germany regarding the whole arc from Poland to the Sudetenland and the Rhineland. The Tribunal, rather than listening to claims of citizens, would even forbid them to open their mouths by preventing itself from doing anything. In particular, this prevented Komaru's non-'tribal' ancestral rights from being implemented as in the case of Te Whanau O Waipareira, which Haki Wihongi had lodged with the Tribunal of 11 January 1994. At any rate, Komaru would have refused even to acknowledge his rights, for Ao Tea Roa in his opinion was not to be parcelled out as a carcass from which to toss pieces of flesh to starving dogs.

It did not take long for Komaru to convince himself that the occupation was destined to fizzle into a 'chronic' tradition of *laissez faire* Pakehanism watching the *feu de paille* until it became extinguished for lack of popular support. This feeling of impotence became more evident when, utilizing the radio scanner brought as a gift by Mahina to her father on his deathbed, Komaru monitored most of the conversations between the unarmed police and government officials. He also listened to the newspaper reporters waiting in the wings with the sinister hope that the 'armed offender squads' would cross the Marina Whanganui bridge from the east and intervene with force if necessary. The *New Zealand Herald* had become the non-official spokesman for all the pussy-footing over Moutoa as reported on 28 March 1995, especially after the Wanganui Council served an eviction notice a few days earlier. A crisis was almost ready to develop when on Anzac Day a crowd of about 600 'patriotic citizens' marched by the Gardens singing the national anthem. Komaru, although he knew that 'his' protesters had been instructed not to engage in confrontations, hoped that a mêlée would ensue between lawful citizens and a bunch of latter-day hippies. That kind of hope was rekindled when on 10 May the police stormed the gardens with the excuse of looking for drugs and weapons. Arrests were made. The next day the Mayor of Wanganui had his way by declaring the protesters trespassers since the Moutoa Gardens were the legal property of the Wanganui District Council. *Also sprach* the High Court on the 16th. Two days later, in the dark of an early, cold morning, some fences came down, tents were rolled up and utensils were packed, while a bonfire gave light and heat to the last *Dämmerung* of the 79-day-long vigil for justice. Niko Tangaroa had a few faithful comrades-at-hope gathered around the bonfire for a *karakia*. Before noon, the police escorted the remaining brothers and sisters a few miles downstream toward the Putiki Marae. Silent tears flowed along the way, but the Whanganui river flowed noisily, complaining against another act of injustice. The Maori 'protesters' had been kicked out of their home, their temple, their ancestral *whenua*. Over the police scanner, Komaru heard a comment by someone apparently in charge of the whole operation.

'W-One to Council. Over.'
'Council to W-One. Ten fifty-five.'
'Mission accomplished. Over.'
'Ten fifty-six. Any stragglers?'
'A few. Apparently Chas Poynter is supposed to inspect later. Henry Bennett still at location. Over.'
'But, what about the Weasel?'
'No sign of him, probably still cooking for the few gang members lingering in the area.'
'So, that is not Henry Bennett?'
'Apparently not. But we have a few officers left for a mop up visit. Over.'
'What about Ken?'
'He is being interviewed by the *Herald*. Still bellicose. But, you know, I have seen these paper tigers so many times since Bastion Point. Over.'
'Ten-four. Eleven-o-one. Over and out.'

In fact, the following day, the *New Zealand Herald* reported Ken Mair's statement *in extremis*: 'As long as the Crown buries its head in the sand and pretends that the issue of *tino rangatiratanga* and our land grievances are going away, well, I don't want to shock anyone, we are going to stand up and fight for what is rightfully ours.'

Poor, wonderful, idealistic Ken, thought Komaru. He thinks like father. He never gives up. Komaru knew that the occupation had succeeded tactically, but had failed strategically like all the previous 'occupations' since the cutting of the flagpole more than 150 years before. Was then Maoridom doomed to slide into oblivion? He removed the earpiece, left the kitchen, and entered the dining area, where a hungry crowd seemed to be in a jovial mood. He also observed that a couple of individuals wearing dark glasses had taken their place in the queue at the salad bar. Never seen before, he thought. Trying to act normally, Komaru removed a nearly empty tray of *penne all'arrabbiata* in order to replace it with a fresh one.

'I shall be back in a moment, gentlemen.'

'Take your time, my dear fellow. We are in no hurry. We know that you have good food. Oh, what is this dish?'

'*Penne all'arrabbiata*. Quills in an angry mood.'

'Oh, my goodness,' said the older of the two visitors. 'But why so?'

'Well, sir, you should ask the Italians who invented this dish. Probably they were mad at the cook for being mistreated.'

'But you are not, are you?'

'No, sir, not at all. And our cook is a real chef. She has captured the very soul of Italians at table.'

'A rather flighty dish, then? I think I will like it. Would you not, Jonathan?'

'Absolutely, mate. I think that only Maoris can cook as well as the Italians. They are the spice of culinary ... life. They add a rather exciting dimension to a standard fare of kidney and pork pie. Wouldn't you say, oh, what is your name?'

'Komaru, sir.'

'Quite a name for an Italian. Are you from Sicily?'

'Not quite, sir. I ... am actually a New Zealander. But, sir, sorry, let me bring a fresh tray. I'll be right back.'

When Komaru came back, the two blokes were nowhere in sight. Melissa informed him that they had left immediately after radioing a message from the kerb.

Chapter 40

The Austral winter of 1995 was closing in fast on Ao Tea Roa after two-and-a-half months of a 'pacific disturbance' that was supposed, or hoped, to become a 'Pacific revolution'. Komaru had high hopes that the Maori people would finally rise consciously from atavistic lethargy and stand up for their rights. The global climate of opinion was clearly in favour of 'nativism', of 'indigenism', of activism. He knew, of course, that the road leading to anything satisfactory was sprinkled with obstacles, but, by taking a look at what had been accomplished within a century of fighting for genetic freedom, the balance was visibly in favour of people who, merely a couple of generations ago, had never thought of becoming independent nations. In the case of South Africa alone, who would ever have dreamed that a political prisoner for a whole generation would become the president of a country kept in bondage for centuries? Thus, for how many more years would Ao Tea Roa continue to suffer the indignity of being kept a slave of a master race?

Komaru felt a certain sense of the impending, but he was not a fool. He knew that palliatives such as the Waitangi Tribunal could act only as a magic smokescreen, if not a mesmerising distraction, luring simpletons into accepting temporary solutions for the sake of immediate gratification. The fools!, he thought. Their political blood had been sucked by the last vestiges of colonialism disguised as a sudden *au pair* comradeship. And, as the autumn of an astronomic year anticipated a winter of unknowns, so the autumn of the 20th century was also forecasting a new century of larger unknowns. Komaru sensed that the political dimension of his *whenua* was inseparably tied to the end of the Industrial Age, an age that had affected the dominant nation, New Zealand, only in theory. The factor of Industrialism had performed wonders even in Third World countries until recently regarded as 'economically retarded' as in the case of China, or even Taiwan, but The Hermit Islands were still floating barely above the water of survivalism exactly as they were a century earlier. In fact, the gaoler New Zealand was still regarded, as it were, as a complex of islands populated by shepherds who kept on exporting, as did their grandfathers, unprocessed wool, artery-clogging butter, and tasteless frozen meats on the one hand, and childish naïveté, conceited beliefs of social superiority, and repressed despair on the other.

Was it possible that the new millennium, carrying in tow the deceptive bi-frontal Age of Information and Age of Communication, could generate an Age of Freedom? Komaru had deep doubts, for, after all, both 'Blitz' Communication 'Overload' and Information seemed to efface each other. They acted like a *kuri* biting its tail of Communication with Information, or vice versa. What was it within Man's psyche that could not be communicated with knots tied on a string? Yes, he admitted to himself, communication could be accomplished in nanoseconds among humans and things, but how would that change the global social condition for the better when in the half century after the end of the Second World War one had witnessed the most atrocious in-fighting among Europeans alone, much worse than that among 'primitive' tribes, as the Maoris were regarded a couple of generations earlier? Komaru desperately tried to understand any positive correlations between Information and Communication, but he found only a frightening wall of impersonality surging among humans quickly bound to obliterate any way of looking each other in the eye, for obviously the dyad 'InfoCom' did not warrant either knowledge or wisdom. Besides, he feared that the pan-globality, impersonality and rapid diffusion of communication had the potential to spread unchecked information without any chance to check its veracity. In essence, both Communication and Information were bound to work as two antithetical furies destined to efface each other through their means of existence. Once more, the electronic medium was the message, and this was operating in a vacuum where new generations of Terrestrials would have their capacity for thought reduced to the level of moronity. Everything would fall out of a square screen of hardware onto the insecure and atrophying mind of computer-literate biological entities destined to share their lives with software. As a matter of fact, Komaru concluded that humans were paradoxically condemned to become software in reverse, and thus destined to 'live' in a pre-programmed climate of zombiness for lack of a genetically ingrained purpose. In a way, computer-designed life would lead to the death of intelligence, and thus of the spirit.

Even in his own political microcosm within Wanganui, Komaru had found the validation of macrocosmic parallels between the 'disturbance' taking place at home, for, in comparison with geographically unrelated cases of social, religious, political or economic centres of eruption 'in the field' as in Bosnia, Ireland, Russia, Burundi, Rwanda, Somalia, Zaire, Algeria, Iraq and its nearby X-stans, the Occupation of the Moutoa Gardens had been simply another 'Maori fart'. Once the noise and the stench of that political constipation had vanished under the watchful eyes of police power, the Crown would shine as usual on the empty head of a mythological monarch. If any cloud of insecurity cast a shadow of concern on the fate looming on the Jewel of the Pacific, well, that was dispelled by the policy of psychological control subtly injected into the minds of 'natives' by *laissez-faire* waiting in the wings of time. And time was clearly in favour of Pakehas even if it took 2,000 years *more Vaticano*.

Sadly, Komaru could not help but accept the fact that Ao Tea Roa had died of ideological asphyxia on the morning of 19 May. Unlike any 'social disturbances' reported instantly thanks to living in the Age of Communication/Information, the one taking place on The Hermit Islands had been ignored by everybody in control of reporting, recording, analysing and transmitting political events throughout the World. The Fourth Estate, the United Nations, the Embassies, the Intelligence organisations, the Words of Mouth and analogous sources of divulgation had simply refused, and laughed at, acknowledging anything Maoris engaged in as frolicking at a 'summer picnic ground'. In the eyes of the various government agencies, and even Maori turncoats, drugged youth, petty thieves, drunken dole recipients, ragtag gangs, dirty 'coconuts' and a whole rosary of 'un-British' populace had failed to pull Maori consciousness from the doldrums of political callousness. The whole camp had assumed on the pages of the white press and on the benches of local government representatives an atmosphere similar to that of Waco, Texas.

By mid-April, Komaru had recalled what took place in Waco two years earlier, and he did not want to see a repetition of a useless 'holocaust' involving women and children. On the evening of the 20th the news of an Oklahoma act of 'terrorism' hit him hard. Two years to the day after Waco. Was the camp at the gardens going to be next to have blood spilled? Suddenly, he realised that his people camping by the Whanganui could become casualties in a confrontational situation. Those people in the gardens were alive, but the rest of Maoris inhabiting The Hermit Islands were already among the living dead. The Treaty of Waitangi, in fact, had been the *Dies irae, dies illa* recited by Governor Dobson so long ago that not even bone scraps could be dug out of the caves of memory. When the news of the Oklahoma City bombing reached him a day later, it became apparent that just one individual could accomplish more than a whole group of protesters. He thus decided to coast along with the protesters in a 'ping-pong' game of useless negotiations, and intentionally allowed himself to wait for a month of wait-and-see developments. Accordingly, he gave instructions to hang on for a month counting from 20 April just to save face. If nothing happened in the meantime, then the 'protesters' would abandon camp.

And so, a month later, Komaru entered the date '19th May 1995' onto the annals of his private history as the day in which all abstract concepts of freedom fell into oblivion. And, with it, time too. When history and time fail to stay together in any social connubium, what remains in the bowels of Polynesians is despair sprinkled with a heavy dose of bitterness, impotence and alienation. The essence of *Homo semeioticus*, barely discerned on the blackboard of a fooled Humanity, becomes self-effaced as if an invisible hand held a giant felt eraser, wiping out any vestige of intelligence, humanness, consciousness. Everything reverts to a pre-*signum* stage of what was supposed to allow marine creatures to create a social community on dry land, arboreal biological entities to descend onto the grounds of enlightened lives, quadrupedic brutes to emerge on two limbs from the dark caves of physical security into the dazzling ambience of exciting novelty, of living progress, of cultural developments, the whole leading to the first stage of so-called civilization. And freedom! Komaru was now convinced that humans had conceived of and labelled that vague notion of psychological liberty in order not to go insane, for freedom was a joke. After all, why would Maoris need to complain? Most of them were well fed, owned real estate, possessed most modern amenities, had no need to fight each other. A century ago they were still 'savages', weren't they, engaged in primitive activities of survivalism. Nowadays, thanks to the British, they were enjoying life as never before in the previous millennium. Why complain?

For Komaru, who had given his word to a dying father, however, even at the most elemental level of social interaction, everything had become a mockery of dignity. As metaphorically concluded by Paul Moon in relating the swan song of Maori activism, the *Götterdämmerung* of Ao Tea Roa had not been grasped even by the retreating rear guard of history, for history itself had fallen off the edge of *whenua* as at Wounded Knee Creek: 'The protesters' claim for the

Moutoa Gardens represented that of a mother whose child had been give(n) up for adoption [to the Pakehas]. While the child may legally be the responsibility of someone else, the birth mother will always feel a bond with the child that transcends legal definitions, and that can be easily articulated or explained.' Once more, the dog was biting its tail by giving its shadow to the Queen and the substance to its puppies on paper, but in practice the Queen had become a monarch for all in the islands. In fact, was she not supposed to visit her estate in a few months on the occasion of a reunion of Commonwealth nations?

Komaru had witnessed, once more, and this time *in vivo*, the giving up of too many children for adoption, beginning with Bastion Point. Yes, the gardens of a 'primitive' and sacred *whenua* were like the one where Eve had been left as a prisoner of white oppression for future generations to weep on masochistically, in spite of all artistic tangibles and *whakamaharatanga* therein erected by sculptor Matt Pine. Yes, the Gardens of Hope had been fenced off as a showplace for past patriotic exploits like those of Monte Cassino, but nothing else had been left, not even infertile seeds of moral *Kumara*, for future planting.

And the concept of time, now fallen into the Pacific Ocean in its attempt to reach the first rays of Earthly sunshine, triggered in Komaru the formulation of his last theory, a sad one revolving around the periodical 2,000-year segment imposed on, if not concocted by, humans simply not to lose a sense of chronological orientation. Thus, he tried to re-orientate himself on the basis of what he had read and analysed during his research years within the giant paradigms of Mankind. He recalled only a few historiographic landmarks at random, the latest being a synthetic presentation in William Irving Thompson's *The Edge of History*, followed by his *Passages About the Earth*. Thompson had avoided diachronic speculations limited to numerical data. But Oswald Spengler's *Der Untergang des Abendslandes* made him feel willing to reinforce more specific cases of people who had vanished during the 2,000-year life span of civilization. Komaru just could not believe, nor escape from, realising how at the age of 29 he had grasped that kind of time-curse connected with live, anthropologically defined cultures on the verge of becoming dead civilizations. And Maoridom could not escape that fate. From Spengler's list of cultural stations in Europe, Komaru borrowed the concept of an *envoi*, namely, 'der Kreuzzüge oder von derinneren Glut des *"Dies irae"* jenes Thomas von Celano.' In lamenting the demise of Ao Tea Roa, Komaru had titled that *envoi* 'The Polynesian Book of the Dead.'

So, there was nothing new in the recurrence of that two-millennium periodicity in accounting for the existence of dynamic intelligence on Earth. The world itself had been indoctrinated by the Gregorian calendar, regardless of other calendric systems, to the point that everything electronic had taken over in every organised corporate structure at a price – in the process of saving digital space in earlier models, the hardware configuration had been contaminated endemically by the double-0 factor. And this had become a gene in the DNA structure of Mankind at the end of the second millennium carrying away 2,000 years of Aotearoan culture into the *waka* of civilisation. After all, Spengler had been clear and prophetic in his analysis of the eight 'epochal paradigms'. There is no question that Spengler's EIGHT EPOCS were not his invention, for he had obtained them from the mythological sketch appearing at least sixteen centuries earlier in the *Symposium* by St Methodius ('Eubulius'). Was it a coincidence that Methodius's 'Day 8', that is, the Eight Millennium, was equated with 'Eternity', so similar to the value of '8' in Chinese numerology? The meaning of '8' in China before Greek Christian visionary epochs is simply uncanny for, in both cultures, that number designated Heaven as a vision of immortality, namely the 'heavenly medows with the trees of truth.' The fact that the mythological 'Nine', from Deucalion's ark, suggested by Prometheus, to Milton's Gates of Hell to the Scandinavian worlds of Niflheim, was missing in each of his three Tafeln (namely, the *Geistesepochen*, the *Kunstepochen* and the *Politischer Epochen*) as it did not in Methodius, did not mean that Ao Tea Roa did not exist. Simply, Polynesia and Maoridom, in particular, had fallen into the *case vide* of Cromwell's *Umgebung* that could be expressed as 'die das britische Kolonialreich ins Leben gerufen hatte', as well as paraphrased through Cumming's view at the beginning of the 19th century in the ante-Waitangi era: '*Ao Tea Roa frei – und wömoglich englisch!*' Thus, Ao Tea Roa, after nearly two centuries of British indoctrination, had become 'free' and English, but the Maori language carrying 80 per cent of semantemes from Anglo-Saxon transphonation had become bastardised by its adaptation to Polynesian phonematics. Without genetic langauge, freedom was simply a myth. The phenomenon, ironically, was not without precedent, for English itself had become bastardised by a similar process – 85 per cent Latin either directly from a parent stock or indirectly via daughter languages, particularly French.

It was also baffling to Komaru that the missing '9' in Spengler's structural classification, as in St Methodius' millennia charts, had been entered into the periodic table of culture versus civilisation, that is, the dynamic versus the static, as the latest parvenu, namely, Ao Tea Roa, in the chrono-dichotomous analysis. Thus, almost self-gratifyingly, Komaru's 'Theory of Nine' had been validated by default, though not phenomenologically in the 19th and 20th centuries, but in the Etruscan period preceeding Rome's genocide to the point that all written records were systematically destroyed. The few extant titles of evidence and direct references by contemporary Greek and Roman writers give an inkling of how a whole civilisation had been 'absorbed' through planned effacing. The destruction of the three libraries in Alexandria contributed to obliterating the most important culture of pre-Roman 'Italy'. Of course, false theories discount cultural genocide by not adducing, as for Ao Tea Roa, the imposition of an alien power over another, and so Etruria's disappearance is conveniently viewed as the result of a natural absorption by a generous new emerging culture, such as that of Rome. Analogically, Ao Tea Roa is being deceptively and subtly 'absorbed' by invisible and silent British politicisation exactly as Rome had done with Etruria. The problem is that facts demonstrate this alleged 'absorption' otherwise, for Polynesian dignity had not yet died.

Without collating similar events in both Etruria and Ao Tea Roa, respectively sponged out by Rome and England, Komaru reviewed the history of Europe, and he just could not believe his own eyes in seeing how the mythical bitch seemed to repeat herself at the antipodes during the ninth, and the last, component beyond Spengler's octohedral classification. 'Nine' for Komaru was the last digit of history before this fell out of the arithmetic of Mankind. Chinese cabalistic numerology could not have been more prophetic in wrongly assuming 'nine' as the Etruscan mantissa for the attainment of perfection and, consequently, for stasis and extinction.

The Etruscan lesson was easy to follow and understand. In both Etruria and Ao Tea Roa, by adding another 'natural century' to Spengler's eight, Komaru saw an inexorable law, perhaps even a cosmic one, binding the Mediterranean to the Tasman Sea. And, although resigned to the fate of defeat stemming from factors beyond his control, he nevertheless went over 'The Theory of the Natural Century' almost as an act of penance before resolving to do something desperate about it for the sake of dignity. Yes, all the battles had been lost. And now also the traditional war. But, before dying on the battlefield, he decided to be remembered. He had to do something alone, for it was clear that the Maori people, the *kumara*-raised populace, and the newly created middle class basking in government jobs, had become and would remain indifferent *vis-à-vis* the Gardens. 'Once were warriors,' and 'Now are sheep'. Two years of preparation during 1993–95 had been wasted, and he himself had meanwhile been tagged by the forces of law and order as a dangerous individual, undermining the security of New Zealand. There was a mole somewhere. He knew he had been betrayed, but by whom, and why?

The day after the last 'protester' left the Gardens of Hope, Komaru took a whole week off, away from the restaurant. What had happened at Oklahoma City gave him food for thought. He had to collect himself in order to do something with the rest of his life. He wanted to study and understand the 'Etruscan syndrome' applied to Ao Tea Roa. Then he promised himself to 'return to Mahina' almost as a means of purification under the drive of a powerful sense of conscience screaming loudly in the back of his mind. For the last two years he had left her alone in spite of the fact that she wrote faithfully describing, in non-intimate terms but vividly in geographic and motivational language, most of her Novitiate after moving from Portland to the Denver area. He reserved the last part of the week to dedicate himself to the memory of his sister. He felt like a latter-day William Wordsworth receiving 'tourist' affection after the intimacy of a Dorothy's hidden life settling in a utopistic home with his sister. Why had he not settled in an Austral Grasmere, even having Ling-ling as Mary and Bill as Coleridge, after relegating Melissa to the rôle of Annette? Yes, of course, he risked being investigated for 'political treason' by a government agent, but would New Zealand police dare to do anything to him without any proof? Would the forces of law and order risk creating an atmosphere of journalistic 'propaganda' by arresting him in the wake of 'botanical disturbances'? How could a latter-day agent James Walsh proceed in an attempt to silence a potential nuisance? Would the Oklahoma City episode enter the preventive branch of MI5-trained police in order to pre-empt manifestations of protest on the occasion of the Queen's arrival in a few months? The egg episode of 1986 had not been forgotten as an impromptu farm implement of offense, but after nearly a decade another American farming tool of production had created quite a 'body count' after the sudden splash of an agrarian fertiliser. Then what?

Before returning to Mahina in spirit, for she had died for him, he started to analyse the Etruscan's phenomenon among so-called civilised nations. Since time immemorial, these had waged wars and revolutions in order to settle sticky matters. In the process, confrontational activities involved masses of humans properly organised to efface each other. Was there any way to perform similar tasks on a one-to-one basis? Even the arrangement between Curatii and Horatii was too crowded. Then, what? To receive inspiration and to avoid emotional rushes, he had to be sure that the Etruscan syndrome could be dealt with properly. Actually, Etruria had already reached the zenith of its culture before sliding down into the doldrums of civilisation. In Komaru's mind, Ao Tea Roa could not compare with Etruria quantitatively, but qualitatively there was no difference, for the psychological life could be considered equipollent as a function of a people's need. Rome, the *parvenu*, was already beginning to climb the steps of acculturation at the expense of Etruria, then of Greece, and then of the entire known theatre of political accomplishments within the triangle of Europe–Africa–Asia.

By the end of the week following the 19 May, Komaru had individualised, synthesised and sharply compared the Etruscan syndrome with the social organisations of people who had been effaced from the Earth. At that point, he realised that there was no escape from what seemed to be a 'natural' millennium life span for any civilisation on Earth, except perhaps the moral equivalent of a V–2 in action, well, if not as a last desperate attempt, at least as an act of sealing a historic period with a bang to save the dignity of a people in the cryogenic-type urn of a cosmic cemetery. It was a feeling that emerged surreptitiously as an act of retribution, perhaps of a super-utu whose seeds would germinate 1,000 years from now, thus initiating a ninth symphony beyond what Spengler had constructed as an Earthly production of eight. Komaru doubted that Spengler had secretly reserved the *case vide* of the ninth millennium for Hitler's dreams. And even if he had, who would be around on Earth to verify that hypothesis?

He went through his notebook in search of some data he had jotted down at random here and there, perhaps in the early 1990s, when researching 'history' at the Turnbull Library. Unfortunately, in those pre-personal laptop computer days, he had not entered complete source data. He had just written a name and a title, Raffaella Paoletti, 'The Etruscan: Myth and Civilization of a People.' That was not in the original language, but a translation from Italian into English. But by whom? Oh, the mistakes of youth! Now he was fussy about entering all the possible details. So, he thought, sorry Ms Paoletti for not giving you exact credit. And the same to the translator, whom he had at times paraphrased, but mostly transcribed in the process of having in mind an elaboration of the 'millennium theory'. Later, after discovering a similar theory in Spengler, Komaru wondered that there was indeed nothing new under the sun, for the Etruscans had already formulated the same, and they even attributed it to 'Oriental' sources. Was it possible that before departing from Hawaiki, Maori navigators were already aware of that myth? Strangely, on the occasion of the sesquicentennial 'celebrations' of the Waitangi Trick, Pakeha sources had assumed a similar period ascribing the arrival of Maori people to merely 1,000 years before. Was there anything magical about the number '1' followed by zeros? After all, the Etruscans had conceived their mantissa on a base of '10', though, of course, that was the first step toward infinity.

It was quite a revelation for Komaru to re-read, with more maturity, what he had transcribed at the inception of his university life having in mind to study history. He started with Censorinus in midstream, ironically a grammarian, thus a student of language, and not a historian.

Censorinus, who lived in the third century AD, at least a century before St Methodius, narrated in the 17th chapter of *Liber de die natali* how Marcus Terentius Varro, another grammarian, had been intrigued by a specific topic that occurred both in the *Tuscae Historia* and the ritual book of the *Disciplina*. They both treated the famous theory of the '*saecula*', the periods obsessing a whole segment of scholars from Vico to Spengler in modern times. Censorinus, as the avatar of 'secular' periodicisation, tried to understand why and how the mere digits of 1 plus three zeros (an *ante-litteram unum et trinum*?) would have influenced the fate of Etruria over a millennium! Komaru wondered whether, by any chance, Hitler may have been influenced by Spengler, though the latter was relegated to oblivion by Nazi historians. The origin of this bizarre belief could have been inspired by some cosmogonic theories of a distinct 'Oriental' origin, perhaps Chinese, for only Chinese people may boast of recorded data going back at least 6,000 years. Or was it possible that Censorinus was referring to Egyptian sources, or both, as 'Oriental?' How could it be that, by basing the life of the pre-Bruno, if not Pythagorean, universe on millenarian cosmic cycles, one could also specify the irrevocable limits placed by gods on humanity and its activities?

Of course, a similar theory had been formulated at least 300 years earlier by a poet, namely, Hesiod. That was the time when thinkers were only poets, before being split into philosophers, dramatists, historians and so forth. And that poet had imagined a cosmic temporal division into millennia, each of which he identified with the name of a metal: the gold, the silver, the copper and the iron ages. The problem for Komaru was that those eras may not have applied, not even in Hawaiki. In Ao Tea Roa they were absurd, for there one could only conceive of eras based on bones, stone and wood, with the difference that all these eras may have coincided and merged into one, so that the Bone People also knew of the other means of recording. And even without the metal, all these eras reflected different periods of spirituality attained by the human race during the course of its existence on The Hermit Islands. The progressive decadence of their quality revealed the inarrestable deterioration that occurred in the customs of mankind in its ever-increasing separation from the happy world of the gods. That is why, *nach* Annemarie de Waal Malefijt, 'Maori priests told how the original state of the universe was one of chaos.' To avoid freedom-restrictive monotheism, at the same time Maoris devised a variety of religious despots, namely, 'at least ten classes, ranging in hierarchical order from high priests, whose duties concerned the whole of the social group, through acolytes, seers, magicians of various sorts, and on to experts in astronomy at the lower stratum,' according to Edward Norbeck, basing his tenets on E.S.C. Handy's *Polynesian Religions*. Talk about 'primitive' people, thought Komaru. The Vatican's classification of pastoral charlatans was, in comparison, more primitive than the Maoris'.

It is not difficult, thus, to accept Etruscan cosmogony as derived from archaic Oriental myths. It was undoubtedly based on the millenary theory and, again, according to Paoletti, it is remarkable how Etruria was able to know the alpha and the omega of its national life deduced from the revelations dictated by Tages and collected in *Libri fatales* by priests. This view is reinforced by reading the chapter dedicated by Plutarch to Lucius Cornelius Sulla, containing a note that the Etruscans already knew of the millenary theory in the eighth century of their existence. This Etruscan millennium was divided into 10 so-called 'natural' centuries. However, they were not based on a conventional period of 100 years, but on a segment of time arbitrarily determined by the will of the gods, who marked the end of the 'century' on the basis of a phenomenon carrying a dramatic effect. That is why even nowadays there are people who believe in events such as the end of the world, or whatever, announcing a change and thus a new age at the end of a century of or a millennium. Consequently, even the Romans, and Hitler, originally adopted the Etruscan tradition nowadays known as 'millenarism'. Censorinus wrote in *Liber de die natali* that the proper procedure of calculating the non-astronomical century was based on the longest duration of human life and had as a limit the birth and the death of a man. Such a selfish assumption, thought Komaru, deriving from the Greek concept of man as the measure of everything. Amazingly, in spite of assumptions that the life of an average man was not as believed nowadays, some persons could live to 100 years of age. According to Censorinus, his ancestors had observed that a good number of their citizens lived to that age. That singular custom of basing a century on the longevity of a model 'calendar citizen' was at a certain moment abandoned, probably as a consequence of 'tribal' wars, and they preferred to deduce the end of each century from signals sent by gods, such as Celestial upheavals, natural calamities, tragic facts of human history such as, nowadays, the inception of the atomic age. In the case of the Etruscans, the end of their sixth century may have coincided with the fall and destruction of the Volsinii, the moral capital of Etruria. Analogically, the end of the 20th century could be reckoned as that of the disappearance of the Red Scare, or perhaps even the inception of the *saeculum Sinense*, and consequently the disappearance of the *saeculum Americanum*. Calculations for a 'historical' and not astronomical century were not numerically standard, but logical enough to assume that the 21st century will not be an American one if the USA persists in assuming that it is at the centre of the Universe. Unlike the most destructive, organised evils ever affecting Man, that is, War, there will emerge a new spectre of chaotic social derangement that no political, military or religious power can stop. This is called, wrongly, 'Terrorism'. It is, in fact, a return to tribalism reduced to its most minimal component, individualism. And Komaru resolved to consider it as a possibility at home.

On 21 June, winter arrived in Wanganui, dumping cold rain throughout the region. The summer tourist season had ended in conjunction with the evacuation of the Moutoa Gardens. Both tourists and members of the Fourth Estate, as well as curiosity seekers, political representatives and many other people, had gone home. The *New Zealand Herald* on the morning of 18 May sealed the urn of discontentment by writing its epitaph with the anonymous excerpt of a good-bye: '... We know that we can't battle the system if we are forcibly removed. We are going out of the way, we want to go out the way our people came in ... with integrity and under our own *tikanga*.' Surely, the government had not rolled out a red exit carpet, for in clear terms it had announced that it was honour-bound to intervene following the High Court ruling. This meant force at any cost, for no one wanted to prolong the impasse of 'disturbances' a few months from the arrival of the Queen of The Hermit Islands. Wanganui was a model city, the expression of Albionism overseas, and its Council would not tolerate any infraction to the spirit of Thatcherism as manifested in the Islas Malvinas. Just as those equidistant islands, at the antipodes of Mommy Britain, had been taught a lesson, so The Hermit Islands would suffer the same fate of harsh punishment. The Wanganui Council had spoken via business tycoon Chas Poynter. As the mayor of Wanganui for 9 years, and a member of the local Council on and off for a total of 18 years, and here Komaru wondered at the number 'nine' and its multiple, Poynter had pushed for positive action with a warning: 'I hope those people who are down there will see the opportunity to move off the gardens without any trouble.' So, a New Zealand Waco had been avoided. Komaru felt relieved at the peaceful departure of protesters, including not only women and children, but also nuns and monks acting along the trail of compassion blazed by Florence Nightingale, Sister Mary Aubert and Brother Emilio Faccioli.

It was still a bit early for the ski season to begin, and thus the month of July created a slack period for the local Chamber of Commerce. Chas Poynter was furious. Even Northern Maoris avoided Wanganui. And the Mediet restaurant suddenly suffered a decrease in business. But Melissa was nevertheless optimistic to the extent that she suggested, as she had done in the past, that Komaru open the first in a franchise chain in Auckland. Komaru agreed to meet with her and Bill at their home in a few weeks on the occasion of Mahina's 26th birthday on the 27th. It was puzzling to Komaru that Melissa remembered Mahina out of nowhere. When he mentioned that Ling-ling should participate as well, Melissa matter of factly replied with a perfunctory 'Of course,' almost as an afterthought. Komaru sensed that Melissa, whom he had not visited in a long while, was trying to create an encounter of some kind, so as to reassure herself that the reason for Komaru's absence was entirely due to political activities.

Thus, Komaru, in a quasi-act of expiation, decided to combine a retreat period at home, in preparation for the July meeting, with a dissection of the Mahina situation lingering at the door of his conscience, for he had virtually abandoned her for nearly two years. Ironically, the two extremes of intensely felt attraction, Mahina and Melissa, were like two parallel lines meeting in infinity. The spirit and the flesh were running along those two lines in both directions, though carefully, not to cross each other, for they carried with them powerful charges of emotionalism. Ling-ling seemed to keep those two lines apart, for Komaru had even refrained from entering Mahina's room, except for adding her missives into the *waka reta* in chronological order of arrival since his sister at times forgot to date her correspondence. Only through Ling-ling could Mahina know that her brother was still alive and busy in Wanganui trying to change the world of injustice.

Mahina's room was nearly a duplicate, actually a recreation, of her original Papakura quarters. The setup developed itself almost by accident when furniture and personal effects had been transferred by the Wanganui Moving Company from a storage building as soon as Komaru purchased a house. At that time, Ling-ling moved into Komaru's dwelling permanently as what the neighbours called a 'Chinese concubine'. So, each and every time Komaru felt miserably despondent, he entered the 'M-room' where he tried to recapture remembrances of the past. Mahina's image had become a *petite Madelaine* exuding the gentle fragrance of recalled pristinity, the malleable structure of barely baked pastry, the tartish sweetness of crumbling wholeness. For that *mise-en-scène*, Komaru had placed Mahina's furniture in nearly identical places: the work desk, the fax table, the computer table in the corner, the easy chair, the book ... oh!, the books. But these were to integrate themselves at random with those which had arrived from Portland. What a discovery! Komaru had even designed the bookshelves as they were in Papakura, around the window looking out on the viaduct. In Wanganui the corresponding window looked, however, toward the grey mist of the Whanganui River on its way to the Tasman Sea.

There was one difference in the whole design. The *kauri* wall was missing. How could he tap a good-night greeting on a white and hollow wall covered with gypsum sheet nailed between four-by-twos? In addition, between him and the tract-home wall dividing the 'marital' bedroom from Mahina's single room, Ling-ling had placed herself *sans le savoir* as a screen between Komaru and his sister. Many a time, when Komaru hungered to tap a double good-night on the echoing *kauri* of the *tapu* wall, this presented itself either as a plaster one or as the toy body of languid Ling-ling mistaking his wishes as tit for tat. She even wondered why Komaru would prefer to be mounted by her rather than settling for a sidekick or a scissors position allowing a deeper, though painfully pleasurable penetration. And for that, she had often asked to be taken conventionally, if not 'royally', at the edge of the bed. The various buildings of the Forbidden City still contained a few illustrations left by the Chiang Kai-shek government on its flight to Taiwan. And Komaru obliged without realising that he nearly compressed her ovaries into a bloody, scrambled dish until he became more careful, slowing down the adaptation of his All-Blacks organs to her Red Chamber literary traditions.

As to his preference for being used as a saddle, he had answered that he did not like to put the weight of his large and smothering body on top of her. Of course, the real reason was that he was imagining Mahina climbing on top of him while he closed his eyes and recreated her careful ride in the insertion of a vertical shaft into a narrow and tight receptacle. He even compared timing, viscosity and stroking style. In Mahina's performance, the little he had shared during a single encounter like a *jus primae noctis*, she had slowly pressed for position as if a Lunar Module trying to 'moon' without bouncing back. This was particularly engaging when Mahina allowed herself to disperse the petals of her first full blossoming lotus into the gale wind of fulfillment. She was even surprised when Komaru followed in tow, moaning in synchrony with a torrent of lava interspersed by intermittent jets of pellets spending themselves into a puddle of dark purple and ruby red blood running toward his navel. The only missing element in re-enacting a unique type of encounter was the Maori bed, that is, a quasi-futon structure onto which Mahina had become, purposelessly to her, a full female. For Komaru, that futon had become a symbol of sacrifice on his behalf, and as such it was not to be contaminated under any circumstances by surrogate exploitations.

It was hard for him to formulate a logical explanation when once Ling-ling had seen him 'resting', actually daydreaming, on that futon in the M-room. In a bout of affection prompted by desire, she had joined him on the futon, trying to land Mahina-style. No, he would not have it, but he carried her to their bedroom where she topped him furiously as if following the musical score of Rossini's overture for *Guillaume Tell*. Was Ling-ling aware of something unspeakable? Had she detected in his eyes that far-away look that only the Chinese can detect and dissect as through a window to one's heart and mind?

If so, she outperformed herself when Komaru, almost paralysed by the transfer from a futon to a European bed, took a long time to function while Ling-ling engaged in a tight quarter dance made mostly of side steps, of gyrating contra dances, of alternating tempos from a slow Argentinean tango to an Italian *tarantella* to a frenetic Irish tap rhythm. When he was ready to squelch the terrible pain around his groins, he still could not succeed. It seemed that there was a safety valve somewhere blocking the way to the end of the home stretch. Then he remembered – the *tertium quid*. Where was it? That must have been the nexus. And so he bent his head, raising it toward Ling-ling's bosom and, by pulling her up to his mouth, sought the *locus libidinis* (O Horace, he thought, did you really say that 'Dulce est desipere in loco?'). He reached it by placing his lips between Ling-ling's teats, and there he sucked the skin on top of her breastbone so hard that he rendered it black and blue. Ling-ling felt as if a giant silkworm had eaten a circular section of her skin, leaving a mark that lasted for a long time in spite of her applying a daily dose of Suchow silk cream to the area. It had turned on a psychological switch that even Ling-ling learned to like, at the risk of developing breast cancer, as an alternate erogenous zone in competition with the sensitive cleavage between her toes.

Now Komaru was in the M-room as if in the alcove of an invisible goddess who had moved her quarters from Mount Olympus down to Earth next to his room. The M-room was now *tapu* to erotic enterprises. But the *waka reta*, still untouched on Mahina's desk, was full of missives ready to be fingered and opened in a process of masochistically recollecting what he had missed by not replying to any of her letters. He was now ready to peruse, browse, reminisce those two years of self-punishment when in reality it was he who had chastized the quintessence of siblinghood and siblingness – love. At that point he realised that, whatever 'love' was or could be, it could exist, manifest itself, and perform only through incest, a concept so 'young' among civilised humans that it could be accepted only as a sin. In no other relationship, be it Oedipal or otherwise, could love become total love for, if any two humans felt any guilt ever, how could this be sidestepped except by proffering and accepting love as the supreme sacrifice? There was only one synonym for love, and it was undeniably incest. Every other association was prompted by a host of reasons, from procreation to athletics to boredom. In the final rational and emotional analysis, was incest not then the validation of love beyond any other level of affection? And this could not have been closer than that between siblings. Even St Augustine had sanctioned it in *The City of God* before human 'laws' were formulated. But those had been enacted too late! All the aeons of human interaction had gone by since Ops had received Saturn as sister first, and then wife.

Even in Maori tradition it was possible to retrieve pristine and unadulterated love through the scholarly efforts of Elsdon Best's work. In one text alone, namely *Tuhoe*, the original coupling leading to sex had been performed by a brother and a sister, named Te Pu and Te More respectively. They were the creators and the first inhabitants of the Universe. Amazingly, if not amusingly, Te Pu was above, and Te More was below him. They did not have to wait for the arrival of missionaries to adopt their position. And, even more strange, they had devised a copulation position beyond those of humanoids *à la Quest for Fire*. Their first act of pure love had been possible through what was later labelled incest. When this was banned by human law, not by Gods, love had already died by becoming merely sex.

In conclusion, Komaru wondered why, among the books Mahina had despatched from Portland to Papakura and then to Wanganui, he had found a heavily marked tome titled *The End of Kinship: 'Measure for Measure', Incest and the Ideal of Universal Siblinghood* (Stanford University Press, 1988). Its author, Mark Shell, in defending Christine de Pisan's view on women's liberation, had exploded a shell in Komaru's bowels. He suddenly understood how and why some human beings could come to love an idea, a cause, or even a fetish by allowing a charge of explosives to blow up in an act of martyrdom vulgarly called 'Terrorism.' After all, most saints had been beatified by first engaging in what Bill McTavish labelled 'holy suicide.' And history was full of instances of self-immolation, from political to religious to personal reasons, either by single individuals, groups or *en masse*. What was new under the sun as a sacrifice? And why had this now been mislabelled as 'terrorism?'

Chapter 41

'Meditation' was a Classical Latin blanket term under which Komaru spent a whole week away from nearly everybody. Cicero's *'meditatio atque excercitatio'* as well as *'meditatio mali'*; Seneca's *'meditatio mortis'*; Pliny the Elder's *'meditatio campestris'* furnish examples of the range of meanings assigned by the Romans to physical and abstract engagements connected with *meditor*, a verb the Latins had borrowed as a concept from the Greeks and their μελετάω, in relation to *lacrima* 'tear' from δάκρυον. For a moment, Komaru felt like connecting its roots with Melissa's onoma, but he had other things in mind beyond speculations within Indo-European history. Rather than retracing the -tt- and -ss- Greek dialectical variants perhaps leading him to tears of crying and of honey, he briefly concentrated on English, the language that had welcomed a non-nominative form of *meditatio, -onis* through Old French. Chaucer had used it in his Prologue to *The Parson's Tales*, followed by Shakespeare in *A Midsummer Night's Dream*, down to other writers such as John Donne in *Letters* and Byron in *Childe Harold*.

In his isolation, Komaru put aside the practice of meditation when interrupted only by contacts with Ling-ling. He, however, reserved his intention to analyse the various contemporary meanings of the term to ascertain what was afflicting him during this search for himself. He had compared the eviction of his people from the Moutoa Gardens with the episode of Adam and Eve expelled from the Garden of Eden by an asexual God.

Ling-ling was allowed to interact with him desultorily on matters regarding the Mediet Restaurant. She had been gradually entrusted with all the aspects of running the establishment, from the managerial responsibilities to the daily supply of fresh victuals to its stressful culinary implementation. As a matter of fact, without Ling-ling the operation would have encountered serious difficulties, especially during the distracting manifestations at the Moutoa Gardens. Ling-ling was the brain behind all the invisible operations, while Melissa acted mostly as a flamboyant 'lady-in-waiting' for public relations.

During the Occupation of the Gardens, the clientele had become a motley crowd of patrons ranging from invading Fourth Estate members to curiosity-seekers to mysterious personalities appearing and disappearing without rhyme or reason. It was the period during which Komaru began to develop toward Ling-ling a mature sense of affection stemming from his analysis of an individual strong enough to immigrate from China to New Zealand, a country basically at the antipodes of cultural geography, for, in relation to Pakehas' *bagage culturel*, Kiwis were Johnny-come-latelies on the global scene of human accomplishments. In spite of overt racial discrimination, of initial language difficulties, of non-legal shacking up as a 'concubine' with a British 'subject', Ling-ling had succeeded in integrating herself into a complex social structure through sheer persistence by proffering smiles instead of tears, faithful cooperation with the watchdog Melissa acting as a Dowager and silent dedication to Komaru.

Besides, she loved Komaru, and he suddenly became aware of that bundle of tender human ties with which he felt surrounded and bound by her every day. She never told him anything about her feelings, and neither he to her regarding his own for, in part, he did not want to acknowledge his being dependent on her. But lately he kept wondering what he would do if by any chance Ling-ling would disappear from his life. It was almost as if, once people caught a disease, the first reaction to it was one of total denial until, by overcoming all the transitional stages toward reality, one would finally accept it in a resigned manner.

The 'meditation' week was for Komaru, indeed, one of introspection that took him back to his childhood, when appearances of the external world projected themselves in one way, but at the same time they could be in reality so different, even antithetical, if not synchronically dualistic, moot and baffling. The very term 'meditation' triggered in him a string of semantic variations, for its very Latin root displayed a polysemeiotic range of connotations undoubtedly confusing and bothering. Again, as derived from the verb *meditor*, 'meditation' could be interpreted on at least three levels. The first had to do with 'to reflect', and thus its whole range of synonyms from 'to muse', to 'to consider', to 'to meditate' as understood in the *sermo cotidianus*. The second level displayed an analogous range, though stressing 'to plan', 'to devise', 'to contrive'. And, finally, the third suggested 'to study', 'to practice', 'to rehearse'. Komaru, aware of most nuances in association with his 'reflection', concluded that his 'meditation' week included all three levels, and even more than those, for he recognised several mental manifestations in nearly all the possible directions.

Komaru needed that week of self-analysis, since he felt psychologically destabilised. He anticipated momentous decisions about drastic measures that had been lingering in the back of his mind. Too many things had taken place, and for the first time in his life he fell into a bout of emptiness with all the symptomatic characteristics of depression, namely, fatigue, insomnia, anxiety, an inability to concentrate, and others. Actually, he did not feel like individualising and classifying those nauseating signs in an orderly fashion of some kind. One thing, however, emerged clearly above the scum of bitterness, a feeling of painful doubt about the nature of reality, of truth, as a function of 'knowing', or at least sensing that someone had betrayed him by revealing something relevant or imaginary to the police. Although he had always covered every possible step of activity on behalf of his cause, he also knew that even a supposition of 'guilt by association' could give him plenty of trouble. And, thus, he began to doubt, a nauseous feeling that gave him a sickening pain in his stomach, because whoever may have, intentionally or accidentally, revealed anything about him, must have been either a relative or a close friend.

Well, he doubted that Mahina had been the culprit. Perhaps some correspondence between the siblings had been intercepted. But, to the best of his recollection, he had never written anything compromising beyond what the press published daily. Or perhaps Mahina had asked questions in missives that he never received. That is why Komaru planned to go over the 'American' letters lying in the *waka reta*, 'the letter box', to look for possible gaps.

Could it be a friend? He had no wife. But he had been associated with Melissa and, of course, with Ling-ling. And Whina at the sanatorium. And with Bill. But he trusted Bill totally. Had Komaru's father opened up to Whina about himself *vis-à-vis* his son? At any rate, Komaru knew that, well, betrayal can be expected from a family member because of genetic dysfunctions and even from a wife, the first one expected to betray a secret of any kind, including the most personal. But, from a friend the anguish of doubt is more intense because friendship is something acquired by faith, as a mutual contract between and among members of a human consortium validated the humanness of former *insensata animalia*. How else could a brute biological entity became *animal rationale*? Failing that, the Earth would fail to detach itself from the nether status of chaos and return, as per Maori beliefs, to the original stage of pre-Mankind.

Komaru remembered that once Bill had quoted La Rochefoucauld on the occasion of a discussion on human relations: 'Il est plus honteux de se méfier de ses amis que d'en être trompé.' At the time, Bill did not know that Komaru had a most felt antipathy for the French language, and for its speakers, preferring to it German, the language of 'consistency'. Thus Bill interpreted it himself, literally as 'it is more shameful for one to doubt of his friends than of being (actually) deceived by them.'

Komaru felt relieved that the week of reckoning was over, although he was still coping with the meaning of reality, if this existed at all as something tangible. And this took him back to his first year of Latin, when he had not yet begun to study philosophy. He was about 10 or 11, but he clearly remembered the shock he felt in discovering the concept of deception associated with *meditor*, for this verb was 'deponent'. How could it be that its form was passive, but its meaning was active?

He later learned more complex signs of linguistic nature, particularly those revealing the nearly infinite variations showing one thing on the surface, but functioning otherwise at their very core. The Latin 'deponent' verbs had an Indo-European history that only a computer-minded grammarian could describe, especially since it was not only a matter of one extreme versus another, no! It seemed to Komaru that between the two extremes there was the intriguing *tertium quid*, called 'semi-deponent', that is, neither fish nor fowl popping out of nowhere as a function of the 'mood'. That is why a form of 'semi-deponent' like *fido*, 'I trust', in the present indicative, innocently looking like, say, *audeo* as active, unexplainably becomes *fisus sum* in the perfect tense, with a passive face, though deceptively functioning as active. That was not unlike some human relations between same-form biological entities who by appearance were assumed to be active by nature, but in practice they preferred to be passive *contra naturam*. Thus, Komaru thought that, *mutatis mutandis*, and here he laughed at his own involuntary pun, *fixus sum*, 'I have trusted', manifests an extrasemantic face of distrust if referring to the past when one thinks that friendship is still in the present, but subject to betrayal when assumed differently for the past.

Komaru had heard of the practical application of grammatical forms to human relations, and finally understood why prospective husbands and wives, disgustingly, have an attorney prepare prenuptial agreements that anticipate the morphological shape of a break-up involving a 'semi-'. How shocked Komaru was when a friend at Victoria University refused to learn Komaru's password for his website just in case there would be a falling out between them. It seemed to him that language, through verbs, reflected an intricate network of moot relationships. Of course, humans had concocted spoken language to hold mental reservations, and even Roman Law, so much trumpeted as the eighth marvel of the West, must have been based on grammatical categories reeking with deception. How else could one state that in English 'in' was classified as a preposition, when in reality it could be (or function as) a noun, an adjective, a verb or an adverb? Undoubtedly, Latin grammatical categories, and their subsectional forms as multi-signforms, allegedly an index of civilisation, in practice, carried the potential for the demise of language, or at least accounted for the proliferation of attorneys, barristers, lawyers and the like to perpetuate the dissonance between form and meaning. Komaru was happy to recall that Maori verbal forms were among the most simple, not unlike the Chinese. Hawaiki, as a point of departure, could furnish an explanation for a sharp Occam's razor operating in both cultures.

The second week of July, nevertheless, gave Komaru the opportunity to 'dig' into the letters sent to him by Mahina desultorily during the previous two years. She had become an obsession for him, something beyond 'love'. He felt that he had not fulfilled whatever he could through his sister as a means of having a purpose in life. Time had prevented him from showing himself to her, but he rationalised that the abyss created by an *atua* was better for both of them in order not to become insane. Yes, he could have given her more than he did, and likewise received from her much more. But, to what avail? Thus, he came to appreciate Ling-ling as a 'semi-'deponent form. It was not something to be construed in a negative way, as a cop out. It was perhaps nature's way of keeping humans at the lowest earth level to remind them that they are no different than worms. The *reductio ad primordialem originem* was simply a reminder of the constant *umbra futurorum* enveloping everything *sub sole*. So, his sister was regarded by him, and sadly so, realistically for what she was – not the still 'active' form of a Melissa, but as the vanished 'passive' one of a Mahina. The two *M*'s had performed their voluntary duty of allowing him to grow up as a Man. The adjacent letter of the alphabet, *L*, was next in line to occur doubly, as if to furnish a comparative connection with each for the previous *M*'s, a potential 'semi' that the other two women could never produce for different reasons.

In browsing through Mahina's letters, Komaru realised more consciously that they were all in Maori. He had not thought about that before. The message had been superseded by the medium, which had become invisible, if not irrelevant. And Maori gave him plenty of trouble linguistically because Mahina transliterated concepts of American life and culture *impromptu*. Most terms looked and sounded as if dished out from *latinus macaronicus*. In addition, many items of a religious nature were baffling, though on occasion Mahina used Republican, Medieval and modern Vatican Latin, mostly based on lengthy paraphrases of ancient Latin.

For Komaru it was a journey criss-crossing the geography of Christian riddles, Medieval beliefs, American life, monastic rituals and a whole inventory of daily activities completely alien to him. Moreover, Mahina often alluded to past events although written in Maori, common to each of them, in order to baffle intruders, protect him and trying to obey the Rule at the same time.

What Komaru had designated as 'waka reta' was actually a topless cardboard shoebox containing Mahina's assortment of pencils, pens, crayons, erasers, elastic bands, paper clips and other items employed by anyone writing at school, at home or even in a small business activity in precomputer days. She had brought that box from the States and, after being emptied of its contents, it had remained on a shelf waiting to be utilised for some practical purpose. Komaru had used the container to file all the letters, cards, photographs, newspaper clippings and random documents as relics of a past left stalled on a one-way street.

Actually, those relics had become a trove of tangible memories, and thus the *waka reta* had acquired the status of a *waka huia*, the most valuable house possession of *whakapapa* inheritance from one generation to another, not dissimilar from a Pakeha family loom. In Komaru's case, however, he wondered what to do with those reminiscences. Destroy them? Or leave them to an imaginary posterity? He had none, and neither did he intend to create any, for no one else in the entire world would have benefited from knowing what went on between two human beings possessing a soul in common. For the time being, he decided to utilise them as a temporary bridge, like those made by magpie wings once a year in some Asian cultures, not excluding the Hawaikian one that had been lost in transhemispheric migrations. He sensed that even an Austral winter bridge connecting two lovers once a year would be the last. Thus, he decided to read all the items and then toss them in a paper sack before burning the contents in the backyard incinerator.

One of the oldest missives had arrived nearly two years earlier. There was a place and a date: Boulder, Colorado, 10 August 1993. The letterhead showed something new to him, especially since he had no idea whatsoever about Colorado. He vaguely remembered having read of it as a backwoods area where the US government processed uranium to create plutonium for nuclear bombs, the most up-to-date weapons of mass destruction, first used at Hiroshima almost 50 years earlier. Oh, yes, another toponomastic reference had surfaced onto the screen of recollection. That was when, in Shanghai, he had been asked rather facetiously by a Chinese student whether Maori islanders had discontinued cannibalism. Komaru took that question in stride, particularly when an American student informed the Chinese that, yes, the Maori had given up human flesh, though in Colorado the practice persisted for political reasons. In fact, the University of Denver exchange student had informed that at a nearby sport-minded institution an anthropophagous ceremony is faithfully re-enacted at its Memorial Center. Well, nothing morbid, of course, for it sounded like students eating corned beef on St Patrick's Day a few weeks apart from a celebration in memory (that is why the assembly building had been named a 'memorial' centre of a certain Alferd Packer, a Republican, who had fed on the frozen carcasses of four or five fellow travellers who happened to be Democrats. In the process, half the constituency of whatever county had been eliminated by digestion. To give Komaru a geocultural background of Colorado, and Denver, its capital boasting of a capitol with a dome covered in gold leaves, Mahina had sent him an old issue of *Atlantic Monthly* acquired at a used book store on Boulder's Pearl Street. Surely, it was a generation old, for it carried the date of April 1978, but, after all, what drastic change can take place in less than a generation? Referring to Colorado's capital, the article on page 82 was introduced by the title 'No Mean Cow Town', and cited one of the most cultural events recently taking place there, 'an Elvis Presley concert at the fairgrounds ...'. The city, a bleak outpost of racial violence, seemed not to differ much from Dunedin at the bottom of the Earth, for 'there was *nothing* ever happening in Denver. You could see all you wanted of it as you bypassed it on Highway 6 heading West toward Aspen.'

However, Boulder County, where Mahina had been transferred, was another matter for, in addition to her Convent, it boasted of a buffalo bull at the homongmous county seat. This was actually a bison named Ralph, in whose honour the city fathers had erected a monument at the entrance of the university campus. The bull is still the most honoured guest paraded on the football field just before the American national anthem is played at the same time as a squad of sanitary workers cleans up the home end-zone normally peppered by digested hay balls as a good omen. When the bull performs its propitiatory rites, the chances are that the Colorado team wins the game. If it loses in spite of the evidence left on the turf, then the animal is tested for drug-induced diarrhoea.

Collaterally, the name 'Buff' spread out as a password to cultural identification sported on motels, clubs, restaurants, academic insignia, credit cards and even documents required for an entrance pass to libraries, busses, supermarkets and football games. Mahina, however, was not impressed by the buffalo myth because she knew it was a phoney name for a bison, that is, the '*moa*' of the American Indians as resurrected from near extinction a generation earlier. In addition, no one raised bison to make mozzarella as in Italy, since the animal was simply a wild ox. Ergo, the label of 'Cow Town' for Denver, the Metro corral for January festivities where the Boulder 'Buff' mounts prize cows at the Coliseum for the propagation of the species under the blaring lights of Japanese TV cameras from Kobe.

The description of Mahina's convent, north of Boulder on the highway leading to Estes Park, took almost two pages. Named the 'Rocky Mountain Sisters of St Francis,' it was designed to welcome any qualified female to become a Sister of St Francis of Penance and Christian Charity. The training organisation includes three 'academic-like' levels, not dissimilar from a curriculum leading to a PhD in 'Clarehood'. The first level is like an undergraduate programme, namely, the Candidacy, which Mahina had completed in Portland. The second, just begun, is called the Novitiate and lasts at least two years, during which, among other things, the Novice studies the history of the Congregation, the social thoughts of its Foundress Mother Ruth, and a comprehensive preparation for profession of first vows. During this period, the Novice blends theory and practice by working in the 'open world' of social injustice, dejection and anguish. Komaru thought how those two years coincided with his own time segment of 'political' novitiate that had ended in failure. He hoped that at least his sister would succeed in her efforts to cope with a tiny portion of humanity. Finally, the third level, completed after 3–9 years, would confer on the Novice the title of 'Sister,' when final vows are professed upon inalienable conviction of the candidate as discerned by the whole Congregation. The final 'examination' consisted of a review of 'exposure' undergone by the Sister-to-be to the 'temptations of the world.' Certain publications were even required readings so that the Novice would anticipate possible tendencies to regret her decision before the final jump. For example, one of these readings was Elizabeth Upton's *Secret of a Nun, My Own Story* (1985). When entering too young into religious life, some women are not usually exposed to the physiological drives of the flesh. Mahina had apparently overcome that incipient natural tendency. And she did not regret that the recipient of that propensity was her brother, the party to whom she could never revert had she stayed freely within laical society. In a way, she had been burnt enough by a flame so close to her that nothing else could tempt her to a longing for bodily interaction with any other biological entity on Earth. Of course, her Father Confessor did not need to know of her internal resolution since her mental dysfunction, as she referred to it in talking to God, had occurred before officially beginning the long climb to Sisterhood.

Mahina had sketched for Komaru a short history of her 'family' organisation, almost to reassure him that she was in good hands. Established soon after the First World War, the convent had changed between the wars, Rather than emphasising original 'cloistered' functions, it now spread into mission activities along Clarissean traditions, reaching out to humans who struggled to create for themselves a wholesome life of peace and tranquillity.

After the Second World War, among various programmes instituted in the Denver area, the convent organised the so-called Heva House as one of the social work infrastructures within the region bound by ecclesiastic superiors. Mahina elaborated a little on the name 'Heva', that is, Eve, Adam's sister. It had created quite a fuss in the beginning, since even the local bishop had opposed it on grounds of the original sin incurred by the first female terrestrial. However, when the nonagenarian Mother Foundress Ruth reminded him that he often referred in his *Salve Regina, Mater misericordiae*, to humans as being 'exsules filii Hevae,' he relented, particularly since Heva House was to be a Safe House and Place of Hope for Homeless Women and Their Children. After all, Eve or Heva was the first mother of the human race according to the account of the Creation in Genesis. As the first female on Earth, she had, through no fault of her own, suffered the first abuse, perhaps even an environmental alteration of her 'natural' creation for being born without a belly button. Poor Heva did not have anyone to help and comfort her. She had been left out in the 'cold' to fend for herself without even a coat during the severe winters, and in Denver it was not unheard of to incur in inclement weather temperatures of 20 degrees Centigrade below zero.

Mother Ruth, in order to help her own Sisters, had often left the convent in a metre of snow and descended onto the 'killing' fields of abused and homeless 'children', including grown-ups, when she found out that, in spite of theoretical social programmes decided upon by Denver's KKK members, most 'coloured' women were a step away from dejection, desperation and suicide. In essence, Mother Ruth had become the silent 'Mother Teresa' *avant la lettre* of the Rocky Mountains. It had been a long journey to create a 'Search and Rescue' service among the derelict for the Metro Denver area, and Boulder furnished an ideal place because of its rural setting.

Particular attention was paid to abnormal human interaction for victims of rape, domestic violence and incest, these often being shoved under the rug in police records in order not to taint the inflated reputation of Boulder as the ideal town to raise a family. Cases of crimes related to both alcohol and drug abuse were relegated by the local press to back pages since apparently their frequency was directly proportional to the police's inability to cope with disorderly events except for the usual ones involving typical drunkenness by students trying to place Boulder on the national map for 'playboyism'. And Mahina, for reasons not mentioned in her letters, was assigned to Sister Margaret as her supervisor in handling cases of women rescued from the psychological pit into which they had been tossed by 'kai-whiore,' which Komaru interpreted as 'incest,' though it literally carried the meaning of anyone eating his own tail. So strange, thought Komaru, the letter ended abruptly in mid-page without any details, and he wondered how his sister had been assigned that particular task, and why. Had she volunteered for it? Apparently, Metro Denver registered the highest percentage of incest cases between brothers and sisters, a plague being spread not so much among 'Latin' immigrants as among affluent members of a white society. Regardless of the type of victimisation, the aim was the same for all women, regardless of social status or religious affiliation, for it was not uncommon to see a Mercedes Benz or a Ferrari in the car park fronting the convent on a Monday morning. Heva House offered a long-term stable environment for both mothers and their offspring under the age of 12, until they were able to secure a home and a job in order to become normal members of Colorado society, one of the most fluid and kaleidoscopic masses in urban America. For whatever reasons, climatic, economic or utopistic, Denver, the former 'Cow Town,' had become a dynamic Mecca for young people to start a quick life in a rush to grow up beyond the parameters of sane and safe living. The old 'Cow Town' had suddenly become the potential 21st century Sybaris at the moral edge of the American dream astride the Rocky Mountains.

The next letter read by Komaru was dated, American style, '15 August 1995,' celebrating the Assumption of the Blessed Virgin Mary. Mahina was so 'high', as if she herself had ascended into Heaven. First she wrote Komaru 'Hodie Maria Virgo caelos ascendit: gaudete, quia cum Christo regnat in aeternum.' She even transcribed the six vowels punctuating the envoi with high notes: '*E u o u a e.*' But the bulk of the letter contained, in an excited manner, her experience on the occasion of the International Youth Festival held in Denver that summer. However, most of Mahina's account skipped the Denver ceremonies, basically an exalted 'Tanglewood' astride the Rockies, and concentrated on her encounter with the pope at St Catherine's Church in St Malo, at whose Spiritual Retreat Center His Holiness had rested and celebrated a Mass on 13 August. This similarity in construction, material, style and natural setting between St Malo's church and that of the Good Shepherd in South Island gave Mahina the shivers. She wrote Komaru that she felt at 'home' immediately.

On that morning, Mahina and other Novices had been 'lent' by her Boulder convent to assist in the logistics of the papal horde descending on that idyllic mountain complex. The few residents in the area, although allowed to meet the pope smack in the middle of Highway 7, for security reasons had not been allowed to enter the premises. Mahina had been chosen, because of her knowledge of both British English and 'literary' Italian, to serve breakfast. Noticing her excitement, the pope asked her where she was from, and Mahina tried to quote from memory for Komaru the short dialogue that took place by the north-east window of the refectory on top of the central building overlooking the stream and the little ponds between the church and the residence. After a strenuous celebration in Denver the previous day, the pope began to relax. His late morning Mass at the church had been short.

'Thank you, Sister, this breakfast is heavenly. Did you bake the buns yourself?'

'No, *Sua Santità*, I am only serving them.'

'Oh, you address me in Italian. Are you from Italy?'

'Sorry, Your Holiness, I am from New Zealand.'

'You mean, Aotearoa? *Ma tu parli italiano. Come mai? Io sono stato lí. Lo sai?.*

'*Sí, Santo Padre, ma ero ancora bambina. Avevo solo dódici anni. E non ero ancora cattòlica.*'

'*Ma allora sei ancora ... in fasce?*'

Mahina did not understand the last idiomatic reference to a baby wrapped in swaddling clothes to indicate a new arrival to Catholicism. Under the nervous eyes of the pope's personal nun and doctor watching in the background, His Holiness spent nearly 15 minutes eliciting not only Mahina's background, but also information about her ancestors. When Mahina told the pope of her Slavic mother, he nearly invited her to sit down at the table. She retreated a little so as not to become too invading. After a few seconds, the pope went into a recollective mood, enchanted by the mountain range between the dining area and the sun rising majestically through a forest of young aspens and lodgepole pines. He seemed to reflect for a moment on that dawn, especially when looking at the statue of Christ the Redeemer erected on a rock at the entrance of the car park. The sun was peaking above Christ's head as if crowning him with its rays. Mahina was fascinated by the spell of silence and reflection. The pope had stopped eating half a banana.

'*Oh, le montagne, e quelle cime che fanno da gradini al Cielo.*'

Then, he switched to English.

'Upon arriving in Denver, I lifted my eyes toward the splendour of the Rocky Mountains and ... the Lord, who had made Heaven and Earth.'

At that moment, the papal secretary casually intervened in the fascinating interlude, rudely whisking Mahina away while in the process of removing a pitcher of hot milk, she dropped it on the floor. The pope laughed, blessed Mahina nearly in tears and said, '*Il sole del Colorado avrà bruciato i tuoi begli occhi.*' She exploded in tears, and rushed to the door under the cerberean eyes of the 'nun-in-waiting.' When she turned around apologetically, the pope told her, 'Arohanui!' That did it.

It had been too much for her in a single day, actually a morning. The altitude must have also affected her. Coming from Boulder at the 1-mile altitude, the rarefied air at more than 9,000 feet had gone to her head. Only the following day was she told by the abbess, to whom Mahina had related the entire episode, that, in looking at the Denver sky, the pope had quoted from Psalm 121:1.

Mahina, however, did not tell the abbess what went on in her mind when the pope became transfixed looking at the east side of the front range mountain section. Even a casual observer, beholding it from either the car park or the steps of the chapel, can see three perfectly shaped peaks like truncated cones of brown rock. For whatever geological reasons, the terminal part of the peaks were treeless, and at the centre of each a round rock projected itself under the pink colour of early morning sunshine. The lateral ones were almost identical, and the central one, a bit off centre to the right, was smaller. There, with the pope two feet away from her, and carrying a pitcher of frothy hot milk, Mahina saw herself lying on the Rocky Earth in the nude and imagined the profile of her bosom with the *tertium quid* palpitating in the light morning mist rising from Boulder Valley as if being pushed away by the August heat. In that sun, Mahina thought of Komaru when he once remarked that in Wanganui the highest peaks were not Durie Hill and Bastia Hill, but her own, like a St Agatha of the southern hemisphere. She had left them for him to see from the window of her 'artificial' room facing the Whanganui Riverboat Centre. Oh, how she wished to spend just one night there, even blocked by a *kauri* wall. Komaru's description of her Papakura room transplanted to Wanganui had fired her imagination, especially when her brother wrote her that not even Ling-ling was allowed to enter the 'Moon' room.

The entire account in Maori relating to the encounter with the pope was interspersed by recollections including the reference that, the previous day, St Clare of Assisi had died a virgin, a fact that the canon at the Boulder convent chapel had mentioned by saying:

> Exaudi nos, Deus salutaris noster, ut sicut de beatae Clarae Virginis tuae festivitate gaudemus ...

Mahina wondered if Clare had any brothers and, even if she had just one, she doubted that he could be a child of the Umbrian 'misty hills.' She, of course, referred to Eldson Best's 'children of the mist' in the far northeast of the North Island, where kingship was nebulous when, *in principio*, it came to keep apart a brother from a sister through the Arawa concept of *weke*, 'separation,' like Rangi and Papa.

After that reference to a mountain range, Komaru simply leafed through the rest of the one-way correspondence. He did not like to indulge in painful recreations of what could have been and was not. Everything else was prosaical, for world events were known to Komaru nearly instantly in the so-called 'informational' world. Mahina at times elaborated on her routine life according to the Rule. One thing seemed to have shocked her – the Oklahoma City bombing, so 'close' to Colorado in her last letter dated on ANZAC Day. She simply could not grasp the impact of 'terrorism' at home, and she referred to 'home' as the USA. Apparently, for her 'terrorism' was something taking place against America or American 'links.'

Whether the place of action was on the North American continent or outside it did not seem to affect her, thought she hoped that New Zealand would never be involved in violent acts leading to the destruction of lives and property. However, she asked 'why America?' What had America done to the world to deserve that kind of retribution? Of course, Mahina was too young to recall that one early act of global terrorism had taken place in Auckland, where the *Rainbow Warrior* had been sunk by explosives. Ironically, New Zealand had done nothing wrong to anyone, and no minorities, no activists, no fanatics, no Maoris anyway, had done anything despicable to attract terrorism. Yes, it was the action of a 'civilised' country, a producer of weapons of mass destruction, France, that had shaken New Zealand from the very foundations of trust toward a nation of Cartesians. Ironically, no one accused France of acts of terrorism, even after the death of the photographer aboard the ship.

Mahina's observations on terrorism affected Komaru a great deal, for he was undergoing a terrible crisis of conscience. Had anyone ever traced a demarcation line between terrorism and anything else such as sabotage, anarchism, raid, covert attacks, destructive immolation, behind-the-lines 'surprises', mine-laying on earth and in water, and the like? What about an operation like 'The Bridge on the River Kwai'? Oh, yes, of course there was a war, a war between groups called nations. Then, could there not be a war between individuals or an individual against a group? Who sanctions the morality of a war? Komaru's somber mood intensified when he went to a lecture at the Wanganui Polytechnic Institute. Melissa had actually suggested that they attend the lecture, sponsored by the Mayor of Wanganui almost as a warning to those protesters who had created a 'climate of terrorism at the Moutoa Gardens effectively defused by common sense directed towards realistic race relations.' Komaru felt that the term 'realistic' reeked with hypocrisy, for that meant to him falsely 'better' as long as Maori activists succumbed to the threat of force by police.

The title of the lecture, delivered in the main hall of the Institute, was 'The Terrorism of Politics and the Politics of Terrorism: The War to End War,' undoubtedly a cryptic statement that Komaru analysed as a catchy one by the assumption that for the speaker, Dr Paul Peterson of the Sydney University Department of Political Sciences, 'terrorism' superseded 'war'. How could it be so? Wasn't war a noble enterprise supported even by chaplains praising the Lord on either side of the battlefield? And, better than that, was not war a chivalrous solution to human conflicts properly codified by the Geneva Convention like a business contractual guideline?

Thus, Komaru and Melissa entered the auditorium where, surprisingly, they saw that Bill was seated in the front row. They joined him to act as devil's advocates, for they knew that he regarded himself as the only 'psychiatrist' specialising in mass suicide as organised by deranged leaders. The fact that he was an employee of the social services department for the Ministry of Health did not seem to generate any conflict, for his work with 'suicide teens' was nearly identical to that considered by nations at war. In other words, the whole methodology of analysis, the technique of data gathering, the correlation of intraconflicts among humans, led Dr McTavish to identical conclusions – in behavioural terms, nations are like suicidal children committing individual, irresponsible actions.

Bill seemed to be rather amused listening to the opening remarks by Dr Peterson, for he did not begin with the customary *captatio benevolentiae* to seek the audience's attention. He paused at the lectern for a full minute of seemingly theatrical reflection that made the public nervous and moody. Then he moved to the front of the stage, and in angry tone screamed:

'Ladies and gentlemen, rejoice! War is dead! We have a new chum in town. Terrorism!'

Then he returned to the lectern and reminded the audience to refer to the handout available at the entrance to the auditorium. There were two sheets containing an outline of the speech that Komaru interpreted, rather selfishly, as if it had been custom-made for him. The two pages might as well have been two tablets delivered from the top of the political Sinai. He simply became spellbound to the point that he wrote a lot of notes in the hope of recording graphically most of the lecture, plus his own impromptu interpretation of terrorism.

That evening, at home, without waiting for the usual unilateral interpretation of public matters by the *Wanganui Chronicle*, Komaru synthesised the contents around a few key points, namely:

1. Origin. From the Greek verb through Latin to the 'Reign of Terror'

instituted by Robespierre from 1793 to 1794 to save the accomplishments of the French Revolution.

2. Function. To leave a calling card in order to be heard as a court of last resort. It seems that callousness is melted only by blood and not by reason.

3. Structure. Nothing codified, everything loose. The only 'constant' symbolized by '*u*' meant 'unexpectedness'.

4. Application. To any material or symbolic entity reeking with oppression of rights, be they religious, political, economic, and even philosophical.

5. The End of War. The 20th century, as the centennial incubation of terrorism, beginning with the assassination of a queen and perhaps ending likewise, as the obverse of the most destructive human period among suicidal nations. The inception of individual action 'millenarianism' – from the frustrating failures of conference tables to the destructive successes of target actions. From *Homo belligerens* to *Homo territor*.

At the end of his long night writing session, Komaru had not only transposed into organised programmes his auditorium notes from the speech, but also had sketched guidelines for what a week later he rewrote after researching the topic through reference materials at the Wanganui Public Library. He concentrated actually on Item 5, which contained *in nuce* a whole prophetic patchwork of procedures. At the end of his research, he had enough material to compile a mini-encyclopaedia, but he thought it useless to him except for corroborating his spirit of defiance against the 'system'. Indeed, the final product had almost little to do with Professor Peterson's speech, for Komaru suddenly found himself in an international kitchen where the first reference tool was not Elisabeth David, Graham Kerr or Eric Rolle. In fact, the first volume of his new encyclopaedia was titled *The Anarchist's Cookbook*, a product of American democracy. Although listed in the general computerised catalogue under its title, the book was not to be found anywhere on the shelves of the library. Amusingly, its physical space had been 'occupied' by *The Mediet Cookbook*, by a certain Ling-ling Chu, a product of the Wanganui Nutrition Council for Healthy Life. It was a self-published booklet containing most of the recipes used at Komaru's restaurant.

A casual reader of Dr Peterson's vision of terrorism, as interpreted by Komaru, would notice that it embodied a 'global' re-interpretation of human societal conflicts through a projected *coupure épistémologique* burying the Industrial Age that had died in the process of giving birth to a set of twins – Information and Communication, ready at the push of a button to cause mass destruction at the push of another button. Eventually, the Info/Com era would come of age by creating a deadly monster, terrorism, a loose term signifying several things to many people having in common the wish to destroy not only other people but also themselves. Basically, it was a process similar to deconstructing' what 'civilisation' had built in millennia of toil and sweat, like running the records of a hypothetical movie of accomplishments backward to square one. Should that process of annihilation proceed unchecked, the final result would be the end of 'War' by pushing the cradle of civilisation, the Earth, into premature selenisation. In reality, and here Komaru laughed at some 'cult' leaders announcing the End of the world, the End was near. And, if so, Komaru decided to hasten it, for he had nothing to lose except a few people who, surviving him, would add another link of history along the chain of their *whakapapa*. Of course, he said nothing to anybody, but, still attached 'filially' to Melissa as when working on his MA thesis, he presented his 'terrorism' notes to her for constructive criticism on a destructive topic. A few weeks later he began to think that perhaps he had made a mistake. He also realised that it was too late to change the course of events, but said nothing and did nothing to prevent possible, even involuntary, leaks carrying Info/Com to the wrong party.

The typescript given to Melissa contained what probably no one in New Zealand had ever conceived of as a function of living on a few small islands where, unlike large continents, a simple act of terrorism would cut life from the rest of the 'helping' world in case of need. Potential social dysfunctions could not be coped with at the edge of the Earth. No American neo-Marines would be able to help, even if they were willing to whisk hospital ships to Wellington or build airstrips in Kaikoe.

There were several reasons in Komaru's opinion, for, ironically, the whole thing looked historically like a 'reverse' holocaust. For Komaru, terrorism appeared genetically as a 'Jewish' phenomenon, a success story as in every great Western paradigmatic shake-up from Jesus Nazarenus to Karl Marx, from Freud to Einstein. It was basically an Archimedean process of Machiavellism involving a fulcrum device not necessarily *ad litteram* when material implementation was impossible for a 'minority' to fight successfully against a majority. Thus, in terms of protohistory, Komaru recorded the episode of David against Goliath as the first one in Judaeo-Christian society. The inception of the modern history of 'terrorism' was marked by Komaru with the actions of Menachem Begin, leader of the Irgum Zvai Leumi, who conceived the destruction of King David Hotel as per his book *The Revolt*. The avatar of terroristic analysis based on faith. Mr Begin, a consonant away from Mr Bevin, who hated the Jews passionately to the point of dying of self-injected 'hebraicitis', had applied Cartesian logic: 'We fight, *ergo* we are.' And, in fact, the death of the British Foreign Secretary in 1945 marks, ironically, the foundation of the Israeli nation. Komaru was particularly impressed by Mr Begin's desperate views: 'There are times when everything in you cries out – your very self-respect as a human being lies in your resistance to evil.'

'Terrorism', after the 'milk cans' subterfuge causing the King David Hotel to split in two, cannot be accounted for to end its original function, since Dr Peterson had to define the term several times during the cycles of its existence as a concept. Komaru remembered a few basic situations but, once in the Wanganui Public Library, he covered the historical aspects of the term from Greek to Latin to French and English. He soon found out that the wide meaning of 'terror' as fright, fear, anxiety and the like had lost its pristine meaning as covered extensively in the *OED*. It later changed to a 'mood' and to a concept of action for which entire encyclopaedias could be written along religious, political, economic and even organised crime lines. Amazingly, Komaru realised that what had begun as a 'Jewish' paleo- and modern phenomenon during Bevin's favouritism toward Arab nationalism, had turned around 180 degrees and, thus, it is now the Jewish nation fighting terrorism in the form of complex Arab religious and political tenets displaced by and inherited from British colonialism.

The *coup de grâce* came when, under Professor Peterson's influence, the American view of terrorism hit him suddenly. Simply, he found out that the term is now understood as anything done violently against the USA. What was originally called an act of war is now one of terrorism. In the good old chivalrous days, when the German Kaiser had complained that it was not fair unilaterally to use British tanks on the Somme, a war used to be declared according to protocol and implemented in an organised fashion, but the defeat of America by a ragtag bunch of Vietnamese animated by political faith against a monster created an atmosphere of re-evaluation. Basically, anything unexpected as an act of violence anytime, anywhere, in any manner, against any obstruction of 'moral' justice, is considered an act of terrorism. That is why Professor Peterson concluded that the Vietnam 'conflict' was an organised attempt to squelch a genuine reaction of evil on either side, and opened the door to what the States sees as a treacherous enterprise when a 'minority' does not conform with official policies of 1,000 year-like envisioned dominance *more nazista* within and without the Earth. How else, however, could David bring Goliath to his knees? And for how long can a modern superpower be brought to 'global reasoning', whatever Dr Peterson meant, except by terrorism? Had Mr Begin not sent a milk lorry full of 'milk' to squelch the thirst of British power in the Middle East, the State of Israel would have remained a dream carried over into the third millennium of exile.

At the end of the lecture, Komaru felt as if a charge of explosives had been ignited in his bowels. When he and Ling-ling met a few times during September at the McTavishes in order to outline a business expansion in Auckland, the mood was not particularly conducive to positive action since Komaru had been distracted by the imminent arrival of her Majesty the Queen during the late spring on the occasion of the periodical congress of Commonwealth nations to be injected with a few more puffs of political oxygen to last another 4 or 5 years. Coincidentally, Ling-ling had announced the arrival of something else that shocked Komaru's normally envisioned life when she said almost casually, 'Komaru, I have just learned a new English term after visiting with the Karitane nurse. The cook told me that, when I passed out in the kitchen, the reason was not fatigue, but ... simply ... I had been visited by Annie Brown.'

Chapter 42

'I was exactly 10 years old when she was crowned. I vividly remember her smiling by the left window of her carriage. She was wearing white gloves, a gold wrist watch, and tear-drop earrings so long that they nearly touched the tips of the fur stole. Forty-two years ago, just imagine!'

Then, as an afterthought, she added: 'We had just heard that Mr Hillary had climbed to the summit of Everest on May 29th. What a day! My mother was so touched by the combination of the two events that she felt England had reached the peak of glory. My father, who reluctantly had taken us down to London from Cambridge, reminded mother that India was no longer the Jewel in the Crown. And Nepal had barely emerged from the 1950 revolution, placing a royal family in power after disposing of the local nobility. The situation in Nepal was similar to that existing in England just before Elizabeth I became a queen. Unlike her, however, Elizabeth II had not witnessed any internal strife. Actually, the first executive action was that of knighting a beekeeper as Sir Edmund as soon as he could reach Europe.'

Melissa was reminiscing as a way of injecting a touch of familiarity into the royal event in order to celebrate. She suggested toasting to the health of the Queen, Her Majesty Elizabeth II. However, Bill proposed that Melissa should not offend her by employing a nationalistic alcoholic conveyance. Cardhu was hardly a liquor to be used for that toast. Of course, gin was out of the question, though much more patriotic than scotch even though the Beefeater brand may have appeared mildly insulting to the average British citizen whose historical knowledge included Elizabeth I's imprisonment in the Tower of London.

In the absence of champagne, Melissa proposed a drink she had learned to savour in Brazil. Bill approved it since at least it contained some vitamins. Did Melissa have any *cachaça* left in the bottle she brought from Brazil so long ago? Yes, just enough for two cocktails called *Caipirinha*. She had purchased the best brand, in Dr Tavares' opinion the *Pitu*. So Melissa cut a lime, including the peel, into small wedges, placed them in an American-type glass called an 'old fashioned,' added two teaspoons of caster sugar and, using a wooden pestle, squashed the lime pieces with the sugar. Next, she filled the glasses with cracked ice, poured two stiff jiggers of *cachaça* into each of them, and served them immediately saying 'Saude!' Well, a Brazilian drink to honour a British monarch was diplomatically a tolerable compromise since Brazil had once been the first and most powerful monarchy in South America. Whether it had succumbed to the consequence of *caipirinhas* was another matter. Probably one day that could happen in Scotland if it was allowed to have its own parliament as the first step to an independent form of government, though Bill was not sure of its advantages since Scotland had the lowest percentage of suicide in Europe after Italy. Switzerland, the freest nation, had the highest. Was there any correlation between scotch whisky, possibly single malt, and longevity?

Undoubtedly, Elizabeth II had been born under the auspices of the foundation of Rome – same day, same month. The Holy Roman Empire had lasted for about 1,000 years. How long would the British Empire, or what was left of it, last? As regards the year of birth, well, astrological signs seemed to guarantee a reasonable longevity to leaders, but that was mainly for men, not women. In fact, not many distinguished females had been born in 1926. Melissa could only think of two men. One was Fidel Castro, the revolutionary of minds at the antipodes of a traditional governmental system, though nevertheless a leader. And the other? Oh, yes, Hugh Hefner, another revolutionary of sexual mores via American crassitude reeking with Sybaritic laxity.

As a consequence, the populace of the United States sported per capita the highest frequency of promiscuous penetrative interaction between and among humans, animals and things in all possible combinations, not counting incest. There were a few more people of rather modest ambition and accomplishment. Even Elizabeth II could be regarded as a person of minimal impact on Brits – no philosophical, political or ethical maxims had ever been manifested. As a mother, well, she had tried hard to stem the flood of scandal erupting as in every European family of monarchs. As compared with Elizabeth I, the Queen had kept a low profile after succeeding her father, George VI, and had so far left nothing iconic except her profile on coins. On the other hand, she had never ordered the execution of anybody, even of a sister. The auspices of her birth, however, had saved her from 'moral' execution, the last being attempted in 1986, when eggs had struck her royal image in New Zealand. And New Zealand seemed to pop up here and there in connection with her physical person even before she became a queen. She had to interrupt her voyage to New Zealand when the news of her father's death reached her in Sagana. Now, one more month, and she would be back in Auckland for the meeting of Commonwealth nations. Already at Antoine's in the Parnell district, the restaurant was being refurbished and 'security-cleared' in case Her Majesty would eat Maori food, such as her favourite *toheroa* soup, as a gesture of good gastronomic relations.

The 'business' meeting at the McTavishes was, in a way, a 'first' since, in addition to Melissa, Bill, Komaru and Ling-ling, there was one still in embryo. Etymologically, there was nothing yet visible around the latter, but signs of morning discomfort had become manifest, as well as adduced as *aegrotat*, when Ling-ling failed to appear in the kitchen for the usual meeting to plan the activities of the day. Melissa, who had never shown any signs of nausea except when mixing Cardhu with an assortment of drugs such as Klonopin, Depakote, Lithonate and Thioridazine among others, at first refused to accept the 'good news' from the cook. It could not be so. How could that little Shanghainese structure do that to Komaru? Why had she not taken prophylactic measures? Not that Melissa discriminated against Chinese. It was just that Ling-ling's indiscretion had created an unwanted and unexpected paradigmatic dysfunction in human relations. And that meant a lot of conflicting feelings in Melissa, for, although she knew that Ling-ling 'lived' with Komaru, it had not occurred to her that under the Reti roof two humans could engage in enterprises beyond those of pragmatic reasons. Melissa felt betrayed, or at least shocked, in admitting to herself that romantic interludes existed not only in books of missionary records such as *My Lady of the Chinese Courtyard*, written by another 'Elizabeth', this time a Cooper, in 1914, but also in New Zealand bedrooms. At that time in China, the Manchu empress had been substituted by a democratic government a few years earlier, and Melissa's knowledge of history had started at that date in connection with literary activities influenced by Byron's poetic works via a Spanish woman whom Su Man-shu had met on a boat between Shanghai and Singapore. Apparently, actually for sure, Ling-ling had gone beyond discussing Chinese poetry of the Republican era. She even informed Komaru that one of the modern Chinese poets was Mao Ze-dong, who was interested, among other things, in the rôle of the number Nine, as in his poem 'Song of Picking Mulberry,' composed on the occasion of the Double Ninth Festival. Ling-ling used to read that poem to Komaru on his birthday.

Komaru announced the impending change in the Reti ménage even before business topics were presented for discussion. He had said that the restaurant would soon welcome another 'corporate' partner. Melissa's reaction to that statement did not escape Bill's scrutiny. The same for Komaru's, but his thoughts were still frozen on Ling-ling's body, for during the first month or so he saw how her breasts had swollen almost to Melissa's size ante-Brazil, and undoubtedly to Mahina's size. They had become more sensitive to the touch, well, at least there was something to touch. Komaru noticed for the first time that Ling-ling's breasts had both a longitudinal and latitudinal projection similar to Mahina's, while Melissa's were set a few degrees closer to her abdominal equator. As regards shape, there was no need to make a comparative analysis with Melissa's protuberances because of her pronounced pendular propensity. And Ling-ling's had changed, too, since a light brown hue had spread from the base toward the nipples, which had become almost white in contrast with the surrounding golden skin. They appeared like water lilies ready to bloom in a pond bathed in early morning sunshine. They even smelled sweet. Komaru felt that the whole olphacto-chromatic and tactilo-topographic blend of natural *primitiae* offered an opportunity to regard Ling-ling as a vehicle of continuity in the chain of life, besides deriving aesthetic pleasure through visual and dactylic inspection.

Ling-ling's heightened erogenous zone confirmed a Manchu *whakapapa*. There was no question that her breasts and her genitals were more sensitive to the touch than her lips. It seemed to Komaru that touching her nipples released pleasure-inducing hormones in her much more than in handling her genitalia. A thought occurred to him. Was this touch reaction similar to Mahina's? Apparently, yes, even more than in handling Melissa, but of course she had been injected with an artificial compound. Besides, Melissa did not react to touch in concomitance with smell. Ah, was it a coincidence that both Ling-ling and Mahina possessed a symbiotic duality involving both touch and smell? He vaguely remembered having read somewhere that in Classical Egyptian the semanteme *sn-* meant both oscular touch and smell. In essence, that combination had merged into a *hongi*, a means for humans to touch and smell, via the nose, each other as a manner of establishing trust. Yes, he thought, Mahina and Ling-ling could be trusted for two different though complementary reasons, the former genetic, the latter cultural. There was no question that Melissa's sensitive areas were to be found only below the navel, *intra coxas*. Both Terence and Horace had attested that reaction respectively for a *virginem* and a *matronam* beginning with the face (*buccam*), then the bosom (*mammillas*), and finally the outer *labia* as a preliminary exploration of the vulval area, literally in that order.

For Komaru, the idea of 'seeing' something germinating in the womb of a Chinese woman after the chance encounter of a sperm with an ovum ('Dr Livingston, I presume?') was not only a physiological event but also a generic Maori symbol of returning to Hawaiki after thousands of years of navigation. Thus, Komaru felt stronger, even bolder, for now he did not care about what would happen to the restaurant, the 'cause', or to himself. As a matter of fact, in the ensuing conversation regarding the Queen's arrival, Komaru was suddenly struck by a wild idea. Ah, he thought, what an opportunity to send a message to the world at large from its very bottom! But, when, what, how? The order of those three adverbs was not casual. The 'when' was upon the queen's stay in Ao Tea Roa; the 'what' was undoubtedly not eggs; but the 'how' presented difficulties. He just could not enter a Pacific training camp in Islamic fashion. Abū al-Qāsim Muḥammad ibn 'Abd Allāh ibn al' Muṭṭalib ibn Hāshim was too long a name to obtain a tourist visa from the Ministry of Immigration. The 'how' was closely tied to 'where', and this meant Auckland.

Yes, of course, Auckland. Who remembers now the original seven-hill Maori settlement displacing the ancient names of the Ngati-Whatua? The Etruscan parallels with Rome's seven hills was uncanny. That the modern designation of Auckland was given in honour of George Eden, Governor-General of India, indicated how toponomastics was created on the basis of Pakehas, who, in most cases, had never heard of Ao Tea Roa. The name of the Nga Marama chief, Kiwi Tamaki, barely survives in myth and legends centering not on battle records, but on exploits involving a hundred lovers who believed in making love, not war. Polynesian onomastics had been emasculated by Anglo-Saxon philology to the point that British heroes, forgotten at home, needed an antipodean foothold to extend their colonial fame.

For Komaru, however, Auckland immediately assumed an operational rôle. Even Melissa was somewhat surprised when he, originally adverse to opening the first of a chain restaurant on the Isthmus (he thought a better place would be Christchurch), agreed to travel there on the occasion of Armistice Day, 11 November, no longer printed in 'red', and not even in 'blue', as Marlborough Anniversary Day and Canterbury Anniversary Day for November on the Calendar of Festivities. Yes, Melissa and Komaru would spend a week of discussion in Auckland, explore leaseholds, seek capital from Maori-sympathetic sources, and the like. The fact that Elizabeth II would be in town around Armistice Day was simply a coincidence. Not for Komaru.

Melissa in particular was ecstatic, for Ling-ling had decided to remain in Wanganui for 'health' reasons. Bill would do likewise for similar reasons, though on behalf of teenagers whose suicide attempts seemed to be higher during the Austral Spring. Thus, the prospect of having Komaru to herself had become an exciting *idée fixe*, almost a re-creation of the 'Friday seduction' that lasted a whole weekend. After all, she was not getting any younger at 52. And she even imagined that Komaru could not possibly squeeze out of Ling-ling all the erotic pleasure that only she could dispense. In Melissa's self-centred belief, Ling-ling just did not look like a female capable of erotic refinements that only a European could offer, like the best meal on the eve of an execution. And, indeed, Melissa thought about that, especially when Komaru announced that he and Ling-ling would soon get married. That shocked everyone, Ling-ling the most, since she had not been informed of Komaru's sudden decision. What he had intended to say was that he planned to get married in order to legalise a social situation that was becoming more 'evident' by the week. After all, it was not a tolerable Maori–Pakeha liaison to improve race relations. Any race connubium did not count unless it involved a white. An 'Oriental' did not seem to contribute anything 'political', which meant survival for the Pakehas.

Ling-ling became red in the face, but said nothing, though she was pleased. Bill, observing her, thought that the myth of 'Oriental' inscrutability, for 'Asian' did not seem to trigger any such views, was real to the point of defying a century of traditions from Paolo Mantegazza's anthropological studies to Paul Ekman's scholarship. By accepting Darwin's statement that there is 'no distinctive facial expression for love,' Ekman regards love as 'an affective commitment, in which many emotions are felt, though not manifested.' Who was, then, showing 'love' for Komaru, Melissa or Ling-ling?

Melissa became silent, particularly when Bill stated: 'Well, can you imagine how our dear fellows feel at the prospect of witnessing the results of an ... unexpected race relation?' Probably he felt that for the subtle Pakeha policy of maintaining white supremacy it was bad enough to envisage a palliative Maori–Pakeha miscegenation. Surely, the white would become 'browner', fine, but now mixing yellow with brown? Not even Margaret Mead would have been wild enough to invent that possibility in Samoa, where she had concocted the most fertile fabulistic theory of coming of age as she herself may have hoped for vicariously. That was a new dab of colour on the palette of 'physical' anthropology, straight impasto from the oil tubes, for no one thought of dynamite-proof cultural aspects permeating Maori traditions. Yes, a white may go 'native', but a Maori can never become a Pakeha. This had nothing to do with skin colour since, in the case of Chinese and Maori, one could uncover under the skin a most powerful substratum of genetic affinities. In essence, Bill felt that it was possible for a white and a Maori to mingle at the superficial level, but the Chinese 'card' could never become part of the genetic game. That would create baffling results in spite of the Macao experimentations leading to the absorption of whites by yellows. In practice, the Asian–Maori potential blend would validate physically that New Zealand was an Asian country like Australia, and not an 'albo-Pacific' abode.

Melissa asked about a projected wedding date, of course, that was to be expected upon returning from Auckland, since there were several immigration procedures to be followed step by step. The ceremony would be simple, informal in one way, but formal in another, because it was assumed that Ling-ling would invite a few relatives from Shanghai, Canton and Hong Kong. The wedding would be performed in Wanganui, preferably at the Mediet, Komaru added as an afterthought.

Well, there was time for that, just enough for Melissa to vocalise her swan song in Auckland. Although Ling-ling may have imagined past connubial ties between her and Komaru, she never made any comments, for Komaru had refrained from engaging in synchronic dualistic relations with the two women. Komaru saw an opportunity abruptly to detach himself from Melissa's sexual oppression. And, in fact, he had never participated in any 'club' activities, particularly to avoid having Melissa as an eyewitness offering arrangements for younger 'chicks' under her voyeuristic rôle. That was a way of enticing Komaru's diminishing interest in her into a sexual revival, especially after Melissa had accepted the Italian 'fine hand' proffered by a Sicilian *cicisbeo* during the period when Komaru was engaged in the Moutoa Gardens 'disturbances'. He simply could not think of wasting time feeding Melissa with his energies. The 'white lust' he had acquired during the historic research for the MA thesis had been wiped out by the defeat suffered at the Gardens. Too many things had occurred to bring him in line with other more valuable experiences acquired while growing up. He was not 'hooked', he had not become subject to acquired satyriasis. Yes, he had enjoyed being played as an instrument of hedonism, normally absent in the monotony of a marriage. In the end, he knew that love did not enter into lust at all. He was even sure that Melissa loved Bill, no question about it. But, at the same time, he was convinced that a bout of lust could affect seasoned wives sooner or later, perhaps as an index of vitality sought by them, consciously or not, either at the sunset of eroticism, after a trauma, or even watching a movie, if not reading a book. His theory was reinforced by a study on female sexual life indicating that the most enjoyable period of their lives was, for most women, in their 50s when menopause created havoc. The lack of worry about becoming pregnant could become an incentive to assert the uniqueness of non-restricted femininity.

In turn, Komaru thought of utilising Melissa as an instrument of political purpose. The whole scheme surged in his mind and began to develop slowly after Melissa suggested booking a reservation in Auckland as soon as possible because of the Commonwealth meeting rendering accommodations at a premium. Melissa was even tactful enough to ask for two separate rooms, of course, under business expenses. In a modest place such as the Imperial Hotel on Hobson Street, it was *de rigueur* to maintain a certain modicum of formal detachment between a 52-year-old Pakeha lady, the rather easily identifiable wife of a nationally known psychiatrist, and a 29-year-old Maori bull, a school dropout. Probably at the *Hyatt*, as a more 'internationally' tolerant establishment, no one would raise an eyebrow, but, of course, that was more expensive and probably already full. Komaru, amazingly, would not have minded paying more if he knew that the queen would be staying there during her Auckland sojourn. However, he did not inquire about that, not even of Melissa, for she would smell a rat. In her mind, a photograph had been taken when she was 10 years old. That was her first trip to London, and London was Queen Elizabeth II, the first woman who had imprinted in her memory the most romantic notion of a life to be lived as in a fable.

Melissa was excited about the trip because she hoped to relive the emotions of a pre-teen dream when in 1952 she saw the queen on her way to Westminster. Komaru saw the opportunity to be near Melissa somewhere, particularly if tickets were to be given by the British consulate to trusted Brits welcoming their queen. After all, Melissa had impeccable credentials, and her Maori chauffeur could be regarded as loyal as she was simply by association. Was the queen in any danger stemming from those holding a grudge for having been forced out of the Moutoa Gardens, a 'sacred' Maori place, just months before her visit? Komaru knew well that he was a suspect with regard to the Wanganui 'disorders' but, of course, no one could prove anything. He was a business partner with Melissa and, as such, he tried to behave, though with a devilish plan inspired by the lecture delivered by Professor Peterson in Wanganui. Komaru had simply decided to become the Menachem Begin of 1995. Although Komaru reviewed the history of what is now called 'terrorism', he dismissed everything as incidental and irrelevant terminologically, for in each and every case, although the variables were several, the ultimate result would be like a particular war, like the 1955 *fedayeen* attacks into Israel (a counter-*utu* operation) or the 1972 Olympic Games or the 1983 attack on the US Marines barracks in Beirut.

Komaru had even read David Hirst's *The Gun and The Olive Branch*, one of the books listed by Professor Peterson on the bibliographical reference page distributed to those who attended his lecture. The author had actually, and brilliantly, made an equipollence between an act of war and acts of so-called 'terrorism' by retrieving from the Movement 'Black September 1970' (when Palestinians were removed from Jordan by King Hussein), a general definition on which Professor Peterson based his interpretations of the new 'war' emerging from the death of the old war. Apparently, it had been described impromptu by a teenage terrorist who had nothing to lose except his own life: 'It [terrorism] cannot be pinpointed, tracked down, or crushed. It has no name, no flag, no slogans, headquarters, or base. It requires only men who have the determination to fight and succeed and the courage to die.'

That statement, much less than a formulation of a program, and undoubtedly not consonant with a traditional declaration of war, shocked Komaru for something beyond its immediate purpose. Within the general framework of humanity, Komaru saw the end of civilisation as a consequence of advances in technology, communication, information and so forth. Spengler could never have imagined that new dimension in his formulation of the decline of the West. Humans had now reached the apex, or the stage, of resourcefulness that made war impossible, unnecessary, and futile through concocting the quintessence of self-destruction for the purpose of righting wrongs in religion, politics, economics, and other ideals that were always different in each nation seeking them.

Ironically, Komaru noticed how this new twist in resolving conflicts had not appeared in the immediate past. For example, nearly, if not all, African nations, including South Africa, had emerged not from acts of terrorism, but from either public opinion or conventional guerrilla wars. In the case of the US, no one had done anything beyond brewing tea in the Boston pot. America was later invoked as the ideal for making slave nations free. Yes, there had been cases of guerrilla warfare, but still as part and parcel of war. Humanity, however, had entered a sudden paradigm that had become the scourge of everything built during a dozen centuries of traditions. Innocent victims such as bystanders, children, aliens to the cause and others were indiscriminately killed without rhyme or reason anywhere, anytime. This scourge was worse than Nazi genocide in method, AIDS in diffusion beyond all frontiers, nuclear annihilation and natural upheavals, totally out of control even on the part of leaders who would later assume responsibility after acts of 'terrorism' whether they were involved or not.

And, sadly, no one could do anything to avoid or destroy the new germ of impending Armaggedon. What nation on Earth, including the most powerful such as the United States, could constantly prevent, fight and contain 'terrorism', even if all its resources were directed against that plague? That would be tantamount to engaging in a constant and continuing war against war. What could humans do if they saw themselves on the Medusa raft of precarious life in order to survive peacefully in a troubled world? How long could a superpower keep on sending WMD to the four corners of the world for the sake of destroying other WMD? What was the purpose of quelching a local fire of destruction by a counter fire of larger proportions? Had no one begun to see the Earth as a giant theatre of 'Vietnamisation' magnified by advances in technology? Had anyone ever thought of dropping not bombs but parachuting food, medicine, books, or even landing agricultural experts, engineers and teachers, rather than camouflaged, weapon-holding, impotent UN peacekeepers? Had anyone ever hoped of forbidding the making and exporting of ammunition, or even of destroying all its factories in place of destroying humans?

Surprisingly, Komaru received a 'yes' to most of his questions, one of them lost in the annals of history by those powers who had become such through terrorism, like Israel. In talking with Bill in general about the psychological dimension of terrorism, Komaru had come across the 1932 correspondence between Einstein and Freud, published in *Why War?* in 1933, the same year Hitler ascended to absolute power. Well, in certain cases, it was a matter of terminology. Freud had asked Einstein to substitute *Macht*, 'power', for *Gewalt*, 'violence'. In spite of several attempts to rationalise, Freud subtly admitted the inevitability of war, perhaps in connection with his view of Life in addition to ethical inevitabilities that, on the one hand, teach a citizen along moral and religious duties ('Don't kill!'), and then the same individual is suddenly trained to kill by looking into the eyes of the 'enemy' across a trench. What happens to the psyche of such an individual? Even Einstein, though agreeing with pacifism, was the first to sign the letter asking Roosevelt to built an atomic bomb. He was simply afraid that the Nazis would built and employ the bomb before the Americans. Komaru felt that the mere dropping of the bomb over Hiroshima was the avatar of terrorism that checks in part with its definition given by the Palestinian youth. Yes, Komaru knew all those cogitations intellectually, but emotionally he put them aside. He simply could not understand how the British had been evicted from the four corners of the Earth, except from his own home.

When Komaru heard that, in order to create an atmosphere of good will before her arrival, the queen, not the Crown, was to apologise to the Maori people for all the 'discomfort' created in New Zealand (not in Ao Tea Roa) during two centuries of 'involuntary' conflicts created by the spirit of times past, he got mad. He thought that an apology from a person in power without the implementation of retribution for moral and physical damage to the 'natives' actually constituted a reinforcement of superiority toward a minority, as if God itself would apologise for having created a world of injustice without trying to change it. The status quo would still be the same. Apologies do not reinstate dignity in a people under chronic oppression. The very fact that the queen was coming to New Zealand, one of her 'subjects', was an affirmation of her 'rights' as the sovereign of those hermit islands. Thus, every day that passed reinforced Komaru's determination to do something unique in the history of the Commonwealth. And Melissa would unknowingly help him to send a message to the world at large.

The plan in sending that message included self-immolation if necessary. Thus, not having any time to get married to Ling-ling, he made a Last Will and Testament leaving everything to her. Second, he wrote a letter to Mahina, but he entrusted it to Whina, who had called Komaru expressing fear of right wing elements connected with the unrest in Wanganui. Third, he planned to burn all correspondence in the *waka reta*. Finally, he started the delicate mission of securing what he needed to be remembered as the first Maori to immolate himself for a cause. He knew that dousing oneself with petrol and then igniting it in a public square was simply a useless romantic gesture. Something else, more drastic and direct, had to be devised and acted upon. Thus, he postponed his plan until he went to Auckland with Melissa, for in Wanganui any departure from his routine would be known immediately.

The group tone of the meeting at the McTavishes had slowly changed from the business to a 'family' one. In fact, at supper, the atmosphere was relaxed, even jovial, on the part of everyone except Melissa. Whether under the influence of the *caipirinhas* or the planned excursion to Auckland, she had become morose and pensive, as if her mind was somewhere else. At her suggestion that the 'Retis' would be welcome to spend the night at the McTavishes, Bill concurred with Komaru that Melissa needed a good night's rest after such a full meal prepared by her, like one enjoyed by Charles Dickens on Sunday at Broadstairs before he became an alcoholic. Melissa's idiosyncrasies and diets were not dissimilar from Dickens' as a consequence of manic depression affecting both of them. The dinner consisted of a bloody beef roast with potatoes and carrots. It ended with an English trifle dish with rum soaking the ladyfingers, and topped with whipped cream. Nothing spectacular, and everyone except Komaru enjoyed it.

At the conclusion of the repast, Melissa and Ling-ling left for the kitchen to do the dishes. Bill and Komaru moved downstairs to the rumpus room. There Bill did not waste any time in eliciting from Komaru what he had detected in the air.

'Your interest in the queen seems rather, well, I should say ... puzzling. The questions you have been posing to Melissa about the CHOGM have perturbed me somewhat for ... your own safety, and Melissa's. Komaru, tell me, by any chance are you planning to create a disturbance on the occasion of the ...'

'No, well, Bill, I can't lie to you, but I am thinking in terms of a perfectly democratic demonstration as in England. Would it be impolite to express a political opinion at home, my home?'

'Of course not, but, you see, nowadays there is a thin line between a simple demonstration and an act of terrorism.'

'And, how do you know where this line is? After all, you are aware of the fact that terrorism may be a misnomer for something vocal. Besides, it reflects many facets of protest, and, at any rate, is not new. It may be traced to ...'

'Please don't lecture to me. Historians never can get out of classrooms ...'

'Sorry to interrupt, but, after the actions taken by religious fanatics all over the world, no internal security organisation is going to be finicky, as Mahina would say in Americanese, about deleting that line for whatever reason.'

'There are no dividing lines for fanatics.'

'Rather intriguing, Bill. You refer to fanatics. Do you mean what, Islamic? I do not know of any other wider religious movement, even in India. By any chance, do you equate "Islamic terrorism" with religious fixation, if I understand it correctly?'

'Sadly so!'

'How revealing! But I am sorry to say that you are wrong. And please forgive me if I may presume to have the opinion of an amateur, for I know you are older and wiser than I. But studying history has created in me a vacuum of sorts regarding traditional views. If you equate 'terrorism' with Muslim Holy War, that is 'Jihad', in any degree. As a historian I can state that this war has been waged since before Charlemagne was crowned. By the time Pakehas celebrate the 200th anniversary of the Waitangi Trick, terrorism will be more than 13 centuries old. Does that surprise you?'

'I am sorry, I don't quite ... read you. For ...'

'Bill, please, you know that number "711" is not an American sign on a dairy by a petrol station. It marks the date when al-Tarik began the conquest of, well, not of Europe, but of Christendom that happened to be located in Europe. How, sending missionaries, like Ireland? No, of course, but by dumping hordes of exalted Arabs drunk with the mesmerising sounds of drums in order to increase the adrenaline level of the attackers. If you study what the Muslims have been doing since then through bloody brutality, what the Crusaders did later, including cannibalism, was child's play. And, literally, the "Children's Crusade" proves my point.'

'Rather intriguing, I should say. Your account is like the fable in which Red Hood meets not a wolf but a rapist.'

'In fact, Bill, I think that it was Jihad landing on ... Gibraltar, exactly on 711 AD, not hordes of merchants raiding orchards in South Spain. And that "religion", beginning with a military operation, signalled the inception of eternal war branching out on different levels, from the psychological via indoctrination to contemporary actions through WMD. From al-Tarik to Ayatollah Khomeini the only difference is chronological time. Everything else is a matter of details. The Crusades were just, as I said, temporary palliatives lasting only about 200 years, namely between 1095 and 1291. The Holy War against Christians has never stopped and never will until humans perish like dinosaurs ironically believing in a sadistic god.'

'Then what has Christianity done so far? Waiting in the wings for … ?'

'Ah, Christianity has only been able to associate itself with the West and its descendants as "civilised" nations. Well, my adjective "civilised" is a vague term, for you know well that, after the Crusaders lost their military mission, something else developed in tow to Jihad among Christians.'

'I am afraid I can't grasp your line of reasoning. You just can't …'

'What I mean, Bill, is that another Holy War, an eye for an eye, was waged by Christianity in Europe not only against "pagans", but also against Europeans and other people suspected of heresy. This "war "actually was the personification of "pure terrorism" *avant la lettre* surpassing in scope, means of implementation, and final objective, even Jihad.'

'Komaru, perhaps the *caipirinhas* I drunk have obfuscated my brain, and …'

'Bill, can you tell me what Christian organisations, or I should say Christ's *Armadas*, did soon after the Muslims were evicted from Spain along with the Jews in 1492? Have you forgotten a most base and repressive activity called "Inquisition"?'

There was a long silence. Bill looked intensely at the parquet floor, then at Komaru, and stood up. Presently he sat down, nearly transfixed, as if afraid of being absorbed by the soft seat of the armchair. And there he remained, silent.

'Even before the Crusades abroad and the Inquisition at "home", the Church was always ready to strike against anyone trying to destabilise its pyramidal organisation. Amazingly, it was against its own followers that the Church fought more fiercely than during the Crusades and the Inquisition. The whole activity of repression started slowly during the time of Augustine, who at first was reluctant, but later agreed on "inquisitive" methods of defense. After the death of

Charlemagne, when our *waka* fleet was coming down the Pacific from Asia, the Church's die was cast for the foundations of physical elicitation. One could assume, for the sake of chronology, that the institution of the Holy Roman Empire, with Otto I, marks the beginning of psychological "terrorism" lasting 1,000 years until it was taken over, through the Unification of Italy, by the politicisation of the Vatican, along with Fascism and Monarchy.'

'I simply can't grasp the magnitude of your assumptions.'

'Bill, at that time, as the end of the first Millennium was approaching, anything new from philosophers, ascetics, mystics, preachers and so on was regarded as deleterious to the Church. In essence, any time its boat was rocked, a culprit had to be found and designated as heretic. It is not coincidental that most, if not all, "heretics" developed in Southern Italy for historical reasons based on Greek culture, and particularly in the region that later was ascribed the name of Calabria, a land of thinkers who never accepted any dogma imposed by anyone. Even Napoleon was afraid of Calabrian "minds". One of these minds could be individualised in Gioacchino da Fiore.'

'Do you mean Joachim of Floris?'

'Exactly so.'

'But was he not placed by Dante in *Paradiso*? Sorry, I don't know the details.'

'I came across him through Mahina's interest in Francis of Assisi, who, together with St Dominic, could be considered as Johnny-come-latelies with regard to the Calabrian abbot. You see, Joachim was a prophet, and when the Church was told of the impending fall of Jerusalem to Saladin in 1087, that was too much. He had become suspect, even after it was known that he had prepared the way for Francis of Assisi's novel views. Who in the world were these lowly friars preaching a new "gospel"? In fact, Francis converted to Christianity after Joachim's death. Thus, Joachim left behind, according to Spengler, a "new" Christianity, that later "moved" the best of the Dominicans and Franciscans ... in their utmost souls, and awakened a world outlook that took possession of the historical sense of our own culture; the sense of mankind as an active, fighting, progressive "whole". As a historian, even a failed one on the books of Victoria University, I can state that the Medieval soul had died with Joachim and at the same time the Renaissance of the human spirit had begun.'

'Simply fabulous, my dear fellow!'

With that admission, Bill had accepted Komaru au pair intellectually. More than that, Komaru had become a trusting friend by speaking his mind, unafraid of consequences.

'And that is why the Church, shaken to its very foundations, at first did not know what to do, particularly as the end of the first Millennium approached, preceded by the scourge of the Antichrist, not dissimilarly from Communism and its evil empire dying at the end of the second Millennium. Thus, Joachim generated the condemnation of the Church and the apprehension of the University of Paris. Consequently, after Joachim's death, the Joachites, with their pacifist-international-democratic ideas, became "doves", hardly welcome by the militarism that was needed for the Crusade. Joachim's writings were eliminated from each and every monastic institution in Europe, except in Northern Italy and France, where ironically they became the seeds of the French Revolution seven centuries later. George Sand's *Spiridion*, though a "quavel" *avant la lettre*, related exactly the long incubation of an idea conceived in the 'new' Calabria.'

'And now he is a saint, isn't he?'

'No, of course not, for his doctrine was condemned by the Lateran Council in 1215. However, he should be named the patron saint of "terrorists". Come on, Bill. You know, if you can't fight them, join them. So, Joachim should be canonised in order to quelch his "heresy" like that of Fra' Dolcino of Novara. For me, this technique is not unlike an act of terrorism of the mind imposed on believers, as in the case of Galileo. Unfortunately, other thinkers throughout history, such as Michael Servetus and Giordano Bruno, were not so lucky. Things had changed, and the Inquisition took over *In nomine Patris, Filii, et Spiritus Sancti*.'

'Amen.'

'Well, not quite, unless the Church, through its popes, recognises its mistakes. Pope John Paul II seems to have initiated a revolution of atonement. Is it because he is the first non-Italian pope in centuries, and thus perceptive enough to analyse an alien culture as a social anthropologist? When visiting the Czech Republic, he, as a Slavic soul, asked forgiveness for what the Catholics did to the Protestants durign the Counter-Reformation. No self-centred prelate would ever dream of doing anything similar before. Then, when in Africa, the pope apologised, on the quay of the island that had anchored slave ships, for those believers who traded in Black souls taken away to Christian America. Even in a stadium built by Hitler, the pontiff regretted that only a small group of Catholics resisted the Holocaust.

I wonder what he thought of Teutonic-minded Pope Pius XII. But, you see, the pope still has done little at "home". What I mean, will he have the intestinal fortitude to take a similar stand of apology against the horrors of the Inquisition? Will he ever open the secret archives of the Inquisition to scholars and citizens who hunger to know the truth so far covered up by the corporate Vatican as a trademark of oppression? And, finally, do you think that, on the 400th anniversary of Giordano Bruno's barbecuing, on the 17 February 2000, John Paul II will deposit a bouquet of flowers, as the first step towards canonisation, at the foot of Bruno's statue in Campo dei Fiori as Willy Brandt did at the mausoleum for victims of the Holocaust? You see, Bill, the physical distance between the Vatican State and Campo dei Fiori is short enough even for an ailing pope to cover on foot as he does at Easter in the pagan Coliseum, but the moral distance is antipodean. I bet that he is afraid of being killed by the forces of tradition, the same ones who killed another pope a generation earlier ...'

'No, Komaru, I doubt it, but if John Paul II will ever kneel in front of Bruno's place of holocaust, this being the most correct term etymologically, then I myself will convert to Catholicism.'

'So, Bill, don't you think that Christianity has survived and even thrived through "terrorism"? Or do you equate it with bombs only? Can't you, as a psychiatrist, see that explosives can be implanted not only into bodies and buildings, but also into the minds of free thinkers? What was more deleterious during so many centuries of Inquisition, the psychological cleansing of a man's belief through brute force or just a few kilograms of plastic explosives attached to the waist of a "fanatic" youth?'

'Please, Komaru, you are disturbing me quite a lot, I ...'

'Tell me, Bill, as a specialist in suicide, how do you view the fanatical youth carrying a satchel of mass destruction, as a terrorist or an individual who needs some Librium? Don't you see that militarism is just a cover-up for Christianity as terrorism is for Islam in general? Don't you believe that whatever began in 711 has never stopped, just changed hands in one direction or another? What is the difference in anything deleterious either in Mecca or at the Vatican as directed by people blinded by fanaticism? You are a psychiatrist. Tell me, how deranged am I for trying to synthesise 20 centuries of World History *vis-à-vis* terrorism on the studio couch of the West? Can you think of anything similar taking place among Buddhists and Confucianists? Don't you see that the Torah and the Bible are the

Father and the Mother of a rebel child, the Koran, against which no one can do anything to slow down the selenisation of the Earth through what you label collective suicide? Are you afraid of reneging on Freud and his seminarists dispensing drugs from offices organised by pharmaceutical companies? Or ...'

'Please, Komaru, I am lost. Give me a breather. It is amazing that 20th-century "Freudian experimentation" coincided in large part with the failure of American psychiatrists to understand the counter-"Freud" of modern culture. I refer to a man who allegedly had lost his mind meandering through the civilisation of Man, namely, Ezra Pound. I came across his ideas and the "problems" he created for the United States after he was released from his iron cage near Pisa. In any mature culture, by now Pound would have been sanctified or elevated to the status of a national hero. Of course, his mind never changed in spite of all the tangible and intangible correctives forced on him. And he never shed anything "Freudian" along his way to the quintessence of "genius integrity". How could an inferiority-complexed Roosevelt understand the revolutionary ideas of a Pound to rescue mankind from disaster? We psychiatrists may be charlatans, but American leaders of post-World War II are simply ignorant of economics, politics, and "world management".'

'And we historians, Bill, intentionally change facts into excuses for reneging on them. The more we read about history, and even looking synchronically at events, the deeper we are submerged by the so-called "Heisenberg effect".'

'The ... what?'

'I refer to Karl Werner Heisenberg, who had his brain split into two parts and no corpus callosum between them, namely one for philosophy and another for physics. It was Mahina who explained to me Heisenberg's "indeterminacy principle" for which he was awarded the Nobel Prize in 1932. Basically, Heisenberg, according to Buckminster Fuller's "general law", stated that, when one observes a phenomenon (probably he meant beyond physical recording such as an internalised reasoning process undetectable by physics), this, I mean the phenomenon being observed, is altered by the very act of observation. That is why it is impossible to formulate any general truths. All pseudo-truths so far can be tossed into the refuse bin of "temporality" until another empty bin is brought to be filled with unfreezable observations capable of lasting long enough to reach any "cosmic" (and allegedly "eternal") conclusions. Only the poet can cut across the maze of apparent contradictions and, indeed, even before

Pound it was another poet, T. S. Eliot, not a historian, who concluded that the study of history, a baffling activity, always alters history itself.'

'Komaru, yes, I recall and understand what we psychologists tried to uncover in Pound's mind when he used to mock us. I was an intern and an assistant to one of the four psychiatrists officially appointed by the American government to "treat" Pound at Washington St Elizabeth's Hospital. How could one cure a genius, a prophet, a spelunker of never-before reached corners of the human mind? He told us, quite clearly, that the more we think, the more our thinking "metamorphosed" what was being thought about. He used to employ Greek terms, and at times he drew Chinese characters in the air with his hands. We simply concluded that he would never be cured. We were not prepared to treat, what analogy can I give you, the Einstein of the mind, and too bad that he did not concentrate on studying the mind *per se* through poetry or, actually, what we call poetry. In retrospect, I think, and here I hate to use this analogy, he thought of the mind as a cold mechanism devoid of intelligence. Once he told me, probably because I was the youngest in the group and never said anything, shuffling papers for my professor, that actually the mind did not exist as an independent entity. For him, it was made of amoebas changing so fast that it was impossible to detect any "rhyme or reason" to their function. And here he laughed at his own pun, probably thinking of traditional poetry. He was convinced that early Greek philosophers invented the concept of the mind in order not to become deranged.'

'So, who is afraid of becoming deranged? Aren't we all, daaaling.'

Chapter 43

Melissa had stormed in from the kitchen with Ling-ling in tow. She collapsed on the sofa as if exhausted. Ling-ling sat by Komaru as if she had not seen him in a long time. Her eyes displayed something new that could be termed 'marital happiness'.

'Oh, Kom, you will have the best housekeeper in New Zealand. Much better than a Filipina. Ling-ling is so organised, so thorough and fast. My kitchen has never been so clean.'

Bill chuckled at hearing 'my' kitchen. As long as she remembers to turn off the stove, he hoped.

'Thank you, Melissa. Yes, Ling-ling applies Chinese methodology of simplicity to Western complexity. Her world is made of little things ready to be utilised without interruption. Did you notice that we had already eaten our slice of beef while she was still cutting hers into bite-sized pieces?'

'I, Komaru, actually we, have to be careful not to cause indigestion to ... who knows? Will it be a boy or a girl?'

'What do you mean? It had better be a boy, otherwise I'll send you back to Shanghai.'

'Meanwhile, please send me home. Melissa, Bill, I beg you to excuse me,' said Ling-ling. 'We must be tired.'

At home, Komaru found a letter from Mahina. As soon as Ling-ling went to bed, he put all other mail aside, sat at the kitchen counter and read, or tried to read, the letter bearing a canceled US 60-cent stamp under the round black ink showing 'Boulder, CO 80306. US Postage.' And in the centre, '11 3 1995 one day after All Souls' Day.'

The letter, in Maori, had been written in several installments, the first being dated 1 November. In trying to send general news items, perhaps as a means of relaxing, Mahina mentioned a disgusting celebration of skulls and bones called Halloween. She was horrified at the way even young children handled what in Maori culture would be a serious and spiritual topic in remembering a *whakapapa*. The little she saw in the streets, the offices, and even at the Estes Park hospital, was beyond her comprehension, mainly because of the jubilation and phoney euphoria like that of a carnival, including the masquerading of dogs and cats. Her Sisters explained that the whole thing was just the first step to a year-end consumerism beginning at Halloween, picking up speed at Thanksgiving, exploding at Christmas, and closing at New Year's in a country suffering from the psychological impact of abundance. She wondered how *Homo americanus* is biologically equipped to exist in an Age of Plenty. She was also told that, as a small city near-by, Boulder, being a university town with the highest concentration of PhDs per capita in the States, availed itself of any opportunity to place the town on the map of national notoriety, not only with senseless riots and the destruction of shops and public property, but also by attracting 'flat-land' people to generate some of the most baffling murder cases in the annals of criminality.

Among other news items, Mahina mentioned that she had begun to study American history to prepare herself for the examination previous to acquiring US citizenship in two years. She even thought of considering the continuation of her academic life by applying for admission to graduate school in comparative literature. This baffled Komaru, for a change from an 'abstract' discipline, such as philosophy, to a more creative one, such as literature, seemed to indicate a wish to give birth to something mental as a subliminal palliative in place of physiological normality for a young female. He realised that subconsciously he was being influenced by Ling-ling's proximity. Mahina had even thought of a PhD dissertation exploring the roots of Franciscan thought beginning with Joachim of Flores and centring around the three lines describing him in Dante's *Paradiso* in the company of two saints. At the coincidence of the topic just discussed with Bill a few hours earlier, Komaru nearly became frightened. Had he 'read' his sister's letter before even receiving it? Who was the prophet, he or Joachim? But fate had decided otherwise, for, as related by Mahina, four days after her first meeting with an *ad hoc* advisor in a decrepit building near Norlin Library, she heard that the professor had died after receiving a flu shot recommended for people near retirement age. This Mahina took as a sign of having had enough of academia. Besides, commuting to the University of Colorado campus, even on a part time basis, was not an activity she looked forward to, for her psyche was alien to snowstorms. She had been told that Boulder was the only city in the US where snow plowing was left to the whims of solar maintenance, that is, no one thought of plowing the murderous streets of the 'Hill', the area surrounding the campus. When the sun failed to appear 'after five minutes,' the department of physical education let its ski team practice slalom around the Sink, a Medieval-type of watering hole, rather than at Eldora, an old mining survivor community half an hour away from campus. The traffic jams sported by Boulder drivers even without icy roads competed with those of Los Angeles, Houston and New York, but the city fathers felt that, the town being inhabited mostly by PhDs, these could solve all the problems of navigating through streets whose intersections displayed signs hidden among the foliage of a 'Tree City USA' How drivers read those signs is a mystery, though an IBM executive boasting two doctorates explained that he always read the street signs in the rear view mirror AFTER crossing the wrong street or making the wrong turn.

Komaru wondered why Mahina would waste time and effort relating inconsequential news items. Who cared about a city full of complexes? Was she intentionally trying to tire out any possible reader other than her brother? Her day started at 05:15, she took one minute and 17 seconds to dress – did she not take a shower? – spent half an hour in the matutinal Lauds, then a quick cup of tea – the other Sisters coffee – and so until Mass, communion and breakfast. In writing her letter she elaborated on All Souls' Day, following All Saints' Day, and so forth. Then, suddenly, obviously she had been interrupted by something making her forget her train of thought, soon after Vespers, just as she was beginning to sing 'Magnificat animam meam, Domine!', she was approached by her abbess, a rather unusual occurrence, smack in the middle of the prayer-hymn. Mahina's help was needed to assist a 'drop in'. An intelligent woman in her early 20s had rung the carillon at the Heva House. The receptionist had summoned the Resident Services Director, Sister Renée, and she in her turn the abbess.

Mahina did not elaborate and did not give any specific details, though the Maori language conveyed between the lines something closer to a third-party experience. In short, the young lady was on the verge of committing suicide, and had actually attempted it by conveying carbon monoxide from the exhaust pipe of her car with a vacuum cleaner hose. Ironically, the Toyota petrol tank had run out of fuel after a few minutes, not long enough for her to pass out and die, for it requires about a quarter of an hour for a 50-kilogram person to become poisoned. It had merely given her a terrible headache. What else could Beverly do in North Denver among 'Mexican' homes? She took the bus to the 17th Street 'San Marco Square' tower, though actually she did not know, like most Denverites, that the tower was a stronger copy than the one sinking slowly in Venice. No, no dice, the door was locked. She proceeded on foot to the 16th Street bridge over the Platte river. The water was frozen. Then, perhaps, jump under a train? After half an hour no train appeared from the nearby station. Actually, the yard was empty. Just then, a bus stopped by the bridge entrance where a sign showed various routes throughout Metro Denver. The first bus sign displayed 'Boulder-Estes Park.' Oh, Beverly thought, the mountains, a trail into the sky, rest by a lake, and there wait for nature to take over. That was a favourite cop-out by many PhDs populating the Boulder Valley. But then something attracted Beverly's attention. A pamphlet had obviously been left by someone who had either changed her mind or forgotten it on a previous bus run. The brochure was folded into three pages. The second one read: 'Heva Home ... Where there is hope ... Where there is help ... Where there is a home.'

Komaru skipped a few paragraphs. He was becoming bored. So what, he thought. Women still pay the price for lingering in apple orchards like Eve. What does one know about her? By switching to English she asked herself, Was she a vamp, a mermaid, a witch, a temptress or a lunatic? Komaru thought that those five possible designations contained all the vowels and consonants to compose a noun like 'W-O-M-A-N.'

But then Mahina had underlined a lot of words, traced vertical lines on both sides of certain paragraphs, inserted large asterisks here and there, and drawn arrows in a bundle like Franco's *Falanges* for cross reference. Komaru slowed down and it did not take long for him to grasp the essence of the narrative. Beverly had spent her weekend in Frisco and her brother had joined her on his way back from the Gulf Area, where he had patrolled the 'no fly zone' as leader of a squadron. She had not seen him since she was 10 years old, a 'kid sister.' Now she was a woman nearly ready to get married in June 1996, just a winter away. But in Frisco, a bleak lake community for international shoppers willing to break a leg on murderous ski runs nearby, Beverly had succumbed to the idea of practicing for her impending wedding, for she was a virgin. She thought that her brother, already married and with two young children, was the ideal man to perform the avuncular operation about which, as a major in anthropology, she had first read with clinical detachment, and then with personal interest. Who else in the whole world could help her to surmount that once in a lifetime barrier, both psychologically and anatomically? Whom else could she trust for the sake of safety, security, health and genetic compatibility? The fleeting encounters at sports or academic centres always presented potential dangers of all sorts, she thought. And, thus, over the Halloween weekend, consciously disguised as one of the odaliscas whom her brother had seen dancing in Kuwait, she seduced her brother. For her it had been an exhilarating experience, for she compared her initiation to the flowing of the river under the little bridge dividing Frisco from its shopping centre and the townhouse south of I-70. The river was frozen, but a thin stream was flowing on the north side of the embankment, in full sunshine. The problem surged after she returned to Denver, for there she began to think about the condition in which she had left her brother. Had she seen in him a father from whom, because of a divorce situation, she had been away all of her life?

Mahina continued her story, though not in the style of a social worker or a spiritual assistant. After Beverly took her brother to Stapleton airport, a crisis developed nearly immediately. A profound feeling of wrongness had descended upon her, particularly after waiting in vain for a telephone call from San Diego, where 'Kurt' was going to meet his family. The fictitious name beginning with a 'K' left no doubt in Komaru's mind about the identity of the people involved in the Beverly case. The rest of the story was rather trite. Mahina had felt sorrow, not so much for Beverly as for Kurt. She wondered what kind of scars she had left in his psyche, and how she could get out of his conscience for the rest of his life. At this stage of the narrative, people and places had superimposed themselves in a rotating manner, so that Komaru did not know who was who. After all, he had not replied to any of Mahina's letters in two years. Why? Who was Mahina and who was Beverly? Well, so what? Wasn't Mahina going to get married, too, like Beverly? Was not Jesus waiting in the wings according to a scheduled event for which he had been born a few years *ante Christum*? The problem was that Beverly's case was real, though almost a copycat of Mahina's life nuptials. At the same time, Mahina felt intrigued by the fact that the abbess had entrusted Beverly to her care. She had obeyed without hesitating, though once she timidly asked the abbess why she, Sister Mary, had been chosen to help Beverly through spiritual counseling until a proper programme of rehabilitation from deep depression was to be formulated and initiated. The abbess replied that, from among the Sisters able to assist Beverly, she was, first of all, of a similar age, and thus possessing feelings of 'generational curiosity.' That astounded Mahina. Besides, the abbess continued, Mahina had a brother, did she not, a helpful coincidence. Finally, Mahina had not yet taken her final vows. So the Beverly case could help her, as a novice, analyse both sides of the emotional coin just in case the 'distance' from New Zealand became shorter via faxes and e-mail. That did hurt Mahina because in two years she had not received a line from her brother, though she had heard about him via Melissa, Whina and Ling-ling. Bill did not like to put anything on paper, except professional matters. He knew that 'verba volant, scripta manent.'

That night, Komaru could not sleep at all. He decided, because of his imminent departure for Auckland, to write something to his sister to be mailed later, depending on the outcome of his mission. The power of the mind!, he thought. Also, he felt so inert near the softly breathing body of Ling-ling lying nearby as she would for the next 9-month *whakapapa* of expectant postulancy and many years of motherly novitiate.

The trip to Auckland was a routine one for Komaru regarding the typical stops here and there to check the tyre pressure, refill the petrol tank and perform related operations. Summer had exploded, and thus traffic was more intensely felt on a Friday afternoon. Australian car plates indicated tourist interest along Motorway 4. The eruption of Mt Ruhapehu just two months earlier had been viewed by him as a premonition, at least from an etymological and historical angle. During the last few months he felt as if carried away ('riro') by the southern wind ('tonga') of defeat at all levels, for the southern wind brings the most penetrating cold into the bowels and the head of anyone attempting to do anything noble and sublime. This had happened to Ngatoru-i-rangi, who nearly died of exposure on top of the volcano. If Komaru ever attempted to do something similar, unlike Ngatoru who called for help from his sister in Hawaiki, he could not call Mahina. She was so far away, so detached from him, that no one could cover that distance of solitude, depression, and infinite sadness.

Melissa seemed to enjoy the journey though, as she told Komaru, she did not feel 'right'. That was because the condition dictated by Komaru was complete abstention from alcohol, regardless of the fact that she did not like to drive on open motorways. And that put her in a state of morosity, a welcome situation to Komaru for he did not like to listen to the usual comments made by backseat drivers.

At the hotel, Komaru made a reservation for supper the following day at *Antoine's*. He was told that on that day the restaurant served only dinner, and an early one, no after theatre booking, for the establishment had to be ready for a private party on Sunday. Fine, he thought. He also guessed that, since the establishment was never open on Sunday, it must be readied for a celebrity.

That evening, after supper at the *Dragon Boat*, a good Chinese restaurant on Elliot Street, he pleaded a headache and retired early for 'a good night's sleep'. Of course, that was a good excuse to fend off Melissa, who had invited him for a cup of tea in her room. In spite of his refusing the cuppa, she tried to storm into his room, but he did not answer her knocks. Besides, Komaru's telephone was constantly busy. And, indeed, he was on the phone for several hours, mostly contacting a few trusted friends on K-Road. He needed a lorry carrying a sign like one of the food suppliers for *Antoine's*. No problem, that could be done by stealing one of the vehicles from the New Zealand Co-Operative Dairy Co. Ltd directly from its car park on Maurice Road in Penrose. The delivery lorry was needed by Sunday afternoon. No one would miss it until the next day. A problem could arise from the fact that the Dairy supplied the richest butter and the sweetest cream in the whole world only on Monday mornings, but Komaru had to take a chance on routine delivery a day earlier in order to furnish the freshest products for the exigencies of a queen. Komaru counted on the next day's dinner at 333 Parnell for the topographic and strategic details involving parking and access routes to both the main entrance and the 'private' one leading to the dining area.

As regards other details, Komaru was to meet some people on Sunday morning, while Melissa would go to church wherever she liked nearby. Komaru, after contacting his local sources by phone, left it off the hook and informed the service desk that he did not wish to be disturbed. Then he spent several hours working with his radio scanner to retrieve any frequencies used by the police and other security operations. It was a tiresome activity, particularly since he used an earpiece for privacy. It was even hilarious when the first transmission he picked up was a semi-coded conversation between a dispatcher and a field officer for the Police Dog Section on Vincent Street. The officer was speaking about a 'canine dog unit,' and the dispatcher was at a loss to identify that particular breed of dog. Finally, Komaru was able to retrieve a few frequencies for the Panmure Patrol Base on Queens and the Ellerslie Patrole Base as well. He doubted that the queen would expose herself to eggs again, but, just in case, some itinerary data might transpire here and there, for, unlike at her last visit, the press was completely mute on the topic.

The following day, Saturday, a preliminary meeting was set by phone for a Tuesday discussion at one of the hotel conference rooms. Melissa went shopping, promising to be back by early afternoon. Komaru took the opportunity to visit some bookstores. It was a matter of killing time, as well as evading being spot-checked at key locations, as he felt he was. Too many coincidental signs, he thought, that indicated plainsclothesmen following him or simply bumping into him apologising profusely. At noon, he entered the *Crescent* eatery on Ward Street. It was a small and crowded joint, the salient feature of which was a display of camel art. In waiting to be seated, Komaru lingered by the corridor leading to the kitchen, a place redolent of spices that reminded him of Shanghai open air lunch bars.

'Good afternoon, sir, do I presume you are interested in ships of the desert, or in some of its fish? We have just received a shipment of super dates from Iraq, you know, the war is over.'

'Oh, thank you, do you stock any other artwork besides this on the walls?'

'Of course, we do, for the connoisseur. We would be delighted to show you several possibilities, if you wouldn't mind stepping into the storage room. However, you know, shoes have to be removed between rooms, before entering the display area.'

Komaru removed his Chinese tennis shoes while sitting on a bench in the small entrance way.

A man came in immediately and introduced himself.

'I am Habib. Please come in ... oh, they look comfortable. May I?'

Without even waiting for a reply, Habib took the right shoe, removed its thin lining, and retrieved a message.

'How coincidental! The initial letter of your name matches the first of Karangahape Road. Welcome! Let's take care of business.'

Whatever went on during that short meeting between Komaru and Habib was unique. No sounds were heard. The few words exchanged were printed temporarily in capital letters on the screen of an electronic organiser. Each time they were read, they were erased, not by touching 'D' for 'Delete,' but by shutting off the power supply.

Upon returning to the hotel, Melissa heard Komaru's door being shut, and called him on the phone.

'Well, Kom, what an exciting day! I could not believe how this city had changed in a few years. No way for that fishing village on the strait ever to compete in city life, except perhaps for wind. What kind of day did you have?'

Komaru remained evasive and gave her detailed 'generalities'. She then mentioned that half an hour earlier the maintenance manager had checked the east side of the corridor for a water leakage. He apologised for the inconvenience. He had not realised that she would return in mid-afternoon. Then the reservation desk of Antoine's called to confirm a booking for dinner at 18:00 sharp. For a while she was confused, for the manager had mentioned two seats for Mrs McTavish and Mr Kornarich. She explained that Komaru's family name was Reti. Komaru said nothing, though of course he wondered how easily those calls might have been traced to his room and Melissa's.

Thus, although tempted to cancel the dinner engagement, obviously so-called 'American style' in place of supper as listed in *Gourmet*, Komaru and Melissa spent a bittersweet early evening at the only restaurant listed in the American magazine. Night had descended late, after a meal that took more than the usual time to be served, Melissa chose salmon with lemon sauce as a main dish. Komaru opted for the rack of lamb with potatoes. She had drunk a whole bottle of Australian wine from the Barossa Valley. And when she started vociferously to reproach Komaru for being so distant from her lately, he simply paid the bill, stepped out and gave the valet the ticket for his Toyota.

Komaru's Toyota was never delivered, for, as soon as the parking valet disappeared with the identification ticket, a black Mercedes Benz stopped by the kerb and two men in black suits came out of the automobile. One of them, who resembled the one milling around the cemetery at his father's funeral, went straight to Komaru and flashed a disk of some kind.

'Mr Reti, Komaru Reti?'

'Yes, sir.'

'I am Assistant Superintendent John Mills. Please follow us.'

In a second, Komaru sensed the inevitable. The bottom of the world had collapsed under the weight of a feather. There was no point in resisting or making a scene. Had he been alone, he would have gone back into the restaurant and from there called the press. But Melissa's presence, plus some non-uniformed policemen obviously standing by in strategic places, including the restaurant's entrance, made him decide to play dumb. He only asked why he should follow the Assistant Superintendent and where.

'To our office. Just a formality. Incidentally, the lady may go home.'

Komaru thought of informing the inspector that the lady was in no condition to drive after drinking a bottle of wine. He was afraid that she would get involved in an accident, not so much for her sake as for that of the car. He still had three years of monthly payments. However, he said nothing.

'Constable,' she articulated slowly, 'I cannot leave my business partner alone. I will come along, if you don't mind.'

'By all means, Madam.'

And so they were taken to the Central Police Station. Komaru was frisked perfunctorily, and Melissa's purse was inspected by a policewoman before they were introduced to the police superintendent. On his desk, Komaru's radio scanner was 'ON' and tuned to one of the frequencies related to the police station. Rather amusingly, Komaru heard his car plates from Wanganui being spelled out in 'phonetic code'. His car was being taken away for storage at a holding garage.

The inspector did not waste any time informing Komaru that, because of the Commonwealth Heads of Government Meeting, he was to leave immediately for a week's vacation on a nearby island. At the useless complaint raised by Komaru, the Superintendent told him that all his personal effects had been checked out of the hotel, the bills had been paid and an airplane was ready to take him to Great Barrier Island. Just a matter of 5 days absence from Auckland. His Auckland business partners had already been informed of a *contretemps*. A new meeting had been scheduled in exactly one week, and in the meantime Mrs McTavish could stay in Auckland to work on preliminaries for the franchise. When Melissa objected that the extra expenses alone would be quite an inconvenience even if her husband agreed to an extended sojourn, the Inspector assured her that the tab was included in the overall heads of government meeting policing budget. Besides, Dr McTavish had agreed that she was free to decide on her own. At that, Melissa told the Superintendent that she could not leave her partner alone for several reasons, particularly because in Wanganui the separation could be construed as a business split or takeover. Well, the Superintendent agreed to take both of them wherever they were supposed to be taken on the honour system. Before Komaru left the station in good company, the Superintendent wished the couple a good holiday trip, and to Komaru in particular he mentioned that, if he had time to read, there was a very small library on the island with a varied assortment of books including a Koran and many treatises on psychology. From the Air New Zealand Domestic Terminal, a special commuter plane departed in a north-east direction. In half an hour it landed at Claris airstrip, not far from Kaitoke Beach on the Great Barrier Island. There the exiles were consigned to the local constabularies in charge of 24-hour surveillance, who drove them to the Pohutukawa Lodge in Tryphena.

The moon had just set in the direction of Cape Reinga. The owners of the lodge welcomed the guests like any of the other tourists who had just begun to pour onto the island from mid-November to Easter. They had each been assigned a room facing the Shoal Bay where in the south one could see the busy Tryphena Harbour and its wharf. Just before retiring, they were informed that 500 metres away was the only bar on the entire island. All their personal effects had already been delivered to their rooms. Melissa perked up at knowing the location of the bar, Tipi and Bob's. She needed to have a drink. However, there was no need to change clothes and go out, for on her nightstand someone had left a bottle and one glass. Although wrapped in a paper bag, Melissa guessed that, by its shape, the bottle could only contain Cardhu. And she was right. Ten-year-old vintage. She thought that, even against her husband's wishes not to use scotch, it was perfectly all right to toast to Her Majesty Elizabeth II. She had even forgotten that Komaru was in the next room listening to a battery-operated radio, for there was no electricity on the island. The Queen was in town, and the *Britannia* anchored safely near the quay where the *Rainbow Warrior* had been blown up by French 'terrorists' 9 years before.

It was at breakfast the next day that, being sober at least for a while, Melissa was told a few things by Komaru without any bitterness, at least not outwardly. He had planned to take it easy, for he knew that there was nothing he could do. Escape was impossible. Police were in close contact with all possible means of transportation to and from the island. The quay was monitored around the clock in case Komaru had any wild ideas. So, on Sunday they decided to explore the immediate neighbourhood. On Monday afternoon, after a heavy lunch of minnow fritters prepared by Tipi, Bob's wife, Komaru and Melissa walked to the wharf, where a couple of German tourists had anchored their motorboat near Pigeons Lodge. Melissa and Komaru sat nearby in the sun making small talk while watching some repairs being made on the boat engine. It was Melissa who started eliciting from Komaru some information, or actually some speculation, on how the police had concluded that Komaru posed a risk to the safety of the queen and her family. Komaru played the game as long as he could, and in the interior process of discovering where a leak had happened, it occurred to him, to his horror, that only Bill could have given information to the superintendent. Bits of sentences and words, such as the mention of the Koran, books on psychology and other real or imaginary reasons convinced him that Bill, whom he had just recently accepted as his friend outside the Movement, had betrayed him. But, why? To protect Melissa, himself by association, the queen, or what?

While Melissa slept soundly in the shade of native bushes, Komaru spent a long time trying to understand Bill's behaviour. Why? he kept repeating to himself.

'Hello, *kia ora*, *tena koe*, speak English?'

Who was saying what? And to him?

The man working on the engine, probably a German speaking tourist, was trying to engage Komaru in a conversation. Komaru refrained from trying his school German. The engine did not seem to perform well as he understood in good English.

'I'm Hans. Brigitte, my woman.'

'I'm Melville.'

The German laughed at Komaru's sense of humour.

'You know anything about engine?'

'Not much. Let me see. Do you have plenty of petrol?'

'Ja, just refuelled at the quay.'

Komaru jumped aboard. Melissa had just woken up and had been informed by Brigitte of his attempts to help. The outboard motor was a powerful one to get in and out of coastal areas. Komaru immediately noticed that a spark plug was dirty to the point of showing no space between the terminal and the end of the hook. Simply cleaning it with a spray solvent would solve the problem, which he did in a few minutes after delicately inserting a small file. At the second pull of the cord, the engine started beautifully. He adjusted the choke, twisted the speed handle and kicked Hans into the water. In a few seconds he had rounded the northern point of Shoal Bay and turned south to Cape Colville on the Coromandel Peninsula. He knew he had plenty of fuel and enough sunlight to reach, if not the Thames area, at least one of the small campgrounds where a telephone would be available in the manager's office. He had to call someone and inform him or her of his predicament, but whom? The professor? The way he had been exiled could rival the most dictatorial nation in the Third World. He also wanted to alert Whina as the only trusted person working in the background of activism, and through her inform Ling-ling, whom he did not want to contact directly for obvious reasons, with regard to his virtual abduction. She knew nothing of his political background except generalities, but he was worried about her being implicated in anything by association based on business ties and close friendship.

Oh, yes, Whina. She could be trusted. She had to be told of the double cross he had suffered. There was no question that Bill had informed Auckland police. Who else would know about recent details, not to mention Melissa's favourite drink? Now he remembered other innuendoes casually dropped by the superintendent in his office. How was his sister's novitiate proceeding in Colorado? Of course, that information could have been gathered from intercepted letters, but not Komaru's views on Church matters and medieval crusades. Yes, Bill deserves to be killed, he thought in a cold spell of reasoning. But how could he reach Wanganui?

Near the northern tip of the peninsula, Komaru remembered to avoid the eastern coast. Too dangerous and not many centres of 'civilisation'. Thus, he steered westward, and then south. He would probably have another hour of sunlight. Without charts he could not be sure of distances. Then he saw the group of islands west of Coromandel, and thus he knew he could reach either Kereta or any of the campgrounds farther south. Past a wide opening which he guessed could be Manaia Harbour, he decided to speed south for another 20 kilometres or so along the Firth of Thames coast. It was beginning to get dark and he nearly entered a small river mouth, when he noticed two communities, one on the north side and one on the south. He slowed down and took the latter beach, following it to a deserted wooden jetty where he tied the rope that had been dangling from the stern all the way from Shoal Bay after he had quickly removed the end from the beach pole while Hans tried to climb aboard. The campground turned out to be near Tapu. The meaning of the word was ominous enough for anyone to stay clear of the community centre. On its fringes, a lighted sign showed Te Mata Lodge, a rather primitive-looking type of hostel in the middle of dense vegetation.

When Komaru entered the registration room, he saw a semi-stupefied attendant with the look of either a moron or a drunk chewing on a toothpick. Komaru asked for a public phone, which he located near a vending machine. Oh, how happy he was to feel coins in the back pocket of his chino pants! He spent some time finding Whina at the sanatorium, but once located he switched to Maori and, without giving her a chance to say anything, briefed her on his situation, stressing Dr McTavish's betrayal. Then he begged her to get in touch with Ling-ling in person and protect her. Finally, he asked her to mail the letter in her possession to Mahina as soon as possible, but not from New Zealand. The letter would be entrusted to a 'safe' messenger stopping in Australia.

While winding up his instructions to Whina, the office desk phone rang. He hung up his receiver quietly, without even a good-bye, but feigned talking in Maori while paying attention to the desk.

'Yeah, Jack here ... yes, this is Jack.' He then removed the toothpick from his mouth. 'Yes, the Tapu Motor Camp ... yes, 868–4837 ... no, no one under that name ... no, no automobile ... a boat? A hamster? Oh, lamster, what is that?'

At that Komaru casually left the reception area by a side door leading to a patio. Then he ran straight to the beach. According to Jack, yes, there had been the sound of an outboard engine, when an hour later a constable from Thames came to interview him. Yes, from the patio he had heard the sound of a powerful engine fading away. The Moon had just cleared the top of a *pohutakawa* bush.

'Hard to say, sir. There are only three directions from here. Either north, south, or west.'

'West whither? In the middle of the night? With just a little moonlight?'

'Well, sir, who knows? I reckon the crescent Moon may be enough for him to head westward towards the mainland, or perhaps one of the gulf islands. Actually, that bloke did not seem to be in a hurry. He took his time on the telephone, and ...'

'He used the telephone?'

'Yes, he did.'

'Did you hear anything?'

'How could I? He talked in Maori. You know, there are still a few natives speaking foreign jargon, but ...'

The constable did not hear the rest of the story. A noisy helicopter approached the camp shining a powerful beam of light on the area. He went out on the patio and signalled 'all clear' to the pilot. Then the 'copter headed west, flying straight into the tiny Moon. The Southern Cross was still low on the horizon, but high enough to remind humans that its presence guaranteed the continuation of a symbolic guidance to lost souls in the cyclical darkness of baffling existence.

Chapter 44

As Dr McTavish told Ling-ling a couple of times, psychiatry has failed so far to create a branch for an inquiring mind to analyse, and perhaps even attempt to treat, humans suffering from, if not enjoying, the mental derangement triggered by the learning of a 'foreign' language. The stress of the pedagogical process becomes acute especially when pupils are assembled in close confines under the guidance of a teacher who may even possess and exhibit linguistic abilities. These are often antithetical to the operational psychological framework present within an assumed homogeneous group of learners willing to absorb new abstract codes next to or in place of existing ones.

When such a didactic activity is compared with any other in academic fields of learning, from basketball to basket-weaving to astrophysics, the rate of efficiency in terms of time, money, effort and other factors is barely detected at the bottom of any statistical chart. The reasons are several and the inferences are disheartening, for the whole learning process is infected by subtle chaos insidiously permeating the very fabric of the two-way theoretical exchange of information between a giver and a recipient. Statistically, the chances of hitting a bull's eye in absolute darkness with a stone, an arrow or a gun are far more satisfactory than those derived from the average exchange performance between a source and a target language.

It follows apparently that a 'foreign' language teacher is the quintessence of a masochist exploited by an organised society basking in the illusion of providing quality instruction to generations of innocent zombies. These glottic recruits normally learn first, particularly in the United States, the grammar of English permeating 85% of a 'foreign' language textbook. The rest is grammar of the 'other' language which, *per se*, vaguely manifests itself in the expression of greetings at the 'second' person pronoun level. No wonder that instructors engaged in sinful activities of that sort at times need an outlet to maintain a functional level of mental sanity by using language in some other way, almost as if subconsciously seeking revenge for having taught a most baffling subject-matter. The history of so-called scholarship in Western society alone is replete with cases of humans who, before or after radically changing the course of their lives, had to cope with the teaching of language, this being either 'native' or not, in many degrees of 'foreign-ness' across the lectern. James Joyce is but one of those who in the 20th century alone had to cope with English versus Italian in Trieste. A couple of centuries earlier, Lorenzo da Ponte did the reverse by teaching Italian to American speakers at Columbia University in New York.

Even by teaching a language in a 'homogeneous' atmosphere, such as 'Neo-Zealandese' by an Englishman to a Chinese who already *speaks* American, the futility of organised instruction in a classroom emerges clearly in connection with the exposure of a monolingual to a foreign language. To start with, the very term 'foreign' is not only inappropriate but also deceptive to describe a switch from a 'naturally' acquired system of communication to a different one, particularly when the change from a 'source' language to a 'target' one requires a revolutionary re-adjustment of neurological paradigms in contrast with those learned during childhood. Ling-ling had to reduce her Cantonese tones from five to four during her stay in Shanghai, where her family had been dislodged by the Cultural Revolution. Her father, a doctor, had been sent to work in a beer plant. Her mother, a teacher of American English in a middle school, had been forced to work in the 'dorm' laundry located on the first floor of the 'Foreign' Student Building at East China Normal University. A speaker of American acquired at home, in addition to several Chinese 'dialects', Ling-ling had performed several mental somersaults, including the last one to Neo-Zealandese English permeated by Maori, the 'native' idiom still struggling to survive in an ambient of deception worse than what the Romans had done by imposing Latin on the Etruscans.

Thus, rather than 'foreign', Bill would say, one should think in terms of 'another' language, for anything new, as in Ling-ling's case, is socially alien, psychologically destabilising, and functionally bewildering. Of course, the more 'different' the target language is, the more complex the problems are of mutual interaction, of subconscious parallelism, of intentional transfers at all levels of 'grammatical' analysis to render identical, even minimally, culturally similar thoughts through diverse forms of expression. It would seem at the superficial level that the narrower the genetic gap between the source and target language, the easier the effort to collate linguistic structures in terms of kinship either vertically, as from a parent to one or more offspring, or horizontally, as between and among siblings within a close area of proximity.

Therefore, it might appear that it is more facile to switch, say, to English from German rather than from Anglo-Saxon, not to stretch Western Indo-European, or even crossing language-in-contact boundaries as, for example, from Latin to English, or vice versa. The degree of 'relativity' depends on the level of analysis as a function of the building blocks of a language, assuming that the system as a recipient does not reject incompatible structures. In terms of components, perhaps a student of English would be more at home lexicologically shifting the analysis from Latin to English in both directions because of historical accidents. So it would seem on the surface under an impulsive conclusion even at the morphological level. But this often meets a barrier of false deductions, particularly when one encounters a spurious 'parent' or an adopting one as in the case of Latin dispensing an imposed 'colonial' system, such as parts of speech from Greek and Latin onto 'modern' English.

In this connection, English became more chaotic to Ling-ling by allowing itself to absorb 'politically correct' terminology, though 'grammatically incorrect' descriptive structures. She belabored to grasp, among other things, the concept of the present participle and of the gerund, through an identical bound morpheme (-*ing*), not to speak of structures differentiating only paradigmatically what in Latin was syntagmatic as in the case of an absolute phrase or absolute construction.

Paradoxically, these quixotic ingrafts between incompatible species seemed to occur when totally unrelated languages, if they ever existed for a 'general' philologist, are taken back to an 'Adam and Eve' stage in the Garden of Eden at the foundation of the Tower of Babel. The result is that the more 'distant' a language is from another, the fewer the traps of false logicality encountered in learning and using another language. In essence, for Ling-ling there were no 'foreign' languages, just other languages. This she found out in coping with the term 'exiled' when it appeared on the very first page of the *New Zealand Herald* on Saturday, 1 February 1997.

The article authored by 'Naomi Larkin' contained 'exiled' twice, namely, once as the second word in the lead title 'Man exiled in operation to protect Queen' in bold letters, and again as the second word of the first paragraph:

Police exiled a man to an island hideaway during the Commonwealth Heads of Government Meeting (CHOGM) because they feared for the Queen's life.

A 6 by 6 centimetre picture insert in full colour atop the second column of the article enlivened the traditional black-and-white presentation of newspapers printing style, for the *Herald* had 'gone American' *à la USA TODAY* hoping to boost its readership. The graphics department had sketched an area of approximately 6400 square kilometres to illustrate the location of the 'Great Barrier Is' in relation to Metro Auckland. The dotted itinerary between Auckland and the Pacific St Helen had been detailed on one side by a speedboat, creating white water in its wake, and a two-engine aircraft on the other. An effort to confer a realistic aerial view included the airplane's shadow on the Hauraki Gulf water, though astronomically erroneous because, regardless of time of day and solar season, the craft's shadow could not possibly be shown ahead toward the island of its destination, but behind on the mainland. After all, at that penguinal latitude, the sun is always north, casting a shadow south.

Ling-ling, however, paid little attention to the insert, except to read the caption over it, 'Security scare hideaway' in small bold characters. She then tried to correlate it with the term 'exiled.' The word did not appear in any dictionary at her home, though 'exile' had been entered many times in different contexts. Then she tried to understand as much as she could after reading a lot, beginning with the *Oxford English Dictionary*. The third paragraph was clear:

> Former police superintendent Bryan Rowe yesterday confirmed to the *New Zealand Herald* that the man was sent to Great Barrier Island for security reasons during the 1995 November summit conference.

After more than a year of anguishing investigation, she had finally found out that New Zealand was far worse than Communist China during Mao's Cultural Revolution. Even at that time the names of people being exiled for whatever reasons were written not only in official Party newspapers, but also on local bulletins and public building walls.

In New Zealand, Ling-ling thought, there must be some kind of unique state police that can dispose of a human being in a manner that does not exist, at least officially, anywhere else in the world, even in the People's Republic of China. Her shock was compounded by the fact that, within the Commonwealth, criticism had always been made, and concern had been expressed, with regard to Human Rights and similar luxuries. Yes, of course, it was not long ago that Nazi Germany disregarded basic concepts of personal freedom. Was New Zealand still harbouring Nazi expats in its police force? Even in post-Soviet Russia, there is some mechanism to account for the disappearance of people under the watchdog activities of organisations like Amnesty International. To bring into the picture cases of abduction as in Chile *à la* Pinochet would be futile, for south of the Rio Grande anything like a Magna Carta could only be used in place of dry corncobs. But in New Zealand! The country that was the first to declare war against Nazism?

Ling-ling made an effort to understand, first semantically and then politically, what 'exiled' meant in contrast with euphemisms such as 'protective custody,' 'being held for investigation,' etc. How was the whole mystery related to the disappearance of her fiancé, or actually, *de facto* husband? Even in Argentina, the land of the *desaparecidos*, there were devious ways to find the graves of dissidents, unless they had been dumped into the Rio de la Plata in concrete barrels or tossed into the Atlantic from helicopters. Perhaps she could find some psychological relief by finding some antecedents in England. Well, that was a dead end, even during hard times such as the Second World War. After all, Britain had never had any Inquisition. That refinement was a privilege of the Catholic Continent. However, England had produced a monument to printed verbiage, namely, the *Oxford English Dictionary*.

And she started from that stage without wasting much time in historical attestations. She concentrated on the grammatical values of Western tradition, on labels that did not exist in any Chinese structures. Sino-Tibetan languages for her were 'free' languages, not chained to what the English language had to do to adapt itself to Greek and Latin concepts. Thus, she began to investigate the past participle and preterit(e), without bothering to waste time on variations connected with modalities and other linguistic phenomena. After all, Greeks and Romans spoke a very complex language without caring about regimented forms that were illustrated 23 centuries later after William Jones translated Pāṇini's sutras. She knew that 'exiled' was a function of the verb 'to exile.' That was the only way to 'read' in it what she could not in any classical language. In Latin, to the contrary of what happens in English, no part of speech can become a transvestite. A verb is always a verb. And a noun is always a noun, from which she could not infer a derivation. If any problem existed in genetic terms, that was for English to solve in parallel fashion with the riddle of the chicken versus the egg.

Oh, how beautiful! Latin was straight-laced, like the 'standard' Neo Zealandese frozen by intellectual disabilities. Unlike English, the language of compromise camouflaged as lexicological wealth, Latin had 'exsul' as a noun, but not a synthetic verb from the same root correlating 'exile' with 'to exile.' Ling-ling was convinced that *Homo loquens* var. *Britannicus* must have built an empire of riches not only by 'borrowing' from any political idiom that came across his path, but also, and mainly, as an inbred mechanism producing *Partes grammaticales* as underground aliases. Thus, say, 'right,' initially a 'noun' according to her theory, could become a verb, either transitive or intransitive, as well as an adjective and an adverb. No wonder that English can be considered the 'richest' language on Earth by virtue of its schizophrenic behaviour.

Once Ling-ling understood the English situation, she went back to its source, Latin. This had its own correlation of terms between 'exsul' as a noun, but amazingly not a synthetic verb from the same root. It seemed that paleo-Latinophones had a phobia about adulteration, or at least excessive respect for property rights, if not personal integrity. They solved, however, their lexicological parsimony by exceeding in analytic constructions and by allowing their imaginations to roam over the border of poetry. Dozens of constructs popped up in analytic strings such as *agere, mittere, pellere, depellere, relegare ... in exsilium*. Oh, yes, at least one of these 'verbs' furnished, probably via an initial past participle such as *relegatus*, a non-Classical expression for *exsul*. But this *sermo cotidianus*, or *sermo vulgaris* term, came later in Roman law, after Tiberius had introduced the *capitis deminutio media* in the first century AD. It had been a long time, perhaps seven centuries, since Zaleucus from Locri, a 'Calabrian', codified some laws among civilized humans. Ironically, it took the Romans some time to send a delegation to Greece around 450 BC to learn what the Greeks had done in the codification of social idealistic traditions, later humanised by Epictetus in his *Encheiridion*. That both Zaleucus and Epictetus were Greek ex-slaves might indicate that fairness in justice emerged from the ranks, not from a throne or an altar. When this happened, as in the time of Augustus, well, more 'civil rights limitations' were conceived as he applied the form of *deportatio in insulam*, exactly what New Zealand state police did to Komaru without any trial, or even a specific accusation based on real or imaginary transgressions of Pakeha law. The common joke among

Kiwi expats from Pennsylvania to California is *Nemo propheta in patria*, though undoubtedly one can become *Exsul ... in insulam* in spite of being a 'native' whose *whakapapa* was older than that of the Germanic tribes who crossed the channel 15 centuries earlier. The Pennsylvania Akiko, http://nz.com/ seems to imply that, yes, Virginia, everything in New Zealand is topsy-turvy.

Ling-ling was lucky, however, since she was able to get some information from www.tvnz.co.nz/maori for Komaru had been taken away under a milder form of *deportatio*, one different from that used by the British who sent Maoris to perish in Chatham. It was superficially a 'benign' *relegatio* that, according to Larkin's article, implied a jolly good time. Apparently, 'Mr Rowe said that the [State] police had "discussed" their plan with the man before the conference and he agreed to go.' What else could Komaru do with a woman in tow? Compromise Ling-ling and his future child, especially if the SIS were to invoke the 'no knock' law, then concoct a way through the Crown High Court, and decree a *capitis deminutio media*, that is, the 'freezing' and removal of Komaru's real estate, the restaurant business and even his vehicle after a 'proper' and lengthy trial and conviction, if he had not 'agreed' to go? In New Zealand, as Komaru knew from what he had proposed as a history of his people in the manuscript for the MA at Victoria University, the SIS would proceed to take a hard line regardless of the fact that the covert entry of private property is illegal. Attempts, however, have been made to legalise it. Civil liberties Vice-president Margaret Lewis knows how things can be broadened, as done soon after the Komaru 'incident', to protect New Zealand's economic or international 'well-being.'

Ling-ling concluded that, to escape a potential accusation of sedition, Komaru accepted the *solum vertere exsilii causa*, namely, a state of 'voluntary' exile. As in Roman times, 2,000 years past, before Caesar crossed the channel, that type of *relegatio* did not carry the loss of *civitas*. How could a Maori 'native' be deprived of citizenship overtly? A hundred years ago, yes, but not nowadays, with the Pakehas inching their way into 'Waitangi-Tribunalizing' the minds of washed out Maoris. The recent 'commemorations' of the yearly Waitangi charade, the 'Fiscal Envelope' *mise-en-scène*, and the Moutoa Gardens 'trespassing' episode were, in Komaru's view, merely the shadows of things to come.

The only palliative left to Komaru, in a deep depression that was getting more out of control by the day, was to console himself in knowing that he was sharing a fate with Ovid, exiled to Tomi, as he wrote in *Tristia*, V, xi, 'he [i.e. the emperor] had not deprived me of life, nor of wealth, nor of the rights of a citizen ... he has simply ordered me to leave my home.' Komaru wondered. Yes, the empire had disappeared. But, had the SIS changed any to protect the daughter of the ex-Empress of India? Yes, Komaru has become a *relegatus*, and not an *exsul*. However, Naomi Larkin had written the term 'exiled' in typical British tradition, that is, encompassing all three of the Roman law forms, namely, *aqua et ignis interdictio* (at times even *et tecti*), 'deprivation of (the basic necessities of life) such as food, heat, and shelter.' These had been provided, according to Larkin, at taxpayer expense in 'a lodge in Tryphena.' The classic analysis of 'missionary' generosity toward 'our Maoris' had been dispensed exactly the same way as described half a century earlier by J. C. Furnas in the still unsurpassed *Anatomy of Paradise*. Had Michener read that eviscerated work of a White conscience, he would probably have changed his *Return to Paradise* into *Return to Hell*. Well, the Crown had done similar things in rerouting convicts from America to Australia and Norfolk. There was no need to export cheap labour to New Zealand. It was already there for the grabs in Melville's parlance. Queequeg was not really a fictive character among whalers.

So, Komaru was relegated *in insulam* without having the pleasure of being traditionally 'transported' by ship in his own waters. Airborne 'transport' saved his face. He wondered how Professor Bettina Knapp would classify his particular type of 'exile', for his writings in the failed MA thesis had not been published and, besides, 'They ... ['the man ... with a woman companion'] just blobbed out and relaxed – had a good holiday.' That, of course, was the official version. The Crown, however, after initial inquiries by Ling-ling and Whina, did not leave the 'exile' loose. An 'exsul' is a potential criminal in the eyes of State police and, accordingly, 'he has consequently been arrested and, after a long police investigation, is now facing criminal charges unrelated [!] to the high powered conference that brought leaders from around the world to Auckland.'

Ling-ling was more baffled than ever. She reviewed all her tribulations as a function of the long months spent in agony while waiting for an official verdict on Komaru's fate. The mystery began to unravel after the 1997 Waitangi 'celebration', for no one wanted to tie a 'single case of crime prevention' with the larger problems of Maori independence, freedom and similar dreams. Even *Mana*, 'The Maori news magazine for all New Zealanders,' except for some courageous editorials, refrained from detailing events bearing the importance of the Moutoa Gardens fiasco. Yes, an attempt was made to integrate abstract hopes, but would it have been so difficult to subtitle *Mana* as 'The Maori news magazine for all Aotearoans'? Or are Aotearoans supposed to be Maori only? It is a fact that attempts made by Kuru Waaka on the occasion of the 1993 Waitangi 'celebration' to change the name of the country from New Zealand to Ao Tea Roa (or AOTEAROA) fell on the deaf ears of Prime Minister Jim Bolger. The problem is clear. The Brits who conquered The Hermit Islands did not regard themselves as those who had done similar things in Africa, where changes produced countries from Botswana to Zambia to Zimbabwe. Why? Because Pakehas assume that, numerically, Maoris do not have the potential to do anything as imagined in Africa. But, then, how does one explain the Israeli phenomenon as a result of a game played by Bevin and Begin. Was it only because of a consonantal change? Or a change in settling matters in a desperately unique way? How could a Chinese immigrant ask for help from Tame Iti at the theatrical Tuhoe Embassy, or apply for relief through Winston Peters who, according to Whina, had a metre-long record of Maori bashing in spite of having Polynesian blood coagulated in his veins? Denes Henare was right in saying that 'political correctness ensures that Maoris are kept in a state of dependency.'

A letter left by Komaru, attached to the cheque book in both his name and Ling-ling's, now began to make more sense after she read it more carefully. And Whina helped to inject historical dimensions into something purely ethical and moral. On the envelope, Komaru had written in block letters:

TO BE OPENED ONLY WHEN I AM PRESUMED
TO BE OFFICIALLY DEAD

Wanganui, 2nd November, 1995
Dear Ling-ling,

Christianity, so alien to both of us, deserves the praise for reminding its followers, at least once a year, that we are mortal, and that the Dead should be remembered today. Even the *Wanganui Chronicle*, so faithful in publishing church activities, tells us of the 2nd of November as the day for the Commemoration of All the Faithful Departed. As a matter of curiosity this morning I entered Mahina's room, where I found among her religious books a *Liber usualis* regulating, almost by the minute, the daily life of devoted believers.

This way, as she agreed at the inception of the business, inheritance rights would not create delays in the dissolution of the partnership. It may sound strange, but Melissa has no heir, and she felt that her help in the restaurant was only a means for her not to go insane.

4.   Everything else deriving from the business has been assigned in trust to our child. Whina has been named personal representative, should that be necessary for odds and ends. She has a key to the bank box, to be opened under the supervision of a third party.

5.   For other tangibles and intangibles, the majority rights are in your name or, failing that as a recipient, in our child's. But there is a contingency clause. If our child is a girl, please dispose of her as soon as possible in the Chinese style. Do that yourself, 'accidentally.' Do not trust, do not involve anyone, not even Whina. Why? Because a woman in my country has no future, no rights, no chance to excel in anything. What can a girl do when she realises that she is 50% Manchu and the rest Maori, as, for example, Jean de Huia (50%)? If she were 100% Maori, and even if elected to Parliament like Alamein Koopu, it would be a hell of a life for the free amusement of Pakehas. What a mess ... but only for a woman. If the child is a boy, as I hope, he will always be a *maori* Maori. Like me, regardless of qualitative and quantitative genes. I myself, 50% Maori, and for the rest a minestrone of Slavic-Venetian, have always been tied to the highest duties of fighting for justice, righteousness, and the dignity of freedom. The *whakapapa* of a *maori* is Polynesian forever as far as his psychological roots can go, that is, Hawaiki. This is more a state of conscience as a human being.

6.   If a boy, then, please do the following. Starting from the very first day, teach him Cantonese. Do not expose him to anything Maori or English until he is completely aware of his 'Hawaiki' heritage. And, for as long as you can, play the game of raising him later as a phoney Pakeha in 'NZ' as part of the so-called race relations myth, until you take him to China. Do this as soon as possible, perhaps to Shanghai, to be in touch with your parents, or even Canton with your grandparents. Shanghai would be better because of your local contacts as a teenager before the fracas of Tiananmen when you went to Beijing to obtain the emigration visa.

Yes, I know, you are naturally afraid of returning 'home,' but things have changed. As you know, there is a programme of 'political rehabilitation,' basically a way for China to get her children back after they have acquired Western skills. In China you would become a business executive because of your acumen in dealing with the Pakeha mentality through your superior knowledge of English. I am confident that you would be welcomed back. You were so young, idealistic, etc., and infatuated with the notion that a *papier mâché* Statue of Liberty would suffice to bring Taiwanese 'democracy' to the largest population on Earth. What foolishness! As if this were a homogenised political system, valid for all cultures in the world. You well know that 'American-style' democracy, tied to an overblown belief in God-given tablets of ethical principles, is supposed to be valid for all cultures on Earth. The way I anticipate developments on our overcrowded planet, American democracy will be not only counterproductive but also suicidal within a finite living room in space such as ours. Take your own country. How do you think that it has survived, as China, for so long, the only continuous nation at the centre of the Earth? I believe that even the graphic symbol is undeniably tied to the concept of centrality, though not politically, but culturally. And centrality means pyramidal, an institution favouring the climbing to the top of the best leader, though leaders usually are the most tragic species among humans. Sorry for diverging, but democracy has clay feet and is incompatible with human nature. Whatever political exists in America is racist democracy controlling opiate masses through an abundance of riches and sports games, as in ancient Rome.

7. Do your best to go back to China with our child. There he will absorb life, realistic life, among psychological 'compatriots' that have never detached themselves from their ancestors' past. Nowadays, in the Christian West, people vaguely honour their Dead, but in your culture it is still done all the time. You do not know how touched I was, particularly in the Confucian temples around Qufu and in Buddhist monasteries in Xi'an, when I grasped the essence of cosmic continuity, even by burning a few incense sticks and bowing my head in front of the graves alongside the road between Xi'an's airport and the walled city centre. I am convinced that the Chinese, and here I imply most of the Asiatic people, have survived for so many millennia through their relationship with their ancestors.

painting the water lilies that grew on the surface of that pond. If you ever can, take a look at the painting and try to understand why Melville thought of lilies and its leaves. Monet painted them in sparkling colours, dabbing bits of hues side by side to take the shape of flowers and water when looked at from far away. I wonder whether Monet tried to symbolise love through flowers, only to be seen from a distance through the mirror of a pond, and not too close to spoil the beauty through details. After all, Monet is thought of as an impressionist. And probably love, like a lily in a pond, is merely an impression that can vanish as soon as one is too close to it. Mahina, of course, is gone, but if she can help you, even though lost among the Vatican wolves, she will see in our child the link that she cannot provide as a nun, except morally and even spiritually. I do not know how she can conciliate Catholic tenets with yours, but rest assured that, as I feel, she will never forget the tremendous burden of a Maori *whakapapa*.

11. To Whina I have left all Maori memorabilia belonging to the Reti family hoping that, when our boy (what could his name be?) returns to his birthplace as an adult, he will find a link with his past through those items. I trust that all mementos, though so ephemeral *sub specie aeternitatis* (this is Mahina's favorite view of 'history' reduced to minimal terms), will not be destroyed by the forces of 'law and order.' Ask Whina to keep them safely for our boy when he will return as a new Maui to fish our *whenua* out of an ocean of oppression. Whina spent many hours in conversation with my father when he was being treated for alcoholism. Ask Whina to one day send all Reti relics to you in China if this is possible. It will balance, though minimally, what Rewi Alley did by bringing into Ao Tea Roa a token treasure of Chinese culture. Well, it is high time that Maori culture be welcomed, as I hope, into a safe place until a new *waka* will depart during the 21st century with a rudder in the hands of our boy steering the leading canoe. Ask him to disembark at Waitangi in order to raise the flag of Maori independence, freedom, and dignity forever.

Now, to you what can I say? Without you I would not have been able to understand your traditions, your culture and, above all, the principles of human ethics that only your people have developed and kept intact at the highest level of integrity above the whole human consortium.

My dear wife, through you I have married not only the most

noble people on Earth, but also the hope that The Hermit Islands, *de jure* Asiatic in all aspects of terrestrial life, will also be *de facto* the ones to efface colonialism, despotism, and racism in the last bastion of colonial shame.

Now, I sign forever, and with my expression of unending gratitude for taking care of our boy as you did of me both in your country and in mine. May you always bask in my Maori name's full sunshine, and your shadow never grow less in protecting our child from evil.

Komaru

P.S. I have left the family *hei tiki* in the bank safety deposit box for our boy. If we have a girl, please give it to Whina.

Ling-ling's re-reading of Komaru's letter after Larkin's article in the *Herald* functioned as a key to introduce '1997' as a year to be remembered more vividly than the other years spent in New Zealand. Several puzzling questions began to yield fragmentary responses, but these were not enough to satisfy her queries, an attempt to delineate a complete picture revealing Komaru's disappearance from her life. With Mahina so far away, as well as difficult to reach within a highly structured monastic environment, Ling-ling could only rely on Whina to cope with daily demands and business tasks. As the year progressed, however, some hope surged in her heart on the basis of events that on the surface did not seem to carry any immediate explanatory weight. When pondered through suppositions and even articles in Auckland and Wanganui newspapers, well, Whina and Ling-ling were able to acquire basic knowledge as if a transfusion of white blood had been made into the 'foreign' one running in their veins.

Ling-ling and Whina learned that, for the first time ever in New Zealand, a Maori had been appointed as coroner. This made quite a change in the routine handling of suicide, murder, accidents and other violent deaths among Maoris. Whites' insensitivity and ignorance in the past had compounded the grief of survivors by processing post-mortem according to non-'native' traditions. The returning of the *tupapaka* to the family, the retrieval of body parts, the presence of relatives at an autopsy and the whole inquest for *desaparecidos* often created racial tension and accusations of callousness among Pakehas. The appointment of Gordon Matenga as coroner, although based in Hamilton, opened a small window of opportunity for Whina to solve and 32. However, the discovery was not reported immediately by the police to anyone, with the excuse that the relatives of the deceased had to be informed first. The logic of that procedure defied even the whole pharisaical apparatus for the establishment of the Waitangi Tribunal.

4. Months later, Dr McTavish and Melissa accompanied Whina to Oneroa, on Waiheke Island, where they were shown a frozen corpse at the local morgue. It was a very difficult situation for all, since some of the flesh was gone. Bill's observations were clinical, stating that a body kept in water decomposed four times faster than one in soil. Softened by water, body tissues are eaten by fish and insects that first attack the eyelids, lips, and ears. That is why Komaru's face was unrecognisable. Melissa uncovered the lower part of Komaru's body in an attempt to recognize what she alone in the group could identify, but both the penis and the scrotum were gone. However, she stated that the corpse was Komaru's in an affidavit left with the coroner. That created quite a sensation at police headquarters, leading Auckland authorities to accept Dr McTavish's statement that his wife had 'known' the Maori bloke for a long time. What Melissa knew was unique, something that only Mahina could corroborate. Komaru had been born with an extra small toe, an appendage that had intrigued Melissa at the very onset of her osculations beginning at Komaru's bottom and ending at the convergence of his lower limbs. That presented to Melissa an additional part of a human body, which she found extremely exciting, as if the extra time necessary to lick one more toe kept her in suspension. Yes, indeed, Komaru was 'special,' as she used to tell him. No question about that detail, although Dr McTavish also remembered the podiatric anomaly because, during the first beach outing on New Year's Day in Wanganui, he casually observed Komaru's feet and noticed a common case of podasteroid extremities compounded by the sixth small toe, not a rare case in some Indo-European polydactylism that normally runs, like polymastia, in the family.

5. Dr McTavish, however, detected two strange body marks that made him not only uncomfortable, but also restless, a condition that Melissa attributed to feelings of guilt. On Komaru's upper shoulders were some spots that could be interpreted as evidence of bullet holes, as if he had been either lying face down or standing up with his back to a high-powered rifle. At the same

time, the flesh remnants around Komaru's neck displayed heavy bruises typical of one who has hanged himself. When Dr McTavish asked for a copy of the forensic report indicating a possible broken spine, he was given the runaround. The coroner had not yet completed his examination, quite a stupid excuse for a case like Komaru's. Finally, at the McTavishes request to see the speedboat, the Auckland police replied that it had been repossessed by the Marine Assurance Company and taken back to Tryphena for documentary evidence in a damage recovery lawsuit. And was there anything missing from the boat? Yes, only the rope used to moor the craft to the quay. Either the police had botched the entire process of collecting evidentiary proof, or there was an intentional cover up regarding the incident.

6. In remembering the telephone call from the Coromandel campground, Whina had no doubt that someone who knew Komaru rather well had furnished the police not only detailed information on his behavioural patterns, but also probable intentions of leaving a terroristic 'message' in the area at any cost. Whether McTavish's actions stemmed from political reasons or simply for the sake of protecting his wife is something that will never be known. Melissa, however, after grilling Whina on Komaru's ideology, had no qualms about openly accusing her husband of murder. During a drinking binge she told Bill that she was going to remove all the skeletons in his closet in connection with the suicide of a 17-year-old boy under his professional supervision. Apparently, McTavish had tried sexually to abuse the youth, whose body was found one morning under the Bull Bridge, a clear case of suicide. Only Melissa knew that, during the preceding night she had heard a series of screams, as if the boy were trying to defend himself from a haunting attack of some kind, not necessarily physical. Melissa even illustrated her husband's technique of seducing boys for later induction at the WWW Club. The classical procedure for such a sexual attack followed what the good doctor knew about Roman norms for seduction, namely, what Terence had codified in his *Eunuchus* in five stages as 'quinque lineae perfectae sunt ad amorem: prima uisus, secunda alloquii, tertia tactus [tango], quarta osculi, quinta coitus.' Melissa wondered whether what her husband failed to elicit in Komaru had been tried on the youth. Now she remembered the heated discussion about the derivation of 'tango' as imported from Italy, which, of course,

from Boulder had not yet restored electricity. The legal recognition of the death certificate signed by a Pakeha so easily in order to close an annoying incident in a way had been a blessing in disguise. Accepted by the police quickly and satisfactorily, the certificate favoured a fast testamentary process involving Komaru's possessions in Wanganui.

10. The day after Mahina was awakened in the middle of the night, the Abbess called her into her studio. There was a letter for Mahina, who, stupefied by the announcement, timidly asked when the missive had arrived. She was informed that it had been in her trust for about 2 years and had not been released because on the envelope the instruction was clear:

THIS LETTER IS TO BE DELIVERED TO MY
SISTER MAHINA RETI ONLY AFTER MY DEATH

Mahina, by adhering fully to one of the three vows, Obedience, although not yet taken in final form, accepted the instructions blindly. She was so well thought of by her Sisters for working hard and efficiently among the Colorado *desesperadas*, that no one would have dared to hurt her even indirectly. The abbess suggested that Mahina could take the letter to her cell and read it in private. She refused that privilege. She wanted no special favours because it was the abbess' duty to read all correspondence at her discretion, as well as to listen to all telephone conversations. Mahina begged her to open it and read it herself. Thus, the abbess opened the envelope, retrieved several pages and ... became red in the face. The letter was in Maori. Mahina volunteered to translate it for her impromptu. The entire contents were not only painful, but also extremely difficult because Mahina had not used Maori in years. Besides, there were several innuendoes and references to a past that she just could not totally conceal. But the abbess was maternal and magnanimous in allowing Mahina to express herself among tears and sobs. The apprehension felt by Mahina not to betray her brother, on the one hand and, on the other hand, the trust the abbess had proffered to her during her years of novitiate was dispelled when the abbess took her left hand and kept it in hers until Mahina finished the reading. After all, Mahina was nearly a full-fledged Sister. In fact, plans had already been made for her to take her final vows on the 6 January 1999, on the occasion of the Epiphany for the little Jesus and for Mahina herself.

There was no date on the letter. It took nearly an hour for Mahina to read the following:

Dear Mahina, my dear sister, and my very dear Sister, [he capitalized the 't' of the second Tuahine to indicate the religious 'Sister' ... I myself don't know it in Maori ...] *Your being away physically from me ... frees my thoughts somewhat away from the immediate ... anguish I feel ...* [I sense?] ... *in conveying to you these final words ... last thoughts ... in writing, for, were you here could probably be strong enough ... mentally* [he means 'psychologically', perhaps] *to detach myself from you as a brother. Now that I am dead I don't know where, how, and when exactly, the distance* [actually the lack of contact] *makes it easier* [simpler] *for me to depart for my Rangi* [that is the Maori heaven], *away from you, but this separation is a wrong word for a new relationship* [connection?] *between me and you. Since you are 'clarid'* [he means 'clear', 'lucid', a term borrowed from an American historian. I still have the book Komaru sent me to prove his point] *you can interpret our temporary separation as the formalization of a previous situation* [... status quo?] *for, since we have been apart for ... certain things one being our unique hongi* [our Maori greeting by ... touching noses . . .] *which I miss so much, though I can close my eyes and, even in the dark, I can find you* [he means my face, my nose] *to breathe the last puff of our joint* [... common] *wairua* [oh ... perhaps 'spirit' or he may have meant *manawa*, still 'spirit', live 'soul' tied to a body, but for only him and me ... I frankly can't guess what he means].

Yes, the *wairua* that bound us on the eve of your last birthday at home the ... *night* [sorry, he means day] *you chose to ... immortalize our whenua.* [Now I know for sure, he refers to 'soul' you see, maybe I am carrying my own interpretation of *wairua* into my mind ... blending it with *manawa*] *I can assure you that if upon dying I am conscious enough to recall anything at all, well, the ... pakoko?* [he may mean 'image'] *of you* [yes, image], *including the tertium quid, will be the last realistic link in our whakapapa. But I know I may die a violent death* [yes, he writes *mate kiatu*, 'death by violence'] *either myself not intentionally or by Pakeha ... agents. Please, I do not whakamorimori* [die or commit suicide] *as a weakling* [pusillanimous? Sorry Sister ... I know Komaru would not do that] *per se, but for a cause.*

I am convinced that there is nothing [more] *I can do for our*

~ 685 ~

whenua [... Motherland ...], *my Father, our iwi* [... people ...]. *I now feel impotent, and I am at the end of,* [of, yes] *of the rope, but not before sending a message to the world.*

Mahina, my little Moon, at times even the Sun has no more mana [force, power ...] *to perform its duties. This year has already seen* [witnessed] *nothing but failure starting with Waitangi Day for the insult of being bought off for cash ... one billion dollars merely five hundred million American dollars as if Mr Bill Gates would buy 50 New Zealands through the ... stock market in Auckland as if they* [the Whites] *were thinking of us as perishable goods, what?, 'lobster' tails from Stewart Island. Tragedy is in the air. Do you remember Tame Iti? We would be better off to be bought in yen, no in ... yuan. As a Maori nationalist he feels that we cannot do anything as a group, and I concur. We Maori have already been ... fragmented,* [well, divided] *forever ... divide et impera, how right! The only dignity we have left is for each of us to fight back alone, as I have done, and am doing.*

But, even so, I give up, because I know [I realize] *that no one in Ao Tea Roa whether alone or as a group, can remove* [dislodge] *the oppressor. Total failure – the Waitangi Day ... charade according to Pakehas. The Fiscal Envelope ... a slap in the face. The Moutoa Gardens invasion* [sorry, occupation] *a 'Maori picnic', the Tuhoe Embassy a ... carnival* [mockery] *among the diplomatic corps of windmill nations. I feel so sorry for Tame. He means well.*

As for myself I prefer to die, but by sending a letter [message] *to the world first. I wish I could survive as Hone Harawira has done for he is a pacifist in comparison with a Corsican, a Basque, or a Chiapan. No, my dear little Moon. The Sun is going into hibernation* [retiring]. *Future warmth will come one day from other shores, from another spiral* [galaxy?].

I am sorry to leave you alone on Earth, though I know that you have been adopted by a new whanau [family, or actually extended family] *that cares for you all over the world. How many Sisters do you have – thousands, hundreds of thousands? Together you can help women who, like you, went through the* [effort? no, the case history? can't understand] *problems of life at the emotive level. Once you spoke of a young woman on the eve of ... suicide ... sacrifice and you helped her. I am sure that whatever she may have done was simply a human* [normal] *way of finding herself in a world of stressful unknowns, particularly in such a tense society as America: increased gaming* [he means gambling], *an uncon-*

trollable mania for sex in all its perversions, the spread of drugs among children, a fascination for speed, the substitution of computer chips for human brains, the love of noise called music, and, above all, violence as a panacea even among school children. That young woman did well and laudably [?] to seek help from her brother. I would have done the same to help her because if a brother can't then who on Earth could [help, I assume]. The bond established between the Moon and the Sun will never be dissolved [destroyed] *even if the Sun retires* [dies, falls through] *into a dark hole* [black hole?]. *I regret nothing except my inability to set our whenua free. But, as the old Gregorian millennium begins to die after 1.1.1999, please remember me one more year after that in order to verify that stupid* [childish] *theory of mine. I had been influenced by the astro-philosophical works of thinkers from St. Methodius to Spengler – two thousand years of useless speculations, not to mention the* [let me think, please] ... *the preceding millennia of Chinese suppositions on numerology. Humans are so* [credu ...] *gullible, but if they want to believe in witchcraft, why not? I fell into the same effect* [no, trap, syndrome?] – *it was a way of fooling myself as an antidote to despair even knowing that counting years in one particular calendric system - why not the Jewish, it is older, or Muslim, it is younger – repeats itself with all possible Nines to be generated until no more light and warmth will be poured* [shined] *onto human tragedies.*

Now I close on the evening of my last Night [darkness?], *as if I cannot see the Moon on one side and the Earth on the other but I first want to knock on our kauri* [a large native tree] *wall with three taps multiplied by three total sequences ad infinitum, so that, even without receiving a reply, I know that within eternity the Universe will be replete with Nines, the last digits of our own intimate decimal system filling our bowels* [sorry, he means 'hearts'] *forever.*

This 'for-everness' is the only belief I can now carry [conceive], *especially if a boy is born to Ling-ling. Incidentally, did you know that Līng* [with a macron on the ī, i.e. an even tone] *is the only single verbal root in Mandarin meaning to 'carry'? Followed by Líng with a rising tone* [i.e. an acute 'accent'] *the total meaning could indicate someone carrying a part of something. So she is bearing a part of myself. If not a boy, then the Pakeha curse* [malediction?] *will end as it did for the 'American Indians', the Black Fellows of Australia, the Moriori of Chatham, oh, I don't have to list them for you. But, if a boy, then he will have the duty* [the chance] *to prolong my fight for another generation, even if it is the last one to succumb under white oppression.*

I have only one hope. Do you remember I wrote you once that I had attended a meeting [a lecture] *on Giordano Bruno? Lately I have been reading much about and by him particularly the 'Second conversation'* [he means 'Dialogue'] *of Della causa, principio, ed uno, printed* [published] *in Rānana* [Rānana? Oh, yes, London] *or Wēnihe in 1584. May I quote him in English (why don't you translate his work in Maori during your old age)? I hope I do not bore you, but as a philosophy scholar you should appreciate* [like] *what Theophilus explains to Aurelius Dixon (I wonder how Bruno injected a British name, yes, after all he was in London and why did he not stay there?) the meaning of Universal Intellect. This is really what binds each other better than aroha* [love, affection, sympathy], *would you not say so?*

> Theo. The universal intellect is the most intimate, real, and essential faculty and effective part of the world-soul ... This is called by the Pythagoreans the moving spirit and propelling power of the universe; as saith the poet (frankly, I don't know who, do you?), 'totamque infusa per artus, mens agitat molem, et toto se corpore mescit.'

Well, I know now, I remember. I relish that our minds have accomplished [perhaps, better, 'accepted'] *the Pythagorean belief. And I hope too that one day, as Virgil wrote 'Lucentemque globum lunae Titaniaque astra spiritus intus alit . . .' when our grains* [sorry, particles of dust? Oh, corpuscles, yes, Lucretius] *will meet again somewhere in the Universe without my knocking on the ... kauri wall.*

Your loving brother,
Komaru.

The abbess released Mahina's hand and hugged her tightly. When Mahina's face touched the Sister's cheeks, they were wet with tears. Then the abbess got up and said, 'Your brother is extremely intelligent. I wonder why he said he did not know who "the poet" was and asked you if you did. That poet was Virgil, in the Sixth Book of his *Aeneid*, between verses 725 and 727. What he did, whether intentionally or not, was to split the three verses into two parts, leaving to you the task of re-assembling them in their proper sequence, with the latter preceding the former, especially if you start with verse 724. The Genesis of Komaru's Universe was not dissimilar from ours. Unless you already know why, one day you will understand, or remember, the last message "Komaru" sent to "Mahina." Personally, Sister Clara Maria, I think it is not my task. Each of us has the right to keep a small corner of our hearts to herself.'

Epilogue

At the Auckland Airport, while Ling-ling was checking in for Flight NZ4842 departing for LAX at 20:15, Whina stood by holding Mao Ri next to her. There was not much luggage, just one medium-sized suitcase. A carry-on case contained the child's clothes and overnight apparel for both him and his mother. Ling-ling's heavy parka and the child's Chinese style quilted overcoat lying over the case looked incongruous during the 'hottest' day of the Austral summer. The weekend weather forecast had been for partly cloudy skies with north-easterly winds between 10 and 30 kilometres per hour and a maximum temperature of 23 degrees Celsius.

When Mao Ri moved next to his mother, Ling-ling followed the routine procedure preceding the weighing and tagging of the suitcase by the conveyor belt. The Air New Zealand employee, a young Pakeha lady, seemed to have some hesitancy in entering data into the computer. She looked carefully at Ling-ling, a Chinese-looking woman carrying a People's Republic of China passport with a one-month US tourist visa. An Inland Revenue document had been attached to it. The other passport, for the child, a New Zealand citizen, was examined in more detail since the Reti family name and Ling-Ling's Chu did not seem to rhyme. In anticipation of that 'discrepancy,' the Auckland US General Consulate had provided an affidavit explaining the relationship between Mao Ri and his mother. Such a strange 'given' name for a Maori displaying 'Oriental' features around his eyes, if not quite an epicanthic fold. But the jet black colour of his hair, brown eyes and 'olive' skin matched the colour photograph perfectly. No Chinese this time could be accused of smuggling a child for adoption into the United States.

Meanwhile, Whina, a bit tired from the long check-in procedure, sat on the closest plastic bench and browsed through the *Weekend Herald* that Ling-ling had bought to read on the plane. She nearly fainted when she casually turned to page A16. The woman in the photograph being 'hugged' by President Clinton, Monica Lewinsky fashion, could be her mother when young, or even herself. The resemblance was so uncanny that she bought another copy of the paper for herself. No question about it, Carol Moseley-Braun must have carried some genes from the same African tribe as the American Marine who was Whina's grand-father. The title of the article, even without a question mark at the end, was more than a declaration of bewilderment: 'Is the White House's recommendation for the new United States ambassador to his country an easy way for President Clinton to sidestep another embarrassment, wonders Roger Franklin.' Whina started reading the article when Ling-ling called her to hold the child since he was getting restless. Finally, the employee detached the first portion of the ticket for the AUK-LAX leg. The case was placed on the conveyor belt, and the group re-assembled on the way to the departure gate. Before leaving Ling-ling and the child, Whina gave Ling-ling her copy of the paper pointing out the blunder made by Clinton suggesting that lady. Did he not know how Black Americans were regarded by New Zealanders? And that included Maoris, of course, who were caught by racial crossfire of 1944 vintage because of some fisticuffs that took place on Wellington streets where US Marines had gotten drunk on DB. After more than half a century, the animosity was still so present among people in their late 60s to the point that, when a New York theatre company toured Australasia just a few months earlier, during the performance of *Porgy and Bess* the audience behaved exactly like the Shanghainese at a Peking Opera.

The plane took off almost half empty on a Christmas weekend, but on time. Flying eastward into the night, Ling-ling watched the sun rise on a day 'earlier' than that in Gisborne. After a hostess gave Mao Ri a toy to play with, ironically a black-and-white plastic panda, Ling-ling began to relax. And not to be distracted by the food being served to some passengers, she preferred to read the paper, for she was not hungry at all. Actually, she was a bit upset at the question fired, perhaps innocently, by Whina. She had asked whether Ling-ling would return 'home.' There was no answer for a few seconds, and then Ling-ling replied that the plan of the journey called for 'repatriation.' In fact, the tourist visa was only for a month, although one could automatically extend that. Of course, Fate could play the usual trick, Ling-ling had added. What else could she do with a British subject, nearly a 3-year-old child, in any other place but New Zealand? He was not a Hong Kong citizen, and not even a citizen of St Helen, surely, but naturally they would return home, no question about it. Besides, she had the restaurant in Wanganui.

After declining supper for the second time, she immersed herself into the reading of the *Weekend Herald*, Saturday–Sunday, 26–27

December 1998, which for her was a novelty in format and content. Normally she would read the *Wanganui Chronicle* for both Saturday and Sunday to study the food specials. Peaches, which were her favorite, cost NZ$5 a kilogram, less than in Auckland. There seemed to be nothing special in the *Herald*. Oh, the first page carried a short article on the fate of chocolate, actually a concern by a 'Cadbury scientific adviser' who was worried that the new proposed product might contain 'no longer the right ingredients.'

Then on page A5 a report on the annual feeding of the needy by the Salvation Army caught her eye. Why only at Christmas? What do the needy do the other 364 days of the year? She wondered whether there was any correlation between the birth of a child 2,000 years earlier and the '2,000 people [who] sat down at a lunch organised by the Anglican Church Mission.' There was no question that the Jewish infant had later caused quite a revolution in the five continents during barely 20 centuries, something that neither Buddha nor Confucius had done. But these two thinkers were not Semitic. She had not read much about Christianity, but she understood the temporal and spiritual leadership of the pope, as she did of the Dalai Lama. Whether Jesus had been born on the 28 August or on the occasion of the Boreal Winter Solstice was really not important. As a matter of fact, whether Jesus was Jewish was irrelevant, too. In fact, once she attended a lecture in Wanganui, a city that could be located in any American trikappa city. The speaker was a professor at the local Polytechnic Institute, a scientist who, as a very young assistant, had worked with Werner von Braun in 1945 before the technicians were flown secretly to America. Professor von Litzen, like von Braun, was a devout Catholic, and as such he was barely accepted as a Christian in spite of maintaining, after Houston Stewart Chamberlain, that almost all pre-eminent and free men, from Tiberius to Bismarck, had looked on the presence of the Jews as a social and political danger. His logic was infallible, like papal dogma: 'Above all it must be clear that Christ was not a Jew. He had not a single drop of Jewish blood in his veins; Christ opposed the Jewish dietary laws, never once mentioned fear of God ... Anyone who regarded Christ as a Jew was ignorant and insincere.' Whether von Litzen can explain why the pope took 19 centuries to launch Jesus' mother into Heaven, well, that was a Prussian secret revealed only to Hitler in the early 1940s. Thus, according to that logic, the first aetheronauta was not Gagarin, but Jesus for a man; and not Valentina for a woman, but Mary. No wonder women complain of being left behind. It had taken a Nazi scientist to open the highways to outer space. But first Chamberlain had to be sure that no Jew was to be admitted to Heaven by simply removing first his citizenship.

It was the article by Ron Taylor on page A17, however, that made Ling-ling extremely agitated, since the headline appeared ominous. Her thoughts were taken back to China during the Cultural Revolution as related to her by her parents: 'The government is changing the law to allow SIS [Security Intelligence Service] to enter your house.' And Whina's question came back to her mind. So much effort to leave China in search of freedom, for what?

She was tired, but not yet sleepy, and, in trying to read some more to kill time, she turned back to page A15, which she had inadvertently skipped. Humans were not different when it came to reminiscing, as if trying to extend their lives on Earth by digging into last year's events. The old Chinese year was about to end, and the new one was not far off – from the Tiger to the Rabbit. Yes, she was going to almost initiate her cultural year in the United States of America, and so how had the Tiger been in New Zealand? According to the reporter, 'The year that made everyone wonder' was being synthesised in a one-page article. Yes, thought Ling-ling, as if Whina's infatuation with Edgar Cayce and the second coming of Christ in 1998 were to happen during the next few days. Whina used to speak about the land of her grandfather as the promised land dreamed of by the genes rattling in the cells of her mind. It was not Africa, but America, the country attracting the material aspects of existence, not any Shangri-la of pre-Second World War vintage hoping for a Utopia of the spirit. Ironically, some thirty Americans who had been born and raised in the States did not feel safe enough to reach their souls' destination and had secretly fled to Israel, the land of the Jew, to die en masse at Christ's Second Arrival. Only Americans could commit religious *harakiri* starting with Jonestown and ending in tow to the Hale–Bopp Comet. But Israeli authorities regarded them as subversive. So they were forced to return 'home' to 'gates'-land, to Monica-land, to IOC-land. This list was so long that it appeared as if generated by all the evils only a 'democracy' could devise in order to counteract the assumption that it was, like New Zealand, God's own. That kind of God was either naïve or sado-masochistic. Sending his Child to Israel to save souls from an original sin! And now Israel was evicting those Americans who believed in him, good religious citizens now being returned home to Denver. Denver? That was where she was going. Yes, Denver, the neo-Nazi-est city in the World. She would ask Tanya about that place as soon as she arrived in L. A. Meanwhile, Ling-ling hoped that, in all fairness to Cayce's prophecies made half a century earlier as related by Whina, all of his 'cataclysmic earth changes' had already taken place, as they did in all continents, and particularly in China, where the Tiger had gone wilder than ever through rains and floods. The temperature alone was the highest ever registered on the planet. That gave Cayce some credibility and some hope to Whina.

By the time she had perfunctorily read about the rôle played in New Zealand by Winter Peters, Sir Robert Douglas, Jim Bolger and Doug Graham, she felt sleepy wondering how a lady PM would fare in a God-owned country afflicted by a chronic political bipolar disorder, thought not as bad as that permeating the United States of America for more than 200 years.

It was Tanya who recognised Ling-ling and her child at the L. A. terminal. For a while, Ling-ling doubted she had arrived in an English-speaking country, particularly in a State espousing the 'English only' policy. What she heard all around her sounded more like Latin. But she also recognised many tones in different languages, unmistakably Asian. Los Angeles sounded like Stockholm, but the colour was much darker. Tanya's West Coast English was re-assuring among a vociferous crowd of Latin Americans that reminded her of the chaotic Beijing Airport. The westerly winds had favored an earlier arrival, thus Ling-ling and Tanya had the opportunity to visit among a Tower of Babel humanity returning home on Boxing Day, while waiting for the connection with the plane for Denver. A copy of the *Los Angeles Times* left on a nearby seat emphasised the cold snap slapping the nation. The price of oranges would triple after the freeze destroyed most of California's crops. Even the impeachment of President Clinton took second place in the series of articles dealing with the weather that had undoubtedly tested the holiday spirit. After all, Americans were celebrating a Christian holiday. The fact that Jesus was a Jew like Monica had perhaps pre-empted the reporting of White House problems caused by a drop of semen. In France, that would simply be regarded as a lack of *savoir-faire*, in England as an opportunity to smack one's lips, in China a waste of precious protein, but in New Zealand that would have been welcomed as good business for dry cleaning establishments. Politics makes strange bedfellows, even when beds were not used at all. There was standing room only in an oval environment.

Approaching Denver International Airport, Ling-ling and Tanya wondered whether they were going to land in the right place for, from the right side of the aircraft, they could not see any city around, just a set of white sails in a frozen white ocean-like plain. No customary buildings like hotels, motels, restaurants, petrol stations or whatever. Tanya was reminded of the ship terminal at Vancouver, British Columbia. Then once inside the building they were confronted with a shining structure that could contain at least ten Mangeres. The passenger lounges were crowded, confusing, rather shifty, as at a large railway terminal, and indeed a neurotic train had to be utilised to reach the luggage area. Because of snow at other airports, many flights had been cancelled, and it was normal for proletarian jet-set families to lie on the floor in a modern version of Andersonville. The toilets were hot and packed, the food stalls were empty of victuals, and some were closed. No one ventured to go out to breathe the 'pure air' of the Rocky Mountains, for the high temperature on Saturday, 26 December, was expected to be 7 degrees Celsius and the low 4, quite a mild day for the Denver area even taking into consideration the wind chill factor that transformed the prairie into an Arctic suburb. After all, the treeless frozen tundra surrounding the airport was nearly 2 kilometres up in the sunless sky. Ling-ling felt a bit dizzy, short of breath. The child did not seem to mind it. As the Airporter scheduled to take them to Boulder, where they would take another minibus for Estes Park was late, they simply waited inside watching the Christmas crowd. Ling-ling mused over her inability to understand what in the world passengers had in those carry-on packages. Tanya replied that most of those items could be gifts, but not for the Holy Child as those brought by the Three Wise Men. No. Gifts were given by people and even by corporations, thus suggesting to humans a vicarious holy birth in addition to the original one. Probably, she thought, a gift to anyone being born is something given to lessen the shock of being tossed on top of a planet for many years of Disneyland wonderment, for no one born has ever asked for it. No wonder that America is the largest consumer of toys for both children and adults. Jesus was the best PR for the American economy through goods 'Made in USA,' though produced in Saipan's sweatshops.

In a way, for Ling-ling Christmas was merely a social phenomenon that had reached a stage of pagan folly. What she witnessed in Shanghai at New Year's had given her an inkling of the splurging festival later observed in New Zealand. It was completely beyond her comprehension. So much emphasis on exchanging gifts, drinking parties and wasting so many trees! Schizophrenia at its best! On the one hand concern for ecology, and on the other the waste of primary resources. Well, Tanya rejoined by saying that affluent nations, and America more than any other in the world, need economic exhibitionism to forget deep structural problems lingering in the winds of impending chaos. Americans are accustomed to replenishing their psychological pantry so easily that if any social upheaval, like the 'Y2K' phenomenon, ever takes places, they would revert to animalism much faster than people in any other culture. They had read in the papers that Russia, China and India had just created an alliance for 'trade.' Even France has left America. Only England continues to pay lip service, as in the bombing of Baghdad under the sponsorship of BP. This should not stand for British Petrol, but Baghdad Petrol. When Tanya told Ling-ling that 'gas' in the Denver area cost 89 cents per gallon, she just could not understand why Americans complained about Iraq. Well, Tanya told her that, if England and America were to control Iraq, the cost of petrol would automatically increase to nearly US$2 a gallon in a matter of months. American patriotism seems to flow from petrol station hose nozzles.

After arriving in Boulder in the early afternoon, the travellers were able to rest a while and refresh at the Boulderado Hotel, smack in the middle of downtown. Its lobby was still decorated with Christmas trinkets in green, red, gold and silver, the colours of the holiday merchant flag. In waiting for the minibus to Estes Park via Colorado State Highway 36, Mao Ri took a nap while the two women observed the shopping crowd returning gifts to stores or purchasing bargains such as next year's Christmas cards and decorations for the 1999 festivities.

In the evening, they checked in at the Big Thompson Estes Village Motor Inn, just south of Estes Park, not far from the convent. On Monday, they would rent a car and wait to see Mahina on several occasions. In the lobby, they purchased some local papers to get acquainted with the 'social' life of northern Colorado. The motels were not as full as they would normally be during that period, for there was not much snow on the slopes, though it was cold and windy. Ling-ling began to read the *Sunday Denver Post*. Coloradoans had elected a new governor, this time a Republican after 26 years of Democratic rule. Mr Romer, the former governor, had survived a 12-year reign along with an alleged concubinage shuttling between Denver and Washington, while happily married to his Colorado first lady *more hispano*. An article about 'International Healing' described the 'free medical care service to desperately sick residents of Nepal' by Dr Jerry A. Schultz of Lakewood and Dr Ward Anthony of Boulder. It seemed that the white community west of the Atlantic had begun to register the fact that James Hilton's 'Shangri-la' existed only in his mind after being influenced by the writings of the Austrian Joseph Rock in *National Geographic* magazine during the 1920s and 1930s. Amazingly, Rock's writings led one to believe that he was describing the western area of Yunnan Province, China, since Mt Karakal corresponds in shape to Hilton's description.

Ling-ling had just finished reading about Italy's backing out of the deal to return the Axum obelisk to Ethiopia. The *Boulder Camera* had a story about a round-the-world balloon voyage ditching near Oahu in Hawaii as in the previous day's *Denver Post*. She wondered why there was a big headline on the very first page. Well, apparently the voyage had been sponsored by a real estate company led by a Denverite, Dave Liniger. My goodness! She thought, after all Denver was not a cow town as Mahina had written to Komaru: 'Mile High, Culture Low.' Nevertheless, preparations were being made for the annual Denver Stock Show with the hope that by that time the local zoo's polar bear would give birth to two more baby bears. Exciting news items, she thought, for mountain people. The wind would take the manure effluvia all the way to Kansas. Then a car arrived to take them to the convent. Where was Mahina? At the last moment, the abbess suggested that Sister Clara Maria stay 'in residence' in order not to upset the religious function of the first Sunday following Advent. Besides, she had been extremely busy with Heva House activities, where women of all ages were welcome for a host of reasons – depression, attempted suicide, domestic violence and all the typical consequences of a hedonistic society affected, particularly at Christmas time, by alcohol, drugs, loneliness and other problems. As was discovered later, the abbess had diplomatically avoided an uneasy 'encounter' outside the convent. The meeting took place in a corner of the visiting lobby, which was packed with the relatives of both Sisters and house residents. Under no condition would anyone, except the child, be allowed to cross the threshold of the grilled wall, and no one was allowed to visit Mahina in her cell. The church, of course, was open to local people for the usual evening functions and benediction preceded by the 'Litany' and the 'Tantum ergo.'

The restriction caused some consternation in Ling-ling because she did not know about certain developments that had taken place after Mahina learned of her brother's death. Yes, the final vows and consecration to the profession were to be celebrated with a Mass on the coming Epiphany, but no details had been announced. When Mahina entered the lobby to meet Tanya, Ling-ling and her child under the initial supervision of the abbess, it was hard for anyone to say anything in front of so many people. Tanya tried to hug Mahina, but she nearly snapped Mao Ri from his mother's hand and took him to her bosom with an embrace that triggered a cry in the child. Then Mahina sat on the sofa, where she calmed him down while trying to hongi him, calling him 'Komaru.' Ling-ling intervened saying that his name was Mao Ri. Maori? No, Mao Ri. And she explained that the first and second given name have nothing in common with Polynesia. How come? Ling-ling illustrated the process leading to the selection of that name, a sequence of two Chinese ideographs. The first was not in honour of Chairman Mao, whose given names were Ze Dong anyway, but was chosen on purely lexicological evidence, as well as coincidental grounds in honour of Komaru. Ling-ling wanted to extend Komaru's memory with the meaning of 'Sun', which in Chinese is *rì*, with a falling tone, one of the very few isolated graphs carrying only one lexeme in the whole Chinese vocabulary. Nevertheless, it is so famous that it was borrowed by the Japanese who connected it to their own flag in isolation as well as in a series of compounds unlike what happened in Chinese. The adjectival *mào*, also with a falling tone, means 'luxuriant,' 'brilliant,' 'exuberant,' and so forth. The coincidence that it sounds also *maori*, 'native,' well, also makes happy the Maori people who may remember his father one day at the 'Second Arrival' of Maui from Hawaiki, a hoped for Polynesian *Parousia*. Actually, there is more in Maori culture for, when Mao Ri was about to be born, it had been raining for a whole week. But, at the moment he was born at the Wanganui hospital not far from the Moutoa Gardens, it stopped raining (*māo* meaning 'to stop raining') that the sudden change in the weather was taken as a sacred sign by Whina to make an event, namely, *rí*. The vowels of those two 'maori' words are long, but in a compound only the first is long with a macron or a double written vowel, since the structure of Polynesian languages rejects two long vowels within one single morpheme. Amusingly, the Maori cook at the restaurant understood that Mao Ri actually means 'umbrella' since the *rí* 'screen' in her dialect 'stops the rain.' Tanya commented that, with a name like that, Mao Ri will undoubtedly become a very well known man during the 21st century.

During the several visits that took place before and after New Year's

Day, a few developments were made known regarding Mahina's situation. The main one was related by her to both Ling-ling and Tanya before the *Octava Nativitatis Domini* functions. The High Mass by Reverend Martin from Longmont was a moving event. The *Introitus* alone was an opening to a year of hope for a better humanity as felt by Tanya, whose mother followed the Orthodox rituals at home, although at the convent the Gregorian Calendar was observed in agreement with the majority of Christian economies all over the world. The nuns on the organ floor above the main entrance of the church sang:

Puer natus est nobis, et filius datus est nobis ... Cantate Domino canticum novum: quia mirabilia fecit. Gloria Patri. Puer.

Mahina finally had her only *puer*, Mao Ri, in all dimensions on Earth in addition to the one now so far away in Heaven. She had immediately recognised Komaru's nose breath on Mao Ri. Although not as powerful, it was identical to Komaru's inebriating flow of life from his very bowels. Her heart palpitated faster each time the child was embraced furtively in the visiting room divided by the screens of the cloister inhabited mostly by older nuns waiting to die and be buried among the ponderosa and scotch pines whose bark smelled like butterscotch, and the aspens that in the fall shine like gold against the blue sky of the Rocky Mountains.

After the Mass, Mahina opened up to the two girls. She felt more comfortable with Ling-ling, whom she barely knew, than with Tanya, who, though properly dressed all the time, nevertheless exuded whatever Mahina wanted to avert. Memories of days and nights fighting the flesh and its drives particularly in Copenhagen on two occasions, but especially on their trip to Kòrčula. At a bookstore near the railway station they had bought, out of curiosity, an underground English translation 'published' as a pirated edition through a Xerox reproduction from a book by Ane Schmidt. The English 'translation' of two original Danish works, namely, *Jeg* and *Ham*, had been rendered as *In the Flesh*. And in their hotel room, Mahina and Tanya read the whole work in a single night. Tanya did not have a brother, but Mahina did, and so the two girls exchanged gender in trying to actualise the writer's imagination, with the difference that Mahina always beamed her thoughts onto Komaru. But Tertullian's *Ad uxorem* helped her, particularly section 4, to find a balance in her psychological system: 'the flesh is weak ... but the spirit is strong ... The flesh is of the earth, the spirit is of Heaven.' Now, in the waiting room of a convent, under the stressful weight of that recollection, almost as an expiatory penitence of a sort, Mahina explained to Ling-ling and Tanya what she had tried hard to convince the abbess to accomplish. She had decided to abandon the 'public' and social activities outside the convent, for which no habit was required, in favour of cloistering herself in the northern portion of the institution. That would take place soon after her final vows on the Epiphany. The cloistered section was barely alive since there were only seven old nuns who had entered the convent before the Second World War. It was a fight to convince not only the abbess but also all the ecclesiastic authorities to approve Mahina's idea. James Francis Stafford, the former Archbishop of Denver, had approved Mahina's wish since she possessed excellent qualifications to work on research projects in Clarissism. Her knowledge of Italian and Latin alone would guarantee first-class scholarship in the region, like the research center at the Convent of St Clare in Minneapolis. There, a Sister had plowed new ground going back to the very origin of Franciscan thought, including a study on Isabelle de Longchamp. The fact that a social worker was 'lost,' well, was offset by the necessary scholarship to keep alive the wishes of Clara of Assisi where, after the earthquake, every stone of every structure was being picked form the rubble and re-assembled.

There was only regret involved in Mahina's plan. On the 21 February 1998, the archbishop had been elevated to the most élite brotherhood, namely, to the rank of cardinal by Pope John Paul I. Mahina accepted the absence of a 'friend' as an act of humility, for she had hoped the archbishop would be present at her Epiphany function. She had even dreamed of flying to Rome, where about 400 Denverites had travelled to witness the event. One never knows how long a potential American pope can wait in the wings of the North American College. Mahina experienced some vicarious pleasure through the news given on the phone by Sister Maria Dolorosa Simones, who attended the event after taking leave of absence from her teaching post at Denver's St Vincent de Paul School.

By the eve of the Epiphany, Mahina was ready. She had digested *The Gospel Way of St Clare* from page 1 to page 167. She was totally convinced about two of the three rules already, Poverty and Obedience, as she was also about Chastity, but for this she asked the abbess to insert into the church ritual something she had studied and learned in St Methodius' writings. Meanwhile, of the three formulas of profession she had suggested and obtained permission to follow the guidelines formulated by Pope Urban IV, according to the Constitution confirmed by the Holy See:

> In the service of God and the Church, I entrust myself with my whole heart to this religious family, so that by the grace of the Holy Spirit, through the intercession of the Immaculate Virgin Mary, our holy Father St Francis, our holy Mother St Clare, and all the Saints, and with the help of my Sister, I may fulfill my consecration.

As for the thorny issue of the third vow, Chastity, Mahina had already sublimated most of it in herself and all of it through a second person. Moreover, by looking at the crucifix she would see Komaru suffering a death such as that, like Christ's, triggered only by compassion, forgiveness and pure love. But to be sure about herself, she wanted to formalise the occasion by asking her Sisters to recite and sing together with her what Thecla had done in Greek with Paul. The Greek text of the epithalamium was taken from W. Christ and M. Paranikas, *Anthologia Graeca carminum christianorum* (Leipzig, 1871). Mahina had taken almost a year to translate it into English, for no one in the convent, except the abbess, knew Greek.

Finally, in the convent church everything was ready for the first manifestation of Christ to the Gentiles for Mahina and for the commemoration of the baptism of Christ for Tanya. For Mahina, it was her wedding day at age 30. She was nearly a spinster, but soon she would be in the arms of her spouse forever. The church was brilliantly lit and decorated with flowers. At 8:00 a.m. it was still dark at the bottom of the front range, but the peaks of the National Park were turning pink under the first rays of sunshine. The high for the day would be 48 degrees Fahrenheit, and it would be more windy than in Wellington. By noon, the clouds would take over and darkness would cover everything by 4:00 p.m. But in Mahina's heart everything was shining in the glory of embracing the life that could give her peace, tranquillity and a feeling of security among her Sisters. Tanya, Ling-ling and Mao Ri were seated in the front row of the section reserved for the general public. Father Mancini had come all the way from Denver together with his assistants. And so the Mass began according to Fulton J. Sheen's *Missal* for *Die 6 Januarii in Epiphania Domini*, with the *Introitus*:

> Ecce advenit dominator Dominus: et regnum in manu eius et potestas, et imperium ...

To Tanya it sounded like Roman government terminology but, after all, even the title Pontifex was taken from the Caesars. Only the details had changed in 2,000 years. The system of ruling a peninsular population was the same. The Gospel according to Matthew was a refreshing account for another Maori *metua*. It was after the 'Ite missa est' that the *intermezzo* placed Mahina at the centre of attention. She had to get rid of her last remnants of burned flesh to feel purified. Thus, the chorus singing by the organ began to intone the refrain:

> From now on, I shall live for You chastely, and, by preserving forever my lamps lighted, O my Spouse, I proceed freely to embrace You.

There followed twenty-four identical repetitions of this *cantus responsorium* followed by Mahina's affirmation of diverse instances of what a bride recites as a *precentrix*, similar to a wedding ceremony listing promises of faithfulness, succor, etc., that in the United States are broken in 50% of cases. Tanya felt that the third promise was the most human of the sequence, since a long time ago she herself had also decided not to get married ever:

> O my King, for You I have declined a terrestrial marriage and a home full of comfort. I prefer to come to You in white garments so that I may enter under Your guidance Your sacred epithalamium.

Then, at the risk of being rude, Ling-ling asked Tanya in a whisper what the meaning of the last word was. Tanya replied that normally it was a motel room on the newlyweds' trip to Disneyland during the summer or Aspen during the winter.

At the conclusion of the Mass, Ling-ling and Tanya were invited to join the abbess in the Discretorium office, not far from the sacresty. There a Sister in charge of conventual events and the Order of St Clare introduced the portress, who brought a suitcase containing all of Mahina's personal effects. She had already given most scholarly books to the convent library where, for the first time in the history of the elementary school, a corner of the reference section included Maori and Polynesian language publications. Among them, the place of prominence was the venerable *Maori–Polynesian Comparative Dictionary* by Edward Tregear (Wellington: Lyon and Blair, Lambton Quay, 1891), a tome older than the convent itself. Sister Clara Maria did not possess anything worldly any longer, and whatever she had from a former life was replaced by the religious habit and standard clothing for all Sisters not engaged in out-of-convent activities. The only exceptions to 'personal' items were a golden rosary and a bronze crucifix. The rosary was not for daily use, for gold was against the vows of poverty. The abbess had allowed her to have it 'on loan' along with the crucifix already hanging on the wall above the prie-dieu in Sister Clara Maria's cell. Those were the only two contacts with the memory of her mother and brother.

Sixty days earlier, on All Saints' Day, Mahina had prepared a written statement renouncing any property she actually owned, or that would come to her, both in the States and New Zealand, and had conveyed everything in trust to Mao Ri Reti. Consequently, as all Sisters were one in mind and heart, they were to share all material things with each other as at the early Church of Jerusalem where 'all who believed were together and had all things in common.' Karl Marx and Friedrich Engels were almost nineteen centuries late to appear on the scene of economic socialism.

In her new habit, parts of which formerly 'belonged' to a Sister who had died a few years back, Sister Clara Maria looked simply stunning, displaying only part of her face and resembling an oval cameo of ivory carved by the jewellers near the little bridge leading to the Academia Quay in Venice. Even deprived of lipstick, her lips looked like the petals of a unique rose blooming in snow as her face reflected the white pectoral. Only the deep brown eyes, part of the brows, and the nose adorned her semi-hidden cheeks – the minimum traits of the human figure still betrayed a classical beauty. At least she so appeared to Tanya who tried to contain her constant dizziness triggered by the reminiscence of having showered her in Milan with the hottest kisses after Mahina translated Labé's sonnets for her.

The legal formalities for the recording of the Act of Profession were expedited quickly and as a matter of fact as in the office of a notary public. The document was signed by Mahina as Sister Clara Maria and witnessed by Chu Ling-ling, who signed in both English and Chinese, and by Tanya Halisky. Finally, the Abbess affixed her own signature by the sign of the Cross. As the Profession was already solemn and perpetual, the Abbess was to be sure that it be known to the parish priest in Portland, Oregon, where Mahina had been baptized.

It was nearly noon, time to go. The world was now divided into two parts by a screen wall between a parlor and lay reality. On that threshold Sister Clara Maria first embraced Ling-ling 'professionally', almost as in the fashion of a priest doing similar things to his assistants on the altar of a High Mass. She then tried to do the same with Tanya, but Tanya got hold of her so fully and tightly that the former Mahina trembled visibly while her face first became red and then pale after Tanya, either accidentally or intentionally, brushed Sister Clara Maria's tight lips with her hot and open mouth. And, finally, Mahina knelt by Mao Ri who, not knowing a word of English except 'excuse me' and 'thank you' did not hesitate to make an impromptu speech in Chinese, ending with 'zài-jiàn' 'good-bye' innocently followed by 'yì-huĭr-jiàn,' 'see you soon.'

The internal door of the parlor was then closed as Sister Clara Maria stood briefly by the grilled wall watching Mao Ri wave at her, Chinese fashion. She felt like Plato on his deathbed, as she had been 'practicing dying' slowly since Komaru's death. Now she herself had died to the world. In effect, as Komaru had done in his failed attempt to leave a message to a callous world, she had committed virtual suicide, for there are several ways to nullify one's psychological persona among the rest of humanity. She had placed a huge *ri* behind her, the screen of voluntary exile. The physical body did not seem to count any longer, although existing and functioning in all its physiological aspects. The phenomenon is actualised merely by visual and phonic separation, as when a family member dies, or a wife abandons a husband, or even a close friend or a pet disappears from daily life. The survivor remains alive, but often a sensitive one subconsciously commits 'silent suicide' not to offend either society or the system of which one is a component for better or worse. In the final analysis, the process is a cunctation guaranteed by the fact that life is always finite, the best security device encoded at birth. Mahina had chosen the noble way to vanish from a world in which she had nothing left, not even her clothes. Oh, what a relief! How many fortunate people can reach that state of bliss? Whatever may have lingered within, whether in her heart or her mind, was actually an incipient fraction of a cosmic intellect pullulating in the vortex of the past, present, and future specks of the ineffable in seeking each other at random with the hope that each would recognise another as a mutual ingraft for the rest of Eternity.

At the motel, Ling-ling opened Mahina's suitcase. It was full of Retihood, including correspondence, photographs, books, personal articles such as mini-slips, a bathing suit, and even toilet items such as face cream and the like. She decided to take everything with her as Mao Ri's luggage. Among the books, Ling-ling found one titled *The Evolution of Civilization [:] An Introduction to Historical Analysis*, by a Carroll Quigley, published as a paperback in 1979. It was heavily highlighted in green, and on page 424 Komaru had inserted a handwritten note:

> Mahina, you see? *Nihil novum sub sole.* I had thought that Professor Peterson was original in his speech regarding the end of War as a process, as old as *Homo sapiens* itself, to settle injustices. Well, the Australian lecturer may have just expounded on Professor Quigley's 'clarid' views of things to come, as he had done in his own speech delivered at the School of Foreign Service, Georgetown University, Washington, D.C. Professor Quigley died a few weeks later. It is amazingly that the concept of 'military impotence', in spite of all the internal armament including weapons of mass destruction held in storage by the Pentagon, versus 'uncontrolled individual behavior' through terrorism, was born in the '60s along the Potomac river, in the political heart of America, a nation that, like Rome, began to commit suicide a generation ago by entrusting brute force into the hands of people who do not possess 'the internalized control of the civilization.' Korea, Vietnam, Lebanon, Iraq, Bosnia, and similar theaters of Wagnerian Götterdämerung operas, are just overtures to chaotic global upheaval.

Thus, on Thursday, the 7 January, they took the minibus back to Boulder, which they had visited a couple of times in order to shop at the downtown mall on West Pearl Street, an artificially narrow gully of bazaars and all-American shops swept by the icy winds rolling down from the front range like a hurricane to test aircraft. They also visited the other mall at Crossroads, where they stayed only a short time since it was in the process of remodelling or expansion, but they checked a couple of bookstores to warm up, and also because Tanya was trying to get some books she could not find in Walla Walla. No luck! Just before Christmas she heard that her favourite writer, William Gaddis, had died. She had planned to buy a copy of his books as a small present for Whina, since in New Zealand no one had ever heard of Gaddis. Well, apparently not in Boulder either. Gaddis, the American 'James Joyce', had never crossed the South Platte River. Tanya promised to send Whina at least *The Recognitions*, published nearly 40 years before, quite a long book of about 1,000 pages. Tanya herself had not yet read *A Frolic of His Own*, but the previous book, *Carpenter's Gothic*, published in 1985, had opened her eyes to the real America, a society reeking with lies, political paranoia, religious corruption, sexual permissiveness and dissolution of morals at home, not to mention polluted academic standards at universities, and the like. Tanya had naïvely commented that the same kind of litany about the disintegration of materialistic America was already being covered by the daily newspapers. Indeed, that morning Ling-ling had read the *Boulder Daily Camera* as if it had been published on the Moon. The front pages showed in block capitals three words, 'PRESIDENT ON TRIAL,' followed by a facsimile invitation ticket to attend the '106th Congress – First Session, United States Senate, Impeachment Trial of the President of the United States.' For whatever reason, no one thought of adding 'of America,' for there are other nations organised as United States, such as Mexico. The second item on the front page was a request for money to fund the solution of THE SHAME OF BOULDER as labelled by most people. The city seemed to be ideal for a perfect murder. Two years earlier, a six-year-old girl had been killed on Christmas night in her own home, just a few feet away from her parents. With all the PhDs working in Boulder to design and build gadgets to explore Mars, no one seemed to be really able, it not concerned enough, to unravel the mystery afflicting the inflated ego of a city trying to be known at any cost through the exploits of a football team. In fact, during the shopping trip to Boulder in order to buy something 'American' for Whina, they could not find anything 'original.' Perhaps that was the excuse adduced by Ling-ling. She must have a mental reservation.

On another occasion, while killing time in Boulder, they went to visit the Norlin Library at the university. It was closed for the holidays. So, what else to do in the area? Someone suggested climbing another mile toward a mountain community called Nederland, where murder is a cultural event occurring from time to time. Sometimes it takes a whole generation to solve a mystery, for the most notorious murder had been committed by the local Marshal himself to keep the village free of transients. Of course, he had never been caught by the justice system from which he received a salary. Only recently, as a terminal cancer patient, had he confessed. A shallow grave had been found, on which the victim's sister placed the customary flowers of remembrance, which were eaten during the night by deer. Actually, the real cultural monument of the community stemmed from a scientific enterprise. Nederland is the only former mining community in the United States where an alien, popularly known as 'The Frozen Dead Guy,' is kept in cryogenic suspension under a pile of dry ice which is replenished twice a week. It seems that a Mining Museum is being organised 'downtown,' but whether the alien is to be housed there has not yet been decided upon by the town's Board of Trustees.

On 8 January, after the Airporter practiced bobsledding on the frozen highways leading to DIA, the weary travellers checked in for their flight to LAX and lounged at the concourse in terminal B. There, Ling-ling found a free 'local' newspaper on an empty seat. It was mostly advertisements from Russian and Filipina women desirous of marrying American men. Apparently, the marital traffic was booming since single men, especially divorced, had been 'burned' by American women. The Thai women fad had vanished in view of the AIDS scare. The Internet was now favouring a fast way to try again. Ling-ling wondered whether William Gaddis had been more than a writer. Had he prophesied in *Carpenter's Gothic* what was now reality? And, finally, as a consequence of the official papal position on the death penalty in America, the most civilised country and a leader of the free world, an article had been written on the status of Timothy McVeigh's impending execution. Ironically, his trial had been held in the same Denver downtown Federal Building where Mahina, between sessions, had pledged allegiance as a new citizen of the United States. Well, it seems that the army had trained him properly to kill. Whether blowing the head of an Iraqi with a 25-mm cannon or more than a hundred people with a mixture of oil and fertilizer, could be answered in two ways: If America needs a martyr in the 21st century, fine. He could be executed British style as done to Hindus tied to the bore of a cannon. The other way would be to rehabilitate and pardon him, for who would gain anything otherwise? Terrorism cannot be cured with an eye for an eye policy, ironically in Biblical fashion, wrote the reporter. Would it not be better to demilitarise the brute armed forces through which America naïvely believes she can police the whole world by dialling a global '911'? Tanya was happy to be away from Denver, where during the McVeigh trial, at a cost of $15 million and conducted in an emotional circus atmosphere rather than in a climate of understanding and forgiveness, the local merchants had made a mint. And Ling-ling concurred, for New Zealand, although officially a pacific 'democracy,' had, in her opinion, a government that was worse than that of the United States. She was tempted to disclose to Tanya what she had in mind once she reached Los Angeles, but she refrained from doing so for a few more hours. She wanted to be sure that the year of the rabbit would be about to begin, at least in China. Whether it was a superstition or not, it is always better to be cautious. The NZ flight for Auckland was scheduled for 8 January and Tanya's to Seattle for the 9th. So, they checked into a hotel in Santa Monica for a day of relaxation, though Ling-ling put into action a different plan to spend her last hours in the States.

The following morning, Ling-ling woke up early and knocked at Tanya's door. No, she was not going back to New Zealand, and needed Tanya's help for the last time. They went together to the General Consulate of the People's Republic of China two blocks off Wilshire Boulevard. Ling-ling mentioned Komaru's wishes in his last letter. She had a unique chance to implement those wishes now, before any political or social upheaval had developed. But, the business in Wanganui, the house and all the rest? And her own 'political' stigma stemming from her innocent participation as an observer in Tiananmen Square when she was not even 18 years old? She took a chance and, besides, she did not care what would happen to her. The child came first no matter what.

The Vice-consul, Xu Hao, was delighted to listen to Ling-ling's plea. Mother China is always happy to welcome a good brain back from Western training. There was no problem regarding Mao Ri because the proceeds from the restaurant and the house would guarantee a comfortable education both at 'home' and abroad. Ling-ling could be easily 'debriefed' Japanese style as done for all Asians indoctrinated with materialism. Besides, her knowledge of English and of business practices would guarantee her a good job anywhere in China, even in Hong Kong. China was going to become the most capitalistic nation in the world. Whether the West considered the Middle Country as Communist was simply a way to fight the potential economic supremacy looming astride the 21st century. Finally, a telephone call to Shanghai verified that Ling-ling was the prodigal daughter of Dr Chu Hang, in charge of Shanghai Hospital No. 2, and of Professor Cao Jin, director of the Department of American English at East China Normal University. They would guarantee housing for her until a permanent solution could be found later, perhaps in some of the apartments being built around the railway station in place of the old wooden shacks.

Arrangements were made for Ling-ling to depart that very evening on an Air China airplane. In her case, she was still a Chinese national; thus, there was no problem. The child obtained an immigrant visa on his New Zealand passport, quite a feat for anyone allowed to enter China as an immigrant, but it was faster to process a visa than to issue a new Chinese passport. Once at 'home,' Ling-ling could take her time in resolving pending issues, including entrusting Mao Ri to her maternal grandparents in 'Canton.' In the taxi to the airport, Ling-ling asked Tanya to send a fax to Whina in Wanganui as soon as possible from the airport branch of Mail Boxes, Etc., so that she would not drive to Auckland International to wait for her and the child. And Tanya herself decided to take an earlier flight on a stand-by basis for Seattle that very evening.

Waiting to board the plane, Ling-ling did not want to read anything this time, particularly newspapers carrying articles of doom from the first to the last page. The Monica Lewinsky 'spillover' alone had assumed the proportion of a Universal Deluge. Whatever happened in the West took second place in her life now. She was anxious to see her child in the land of her ancestors, for she was afraid that, if she were unable to leave America now, anything could happen at any time. She was afraid that Mao Ri could even die in America. Besides, news relating to Iraq, Kosovo, the Kurds invading Italian shores, Pinochet's extradition, and a host of other 'democratically' induced pleasures could ricochet even into Los Angeles.

The embrace between Tanya and Ling-ling was quick and business like when the attendant announced that passengers with children could board the plane immediately. Ling-ling, however, made a point of thanking Tanya warmly and suggesting that perhaps they could get together in China next ... millennium. That remark broke the uneasiness of the separation and puzzled Mao Ri with the sudden explosion of laughter that Tanya released nearly hysterically.

It was a glorious Sunday morning in Wanganui. The sun was already warm. Tourists had been arriving from all corners of the world to take advantage of the dollar exchange, NZ$2 for US$1. Unbelievable. That had not taken place since pre-Rogernomic times. In waiting for the arrival of the cook, Whina sat down at a table in the empty salon that would open at 11:00 for Sunday brunch. She had a hearty breakfast and a cuppa in front of her, but did not drink the tea that had become cold and stale. Her thoughts were lost on three continents. Her vagaries were interrupted by the arrival of the *Weekend Herald, Metro Edition*. She took a perfunctory look at the *Herald*, undoubtedly more worldly than the parochial *Wanganui Chronicle*. While trying to browse through the paper, she re-read the fax received during the night. It was rather sibylline, but clear enough even for a moron in spite of the fact that there was no addressee:

PLEASE CANCEL RETRIEVAL MERCHANDISE AUCKLAND INTERNATIONAL DUE TO FREEZE. WAIT FOR FURTHER

INSTRUCTIONS. MEANWHILE TAKE CARE OF MEDIET AND OF THE HOUSE AS IF IT WERE YOUR OWN.

The telegraphic-style message had been jotted in capital letters by a feminine hand, of course, but the writing was 'American.' Whina knew that Ling-ling and Mao Ri would not come back to New Zealand. And in order to kill some time she automatically separated the unwanted sections, such as sports and automobile adverts, from the rest of the paper. In the process, a small cartoon caught her attention at the bottom of the very first page. Under 'Body language' the scene represented presumably the Anglican Archbishop of Canterbury asking a couple, 'Prince Edward, do you promise to wed this woman, at least until the tabloids get a whiff of something saucy?' In spite of the sick Kiwi humour, Whina laughed. That compensated for the concern she felt in reading the caption 'Intruder terror turns homes into fortresses' by Darrell Mager and Naomi Larkin. Well, this time Miss Larkin shared reporting on doom matter with a colleague, and amazingly the date was not the first of the month.

Whina thought that the world was shrinking. The Pacific lake had become a narrow river crossed by pan-suburban fear among 'Frightened householders, many of them immigrants ...' Whina felt that specific reference to a particular social group was more than gratuitous. She wondered. In all fairness to Miss Larkin, the second article on page A2 dealt with a serious socio-aesthetic topic, an exciting one, namely, the symbolism and tyranny of the tie. She must be rather naïve, for she avoided a Freudian, and semiotic, interpretation pointing out and down to a phallus, constantly reminding women that men were the rulers of society. And, indeed, her supposition was confirmed by the article on page A6 – the improbable meeting between President Clinton and PM Jenny Shipley, compounded by the 'airport welcome unlikely ...' between Josiah Beeman, the New Zealand ambassador, and Miss Shipley. That was contrary to tradition. The ambassador had always received Jim Bolger with a red carpet. But this time the ambassador must have remained at home to peel carrots for the evening dinner. The new PM, who had displaced Bolger, happened to be a woman, the only one to become 'first lady' of New Zealand.

It was time to double check the tables and the salad bar for the usual high service standards. She missed Ling-ling. Before dropping the paper into the refuse bin, she took a look at the STARWatch for Sunday. She was not superstitious, but it would not hurt her to read what the stars had in mind for the day. 'You will find it hard to return to a weekly routine. Soon enough you will click back into gear for a month, indeed a year, of courage and commitment ...'

She then opened the front door of the restaurant. There was already a long queue. The very first 'couple' consisted of two gentlemen who, in spite of the 'equatorial' climate, for it was already 23 degrees Celsius, were wearing dark suits, black ties and dark sunglasses, even inside the restaurant. She wondered if those ties were Christmas gifts. Oh, if Naomi Larkin were at hand! Probably she would know whether the ties had been purchased for corporate employees at the 'mecca of Auckland sophistication – the Smith & Caughey department stores' for 'a price tag of around $200. Paying so much for a length of fabric that hangs there ... seems criminal.'

The two gentlemen who were at the front of the queue had meanwhile entered the premises and were standing by the sign indicating seating options. Whina approached them, imitating Melissa's hostess intonation.

'Good morning, gentlemen,' said Whina. 'Please be seated any place you like.'

'Oh ... thanks. We are Criminal Intelligence agents. May I ask you a question?' whined the older man.

'By all means!'

The agent showed her a photograph. 'Have you ever seen this ... gentleman?'

Whina glanced at the smiling face of an athletic-looking blond man wearing a flamingo-pink polo shirt. No tie.

'Yes, indeed!' she replied.

'It's not funny! Where, when?'

'A few minutes ago on the first page of the *Herald*. May I ask why?'

'Just routine. Thank you, madam. *Kia ora!*'

Whina hesitated, not knowing what to say. The Maori greeting proffered with an atrocious pronunciation hit her like a slap in the face. She felt insulted. Then she retrieved the *Herald* from the bin and glanced at the article. According to Detective Nevil Shirley of the Auckland police organised crime squad, the details of the passport allegedly held by the man shown in the photograph 'belonged to a dead British man.' His hair, however, had been described as jet black. He was now in prison waiting to be extradited 'home'.

Home! Where was her home? In Africa, in America, in Britain, in

New Zealand, in Aotearoa or in Hell? She felt dejected and lonely in the midst of the jolly crowd standing by the salad bar tables. The strong fragrance of melted parmesan over the baked eggplant mingled with the roasted garlic of the popular bruschetta. Then her heart beating fast made her stomach very sick. She rushed to the staff lavatory, dropped on her knees and, bending over the stool, vomited her very *manawa* into the cesspit of Humanity.

Postscript

On the 6 February 1999, the *Mediet* restaurant crowd was lighter than usual. The weather had been very fine, with all-day sunshine yielding a maximum temperature of 25 degrees. Whina attributed the lower-than-usual patronage to the fact that Waitangi Day fell on a Saturday. People were simply eager to watch TV in anticipation of what Titewhai Harawira would do at the annual ceremony. In 1998, she had fought for her right to speak as a Maori woman. That right had been denied, while the Tai Tokerau Kaumatua preferred a Pakeha woman. In spite of the tears shed by Helen Clark, Leader of the Opposition, the 1998 meeting had favoured the 'Establishment'. Nevertheless, a few activists were still dreaming of justice. The Tuhoe spirit was lingering through the lifetime activities embodied in Tame Iti.

As usual, the Fourth Estate was ready to utilise the occasion for filling out the pages of the various newspapers and TV scripts for the evening news, but, for whatever reason, the expectation for Tame Iti's exploits seemed to have subsided. There was, thus, a near-hungry wish for any manifestation on the part of the young woman who had spit on the Governor's face and consequently had been 'fined' with six months in gaol.

It was dark when Whina reached Komaru's house. The third quarter moon would not rise until 23:30, just before the BBC World News, to be followed by 'This Week' on Channel One. She had an inkling, via the radio in the restaurant kitchen, that something 'different' had taken place in Northland. She sensed that the 1999 Waitangi Day was unusual. The last time it had fallen on a Saturday had been in 1993.

That year she was hopeful, dreaming of freedom and independence for the last outpost of British colonialism. The Fiscal Envelope and the Moutoa Gardens Occupation were not yet conceived of as tools of political protest. Only Komaru was planning to organise something to be remembered by future generations of Maori free spirits. Thus, Whina tried to understand what must have been a disappointment for the press. Nothing really historical seemed to have taken place, at least according to fragmentary news items appearing on the screen.

It was a long and restless night for Whina. She tossed and turned, trying to recollect the 'non-news' day at the surface level, for there was plenty brewing at the deep structure of the historical ceremony. Her attempt to understand the implications of the lack of sensationalism for the Pakehas made her sense that she was witnessing the death of History itself.

She mentally reviewed some of the images flashing on the TV screen in a non-sequential manner. There was a shot of the *Norwegian Star*, a cruise ship, anchored in the Bay as a background of a Maori *waka*, for the bemusement of American tourists. Another camera panned slowly on a group of youngsters climbing the steel pole to fly the Maori flag. Whina was able to read a large white cloth sign inscribed hastily in red paint. She interpreted it as 'Pakehas got the loaf, Maoris got the crumbs, it is time for a change, Waitangi 1999'. Another group of pathetic demonstrators waved some flags with the letters 'TE MANA MOTUHAKEO...'. She could not read the rest, asking for a special status of someone or something, unless understood as Matiu Rata's political party born after the demise of the Labour Party.

In the most intriguing sequence, Whina saw Titewhai Harawira standing at the side of the PM Jenny Shipley as if the two women were college girls attending a weekend picnic. The most baffling inference was that Titewhai acted like a Maori guide to a Pakeha visitor, much in the spirit of Maggie Papakura. But what had happened meanwhile in two hundred years of fighting? Whina hoped that the TV images would not break through the Rangi walls. What would an Apirana Ngata say if he were to watch the evening news? And the 'warriors' of all the white wars all over the world ending with Sir James Henare? Whina was glad that, with the death of Charles Moihi Bennett on 26 November 1998, no Maori Battalion officer was left to report on the disappearance of an entire way of life. And what would a person like Timoti Karetu think of the ensuing disappearance of Maori *reo* as the next stage in the obliteration of Polynesian culture still lingering in Tuhoe?

The very name of Tuhoe punched Whina in the stomach. Had the camera shot shown Tame Iti honging the Prime Minister? No, it could not be possible. It must have been a trick of her sick imagination. Thus, she decided to wait until the next day to verify what took place. Undoubtedly, the newspapers would report on the episode that she construed as something that only a *kupupa* would participate in with a deranged mind. Could it be that Tuhoe had cut all bridges with its *whenua*? She remembered a proverb that made no sense any longer: 'Kotahi na Tūhoe ma te pō e kata'. How could there be amusement in the underworld if no Tuhoe 'once warrior' was left to die in battle?

The next morning, as she woke up, Whina knew that Ao Tea Roa had finally been buried at sunset on the 6 February 1999 in an unmarked grave at the bottom of the Waitangi flagpole. Komaru, who had witnessed the death of his country on 19 May 1995, could now have his bones removed and polished before his spirit could take off for its final resting-place. Still, Whina could not believe what she had seen the previous night. She would wait for the arrival of the *New Zealand Herald* at the restaurant.

Later in the day Whina was finally able to sit down at the cashier's corner to read the *Weekend Herald* at the completion of the kitchen clean up by her trusted cook's helper. On page one, a large colour photograph contained several remarks authored by RICHARD KNIGHT. The first, on the top left, read 'Odds on the Crown's gamble with the fate of our [British] national day will pay rich dividends [to Pakehas]'. The words within brackets surged subconsciously in Whina's mind automatically after nearly one hundred and sixty years of Polynesian agony.

Under the photograph she then read, 'Veteran Tuhoe activist Tame Iti joins Prime Minster Jenny Shipley in a symbolic coming together of the Crown and critic as Government and Maori leaders met at Waitangi yesterday...'. Whina could not believe her eyes, for Tame, her idol, looked so tame he reminded her of a most appropriate proverb, 'Hohonu kakī pāpaku uaua'. At the bottom right an inset titled 'Payout tipped to exceed $2 [NZ]b' led Whina to read, '...Waitangi Tribunal historian Alan Ward said he expected the settlement of claims would take until 2010 and would cost about $2 [NZ] billion.' That amount, she thought, corresponds to about US$1 billion, less than the cost of an 'atomic' submarine. She calculated mentally that the entire Hermit Island would be paid off under duress at the rate of US$15 per acre just for the land.

The whole charade was encapsulated by 'RodY' in the usual 'Body language' cartoon at the lower left. It depicted, under the lead title 'NEW START BETWEEN MAORI AND GOVT...', what Whina understood as a long-nosed *kaikaiwaiu* holding a small piece of paper, the Waitangi Trick, and saying 'YOUR INVITE TO WAITANGI...' to Jenny Shipley. She also held a larger piece of paper containing some data as 'YOUR UNEMPLOYMENT FIGURES...'. Whina, as a woman, could not refrain from observing the designer-made glasses worn by the Prime Minister. Their 'precious' stones seemed to match her classic-style earrings hovering over a flower brooch. She thought, the beauty and the beast exchanging germs. But she was not sure who of the two was who.

In the action of tossing the daily into the dustbin, she felt as if life itself had assumed the value of another Pakeha tool of deception. Intrinsically, the Sunday paper was simply the result of tree pulp, yes, but it was also a weapon that no Maori could ever forge and use against the forces of fate. She wondered whether Komaru, the last Maori 'warrior', would ever have the stomach to *hongi* a female executioner. She knew that he would have felt demeaned in his very *manawa*. There was nothing else to do except try to exit herself from the deep state of depression into which she had fallen. Not even dignity had been left anywhere, for Ao Tea Roa had got off the Earth forever. Now only the vestiges of The Hermit Islands remained as a geographic expression named New Zealand in the atlas of despair.

It was time to go home. But, before closing the establishment, Whina had to act. Her body had to do something drastic during her last day on Earth, for her soul had died along with Ao Tea Roa. The white cloth covering one of the long tables between the kitchen and the dining area attracted her attention, for it was stained with tomato sauce spilled from a tray of vegetable lasagna. That gave her an idea. She got hold of her lipstick and wrote on it in block letters: THIS RESTAURANT IS NOW OUT OF BUSINESS. CLOSED PERMANENTLY. Next, using a stapler, she affixed the sign inside the street window and turned all the lights off.

She drove to the Reti house, where she had been living pending its sale. Lately, Komaru's presence was being felt so heavily that she simply could not stay there any longer. She had detected in the air the old Maori atmosphere of his *wairua* fighting to escape through a ritual of purification. So, she retrieved from the garage two reserve jerry cans of diesel fuel and a tin of petrol from the restaurant lorry. She next filled the bathtub with hot water, poured the fuel around the internal perimeter of the house, and finally selected a sharp knife from the kitchen.

Before stepping into the tub, she lit the petrol trail leading to the diesel fuel, slashed her wrists, and allowed her blood to flow freely into the water. It took the poisonous fumes only a few seconds to make her pass out, mercifully before her body collapsed at the bottom of the tub in the ensuing natural gas explosion. The Tasman Sea breeze gently blew the smoke of the burning house toward the Moutoa Gardens. Then the rain came to wash out every trace of Retihood from the *whenua* once inhabited by the last warrior eaten by the angry gods of oblivion.

That night, having waited for years next to Cape Reinga's *pohutukawa* tree on Hicks Bay, Komaru's *wairua* felt free enough from Maori shame to make a desperate move *in extremis*. He looked for the *kauri* door blocking him from eternity, and knocked on it hesitantly. He was happy to see his father on its threshold welcoming him, with a long-held *hongi*, to his ancestors, Rangi.